Transdimensional Invasion: The Déjà Vu Factor

I0564570

By
Daon Daniels

Front Matter

To the countless minds that have felt the alien whisper, that have experienced the disquieting tremor of déjà vu and dismissed it as a trick of the mind, a glitch in the familiar flow of time. To those who have looked up at the stars and felt not just wonder, but a deep, unsettling premonition, a sense that humanity is not alone, but perhaps, not entirely welcome. This story is for the lonely sentinels in the quiet observation rooms, the brilliant minds who wrestle with data that refuses to conform, the brave souls who dare to question the established order when their own perception screams a different truth. It is for the unsung heroes who fight battles on planes unseen, who defend realities not yet understood, and who hold fast to their humanity even when the very foundations of it are being systematically dismantled.

May this narrative serve as a testament to your courage, your resilience, and your unwavering commitment to the light of truth, even in the deepest, darkest encroaching shadows, to all those who have felt the echo of the impossible and refused to let it fade. Your vigilance is our hope.

Table of Contents

Front Matter.. iv

1: Echoes of the Familiar... 7

2: The Bureaucratic Wall.. 30

3: An Old Friend's Faith 55

4: Rogue Mission 81

5: The Nexus Point... 115

6: Whispers of Compromise.. 150

7: Unraveling the Objective 181

8: Political Puppets 213

9: Severing the Connection 243

10: Infiltration and Sabotage 271

11: The Psychic Cascade 303

12: The Counter-Offensive.. 332

13: Humanity's Awakening.. 509

Back Matter... 541

1: Echoes of the Familiar

The laboratory was Aris Thorne's sanctuary, his gilded cage. The sterile white walls, meticulously maintained to reflect every lumen of the overhead LED lights, seemed to absorb all ambient sound, leaving only the low, resonating hum of the complex machinery that served as his constant, inanimate companions. It was a symphony of advanced science, a testament to his dedication, yet it echoed the profound emptiness that had become the foundation of his existence. Days bled into nights, marked only by the shifting intensity of the artificial illumination and the relentless pursuit of a theoretical Holy Grail. He existed in a state of perpetual anticipation, teetering on the precipice of a paradigm-shattering discovery, a breakthrough that promised to redefine humanity's understanding of the cosmos. Yet, this intellectual ascent was shadowed by an increasingly debilitating internal struggle, a private war waged within the labyrinth of his own mind.

The episodes began subtly, insidious whispers at the edges of his perception—fleeting sensations of having lived this precise moment before, a phantom echo of experience. At first, he dismissed them as the occupational hazards of prolonged intense focus, the mind playing tricks when pushed to its absolute limit. But the déjà vu incidents grew in vividness and frequency, evolving from fleeting whispers to jarring, almost prophetic pronouncements. They were no longer mere cognitive glitches; they were immersive, disorienting replays of events that had not yet transpired. One moment, he'd be meticulously calibrating a quantum entanglement array, the next, he'd find himself reliving the calibration, complete with the precise angle of the laser, the exact flicker of a dial, and a phantom sensation of success or failure that defied the present reality. These jarring temporal intrusions left him reeling, his grip on his own sanity loosening with each recurrence. He would stare at his hands, the very instruments of his research, and wonder if they truly belonged to him, if the thoughts that coursed through his mind were his own. The isolation, once a chosen crucible for his work, had become an inescapable facet of his reality, amplifying his disorientation and feeding his growing unease. His current research, delving into the volatile and largely unexplored realm of unstable quantum fluctuations, was a field so esoteric that few colleagues possessed the inclination, let alone the courage, to follow him into its theoretical depths. It was a lonely frontier, and the anomalies he encountered there seemed to mirror the increasingly alien landscape of his own consciousness.

The sterile environment of his lab was more than just a workspace; it was a deliberate construct, designed to minimize external stimuli and maximize internal focus. Every surface was polished to a high sheen, every wire meticulously routed, every piece of Equipment calibrated to perfection.

It was a testament to his drive for order, a bulwark against the chaos he perceived in the universe, and perhaps, the chaos he increasingly felt within himself. The hum of the machinery was a constant lullaby, a soundscape that had become as familiar as his own heartbeat. He sought solace in the predictability of scientific law, in the elegant equations that governed the fundamental forces of existence. Yet, the more he delved into the esoteric nature of quantum fluctuations, the more the universe seemed to fray at the edges, revealing inconsistencies that defied his carefully constructed understanding.

The pursuit of knowledge in this uncharted territory was a solitary endeavor. His theories, often dismissed as too abstract or speculative by the mainstream scientific community, kept him at the fringes. He was a theoretical physicist, yes, but his theories danced on the precipice of what was considered possible, dipping into realms that bordered on the metaphysical. Space-time anomalies, quantum entanglement across vast distances, the very fabric of reality itself – these were his obsessions. He saw the universe not as a static entity, but as a dynamic, mutable tapestry, capable of being warped, torn, and perhaps, even influenced by forces beyond human comprehension.

His current focus was on the inherent instability within the quantum foam, the theoretical substructure of the universe. He believed that at the most fundamental level, reality was not a smooth continuum, but a turbulent sea of quantum fluctuations, constantly bubbling and popping into existence and then collapsing back into nothingness. While most physicists acknowledged this theoretical construct, Aris posited that under certain extreme conditions, these fluctuations could become amplified and stabilized, creating brief, ephemeral breaches in the fabric of space-time.

These were the anomalies he was hunting, the whispers of a universe far stranger and more interconnected than anyone dared to imagine.

The isolation, however, was a double-edged sword. It allowed him unparalleled freedom to explore his radical ideas, unburdened by the constraints of conventional thinking or institutional dogma. But it also meant that when the inexplicable began to manifest, he had no one to turn to, no peer to validate his burgeoning fears. The sterile white walls of his laboratory, designed to promote clarity, now seemed to mock him with their blank impassivity, offering no answers, no comfort, only the incessant hum of his solitary pursuit. He was a man adrift in a sea of his own theories, the shores of accepted reality receding with every passing moment.

The déjà vu wasn't just a feeling; it was a visceral experience. It would strike without warning, usually when he was deep in concentration, the lines of code on his monitor blurring, the intricate diagrams on his whiteboard swimming before his eyes.

Suddenly, he would be elsewhere, yet still him, seeing his own hands move with a practiced, fluid grace that was utterly alien to his current, hesitant movements. He'd know the outcome of an experiment before he'd even set it up, the triumphant reading on a spectrograph or the chilling anomaly on a waveform. These were not memories, not in the conventional sense. They were too vivid, too detailed, and too future-oriented. It was as if a sliver of his future self, or perhaps another version of himself entirely, was bleeding through the veil of time, leaving behind these potent, disorienting imprints.

He tried to rationalize it, of course. He was a scientist, after all. He meticulously documented each episode, noting the time, the prevailing external conditions, his current mental state, and the specific task he was engaged in. He cross-referenced these personal logs with his experimental data, searching for any correlation, any pattern that might suggest a scientific explanation. Was it a byproduct of the intense gravitational fields generated by his experimental temporal projectors? Or a side effect of his work with exotic matter, something that subtly altered his perception of causality. He even considered the possibility of latent psionic abilities, a concept he'd always relegated to the realm of science fiction, but which now seemed disturbingly plausible.

The isolation gnawed at him. He was a man on the verge of something monumental, something that could fundamentally alter humanity's place in the cosmos, yet he was utterly alone. His colleagues, those few who even understood the abstract nature of his research, treated him with a mixture of awe and pity. They admired his brilliance but were wary of his increasingly unconventional pronouncements, his growing obsession with the inexplicable. They saw the toll the isolation and the relentless pursuit of the unknown were taking, the subtle tremor in his hands, and the shadowed circles beneath his eyes. He was becoming a recluse; his lab was his universe, and his theories were his only companions. The sterile white walls, once a symbol of his controlled environment, now felt like the confines of a self-imposed asylum, a place where his groundbreaking work was slowly, inexorably, unravelling his sanity. He was a prisoner of his own genius, haunted by echoes of a future he couldn't quite grasp, a future that seemed to be unfolding not through his own agency, but through some unseen, external manipulation. The hum of the machinery was no longer a lullaby; it was the thrumming pulse of a hidden engine, driving him toward an unknown destination.

The humming of the servers had always been a comforting drone, a sonic manifestation of order and logic within Aris Thorne's meticulously controlled universe. It was the sound of data being processed, of raw information being sculpted into understanding. But lately, that hum had begun to feel like a prelude, a low vibration that resonated with the unsettling tremors in his own perception. He found himself drawn back to the vast archives of the Kepler and Hubble deep-space observatory datasets, not for any specific research goal, but out of a gnawing, inchoate sense of seeking. He'd sifted through these cosmic records countless times, mapping nebulae, cataloguing exoplanets, searching for the faintest whispers of extraterrestrial life in the predictable language of electromagnetic radiation. Now, he was looking for something else, something that defied categorization, and something that felt like an echo of the unsettling premonitions that plagued his waking hours.

He initiated a broad-spectrum analysis, a brute-force query designed to flag any deviation from established physical models. It was a task that would normally consume days, the processing power of the laboratory's supercomputers churning through petabytes of raw observational data. But Aris was driven by an urgency that outstripped the usual protocols. His fingers flew across the holographic interface, his mind a whirlwind of algorithms and hypotheses. He was searching for the impossible, for anomalies that shouldn't exist, for signals that spoke of physics yet undiscovered, or perhaps, actively suppressed.

Hours blurred into a familiar rhythm of focused intensity, punctuated only by the soft click of his stylus against the projection surface. The results began to trickle in, a cascade of spectral analyses, light curve deviations, and gravitational lensing distortions. Most of it was noise, the expected imperfections of cosmic observation. He'd almost succumbed to the familiar sense of futility when a cluster of unusual readings caught his eye. They were subtle at first, anomalies buried deep within the noise, flagged not as significant discoveries, but as statistical outliers. He zoomed in, his brow furrowing in concentration. These weren't the gentle undulations of a planetary transit or the predictable redshift of a distant galaxy. These were sharp, almost violent spikes, brief but intensely energetic fluctuations in the space-time continuum itself.

He cross-referenced the timestamps of these anomalous readings with his personal logs of the déjà vu episodes. A cold dread began to coil in his gut. The correlation was too precise, too consistent to be a mere coincidence. The spikes in energy signatures, localized and fleeting, often coincided with the moments his own sense of reality seemed to fragment, moments when he felt an inexplicable foreknowledge of events, a phantom memory of something that hadn't yet happened. He remembered the first time he'd noticed the pattern. It was during a routine calibration of his temporal displacement field generator. He'd experienced a vivid flash of himself dropping a critical component, the metallic clang echoing in the sterile silence of the lab, followed by the sharp sting of reprimand from a superior he hadn't even encountered yet. Moments later, while adjusting a micro-capacitor, his hand had slipped, and the very component he'd seen in his vision had tumbled from his grasp, the clang a chilling replica of his psychic echo. At the time, he'd attributed it to the immense gravitational forces his experimental device was generating, a localized distortion of causality. But now, seeing these extraterrestrial energy signatures mirroring his internal disarray, he wondered if the source was far more alien, far more deliberate.

He began to meticulously isolate these anomalies, creating a dedicated database that tagged each event with its precise coordinates in space and time. He correlated it with his documented episodes of precognitive déjà vu. The data painted a disturbing picture. These weren't isolated incidents scattered randomly across the cosmos. They were clustered, appearing with an unnerving regularity, and disturbingly, many of them originated not from the distant reaches of space, but from points alarmingly close to Earth, some even within the terrestrial atmosphere. The signatures were characterized by a unique energetic profile, a rapid oscillation that seemed to tear at the very fabric of space-time, creating transient, localized rifts. They were whispers of an impossible physics, a reality being systematically, subtly, disrupted.

The complexity of the signatures defied any known natural phenomena. They weren't the predictable energy emissions of pulsars or the gravitational waves from merging black holes. These were sharp, coherent bursts, too brief to be thoroughly analyzed by existing instruments, yet too distinct to be dismissed as sensor noise. They suggested an intentional manipulation, a deliberate, albeit fleeting, breach in the established order of the universe. Aris found himself staring at the holographic projection of these signatures, the jagged lines representing impossibly energetic events, and felt a visceral connection to them, as if they were the physical manifestation of the internal schisms he'd been experiencing for years.

He decided to approach Dr. Lena Hanson, a colleague in astrophysics whose pragmatism was matched only by her intellectual rigor. He knew she'd be skeptical, that she'd likely attribute his findings to stress, to the isolation of his work. But he needed an outside perspective, a sanity check, even if he suspected the sanity he was seeking was already compromised. He arranged a meeting in a small, neutral observation room overlooking the central data processing hub. The room was deliberately nondescript, a stark contrast to the controlled chaos of his own laboratory.

"Aris," Lena began, her voice calm and steady as she entered, her gaze assessing. "You sounded... urgent on the comms."

Aris gestured to the holographic display he'd pre-loaded with his findings. "Urgent doesn't quite cover it, Lena. I think I've found something. Something... impossible."

He guided her through the data, explaining the energy signatures, their unusual characteristics, and their unsettling correlation with his own experiences. He presented the graphs, the spectral analyses, the temporal alignments, careful to maintain a detached, scientific demeanor, though the tremor in his voice was betraying his inner turmoil.

Lena watched, her expression evolving from polite interest to a focused intensity. She asked precise, probing questions, her mind dissecting his data with an efficiency that was both reassuring and daunting. "These deviations, Aris, they're unlike anything I've seen cataloged. The energy levels are off the charts, and the duration... It's microseconds. How are you certain these aren't artifacts of the data acquisition process? Contamination from atmospheric interference? Or perhaps a miscalibration in the deep-space array optics?"

"I've accounted for all of that," Aris replied, his voice firm. "I've run diagnostics on every instrument, cross-referenced with multiple independent observatories, and analyzed atmospheric data for each instance. The signatures are too consistent, too localized. They appear as coherent disruptions, like tiny, violent tears in the fabric of space-time itself." He paused, gathering his resolve. "And the temporal correlation with my own... episodes. It's too strong to ignore."

Lena's eyebrows lifted slightly. She knew about his "episodes," as he'd vaguely referred to them in the past, dismissing them as perceptual anomalies brought on by intense focus. "Your déjà vu experiences, Aris? You're suggesting a direct causal link between these astronomical energy spikes and your subjective temporal distortions?"

"I don't know if it's causal," Aris admitted, running a hand through his already disheveled hair. "But the correlation is undeniable. It's as if these... tears in reality... are somehow bleeding into my consciousness, imprinting themselves on my perception before they occur." He looked at her, his eyes pleading for understanding. "Lena, I've spent years studying the theoretical limits of space-time, the quantum foam, the potential for instability. These signatures fit the theoretical models for localized transdimensional breaches. Brief, violent ruptures where reality itself is momentarily... permeable."

Lena leaned closer to the holographic display, her scientific skepticism battling with the sheer strangeness of the data Aris was presenting. The patterns were indeed compelling, almost too persuasive. "Permeable," she echoed, a thoughtful frown creasing her brow. "But to what end, Aris? What would cause such localized, high-energy space-time disruptions on Earth, or in proximity to it?"

"That's what I'm trying to figure out," Aris said, his voice tight with a mixture of fear and exhilaration. "The implications are... staggering. If these aren't natural phenomena, then they're artificial. And if they're artificial, someone or something is manipulating space-time. And the fact that they're happening here, now, in our solar system, suggests a purpose. A very immediate one."

He projected a world map, highlighting the locations of the most prominent energy signatures. They weren't confined to remote deserts or deep oceans; they appeared in densely populated urban centers, in major industrial hubs, even in proximity to critical infrastructure. The distribution was almost... strategic.

Lena traced a finger over the projected map, her expression grave. "This is... deeply concerning, Aris. If this data is accurate, it suggests a level of technological capability far beyond anything we possess. And the implications of a civilization capable of intentionally manipulating space-time... It's almost unimaginable." She turned back to the energy signatures, her analytical mind already grappling with the sheer impossibility of it all. "But even if we accept this premise, the mechanism remains obscure. What could generate such focused bursts of energy without collapsing into a black hole? What kind of technology could achieve that?"

"That's the million-credit question," Aris replied, his gaze fixed on a particularly sharp spike originating from the Pacific Ocean. "It suggests a form of energy manipulation that's fundamentally different from anything we understand. Perhaps it's not about brute force, but about resonance, about exploiting inherent instabilities within the quantum field. Think of it like striking a tuning fork at precisely the right frequency to shatter glass. They're not breaking space-time with a hammer; they're finding the precise harmonic to cause a momentary, controlled fracture."

He zoomed in on another cluster of anomalies, this time originating from the orbital path of several defunct satellites. "These aren't just terrestrial phenomena, either.

There are signatures originating from low Earth orbit, from decommissioned orbital platforms. And the patterns, Lena, they're not random. They show a progression, a deliberate deployment of this... technology, or whatever it is."

Lena remained silent for a long moment, absorbing the weight of his words, the chilling logic that underpinned his increasingly desperate assertions. She knew Aris, knew his brilliance, his dedication, and his inherent integrity. If he was convinced of something, it was because he had meticulously, painstakingly, convinced himself. And while her scientific training screamed caution, a deeper, more primal instinct urged her to listen.

"You need to report this, Aris," she said, her voice firm. "To the highest levels. This is beyond anything that can be dismissed as personal eccentricity or research-induced delusion. This is... potentially world-altering."

Aris scoffed, a bitter sound. "Report it? Lena, I've tried. I've presented fragments of this data to my superiors and to the oversight committees. They waved it away as sensor anomalies, as 'mathematical ghosts.' They said my research was becoming too esoteric, too detached from observable reality. They're not ready for this. They can't comprehend it. They're too steeped in the old paradigms, too afraid of the implications." He looked back at the map, his expression hardening. "If I'm right, then these disruptions are a precursor. A prelude to something far greater, far more insidious. And if I can't make them understand, then I have to find another way."

He began to systematically categorize the data, not just by location and time, but by the specific type of energy signature, the intensity of the correlated déjà vu episode, and the perceived nature of the precognitive flash. He was building a lexicon of these impossible events, a Rosetta stone for a language of cosmic disruption. Each anomaly was a word, each temporal tear a syllable, and together, he believed, they were forming a sentence, a message from a force that was slowly, deliberately, unraveling the reality he'd always known. The hum of the servers continued, a steady rhythm beneath his agitated thoughts, a soundscape that was slowly transforming from the symphony of scientific pursuit into the overture of an unimaginable threat. He felt a growing certainty that these weren't just whispers in the data stream; they were the first, faint signals of a new, terrifying reality.

The low thrum of the quantum entanglement apparatus, a familiar lullaby of oscillating particles and probabilistic fields, suddenly felt like a discordant note in Aris Thorne's carefully orchestrated reality. He was in the observation chamber, the air thick with the sterile scent of ozone and the silent anticipation that always accompanied the delicate dance of entangled photons. Before him, the holographic projection shimmered, displaying the complex waveform of his latest experiment, a meticulous demonstration of quantum superposition. His audience, a small delegation of visiting dignitaries from the

Interstellar Science Consortium, watched with a polite, academic detachment, their faces illuminated by the ethereal blue light of the display.

Aris began his explanation, his voice steady, detailing the principles of quantum entanglement, the instantaneous correlation between two particles, regardless of the distance separating them. He spoke of quantum teleportation, of the potential for instantaneous communication across vast cosmic gulfs. It was a topic he knew intimately, a landscape he had navigated countless times. Yet, as he reached for a holographic control to adjust the entanglement parameters, it happened.

A wave, potent and suffocating, washed over him. It wasn't just déjà vu; it was a complete sensory immersion into a past that hadn't occurred, yet felt irrevocably real. His hands, poised over the controls, froze mid-air. The laboratory, the dignitaries, the humming machinery – it all flickered, replaced by a phantom sensation of stark, cold observation. He saw himself, or rather, a spectral echo of himself, standing at the periphery of his vision, a figure cloaked in shadow, the edges of its form indistinct, wavering like heat haze. And then, a whisper, barely audible yet seeping into his very bones, a sound that wasn't sound but pure intent: "They are here. Not ships. Within."

The whisper was followed by a visceral jolt, a surge of adrenaline that sent a tremor through his limbs. His eyes snapped back to the present, to the holographic display and the startled faces of the dignitaries. His own hands were trembling, his breath catching in his throat. The feeling was overwhelming, a suffocating certainty that he had just witnessed a prophecy, a warning from a future that was already seeping into his present.

He managed a shaky smile, attempting to regain his composure. "A momentary... recalibration," he stammered, his voice rough. He forced his trembling fingers to resume their task, manipulating the controls with a newfound, desperate urgency. The quantum waveform stabilized, but the tremor in his hands remained, a physical manifestation of the profound disruption he had just experienced. The dignitaries exchanged curious glances, their polite interest tinged with a hint of concern.

"Are you quite alright, Dr. Thorne?" asked the lead delegate, a stern-faced woman with eyes that seemed to pierce through his carefully constructed façade.

"Perfectly," Aris replied, though the lie tasted like ash in his mouth. He forced himself to meet her gaze, to project an image of scientific focus, of unwavering control. But inside, a storm was raging. The spectral figure, the whispered warning – it was too vivid, too chillingly precise to be dismissed as a mere neurological glitch. It was a ghost of a memory, a premonition etched into his very being, and it confirmed the terrifying hypothesis that had been lurking at the edges of his consciousness for weeks. His lifelong episodes of déjà vu weren't random quirks of perception; they were something else entirely. They were echoes, faint but persistent, of an alien presence that was already among them, not arriving in ships, but… within.

He continued the demonstration, his scientific explanations flowing on autopilot, his mind, however, was a maelstrom of analysis. The alien whisper, "Not ships. Within," replayed endlessly, each iteration tightening the knot of dread in his stomach. It spoke of an infiltration so subtle, so insidious, that it bypassed physical detection entirely. It implied a conquest of minds, a silent subjugation that began not with explosions and invasions, but with a whisper in the mind, a subtle shift in perception.

He remembered the earlier anomalies he'd uncovered in the deep-space data, the fleeting, violent tears in space-time that coincided with his own episodes of precognitive déjà vu. At the time, he had theorized about transdimensional portals, about brief breaches in reality. But the whisper… it suggested something far more intimate, far more terrifying. These weren't just tears in the fabric of the universe; they were conduits, pathways for something to seep through, to take root. And if his own experiences were any indication, the first point of ingress was the human mind itself.

As he spoke about the practical applications of quantum entanglement – secure communication, advanced computing, even the theoretical possibility of quantum teleportation – his words felt hollow, laced with a bitter irony. He was demonstrating the pinnacle of human scientific achievement, while simultaneously being confronted with evidence of an alien intelligence capable of subverting reality at its most fundamental level. And the mechanism of their arrival, as the spectral whisper had suggested, was not through the grand spectacle of starship fleets, but through the quiet, internal landscape of the human psyche.

He glanced at the dignitaries, their faces a mosaic of intellectual engagement and polite skepticism. Could any of them, he wondered, be already compromised? The thought was chilling. If the infiltration was indeed internal, a corruption of consciousness, then the enemy could be anywhere, anyone. His own colleagues, his superiors, the very people he needed to convince – they might already be under alien influence, their minds subtly re-written, their loyalties warped. The weight of this realization pressed down on him, a suffocating blanket of isolation.

The demonstration concluded, and Aris offered his thanks, his voice betraying none of the internal turmoil. He watched the dignitaries file out, their footsteps echoing in the corridor, each echo a reminder of the fragile normalcy he was desperately trying to cling to. Once they were gone, the chamber felt cavernous, the silence amplifying the frantic pounding of his heart.

He turned back to the holographic display, the quantum waveform now quiescent. He ran a diagnostic on the entanglement apparatus, checking every sensor, every calibration. All systems were functioning within optimal parameters. There was no physical explanation for the vision, for the whisper. It had originated from within him, a phantom experience triggered by the very act of observing and manipulating the fundamental forces of the universe.

He walked over to his personal terminal, his fingers hovering over the holographic keyboard. He needed to re-examine the data, to look for patterns that might explain the internal nature of this alien presence. He pulled up the files related to his déjà vu episodes, cross-referencing them with the energy signatures he'd cataloged. The correlation remained stubbornly intact. The more he looked, the more he saw. The anomalies weren't just localized space-time disruptions; they were intricately linked to moments of heightened consciousness, to instances where his own mind was operating at peak capacity. It was as if the alien presence was drawn to, or perhaps even amplified by, moments of intense cognitive activity.

He began to formulate a new hypothesis, one that was far more terrifying than he had previously imagined. The transdimensional breaches he had detected were not mere portals for physical entry; they were points of psychic resonance. They allowed for a form of non-corporeal infiltration, a subtle hijacking of consciousness. The déjà vu, the precognitive flashes – these were not random neurological events, but the echoes of the alien influence, the faint signals of minds being subtly altered, subtly reshaped.

He remembered the spectral figure at the edge of his vision, its indistinct form, its whispered warning. It hadn't been a threat; it had been a desperate plea, a fragment of a consciousness that was fighting to assert itself against an encroaching darkness. The message, "Not ships. Within," resonated with a new, chilling clarity. The aliens weren't invading Earth with armies; they were infiltrating it from the inside out, using the very fabric of human consciousness as their battlefield.

He thought of the pervasive sense of unease that had settled over the populace in recent months, the subtle shifts in social dynamics, the growing polarization of public discourse, and the rise of inexplicable anxieties and paranoia. He had dismissed these as products of societal stress, of political upheaval. But what if they were symptoms?

What if the alien presence, by subtly altering minds, was already beginning to destabilize humanity from within?

Aris leaned back in his chair, the sterile air of the observation chamber suddenly feeling heavy, claustrophobic. He was a scientist, a man of logic and empirical evidence. Yet, the evidence he was accumulating defied all conventional understanding. He had stumbled upon a truth so profound, so terrifying, that it threatened to unravel his entire perception of reality. The ghost of a memory, the whisper of a warning – they were no longer abstract anomalies; they were the harbingers of an unseen war, a war waged not on battlefields, but within the minds of humanity. And he, Aris Thorne, was perhaps the only one who truly understood the nature of the threat. The thought was both a terrifying burden and a stark, terrifying call to action. He knew, with a certainty that chilled him to the bone that he could not afford to be disbelieved, not any longer. The fate of Earth, he now suspected, depended on it. The hum of the machines around him no longer sounded like a lullaby; it was the ominous ticking of a cosmic clock, counting down to an unknown, terrifying future.

The sterile hum of the observation chamber had receded, replaced by the gnawing silence of Aris Thorne's private study. The holographic displays, once showcasing the elegant dance of quantum particles, now projected a stark, chaotic tapestry of data. He had spent the better part of the night sifting through the archives, his eyes burning, his mind a frenetic engine of correlation. The energy signatures, those fleeting, violent tears in the fabric of space-time he'd detected, were no longer isolated anomalies. They were patterns. Disturbing, terrifying patterns that mapped not onto astronomical phenomena, but onto the very historical record of humanity itself.

He traced a line on one of the projections, connecting a violent surge of energy recorded six months prior with a sudden, inexplicable wave of mass paranoia that had swept through Neo-Alexandria, a city renowned for its placid populace. The paranoia had manifested as baseless accusations, a descent into suspicion that had nearly fractured the city's delicate social order. It had passed as quickly as it had arrived, leaving behind a residue of distrust and confusion. Aris had initially filed it away as a socio-political anomaly, a predictable reaction to the anxieties of the era. Now, the energy signature pulsed beside it, a silent, damning indictment.

Then there was the cluster of disappearances in the Kepler Belt colonies two years ago. Entire outposts, gone. No distress calls, no salvageable wreckage... absence. The official explanation had been a catastrophic environmental collapse, a sudden atmospheric breach. But the energy readings from that period, meticulously logged, showed a localized space-time distortion, a ripple that was far too precise, too deliberate, to be natural. It coincided with a series of Aris's own more intense déjà vu episodes, flashes of a chillingly alien architecture, of impossibly cold landscapes. He hadn't understood them then. Now, he saw the terrifying correlation. These weren't just energy bursts; they were conduits, fissures through which something was subtly influencing Earth, a silent, insidious seep into the collective consciousness.

The déjà vu, those moments of unsettling familiarity, weren't random neurological quirks. They were echoes, residual psychic imprints left by these transdimensional incursions. Each vivid flash of memory that wasn't his own, each phantom sensation of a life unlived, was a tiny psychic scar tissue, a testament to something brushing against his mind, leaving its trace. The whisper, "Not ships. Within," echoed relentlessly in the confines of his skull, a constant reminder of the terrifying reality he was uncovering. The enemy wasn't approaching in lumbering vessels that defied detection; they were already here, a contagion of consciousness.

He pushed himself away from the terminal, the sterile light glinting off the smooth chrome of his desk. The sheer magnitude of the problem was beginning to dawn on him, a chilling realization that settled deep in his gut. How could he possibly convince anyone? He, Aris Thorne, a physicist, was now delving into realms that bordered on mysticism, poring over ancient texts and fringe theories as if they held the key to unlocking an extraterrestrial invasion. It sounded like madness. But the data, the relentless, quantifiable data, pointed to a truth far stranger and more terrifying than any science fiction novel could have conceived.

He remembered a forgotten anecdote from his grandmother, a woman who had lived through the tumultuous mid-21st century. She spoke of periods of collective irrationality, of outbreaks of unshakeable beliefs that gripped entire populations, only to dissipate as mysteriously as they had appeared. At the time, Aris had dismissed it as the unreliable recollections of an aging mind. Now, he wondered. Could those events, too, have been the faint tremors of these incursions, the early stages of a subtle manipulation?

He pulled up another data stream, this one compiled from obscure sociological journals and forgotten historical archives. He was searching for historical precedents, for any whisper of a similar phenomenon across millennia. He found accounts of mass hysteria throughout human history, including the dancing plagues of the Middle Ages, the Salem witch trials, and the sudden bouts of inexplicable fear that had gripped communities in various eras. They were often attributed to disease, to mass delusion, to religious fervor. But what if they were something else? What if they were the ripples left by an ancient, recurring influence? What if humanity had been subtly infiltrated, again and again, throughout its history, each time misinterpreted as a terrestrial event?

The thought was overwhelming. The idea of an invasion, silent and unseen, meticulously orchestrated not through brute force but through the delicate, intricate pathways of the mind, was no longer a vague hypothesis. It was beginning to feel terrifyingly, undeniably real. He found himself drawn to conspiracy theories, to the dismissed ramblings of those who spoke of unseen forces guiding human events. He'd always dismissed them as the product of fractured psyches, of a desperate need for order in a chaotic universe. Now, he felt a perverse kinship with them, a chilling understanding of their underlying anxieties. They had glimpsed a truth, perhaps only in fragments, a truth that he was now painstakingly piecing together.

He navigated to a secure, encrypted corner of his personal network, a digital sanctuary he had created for his most speculative research. Here, he began to cross-reference the energy signatures with instances of unexplained technological leaps, periods of rapid societal advancement that defied logical explanation. Were these moments of alien intervention, subtly guiding humanity's progress, shaping its development for their own unknown purposes? Or were they simply byproducts of their presence, energy leaks from their transdimensional activities? The ambiguity was maddening.

He recalled a specific incident from his own childhood, an episode of vivid precognition that had saved his younger sister from a freak accident. He had foreseen a structural collapse in their home, an event so improbable that he had struggled to articulate it, yet the certainty had been absolute. He'd dragged his sister out of the path of falling debris, an act that had earned him accolades for his quick thinking, but which he knew, deep down, had been more than just intuition. Had that, too, been an echo? A subtle nudge from an alien consciousness that had chosen, for reasons unknown, to spare him? The thought was deeply unsettling, the idea that his own existence might be a result of their influence.

Aris's gaze fell upon a dusty tome on his shelf, a gift from his mentor, an eccentric xenolinguist named Dr. Elara Vance. It was a collection of ancient Sumerian tablets, meticulously translated and annotated. He had never delved deeply into it, finding the mythological narratives more fanciful than factual. But now, an impulse, a desperate need for any kind of corroboration, drove him to retrieve it. He settled back into his chair, the weight of the ancient book surprisingly substantial in his hands. He began to scan the translated texts, his eyes darting across the intricate cuneiform. He was looking for anything that spoke of sky-gods, of watchers from beyond, of beings who influenced human destiny from the shadows.

And then he found it. A passage describing the Anunnaki, beings who descended from the heavens, who "shaped man from clay," and who "knew the secrets of the stars." The text spoke of their subtle manipulations, of their influence on early human civilization, and of their whispered guidance that had led to the dawn of agriculture, written language, and organized society. It was couched in myth, in religious allegory, but the undertones of intelligent, purposeful intervention were undeniable. He found more. References in Egyptian hieroglyphs to entities that "guided the Nile's flood," in Mesoamerican codices to celestial beings who "whispered the calendar into human minds."

These weren't merely stories of gods. They were fragmented historical accounts, passed down through generations, distorted by time and belief, but hinting at a recurring pattern of external influence. The Anunnaki, the Elohim, the Watchers – were these simply different cultural interpretations of the same fundamental phenomenon? The aliens he was detecting now, the ones causing these space-time distortions and psychic echoes, were they the same beings, or their descendants, or something even more ancient?

He returned to his data, overlaying the historical periods mentioned in the ancient texts with the energy signature readings. A startling convergence emerged. Specific periods of significant cultural upheaval, of rapid societal change, coincided with spikes in the energy readings, with temporal anomalies that mirrored those he had recently documented. It was as if these ancient texts were not mere mythology, but a historical record of these very incursions, albeit cloaked in the language of the divine.

The implications were staggering. This wasn't a new threat; it was an ancient one. Humanity had been under observation, and perhaps manipulation, for millennia. His own déjà vu episodes were not unique, but possibly intensified manifestations of a phenomenon that had been subtly influencing human consciousness for eons. The whisper, "Not ships. Within," took on an even deeper resonance. They hadn't just arrived recently; they had always been here, woven into the very fabric of human experience, their influence subtle, pervasive, and utterly invisible to all but those who knew how to look.

He felt a profound sense of isolation, yet also a strange, burgeoning sense of purpose. If this influence had been shaping humanity for so long, what was its ultimate goal?

Were they benevolent guides, or something far more sinister? The paranoia, the societal shifts he had observed, felt like a shift in their strategy, a move from subtle guidance to overt manipulation, or perhaps even a more aggressive form of infiltration.

Aris leaned back, the weight of millennia pressing down on him. The scientific principles he had dedicated his life to understanding, the fundamental laws of the universe, now seemed like a fragile veneer, easily breached by forces that operated on principles he was only beginning to grasp. He was no longer just a physicist; he was an archaeologist of consciousness, unearthing the hidden history of humanity's silent, unseen masters. The task ahead was immense, the enemy intangible, but the echoes of the familiar had become a deafening roar, demanding his attention, demanding action. He knew, with a chilling certainty, that his life's work had just taken a terrifying, irreversible turn. He was no longer just studying the universe; he was fighting for the very definition of humanity. The quiet hum of the laboratory was a distant memory, replaced by the phantom whispers of an ancient, ongoing war, fought not with weapons, but with thoughts, with memories, with the very essence of consciousness. And he was, perhaps, the only one awake enough to hear the call to arms.

The sterile hum of the observation chamber had receded, replaced by the gnawing silence of Aris Thorne's private study. The holographic displays, once showcasing the elegant dance of quantum particles, now projected a stark, chaotic tapestry of data. He had spent the better part of the night sifting through the archives, his eyes burning, his mind a frenetic engine of correlation. The energy signatures, those fleeting, violent tears in the fabric of space-time he'd detected, were no longer isolated anomalies. They were patterns. Disturbing, terrifying patterns that mapped not onto astronomical phenomena, but onto the very historical record of humanity itself.

He traced a line on one of the projections, connecting a violent surge of energy recorded six months prior with a sudden, inexplicable wave of mass paranoia that had swept through Neo-Alexandria, a city renowned for its placid populace. The paranoia had manifested as baseless accusations, a descent into suspicion that had nearly fractured the city's delicate social order. It had passed as quickly as it had arrived, leaving behind a residue of distrust and confusion. Aris had initially filed it away as a socio-political anomaly, a predictable reaction to the anxieties of the era. Now, the energy signature pulsed beside it, a silent, damning indictment.

Then there was the cluster of disappearances in the Kepler Belt colonies two years ago. Entire outposts, gone. No distress calls, no salvageable wreckage, just... absence. The official explanation had been a catastrophic environmental collapse, a sudden atmospheric breach. But the energy readings from that period, meticulously logged, showed a localized space-time distortion, a ripple that was far too precise, too deliberate, to be natural. It coincided with a series of

Aris's own more intense déjà vu episodes, flashes of a chillingly alien architecture, of impossibly cold landscapes. He hadn't understood them then. Now, he saw the terrifying correlation. These weren't just energy bursts; they were conduits, fissures through which something was subtly influencing Earth, a silent, insidious seep into the collective consciousness.

The déjà vu, those moments of unsettling familiarity, weren't random neurological quirks. They were echoes, residual psychic imprints left by these transdimensional incursions. Each vivid flash of memory that wasn't his own, each phantom sensation of a life unlived, was a tiny psychic scar tissue, a testament to something brushing against his mind, leaving its trace. The whisper, "Not ships. Within," echoed relentlessly in the confines of his skull, a constant reminder of the terrifying reality he was uncovering. The enemy wasn't approaching in lumbering vessels that defied detection; they were already here, a contagion of consciousness.

He pushed himself away from the terminal, the sterile light glinting off the smooth chrome of his desk. The sheer magnitude of the problem was beginning to dawn on him, a chilling realization that settled deep in his gut. How could he possibly convince anyone? He, Aris Thorne, a physicist, was now delving into realms that bordered on mysticism, poring over ancient texts and fringe theories as if they held the key to unlocking an extraterrestrial invasion. It sounded like madness. But the data, the relentless, quantifiable data, pointed to a truth far stranger and more terrifying than any science fiction novel could have conceived.

He remembered a forgotten anecdote from his grandmother, a woman who had lived through the tumultuous mid-21st century. She spoke of periods of collective irrationality, of outbreaks of unshakeable beliefs that gripped entire populations, only to dissipate as mysteriously as they had appeared. At the time, Aris had dismissed it as the unreliable recollections of an aging mind. Now, he wondered. Could those events, too, have been the faint tremors of these incursions, the early stages of a subtle manipulation?

He pulled up another data stream, this one compiled from obscure sociological journals and forgotten historical archives. He was searching for historical precedents, for any whisper of a similar phenomenon across millennia. He found accounts of mass hysteria throughout human history, including the dancing plagues of the Middle Ages, the Salem witch trials, and the sudden bouts of inexplicable fear that had gripped communities in various eras. They were often attributed to disease, to mass delusion, to religious fervor. But what if they were something else? What if they were the ripples left by an ancient, recurring influence? What if humanity had been subtly infiltrated, again and again, throughout its history, each time misinterpreted as a terrestrial event?

The thought was overwhelming. The idea of an invasion, silent and unseen, meticulously orchestrated not through brute force but through the delicate, intricate pathways of the mind, was no longer a vague hypothesis. It was beginning to feel terrifyingly, undeniably real. He found himself drawn to conspiracy theories, to the dismissed ramblings of those who spoke of unseen forces guiding human events. He'd always dismissed them as the product of fractured psyches, of a desperate need for order in a chaotic universe. Now, he felt a perverse kinship with them, a chilling understanding of their underlying anxieties. They had glimpsed a truth, perhaps only in fragments, a truth that he was now painstakingly piecing together.

He navigated to a secure, encrypted corner of his personal network, a digital sanctuary he had created for his most speculative research. Here, he began to cross-reference the energy signatures with instances of unexplained technological leaps, periods of rapid societal advancement that defied logical explanation. Were

these moments of alien intervention, subtly guiding humanity's progress, shaping its development for their own unknown purposes? Or were they simply byproducts of their presence, energy leaks from their transdimensional activities? The ambiguity was maddening.

He recalled a specific incident from his own childhood, an episode of vivid precognition that had saved his younger sister from a freak accident. He had foreseen a structural collapse in their home, an event so improbable that he had struggled to articulate it, yet the certainty had been absolute. He'd dragged his sister out of the path of falling debris, an act that had earned him accolades for his quick thinking, but which he knew, deep down, had been more than just intuition. Had that, too, been an echo? A subtle nudge from an alien consciousness that had chosen, for reasons unknown, to spare him? The thought was deeply unsettling, the idea that his own existence might be a result of their influence.

Aris's gaze fell upon a dusty tome on his shelf, a gift from his mentor, an eccentric xenolinguist named Dr. Elara Vance. It was a collection of ancient Sumerian tablets, meticulously translated and annotated. He had never delved deeply into it, finding the mythological narratives more fanciful than factual. But now, an impulse, a desperate need for any corroboration, drove him to retrieve it. He settled back into his chair, the weight of the ancient book surprisingly substantial in his hands. He began to scan the translated texts, his eyes darting across the intricate cuneiform. He was looking for anything that spoke of sky-gods, of watchers from beyond, of beings who influenced human destiny from the shadows.

And then he found it. A passage describing the Anunnaki, beings who descended from the heavens, who "shaped man from clay," and who "knew the secrets of the stars." The text spoke of their subtle manipulations, of their influence on early human civilization, and of their whispered guidance that had led to the dawn of agriculture, written language, and organized society. It was couched in myth, in religious allegory, but the undertones of intelligent, purposeful intervention were undeniable. He found more. References in Egyptian hieroglyphs to entities that "guided the Nile's flood," in Mesoamerican codices to celestial beings who "whispered the calendar into human minds."

These weren't merely stories of gods. They were fragmented historical accounts, passed down through generations, distorted by time and belief, but hinting at a recurring pattern of external influence. The Anunnaki, the Elohim, the Watchers — were these simply different cultural interpretations of the same fundamental phenomenon? The aliens he was detecting now, the ones causing these space-time distortions and psychic echoes, were they the same beings, or their descendants, or something even more ancient?

He returned to his data, overlaying the historical periods mentioned in the ancient texts with the energy signature readings. A startling convergence emerged. Specific periods of significant cultural upheaval, of rapid societal change, coincided with spikes in the energy readings, with temporal anomalies that mirrored those he had recently documented. It was as if these ancient texts were not mere mythology, but a historical record of these very incursions, albeit cloaked in the language of the divine.

The implications were staggering. This wasn't a new threat; it was an ancient one. Humanity had been under observation, and perhaps manipulation, for millennia. His own déjà vu episodes were not unique, but possibly intensified manifestations of a phenomenon that had been subtly influencing human consciousness for eons. The whisper, "Not ships. Within," took on an even deeper resonance. They hadn't just arrived recently; they had always been here, woven into the very fabric of human experience, their influence subtle, pervasive, and utterly invisible to all but those who knew how to look.

He felt a profound sense of isolation, yet also a strange, burgeoning sense of purpose. If this influence had been shaping humanity for so long, what was its ultimate goal?

Were they benevolent guides, or something far more sinister? The paranoia, the societal shifts he had observed, felt like a shift in their strategy, a move from subtle guidance to overt manipulation, or perhaps even a more aggressive form of infiltration.

Aris leaned back, the weight of millennia pressing down on him. The scientific principles he had dedicated his life to understanding, the fundamental laws of the universe, now seemed like a fragile veneer, easily breached by forces that operated on principles he was only beginning to grasp. He was no longer just a physicist; he was an archaeologist of consciousness, unearthing the hidden history of humanity's silent, unseen masters. The task ahead was immense, the enemy intangible, but the echoes of the familiar had become a deafening roar, demanding his attention, demanding action. He knew, with a chilling certainty, that his life's work had just taken a terrifying, irreversible turn. He was no longer just studying the universe; he was fighting for the very definition of humanity. The quiet hum of the laboratory was a distant memory, replaced by the phantom whispers of an ancient, ongoing war, fought not with weapons, but with thoughts, with memories, with the very essence of consciousness. And he was, perhaps, the only one awake enough to hear the call to arms.

The sheer audacity of it was breathtaking, a form of invasion so subtle, so deeply insidious, that it defied conventional understanding. Aris's meticulously compiled data pointed not to a grand fleet descending from the stars, but to a far more personal, invasive incursion. These beings, whatever they were, didn't need ships that could outmaneuver Earth's defenses or weapons that could shatter cities. Their method was far more profound: they phased. They slipped through the unstable portals, not as physical entities in the traditional sense, but as something akin to pure thought, or perhaps a form of energy that could directly interface with biological consciousness.

He pictured it now, a terrifying mental landscape. Imagine a mind as a vast, intricate city, with its bustling avenues of thought, its quiet alcoves of memory, its sturdy fortresses of logic. These entities, these unseen manipulators, didn't storm the gates. Instead, they found the cracks, the forgotten service tunnels, the ventilation shafts of the subconscious. They seeped in, not with a bang, but with a whisper. A seed of an idea planted in fertile ground, a subtle shift in perspective, a gentle nudge towards a particular emotion or belief. They were hijackers of the mind, not through brute force, but through exquisite manipulation of neural pathways and quantum entanglement within the brain.

His own experiences, the recurring déjà vu, the flashes of alien architecture that felt both foreign and strangely resonant, now slotted into this horrifying paradigm. He wasn't merely observing anomalies; he was experiencing the psychic residue of their passage, the faint scars left on his own consciousness as they brushed past, or perhaps even purposefully interacted with him. Were his intense episodes a sign of his mind's resilience, a subconscious defense mechanism kicking in against the invasion? Or, chillingly, were they a consequence of his own research, his probing into the very fabric of space-time inadvertently creating points of resonance, making him more susceptible to their influence, a beacon in the noise? The thought sent a shiver down his spine, a cold dread that had nothing to do with the ambient temperature of his study. It was the dread of a trespasser within one's own skull.

The historical data he had unearthed, the accounts of mass hysteria and societal shifts, were no longer isolated incidents of human irrationality. They were evidence, stark and undeniable, of their long-term strategy. The dancing plagues, the witch trials, the sudden outbreaks of irrational fear – these weren't random societal maladies. They were carefully orchestrated psychic events, the results of these beings subtly influencing populations, twisting collective thought patterns, sowing discord or unity as it suited their unfathomable agenda. He imagined them, not as aliens with silver suits and ray guns, but as weavers of perception, artists of the mind, their canvases the billions of human brains.

He found himself re-examining the details of the Kepler Belt disappearances. The official report cited environmental catastrophe, a sudden, overwhelming breach of atmospheric containment. But Aris now saw the energy signatures differently. They weren't just ripples; they were signatures of transit, of a direct, localized space-time distortion that allowed for something to pass through, not over. What if the colonists hadn't died from a lack of air, but from something far more profound? What if their consciousness had been accessed, their very sense of self disrupted, leading to a complete dissolution of their existence, leaving behind no wreckage, no trace, because the disruption had occurred at a level beyond physical matter? It was a terrifying thought, the idea that an entire human population could simply cease to be, not through violence, but through a fundamental alteration of their being.

He returned to the whisper, the single phrase that had haunted him, the enigmatic "Not ships. Within." It was the linchpin of his theory, the key that unlocked the terrifying door. They weren't coming. They were already here. They were integrated, interwoven into the very fabric of human existence. This wasn't a foreign invasion in the traditional sense; it was an infestation of consciousness. It was as if a virus had been introduced, not into the bloodstream, but into the very code of human thought, and it had been slowly, subtly rewriting humanity from the inside out, for millennia.

The implications for his own life were profound and disorienting. His entire career as a physicist had been dedicated to understanding the observable, the quantifiable, and the predictable laws of the universe. But this... this was beyond the observable. It operated on principles that skirted the edges of metaphysics, of consciousness studies, of ancient esoteric beliefs. He felt like a scientist who had accidentally stumbled into a forgotten temple, armed only with the tools of a laboratory, trying to decipher rituals and prophecies that defied every scientific paradigm he knew.

He considered the nature of his own déjà vu episodes more closely. He had always dismissed them as odd neurological quirks, perhaps triggered by stress or fatigue. But now, he saw them as potential points of contact. Each flicker of a familiar but unremembered scene, each sudden, inexplicable feeling of dread or recognition, was a ghost in the machine, a sign of his own neural network being momentarily brushed by something... else. It was as if his mind, in its quest for understanding, was inadvertently creating pathways, resonance chambers that allowed these alien influences to bleed through.

He envisioned the process as a subtle manipulation of quantum states within the brain. This non-local entanglement enabled the transmission of information, commands, and altered perceptions without any discernible physical carrier wave.

They were, in essence, broadcasting directly into the human mind, their signals modulated by the very structure of consciousness. The energy signatures he was detecting were merely the byproducts of this transmission, the 'noise' generated by the act of bridging dimensional barriers and interfacing with biological minds.

The sudden surge of paranoia in Neo-Alexandria wasn't an anomaly; it was a deliberate implantation of fear. The disappearances in the Kepler Belt weren't an accident; they were a consequence of a more aggressive, perhaps experimental, phase of infiltration. And his own experiences, the strange intuitions, the flashes of insight, might not be entirely his own. He was a product of his environment, of his upbringing, yes, but perhaps also a product of their long-term, subtle influence. Was his curiosity, his drive for discovery, a natural inclination, or a carefully cultivated trait, designed to lead him to this very point? The thought was profoundly unsettling, the idea that his own life's trajectory might have been nudged, steered, by unseen hands.

He found himself drawn to the more speculative theories he had previously dismissed out of hand. The ancient astronaut theories, the ideas of hidden controllers, the esoteric texts speaking of psychic manipulation and mind control – they weren't just the ravings of the delusional. They were perhaps fragmented, misunderstood accounts of phenomena that had been occurring for eons. The 'gods' of ancient mythologies might have been technologically advanced beings, yes, but their true power might have lain not in their technology, but in their ability to manipulate consciousness itself.

The weight of this realization pressed down on him, a crushing burden of understanding. Humanity, for all its perceived autonomy, might have been a pawn, its progress, its conflicts, and its very evolution, subtly guided by an intelligence that operated on principles so alien they were indistinguishable from magic. The fight, then, wasn't going to be fought with phasers or starships. It was going to be fought in the trenches of the mind, a battle for the very definition of reality, for the sovereignty of individual consciousness.

Aris Thorne, the physicist, was now a detective of the subconscious, an archaeologist of the intangible. The data on his screens was no longer just numbers and graphs; it was a map of an invisible war, a war waged not on physical battlefields, but within the silent, unseen realm of thought. The echoes of the familiar had become a deafening chorus, and he was the only one who could hear their desperate, urgent call to arms. He had to find a way to understand, to resist, and perhaps, to fight back against an enemy that was not only unseen, but intimately, terrifyingly, within. The next step was not to collect more data, but to understand the nature of the influence itself, to learn how to shield his own mind, and how to communicate, or at least, to expose these silent architects of human destiny. The quiet hum of the laboratory felt like a lifetime ago, replaced by the persistent, unnerving hum of something else, something ancient and pervasive, stirring within the collective human psyche.

2: The Bureaucratic Wall

The sterile glow of his study lamps illuminated the stark reality he had painstakingly pieced together. Aris Thorne, the physicist, now found himself burdened with a truth so profound, so terrifying, it threatened to fracture his very sanity. For weeks, he had plunged into the abyss of his own research, sifting through data streams that painted a picture of a subtly manipulated humanity, an existence guided by unseen forces operating beyond the veil of conventional science. The energy signatures, those ephemeral tears in the fabric of space-time, were no longer mere anomalies; they were deliberate intrusions, echoes of a pervasive, transdimensional influence. His own experiences – the unnerving déjà vu, the phantom memories of alien landscapes, the chilling whispers that seemed to emanate from within his own consciousness – were not isolated incidents, but undeniable proof of this insidious infiltration.

He felt an overwhelming compulsion to translate this nascent horror into something tangible, something that could be presented, examined, and, he prayed, understood. Thus began the creation of the report. It wasn't merely a compilation of data; it was a desperate cry into the void, a meticulously crafted testament to years of dedicated, and now terrifying, discovery. He began with the raw data: the precise spectrographic analysis of the energy signatures, noting their unique quantum entanglement properties and their uncanny ability to manifest in proximity to significant societal shifts or individual psychological stress. Each signature was cataloged,

cross-referenced, and contextualized against a backdrop of human history that now, through his eyes, appeared less like a linear progression and more like a carefully curated narrative.

He meticulously detailed the correlation between these energy spikes and periods of collective irrationality. The dancing plagues of the Middle Ages, the Salem witch trials, the sudden waves of mass hysteria that periodically swept through populations – these were no longer viewed as isolated historical curiosities or sociological phenomena. Instead, they were presented as probable instances of directed psychic influence, moments where the underlying consciousness of entire communities had been subtly, or perhaps not so subtly, altered. He illustrated this with specific examples, citing historical accounts of inexplicable paranoia, unshakeable beliefs that seemed to materialize from nowhere, and the subsequent societal ruptures that followed. He highlighted the specific energy readings that coincided with the

Neo-Alexandria paranoia, the uncanny resonance between the quantifiable energy fluctuations and the intangible societal breakdown. The data was presented with a stark, objective clarity, yet beneath the veneer of scientific impartiality lay them palpable terror of its implications.

Then came the Kepler Belt disappearances. The official explanation of catastrophic environmental failure felt laughably inadequate in the face of the energy signatures he had logged. He presented the data showing localized space-time distortions, impossibly precise and confined, occurring precisely at the time of the outposts' silence. He hypothesized, with a conviction born of sheer dread, that these were not accidents, but evidence of a direct, invasive interaction at a quantum level. This phenomenon could effectively erase entities from existence by manipulating their fundamental quantum state. The idea of beings who could unravel reality at its most basic level, not through brute force, but through an intimate understanding of its quantum underpinnings, was a concept that still made his breath catch in his throat.

The report delved into historical texts and ancient myths and legends, which, in his new understanding, transformed from fanciful narratives into fragmented historical records. He included excerpts from Sumerian tablets describing the Anunnaki and their role in shaping early civilizations, Egyptian hieroglyphs referencing celestial beings who "guided the Nile's flood," and Mesoamerican codices speaking of entities that "whispered the calendar into human minds." He carefully presented these not as proof of ancient gods, but as potential, albeit heavily mythologized, accounts of the same transdimensional entities he was now detecting. The convergence of these ancient descriptions with his modern energy readings was, to his mind, irrefutable.

Humanity had not simply evolved; it had been guided, its trajectory subtly altered by an external, intelligent force for millennia.

His own experiences, once a source of private confusion and concern, were now woven into the fabric of the report as case studies in potential psychic infiltration. He detailed the recurring instances of déjà vu, the precognitive flashes, the phantom sensations, presenting them as possible residual effects of direct mental interface. He theorized about the nature of these incursions, suggesting that these entities didn't possess physical bodies in the conventional sense but existed as some form of consciousness or energy that could directly interact with biological neural networks. The whisper, "Not ships. Within," became the cornerstone of his hypothesis: this was not an external invasion, but an internal one, a subtle hijack of the human mind itself.

The process of compiling the report was an ordeal in itself. He worked with a feverish intensity, his study transforming into a sanctuary of dread and determination. Sleep became a luxury he could barely afford, his nights filled with the phantom echoes of his own research and the gnawing fear of what lay undiscovered. Each word he typed, each data point he meticulously cross-referenced, carried the immense weight of his conviction and the sheer terror of his findings. He felt an overwhelming sense of duty, a responsibility that pressed down on him with the force of a collapsing star. The fate of humanity, or at least its continued autonomous existence, seemed to hinge on his ability to communicate this unthinkable truth to those who possessed the power to act.

He knew, with a certainty that chilled him to the bone, that this report would be met with skepticism, with outright disbelief, perhaps even with ridicule. The idea of an invasion waged not with armies or fleets, but with subtle manipulations of thought and perception, bordered on the fantastical, the realm of science fiction, not established physics. He, Aris Thorne, a man of empirical evidence and rigorous scientific method, was now presenting a theory that drew heavily on anecdotal evidence, historical myths, and his own subjective experiences, however quantifiable they might have become. It was a precarious position, a tightrope walk between groundbreaking discovery and perceived lunacy.

Yet, the data was too compelling, the correlations too striking, to be ignored. He couldn't unsee what he had seen, couldn't unlearn what he had discovered. The universe, as he understood it, had been irrevocably altered, its perceived reality exposed as a carefully constructed illusion, subtly influenced by beings who operated on principles so alien they defied comprehension. His years of dedicated research into quantum physics, into the very fabric of space-time, had inadvertently equipped him with the tools to perceive a threat that had been hidden in plain sight, woven into the tapestry of human history and consciousness.

He meticulously reviewed the concluding sections of the report, his fingers flying across the holographic interface. He outlined the potential ramifications of this prolonged infiltration, the possible long-term goals of these unseen entities, and the urgent need for further research into methods of detection, communication, and, if necessary, resistance. He considered the ethical implications of his discovery, the potential societal upheaval that could arise from such a revelation, and the necessity of a measured, strategic approach to disseminating this information. He debated whether to approach governmental bodies, scientific institutions, or perhaps even more clandestine organizations that might be better equipped to handle such an unprecedented threat. The sheer enormity of the task ahead was staggering, the path forward fraught with peril.

He felt a profound sense of isolation, a chilling awareness that he was likely the only person on Earth who truly grasped the magnitude of what was happening. The echoes he heard, the patterns he saw, were invisible to everyone else. He was a lone sentinel, armed with a terrifying truth, staring into an abyss that had been patiently waiting for humanity's collective gaze to falter. The weight of this knowledge was almost unbearable, a constant, oppressive presence that seeped into every aspect of his existence. He thought of his sister, of his friends, of the billions of unsuspecting lives being lived out under the silent, pervasive influence of these transdimensional manipulators. A wave of protectiveness, coupled with an overwhelming sense of responsibility, washed over him. He had to succeed. The alternative was unthinkable.

He stored the report on a highly encrypted, multi-layered secure server, a digital fortress built to resist any intrusion. He understood that simply the existence of this report, if it fell into the wrong hands, could be as perilous as the phenomenon it described. The knowledge itself was a weapon, and weapons, he realized, were often sought after and misused. He then began the painful process of deciding whom to approach first—those who might possess the intelligence, openness, and power to understand his findings and respond meaningfully. The journey from discovery to action was about to commence, and he suspected the bureaucratic barrier was only the first of many he would need to breach. The fate of his world, he now understood, depended not just on his scientific skill but also on his ability to navigate the intricate systems of human authority and belief, convincing them that the greatest threat humanity had ever faced was not a distant enemy but an unseen, intimate passenger. The sterile hum of his study now served as a constant reminder of the silent, pervasive hum of an alien consciousness, and he was its reluctant, terrified herald.

The sterile hum of the study lamps had faded, replaced by the cold, impersonal illumination of sterile government offices. Aris Thorne, clutching his meticulously compiled report like a shield, found himself navigating a series of imposing environments, each one a testament to the impenetrable nature of the bureaucratic wall he had anticipated, but still underestimated. His journey began not with a bang, but with a deferral.

The Pentagon, a monolithic symbol of terrestrial power, offered an initial, almost glacial reception. He had managed to secure an audience with a mid-level analyst within the Department of Advanced Research Projects Agency (ARPA), a man whose office was a testament to organized data: neatly stacked folders, a holographic display cycling through schematics of advanced weaponry, and a palpable aura of detached efficiency. Aris, still buoyed by the sheer conviction of his findings, laid out his case with the precision of a seasoned presenter. He spoke of quantum anomalies, transdimensional energy signatures, and the subtle, pervasive influence on human consciousness. He presented the spectrographic analyses, the historical correlations, and the chilling implications of an invisible, intelligent force subtly guiding humanity's destiny.

The analyst, a Mr. Henderson, listened with a practiced patience, his gaze occasionally flicking to the data streams Aris projected onto a nearby wall. There were no gasps of shock, no exclamations of disbelief, only a polite, almost imperceptible nod. When Aris finished, a heavy silence descended, broken only by the soft whirring of the holographic projector. Henderson steepled his fingers, his expression unreadable. "Dr. Thorne," he began, his voice even and measured, "your work on quantum entanglement is... noteworthy. The energy signature analysis you've presented is certainly novel. However." Here the familiar, dreaded word hung in the air, "the leap you're making from observable quantum phenomena to a form of directed, transdimensional influence lacks a sufficient causal link. We deal with empirical data, Dr. Thorne, quantifiable threats. What you've presented here borders on... speculative."

Speculative. The word landed like a physical blow. Aris tried to interject, to emphasize the sheer confluence of evidence, the historical parallels, the personal experiences that corroborated his findings. But Henderson raised a hand, a subtle but firm gesture that halted his impassioned defense. "Our mandate, Dr. Thorne, is to address tangible threats to national security. Cyber warfare, kinetic engagements, geopolitical instability. While we appreciate the theoretical frameworks you're exploring, they do not currently align with our operational priorities. We'll keep your report on file, of course. Perhaps in a future iteration of our threat assessment models, these... anomalies... could be integrated. But for now, thank you for your time." The dismissal was polite, professional, and utterly devastating. Aris left the Pentagon feeling the chill of that sterile office seep into his very bones. His meticulously crafted report, his desperate plea, had been relegated to a filing cabinet, an academic curiosity rather than an urgent warning.

Next, he sought an audience with a national security advisor, a woman whose reputation preceded her as a sharp, analytical mind. Her office was less ostentatious than the Pentagon's, but no less imposing. The walls were adorned with framed commendations and photographs of her meeting with world leaders. The air was thick with an unspoken gravitas. Aris felt a flicker of hope; surely, someone in such a position of influence would possess the breadth of vision to comprehend his findings.

He began again, his voice perhaps a little less steady this time, the memory of Henderson's polite dismissal still fresh. He focused on the potential destabilizing effects of such an influence, how mass hysteria, irrational decision-making, and societal breakdowns could be exploited or even engineered by an unseen force. He drew parallels to historical events, not just the Neo-Alexandria incident, but other periods of inexplicable societal shifts that had plagued human history. He spoke of the potential for these entities to manipulate global markets, to sow discord between nations, to subtly erode the very foundations of civilization from within.

The advisor, a Mrs. Albright, listened intently, her brow furrowed in concentration. She asked pointed questions, probing the methodology, the statistical significance of his data, the potential for misinterpretation. Aris answered with as much clarity and conviction as he could muster, his mind racing to anticipate her every query. He presented the Kepler Belt disappearances, not as a simple accident, but as a potential demonstration of the entities' ability to manipulate reality at a fundamental level, to simply... unmake.

When he concluded, Albright leaned back in her chair, a thoughtful expression on her face. "Dr. Thorne," she said, her voice carrying a weight that suggested she was genuinely considering his words, "your insights are... thought-provoking. The concept of indirect influence, of shaping societal vectors rather than direct conquest, is certainly a paradigm shift. However, the evidence you've presented remains largely correlational. While the patterns are intriguing, proving intent, proving agency, in the way you describe, requires a level of certainty that is, frankly, unattainable with the current observational tools available to us. We need actionable intelligence, Dr.

Thorne. Something concrete that we can verify, something that poses a direct, immediate threat that we can counter."

She paused, her gaze fixed on him. "To put it plainly, Dr. Thorne, you're asking us to believe in an enemy that, by its very nature, is invisible, intangible, and whose actions are indistinguishable from human error, societal evolution, or even simple coincidence. We are designed to combat tangible threats, threats that can be identified, analyzed, and neutralized through established protocols. Your hypothesis, while intellectually stimulating, falls outside our operational parameters. We cannot, in good conscience, allocate significant resources to investigating a phenomenon for which we have no verifiable proof of existence, let alone any clear strategy for engagement."

Aris felt a cold dread begin to spread through him. He had anticipated skepticism, but the sheer, unyielding adherence to their established frameworks, their inability to even entertain the possibility of a threat that didn't fit neatly into their pre-existing categories, was crushing. It was as if he were trying to explain color to someone who had only ever known black and white.

His attempts continued, a frustrating cycle of hope followed by polite, unyielding dismissal. He met with representatives from intelligence agencies, from scientific advisory boards, even from private research foundations ostensibly dedicated to exploring frontier science. Each encounter was a variation on the same theme: his data was intriguing, his intellect undeniable, but his conclusions were too outlandish, too unsubstantiated by the kind of hard, irrefutable evidence they demanded.

He found himself rephrasing, decontextualizing, trying to find an angle, a specific piece of data that would resonate, that would break through the ingrained skepticism. He highlighted the psychological impact of the energy signatures, suggesting that these entities might be exploiting human cognitive biases, amplifying negative emotions, and subtly altering decision-making processes on a massive scale. He argued that this was not just a theoretical threat, but a clear and present danger to human autonomy and self-determination.

One meeting, with a senior official from a clandestine intelligence branch, offered a glimmer of what felt like understanding. The man, whose name was redacted from Aris's notes, listened with an unnerving intensity, his eyes never leaving Aris's face. He asked detailed questions about the potential for these entities to influence technological development, to subtly steer human progress in directions that served their unknown agenda. He seemed particularly interested in the Kepler Belt disappearances, probing Aris for any additional details, any subtle anomalies he might have overlooked.

"You speak of 'whispers,' Dr. Thorne," the official said, his voice a low rumble. "Of internal voices. What if these aren't internal at all? What if they are direct data injections, bypasses of our sensory apparatus, directly into the neural network? If that were the case, how would we even detect it? It would be indistinguishable from our own thoughts."

Aris felt a surge of desperate hope. This man, at least, seemed to grasp the terrifying implications. He elaborated on the concept of "not ships, but within," explaining his theory that the entities were not physical beings in the conventional sense, but consciousness's that could interface directly with biological systems. He spoke of the subtle distortions in quantum states, the faint energetic resonance that his equipment had detected, suggesting these were the residual effects of such an interface.

The official listened, his expression grave. When Aris finished, he leaned forward, his voice dropping to a near whisper. "Dr. Thorne, your work is... significant. The implications are... profound. However, the very nature of the threat you describe makes it exceptionally difficult to verify, and even more difficult to act upon without concrete, undeniable proof. The channels through which you are attempting to disseminate this information are not equipped to handle phenomena of this... unconventional nature. We operate on actionable intelligence, on verifiable threats. We cannot afford to chase ghosts, Dr. Thorne, however sophisticated they may appear."

He then delivered the familiar, soul-crushing blow. "Your report will be archived. We will, of course, continue to monitor anomalous energy signatures. But to initiate a full-scale investigation based on your current findings would require a paradigm shift in our operational protocols, a leap of faith that, I'm afraid, our current framework does not permit."

Aris left that meeting with a profound sense of despair. He had come so close, had found someone who seemed to understand, only to be met with the same unyielding bureaucratic inertia. Each rejection chipped away at his resolve, each polite dismissal reinforced the terrifying reality: the system was not designed to recognize the threat he had uncovered. It was a system built to defend against the known, the quantifiable, the tangible. His enemy was none of those things. It was a phantom, a whisper, a shadow dancing on the edge of perception, and the world's gatekeepers could not see it.

He realized, with a chilling clarity, that the bureaucratic wall was not merely an obstacle; it was a feature of the system, an inherent resistance to anything that challenged its established paradigms. It was a defense mechanism, designed to filter out the noise, the speculation, the improbable. And Aris Thorne, with his terrifying truth, was precisely the kind of noise it was built to ignore. He was a scientist who had glimpsed a reality beyond the known. He was being politely, systematically, and utterly ignored by the very institutions that were supposed to protect humanity from existential threats. The weight of his knowledge, once a source of profound responsibility, was now a crushing burden, amplified by the suffocating realization that the most dangerous wall he faced was not made of brick and mortar, but of ingrained skepticism and procedural intransigence. He was adrift in a sea of indifference, his desperate message swallowed by the vast, echoing halls of bureaucracy. The silence that followed each failed meeting was louder, more deafening, than any alarm.

The sterile echo of closing doors became a familiar, demoralizing symphony. Aris Thorne found himself adrift in a sea of polite dismissals, each interaction a perfectly crafted performance of professional detachment that masked a deeper, more insidious rejection. The analysts, advisors, and officials he encountered were not outright disbelievers in a belligerent sense; rather, they were guardians of established paradigms, their minds finely tuned instruments calibrated to detect and respond to threats that fit within their meticulously defined parameters. His own meticulously compiled data, the fruit of years of observation and deduction, was too alien, too disruptive, to register on their instruments.

The initial hope that had fueled his persistence began to curdle into a bitter, icy dread. He had presented his findings, his evidence, his terrifying conclusions, with a clarity and conviction that he believed should have resonated. He had anticipated skepticism, of course. He was, after all, proposing a reality that defied conventional understanding. But he had not anticipated this pervasive, almost unassailable tide of polite incredulity, this systematic reinterpretation of his data through the narrow lens of conventional scientific and geopolitical frameworks.

At one particular meeting, nestled within the hushed, mahogany-paneled confines of a prestigious scientific think tank, the skepticism manifested as an almost condescending pity. Dr. Evelyn Reed, a woman whose formidable reputation in theoretical physics preceded her, listened with an air of detached, almost clinical interest. Aris, exhausted but resolute, laid out the correlations between specific energy signature spikes and documented instances of mass societal irrationality, the subtle yet demonstrable shifts in human behavior that, in his analysis, pointed to external manipulation. He detailed the anomalous readings from the Kepler Belt, not as equipment malfunctions, but as evidence of a deliberate, almost surgical pruning of exploratory missions, disguised as unforeseen technical failures.

Dr. Reed, after a lengthy period of silence, during which she carefully perused his projected data streams, finally spoke. "Dr. Thorne," she began, her voice smooth and even, "your analysis of the energy signatures is undoubtedly novel. The statistical correlations you've drawn are… intriguing. However, attributing these fluctuations to an external, conscious intelligence requires a significant inferential leap. We are aware of numerous geophysical and atmospheric phenomena that can produce transient energy readings. Furthermore, the cyclical nature of societal trends, while sometimes appearing inexplicable, is often a product of complex feedback loops within human social systems, amplified by mass communication and psychological contagion. What you are interpreting as directed influence, we might categorize as emergent properties of a hyper-connected, emotionally volatile global populace."

She paused, then offered a small, encouraging smile that felt more like a brand. "Your experiences with what you describe as 'déjà vu' are also fascinating. The human mind, under stress or prolonged periods of intense focus, can indeed create vivid, immersive internal simulations. The brain is an extraordinary organ, Dr. Thorne, capable of generating highly convincing perceptions that are not always tethered to external reality. Perhaps, given the immense pressure of your research and the… extraordinary nature of your conclusions, a period of rest and reflection might be beneficial. We have several excellent research sabbaticals available, or perhaps consulting with a behavioral specialist could offer valuable insights into managing the psychological demands of such pioneering work."

The suggestion, delivered with such practiced sincerity, landed with the force of a physical blow. It wasn't just dismissal; it was a reclassification. He wasn't a visionary uncovering a cosmic threat; he was a stressed scientist on the verge of a breakdown, his own mind playing tricks on him. The energy signatures weren't proof of an unseen adversary; they were faulty readings. The patterns of societal decay weren't orchestrated; they were the natural, albeit unfortunate, churnings of human nature. His own profound, recurring sense of having lived moments before, a phenomenon that had been a cornerstone of his dawning realization, was now reduced to a mere psychological quirk.

Aris felt a cold wave of despair wash over him. The very institutions that were supposed to be at the forefront of understanding and combating existential threats were, in their adherence to established protocols and their inherent inability to process anomalies, becoming the greatest obstacle. The lack of outright hostility was, in its own way, far more terrifying. Hostility implied acknowledgment, a recognition of the threat, however unwelcome. This was something far worse: a systematic, almost passive, erasure. His warnings were not being debated; they were being filed away under 'imagination' or 'stress.'

He tried to counter, to explain that his déjà vu wasn't a delusion but a tangible consequence of the entities' temporal manipulation, a glitch in the fabric of reality itself. He pointed to the consistent, verifiable data logs that corroborated his observations, noting that his equipment had never malfunctioned during these perceived déjà vu episodes, but had instead recorded the associated energy spikes. But his words seemed to evaporate in the well-appointed room, absorbed by the thick carpets and soundproofed walls, leaving no trace. Dr. Reed's smile remained, unwavering, a serene mask of professional concern that offered no ingress for his desperate truth.

The experience was not unique. Each subsequent meeting followed a disturbingly similar pattern. He met with representatives from national security agencies who, while acknowledging the existence of anomalous phenomena, categorized his findings as "low-priority" or "unverifiable." They spoke in hushed tones of potential foreign espionage, of advanced cloaking technologies, but never, not once, did they entertain the possibility of a non-terrestrial, non-human intelligence operating on a scale beyond their comprehension. His detailed explanations of transdimensional energy signatures and consciousness interfacing were met with blank stares or polite redirection to discussions of conventional cyber threats.

One official, from a branch dedicated to tracking exotic technologies, suggested that his instruments might be susceptible to a novel form of electronic warfare, designed to generate false positives. "It's possible, Dr. Thorne," the official had explained, his tone implying a generous concession, "that these 'signatures' are merely a sophisticated form of digital noise. The enemy is constantly evolving its methods. We must consider all possibilities before jumping to conclusions that lack concrete, actionable proof. If this is indeed a sophisticated deception, its goal would be to waste our resources, to distract us. And frankly, your current hypothesis, while... creative, plays directly into that strategy."

Aris felt a chilling realization dawn. They were not just dismissing his findings; they were actively reframing them to fit their pre-existing threat models, interpreting his evidence as confirmation of existing, understood dangers. The very intelligence designed to perceive the unknown was instead twisting the unknown into a distorted reflection of the known. The concept of an enemy that operated outside the established frameworks of warfare, of technology, of even material existence, was fundamentally unassimilable.

He found himself increasingly isolated. Colleagues he had once confided in now met his gaze with a mixture of apprehension and discomfort. Whispers followed him through the corridors of scientific institutions – whispers of "obsessed," "overzealous," and, most damagingly, "unstable." The very people who should have been his allies, his fellow travelers in the quest for truth, were now treating him with a cautious distance, as if his conclusions were contagious.

He continued to refine his presentations, to search for that elusive piece of data, that irrefutable artifact that would shatter the wall of disbelief. He focused on the subtle, almost imperceptible shifts in global economic markets that preceded major geopolitical events, correlating them with spikes in the energy signature. He argued that these entities weren't just observing; they were subtly nudging, manipulating the currents of human activity to achieve their unknown ends. He presented a chilling hypothesis: that humanity's rapid technological advancement, rather than being a product of its own ingenuity, was being subtly guided, its trajectory being steered by an unseen hand.

During one particularly disheartening meeting with a representative from a prominent philanthropic foundation that funded "cutting-edge scientific inquiry," the man, a Mr. Davies, listened with an air of profound boredom. Aris spoke of the potential for these entities to influence not just individual minds, but also the collective consciousness, to sow seeds of discord and amplify existential anxieties that would then manifest as geopolitical tensions.

Davies interrupted him, not with a question, but with a sigh. "Dr. Thorne," he said, leaning back in his plush leather chair, "your passion is evident. But what you're describing sounds like... well, like science fiction. Our funding priorities lie in areas that have tangible, measurable outcomes—advancements in medicine, sustainable energy, and AI ethics. While your theories are... imaginative, they lack the fundamental applicability that our benefactors expect. Frankly, the concept of invisible entities manipulating global consciousness is not something we can present to our board with any credibility. Perhaps you would be better suited to a different arena. Have you considered writing a novel?"

The suggestion, delivered with a dismissive wave of his hand, struck Aris with the force of a physical blow. It was the ultimate categorization: his terrifying reality was mere fiction, a figment of an overactive imagination, suitable only for entertainment. He left the encounter with a hollow ache in his chest, the weight of his knowledge feeling heavier than ever. The world, it seemed, was not ready for his truth. Or perhaps, it was actively, systematically choosing not to be. The silence that followed each meeting was not a passive void; it was an active, deafening negation of everything he had discovered. He was shouting into a void, and the void was politely, efficiently refusing to hear. The bureaucratic wall was not a barrier to be overcome; it was a manifestation of a collective, ingrained refusal to acknowledge a reality that threatened to dismantle their entire established order. And in that refusal lay the actual, terrifying danger.

The polite dismissals, once merely frustrating, began to take on a more disturbing quality. Aris found himself cataloging not just the logical inconsistencies in their arguments, but the subtle, almost imperceptible cracks in their carefully constructed facades of normalcy. It started with the eyes. A certain vacant stillness, a disconcerting lack of the micro-expressions that betray genuine thought or emotion. He'd first noticed it in an aide to a Senator he'd attempted to brief – a young man whose practiced deference seemed to falter, replaced by a brief, unnerving vacancy, as if his underlying programming had momentarily glitched. The aide had blinked, a slow, deliberate movement, and then resumed his professional smile, but the moment had lodged itself in Aris's mind.

He started to pay closer attention, his heightened state of alert, honed by years of vigilance against the inexplicable, now focusing on the human element of the resistance. It was in the unnervingly precise repetition of phrases. During a meeting with an undersecretary in the Department of Defense, the man had used the same condescending analogy about "chasing phantoms" that Dr. Reed had employed weeks earlier. It wasn't a shared professional idiom; it felt... rehearsed. A script is being followed with too much fidelity. Then there was the unsettling synchronicity. He observed two individuals in a waiting room, strangers to each other, both idly tracing the same pattern on their respective tablet screens, a subtle, repetitive gesture that felt more like a coordinated signal than a shared habit.

The bureaucratic wall, he began to suspect, wasn't simply a construct of inertia and ingrained skepticism. It was a deliberately erected barrier, manned by individuals whose minds, or perhaps even their very wills, had been subtly compromised. The stonewalling wasn't born of ignorance, but of a directed suppression. The aliens, the entities he was trying to warn humanity about, weren't just distant manipulators of global events; they were far more insidious, their influence seeping into the very fabric of human interaction, tainting the minds of those in positions of power and authority.

He recalled another encounter, this time with a senior analyst at a clandestine intelligence agency, a man named Sterling, whose office was deliberately nondescript, devoid of personal touches, as if to emphasize his institutional role above all else. Sterling had been particularly dismissive of Aris's data regarding the coordinated disruption of interplanetary probes, presenting a neatly compiled dossier of "equipment failures" and "unforeseen atmospheric interference." But as Aris pressed, detailing the precise energy signatures that accompanied each "failure," Sterling's composure wavered. His gaze, fixed on Aris's projected schematics, seemed to drift, losing focus. For a fleeting moment, his pupils dilated unnaturally, a rapid, almost insectile flicker that Aris had seen in footage of particular deep-sea creatures adapted to extreme pressure.

"Your equipment is highly sophisticated, Dr. Thorne," Sterling had said, his voice unnervingly calm, but with a subtle, tonal flatness that felt alien. "It's designed to detect anomalies. But sophisticated equipment can also be... susceptible to sophisticated deception. The human mind, for instance, can be subtly influenced, its perceptions altered without conscious awareness. We've seen evidence of such techniques, employed by various state actors, to sow confusion and misdirection."

The implication was clear: Aris was being accused of being a pawn in a sophisticated disinformation campaign, his own advanced technology being turned against him. But Aris felt a chill crawl down his spine that had nothing to do with the efficiency of Sterling's argument. It was Sterling's eyes again. As he delivered the fabricated explanation, his gaze met Aris's for a microsecond, and in that brief contact, Aris saw not the practiced skepticism of a seasoned analyst, but a profound, chilling emptiness. It was the same emptiness he'd glimpsed in the aide, the same vacant stillness he was beginning to associate with... something other.

He remembered an incident during a debriefing with a panel of astrophysicists, supposed experts in the field of extraterrestrial intelligence, though their focus was rigidly confined to SETI's conventional parameters. Aris had presented his findings on the deliberate sabotage of the Kepler missions, emphasizing the identical nature of the energy signatures recorded immediately prior to each probe's inexplicable demise. One of the astrophysicists, a Dr Aris, whom I knew casually from conferences, a man usually brimming with intellectual curiosity, had stared at the data, his expression unchanging. When Aris asked for his opinion, he'd responded, "It's... a lot of data, Aris. Very dense. We'll need more time to... process it." But his eyes hadn't moved from the screen; they'd remained fixed, unblinking, reflecting the glowing data points as if he were a sophisticated scanner himself, not a human interpreter. Later, Aris saw him speaking quietly with another panel member, both of them sharing a brief, shared glance that seemed to convey a silent, unnerving agreement. This mutual understanding bypassed verbal communication entirely.

This growing awareness of subtle anomalies wasn't born of paranoia, but of a dawning, dreadful comprehension. The entities were not merely observing or influencing events from afar; they were actively and deliberately seeding their presence within human society, co-opting individuals, corrupting their minds, or perhaps even replacing them entirely, turning them into unwitting or willing extensions of their own alien agenda. The bureaucratic wall was a facade, a carefully constructed illusion of normalcy designed to obscure a far more profound infiltration.

The evidence began to accumulate, like a series of tiny, almost imperceptible chips in a vast, seemingly impenetrable edifice. He noticed how specific key phrases, used by officials to dismiss his concerns, often bore an uncanny resemblance to linguistic patterns he'd observed in encrypted alien transmissions he'd managed to decipher partially. It was as if these phrases were being fed to them, implanted directly into their thought processes, or perhaps downloaded, like software updates for the human operating system.

He found himself scrutinizing every interaction, dissecting every word, every gesture, searching for that tell-tale sign of alien influence. He saw it in the unnervingly synchronized nodding of agreement from a group of advisors, all turning their heads in unison, their expressions identically blank. He heard it in the perfectly modulated tones of reassurance from a government liaison, a voice that, while professional, lacked any genuine warmth, any flicker of empathy. It was a performance, and the actors were flawless, chillingly so.

Aris began to record these subtle observations, meticulously documenting them in a separate, encrypted journal. He noted the precise timing of the vacant stares, the specific phrases that seemed to recur with unnatural frequency, the shared, almost imperceptible shifts in body language between seemingly unrelated individuals. He was building a case, not just for the existence of the alien threat, but for the extent of its insidious reach into the very heart of human governance and scientific inquiry.

The implications were staggering. If the entities could infiltrate and influence human decision-makers, then the bureaucratic wall wasn't just a testament to human ignorance, but a deliberate creation of the alien presence itself. The resistance wasn't organic; it was orchestrated. His warnings weren't being ignored because they were too outlandish; they were being actively suppressed by individuals who had, knowingly or unknowingly, become agents of the alien agenda.

He thought back to his meeting with Dr. Reed at the think tank. Her calm, reasoned dismissal, her suggestion of a sabbatical, her gentle redirection towards psychological evaluation – it all seemed less like genuine concern and more like a programmed response. The way she had so precisely dismantled his arguments, using terms and concepts that felt almost... borrowed, as if she were reciting from a prepared script.

Had she, too, been compromised? The thought sent a shiver of dread through him. The people he had believed might be his allies, the minds he had hoped would grasp the enormity of his findings, could very well be the very individuals tasked with ensuring his silence.

He remembered a particularly galling interview with a journalist, someone he had hoped would amplify his message. The journalist, a sharp woman named Sarah Jenkins, had listened intently, taken copious notes, and then, with a polite smile, had asked him a question that felt like a trap. "Dr. Thorne," she had said, her tone deceptively casual, "you've mentioned the similarities between these energy signatures and certain... anecdotal reports of psychic phenomena. Are you suggesting that these entities operate on a purely mental plane, or that they possess some form of telepathic ability?"

The question was designed to pigeonhole him, to reframe his scientific observations into the realm of pseudoscience, to make him sound like a fringe theorist chasing ghosts. He tried to steer the conversation back to the empirical data, to the quantifiable energy readings and the statistical correlations, but Jenkins skillfully, almost surgically, redirected him, her questions becoming increasingly focused on the subjective, the psychological, and the anecdotal. By the end of the interview, Aris realized with a sinking heart that the article would likely portray him as an eccentric, perhaps even deluded, scientist whose theories were more suited to speculative fiction than serious scientific discourse. He later learned that Jenkins had a

long-standing professional relationship with a certain defense contractor known for its advanced, proprietary surveillance technologies – technologies that might, he mused darkly, benefit from the widespread dismissal of truly alien threats.

The subtle anomalies began to coalesce into a pattern, a terrifying mosaic of compromised minds and controlled narratives. He saw it in the uncanny ability of certain officials to anticipate his arguments, to preempt his objections before he even voiced them. It was as if they had access to his thought processes, or at least to the trajectory of his investigations. He remembered a meeting with a high-ranking diplomat, a man whose entire career had been built on navigating complex international relations. Aris had been about to present his latest findings on the temporal distortions observed around certain "unexplained" disappearances of advanced research vessels. Before Aris could even open his mouth, the diplomat had calmly stated, "Dr. Thorne, while we appreciate your dedication to exploring... unconventional theories, our current diplomatic initiatives require us to focus on tangible threats, on established geopolitical realities. Speculative scenarios, however intriguing, do not align with our strategic objectives at this time. We must maintain a clear focus on the known." The phrasing was so precise, so perfectly calibrated to shut down any further discussion that it felt less like a policy statement and more like a pre-programmed response, delivered with an unnerving, robotic finality.

He started to notice a recurring, almost subconscious tic among some of the officials he encountered: a brief, nearly imperceptible flexing of the jaw, or a subtle, rhythmic tapping of a finger against a desk. These weren't nervous habits; they felt like unconscious neurological impulses, minor disruptions in the sophisticated control systems that governed their outward behavior. He began to wonder if these were the very individuals who were being subtly influenced, perhaps through low-frequency sonic emissions or targeted electromagnetic pulses, designed to alter their cognitive functions and ensure their compliance in a subtle manner.

The realization that the alien influence was not just external but internal, embedded within the very institutions meant to protect humanity, was a profound and terrifying one. The bureaucratic wall wasn't just a passive barrier; it was an active, sentient defense mechanism, operated by compromised human agents. The skepticism he had encountered wasn't mere ignorance; it was a weaponized form of denial, expertly wielded to maintain the illusion of control and to suppress any truth that threatened to unravel the established order. His fight, he understood with a chilling clarity, was not just against an alien intelligence, but against a subtly enslaved humanity. This humanity was, in its most powerful positions, already being controlled. The true danger wasn't just the aliens; it was the insidious corruption of the human will itself, the quiet, almost imperceptible erosion of free thought and independent action, leaving behind a hollow shell of obedience, a perfectly functioning cog in an alien machine. His warnings were not just falling on deaf ears; they were being actively silenced by the very people who should have been listening.

The silence that descended upon Aris was more profound than any audible sound. It wasn't a mere absence of communication, but an active, palpable void. His emails went unanswered, not with polite rejections, but with an unnerving lack of any response at all. Phone calls were met with automated voicemails that abruptly disconnected, or worse, with the chilling silence of a ring that never found a recipient. Colleagues, once eager to discuss his groundbreaking work, now actively averted their gaze when he entered a room, their hurried footsteps echoing the growing chasm between his reality and theirs. Dr. Evelyn Reed, a scientist whose intellectual rigor Aris had always admired, now met his attempts at contact with a series of increasingly strained and evasive excuses, culminating in a curt, almost apologetic email stating that her current research commitments made collaboration impossible. The implication hung heavy in the air: he was no longer a valued colleague, but a potential contaminant, a disruptor of the established order.

Funding, once readily available for his cutting-edge projects, dried up with a swiftness that defied conventional budgetary processes. Grant applications, meticulously prepared and theoretically sound, were returned with generic rejection notices citing "lack of immediate applicability" or "insufficient preliminary data," even though his preliminary data was precisely what had secured his funding in the past. It was as if a coordinated effort was underway to starve his research of resources, to choke it in its cradle before it could gain any further traction. The scientific community, a network he had always relied upon for peer review and validation, seemed to have collectively agreed to ostracize him. Invitations to conferences vanished, his name was conspicuously absent from speaking schedules, and even the forums where he could once freely share his findings became eerily quiet; his posts met with an indifference that was more damning than outright criticism.

He found himself branded, not overtly, but through a thousand subtle whispers and averted glances, as a purveyor of unsubstantiated claims, a man whose groundbreaking theories had curdled into paranoia. The carefully cultivated image of the brilliant, albeit unconventional, scientist was being systematically replaced by that of a deranged Cassandra, a man shouting warnings into an indifferent void. The narrative being spun, he suspected, was that his claims of alien infiltration were not the product of rigorous scientific investigation, but the manifestation of a deeply ingrained psychological distress, a projection of his own anxieties onto the canvas of global events. He was becoming a pariah, his reputation, once a shield, now a target, painted with the broad brushstrokes of scientific deviancy.

This forced isolation, however, rather than crushing his spirit, acted as a potent accelerant. The very act of being systematically silenced, of being systematically discredited, only served to solidify his conviction. If they were going to such lengths to discredit him, to cut him off, to sever his ties to the very institutions he believed he was trying to protect, then he had to be on the right track. The silence from the authorities, the sudden dearth of scientific dialogue, the palpable shift in his professional relationships – it all coalesced into a deafening testament to the insidious nature of the infiltration he had uncovered. The bureaucratic wall wasn't merely a construct of inertia and skepticism; it was an actively maintained barrier, reinforced by compromised minds, and he was now on the wrong side of it, utterly alone.

The realization gnawed at him. The people he had once considered colleagues, intellectual peers, and potential allies were either unwilling or unable to engage with the truth he was presenting. Their silence was a language he was rapidly learning to decipher, and it spoke of fear, of coercion, or perhaps of something far more chilling – a fundamental alteration of their own cognitive processes. He was adrift in a sea of manufactured normalcy, his own perception of reality diverging sharply from the consensus reality being so carefully curated by unseen forces.

He understood, with a certainty that chilled him to the bone, that his efforts to work through conventional channels were futile. The very system designed to facilitate scientific progress and national security was actively working against him. The people in positions of authority, the gatekeepers of information and resources, were either compromised, controlled, or simply too deeply entrenched in their own manufactured reality to break free. He was fighting a war on a battlefield where the enemy controlled not only the territory but also the very minds of those he sought to rally.

The need for new avenues and allies untainted by the pervasive influence became paramount. He couldn't operate within the stifling corridors of power any longer. His mission required him to seek out those who existed on the fringes, those who, like him, might have glimpsed the truth through the cracks in the facade, those who hadn't yet been assimilated into the system. This isolation, this severing of his established connections, was not an end, but a painful, necessary transformation. It was a shedding of the old skin, a preparation for a new kind of engagement, one that would require him to operate in the shadows, to forge alliances in unexpected places, and to trust his own instincts above all else. The paranoia, which had begun as a subtle undercurrent, now surged to the forefront, not as a weakness, but as a vital survival mechanism in this new, terrifying landscape. Every interaction, every overheard whisper, every averted glance, now carried the weight of potential betrayal, and the desperate hope of a hidden ally. He had to find them. He had to rebuild his network, not from the top down, but from the ground up, brick by painstaking brick, in the quiet, unobserved spaces where the truth might still find purchase. The battle for humanity was not being fought in boardrooms or government offices anymore; it was being waged in the unseen, in the subtle shifts of perception, in the quiet acts of defiance that would have to become his new language of connection.

The weight of his predicament settled upon him like a physical shroud. He sat in his sparsely furnished apartment, the hum of the city outside a muted reminder of the world he was fighting for, and the world that was increasingly alienating him. His research, once a collaborative endeavor shared with a network of trusted colleagues, had become a solitary obsession. Each new data point, each corroborating energy signature, each anomalous flight path, was now documented in encrypted files, accessible only to him. The irony was not lost on him: in his quest to expose an alien infiltration, he had become the ultimate solitary operative, an island in a sea of controlled information.

He recalled a conversation with Dr. Thorne, a leading astrophysicist whose early support for his theories had been a crucial validation. Aris had reached out to her again, hoping that the sheer weight of his accumulating evidence might sway her. Her response, delivered via a terse, encrypted message, was devastating. "Aris," it read, "I regret to inform you that our review board has flagged your recent research proposals as exhibiting concerning deviations from established scientific protocols.

While your initial hypotheses were intriguing, the current trajectory suggests a significant departure from empirical rigor. For your own professional well-being, I strongly advise you to seek a period of rest and reassessment. Perhaps consider focusing on areas where your unique insights can be applied without generating such… controversy."

The veiled warning was unmistakable. Thorne, like so many others, had been silenced, her professional integrity seemingly overridden by an external pressure. "Controversy." The word itself was a weapon, designed to isolate and discredit. His "deviations from established scientific protocols" were, in reality, the logical progression of his work, forced by the very nature of the phenomena he was investigating. The aliens, it seemed, were adept at manipulating not just technology, but also the very fabric of scientific discourse, framing any deviation from their desired narrative as inherently flawed or dangerous.

The funding crisis was equally severe. The private foundation that had previously underwritten a significant portion of his work, a foundation established by a visionary philanthropist with a keen interest in extraterrestrial studies, had suddenly ceased all disbursements. The official reason given was a "strategic redirection of resources towards initiatives with more immediate humanitarian impact." Aris had tried to probe further, to understand this abrupt shift in priorities, but the foundation's administrators had become as unreachable as the government officials. Their responses, when they came, were platitudes, polite dismissals that offered no real explanation. It was as if a collective amnesia had descended upon the institutions that were supposed to be at the forefront of discovery and defense.

He found himself scrutinizing every aspect of his former life, searching for the moment the tide had turned. Was it the sudden departure of his research assistant, a bright young woman named Anya, who had cited a family emergency and then vanished from his professional radar entirely? Or was it the inexplicably difficult retrieval of certain crucial data sets from the now-defunct Ares Initiative archives, a process that had been smooth and straightforward just months prior? Each discarded lead, each closed door, added another layer to the suffocating isolation.

The isolation, however, bred a fierce, unyielding determination. He was no longer fighting for recognition or validation from the established scientific community. He was fighting for the survival of humanity, and that fight had to continue, even if he had to wage it alone. The silence was his confirmation. The ostracism was his proof. They wouldn't go to such lengths to silence someone wrong. They were silencing him because he was right. After all, his findings represented an existential threat to their carefully constructed order.

He began to think of himself not as a scientist, but as a fugitive, a rogue element operating outside the system. His apartment became his bunker, his encrypted drives his arsenal. He lived on minimal resources, diverting any remaining personal funds to the essential upkeep of his equipment. The paranoia, once a creeping suspicion, was now a constant companion. This sharpened instinct told him he was being watched, monitored, and perhaps even infiltrated at a level he hadn't yet conceived.

He started to question everything, every interaction, every seemingly innocuous event. Had the friendly barista who always remembered his order been placed there to observe him? Was the late-night delivery driver a potential informant? These thoughts, while extreme, felt necessary, a form of mental self-preservation in a world that had suddenly become a hostile territory. The line between vigilance and delusion was blurring, but he couldn't afford to err on the side of naivete.

He knew he couldn't afford to remain in this isolated state indefinitely. While the solitude focused his mind, it also made him vulnerable. He needed allies, but not the kind he had once sought. He required individuals who were also outside the system, those who had been marginalized, discredited, or overlooked. He needed to find the cracks in the polished veneer of normalcy, the places where dissent and truth could still find fertile ground.

His thoughts turned to the vast, untamed territories of the internet, to the dark web, to the encrypted communication channels used by activists and dissidents. He needed to find the analog to his own situation, to locate others who had experienced similar rebuffs, similar silences, and similar attempts at discrediting their work. It was a dangerous path, one fraught with its own set of predators and deceivers, but it was a path that offered the only hope of rebuilding a network, a resistance, from the ground up.

The isolation was a crucible, forging him into something new. The frustration and paranoia were not debilitating flaws, but the necessary byproducts of his immersion in a reality that the rest of humanity was shielded from, or actively denied. He was on the right track, and the deafening silence from the corridors of power was the most compelling evidence he could have asked for. The game had changed, and he had to adapt to become a ghost in the machine, operating in the shadows, seeking out the few remaining embers of genuine inquiry and courageous dissent. His mission was no longer just about revealing the truth; it was about surviving long enough to reveal it, and perhaps, finding others who were willing to fight alongside him, even if their battleground was now entirely unseen. He was alone, but he was not defeated. He was merely being forced to find a new way to fight.

3: An Old Friend's Faith

The isolation was no longer a shield but a cage, and Aris felt its bars pressing in. Every avenue he'd pursued, every established connection he'd tried to leverage, had either dissolved into silence or twisted into a weapon against him. The scientific community, once his intellectual sanctuary, had become a hostile territory, its pronouncements echoing a narrative he knew to be false. The doors of institutions that had once championed his work now stood resolutely shut, their justifications increasingly hollow, and their evasions more transparently desperate. He was an anomaly, an outlier, a ghost in the machine of progress, his discoveries deemed too disruptive, too... inconvenient. The weight of this solitary battle threatened to buckle his resolve. He needed a lifeline, a tether to a reality that hadn't been so thoroughly corrupted. And in that desperate search, one name rose above the din of disinterest and dismissal: Eva.

Major Eva Rostova. His oldest friend. The bedrock of his adolescence, the constant through the turbulent seas of ambition and discovery. They had met as wide-eyed cadets, brimming with youthful idealism and a shared, almost audacious, belief in humanity's potential to reach for the stars. Eva, even then, possessed a rare clarity of vision, a no-nonsense pragmatism that balanced Aris's sometimes flighty, theoretical inclinations. While he chased abstract concepts and pushed the boundaries of the known, Eva meticulously charted the practicalities, the logistics, the unwavering discipline required to turn dreams into tangible reality. Her ascent through the ranks of the Space Force had been meteoric, a testament to her sharp intellect, her unparalleled dedication, and an innate leadership quality that drew respect and loyalty in equal measure. She was decorated, respected, a woman of action forged in the crucible of rigorous training and tested in the silent, unforgiving vacuum of space.

More importantly, Eva understood him. Not just the scientist, but the man. She had seen him at his most triumphant, buoyed by groundbreaking discoveries, and at his most vulnerable, grappling with the immense responsibility that came with his insights. She had been a silent witness to his anxieties, a steady presence when the weight of his research felt crushing. Her faith in him, even in their youth, had been a quiet, unwavering force, a counterpoint to the inevitable skepticism he faced from others. Now, adrift in a sea of manufactured doubt, Aris clung to the hope that Eva's faith might still endure.

He couldn't risk direct communication through standard channels. The thought that Eva herself might have been compromised, or worse, coerced into distancing herself, was a bitter pill, but one he had to swallow. He needed to arrange a meeting, a clandestine exchange, a conversation unmonitored and unadulterated by the pervasive reach of whatever entity was orchestrating this systematic silencing. His mind raced, sifting through potential locations, discarding them one by one. His apartment was undoubtedly compromised. Any official government facility, any nexus of military or scientific activity, was a minefield. He needed anonymity, discretion, and a buffer zone – a place where the usual protocols of observation and surveillance were either non-existent or easily circumvented.

His thoughts drifted back to his earliest days in the Ares Initiative, before the project had become the monolithic, impenetrable entity it was now. There had been an old observatory, nestled in the remote, rugged highlands bordering the northern territories. It was decommissioned mainly, a relic of a bygone era of astronomical exploration, its powerful telescopes long since superseded by more advanced orbital arrays. But it held a certain charm, a sense of quiet isolation that appealed to him now. It was off the beaten path, rarely visited, and its decaying infrastructure meant it was unlikely to be a priority for any sophisticated surveillance. More importantly, it was a place of shared memories for him and Eva. They had spent countless nights there during their early training, stargazing, debating the merits of hypothetical alien civilizations, and dreaming of the day they would personally encounter the wonders of the cosmos. It was a place imbued with their shared past, a neutral ground where their history could perhaps serve as a foundation for a crucial present.

He spent the next cycle meticulously crafting a coded message, embedding it within a seemingly innocuous academic query about obscure stellar cartography data. The encryption was layered, complex, a testament to the years he had spent safeguarding his own research. He sent it through a series of anonymized relays, bouncing it across secure, independent networks until it reached a designated, low-frequency comm channel known to be monitored by a small, discreet faction within the Space Force intelligence division – a faction Eva had, in the past, been known to liaise with for certain off-the-books operations. It was a long shot, a gamble with the very fabric of his digital footprint, but the stakes were too high for caution to be his primary guide.

The waiting was agonizing. Each passing hour felt like a lifetime. He replayed Eva's likely reaction in his mind. Would she understand the gravity of his message? Would she even receive it? Or had her loyalties, her perceptions, been irrevocably altered? The paranoia gnawed at him, whispering doubts into the hollow spaces of his solitude. He pictured her, immaculate in her uniform, her gaze sharp and focused, perhaps dismissive of what would appear to be an eccentric request from a former colleague. But beneath the polished exterior, he knew, lay the Eva he remembered – the fierce, loyal friend who had once defended him against a superior officer's unfair reprimand, her voice ringing with unshakeable conviction.

Finally, after what felt like an eternity, a single, encrypted ping echoed through his terminal. It was brief, concise, and carried the unmistakable digital signature of Eva's personal secure channel. The message contained only coordinates and a time, along with a single, cryptic phrase: "Same sky, different stars." It was enough. A confirmation. A promise. The embers of hope within him flared to life.

The journey to the old observatory was a study in calculated risk. Aris drove a nondescript vehicle, its registration meticulously scrubbed, its onboard systems wiped clean. He took a circuitous route, doubling back multiple times, utilizing service roads and lesser-known byways to avoid any potential tracking. The landscape grew increasingly desolate as he ascended into the highlands, the air thinning, the silence deepening. The sky above was a vast, inky canvas, already dusted with the first faint stars, a familiar, yet now ominous, spectacle.

He reached the observatory just as dusk began to bleed across the horizon. The structure itself was a haunting silhouette against the fading light, its dome cracked, its once-gleaming metal tarnished by decades of exposure. He parked his vehicle a considerable distance away, a common practice for hikers and urban explorers who occasionally sought out the remote location, and proceeded on foot, his footsteps crunching on the gravelly terrain.

As he approached the main entrance, a figure emerged from the shadows of the dilapidated structure. It was Eva. She was not in uniform, but wore practical, dark clothing that allowed her to blend seamlessly with the deepening twilight. Her posture was alert, her movements economical and precise, betraying her military training. As she stepped into the faint residual light, Aris saw that her expression was serious; her eyes, however, held a flicker of the warmth he remembered —a recognition that transcended the professional veneer she surely maintained in her daily life.

"Aris," she said, her voice low but steady, carrying easily in the quiet air. There was no surprise, no overt emotion, just a calm acknowledgment.

"Eva," he replied, his own voice feeling rough with disuse. "Thank you for coming."

She gave a curt nod, her gaze sweeping over him, a subtle assessment that spoke volumes. "The message was... unusual. And the location. We don't get many coded inquiries about obscure stellar cartography these days, especially not from you.

What's going on?" Her tone was direct, pragmatic, cutting straight to the heart of the matter, just as he'd expected.

They walked towards the observatory entrance, a gaping maw of darkness. The air inside was calm and still, carrying the faint scent of dust and decaying metal. A single, low-intensity beam of light emanated from a hand-held illuminator Eva carried, casting long, dancing shadows on the peeling paint and rusted machinery within.

"I wouldn't have asked for this if it wasn't critical, Eva," Aris began, his voice barely a whisper. "Everything I've been working on... It's true. The infiltration, the manipulation... It's happening. And they're systematically discrediting me, cutting me off from everything and everyone."

Eva stopped, turning to face him fully. The beam of her illuminator settled on his face, revealing the strain etched into his features, the undeniable weariness that had settled deep within him. "I've... heard things, Aris. Whispers. That your work has taken a turn. That you've become... obsessed. Some of your former colleagues have expressed concerns about your mental stability."

Aris flinched inwardly, but he held her gaze. "Obsessed? Yes,

Eva, I am. Because what I've discovered is real, and it's terrifying. And the 'concerns' are manufactured.

They're part of the silencing. They've silenced my funding, they've silenced my communications, and they've blackballed me from every reputable scientific forum. My emails go unanswered. My calls are routed to dead ends. Dr. Reed, someone you know, someone I respected... she wouldn't even meet with me. Just a curt email saying she couldn't collaborate."

He paused, taking a deep breath. "Eva, I know you have access. Access to intel, to resources that I no longer have. Please listen to me, not as a dismissed scientist, but as your friend. Please believe me. Because if you don't, if no one does, then we're all lost."

Eva remained silent for a long moment, her expression unreadable in the shifting shadows. She seemed to be weighing his words, her disciplined mind sifting through the improbable claims. Aris could feel the familiar tension of their early debates, the intellectual sparring that had always defined their friendship, but this time, the stakes were immeasurably higher.

"Tell me everything, Aris," she finally said, her voice devoid of judgment, yet carrying an immense weight of expectation. "Start from the beginning. And don't leave anything out. No matter how... far-fetched it may sound."

Aris felt a surge of relief so profound it almost buckled his knees. He had her attention. He had her ear. And perhaps, just perhaps, he had her faith. He began to speak, the words tumbling out, a torrent of data, observations, and terrifying conclusions, the story of his isolation and his burgeoning certainty unfolding in the echoing silence of the forgotten observatory, under the vast, indifferent gaze of the night sky. He spoke of the anomalies, the energy signatures, the subtle yet pervasive behavioral shifts in prominent individuals, and the chillingly coordinated discrediting campaign. He laid bare the evidence he had painstakingly gathered, the encrypted files, the intercepted communications, the patterns that only he, it seemed, could see. He spoke of his growing conviction that something fundamental had been altered, not just in the human populace, but in the very way reality itself was perceived and understood by those in positions of power. He described his systematic ostracization, the brick-by-brick dismantling of his professional life, the chilling efficiency with which his reputation had been eroded, all designed to isolate him and discredit his findings before they could gain any traction. He confessed his fear, not of his own demise, but of humanity's unwitting capitulation, of a future where freedom of thought and genuine discovery were sacrificed at the altar of an unseen, insidious agenda. He looked at Eva, searching her face for any sign of disbelief, any flicker of doubt that would confirm his worst fears. Instead, he found a stillness, a focused intensity that mirrored his own. She was listening and truly listening. And in that moment, the vastness of the cosmos outside the crumbling observatory seemed to shrink, replaced by the intimate, crucial gravity of their shared understanding. The old friend's faith, he realized, was the most potent weapon he had left.

The air in the hangar bay was thick with the metallic tang of dormant machinery and the faint, lingering scent of propellant. Dust motes danced in the sparse beams of light that pierced the gloom, illuminating the cavernous space like ethereal spotlights. It was a forgotten corner of a remote Space Force outpost, a place where obsolete craft rusted in quiet dignity, far from the gleaming, cutting-edge vessels that dominated the service's public image. Aris had chosen it deliberately. It was a place stripped of immediate association with Eva's current duties, a neutral ground that offered a semblance of privacy in a world that felt increasingly surveilled.

Eva stood before him, a figure of contained stillness. Her dark, practical attire, designed for utility rather than display, did little to soften the inherent authority she projected. Her gaze, sharp and assessing, met his, and for a fleeting moment, Aris saw the ghost of the idealistic cadet they once were, before the weight of command and the unforgiving realities of space had etched their lines upon her.

"You said it was urgent, Aris," Eva's voice was a low, steady resonance that seemed to absorb the ambient silence. There was no preamble, no wasted pleasantries. She was here because he'd summoned her through channels so obscure they bordered on mythical, and she expected a reason worthy of the risk.

Aris took a breath, the recycled air doing little to calm the frantic beating of his heart. He gestured to a grimy, overturned crate, a silent invitation for her to sit. He chose to remain standing, the restless energy that propelled him making stillness an impossibility. "Urgent doesn't begin to cover it, Eva," he began, his voice raspy, the words catching in his throat. He pushed past the polite introductions, the carefully constructed facades. "What I've found… it's not just a scientific anomaly. It's a threat. A fundamental threat to everything we understand about ourselves, about humanity."

He watched her closely. Her expression remained a carefully guarded fortress, her military discipline a formidable barrier against any outward display of shock or disbelief. He knew that beneath the surface, her mind was already processing his words, cross-referencing them with any intel, however tangential, that might have reached her.

"I've been cut off, Eva," Aris continued, his voice gaining a desperate intensity. "My research funding evaporated overnight. My access to data and networks was revoked without explanation. Every avenue I pursued, every colleague I reached out to… they either ignored me or actively worked to discredit me. My papers are being rejected, and my presentations are being cancelled. It's like I've been systematically erased from the scientific community." He felt a tremor run through him, a visceral echo of the isolation he'd endured.

"I understand professional setbacks, Aris," Eva's response was measured, her tone professional. "But this sounds like more than just academic disagreement."

"It is," Aris insisted, stepping closer. He knew he needed to convey the sheer, pervasive nature of the opposition he faced. "It's orchestrated. Every step of the way. They're not just disagreeing with my findings; they're actively suppressing them. And it's not just my work. I've seen… changes, Eva. Subtle at first, but now… undeniable. In people. In their responses, their decision-making, their very essence."

He lowered his voice, leaning in slightly as if sharing a dangerous secret. "Have you noticed anything… off? A strange uniformity in thought, perhaps? A reluctance to deviate from established narratives, even when those narratives are demonstrably flawed? Have you experienced moments where you feel like you've lived through a conversation before, a perfect recall of details that shouldn't be there?"

Eva's eyes narrowed almost imperceptibly. It was a micro-expression, but Aris, who had known her for decades, recognized it as a sign that his words had struck a nerve. He pressed on, his desperation fueling his narrative.

"I've been documenting it. The energy signatures that don't conform to any known physics. The way certain individuals, when exposed to specific resonance frequencies... they change. Their pupils dilate, and their responses become slower and more compliant. It's like a mental recalibration, a subtle overwrite." He pulled a small, encrypted data chip from his pocket, a device he'd meticulously shielded from any network that could be compromised. "This is just a fraction of it. The raw data, the observational logs. I can't show you everything here, but I can prove it. What I'm seeing is not just a scientific phenomenon, Eva. It's an invasion. A silent, insidious takeover of the human mind."

He watched her, searching her face for any flicker of recognition, any sign that she'd encountered similar data or suspicions. The weight of his discoveries, the terrifying implications, felt crushing, and he needed her to share that burden, to validate his sanity and his mission.

"An invasion?" Eva echoed, her voice still unnervingly calm, but with an undercurrent of something Aris couldn't quite decipher. Skepticism? Concern? Or something else entirely? "Aris, the nature of your research has always been... theoretical. Pushing boundaries. But an invasion... that's a profound accusation."

"I know how it sounds," Aris conceded, running a hand through his dishevelled hair. "And believe me, I've fought against believing it myself. I've spent months trying to find a rational explanation, a flaw in my own methodology. But the evidence is overwhelming. I've seen people I've known for years, friends, colleagues... their eyes seem vacant, their opinions strangely homogenous. They parrot the same platitudes, dismiss anything that deviates from the approved doctrine. It's like they're all reading from the same script."

He paused, recalling a particularly chilling encounter from the previous week. "I tried to talk to Dr. Jian Li, remember him? From the orbital mechanics team? We used to debate propulsion systems for hours. I bumped into him in the mess hall, and I tried to engage him in a conversation about the anomalies I was seeing. He just... stared at me. Blankly. Then he said, in this monotone voice, 'The approved consensus on atmospheric displacement remains the most efficient model, Aris. Anything else is inefficient speculation.' He didn't even seem to recognize me, Eva. Jian Li!" The memory sent a shiver down Aris's spine.

"The déjà vu," he added, his voice dropping to a near whisper. "I've been experiencing it with alarming frequency. It's not just fleeting moments; it's whole conversations, entire meetings. I'll be in a briefing, and suddenly I'll have a crystal-clear memory of that exact exchange, down to the precise phrasing of every participant. It's like... like my consciousness is being replayed, or perhaps, overlaid with something else."

Eva remained silent for a long moment, her gaze fixed on the data chip in his hand. Aris could almost feel the wheels turning in her mind, the rigorous logic of her training battling against the sheer audacity of his claims. She was a pragmatist, a woman of action and demonstrable results. Theoretical invasions were not her usual purview.

"You believe this is tied to your research on... extra-terrestrial resonance phenomena?" she finally asked, her tone carefully neutral.

"Not just tied, Eva. It is the resonance phenomena. Or rather, it's the application of it. Someone, or something, has weaponized it. They're using it to subtly influence and control thought patterns, to erase individuality, to create a perfectly compliant populace. And my discoveries about the underlying principles have made me a target." Aris's voice was strained, the raw emotion finally breaking through his carefully constructed composure. "I'm terrified, Eva. Not for myself, but for everyone. If this continues, if they succeed, there will be no more genuine thought, no more progress, no more humanity as we know it. We'll become... automatons, serving some unseen agenda."

He met her gaze directly, his own eyes pleading for her to understand the gravity of his words. "I came to you because I trust you. Because you're the only one I can think of who might have the resources, the perspective, and the integrity to see this through. I need your help, Eva. I need you to believe me."

Eva stood, her movements deliberate. She walked a few paces away, towards one of the derelict spacecraft, her back to him. The silence stretched, taut and heavy, filled only by the hum of distant life support systems. Aris's hope began to fray, replaced by a cold dread. Had he misjudged her? Had years in the service, the pressures of command, eroded even her steadfast loyalty?

Then, she turned back, her expression no longer entirely unreadable. There was a flicker in her eyes, a hint of something Aris recognized as the fierce resolve that had always characterized her.

"Your data chip, Aris," she said, her voice firm. "Give it to me. And then you will brief me—every detail. No omissions. I need to understand the scope of what you're seeing, the evidence you've gathered. My discipline is a shield, Aris, but it is not a blindfold. If what you're saying is true, then this is... a critical threat assessment. And I will treat it as such."

A profound sense of relief washed over Aris, so potent it threatened to steal his breath. He hadn't failed. She was listening. She was willing to look. He handed her the data chip, his hand trembling slightly. As their fingers brushed, a silent acknowledgment passed between them, a connection forged in shared history and a desperate, uncertain future.

"It's worse than you can imagine, Eva," Aris said, his voice hoarse with emotion, as he began to recount the chilling narrative of his isolated struggle, the meticulous data he'd collected, and the terrifying implications of a silent invasion that was already underway. The dust motes continued their silent dance in the dim light of the hangar bay, oblivious to the nascent battle that was about to be waged against an unseen enemy, a struggle that would depend on the faith of an old friend.

The weight of Aris's words settled in the vast, quiet space of the hangar bay, a palpable counterpoint to the echoing silence. Eva turned the small, cool data chip over in her gloved fingers, its metallic surface reflecting the sparse light in a distorted shimmer. Her mind, a finely tuned instrument honed by years of rigorous training and practical application, grappled with the sheer audacity of Aris's claims. An invasion. A silent, insidious takeover of the human mind. The words conjured images of overt warfare, of fleets descending from the void, not this subtle, pervasive erosion of consciousness.

Her professional instincts screamed caution. Every fiber of her being was wired to demand verifiable data, repeatable experiments, and irrefutable conclusions. Aris presented a narrative steeped in paranoia, a descent into the subjective realm of altered perceptions and déjà vu. Yet, the sheer, unadulterated conviction in his voice, the raw desperation etched into the lines of his face, refused to be easily dismissed.

Aris Thorne was not a man given to flights of fancy. His reputation as a brilliant, albeit unconventional, astrophysicist preceded him. He was known for his meticulousness, his unwavering dedication to empirical evidence. For him to present such a hypothesis, to risk his career and reputation in such a public, albeit covert, manner, suggested a level of certainty that demanded attention.

Eva found herself tracing the rim of the data chip, her thumb brushing against the etched circuitry. Aris had spoken of being systematically erased, of his research being suppressed, his colleagues disavowing him. This was not the typical fallout from a controversial scientific theory. This smacked of a coordinated effort, an attempt to silence not just a dissenting voice, but potentially, a dangerous truth. Her own experience within the Space Force, while shielded from the raw, unvarnished reality of Aris's isolation, was not entirely devoid of peculiar occurrences. She'd witnessed, and even filed, reports on certain inexplicable anomalies.

There had been the communication blackout during the Kepler-186f mission, an event officially attributed to a solar flare of unprecedented magnitude, yet the telemetry data had shown anomalies that defied conventional explanations. Then there were the psychological evaluations of personnel returning from extended deep-space patrols. A growing number exhibited a peculiar apathy, a subtle but discernible lack of emotional range, a tendency towards conformity that had initially been dismissed as the psychological toll of prolonged isolation. Eva had personally overseen several of these evaluations, noting the increasingly homogenous nature of the qualitative assessments. The patterns were subtle, almost subliminal, easily rationalized away as statistical outliers in the vast ocean of human behavior.

But now, hearing Aris describe his experiences with uncanny parallels, a disquieting resonance began to hum within her. His talk of "approved consensus" and the dismissal of anything that deviated from established doctrine struck a discordant chord. She recalled a recent inter-departmental briefing on resource allocation for long-range exploratory vessels. The debate had been unusually brief, the dissenting voices swiftly, almost preemptively, silenced by what seemed like pre-ordained arguments for a particular, seemingly unassailable, course of action. It had felt... rehearsed. Managed. She'd filed it away as an example of bureaucratic efficiency, but Aris's words cast a new, unsettling light upon it.

He had spoken of déjà vu, of experiencing conversations before they happened. Eva herself had experienced fleeting moments of intense familiarity, a sense of having traversed the same mental landscape before. She'd always attributed it to fatigue, to stress, to the inherent peculiarities of memory. But what if it was something more? What if these were not mere quirks of her own mind, but tangible symptoms of the very phenomenon Aris was describing?

Her mind sifted through the data chip's potential contents, imagining the raw observational logs, the energy signatures, the behavioral analyses. Aris wasn't asking her to believe in ghosts or aliens in the traditional sense. He was presenting a theory rooted in physics, in energy frequencies, in biological responses. And that, she had to admit, was a language she understood. The question was not if the data could be falsified, but why someone would go to such lengths to suppress it, and what that suppression implied about the nature of the discovery itself.

"You said your research was on extra-terrestrial resonance phenomena," Eva prompted, her voice carefully neutral, her gaze still fixed on the data chip. She needed to anchor herself to the tangible, to the scientific core of his claims, before allowing her mind to drift into the more speculative territories. "How does that connect to influencing human thought?"

Aris stepped closer, his posture radiating an earnestness that transcended the sterile confines of the hangar. "It's not about signals from distant stars, Eva, not in the way we usually conceive it. It's about fundamental universal frequencies, the very energetic fabric that underlies reality. My work focused on understanding how certain complex harmonic resonances could influence atomic structures and how they could be manipulated. I discovered that these same principles, when applied with extreme precision, can interact with the bio-electrical fields of living organisms, specifically the neural pathways. Think of it like tuning an instrument, Eva. A finely tuned resonance can create harmony, or it can induce dissonance. In this case, it's being used to induce a specific, predictable dissonance – a suppression of independent thought, an amplification of compliance."

He paused, gathering his thoughts, his eyes scanning Eva's face for any sign of comprehension, any flicker of connection. "The 'invasion' isn't a physical one. It's informational. It's a subtle, pervasive alteration of consciousness. The energy signatures I've detected are not emanating from a specific source like a broadcast; they are ambient, or rather, they are being subtly amplified and modulated through existing terrestrial infrastructure – communication networks, power grids, even atmospheric regulators. It's genius in its insidious simplicity. It targets the very way our brains process information, creating a feedback loop that reinforces conformity. The déjà vu... that's a byproduct of temporal data recalibration. Your mind is trying to reconcile the 'original' timeline with the 'altered' one. The personality shifts... that's the result of the resonance dampening critical thinking pathways and amplifying the neural networks associated with obedience and groupthink."

Eva absorbed his words, her mind racing to connect the dots. She thought of the increasing reliance on networked AI for decision support, the subtle nudges from curated news feeds, the algorithms that predicted and catered to every known preference. Was Aris suggesting that these were not merely tools of convenience, but conduits for something far more deliberate and sinister?

"You're postulating that these resonance frequencies are being deliberately broadcast, or amplified, to control populations?" Eva asked, the question tasting alien on her tongue. It sounded like something out of a sensationalist vid-drama, not a serious scientific hypothesis.

"Deliberately amplified, yes," Aris confirmed, his voice tight with conviction. "And the 'why' is as chilling as the 'how.' Imagine a society where dissent is not just discouraged, but rendered biologically impossible, where critical thought is replaced by unquestioning obedience. Where every individual functions as a perfectly integrated component of a larger, unseen system. It's the ultimate form of control, Eva. No overt oppression, no visible chains. Just the quiet, willing subjugation of the mind."

He ran a hand over his face, the gesture one of profound weariness. "My research was on the potential applications of these phenomena for advanced propulsion systems, for terraforming through harmonic resonance manipulation. I stumbled upon the evidence almost by accident, while calibrating sensor arrays. I detected anomalies in the background energy readings, fluctuations that didn't align with any known astrophysical models. When I tried to trace them, I found they correlated directly with periods of unusual global social or political stability, or conversely, with moments where significant dissent was effectively quelled. It was the data that refused to lie, Eva. It pointed to an external influence, a subtle but persistent hand guiding the collective consciousness."

He gestured towards the data chip again. "This chip contains the raw telemetry, the spectral analysis, and the predictive models I developed to isolate these frequencies from ambient noise. I've cross-referenced them with publicly available data on global atmospheric compositions, communication network traffic, even seismic activity – areas that, on the surface, seem entirely unrelated. But when you layer the frequency data, a pattern emerges. A symphony of control, played out on a planetary scale."

Eva felt a tremor of unease. The sheer volume of Aris's claimed data, the meticulousness of his cross-referencing, suggested a level of dedication that transcended mere academic curiosity. It spoke of a deep-seated fear, a desperate urgency to uncover and expose a truth he believed was vital. And his fear, she had to admit, felt... earned. His reputation for scientific rigor, his detailed explanation of the mechanism, the unnerving parallels with her own observations of subtle behavioral shifts in personnel – it all began to coalesce into a narrative that was becoming increasingly difficult to dismiss as mere paranoia.

"I've always prided myself on my objectivity, Aris," Eva said, her voice low, the words measured. "My training is to rely on observable facts, on logical deduction. These... resonance frequencies... they're not directly visible. The changes you describe in people are subtle, easily attributable to stress, environmental factors, or even individual psychological predispositions."

"And that's precisely the beauty of the design, Eva!" Aris interjected, his voice rising with a mix of frustration and a desperate desire for her to understand. "It's so subtle, so pervasive, that it masquerades as normalcy. It's designed to be invisible. It's meant to be indistinguishable from the background noise of life. But it's there. It's in the air we breathe, the data streams we consume. I've spent months trying to find an alternative explanation. I've run simulations, I've reviewed every known physical law, and I've even considered flaws in my own sensory apparatus. But the data... the data is consistent. And it's terrifying."

He leaned closer, his eyes locking onto hers. "Think about it, Eva. Have you ever felt a peculiar sense of unease, a feeling that something is fundamentally 'off,' even when everything appears to be in order? Have you ever found yourself agreeing with a consensus opinion, only to later question how you arrived at that conclusion? Have you noticed a growing... blandness in public discourse? A reluctance to engage with complex or challenging ideas, a preference for simplistic narratives and pre-packaged opinions? These aren't random occurrences, Eva. They are the measurable effects of the resonance."

Eva's mind flashed back to a recent news report about a series of coordinated protests that had fizzled out almost as quickly as they had begun, the participants seemingly losing their fervor without any apparent reason. She recalled the official explanation citing logistical difficulties and internal disagreements, but the suddenness of the collapse had always felt... abrupt. Too abrupt. And the subsequent public apathy towards the issues that had initially fueled the protests was, in hindsight, striking.

She thought of the increasing homogeneity in popular culture, the predictable algorithms that seemed to churn out variations on themes that had already proven successful, stifling true innovation. The media landscape, once a vibrant, if often chaotic, marketplace of ideas, had become increasingly narrow, with its narratives converging on a few dominant, and usually unchallenged, themes. It was a trend she'd noted with mild disappointment, attributing it to market forces and shifting consumer tastes. But Aris's theory suggested a far more active and sinister manipulation at play.

"I admit, Aris," Eva said, her voice barely above a whisper, her gaze now fixed on a point somewhere in the middle distance, her mind replaying fragmented memories and observations, "there have been... moments. Disquieting observations. Instances that, at the time, I couldn't quite contextualize. I've always pushed them aside, compartmentalized them as statistical noise, or the natural vagaries of human behavior and perception. However, your hypothesis offers a framework. A terrifying one, but a framework nonetheless."

She looked back at Aris, a flicker of something akin to grudging respect in her eyes. "You're asking me to believe in an invisible force that fundamentally alters human consciousness, a force so subtle it masquerades as normalcy, and that has been deliberately deployed. That's a leap, Aris. A significant leap."

"It's a leap, yes," Aris conceded, his voice softening, sensing the shift in her demeanor. "But it's a leap that the evidence demands. I'm not asking you to discard your scientific principles, Eva. I'm asking you to apply them to data that has been systematically suppressed. I'm asking you to consider that the 'noise' you've been hearing might actually be the signal. My reputation as a scientist is built on empirical evidence, and everything I've gathered points to this conclusion. It's the only explanation that fits all the facts."

He held out the data chip towards her again, his hand steady now. "This is your chance to verify it. To see the patterns for yourself. To apply your own formidable intellect to the data. If I'm wrong, then we've had a very elaborate, and frankly, quite alarming, misunderstanding. But if I'm right, Eva… if I'm right, then this is the most critical threat humanity has ever faced. And your skepticism, while understandable, could be our undoing."

Eva took the data chip. Her fingers closed around it, the cool metal a stark contrast to the heat that was beginning to build within her. She met Aris's earnest gaze, seeing not a raving madman, but a brilliant scientist who had stumbled upon a truth so profound, so terrifying, that it had shattered his world. Her own world, built on logic and order, was starting to feel a little less stable. The faith of an old friend, coupled with the unsettling whispers of her own experience, was beginning to erode the foundations of her carefully constructed skepticism. She could feel the weight of his trust, the burden of his discoveries, settling upon her. And as she turned the chip over in her hand, a single, chilling thought echoed in the vast, quiet hangar: what if he was right?

Eva's quarters aboard the Odyssey were Spartan by design, a reflection of her pragmatic nature. Functionality trumped form, and the limited space was meticulously organized. Yet, as she sat at her personal terminal, the sterile efficiency felt different tonight. It felt like a sanctuary, a quiet space from which to initiate her own clandestine inquiry. The data chip Aris had given her felt deceptively innocuous, a mere sliver of polished metal and etched silicon. But within it lay the potential to dismantle everything she understood about her reality, or to confirm the deepest, most chilling fears of a man she'd known and respected for years.

Her fingers, usually so steady on the controls of a starfighter, now moved with a deliberate, almost reverent slowness as she inserted the chip into a secure, offline reader. The terminal hummed to life, its familiar interface a comforting counterpoint to the unsettling implications of Aris's claims. She initiated a series of diagnostic sweeps, a habit ingrained from years of dealing with sensitive matériel, ensuring no trace of her activity would be left behind. The data unfolded before her—raw observational logs, complex spectral analyses, predictive models that hummed with an alien logic. Aris wasn't just theorizing; he had numbers, patterns, correlations that, if genuine, were damning.

Her first step was to cross-reference Aris's findings with classified reports she had access to through her security clearance. She started with events that had been publicly dismissed or vaguely explained away, incidents that had pricked at her professional intuition even at the time. The Kepler-186f mission, the one officially blamed on a solar flare, was her starting point. Aris's data showed peculiar energy fluctuations during the period of communication blackout, signatures that didn't match any known solar phenomenon. They were subtle, almost imperceptible against the background cosmic radiation, but when isolated and amplified according to Aris's parameters, they formed a distinct, resonant pattern. A pattern that Aris claimed was consistent with his hypothesis of modulated energy frequencies influencing biological systems.

Eva meticulously compared the timestamps, the geographical coordinates, and the spectral readings. The official report cited an "unprecedented coronal mass ejection," a convenient catch-all for inexplicable solar activity. But Aris's analysis suggested something else entirely. His models indicated a localized, highly focused energy wave, not originating from the sun, but seemingly… interacting with the ship's systems in a way that disrupted communication by subtly altering the neural processing of the crew, inducing a brief state of sensory overload and confusion. It was a far more elegant and terrifying explanation for why the mission data had gone dark and why the crew's subsequent psychological evaluations had shown subtle but persistent cognitive blips that were ultimately dismissed as post-traumatic stress.

Then there were the reports of increasing psychological anomalies among deep-space personnel. Eva recalled several debriefings where she had noted a disconcerting trend: a growing apathy, a flattening of emotional responses, a disturbingly uniform adherence to protocol that bordered on the robotic. These were the same observations Aris had made. He had provided data correlating these behavioral shifts with specific periods where his detected resonance frequencies were most pronounced. His analysis suggested these frequencies weren't just disrupting external communications; they were directly impacting the crew's own internal communication networks – their neural pathways. The "unwavering dedication to protocol" that was lauded as a sign of professionalism, in Aris's view, was a direct consequence of a dampened capacity for critical thought and independent decision-making.

A particularly unsettling incident resurfaced in her mind. It involved a high-ranking official, Ambassador Thorne, a distant relative of Aris, though Eva had only known him through official channels. During a critical diplomatic negotiation with a newly contacted alien species, the Xylos, Ambassador Thorne had abruptly. They inexplicably altered the Federation's stance, capitulating to terms that were demonstrably disadvantageous and deeply unpopular with the negotiating committee. Eva remembered watching the televised address where Thorne announced the new policy. His eyes, usually sharp and full of life, had seemed... vacant. Unfocused. He had delivered his lines with an unnerving smoothness, a rehearsed conviction that had struck her as odd at the time, but which she had attributed to the immense pressure of the negotiations.

Now, replaying that memory, a cold dread began to bloom in her chest. Aris's data included spectral analysis of global broadcasts from that period. He had identified a spike in the resonance frequencies correlating precisely with Ambassador Thorne's address, and indeed, with the period leading up to his policy shift. Aris theorized that these frequencies, amplified through the much broadcast networks used to disseminate information, could directly influence neural activity. Thorne hadn't just been under pressure; he had, according to Aris's data, been subtly manipulated. His decision wasn't his own; it was a response to an external, resonant influence.

Eva delved deeper, pulling up encrypted internal memos, redacted incident reports, anything that hinted at anomalies beyond the officially acknowledged. She found a series of reports detailing unusual disruptions in interplanetary communication networks, incidents that were always attributed to solar flares, equipment malfunction, or simple signal interference. Yet, when she applied Aris's filtering algorithms to the raw telemetry from these events, she found the same subtle, resonant signature he had identified. It was like finding a watermark on every piece of paper, proof that a hidden hand had been at work.

She cross-referenced the resonance peaks with periods of significant global policy shifts, moments where public opinion had coalesced with unnerving speed around a particular narrative, or where dissent had been effectively quashed with surprising ease. The data was compelling, a tapestry woven from disparate threads that, when viewed through Aris's lens, revealed a chilling, consistent pattern. He had spoken of "approved consensus" and the suppression of anything that deviated from established doctrine. Eva now saw it everywhere: in the rapid shutdown of a promising research project into exotic energy sources, in the swift dismissal of a scientist who questioned the safety protocols for a new atmospheric terraforming technology, in the way public discourse seemed to have narrowed, favoring simplistic, reassuring narratives over complex, challenging ideas.

She remembered a conversation she'd had with her former mentor, Dr. Jian Li, a renowned xenolinguist. He had expressed frustration about the slow progress of interspecies communication, lamenting a perceived lack of intellectual curiosity within the Federation, a tendency to impose human cognitive frameworks onto alien thought processes. At the time, she had chalked it up to academic pedantry. Now, she wondered if Dr. Li had unknowingly been an early victim, his own cognitive pathways subtly nudged towards a more compliant, less explorative mindset.

Eva's training required empirical proof and reproducible results. Aris had provided the raw data, but the interpretation, the conclusion, was still a monumental leap. She needed to find something more concrete, something undeniable. She focused her search on events where the resonance signature was powerful, cross-referencing them with instances of widespread, uncharacteristic behavioral shifts. One incident stood out: a planetary referendum on interstellar colonization that had seen an overwhelming, near-unanimous vote in favor of a dangerous, unproven colonization plan. The public discourse leading up to the vote had been heavily swayed by what appeared to be manufactured consensus, with dissenting voices drowned out by a chorus of seemingly patriotic fervor. Aris's data indicated a powerful, prolonged resonance event coinciding precisely with the period of intense propaganda and voting.

This was more than just a pattern; it was a narrative. Aris wasn't a madman. He was a scientist who had uncovered a reality far more insidious than any overt invasion. The "invasion" wasn't a fleet of ships; it was a silent manipulation of consciousness, a subtle rewiring of the human psyche on a planetary scale, executed through the very infrastructure of modern civilization. The implications were staggering. If Aris was right, then humanity was not making its own choices; it was being guided, controlled, and steered towards an unknown, perhaps predetermined, destination.

Her fingers flew across the console, pulling up the personnel files for the individuals involved in the analysis and dissemination of the Kepler-186f mission data. She noted the unusual number of individuals who had, in the aftermath, been reassigned to less critical roles or had voluntarily taken early retirement, citing "personal reasons." These weren't isolated incidents; they were clear signs of a systemic effort to silence those who might have noticed something amiss. Aris Thorne was not the only one being systematically erased. He was merely the one who had fought back.

Eva felt a growing sense of urgency, a gnawing realization that the data chip was not just a collection of numbers; it was a desperate plea for help, a testament to a truth that had cost Aris everything. She needed to verify his findings, not just for Aris, but for herself, for everyone. The subtle unease she had felt, the fleeting moments of déjà vu, the growing blandness of public discourse – they were no longer abstract observations. They were data points in a vast, terrifying experiment. The faith of an old friend, coupled with the unsettling whispers of her own experiences, was forcing her to confront a reality that defied every logical explanation she had ever known. She was standing on the precipice of a revelation, and the descent was proving to be far more perilous than she could have imagined. The seed of doubt, planted by Aris, had taken root, and it was rapidly blossoming into a forest of terrifying possibilities. She looked again at the data chip, the weight of it now feeling like the fate of worlds. The quiet hum of her terminal was no longer a comfort; it was the sound of a Pandora's Box beginning to creak open.

The stark reality of Aris's data pressed down on Eva, a tangible weight that settled in the pit of her stomach. The sheer scope of his findings, the chilling consistency with which they appeared across disparate datasets, left no room for denial. He wasn't fabricating; he was excavating. He had stumbled upon a truth so profound, so fundamentally disruptive to the established order, that it was being systematically buried. The thought of Aris, a man she had known for years, a colleague whose integrity she had never once questioned, being silenced, discredited, or worse, sent a cold wave of anger through her. The Kepler-186f incident, Ambassador Thorne's inexplicable capitulation, the creeping cognitive blips in deep-space crews – they weren't isolated anomalies. They were keystones in a terrifyingly deliberate structure of manipulation.

Eva leaned back, the sterile glow of her terminal reflecting in her eyes. The official channels, the very system she had dedicated her life to serving, were compromised. Reporting Aris's findings through the usual chain of command would be akin to handing him over to the very forces he was trying to expose. The data was too explosive, too paradigm-shattering. It would be buried, twisted, or used to further the agenda of those who benefited from the pervasive, subtle control. She saw it now, the invisible currents that had guided humanity's trajectory, steering it away from certain discoveries, nudging public opinion, and smoothing over any rough edges that might awaken the populace to its own subjugation.

A quiet resolution began to form within her. Aris Thorne was not asking for her to validate his research; he was asking for her to believe him. He was reaching out from the abyss, a solitary voice against an unseen enemy, and his faith in her, in her ability to see beyond the carefully constructed facade, was a profound responsibility. She couldn't abandon him. More importantly, she couldn't leave the truth he had unearthed. The threat wasn't an external invasion of warships and ray guns; it was far more insidious, an invasion of the mind, a quiet erosion of free will conducted through the very technologies and systems that connected them all.

Her decision was made not with a dramatic pronouncement, but with a subtle, almost imperceptible shift in her posture, a tightening of her jaw, and a renewed focus that burned brighter than the data streams before her. She would help Aris, not as an officer of the Federation, but as an individual committed to truth. This meant operating outside the established protocols, leveraging her skills and access in ways that would undoubtedly be deemed unauthorized, even treasonous, if discovered. The stakes were unimaginably high. The danger wasn't just from whatever alien intelligence was orchestrating this, but from the very human elements within the Federation, which was either complicit or too blind to see.

The first step was establishing a secure, untraceable communication channel with Aris. Her terminal, while capable of handling sensitive data, was inherently tied to the Federation network. She needed a ghost in the machine, a way to communicate without leaving a digital footprint that could be traced back to her. Eva's mind raced, sifting through protocols and backdoors she had encountered over the years, not for malicious intent, but for the sheer intellectual challenge of understanding systems' vulnerabilities. There was a rarely used, highly encrypted, sub-ether comms protocol, designed for extreme emergency situations where standard channels were believed to be compromised. It was clunky, inefficient, and almost forgotten, but its very obscurity made it ideal for her current needs.

She began by fabricating a series of routine system checks, meticulously documenting each step as if preparing for a standard diagnostic. Under the guise of these mundane tasks, she began to weave her way through the network's deeper layers, implanting a small, self-erasing subroutine that would establish a temporary, encrypted link with a known secure node Aris had indicated in his initial, less compromised communications. It was a delicate dance, a digital tightrope walk. One misplaced command, one unexpected network sweep, and her clandestine operation would be exposed before it had even truly begun.

As the subroutine initiated, a small, green indicator blinked on her terminal, almost imperceptibly. The link was established. Now, she had to transmit her intention without revealing too much. She composed a short, coded message, using a cryptographic key they had devised years ago during a simulated intelligence crisis exercise. It was a long shot, a message buried in the noise of routine data exchange, but it was all she had.

"Thorne, observation confirmed. Initiating independent analysis. Await further directive. E."

She sent the message, her heart pounding a rhythm against her ribs. The transmission was instantaneous, a whisper across the vastness of space. She then meticulously scrubbed all logs of the subroutine's creation and execution, ensuring that not a single byte of evidence remained. The silence that followed was deafening, broken only by the hum of the Odyssey's life support systems. Had he received it? Would he understand?

Eva spent the next few hours in a state of heightened awareness, her senses attuned to every subtle change in her environment. She imagined Federation security protocols, the unseen eyes that constantly monitored network traffic, the algorithms designed to detect anomalies. She knew the risks. If her actions were discovered, she would face court-martial, likely imprisonment, and her career, her life's work, would be irrevocably destroyed. But the thought of inaction, of letting Aris's warning go unheeded, was a far greater burden. The subtle manipulation he described was a cancer, and it was spreading. Allowing it to continue unchecked was a betrayal of everything she believed in, a betrayal of the very humanity she was fighting to protect.

Her mind kept returning to Ambassador Thorne's vacant eyes, to the chilling efficiency with which dissenting opinions were silenced, to the growing conformity that Aris had meticulously documented. This wasn't just about protecting Aris; it was about reclaiming the very essence of human agency. The Federation, founded on the principles of exploration, reason, and self-determination, was becoming something else. Something controlled. Something... predictable. And if the source of that control was an external, non-human intelligence, then humanity was facing an existential threat far greater than any interstellar war.

The need for allies, however limited, became acutely apparent. Aris was a brilliant scientist, but he was also an outcast, his reputation in tatters. Eva, on the other hand, still operated within the system, albeit with increasing discretion. She needed someone she could trust implicitly, someone with a similar analytical mind and a healthy skepticism for the official narrative. The name that came to mind was Commander Jian Li, a brilliant astrophycisist and former mentor of hers, renowned for his rigorous scientific approach and his stubborn refusal to accept easy answers. He was currently stationed on a deep-space research outpost, ostensibly studying gravimetric anomalies, but Eva knew his true passion lay in deciphering the universe's most confounding puzzles.

Reaching out to Jian would be another risk. His outpost was isolated, but still connected to the wider Federation network. She would have to be even more circumspect. She decided to frame her inquiry as a purely academic one, a request for his expert opinion on some of the more complex spectral analyses Aris had provided. She would present it as a theoretical exercise, a thought experiment, carefully omitting any direct mention of Aris or his specific claims of manipulation. The goal was to gauge his reaction, to see if his intellect could recognize the patterns she had identified, without tipping him off to the whole, dangerous truth.

She began drafting a secure, encrypted message to Commander Li. She would need to be subtle, weaving her request within a broader discussion of astrophysics, seeding it with the very data points that had convinced her.

"Commander Li, I hope this message finds you well amidst your gravimetric studies.

I've been reviewing some rather... unconventional data sets related to recent deep-space phenomena, specifically the energy signatures recorded during the Kepler-186f incident. I've encountered some peculiar spectral patterns that don't align with standard astrophysical models. I've attempted to isolate and analyze these anomalies using advanced filtering techniques, but the results are yielding rather... unexpected correlations. I recall your fascination with emergent properties in complex systems, and I was hoping you might lend your unique perspective to these findings. Specifically, I'm interested in your thoughts on the potential for modulated energy frequencies to influence localized atmospheric conditions or even... the subtle interactions within electromagnetic fields that could have cascading effects on sensitive instruments, and perhaps even biological systems. Any insights you might offer on unusual resonance phenomena would be invaluable."

She reread the message, tweaking phrases, softening language where necessary, ensuring it sounded like the genuine curiosity of a fellow scientist rather than the desperate gambit of a conspirator. The challenge was to present the data in such a way that it would spark his analytical fire, to allow him to arrive at the same terrifying conclusions independently. It was a dangerous game of chess, played with incomplete information and the fate of humanity hanging in the balance.

As Eva prepared to send her message, a chime from her personal comm unit broke the tense silence. It was a priority alert, originating from Aris's last known secure location. Her breath hitched. She initiated the comms link, her fingers trembling slightly. The face that appeared on her screen was gaunt, his eyes hollowed with exhaustion and fear, but there was a flicker of something akin to triumph in their depths.

"Eva," Aris's voice was a raspy whisper, strained but clear. "Did you get my data?" "I did, Aris," Eva replied, keeping her voice steady. "It's... significant."

"Significant doesn't begin to cover it," he choked out, a dry cough wracking his frame. "They know I transmitted. I've had to go dark. I'm at a safe house, but I don't know for how long. They're hunting me, Eva. Not just the internal security, but... them. The ones I told you about."

Eva's blood ran cold. "Aris, you need to be careful. I'm initiating my own investigation, but I have to be discrete. I can't risk going through official channels yet. They'll shut me down before I even start."

"Of course," Aris rasped, a hint of understanding in his voice. "That's why I came to you. You're the only one I trusted not to dismiss it. But Eva, listen to me. This isn't just about us. It's about everyone. They're not just influencing events; they're shaping minds. They're steering our entire civilization towards... something. And I don't think it's in our best interest." He coughed again, a ragged, painful sound. "I've managed to secure a secondary data cache. It contains further evidence, more detailed operational logs of their resonance emitters, and… something even more disturbing. It's located at a derelict research outpost, sector Gamma-7, designation 'Echo Station.' It's a long shot, and it's heavily guarded by automated systems that have been reactivated. But if you can get it, it will be crucial. It's the key to understanding the full scope of their operations."

Eva absorbed his words, the urgency of his situation palpable. "Echo Station. I understand. I'll make arrangements."

"Be careful, Eva," Aris's voice was fading, the connection growing weaker. "They're everywhere. They're in the signals, in the broadcast. They're in the very air we breathe. You have to trust your instincts. And if you can't trust anyone else… trust me. I wouldn't have brought you into this if I didn't believe you were our last hope." The comm line went dead, leaving Eva staring at a blank screen, the weight of his words echoing in the silence.

A partnership forged in crisis. That was the only way to describe it now. Aris, a fugitive with a truth that could shatter worlds, and Eva, a solitary officer armed with data and a growing sense of dread. Their alliance was silent, clandestine, and fraught with unimaginable danger. The enemy was unseen, its methods subtle, its reach pervasive. But in that moment, staring at the unyielding truth laid bare on her terminal, Eva knew she had made her choice. She would not let Aris stand alone. She would not allow the truth be buried. She would, against all odds, fight this silent war.

The first move was hers, and it began with a ghost in the machine and a desperate journey to Echo Station. The faith of an old friend had become her burden, and her only guide.

4: Rogue Mission

The sterile, humming confines of the Odyssey's bridge had become a gilded cage. Eva moved through its polished corridors, a phantom in plain sight, her every action meticulously calibrated to betray nothing of the seismic shift that had occurred within her. Aris's fragmented transmission, a desperate plea from the shadows, had irrevocably altered her universe. The Federation, the beacon of humanity's outward reach, was, at best, compromised, and at worst, a willing participant in a conspiracy that reached into the very fabric of consciousness. Her loyalty, once an unshakeable pillar, had fractured, revealing a truth far more terrifying than any interstellar threat she had ever been trained to confront.

Her first priority was resource acquisition. Aris's cryptic mention of "Echo Station" and its automated defenses painted a grim picture of the retrieval operation ahead. She needed specialized tools, diagnostic equipment beyond standard Federation issue, and reliable, untraceable comms for her return trip. The official requisition channels were a minefield, each request scrutinized and logged. To even hint at her intentions would be to invite immediate discovery. Therefore, her approach had to be one of calculated appropriation, a phantom limb reaching into the Federation's vast stores, taking only what was absolutely necessary, and leaving no digital or physical trace.

She began with the deep-space sensor array calibration. It was a routine maintenance task, one that required access to a range of high-frequency emitters and deep-spectrum analyzers. Eva meticulously crafted a false diagnostic report, citing unusual fluctuations in subspace resonance that required a more thorough, hands-on examination of the primary array components. Her argument, couched in the dense jargon of astrophysics and signal processing, centered on the need to identify potential interference patterns that might affect long-range sensor accuracy. The justification was plausible, bordering on mundane for a senior xenophysicist. It granted her access to a secure maintenance bay and, more importantly, allowed her to "borrow" a portable subspace resonator, a piece of equipment far more powerful than anything she'd need for a simple calibration. Its compact size and shielded casing made it ideal for discreet transport.

She logged it out under a classification code that indicated it was destined for a long-term deep-space anomaly survey, a project that would conveniently take her far from standard communication grids for an extended period.

Next, she tackled the communication issue. Aris had gone dark, leaving her with only a vague location. Establishing a secure, two-way channel with him, or anyone else she might need to contact, required more than just her personal comm unit. She needed a dedicated, heavily encrypted relay. The Federation maintained a network of classified deep-space listening posts, ostensibly for monitoring extraterrestrial signals, but many had secondary, even tertiary, secure communication suites designed for covert operations. One such outpost, designated 'Outpost Serpentis,' was currently offline for unscheduled "system upgrades." A perfect opportunity.

Eva initiated a low-level system access request, posing as a network technician tasked with verifying the integrity of Serpentis's secure data conduits before its reactivation. This was a delicate operation, requiring her to bypass several layers of automated security and physical access protocols. She fabricated a series of maintenance logs for a fictional sensor drone that had supposedly suffered a catastrophic power surge near Serpentis, creating a simulated data anomaly that required her direct intervention. The "drone," a piece of digital ghost code she had devised, would generate a low-level, intermittent signal that would draw the attention of Serpentis's automated diagnostics, forcing them to open a specific secure channel for her "remote diagnostic." Once that channel was established, she used her acquired subspace resonator, reconfigured for ultra-low power and directional transmission, to piggyback a tiny, encrypted data packet onto the diagnostic stream. This packet contained a meticulously crafted, pre-arranged set of coordinates for a rendezvous point near Echo Station, along with a request for confirmation of readiness. The entire operation was executed with the precision of a surgeon, her fingers dancing across the holographic interface, each keystroke a calculated risk.

The acquisition of medical supplies was another critical, and equally clandestine, undertaking. Aris had sounded weak, and if he was being hunted, he might be injured or in need of immediate medical attention. Accessing the leading Federation medical stores would be impossible without a direct patient or a documented surgical procedure. Her solution was to exploit the ongoing bio-enhancement trials being conducted on volunteer crews for long-duration voyages. She submitted a request for advanced regenerative med-packs and broad-spectrum neural stabilizers, ostensibly for a simulated deep-space emergency preparedness drill. Her fabricated scenario involved a hypothetical exposure to a novel neurotoxin, requiring rapid cellular repair and synaptic recalibration. The request cited the need for cutting-edge experimental pharmaceuticals that were being trialed on remote research vessels. This allowed her to divert a significant cache of high-grade medical supplies, including advanced diagnostics kits and pain suppressors, which were then discreetly added to the cargo manifest of a supply shuttle scheduled for routine deployment to a sector adjacent to Aris's last known position. The shuttle's manifest would be flagged for a standard, albeit slightly expedited, resupply. No one would question the requisition itself, only its unusual destination.

The disused research outpost Eva had identified was more than just a clandestine base; it was a ghost from a forgotten era of Federation expansion. Designation 'Orion's Anvil,' it sat in a sparsely populated nebula, a relic of a failed terraforming initiative from centuries prior. It had been decommissioned due to insurmountable geological instability and deemed too remote for effective maintenance. This very obscurity was its greatest asset. Its power core was dormant, its communications arrays long since decommissioned, making it a perfect black site, invisible to standard Federation surveillance.

Eva fabricated a personal leave request, citing a need for "personal recalibration" and a desire to pursue independent research on ancient stellar cartography. She attached a carefully constructed proposal for a private expedition to study pre-warp navigational charts housed in the archives of a defunct civilian observatory located on a planet near Orion's Anvil. The proposal was a masterpiece of misdirection, detailing extensive research methodologies and hypothetical findings, all designed to placate the administrative oversight committees. Her request was approved, albeit with a stern warning about the inherent risks of solo deep-space travel.

The journey to Orion's Anvil was a stark contrast to the gleaming efficiency of her usual starship. The Nomad, a small, modified scout vessel Eva had privately acquired and retrofitted, was a stark, utilitarian craft, designed for long-range reconnaissance and devoid of the comforts of Federation vessels. Its exterior was matte black, designed to absorb sensor pings, and its internal systems were heavily shielded. As she piloted it through the swirling nebulae, the weight of her undertaking pressed down on her. Each light-year traversed was a step further away from the life she knew, a plunge into an unknown, perilous reality.

Upon arrival, Orion's Anvil was a desolate spectacle. A skeletal network of ferro-concrete structures and derelict atmospheric processors clung to a barren asteroid, silhouetted against the swirling cosmic dust. The primary docking bay was corroded, its automated systems long defunct. Eva navigated the Nomad through a secondary, smaller hangar, its blast doors half-frozen open. The silence within was profound, broken only by the faint, metallic groans of the station's decaying superstructure.

Inside, the air was stale, carrying the scent of ozone and ancient, settled dust. Emergency lights flickered erratically, casting long, dancing shadows. Eva moved with purpose, her boots crunching on debris. She bypassed the central command hub, its consoles dark and lifeless, opting instead for a deep-level access conduit she had identified from pre-decommissioning schematics. This conduit led to a sub-level research wing that, according to the archives, had been sealed off as a contingency measure.

Her borrowed subspace resonator proved invaluable. It pulsed with a low hum, its beam slicing through the thick layer of dust and debris obscuring a hidden access panel. With a surge of power, the panel hissed open, revealing a narrow shaft leading downwards. Eva descended into the darkness, the resonator's beam illuminating the way.

The sub-level chamber was surprisingly intact, its environmental controls still marginally functional, maintaining a frigid, albeit breathable, atmosphere. This was where she established her makeshift command center. She unrolled the specialized sensor equipment, its advanced filters and deep-spectrum analyzers far more sensitive than anything currently deployed on Federation vessels. She brought online a secured, encrypted communication unit, designed to bypass standard Federation networks entirely, relying on a proprietary quantum entanglement protocol that would allow instantaneous, untraceable communication with her designated contact point, wherever that might be.

The operational justifications she had fabricated for diverting resources were more than just bureaucratic hurdles; they were critical layers in a complex deception. Each diverted piece of equipment, each forged requisition, was a meticulously crafted lie designed to create a narrative that explained away her actions without raising suspicion. The risk of discovery was a constant, gnawing presence. If any of her diversions were flagged, if any of her fabricated logs were cross-referenced with real-time network activity, her entire operation would collapse. The political ramifications alone were staggering. An officer of her rank, engaging in unauthorized acquisition of sensitive technology and operating from a clandestine outpost, would be seen not just as a rogue operative, but as a traitor. The potential alien infiltration that Aris had uncovered was a deeply sensitive issue, one that the Federation hierarchy seemed determined to suppress. Her unauthorized investigation, if revealed, could be interpreted as a deliberate attempt to expose a truth that powerful elements within the Federation wanted kept hidden. This could lead to immediate court-martial, imprisonment, and undoubtedly, a fate far worse than mere incarceration, should the true nature of the conspiracy be revealed. The power wielded by those who sought to maintain this hidden agenda was immense, and their methods of silencing dissent were legendary.

Eva meticulously set up the communication relay, calibrating its directional beam towards Aris's last known trajectory. She then began feeding the initial diagnostic data from her advanced sensors into the system, hoping to establish a baseline understanding of the ambient subspace energies in the vicinity of Echo Station. Her goal was to detect any anomalies, any signatures that might indicate the presence of the alien technology Aris had described – the resonance emitters.

She worked through the silent hours, the only sounds the hum of her equipment and the occasional creak of the old station. The weight of responsibility was immense. Aris had placed his faith in her, and now, with his life and the future of humanity potentially at stake, she was on her own, operating in the shadows of her own organization. The data Aris had provided was a terrifying glimpse into a reality far stranger and more dangerous than any known alien civilization. It suggested a level of manipulation so profound, so deeply ingrained, that it threatened the very concept of free will. The mission to Echo Station was not merely a retrieval operation; it was a descent into the heart of a hidden war, a war fought not with fleets and armies, but with subtler, more insidious weapons that targeted the mind itself. And Eva, armed with stolen equipment and a desperate hope, was now its frontline soldier.

The faint ping of a confirmation signal vibrated through the deck plating beneath Eva's boots. It was a subtle tremor, easily missed amidst the ambient thrum of the Nomad's repurposed engines, but to Eva, it was a thunderclap. The coordinates she'd sent, embedded within a stream of otherwise innocuous telemetry data from a fictional deep-space probe, had been received and acknowledged. Aris was alive, and more importantly, he was ready. The carefully orchestrated illusion of her solo research expedition to Orion's Anvil had served its purpose, providing the necessary temporal and spatial buffer for this clandestine rendezvous.

The "routine supply run" was anything but. The modified cargo shuttle, a nondescript vessel with a surprisingly robust cloaking field Eva had "acquired" through a convoluted series of shell corporations, was currently navigating the outer fringes of the Kepler-186 system. Its destination: a cluster of rocky moons orbiting a gas giant, designated 'Argos Cluster' in official Federation star charts. Unofficially, and known only to a select few who dared to look beyond the sanitized surface of interstellar exploration, it was a known hotspot for gravitational anomalies and subspace distortions. A perfect place to hide, and an ideal place to conduct operations that required a significant degree of discretion.

Eva watched the main viewport, her gaze sweeping over the jagged, rust-colored surfaces of the moons as they drifted past. The atmosphere within the shuttle was thick with a palpable tension, a coiled spring of anticipation and apprehension. Beside her, Aris sat hunched over a custom-built sensor array, his face illuminated by the flickering readouts. His expression was a mask of intense concentration, his brow furrowed, his fingers tracing invisible patterns on the holographic displays. He was a finely tuned instrument, attuned to the subtlest shifts in the fabric of reality, and his current task was to detect the nascent tremors of a transdimensional portal.

"Anything, Aris?" Eva's voice was a low murmur, careful not to disturb the delicate equilibrium of their covert operation. Her own duties were now focused on maintaining the shuttle's stealth and ensuring their trajectory remained within the parameters of their fabricated supply mission. Every deviation, no matter how slight, could attract unwanted attention from any Federation patrols or automated monitoring stations that might be lurking in the sector.

Aris didn't look up, his voice a rasp as he responded, "The background subspace energy levels are unusually high, as expected. But there's a... a harmonic resonance building. Something is pulling at the seams of local space-time." He tapped a sequence on his console, bringing up a spectral analysis. "The signature is faint, almost imperceptible, but it's there. A localized distortion, a sort of gravitational echo. It's like listening to a bell that's just been struck, but the sound is spreading out, becoming a ripple."

Eva leaned closer, her eyes tracing the cascading graphs. "An echo? What kind of echo?"

"It's not a natural phenomenon," Aris explained, his voice gaining a degree of urgency. "The fluctuations are too patterned, too... deliberate. It suggests an artificial manipulation of space-time. The data you provided about Echo Station and the resonance emitters aligns perfectly. This is it, Eva. This is the nexus. The portal isn't fully formed, but the scaffolding is in place. It's being actively maintained, or at least, its residual signature is."

The concept of a "residual signature" of a portal was a terrifying one. It implied that even if the portal itself wasn't currently active, the underlying technology, the very mechanism that allowed for transdimensional transit, was still present, humming beneath the surface of observable reality. This was far more dangerous than a fleeting anomaly; it suggested an entrenched, perhaps permanent, infrastructure.

"How close are we?" Eva asked, her gaze now fixed on the sensor readings.

"Within fifty thousand kilometers. The primary source of the distortion is located on the surface of the third moon of Argos VII. Designation: Argos VII-C. It's a geologically unstable world, characterized by extreme atmospheric turbulence and significant magnetic field fluctuations. The Federation classified it as a Class-D hazardous environment decades ago, and it's been largely avoided since." Aris paused, his eyes narrowing. "Which, of course, makes it the perfect place for them to set up shop."

Eva nodded, making a mental note of the coordinates Aris was now feeding into her navigation system. "So, this isn't just a potential portal site; it's a known entity to them, a place they chose for its obscurity and inherent dangers."

"Precisely," Aris confirmed. "They wouldn't want their gateway to be easily accessible. They'd want it shielded by natural defenses. The magnetic storms alone would scramble most standard Federation sensor arrays. But our modified systems, and your specialized equipment..."

"Should be able to punch through the noise," Eva finished. The thought sent a shiver down her spine. They were not just investigating a potential threat; they were actively seeking out the heart of it, armed with scavenged technology and a desperate hope that Aris's fragmented data was accurate. The very idea of a transdimensional portal, a gateway to other realities, was still largely theoretical even within the Federation's advanced scientific circles. To find one, especially one that was being actively managed by an unknown entity, was a paradigm-shifting discovery, and a profoundly unsettling one.

As they approached Argos VII-C, the shuttle began to buck and sway. The external sensors registered a dramatic increase in atmospheric ionization and electromagnetic interference. Warning lights flickered on Eva's console, indicating minor fluctuations in the cloaking field. "Shields are taking a beating," she reported, her hands steady on the controls. "The magnetic field is fluctuating wildly. I'm having to compensate constantly to maintain our stealth signature."

Aris, meanwhile, was entirely absorbed in his readings. "The portal's resonance is intensifying. It's... it's like a heartbeat, Eva. Slow, powerful, and rhythmic. It's definitely active, or at least, there's a significant power draw maintaining its state." He pointed to a specific region on the moon's surface, a vast, shadowed canyon. "The epicenter of the energy readings is concentrated there. The gravity distortions are most pronounced in that area."

Eva began the descent, her piloting skills honed through years of high-stress maneuvers. The shuttle's exterior cameras provided a stark, terrifying vista. The moon's surface was a chaotic landscape of jagged peaks and deep ravines, perpetually shrouded in swirling, multi-hued atmospheric gases. Lightning, crackling with unnatural energy, arced between colossal rock formations. It was a world on the brink of geological collapse, a testament to the raw, untamed forces of the cosmos.

"I'm initiating a low-altitude approach," Eva announced, her voice tight with focus. "We need to get close enough for your sensors to get a definitive lock, but without triggering any automated defenses they might have in place. If this portal is being actively monitored, a direct approach could be… problematic."

Aris nodded, his gaze never leaving his console. "The resonance readings are spiking in that canyon. There's a localized energy concentration unlike anything I've ever seen. It's not just gravitational; there's a temporal distortion component as well. The very flow of time in that area is being… warped."

The shuttle shuddered violently as it entered the upper layers of the moon's turbulent atmosphere. Eva fought for control, her knuckles white as she gripped the pilot's yoke. Static erupted from the comms, momentarily drowning out the steady hum of their own systems. "Comms are gone," she reported grimly. "We're flying blind on external comms now."

"I expected as much," Aris replied, his voice remarkably calm amidst the chaos. "The interference is designed to mask their presence. However, my internal sensors are still functioning, and the subspace resonator you acquired is picking up the primary energy signature with incredible clarity. It's emanating from a specific point within that canyon. A nexus of… something."

Eva guided the shuttle deeper into the tempest. The visual feed became a dizzying kaleidoscope of swirling gases and intermittent flashes of light. The ground, when it was visible, was a terrifying expanse of fractured rock and ominous shadows. She could feel the shuttle straining against the forces buffeting it, the very air outside crackling with unseen energy.

"There," Aris suddenly exclaimed, pointing towards a deep, shadowed fissure that yawned open in the canyon floor. "That's it. The signature is emanating from directly below us. It's… it's incredible, Eva. The energy readings are off the charts. It's not just a portal; it's a controlled singularity, a nexus point of multiple dimensions."

As they hovered above the fissure, the Shuttle's external sensors registered a sudden, localized surge of energy. It was as if the moon itself had exhaled, releasing a torrent of raw, unbridled power. The readings on Aris's console went into overdrive.

"It's stabilizing," Aris breathed, his eyes wide with a mixture of awe and dread. "The portal... it's manifesting. The residual signature is coalescing into a stable aperture. It's... beautiful, in a terrifying sort of way."

Eva brought the shuttle to a slow, careful descent, hovering just above the opening of the fissure. The air around them began to shimmer, distorting the view of the canyon floor below. A low, resonant hum, felt more than heard, emanated from the depths. It was a sound that seemed to vibrate through bone and soul, a sound that promised passage to realms unknown, and potentially, to unfathomable dangers.

"The data suggests that the portal itself is a temporary phenomenon, a window that opens and closes periodically," Aris explained, his voice a hushed whisper. "But the underlying technology, the emitters, are permanent. They are what maintain the integrity of the aperture and allow for controlled transit. The Federation believes these emitters are of alien origin, technology far beyond our current understanding."

Eva's gaze was fixed on the shimmering distortion below. It was like looking into a warped mirror, the familiar universe twisting and bending into impossible shapes. "And Aris believes that someone is utilizing this alien technology. Someone within the Federation, or perhaps, someone who has infiltrated it."

"The same entity that silenced my warning," Aris confirmed, his voice grim. "They're using this technology for their own purposes, purposes that are clearly antithetical to the Federation's core principles. The implications are staggering. If they can control interdimensional travel, what else can they control?"

The humming intensified, and the shimmering distortion began to coalesce into a distinct circular aperture. It glowed with an ethereal, otherworldly light, a vortex of pure energy that seemed to pull at the very fabric of reality. Eva felt a strange sense of vertigo, a disorienting sensation that suggested their own perception of space any time was beginning to warp.

"We need to gather more data," Eva stated, her mind racing. "We need to understand the nature of these emitters, how they work, and how they're being controlled. This isn't just about rescuing you, Aris. This is about understanding the nature of the threat itself."

Aris nodded, his focus now shifting to a new set of readings. "The energy signature of the emitters is incredibly complex. They appear to be manipulating subspace frequencies in a way that creates localized gravitational distortions, essentially bending space-time to create the portal. The complexity suggests an intelligence far beyond our own, or at least, an understanding of physics that we are only beginning to grasp."

The portal pulsed, and for a fleeting moment, Eva thought she saw glimpses of... something else. Shifting landscapes, impossible geometries, and fleeting shadows that defied comprehension. It was a tantalizing, terrifying invitation.

"I'm going to attempt to deploy a micro-drone," Eva announced, reaching for a console. "It's equipped with advanced spectral analyzers and its own subspace resonator. It can get closer to the aperture, gather more precise data on the emitters without risking the shuttle."

Aris's eyes widened. "A drone? That's... ambitious, Eva. The temporal and spatial distortions around the portal could tear a drone apart before it even gets close."

"This drone is designed for extreme environments," Eva countered, her voice firm. "It's equipped with a reinforced containment field and a self-correcting navigation system. It's our best chance to get a tangible sample of the emitter technology." She initiated the deployment sequence, her fingers flying across the controls.

A small, sleek craft detached from the shuttle's underbelly, its cloaking field shimmering into existence. It began to slowly navigate towards the pulsating aperture. Aris watched the drone's telemetry feed with bated breath.

"The drone is encountering significant resistance," he reported. "The space-time distortions are intense. It's compensating, but it's a struggle. The drone's subspace resonator is picking up a faint, secondary energy signature, almost like a carrier wave, emanating from the emitters."

Suddenly, a cascade of error messages flooded Aris's console. "The drone's signal is... destabilizing. The carrier wave is being amplified. It's... it's a directed energy pulse, Eva! It's a defense mechanism!"

Before Eva could react, the drone's feed went dark, replaced by a burst of static. The shuttle rocked violently as a wave of invisible energy washed over them. Alarms blared throughout the craft.

"We've been detected!" Aris shouted, his face paling. "They know we're here! The portal defenses have been activated!"

Eva's mind raced. Their cover was blown. Their objective had shifted from observation to evasion. The delicate dance of deception had ended, and the actual danger, the one Aris had warned her about, was now upon them. The portal's echo had found them, and it was far more active than they had anticipated. The next move would determine not only their survival but the fate of everything they fought for. The rogue mission had just become a desperate flight for their lives, with the secrets of the cosmos hanging precariously in the balance.

The immediate aftermath of the drone's demise had been a brutal symphony of blaring alarms and frantic system diagnostics. The shuttle, battered but not broken, had clawed its way out of the moon's treacherous atmosphere, the swirling maelstrom of magnetic storms and ionized gases now a receding memory. Aris, his initial shock giving way to a grim determination, worked feverishly to re-establish a stable subspace link, his fingers a blur across the holographic consoles. Eva, meanwhile, wrestled with the shuttle's trajectory, her focus split between piloting through the residual spatial distortions and monitoring the external sensors for any sign of pursuit. They had been detected. The carefully constructed illusion of a clandestine rendezvous had shattered, replaced by the stark reality of an exposed operation.

"They're adapting," Aris announced, his voice tight with

concern, as he finally managed to stabilize a tenuous data stream. "The defensive pulse wasn't just a reaction; it was a sophisticated tracking beacon. They're weaving it into the subspace background, making it almost impossible to filter out without specialized counter-measures." He looked up, his eyes meeting Eva's in the dim, flickering light of the cockpit. "Our cloaking field is still functional, but it's like trying to hide a starship in a supernova. They know our general vector."

Eva's jaw tightened. The drone's sacrifice, intended to gather intelligence, had instead served as an unintentional breadcrumb, leading their unknown adversaries directly to them. The thought sent a fresh wave of cold dread through her. They hadn't just stumbled upon a portal; they had stumbled into a carefully guarded secret, one that its custodians were clearly willing to defend with advanced, terrifying technology.

The implications of their discovery, of this alien technology being wielded by an unseen hand, felt heavier than ever.

"Can we shake it?" Eva asked, her gaze flicking to the tactical display that showed faint, yet persistent, energy signatures emanating from the Argos Cluster. They were ghost signals, subtle ripples in the fabric of subspace, but they were undeniably there.

"Not easily," Aris admitted, running a rapid simulation. "The beacon is designed to be persistent. It's keyed to our shuttle's unique subspace resonance, a byproduct of its modified drive core. The only way to truly break it would be to enter a nebula with a high concentration of naturally occurring subspace anomalies, something dense enough to drown out our signature completely. Or," he paused, a grimace crossing his face, "to engage in a radical evasive maneuver that risks damaging the shuttle beyond repair. We need to consider our options, Eva. Our fabricated supply mission is no longer a viable cover."

The irony was not lost on Eva. She, a decorated officer in the Space Force, was now an unsanctioned operative, racing through uncharted sectors with a wanted scientist, pursued by an enemy whose very existence defied conventional understanding. Her carefully cultivated reputation for efficiency and discretion, built over years of service, now felt like a fragile facade, about to be torn down.

As if on cue, her secure comms channel chimed, a sharp, insistent tone that cut through the low hum of the shuttle's systems. The display flashed with the insignia of the Sector Command's internal affairs division – a grim, skeletal hand grasping a stylized star. Her stomach churned. This was it. The inevitable follow-up to her 'routine' supply request, the one that had allowed her to divert resources and coordinate with Aris. They were already onto her.

"Eva, are you alright?" Aris's voice was a low murmur, a stark contrast to the blaring alarms of their recent encounter. He had a knack for sensing her unspoken anxieties.

"Just a… routine query from Command," Eva replied, her voice carefully modulated, projecting an air of calm she did not feel. She initiated the secure channel, the familiar interface of her personal comms unit appearing on a secondary screen. The face of Commander Valerius, her direct superior, flickered into view. Valerius was a man known for his meticulous attention to detail and an almost pathological aversion to unexplained anomalies. He was also, Eva suspected, the perfect instrument of the subtle, insidious pressures that had been building within the Space Force for months.

"Commander," Eva greeted him, offering a polite, professional smile. "To what do I owe this… unscheduled communication?"

Valerius's expression was unreadable, his gaze sharp and piercing. He was a man who rarely wasted words. "Lieutenant Commander Kestrel," he began, his voice clipped and devoid of warmth. "Your recent requisition for an unregistered subspace resonator and specialized sensor array has flagged several discrepancies.

Furthermore, your flight path deviates significantly from the projected course for your research expedition to Orion's Anvil. Can you provide a satisfactory explanation for these… irregularities?"

Eva felt a prickle of sweat on her brow. The requisitions had been carefully worded, couched in the language of obscure scientific necessity, but clearly, even her most intricate planning had been insufficient. The sheer speed with which the flagged anomalies had been escalated indicated either an exceptionally efficient internal monitoring system, or… something else. Something more insidious.

"Commander," she began, her mind racing, drawing upon years of ingrained training to formulate a plausible, yet evasive, response.

"The subspace resonator was an unforeseen necessity. My initial geological surveys of Orion's Anvil revealed unusual subspace harmonics that necessitated a more sensitive detection apparatus than what was standard issue for my expedition. The complexity of the phenomenon warranted a significant deviation from planned equipment." She paused, letting the technical jargon hang in the air, hoping it would obscure the truth. "As for the flight path, I encountered unexpected gravimetric distortions near Kepler-186, forcing a significant course correction to avoid catastrophic damage to the Nomad. I've been attempting to re-establish the original trajectory ever since."

Valerius's eyes narrowed almost imperceptibly. He was not easily fooled. "Gravimetric distortions," he repeated, the words heavy with skepticism. "And yet, Lieutenant Commander, no other vessels in that sector have reported similar anomalies, nor have your own vessel's logs, before your detour, indicated any such hazards."

The silence that followed was deafening, pregnant with unspoken accusations. Eva's mind flashed back to the unsettling whispers she'd overheard in the mess halls, the hushed conversations about 'anomalous directives' and 'unquestionable priorities' filtering down from the highest echelons of the Space Force. Was it possible that Valerius was not acting on his own initiative, but was instead being subtly influenced, his inquiries directed by an unseen hand? The thought sent a fresh wave of paranoia coursing through her.

"My logs may require... recalibration, Commander," Eva said, forcing a reassuring tone. "The distortions were, as I stated, highly localized and appeared to have a disruptive effect on sensitive chronometric and navigational systems. I've been prioritizing repairs and course correction to minimize further delays." She deliberately avoided mentioning Aris or the true nature of their objective. The less information Valerius had, the better.

Valerius's gaze remained fixed on her, a silent assessment that felt like a probe, dissecting her every word, her every micro-expression. "I will require a full report on these 'recalibrations' and the nature of these 'localized distortions' upon your return, Lieutenant Commander. Any further deviations from your mission parameters will be met with immediate disciplinary action. Is that understood?"

"Understood, Commander," Eva replied, her voice unwavering.

She offered another tight smile. "I assure you, my mission is my utmost priority."

The comms link severed, leaving Eva staring at the blank screen, her heart pounding in her chest. The interaction had been a razor's edge walk. She had managed to deflect the immediate threat, but she knew, with chilling certainty, that her days of operating with relative autonomy were numbered. The scrutiny had intensified, and it was only a matter of time before her actions, or rather, the anomalies her actions created, drew too much attention.

"He's suspicious," Aris stated the obvious, his voice low. "He knows something is off."

Eva nodded, running a hand through her short, dark hair. The feeling of being watched, of being under constant surveillance, was no longer a vague paranoia; it was a tangible, suffocating presence. "Suspicious is an understatement, Aris. He practically read my mind. I'm not sure if it's my own recent activities that have put them on alert, or if... if their influence is already spreading through the internal monitoring systems. Making them flag even the most innocuous deviations."

The idea of alien influence permeating the very fabric of the Space Force was a terrifying prospect. It suggested a level of infiltration far more profound and more insidious than she had ever imagined. It meant that their sanctuary, their base of operations, might not be as secure as they had believed. Every communication, every requisition, every deviation from protocol, was now a potential trap, a carefully laid snare designed to ensnare them.

"We need to be more careful," Aris cautioned, his gaze sweeping over the shuttle's sensor logs, cross-referencing them with her encrypted comms history. "Every interaction, every request for supplies, every data transmission – it's all being scrutinized. They might not know what we're doing, but they're clearly aware that something is happening that deviates from your official mission parameters."

Eva felt a surge of adrenaline, sharpening her senses. She had always prided herself on her ability to blend in, to operate in the grey spaces of officialdom. But now, those grey spaces felt increasingly exposed, the shadows no longer offering concealment but rather, revealing her presence. The subtle nudges and whispers she'd dismissed as background anxiety now coalesced into a chilling certainty: they were being hunted, not just by the unknown entities who controlled the portal, but by the very organization she had sworn to protect.

"The requisitions were standard procedure for a deep-space expedition, even for a solo research mission," Eva mused aloud, replaying the conversation with Valerius in her mind. "But the sheer speed of his inquiry, the immediate escalation... it suggests an automated flagging system that is hyper-sensitive to any deviation. Or, as you said, they're feeding data into the system, deliberately creating anomalies that will draw attention to my activities."

"The latter is more likely," Aris stated, his voice grave. "An automated system would flag the raw data; it wouldn't necessarily trigger a direct comms query from someone of Valerius's rank unless specific parameters were met. Parameters that someone else is setting. They're not just monitoring; they're actively directing the surveillance."

This was a far more dangerous game than Eva had anticipated. It wasn't a matter of outrunning patrols or evading radar sweeps. It was a silent war waged within the very infrastructure of the Space Force, a battle for information and control fought through bureaucratic channels and sophisticated surveillance algorithms. Every interaction with her superiors, every request for resources, became a tightrope walk over an abyss of suspicion.

"My next supply run," Eva said, a new layer of caution settling over her. "I'll need to be even more discreet. Perhaps smaller, more frequent requisitions, spread out across different sectors, disguised as routine maintenance and operational necessities. Anything that doesn't draw a direct line back to this specific mission."

"And what if they've already flagged the pattern?" Aris countered, his brow furrowed. "What if your entire operational profile is now under a red flag? Every requisition, no matter how small, will be scrutinized through that lens. They might not know the specifics, but they know you're a variable they need to control."

Eva gripped the pilot's yoke, her knuckles whitening. The claustrophobic confines of the shuttle suddenly felt like a cage. She was a prisoner of her own success, her ability to operate covertly now turning into her greatest vulnerability. The weight of the mission, the discovery of the portal, the danger to Aris, and now, the potential implication of her own organization, pressed down on her, a crushing burden.

"Then we adapt," Eva declared, her voice firm, a steely resolve hardening her gaze. "We become even more invisible. We leverage the blind spots, the operational gaps that the internal monitoring systems can't penetrate. I'll have to rely on my old contacts, the ones who owe me favors, the ones who operate outside the direct oversight of Command. It's a risk, but staying put is a certainty of capture."

She initiated a silent, encrypted burst transmission, routing it through a series of anonymized relays that she had established years ago. The message was terse, a coded request for specific, high-grade components that would be difficult to trace. It was a gamble, a desperate throw of the dice, but she couldn't afford to be seen to be reliant on standard, traceable supply chains any longer.

"Who are you contacting?" Aris asked, his curiosity piqued by the sophisticated encryption and routing protocols she employed.

"Someone from my past," Eva replied, her expression grim. "Someone who understands the need for absolute discretion. They operate in the grey market, acquiring resources that the Space Force would never officially sanction. They'll be expensive, and the transaction itself will be... complicated, but it's our best chance to acquire the necessary components without raising further red flags with Command."

She knew the risks. Associating with individuals operating in the fringes of interstellar commerce, even for a legitimate cause, was a career-ending offense. But her career was already a secondary concern. The stakes were far too high to be weighed against personal ambition or official protocol. The truth about the portal, and the forces manipulating it, was too critical to be ignored.

"The paranoia is useful, Aris," Eva said, her voice barely a whisper, more to herself than to him. "It keeps us sharp. It forces us to anticipate their moves. Every interaction with Command, every requisition request, is a test. A test of my ability to maintain the facade, and a test of their ability to see through it." She looked out at the endless expanse of stars, the void suddenly seeming less empty and more like a vast, watchful eye. "The feeling of being watched," she concluded, "is no longer a feeling.

It's a fact." The rogue mission had just entered its most perilous phase, not of external threat, but of internal compromise. The enemy wasn't just out there, beyond the stars; it was already within, subtly guiding the hand that sought to expose them.

The hum of the shuttle's environmental controls, once a comforting constant, now felt like a ticking clock. Eva monitored the receding spectral lines on her console, each one a ghost of the drone's final moments. The energy signature that Aris had identified as a 'tracking beacon' was more insidious than a simple signal; it was a whisper woven into the very fabric of subspace, designed to latch onto their shuttle's unique resonance. Their fabricated supply mission, a flimsy shield against scrutiny, had been irrevocably compromised. The stark reality of their exposed operation settled heavily upon them.

"They're adapting," Aris's voice, usually calm and measured, now carried a tight edge of concern. He finally managed to stabilize a tenuous data stream, the holographic displays flickering with diagnostic readouts. "That defensive pulse wasn't just a reaction; it was a sophisticated tracking beacon. They're weaving it into the subspace background, making it almost impossible to filter out without specialized counter-measures. Our cloaking field is still functional, but it's like trying to hide a starship in a supernova. They know our general vector."

Eva's jaw tightened. The drone, meant to be a silent scout, had inadvertently become a breadcrumb, leading their unknown adversaries directly to them. The thought sent a fresh wave of cold dread through her. They hadn't just stumbled upon a portal; they had stumbled into a carefully guarded secret, one that its custodians were clearly willing to defend with terrifyingly advanced technology. The implications of their discovery, of this alien technology being wielded by an unseen hand, felt heavier than ever.

"Can we shake it?" Eva asked, her gaze flicking to the tactical display. Faint, yet persistent, energy signatures emanated from the Argos Cluster. Ghost signals, subtle ripples in subspace, but undeniably present.

"Not easily," Aris admitted, running a rapid simulation. "The beacon is designed to be persistent. It's keyed to our shuttle's unique subspace resonance, a byproduct of its modified drive core. The only way to truly break it would be to enter a nebula with a high concentration of naturally occurring subspace anomalies, something dense enough to drown out our signature completely. Or," he paused, a grimace crossing his face, "to engage in a radical evasive maneuver that risks damaging the shuttle beyond repair. We need to consider our options, Eva. Our fabricated supply mission is no longer a viable cover."

The irony was not lost on Eva. She, a decorated officer in the Space Force, was now an unsanctioned operative, racing through uncharted sectors with a wanted scientist, pursued by an enemy whose very existence defied conventional understanding. Her carefully cultivated reputation for efficiency and discretion, built over years of service, now felt like a fragile facade, about to be torn down.

As if on cue, her secure comms channel chimed, a sharp, insistent tone that cut through the low hum of the shuttle's systems. The display flashed with the insignia of the Sector Command's internal affairs division – a grim, skeletal hand grasping a stylized star. Her stomach churned. This was it. The inevitable follow-up to her 'routine' supply request, the one that had allowed her to divert resources and coordinate with Aris. They were already onto her.

"Eva, are you alright?" Aris's voice was a low murmur, a stark contrast to the blaring alarms of their recent encounter. He had a knack for sensing her unspoken anxieties.

"Just a… routine query from Command," Eva replied, her voice carefully modulated, projecting an air of calm she did not feel. She initiated the secure channel, the familiar interface of her personal comms unit appearing on a secondary screen. The face of Commander Valerius, her direct superior, flickered into view. Valerius was a man known for his meticulous attention to detail and an almost pathological aversion to unexplained anomalies. He was also, Eva suspected, the perfect instrument of the subtle, insidious pressures that had been building within the Space Force for months.

"Commander," Eva greeted him, offering a polite, professional smile. "To what do I owe this… unscheduled communication?"

Valerius's expression was unreadable, his gaze sharp and piercing. He was a man who rarely wasted words. "Lieutenant Commander Kestrel," he began, his voice clipped and devoid of warmth. "Your recent requisition for an unregistered subspace resonator and specialized sensor array has flagged several discrepancies.

Furthermore, your flight path deviates significantly from the projected course for your research expedition to Orion's Anvil. Can you provide a satisfactory explanation for these... irregularities?"

Eva felt a prickle of sweat on her brow. The requisitions had been carefully worded, couched in the language of obscure scientific necessity, but clearly, even her most intricate planning had been insufficient. The sheer speed with which the flagged anomalies had been escalated indicated either an exceptionally efficient internal monitoring system, or... something else. Something more insidious.

"Commander," she began, her mind racing, drawing upon years of ingrained training to formulate a plausible, yet evasive, response. "The subspace resonator was an unforeseen necessity. My initial geological surveys of Orion's Anvil revealed unusual subspace harmonics that necessitated a more sensitive detection apparatus than what was standard issue for my expedition. The complexity of the phenomenon warranted a significant deviation from planned equipment." She paused, letting the technical jargon hang in the air, hoping it would obscure the truth. "As for the flight path, I encountered unexpected gravimetric distortions near Kepler-186, forcing a significant course correction to avoid catastrophic damage to the Nomad. I've been attempting to re-establish the original trajectory ever since."

Valerius's eyes narrowed almost imperceptibly. He was not easily fooled. "Gravimetric distortions," he repeated, the words heavy with skepticism. "And yet, Lieutenant Commander, no other vessels in that sector have reported similar anomalies, nor have your own vessel's logs, before your detour, indicated any such hazards."

The silence that followed was deafening, pregnant with unspoken accusations. Eva's mind flashed back to the unsettling whispers she'd overheard in the mess halls, the hushed conversations about 'anomalous directives' and 'unquestionable priorities' filtering down from the highest echelons of the Space Force. Was it possible that

Valerius was not acting on his own initiative, but was instead being subtly influenced, his inquiries directed by an unseen hand? The thought sent a fresh wave of paranoia coursing through her.

"My logs may require… recalibration, Commander," Eva said, forcing a reassuring tone. "The distortions were, as I stated, highly localized and appeared to have a disruptive effect on sensitive chronometric and navigational systems. I've been prioritizing repairs and course correction to minimize further delays." She deliberately avoided mentioning Aris or the true nature of their objective. The less information Valerius had, the better.

Valerius's gaze remained fixed on her, a silent assessment that felt like a probe, dissecting her every word, her every micro-expression. "I will require a full report on these 'recalibrations' and the nature of these 'localized distortions' upon your return, Lieutenant Commander. Any further deviations from your mission parameters will be met with immediate disciplinary action. Is that understood?"

"Understood, Commander," Eva replied, her voice unwavering. She offered another tight smile. "I assure you, my mission is my utmost priority."

The comms link severed, leaving Eva staring at the blank screen, her heart pounding in her chest. The interaction had been a razor's edge walk. She had managed to deflect the immediate threat, but she knew, with chilling certainty, that her days of operating with relative autonomy were numbered. The scrutiny had intensified, and it was only a matter of time before her actions, or rather, the anomalies her actions created, drew too much attention.

"He's suspicious," Aris stated the obvious, his voice low. "He knows something is off."

Eva nodded, running a hand through her short, dark hair. The feeling of being watched, of being under constant surveillance, was no longer a vague paranoia; it was a tangible, suffocating presence. "Suspicious is an understatement, Aris. He practically read my mind. I'm not sure if it's my own recent activities that have put them on alert, or if… if their influence is already spreading through the internal monitoring systems. Making them flag even the most innocuous deviations."

The idea of alien influence permeating the very fabric of the

Space Force was a terrifying prospect. It suggested a level of infiltration far more profound and more insidious than she had ever imagined. It meant that their sanctuary, their base of operations, might not be as secure as they had believed. Every communication, every requisition, every deviation from protocol, was now a potential trap, a carefully laid snare designed to ensnare them.

"We need to be more careful," Aris cautioned, his gaze sweeping over the shuttle's sensor logs, cross-referencing them with her encrypted comms history. "Every interaction, every request for supplies, every data transmission – it's all being scrutinized. They might not know what we're doing, but they're clearly aware that something is happening that deviates from your official mission parameters."

Eva felt a surge of adrenaline, sharpening her senses. She had always prided herself on her ability to blend in, to operate in the grey spaces of officialdom. But now, those grey spaces felt increasingly exposed, the shadows no longer offering concealment but rather, revealing her presence. The subtle nudges and whispers she'd dismissed as background anxiety now coalesced into a chilling certainty: they were being hunted, not just by the unknown entities who controlled the portal, but by the very organization she had sworn to protect.

"The requisitions were standard procedure for a deep-space expedition, even for a solo research mission," Eva mused aloud, replaying the conversation with Valerius in her mind. "But the sheer speed of his inquiry, the immediate escalation... it suggests an automated flagging system that is hyper-sensitive to any deviation. Or, as you said, they're feeding data into the system, deliberately creating anomalies that will draw attention to my activities."

"The latter is more likely," Aris stated, his voice grave. "An automated system would flag the raw data; it wouldn't necessarily trigger a direct comms query from someone of Valerius's rank unless specific parameters were met. Parameters that someone else is setting. They're not just monitoring; they're actively directing the surveillance."

This was a far more dangerous game than Eva had anticipated. It wasn't a matter of outrunning patrols or evading radar sweeps. It was a silent war waged within the very infrastructure of the Space Force, a battle for information and control fought through bureaucratic channels and sophisticated surveillance algorithms. Every interaction with her superiors, every request for resources, became a tightrope walk over an abyss of suspicion.

"My next supply run," Eva said, a new layer of caution settling over her. "I'll need to be even more discreet. Perhaps smaller, more frequent requisitions, spread out across different sectors, disguised as routine maintenance and operational necessities.

Anything that doesn't draw a direct line back to this specific mission."

"And what if they've already flagged the pattern?" Aris countered, his brow furrowed. "What if your entire operational profile is now under a red flag? Every requisition, no matter how small, will be scrutinized through that lens. They might not know the specifics, but they know you're a variable they need to control."

Eva gripped the pilot's yoke, her knuckles whitening. The claustrophobic confines of the shuttle suddenly felt like a cage. She was a prisoner of her own success, her ability to operate covertly now turning into her greatest vulnerability. The weight of the mission, the discovery of the portal, the danger to Aris, and now, the potential implication of her own organization, pressed down on her, a crushing burden.

"Then we adapt," Eva declared, her voice firm, a steely resolve hardening her gaze. "We become even more invisible. We leverage the blind spots, the operational gaps that the internal monitoring systems can't penetrate. I'll have to rely on my old contacts, the ones who owe me favors, the ones who operate outside the direct oversight of Command. It's a risk, but staying put is a certainty of capture."

She initiated a silent, encrypted burst transmission, routing it through a series of anonymized relays that she had established years ago. The message was terse, a coded request for specific, high-grade components that would be difficult to trace. It was a gamble, a desperate throw of the dice, but she couldn't afford to be seen to be reliant on standard, traceable supply chains any longer.

"Who are you contacting?" Aris asked, his curiosity piqued by the sophisticated encryption and routing protocols she employed.

"Someone from my past," Eva replied, her expression grim.

"Someone who understands the need for absolute discretion. They operate in the grey market, acquiring resources that the Space Force would never officially sanction. They'll be expensive, and the transaction itself will be... complicated, but it's our best chance to acquire the necessary components without raising further red flags with Command."

She knew the risks. Associating with individuals operating in the fringes of interstellar commerce, even for a legitimate cause, was a career-ending offense. But her career was already a secondary concern. The stakes were far too high to be weighed against personal ambition or official protocol. The truth about the portal, and the forces manipulating it, was too critical to be ignored.

"The paranoia is useful, Aris," Eva said, her voice barely a whisper, more to herself than to him. "It keeps us sharp. It forces us to anticipate their moves. Every interaction with Command, every requisition request, is a test. A test of my ability to maintain the facade, and a test of their ability to see through it." She looked out at the endless expanse of stars, the void suddenly seeming less empty and more like a vast, watchful eye. "The feeling of being watched," she concluded, "is no longer a feeling.

It's a fact." The rogue mission had just entered its most perilous phase, not of external threat, but of internal compromise. The enemy wasn't just out there, beyond the stars; it was already within, subtly guiding the hand that sought to expose them.

Aris, his brow furrowed in concentration, was already at work on a new suite of instruments. His fingers danced across the holographic interface, weaving together complex equations and schematics. The drone's data, despite its destruction, had provided a tantalizing glimpse into the nature of the alien energy signatures. It was not merely a field, but a symphony of interwoven frequencies, a deliberately crafted pattern designed to elicit specific responses from sentient minds. His mission, now more critical than ever, was to build a counter-symphony, a discordant note that could disrupt their control.

"I've managed to isolate key components of the energy signature," Aris explained, his voice barely audible above the gentle hum of his jury-rigged equipment. "It's incredibly complex, almost biological in its adaptability. But there are harmonics, predictable patterns within the chaos. If I can replicate these harmonics, I might be able to create a localized subspace distortion, a 'bubble' of sorts that can mask our shuttle's resonance." He gestured to a crystalline structure humming with contained energy. "This is the prototype for the portable quantum resonator. It draws power directly from the ambient subspace field, amplifying and modulating it to match the disruptive frequencies."

He then pointed to a sleek, ergonomic device that fit into the palm of a hand. It pulsed with a soft, internal light. "And this," he continued, "is a bio-feedback monitor. Based on the limited neural scan data we acquired from the drone before its disintegration, I believe their control mechanism extends to influencing cognitive processes. This device monitors for anomalous neural patterns, subtle shifts in brainwave activity that indicate external manipulation. It's rudimentary, but it's a start."

Eva studied the devices, her mind already grasping their potential applications. The quantum resonator, if functional, could be their ticket out of the tracking beacon's grasp. The bio-feedback monitor, however, sent a shiver down her spine. The idea of their minds being subject to external influence was deeply unsettling, a violation of the most fundamental autonomy.

"These are incredible, Aris," Eva acknowledged, her voice filled with a mixture of awe and apprehension. "But they're still... prototypes. We're up against an enemy that can weave tracking signals into subspace and potentially influence our thoughts. These tools, as advanced as they are, feel like flint knives against plasma cannons."

"Crude, perhaps," Aris conceded, a rare smile touching his lips. "But they are our tools, Eva. Developed from our understanding, built with our ingenuity. And they represent our only chance to gather concrete evidence, to find a weakness, or at least, to understand the scope of their control." He carefully placed the bio-feedback monitor into a padded case. "This data, coupled with the advanced sensor technology you've managed to procure, will be our arsenal. The encrypted communication gear you've acquired is also crucial. We can't afford to have our transmissions intercepted or, worse, subtly altered."

Eva nodded, a renewed sense of purpose hardening her resolve. Her contacts, the ones operating in the shadowy fringes of interstellar commerce, had been invaluable. They had provided her with a state-of-the-art, multi-spectrum sensor array, capable of detecting subspace anomalies far beyond the capabilities of standard Space Force equipment. This, combined with a secure, multi-layered encryption system that even Aris admitted was "impressively robust," formed the backbone of their defensive and intelligence-gathering capabilities.

"The sensor array can scan for subspace distortions and energy signatures with unprecedented clarity," Eva explained, activating the device. A detailed topographical map of the surrounding space bloomed into existence on a secondary display, overlaid with faint, pulsing energy readings. "It can differentiate between natural phenomena and artificially generated signals. If this tracking beacon has any subtle variations in its energy output, the array should pick them up."

She then tapped a sequence on her comms panel, bringing up the encryption interface. "And this," she said, her voice low, "is designed to create independent communication nodes, routing our transmissions through a series of defunct satellites and derelict stations. It's a painstaking process, but it makes our communications virtually untraceable by conventional means. They might know that we're communicating, but they won't know what we're saying, or who we're saying it to."

"Excellent," Aris murmured, his eyes scanning the data from the sensor array. "The resonator is still in its experimental phase, but I believe I can calibrate it to target the disruptive frequencies I've identified specifically. It will require precise atmospheric conditions and a significant power draw, which means we'll need to find a sufficiently dense nebula to operate it safely." He tapped a point on the star chart. "There's a Class-4 nebula approximately three sectors away, in the Cygnus Rift. It's known for its turbulent subspace currents and high concentration of exotic particles. It should provide enough ambient interference to mask the resonator's activation and, hopefully, any resulting energy fluctuations."

Eva's gaze drifted to the bio-feedback monitor. "And the thought influence... how can we even begin to guard against that?"

Aris looked up from his console, his expression serious. "That's the most challenging aspect. We don't know the mechanism, the range, or the intent. Is it a form of subtle persuasion, or outright mind control? The bio-feedback monitor is our first line of defense. It will alert us to any anomalies in our own neural patterns. If we detect something, we need to disengage from any complex cognitive tasks immediately, focus on simple, repetitive actions, and try to disrupt the signal by generating a mental 'noise' – focusing on mundane, deeply ingrained memories or routines. It's a mental discipline, a form of cognitive camouflage."

"Mental camouflage," Eva repeated, the phrase echoing the unsettling implications of their situation. The enemy wasn't just a physical presence; it was a psychological one, a silent infiltrator of the mind. This unseen war was being fought on multiple fronts, and their minds were the most vulnerable battlefield.

"We also need to be aware of potential psychological manipulation through our comms," Aris added, his gaze fixed on the fluctuating energy readings. "They might not be able to control our thoughts directly, but they could exploit our fears, our doubts, our anxieties. They could feed us false information, or subtly twist our perceptions through coded messages or altered data streams."

Eva felt a knot of apprehension tighten in her stomach. Her recent interaction with Commander Valerius, the unnerving precision of his suspicions, suddenly seemed less like a procedural query and more like a calculated probe, a test of her mental fortitude. Had they already begun to sow seeds of doubt, to subtly influence her judgment?

"My conversation with Valerius…" Eva began, her voice trailing off as she recalled the commander's piercing gaze. "He was too quick, too precise. It felt less like an investigation and more like… a pre-programmed response to triggers I didn't even know I'd set off."

Aris nodded gravely. "That's precisely the kind of subtle manipulation I'm concerned about. They don't need to control us directly; they need to guide our actions, to steer us towards mistakes, to isolate us. Your attempts to cover your tracks, your reliance on less conventional supply channels – these are all variables they can exploit. They can use these deviations to build a case against you, to paint you as unstable or rogue, even before they fully understand what you're doing."

"So, every requisition, every deviation, every encrypted message," Eva mused, her mind piecing together the intricate web of threats, "is a potential trap. A way for them to gather evidence against me, or to subtly manipulate my actions through the very system I'm trying to circumvent."

"Exactly," Aris confirmed. "It's a war of information, Eva. And our greatest weapons are these tools, our understanding, and our ability to remain disciplined, both externally and internally." He tapped the portable quantum resonator. "This will be our shield against their tracking beacon. Your sensor array will be our eyes, gathering the crucial data on their energy signatures. And my bio-feedback monitor will be our early warning system against psychological infiltration."

He then looked at Eva, his gaze steady and reassuring. "We may be facing an enemy with superior technology, but we have something they don't: a purpose, a clear objective. We're not trying to conquer or control; we're trying to understand, to expose the truth. That moral clarity that drive for knowledge is a powerful weapon in itself."

Eva met his gaze, a flicker of renewed determination in her eyes. The fear hadn't vanished, but a steely resolve now tempered it. They were outmatched, outgunned, and operating under a constant threat of exposure and manipulation. But they were also prepared. Aris's ingenuity had forged them a set of tools, crude though they might be, that offered a fighting chance. The unseen war was upon them, and they were ready to engage. The shuttle hummed onward, carrying them towards the Cygnus Rift, towards an unknown confrontation armed with the nascent technology of their desperate gambit.

The ramp of the modified courier shuttle hissed shut, sealing Eva and Aris within its utilitarian confines. The transition from the sterile, albeit illicitly acquired, docking bay to the cramped interior felt like a symbolic shedding of their former lives.

Outside, the familiar glow of the orbital station was already beginning to recede, a beacon of the ordered existence they were deliberately leaving behind. Eva's hand, still tingling from the finality of her encrypted transmissions, rested on the throttle, the cool metal a stark contrast to the burgeoning heat of her anxiety.

Aris, ever the pragmatist, was already immersed in pre-flight diagnostics, his fingers a blur across the holographic displays. The rhythmic beep of the system checks was a fragile counterpoint to the thrumming silence that had fallen between them. This was no longer a clandestine research expedition; it was an act of calculated defiance, a plunge into the unknown with the fate of billions hanging precariously in the balance. The weight of that knowledge settled upon Eva's shoulders like a physical burden, an oppressive cloak woven from the very fabric of their mission's desperate necessity.

"All systems nominal," Aris announced, his voice a low murmur that barely disturbed the quiet. "Navigational arrays are locked, atmospheric seals are holding. We're clear for ascent." He glanced at Eva, his expression a complex mixture of grim determination and a subtle, almost imperceptible, flicker of apprehension. "Ready to leave the cradle, Lieutenant Commander?"

Eva met his gaze, a ghost of a smile touching her lips, though it didn't quite reach her eyes. "It stopped being a cradle the moment we discovered what they were capable of, Aris. This is just... pushing off from the shore." She engaged the primary thrusters, a deep, resonant rumble vibrating through the shuttle's hull. The slight lurch as they lifted off was familiar, yet amplified by the profound shift in their trajectory, not just in physical space, but in their very existence.

The viewports, once a source of comfort, now displayed a tableau of alien menace. The stars, usually scattered like diamond dust across a velvet canvas, seemed to writhe with a sinister luminescence. The familiar constellations were subtly distorted, as if viewed through a warped lens. This was not the ordered, predictable cosmos of the Space Force's meticulously charted sectors. This was the raw, untamed void, a vast expanse where the rules of engagement were yet to be written, and where the very definition of 'enemy' was fluid and terrifyingly adaptable.

"The tracking beacon," Eva began, her voice tight as she scanned the receding orbital station, searching for any anomaly, any deviation that might indicate their departure had not gone unnoticed. "Has Aris's counter-frequency calibration held?"

"For now," Aris replied, his fingers still dancing across the controls, his eyes flicking between the sensor readouts and the external camera feeds. "The resonance dampener is functioning within acceptable parameters, but it's a passive measure. It masks our signature, but it doesn't erase it. Think of it as a cloak of invisibility; we're still there, just harder to see. And as we've seen, even the most sophisticated cloaking can be bypassed." He paused, his brow furrowed in concentration. "The true test will be how it performs when we encounter their broader subspace manipulation techniques. If they can weave their signals into the fabric of subspace, a simple dampener might not be enough to shield us truly."

The shuttle ascended, the planet below shrinking into a marbled sphere of blues and greens, a stark reminder of the world they were fighting to protect. Billions of lives, blissfully unaware of the existential threat lurking beyond the veil of conventional perception, continued their existence, their destinies irrevocably tied to the actions of two individuals now hurtling into the void. The responsibility was immense, a crushing weight that threatened to suffocate Eva even in the recycled air of the shuttle.

"We need to reach the Cygnus Rift as quickly as possible," Eva stated, her gaze fixed on the navigation display. "Aris, what's the estimated travel time?"

"At maximum sustainable warp, factoring in necessary detours to avoid charted patrol routes and suspected surveillance nodes, we're looking at approximately three cycles," Aris replied, his voice calm despite the urgency of their situation. "However, the drone's last transmission indicated that their network of influence might extend further than we initially estimated. We can't afford any unexpected encounters."

Eva nodded, her mind already processing the implications. Three cycles. Three cycles of being hunted, of being vulnerable, of operating on the razor's edge of discovery.

The knowledge that the very organization she had served, the Space Force, might be compromised, either through infiltration or a deeper, more insidious agenda, gnawed at her. Commander Valerius's unnervingly precise questions, the rapid escalation of her requisition flags – it all pointed to a system that was not merely efficient, but actively directed.

"Have you managed to refine the analysis of the drone's final data burst?" Eva inquired, her attention shifting to the nascent understanding of their enemy. The fragmented information they had gleaned was a tantalizing, terrifying glimpse into a technology that defied their current comprehension.

"Some progress," Aris admitted, adjusting a series of intricate algorithms. "The energy signature isn't just a signal; it's a layered resonance. They're not simply broadcasting a ping; they're subtly altering the subspace itself, creating localized distortions that our standard sensors can't even register. Think of it like this: imagine trying to find a single ripple on the surface of a vast ocean. Our current technology is like trying to measure that ripple with a ruler. What we need is a way to detect the absence of the ripple, or the subtle ways it changes the ocean's fundamental properties."

He gestured to a complex schematic appearing on his console, a cascade of interwoven wave patterns. "The drone's data suggests that their primary method of tracking involves correlating subspace resonance frequencies. Our shuttle, like any ship, has a unique subspace 'signature' generated by its warp core and drive systems. They've found a way to identify and latch onto this signature, effectively marking us for retrieval or... elimination."

"And the resonance dampener is designed to obscure that signature?" Eva pressed, her mind racing to keep pace with the scientific jargon.

"Precisely," Aris confirmed. "It emits a counter-frequency, designed to interfere with their detection algorithms. But it's a delicate balance. Too much interference, and we risk creating our own detectable anomaly. Not enough, and we remain visible." He paused, his gaze drifting to the bio-feedback monitor he had placed on a nearby console. "The greater concern, however, remains the potential for cognitive manipulation. If they can weave their signals into the very fabric of subspace, it's not beyond the realm of possibility that they could extend that influence to our neural pathways."

The implications were chilling. The idea that their thoughts, their decisions, could be subtly influenced by an unseen, alien intelligence was a violation of the most fundamental aspect of their autonomy. It was a form of warfare that bypassed conventional defenses, striking at the very core of their being.

"The bio-feedback monitor," Eva said, her voice barely a whisper, "is our only defense against that, isn't it?"

"It's our first line of defense," Aris corrected, his tone grave. "It's designed to detect deviations in our brainwave patterns, anomalies that suggest external influence. But it's a rudimentary tool. If they're sophisticated enough to manipulate subspace on such a fundamental level, their methods of cognitive influence could be equally subtle and equally advanced. We need to be hyper-vigilant, Eva. Every flicker of doubt, every misplaced thought, every irrational decision – it could be a sign that we're not entirely in control."

Eva nodded, the weight of responsibility intensifying with each word. She remembered her conversation with Commander Valerius, the unsettling precision of his questions, the way he seemed to anticipate her every deflection. Had that been a test of her own mental resilience, or had the seeds of their influence already been sown? The paranoia, once a distant hum, was now a deafening roar.

"We're leaving behind not just an orbital station, Aris," Eva said, her voice heavy with the unspoken realization. "We're leaving behind a system that may already be compromised. Every comms channel, every requisition, every transfer of resources – it's all potentially monitored, potentially manipulated."

"And our fabricated supply mission," Aris added, "was designed to provide us with cover, but it also created a traceable pattern. They know that you're deviating from your stated mission parameters. They might not know what you're doing, but they know you're not doing what you're supposed to be doing. That makes you a target."

The shuttle broke through the planet's upper atmosphere, the transition from the muted blues of the ionosphere to the inky blackness of space a jarring, symbolic severance. The familiar celestial bodies, once markers of safe passage, now seemed like indifferent observers to their desperate flight. The stars, so often a symbol of aspiration and discovery, now felt like the watchful eyes of an unknown, pervasive enemy.

"Our previous context," Eva murmured, more to herself than to Aris, "was about the immediate threat of being tracked. Now, it's about the systemic threat of being infiltrated. The Space Force itself might be compromised."

"It's a terrifying prospect," Aris conceded, his fingers hovering over a diagnostic panel. "But it also means that our understanding of this alien technology is paramount. We need to not only evade their tracking but also gather concrete evidence of their capabilities, and their intentions. The Cygnus Rift offers us the best chance to do that.

The dense nebulae and anomalous subspace currents there should provide sufficient cover for us to calibrate the resonance dampener and, perhaps, even deploy some of my more experimental detection equipment."

Eva's grip tightened on the throttle. The shuttle surged forward, a speck of defiance against the immensity of the cosmos. The weight of their mission was no longer just about preventing an alien enslavement; it was about uncovering the truth within their own ranks, about fighting a war on multiple fronts, both external and internal. The point of no return had been crossed not when they left the docking bay, but in the very moment they had discovered the terrifying implications of the portal. Now, they were hurtling towards the inevitable confrontation, armed with ingenuity, desperation, and the chilling knowledge that the enemy might already be closer than they could imagine. The dark sky was not just a canvas of stars; it was a battlefield, and they had just begun to fight. The silence in the shuttle was no longer one of anticipation, but of a profound, unsettling understanding. They were fugitives, not just from an alien threat, but from the very institutions designed to protect them. The journey ahead was fraught with peril, each light-year a testament to their isolation, their resolve forged in the crucible of a compromised reality. The familiar constellations, once guides, now seemed to mock them, their distant glow a reminder of a universe far more dangerous and unpredictable than the Space Force had ever let on. This was no longer about exploring the unknown; it was about surviving it. And in doing so, they carried the burden of revealing a truth that could shatter their civilization, or save it. The shuttle continued its ascent, a silent declaration of war against an enemy that operated in the shadows of both space and the mind.

5: The Nexus Point

The hum of the modified courier shuttle's deceleration thrusters was a comforting, familiar vibration against Eva's boots, a stark contrast to the unsettling quiet that had fallen over the comms channels. They had maintained absolute radio silence for the final approach, a precaution born from Aris's earlier warnings about subspace resonance detection. Outside the reinforced viewports, the planet's surface resolved into a vista of stark, almost alien beauty. It was a high-altitude plateau, a vast expanse of ochre-colored rock fractured into geometric patterns by eons of unknown geological forces. Strange, crystalline spires, like titanic shards of obsidian, jutted from the ground at improbable angles, catching the dim, alien sunlight and scattering it in fractured, prismatic displays.

"We're approaching the designated coordinates," Aris announced, his voice a low murmur in the confines of the cockpit. His fingers moved with practiced efficiency across the holographic displays, overlaying sensor data onto the visual feed. "Atmospheric density is nominal for this altitude, but the electromagnetic field is... unusually turbulent. My readings are fluctuating wildly, Eva. It's like trying to get a stable signal in a hurricane."

Eva brought the shuttle down with a feather-light touch, the landing gear settling onto the cracked surface with a soft crunch. The silence that followed the deactivation of the engines was profound, heavier than anything she had experienced in the controlled emptiness of space. It wasn't the absence of sound, but a palpable presence, a muffling of the universe that seemed to press in on them from all sides.

Even the whine of their own life support systems felt muted, swallowed by the oppressive stillness of this alien landscape.

"Perimeter established," Eva stated, her voice steady as she activated the shuttle's external sensor grid and deployed a series of low-frequency sonic emitters to create a broad, passive detection field. The emitters, designed to detect subtle vibrational anomalies, would hopefully provide an early warning if anything approached uninvited. "Aris, what are you getting?"

Aris was already outside the shuttle, a compact, portable analysis unit cradled in his arms. He'd donned a lightweight, environmental suit, more for the psychological comfort of a sealed environment than any immediate need, though the readings on his suit's internal display were concerning. "The energy signature here is unlike anything I've ever cataloged. It's not a conventional energy source; it's more like... a dimensional instability. The readings are spiking across multiple spectrums simultaneously. Transdimensional flux is off the charts, Eva. Significant. Very significant."

He gestured towards the sky. It was a sight that defied earthly comprehension. The vast emptiness of space, usually a deep, unfathomable black, was no longer purely that. Instead, a shimmering, iridescent haze seemed to spread across the celestial dome, a swirling tapestry of impossible colors that shifted and pulsed with an inner light. It was as if the very fabric of reality had been stretched too thin, revealing an underlying substratum of pure, vibrant energy. The effect was breathtakingly beautiful, and terrifyingly wrong.

"It's like looking through a warped lens," Eva murmured, stepping out of the shuttle and joining Aris. The air, even through her suit's filters, felt thick, charged with an unseen energy that prickled her skin. "What's causing it?"

"That's the million-credit question," Aris replied, his gaze fixed on the readings scrolling across his wrist-mounted display. "The drone's final transmission spoke of 'tearing reality,' and this... this is visual confirmation. It's localized, too. Our sensors indicate the densest point of this phenomenon is approximately three kilometers north-northwest of our current position. That's where the anomaly is centered." He tapped a section of the display. "And the gravitational readings are equally bizarre. There are micro-fluctuations, tiny gravitational distortions that shouldn't exist in a stable geological formation. It's as if space-time itself is being... flexed."

Eva scanned their surroundings. The crystalline spires, which had appeared monolithic from the shuttle, now revealed intricate, fractal patterns etched into their surfaces. They seemed to hum with a low, resonant frequency, a sound that was felt more than heard, vibrating in the very bones of their bodies. The ground beneath their feet was a mosaic of sharp-edged rock, worn smooth in places by winds that seemed to carry no sound.

"The sonic emitters are picking up something," Eva reported, checking her own tactical display. "Faint, but consistent. A low-frequency thrumming, originating from the direction of the anomaly. It's not a natural phenomenon. It's structured, almost like a signal, but it's too pervasive to be a direct broadcast."

"Resonance," Aris mused, turning his portable sensor array towards the direction Eva indicated. "That's consistent with the drone's data. They're not just broadcasting into subspace; they're resonating with it, subtly altering its properties to mask their presence or, more likely, to anchor whatever they're doing. This whole area is saturated with their influence." He crouched, placing a small, metallic probe into a fissure in the rock. "I'm trying to get a sample of the local sub-atomic particulate. If they're manipulating space-time, there might be residual exotic particles, evidence of their technology."

The silence of the plateau was broken only by the soft clicks and whirs of their equipment and the faint, pervasive hum that seemed to emanate from the very ground. Eva established a defensive perimeter, placing motion sensors and gravimetric anomaly detectors at strategic points around the shuttle, extending outward in a hundred-meter radius. She moved with the practiced efficiency of a seasoned operative, her senses keenly attuned to the unnatural stillness. Every instinct screamed that they were not alone, that this desolate landscape was merely a stage, and the true players were hidden, waiting.

"The readings are incredible, Eva," Aris said, his voice tinged with a scientist's awe, even amidst the palpable danger. "The subspace distortion isn't just localized to the sky. It's affecting the very matter around us. The crystalline structures… they're not just rock. They're infused with exotic particles, particles that exhibit quantum entanglement properties on a macroscopic scale. It's like they're naturally occurring quantum processors, or conduits for whatever energy they're channeling."

He stood up, brushing dust from his suit. "The drone's final diagnostics suggested they were creating a 'Nexus Point,' a stabilized node within the subspace fabric where their dimensional gateways could be anchored. If this plateau is it, then this is where they're emerging, or where they're preparing to emerge."

Eva's gaze swept across the jagged horizon. The iridescent haze overhead seemed to intensify, rippling like disturbed water. She could almost feel a pressure in the air, a subtle warping of her perception. "The 'tearing reality' wasn't just a metaphor, was it?"

"No," Aris confirmed grimly. "It was a literal description. They've found a way to breach the dimensional barriers, to punch holes through the conventional dimensions of our universe. And this... this is the result. A stable tear, a gateway, perhaps. We need to get a closer look."

He indicated a cluster of particularly tall spires in the distance, their obsidian surfaces reflecting the strange sky in a dizzying array of colors. "My readings indicate the highest concentration of subspace flux is emanating from that region. It's approximately three kilometers from our position. We should proceed cautiously."

Eva nodded, her hand instinctively going to the sidearm holstered at her hip. "Cavalry charge isn't exactly an option here. We move slow, we move smart. I'll take point. You stick close, keep those sensors running. We need to know what we're dealing with before we make any... aggressive moves."

As they began their trek across the fractured plateau, the pervasive hum intensified, seeming to emanate from everywhere and nowhere at once. The ground beneath their feet vibrated with a subtle, resonant energy that made their teeth ache. The iridescent haze above swirled with greater urgency, occasionally coalescing into ephemeral, swirling patterns that defied any known atmospheric or celestial phenomenon. Eva felt a growing unease, a sense of being observed not by eyes, but by a pervasive, disembodied awareness.

"The gravimetric distortions are becoming more pronounced," Aris reported, his voice tight with concentration. "They're creating micro-eddies in space-time. It's like walking through a river with localized whirlpools. I'm compensating for them on my readings, but it's impacting our sensor stability. We need to be careful not to rely too heavily on precise measurements right now."

Eva stopped, holding up a hand. "Hold up. Motion sensor just pinged. A definite, solid mass. Approaching our perimeter from the north-east."

Aris immediately shifted his focus, his portable scanner sweeping the indicated direction. "Negative. My scanners are showing... nothing. Not even residual heat signatures. If something is there, it's not registering on any conventional or even exotic energy spectrum I have available."

"It's not on your spectrum, but it pinged my motion sensor," Eva countered, her hand now on the grip of her sidearm. She scanned the alien landscape, her eyes picking out the subtle shifts in shadow and light that might betray movement. "It's large, and it's moving deliberately."

A flicker of movement, almost imperceptible, caught her eye. Near the base of one of the obsidian spires, a patch of shadow detached itself from the natural contours of the rock and flowed, rather than walked, towards them. It was a being of pure darkness, a void given form, absorbing all light that fell upon it. It moved with an unnatural grace, its silhouette shifting and coalescing as it advanced, seeming to possess no solid form, yet leaving distinct impressions on the ground as it passed.

"That's not a creature," Aris breathed, his eyes wide behind his helmet's visor. "That's... a localized absence of existence. It's not absorbing light; it's erasing it. My sensors are going haywire, Eva. It's emitting some anti-gravitational field, and... and it's disrupting my comms. I'm losing signal with the shuttle's perimeter defenses."

The creature, or rather, the void-entity, continued its silent, inexorable advance. Eva raised her sidearm, a pulse rifle, and fired a concentrated burst of energy. The bolts struck the entity, momentarily illuminating its edges with a searing white light, but they seemed to pass through it, causing no apparent damage. The entity flowed around the points of impact, its form undisturbed.

"Conventional weapons are useless," Eva stated, her mind racing. "Aris, anything on your readings? A weak point? An energy signature we can exploit?"

"Nothing I can identify," Aris replied, his voice strained. He adjusted his scanner, his movement's jerky. "It's like trying to analyze a hole in reality. There's no inherent energy to measure, just the absence of it. But... there's a localized gravitational anomaly associated with it. It's pulling space-time towards it. If we can disrupt that, maybe..."

Before he could finish, the entity surged forward with an impossible burst of speed. Eva reacted instantly, pushing Aris behind her and firing a continuous stream of energy bolts, trying to keep it at bay. The pulse rounds seemed to have no effect, but the sheer volume of energy might have caused a momentary hesitation. The iridescent haze above them pulsed violently, a wave of shimmering light washing over the plateau.

Eva felt a sudden, sickening lurch, as if the ground had dropped out from beneath her. The entity seemed to ripple, its form momentarily distending. "It's the subspace flux!" Aris shouted, stumbling as he tried to regain his footing. "It's reacting to the anomaly's energy surge! The entity is drawing power from it!"

Eva saw her opening. The entity was momentarily destabilized, its flowing form rippling uncontrollably. She lowered her rifle, switching its setting to a concentrated sonic blast, a frequency specifically designed to resonate with and disrupt exotic matter. Taking a deep breath, she fired.

A deafening, almost physical wave of sound slammed into the entity. For a moment, it seemed to solidify, its edges burning with a fierce, white light as the sonic energy tore at its very structure. It recoiled, its form flickering and distorting, before dissolving into nothingness, leaving only a faint distortion in the air where it had stood.

Eva lowered her rifle, her heart hammering against her ribs. The silence that followed the sonic blast was even more profound than before, heavy with the weight of what they had just witnessed. "That... was unpleasant," she managed, her voice slightly hoarse.

"Unpleasant is an understatement," Aris agreed, checking his readouts. "That was an existential threat, Eva. And if that's just a scout, or a guardian, then whatever's at the center of this Nexus Point is going to be far, far worse." He gestured towards the distant spires. "We're still going. We need to know what we're up against."

They continued their trek, the encounter with the void-entity leaving them with a heightened sense of dread and a grim understanding of the dangers they faced. The iridescent haze overhead seemed to throb with a malevolent intelligence, and the very ground beneath their feet felt alien and unstable. Every shadow seemed to harbor a potential threat, every crystalline spire a silent sentinel. The Nexus Point was real, and it was far more terrifying than they had ever imagined. The air itself felt like a tangible presence, charged with an unseen energy that vibrated with an alien purpose, a symphony of impossible frequencies that spoke of realities beyond their comprehension, and of an enemy that dwelled not just in the stars, but in the very fabric of existence. The silence was no longer a void; it was a pregnant pause, a moment of terrible anticipation before the true horror of the Nexus Point revealed itself. The planet was not merely desolate; it was a sentinel, a guardian, its strange geological formations and charged atmosphere the outward manifestation of a dimensional breach that threatened to unravel their understanding of the universe.

Each step was a descent into a deeper mystery, a more profound danger, as the shimmering sky above served as a constant, unnerving reminder that the laws of physics were no longer their sole guide. The world they had landed on was a testament to a power that could warp reality itself, a power that had to be understood, and neutralized, before it consumed them all.

The crystalline spires, now closer, seemed to lean in, their jagged facets reflecting the shifting, iridescent sky in a dizzying, disorienting dance. Eva's tactical display, which had been meticulously charting their progress, began to flicker. The familiar green lines of her sensor grid wavered, replaced by bursts of static and garbled data. "Aris, what's happening to the sensors?" she asked, her voice tight.

Aris, a few paces ahead of her, stopped abruptly. His personal resonator, a sensitive instrument designed to detect subtle subspace fluctuations, began to emit a series of sharp, erratic beeps. Its steady hum, which had been a constant companion since they'd left the shuttle, had devolved into a discordant, frantic pulse. "It's... it's going wild, Eva," he stammered, his eyes glued to the device. "The subspace distortion is... it's concentrating. Right in front of us."

He pointed with a trembling hand towards a point about fifty meters ahead, nestled between two particularly towering obsidian formations. At first, Eva saw nothing out of the ordinary. Just the stark, alien landscape, the fractured rock, the silent spires. Then, her eyes adjusted, and she saw it. A faint, almost imperceptible shimmer in the air, like heat haze rising from a desert road, but on a cosmic scale. It was a localized distortion, a ripple in the very fabric of reality. As she watched, the shimmer intensified, coalescing into a distinct, albeit barely visible, aperture. It wasn't a solid opening, but a distortion, a tear. It pulsed with an internal light, not like a beacon, but like a captured star struggling to break free. The colors swirling within it were impossible, shifting through hues that had no earthly names, vibrant and terrifyingly beautiful. This, Eva knew with a chilling certainty, was the conduit. The gateway. The Nexus Point itself.

"By the Void…" Aris whispered, his voice barely audible. He reached out a hand, as if to touch the phenomenon, then pulled it back as if scalded. "It's… it's beautiful."

As Eva's gaze remained fixed on the shimmering distortion, a wave of something akin to profound recognition washed over her. It was more than just a feeling; it was a visceral sensation, a sudden, overwhelming wave of déjà vu that hit her with the force of a physical blow. Images flashed through her mind with blinding speed: herself, standing on this very plateau, dressed in identical environmental gear, observing this exact phenomenon. The crystalline spires, the iridescent sky, the shimmering aperture – it was all there, imprinted on her mind as if she had lived this moment before. She stumbled, gripping a nearby spire for support, her breath catching in her throat.

"What was that?" she gasped, shaking her head to clear the disorientation.

Aris looked at her, his own face pale behind his visor. "I… I think I saw it too, Eva. A memory. Or… something like a memory. Of being here, seeing this. It was so vivid, so real." He gestured towards the aperture. "It's not static. The portals… they're dynamic. They shift. Maybe even… remember."

The implication of Aris's words hung heavy in the charged air. If the portals weren't fixed points, if they possessed a degree of consciousness or adaptability, then their mission just became infinitely more complex, and infinitely more dangerous. They weren't just dealing with an alien technology; they were potentially dealing with something that could learn, that could anticipate.

"If they're dynamic, then the drone's intel might be outdated," Eva mused, her mind racing to process this new variable. "We can't rely on exact coordinates or precise measurements. We need to expect the unexpected."

The aperture before them pulsed again, a more intense surge of energy radiating outwards. Aris's resonator shrieked, its readings spiking to critical levels. "The energy output is increasing exponentially," he reported, his voice strained. "It's drawing from... everything. The ambient subspace, the planet's electromagnetic field, even from us, I think. It's like a siphon."

Eva felt a faint, almost imperceptible pull, a subtle draining sensation. It wasn't physical, but more like a diminishment of her own internal energy. She activated a localized energy shield around herself, a low-level defensive measure, but even that seemed to be struggling against the pervasive pull. "It's affecting us directly, Aris. We can't stay here too long."

"But we need to get closer," Aris insisted, his scientific curiosity overriding his fear. "The drone's final transmission mentioned stabilizing the gateway. If this is the anchor point, there must be a mechanism, a control system, something that's facilitating this... tearing of reality."

He took a tentative step forward, his boots crunching on the fractured rock. Eva mirrored his movement, her senses on high alert. The aperture seemed to draw them in, its swirling vortex of impossible colors a siren call to the unknown. The déjà vu sensation returned, stronger this time, accompanied by a fleeting, almost subliminal whisper in her mind, a cascade of alien thoughts that she couldn't quite grasp, like trying to catch smoke.

"It's communicating," she murmured, her voice barely audible. "Or... influencing."

Aris stopped again, his eyes wide with a mixture of dread and fascination. "The resonance. It's not just a passive phenomenon anymore. It's becoming a resonance field, a carrier wave for... something. Information, perhaps? Intent?" He tapped his resonator, trying to make sense of the chaotic data streams. "The density of exotic particles is off the charts here. They're not just embedded in the spires anymore; they're saturating the air. Macroscopic quantum entanglement on a scale that's thermodynamically impossible according to standard physics."

He gestured towards the aperture. "This isn't just a doorway, Eva. It's a conscious construct. It's actively shaping space-time to maintain its own existence. And it's learning from our presence. The déjà vu... it's not random. It's an attempt to establish a baseline, to understand us by referencing our own past, or a perceived past."

Eva's mind struggled to keep pace with Aris's deductions. A conscious gateway? A portal that could access or manipulate memories? It was a terrifying prospect. If they were dealing with a sentient, reality-bending anomaly, then their carefully crafted infiltration plan was already obsolete.

"If it's learning from us, then it might also be vulnerable to us," Eva countered, her tactical mind kicking into gear. "If it's trying to understand our past, perhaps we can use that against it. What if we project a false memory, a misdirection?"

"A false memory?" Aris repeated, considering the idea. "That's... theoretically possible, if we could generate a strong enough psionic or subspace signal. But we don't have the technology for that, not on this scale. Our own mental states are too unstable in this environment. The resonance field is too disruptive."

He pointed towards a cluster of crystalline formations directly adjacent to the shimmering aperture. They were denser, more intricate than the others, their surfaces etched with complex geometric patterns that seemed to shift and reform as they watched. "Those formations," Aris said, his voice hushed. "They're acting as conduits and focusing the energy. Amplifying the resonance. If we can disrupt those, we might destabilize the gateway."

As he spoke, the aperture pulsed again, and a wave of intense energy washed over them. Eva felt a sharp pain behind her eyes, and the world swam for a moment. The déjà vu sensation intensified, coalescing into a single, vivid image: a vast, alien city, its impossible architecture reaching towards a sky filled with multiple suns. She saw herself, not as Eva Rostova, operative, but as something else entirely, something ancient and powerful, walking among beings of pure light.

"What is this?" she gasped, collapsing to her knees. The image was so real, so compelling, that she could almost feel the alien textures, smell the strange, perfumed air.

Aris was also struggling, clutching his head. "It's... it's implanting memories. Fabricating experiences. It's trying to overwhelm us, to break our cognitive defenses." He managed to pull up his sensor readings, his hands shaking. "The resonance field is being modulated. It's not just energy anymore; it's information— complex data streams. We're being... reprogrammed, Eva. Or at least, they're trying to."

Eva gritted her teeth, forcing the alien city and the phantom memories from her mind. She focused on the task at hand, on the objective. They couldn't afford to be overwhelmed. "Aris, the conduits! We need to disrupt them. Can your resonator do anything? A targeted energy burst?"

Aris nodded, his face a mask of grim determination. "I can try. I can overload it and create a localized feedback loop. It might shatter the crystals, or at least disrupt the energy flow." He began adjusting the settings on his resonator, his fingers flying across the holographic interface. "I'll need to get closer to the main conduit cluster."

Eva rose, her body aching from the psychic assault. She kept a wary eye on the aperture, which was now a swirling vortex of incandescent light, its distorted edges shimmering with an almost palpable power. "I'll cover you. But be careful. If it can implant memories, it can probably anticipate attacks."

As Aris moved towards the nearest conduit, Eva fired a burst of energy from her pulse rifle at the aperture itself, a defiant act of aggression. The energy bolts seemed to be absorbed, vanishing into the swirling light without any discernible effect. But it was enough. The aperture pulsed violently, and the psychic assault intensified. Eva felt a sudden, overwhelming sense of despair wash over her, a wave of hopelessness so profound it threatened to drown her.

Aris reached the base of the crystalline formations. They hummed with a low, resonant frequency, and a visible aura of energy pulsed around them. He raised his resonator, aiming it at the largest crystal. "Here goes nothing," he muttered, activating the device.

A focused beam of sonic energy, far more intense than anything Eva had heard before, lanced out from the resonator, striking the crystal. The effect was immediate and dramatic. The crystal glowed white-hot, then began to crack. A high-pitched whine filled the air, growing in intensity until it became unbearable. The aperture before them flickered, its light dimming for a moment as the conduit overloaded.

But the reprieve was short-lived. The other conduits pulsed in response, drawing power from the destabilized gateway. A deep, guttural roar replaced the crackling whine from the overloaded crystal, and the aperture flared back to life, brighter and more volatile than before. Aris stumbled back, his resonator sparking and smoking.

"It adapted!" he cried, looking at Eva. "It rerouted the energy. It reinforced the structure!"

Eva saw it too. The aperture wasn't just a gateway; it was a living entity, capable of self-preservation, of adaptation. The déjà vu returned, a chilling whisper in her mind: You cannot stop us. We are inevitable. The words echoed not just in her head, but seemed to resonate through the very rock beneath her feet.

"We're not getting through this with brute force, Aris," Eva said, her voice grim. "We need a different approach. If it's learning, if it's adapting, then it's also perceiving. It's aware of us."

She looked at the shimmering distortion, its chaotic beauty now laced with a primal, predatory intelligence. The psychic pressure was immense, attempting to grind down her resolve. She closed her eyes, focusing not on the alien thoughts, but on her own purpose, her own identity. She visualized the courier shuttle, the mission briefing, the faces of her crew. She anchored herself in her own reality, her own memories.

"The resonance," she said, opening her eyes. "You said it was a carrier wave for information. What if we feed it something else? Not a false memory, but... a disruption. A paradox."

Aris looked at her, confusion warring with a dawning understanding. "A paradox? Like what?"

"Like the fact that it's seeing us as having been here before," Eva said, her gaze fixed on the pulsing aperture. "If it's drawing on our perceived past to understand us, then perhaps we can exploit that perception. What if we act as if we've already achieved our objective? As if we've already stabilized or neutralized this Nexus Point?"

Aris's eyes widened. "You mean... pretend we've succeeded? Act as if the threat is already gone?"

"Exactly," Eva confirmed. "If it's trying to learn, to anticipate, then showing it a future where it has already been defeated might confuse its predictive algorithms. It might cause a cascade failure in its own self-maintenance protocols."

It was a desperate gamble, a wild hypothesis born from the

encroaching madness of this alien landscape. But they were out of options. The psychic assault was relentless, and their technological countermeasures were proving ineffective against a force that could manipulate reality itself.

"It's risky," Aris admitted. "If it perceives this as deception, it could retaliate with extreme prejudice."

"We're already facing extreme prejudice," Eva retorted. "This is our best chance." She took a deep breath, centering herself. "On my mark, we'll project confidence, conviction. We'll act as if we're walking away from a completed mission. And we'll head back to the shuttle."

She turned, not directly towards the aperture, but angling away from it, as if preparing to depart. Aris followed her lead, his own actions mirroring hers. The psychic pressure seemed to ease slightly, as if their sudden change in demeanor momentarily threw the entity off balance. The iridescent haze above them shifted, the impossible colors swirling with a new, uncertain rhythm. The aperture itself seemed to flicker, its intense glow momentarily subdued.

"It's working," Aris whispered, a note of cautious optimism in his voice. "The resonance patterns are fluctuating. It's... reconsidering."

They began to walk, slowly and deliberately, back the way they had come. Eva kept her gaze steady, projecting an air of calm resolution, of a job well done. Aris maintained a similar composure, his movements fluid and unhurried. They didn't look back at the shimmering gateway, but Eva could feel its attention still upon them, a palpable, inquisitive weight. The alien thoughts, the whispers of paradox and inevitability, seemed to recede, replaced by a tentative, almost questioning uncertainty.

As they reached the vicinity of their shuttle, Eva risked a glance at Aris's resonator. The erratic pulsing had subsided, replaced by a low, steady hum. The chaotic spikes in the data stream had smoothed out, resolving into something more... stable. Or at least, less actively hostile.

"The readings are normalizing," Aris reported, his voice filled with a mixture of relief and disbelief. "The subspace flux is receding. The resonance field is dissipating. It's like... it believes us."

Eva allowed herself a small, weary sigh. They had faced down a reality-bending gateway, a psychic entity capable of manipulating memories. They had apparently managed to deter it through sheer force of will and a dangerous act of cognitive bluffing. It was a victory, of sorts, but a precarious one. They hadn't destroyed the Nexus Point, nor had they fully understood its purpose or its capabilities. They had merely convinced it, for the moment that its existence had been neutralized.

"Let's get out of here," Eva said, her voice firm. "We have a lot to report. And we need to figure out how to deal with an enemy that can rewrite our own past."

As they boarded the shuttle, the strange, iridescent haze began to coalesce, not into a gateway, but into a vast, shimmering nebula of impossible colors. It pulsed with a soft, internal light, a silent, watchful presence. The Nexus Point was still there, hidden, but the direct threat had receded. For now. Eva knew, with a chilling certainty, that this was only the beginning. The portal's glimmer, once seen, could never be unseen, and its implications for the universe, and for their own understanding of reality, were only beginning to unfold. The journey back to civilization would be a long one, filled with the lingering echoes of impossible visions and the unsettling knowledge that the fabric of existence was far more fragile, and far more complex, than they had ever dared to imagine. The plateau, once a desolate landscape, now felt like a delicate skin, stretched taut over an abyss of unfathomable power, a power that had briefly, and terrifyingly, shown its face.

The shimmering distortion, the Nexus Point, continued to pulse, its unearthly light painting the jagged landscape in shifting hues of impossible color. Eva and Aris had retreated a short distance, establishing a cautious perimeter. Their initial objective – to observe and assess – had been met with a barrage of inexplicable phenomena, from temporal echoes to what Aris now termed "cognitive resonance." The psychic emanations, subtle yet insistent, had been the latest development.

"It's like a broadcast," Aris murmured, his gaze fixed on his console, which displayed a chaotic symphony of energy signatures. "Not direct communication, not yet. More like... background radiation. Psychic static." He adjusted a dial, his brow furrowed in concentration. "The modulation is incredibly complex. It's cycling through frequencies I've never encountered, patterns that defy conventional analysis."

Eva watched him, her own senses on high alert. She had felt it too – a faint, insidious pressure against her mind, a subtle invitation to distraction. It wasn't an overwhelming assault, but a persistent hum, like a siren song sung in a frequency just beyond conscious hearing. She had found herself momentarily losing focus, her thoughts drifting, her attention snagged by fleeting, nonsensical images. A brief flicker of a childhood memory, a distorted fragment of a forgotten dream. Each time, she had to pull herself back, reasserting her mental dominance actively.

"I'm feeling it too, Aris," Eva confirmed, her voice low. "It's trying to... soften our defenses. Make us complacent. Or perhaps," she added, a chilling thought taking root, "make us receptive to something else." She met his gaze, a silent question passing between them. Had their prolonged exposure to this nexus, this tear in reality, begun to alter their own perceptions? Was it an inherent property of the portal, or a reaction to their presence?

Aris ran a diagnostic, his fingers flying across the holographic interface. "The ambient exotic particle density is still off the charts," he reported. "And the subspace distortion isn't just a passive phenomenon anymore. It's actively being manipulated.

I'm detecting feedback loops, self-correcting algorithms operating at a level that suggests... intent. And this psychic resonance? It's not a byproduct. It's a tool. It's trying to establish a baseline of our mental state, to gauge our resistance, our vulnerabilities."

He paused, a flicker of unease crossing his face. "Eva, I noticed you falter for a second there. Just a fraction of a second. Your gaze went distant. Was it... a memory? A thought?"

Eva nodded, her expression grim. "It was. Fleeting, but vivid. Something about a... a meteor shower. From my childhood. It felt incredibly real, but also... manufactured. Like an echo of a memory, but not quite mine." She shook her head, trying to clear the lingering impression. "It's subtle, Aris. Like a whisper. But it's constant. It requires continuous mental resistance."

Aris's fingers stilled on his console. "Continuous resistance," he repeated, the words heavy with implication. "That's what worries me. If this influence is constant and requires sustained effort to ward off, then our operational capacity is already being degraded. And I'm not sure how long we can maintain that level of mental discipline without succumbing to... whatever it's trying to achieve." He looked towards the pulsating aperture, a knot of apprehension tightening in his stomach. "I wonder if my own prolonged exposure has made me more susceptible. Or if the portal's proximity is intensifying the effect for everyone nearby. The energy signatures are too alien, too advanced, to fully comprehend. It's like trying to decipher a language when you only know a few scattered words."

He tapped a series of commands, his focus narrowing on a particular set of readings. "The psychic emanations aren't uniform," he explained, pointing to a graph that spiked and dipped erratically. "There are peaks, moments of heightened influence.

And these peaks seem to correlate with shifts in the portal's energy output, almost as if the mental probing is a precursor to a more direct action. A probing attack, if you will."

Eva considered his words. If the portal was actively probing their minds, trying to find a weakness, then a confrontation was likely to be even more dangerous than they had anticipated. "What kind of action, Aris?" she pressed. "Can you predict what it might do?"

"That's the million-credit question," Aris replied, his voice laced with frustration. "The data is too noisy. The patterns are too fluid. But based on the theoretical models of advanced psionic entities, it could range from direct mental manipulation – full-blown psychic assault – to something far more insidious. It could be attempting to implant false memories, alter our perceptions of reality, or even rewrite our neural pathways to influence our actions. The déjà vu we experienced earlier... that wasn't just a temporal echo. It was a manufactured experience, designed to create a sense of familiarity, to make us underestimate the alien nature of this place. It was an attempt to normalize the abnormal."

He let out a sigh, leaning back from his console. "We're dealing with something that operates on principles we barely understand, Eva. It's not just manipulating space-time; it's manipulating consciousness itself. And our own minds, our own perceptions, are its primary tools."

Eva walked closer to the edge of the plateau, her eyes never leaving the shimmering vortex. The light seemed to ebb and flow, drawing her in with its mesmerizing dance. She could feel the subtle pressure on her mind intensifying, a gentle caress that threatened to lull her into a dangerous complacency. She focused on the solid ground beneath her boots, the familiar weight of her rifle, the rhythmic beat of her own heart. Anchors. They needed anchors.

"If it's trying to establish a baseline, to understand us by creating familiar echoes," Eva mused, her voice barely above a whisper, "then perhaps we can use that against it. It's learning, it's adapting. What if we feed it... inconsistent data? What if we introduce a paradox into the very fabric of its understanding?"

Aris looked up, his eyes widening with a spark of interest. "A paradox? Like what, Eva? We're not equipped for sophisticated psionic warfare. Our offensive capabilities are purely kinetic and energy-based."

"Not a physical attack, Aris," Eva clarified. "A mental one. Remember the deja vu? The sense of having been here before? It was a fabricated memory, designed to create a sense of familiarity. What if we lean into that? What if we act as if we've already completed our mission? As if we've already assessed the Nexus Point, stabilized it, and are now simply completing a final reconnaissance before departing?"

Aris stared at her, a slow understanding dawning on his face. "You mean... we project an aura of success? Of having neutralized the threat? We act as if this whole encounter is a mere formality?"

"Exactly," Eva confirmed, turning to face him. "If it's trying to learn from our perceived past, or our projected future, then showing it a future where its own existence has been rendered irrelevant might be the ultimate disruption. It's trying to understand our intentions. Let's give it intentions it can't reconcile with our current actions. Let's give it a history that contradicts its current efforts to comprehend us."

Aris considered this, his mind racing through the implications. "It's a high-risk strategy. If it perceives this as a deception, it could interpret it as a direct act of aggression. The backlash could be... catastrophic."

"We're already facing potential catastrophe, Aris," Eva

countered, her voice steady. "And our current methods are proving... insufficient. We're being bombarded with psychic static. Our sensors are unreliable. Our own perceptions are being subtly manipulated. We need to try something radically different. Something that exploits its very nature as a learning, adapting entity."

She took a slow, deliberate breath, centering herself. The ambient psychic hum seemed to lessen for a moment, as if the portal itself was sensing a shift in their focus. "We walk away," Eva declared, her voice imbued with an assumed confidence. "Not in fear, but with the quiet satisfaction of a completed task. We project an image of someone leaving a solved problem. We don't look back. We don't hesitate. We simply... depart."

Aris met her gaze, a flicker of apprehension still present, but overlaid with a nascent curiosity. "It's a gamble, Eva. A massive gamble. But... it's the most ingenious thing I've heard since we arrived. If it's trying to understand us by predicting our future actions based on our past and present states, then showing it a 'future' where we've already succeeded might break its predictive models."

"And if it breaks its models," Eva added, a grim determination hardening her features, "it might create the opportunity we need. Or at least, a window of opportunity. We're not looking for a fight here, Aris. We're looking for information. And sometimes, the best way to get information from a predatory intelligence is to make yourself seem like an irrelevant variable. A problem already solved."

With that, Eva turned and began to walk, not directly away from the portal, but at an angle, as if moving towards a predetermined exit. Her movements were deliberate, unhurried. She projected an air of calm resolve, the quiet confidence of someone who had just finished a challenging but successful undertaking. Aris fell into step beside her, mirroring her pace, his own posture conveying a similar sense of finality.

The psychic hum seemed to recede further as they moved. The disorienting kaleidoscope of colors within the aperture appeared to stabilize, the frantic dance slowing to a more measured pulse. Eva felt the pressure on her mind ease, replaced by a subtle, almost imperceptible curiosity. It was as if the entity, faced with their unexpected departure and assumed success, was momentarily confused, its complex algorithms struggling to reconcile their actions with its own predictions.

"The resonance patterns are fluctuating," Aris whispered, his voice barely audible, his eyes darting between his console and the receding spectacle of the Nexus Point. "The ambient exotic particle density is... decreasing. It's as if the portal is... de-escalating. It's not sensing a threat anymore. It's sensing... closure."

Eva allowed herself a faint, almost imperceptible nod. They continued their measured retreat, their steps crunching softly on the crystalline dust. They maintained their facade of confident departure, their minds focused on projecting an image of successful disengagement. The sheer audacity of their strategy was its own form of defense. By refusing to engage, by acting as if the existential threat they faced was merely a procedural hurdle already cleared, they were, in essence, denying the portal the conflict it seemed to crave, the information it sought through direct interaction.

As they neared the point where their shuttle was hidden, Eva risked a glance back. The Nexus Point was still there, a swirling nexus of impossible energies, but its intensity had lessened. The overwhelming psychic presence had subsided, replaced by a more distant, watchful aura. It was like observing a predator that, having lost sight of its prey, was now scanning the horizon for any sign of resurgence.

"Readings are stabilizing significantly," Aris reported, his voice tinged with a mixture of relief and incredulity. "The subspace distortions are resolving. The ambient psychic interference has dropped below critical levels. It... it seems to believe us, Eva. It genuinely believes we're leaving because our task here is done."

Eva allowed a small, weary smile to touch her lips. "We haven't solved anything, Aris," she said, her voice low and serious. "We've merely bought ourselves some time. We've demonstrated that even an entity capable of manipulating reality itself can be... confused. Or at least, misled, by projecting a sufficiently convincing narrative."

They reached the shuttle, its familiar metallic hull a welcome sight against the alien backdrop. As they cycled through the airlock, Eva felt a profound sense of unease settle over her. They had faced down a phenomenon that defied all known physics and psychology, and had emerged, for the moment, unscathed. But the encounter had left its mark. The lingering echoes of manufactured memories, the unsettling awareness of their own mental vulnerabilities, and the chilling realization that they had just gambled with a power that could rewrite their very perception of reality.

"We need to analyze every byte of data we collected," Eva said, as the shuttle's engines hummed to life. "And we need to formulate a new approach. This isn't just about technology anymore, Aris. It's about understanding the very nature of consciousness, and how it can be manipulated on a scale we never imagined."

The shuttle lifted off, ascending into the iridescent sky. Below them, the crystalline spires remained, silent sentinels on a desolate world. The Nexus Point, though no longer directly visible, felt like a presence, a watchful intelligence that had registered their presence and their peculiar departure. They had encountered something profoundly alien, something that blurred the lines between physics, consciousness, and the very fabric of existence. And the knowledge of its existence, and its terrifying capabilities, was a burden they would carry with them long after they left this uncharted world. The subtle psychic whisper, though diminished, still lingered at the edges of Eva's awareness, a faint reminder of the unseen battle they had just fought, and of the new, insidious form of conflict that had just been introduced to their understanding of the universe.

The adrenaline, a potent cocktail of fear and fascination, still thrummed beneath Eva's skin. The calculated retreat, the projected confidence, had worked, at least in buying them breathing room. But the Nexus Point, that shimmering wound in reality, hadn't vanished. It remained, a silent, pulsing enigma, its allure undiminished, its true purpose still shrouded in mystery. They had successfully deceived a consciousness that manipulated space-time and perception, a feat that felt both exhilarating and profoundly terrifying. Yet, Eva couldn't shake the feeling that their reprieve was just that – temporary. The entity behind the Nexus Point was undoubtedly aware of their departure, and perhaps, even more importantly, of their ability to resist its insidious influence.

Aris, his usual scientific detachment momentarily overshadowed by a nervous energy, was already reviewing the data streams from their hasty withdrawal. "The subspace distortions are stabilizing, as predicted," he confirmed, his voice a low murmur in the confined space of the shuttle. "But the exotic particle residue... it's not entirely dissipating. There's a residual signature, Eva. Faint, but definitely present. It's like a faint scent clinging to the air after something powerful has passed through."

Eva nodded, her gaze fixed on the viewscreen as the alien landscape receded. The crystalline spires, once sharp and defined, now softened into a hazy panorama under the strange, filtered light of the distant star. "It's aware we were there. And it knows we saw something. The question is, what does it do now?" She turned her attention from the receding Nexus Point to the immediate vicinity, a habit ingrained from years of reconnaissance. Her eyes scanned the rough, uneven terrain, her mind sifting through the visual noise for anything that didn't belong.

It was then, as they banked for their final ascent, that she saw it. A subtle disruption in the otherwise chaotic pattern of the ground, about a kilometer from the plateau where they had first encountered the Nexus Point. It wasn't a footprint, not in any conventional sense. There were no distinct impressions of boots or appendages.

Instead, it was a series of shallow, elongated depressions, as if something heavy, something with a broad, irregular base, had been dragged or shuffled across the rocky surface. The pattern was intermittent, broken by stretches of undisturbed ground, suggesting a halting, uneven movement, or perhaps, a series of stops and starts.

"Aris," Eva said, her voice sharpening with a renewed sense of purpose. "Hold our trajectory. I want a closer look at that. Sector Gamma-9, approximately 4.7 klicks bearing zero-two-five."

Aris, ever the professional, immediately complied, nudging the shuttle into a slow, sweeping orbit. His brow furrowed as he zoomed in on the designated area. "I'm picking up faint energy readings there, Eva. Residual exotic particles, consistent with the Nexus Point's emissions, but... attenuated. Lower amplitude. It suggests something interacted with the portal and then moved away." He adjusted the optical sensors, his fingers dancing across the control panel. "The terrain disturbance is also evident on our thermal imaging. Recent activity, though the thermal signature is... odd. Not typical biological heat. More like a low-level, diffuse thermal bloom."

Eva's heart rate accelerated. This was it. Tangible evidence. Not just the unsettling psychic resonance or the temporal echoes, but physical traces of something concrete, something that had been there. "Can you get a lock on the specific composition of those energy signatures? Are they identical to the Nexus Point's primary emissions, or are they altered?"

"Working on it," Aris replied, his voice taut with concentration. "The primary emissions are incredibly complex, a multi-layered waveform. These residual signatures... they're like fragments. Like echoes of the main signal, but distorted, as if filtered through a different medium. There are also trace elements... novel compounds, I think. Elements not cataloged in our databases. It's like... like something shed these particles as it moved."

As Aris continued his analysis, Eva guided the shuttle into a low, careful pass over the disturbed ground. The depressions were clearer now, meandering in a loose, almost serpentine fashion away from the general vicinity of the Nexus Point, heading towards a cluster of jagged, obsidian-like rock formations. They weren't uniform; some were deeper than others, some wider, as if the object or entity had shifted its weight or its mode of locomotion. And scattered within these disturbed areas, catching the shuttle's powerful external lights, were glints of something unnatural.

"Aris, enhance visual on those glints," Eva instructed, pointing towards a particularly dense cluster of the depressions. "Are those... debris?"

The magnification optics whirred to life, and the image on the main screen sharpened. It was indeed debris, but unlike anything Eva had ever seen. Not metal, not rock, not any recognizable material from terrestrial or known exoplanetary engineering. It was a collection of fragments, some crystalline, some amorphous, all possessing a dull, metallic sheen that seemed to absorb rather than reflect light. Many of them pulsed with a faint, internal luminescence, a soft, ethereal glow that flickered and died, then reignited with a slow, rhythmic beat. And the energy readings Aris had detected were strongest here, emanating from these strange fragments.

"Incredible," Aris breathed, his scientific curiosity momentarily overriding his caution. "The energy output is minimal, but sustained. It's like a low-level power source embedded within the material itself. And the composition... it's defying spectroscopic analysis. It's as if the atoms themselves are arranged in a configuration that doesn't adhere to our understanding of elemental bonding."

Eva felt a chill crawl up her spine. They had stumbled upon something far more significant than they had initially anticipated. This wasn't just a natural phenomenon; this was evidence of alien activity, tangible proof of a presence beyond their comprehension. "We need to collect samples, Aris. Carefully. Use the manipulator arm. We can't risk direct contact with anything we don't understand."

The shuttle's articulated arm extended, its sensitive manipulators reaching out towards the strange debris. With painstaking precision, Aris guided the arm, carefully plucking a few of the smaller, glowing fragments from the disturbed earth. The samples were deposited into sterile containment units, their faint luminescence continuing even within the sealed environment.

"These are... crystalline structures, Eva," Aris reported, examining the preliminary readings from the onboard analyzers. "But not like any crystal lattice we know. The internal structure is... fractal. It's incredibly complex, and it seems to be shifting, reorganizing itself on a subatomic level. And the residual energy isn't a simple emission; it's more like a contained reaction, a perpetual, slow-burn process. It's self-sustaining."

He then turned his attention to another anomaly. "Eva, look at this. Around the edges of these depressions... there's a fine, powdery residue. Almost like dust, but it's not dust. It's reacting to the shuttle's energy field, coalescing into small, almost geometric shapes before dissipating."

Eva directed the shuttle's sensors towards the ground again. He was right. A faint, shimmering haze clung to the ground where the depressions were deepest. It wasn't easily visible, almost like a visual artifact, but the sensors picked it up. "What is it?"

"I... I don't know," Aris admitted, his voice filled with a rare note of bewilderment. "It's not organic, not inorganic, not mineral. It's... reactive matter. It seems to be composed of exotic particles, the same ones we're detecting in trace amounts, but somehow stabilized into a particulate form. When the shuttle's ambient energy field brushes against it, it seems to... momentarily organize itself. Almost like it's trying to communicate, or perhaps, reconfigure into something else."

He was already activating the collection protocols for the manipulator arm, meticulously gathering samples of this strange, powdery residue. As the arm carefully scooped up the material, a faint, almost imperceptible hum filled the shuttle's cabin, a subtle vibration that seemed to resonate deep within their bones. It wasn't the overwhelming psychic pressure they had experienced at the Nexus Point, but something more nuanced, more intimate, as if the very particles were attempting to imprint themselves onto their senses.

"The residue is volatile when exposed to direct energy," Aris reported, his voice tight. "It's reacting to the arm's internal power conduits. The geometric shapes it forms... they're not random. They're repeating patterns. Complex, but repeating. It's like a language, Eva. A language made of fleeting forms and energy fluctuations."

Eva felt a profound sense of awe mixed with a growing dread. They had come seeking knowledge, and they had found it, in the most unexpected and terrifying forms. This wasn't just a natural anomaly. This was evidence of intelligent, advanced activity.

Whatever had created the Nexus Point, whatever had left these traces, was something utterly alien, something that operated on principles far beyond their current understanding. The residual energy, the strange materials, the reactive residue – it all pointed to a civilization, or an entity, with a mastery of physics and materials science that bordered on the miraculous, or perhaps, the terrifyingly esoteric.

"These samples," Eva said, her gaze fixed on the glowing fragments within their containment units, "are the proof we need. This isn't theoretical anymore, Aris. We have empirical data. We have physical evidence of something here, something that interacted with the Nexus Point. We can move beyond speculation and focus on analysis."

Aris nodded, his fingers already flying across the console, initiating a cascade of diagnostic scans. "The complexity is staggering, Eva. The energy signatures, the material composition, the reactive properties of the residue... it's like nothing we've ever encountered. This debris... it's not just discarded waste. It's information. It's a Rosetta Stone, waiting to be deciphered."

He paused, a sudden thought striking him. "What if the Nexus Point itself is a form of... technology? Not a natural phenomenon, but a deliberately created gateway, and these fragments are... components? Or perhaps, byproducts of its operation? If so, then whatever created it is still active, still utilizing this... nexus."

Eva considered his words. The idea of the Nexus Point being a deliberate construct, an artificial gateway, was both plausible and deeply unsettling. It implied purpose, intent, and a level of technological sophistication that dwarfed anything humanity had ever achieved. "And if it's still active," she murmured, her eyes drifting back to the distant, shimmering distortion that was the Nexus Point, though it was now barely visible as a faint anomaly in the sky, "then we've just announced our presence to it.

Our little charade of departure might have only delayed the inevitable."

"Or," Aris countered, a glint of excitement in his eyes, "it might have given us the upper hand. By projecting an image of completed objectives and successful disengagement, we might have lulled it into a false sense of security. It now believes we are no longer a threat, or perhaps, no longer of interest. These samples, however, tell a different story. They tell of our continued investigation, our persistence."

The shuttle continued its ascent, leaving the desolate, alien world behind. But the lingering presence of the Nexus Point, and the tangible evidence they carried within their hull, weighed heavily on Eva's mind. They had moved beyond the realm of conjecture, into the stark reality of alien presence. The path ahead was uncertain, fraught with dangers they were only beginning to comprehend. But they had taken the first crucial step: they had found proof, solid, undeniable evidence, that they were not alone. And with that proof came a responsibility – to understand, to analyze, and to prepare for whatever lay beyond the veil of the Nexus Point. The universe, it seemed, had just become infinitely larger, and infinitely more complex.

The analysis of the collected samples commenced the moment they were securely transferred to the shuttle's onboard laboratory. Aris, usually a picture of focused composure, was practically buzzing with an almost manic energy. The exotic particles within the debris fragments resisted all conventional categorization. Spectrographic analysis yielded patterns that defied the known periodic table. It was as if the very building blocks of matter were arranged in ways that violated established physical laws.

"It's like the strong nuclear force is behaving differently," Aris muttered, hunched over his console, his brow furrowed in concentration. "Or perhaps, there are forces at play we haven't even theorized about. The way these atoms bond... it suggests a level of manipulation at the quantum level that is... extraordinary. And the embedded energy source within the material itself... it's not radioactive decay, and it's not fusion. It's something else entirely. A contained, perpetual energy reaction."

Eva watched him, a mix of awe and trepidation churning within her. "Can you isolate the source of that energy?"

"I can detect its presence, its output," Aris replied, tapping a few commands. "But isolating it... that would require manipulating the very structure of the material. And given its inherent instability when exposed to external energy fields, I'm hesitant to proceed with anything more invasive than passive analysis. The residue samples are even more perplexing. When exposed to even a minimal energy flux from the shuttle's systems, they temporarily coalesce into complex, repeating geometric forms. I've managed to capture some of the ephemeral patterns, but the underlying mechanism is baffling. It's as if the particles themselves possess a form of rudimentary awareness, reacting to external stimuli by temporarily organizing themselves into predefined structures."

He brought up a holographic display, showcasing a series of intricate, crystalline patterns that flickered and dissolved in rapid succession. Some were reminiscent of snowflakes, others of complex molecular structures, and still others were entirely alien, evoking no recognizable terrestrial analogue. "These aren't random formations, Eva. They are too precise, too repeatable. It's a language, or at least, a form of symbolic representation. And the sheer speed at which these patterns form and dissipate suggests an information processing capability far beyond our current understanding."

Eva felt a cold dread seep into her. They had gone from observing a bizarre temporal anomaly to discovering concrete evidence of an alien presence, and now, they were looking at what appeared to be an alien form of communication, embedded in dust-like particles. "If it's a language, Aris, what is it trying to convey?"

"That," Aris sighed, running a hand through his already disheveled hair, "is the million-credit question. The patterns are too varied, too abstract, to decipher immediately. They seem to be influenced by external factors – the intensity of the energy field, the composition of the surrounding medium, even subtle shifts in the shuttle's own energy signature. It's like trying to understand a conversation by only catching snippets of individual words, without any context."

He zoomed in on one particular series of patterns, a complex, interlocking fractal that seemed to pulsate with a faint internal light. "This one... it appeared when I was cross-referencing our sensor data with the residual energy readings from the Nexus Point itself. It's a direct correlation. So, it is responding to our ongoing analysis. It's acknowledging our investigation."

Eva leaned closer, her eyes tracing the alien geometry. "So, it knows we're studying it. It knows we're analyzing these samples." The implications were immense. This wasn't just passive debris; it was an active, albeit subtle, interaction. The alien intelligence, or entity, that had left these traces was aware of their presence, their activities, and was, in its own strange way, communicating with them.

"This also means," Aris continued, his voice low, "that our little deception might have been... less effective than we hoped. If these residues are a form of distributed sentience, or at least, an extension of the Nexus Point's consciousness, then they might have 'felt' us gathering these samples. They might have perceived our continued investigation even as we projected an image of departure."

Eva's mind raced. The psychic hum, the temporal echoes, the manufactured memories – they were all tools. And this reactive residue, this pulsing debris, was another tool, or perhaps, a different manifestation of the same overarching intelligence. "So, the psychic influence was an attempt to gather information, to gauge our intentions, and this... this is a response to our actions. It's learning from us, adapting to our presence."

"Precisely," Aris confirmed. "And if it's learning, it's also likely capable of predicting. Our calculated departure was a calculated move to disrupt its predictive models. But the fact that it left these residues, that they are still interacting with our systems... it suggests it's still trying to understand us. Or perhaps, to influence us further."

He gestured towards a monitor displaying the raw energy signatures from the Nexus Point, now overlaid with the spectrum of the collected debris. "The elemental composition of the debris, while alien, shows faint harmonic resonances with the primary emissions of the Nexus Point. It's as if these particles are intrinsically linked to the larger phenomenon. They are not merely discarded remnants; they are integral components, or perhaps, extensions of the Nexus Point's existence."

Eva felt a sudden, chilling realization dawn. The Nexus Point wasn't just a portal; it was a manifestation. A gateway, yes, but also a living, or perhaps, a technologically ensouled entity. And these fragments, this reactive dust, were like seeds, or perhaps, like sensory organs, scattered across the landscape. They were tangible proof of an unfathomable intelligence, an intelligence that perceived reality in ways they could only begin to grasp.

"This changes everything, Aris," Eva said, her voice barely a whisper. "We're not just dealing with an anomaly. We're dealing with an agent. An active participant. And it's not just observing us; it's interacting with us, through these traces."

Aris nodded, his gaze now fixed on the shuttle's external sensors, as if expecting something to materialize from the empty void outside. "And the fact that it's still 'broadcasting' these residues, that they are still reacting to our systems, means it's still actively engaged with our presence. It hasn't lost interest. If anything, our continued analysis has only intensified its focus on us. We've gone from being observers to being subjects of its study. And that, Eva, is a far more dangerous position to be in." The implication hung heavy in the air: their calculated deception might have bought them time, but their discovery of empirical evidence had perhaps painted an even larger target on their backs.

The quiet hum of the shuttle's life support systems had always been a comforting sound, a constant reminder of their fragile sanctuary in the vast unknown. But now, it seemed to amplify the silence, making the encroaching mental onslaught all the more palpable. Eva gripped the arms of her pilot's chair, her knuckles white, as the insidious tendrils of alien influence began to probe the edges of her consciousness. It wasn't a loud invasion, no booming pronouncements or blinding flashes of light. It was far more insidious, a creeping dread that whispered doubt into the very marrow of her bones.

Aris, beside her, let out a sharp, involuntary gasp. His eyes, usually sharp and analytical, were glazed, unfocused, staring at some unseen horror. "No," he murmured, his voice strained. "It... it can't be."

Eva forced herself to turn, to break her own intense focus on the perceived threat. "Aris? What is it? What are you seeing?"

His response was a broken sob. "My family... Lena... the children... they're... they're gone. Assimilated. Lost to the... the silence." He shook his head violently, as if trying to dislodge a parasitic thought. "The reports... they said no surface colonies were affected... that the... the Great Silence had spared them..."

The images that flooded Eva's mind were a cruel mirror, reflecting her own deepest anxieties. She saw herself standing before a tribunal, her uniform stripped, her career in tatters. Accusations of insubordination, of reckless endangerment, of treason, echoed in the sterile chamber. Her superiors, faces etched with betrayal, dismissed her findings, her warnings. She was a pariah, her years of dedication and sacrifice rendered meaningless, her very sanity called into question. Her reputation, her life's work, shattered by the same entity she was trying to understand.

"This is not real, Aris," Eva said, her voice firm despite the tremor running through it. She reached out, her hand hovering near his arm, hesitant to make physical contact lest it shatter his fragile grip on reality. "It's a projection. A weapon. It's trying to break us."

"But it feels so real," Aris whispered, tears tracking paths through the grime on his cheeks. "The despair... it's overwhelming. Like a void opening up inside me."

Eva's own mental defenses, honed by years of rigorous psychological training, felt like they were buckling. The subtle manipulation was far more potent than any physical force. It bypassed the shuttle's shields, the hull's integrity, and struck directly at the core of their being. It was a battle waged on the battlefield of the mind, and the enemy knew every weakness, every buried fear.

She focused on the mission. The data, the samples, the very reason they were here. She visualized the sterile confines of their laboratory, the precise movements of the manipulator arm, the objective readings from the sensors. These were anchors in the swirling storm of manufactured emotion. "Aris, remember our training. We are scientists. We analyze, we quantify, we remain objective. This is data, albeit in an alarming form. It's a psychic intrusion, designed to incapacitate us."

He blinked, a flicker of recognition returning to his eyes. He took a deep, shuddering breath. "Objective analysis... right. It's exploiting our emotional vulnerabilities. It's... it's a form of psychological warfare." He squeezed his eyes shut, then opened them again, his gaze meeting Eva's with renewed determination. "The samples... they are real. The data is real. My family... I have to believe they are safe. This... this is a lie."

The intensity of the psychic assault seemed to ebb slightly, as if the entity sensed their reassertion of control. But it was a temporary respite, a brief lull before the next wave. Eva felt a prickling sensation on her scalp, a phantom touch that sent a shiver down her spine. The alien intelligence was not a monolithic entity; it was a pervasive force, capable of nuanced and terrifying manipulation.

"It's adapting," Eva observed, her voice tight. "It's not just throwing random fears at us. It's tailoring the experience. It knows what to target." She remembered the fragmented patterns from the residue, the subtle language of fleeting forms. Was this an extension of that? A more sophisticated form of communication, designed to elicit a specific response?

"It's a test of resolve," Aris said, his voice gaining a measure of its former strength. He was already running diagnostics, his fingers flying across the console. "Not just a passive probe. It's actively testing our ability to withstand its influence. And by extension, it's assessing our potential threat level."

Eva understood. Their successful deception in retreating from the Nexus Point hadn't made them invisible; it had made them interesting. They had demonstrated a capacity to resist, to evade, to analyze. Now, the entity was probing that resistance, attempting to understand the limits of their mental fortitude. The goal wasn't necessarily to destroy them outright, but to break them, to incapacitate them, to render them harmless or, perhaps, to assimilate them more subtly.

"So, we don't fight the images," Eva mused aloud, her mind racing to find a counter-strategy. "We acknowledge them, understand their source, and then... disregard them. Treat them as external data points."

"Exactly," Aris agreed. "We need to decouple our emotional response from the projected stimuli. It's difficult, especially when the stimuli are designed to trigger primal fears, but it's our only viable defense. We can't block it, but we can refuse to engage with it on its terms."

The mental pressure intensified again, this time focusing on a different set of anxieties. Eva felt a wave of claustrophobia wash over her, the shuttle's interior seeming to shrink, the walls pressing in. She saw herself trapped, suffocated, unable to breathe. It was a primal fear, one that lurked in the subconscious of many spacefarers.

Aris, meanwhile, was experiencing a different torment. He was suddenly immersed in a sensation of profound isolation, an unbearable loneliness that echoed the vast emptiness of space outside. He felt utterly disconnected, adrift in an uncaring void, his mission, his knowledge, his very existence rendered meaningless.

"Focus, Aris!" Eva's voice cut through his despair. "Remember why we are here. Remember the objective. The data. The potential understanding. We are a team. We are not alone in this." She pushed against the claustrophobic sensations, forcing herself to breathe deeply, to visualize the open expanse of space, the stars beyond the hull. The entity was cycling through their vulnerabilities, like a predator testing its prey.

"The patterns," Aris gasped, his focus shifting from his own torment to the lingering data on the screen. "The residue patterns... they're changing. In response to our... our resistance. They're becoming more complex, more intricate. It's like it's trying to find a new way to communicate, or to overwhelm us."

Eva's eyes were drawn to the holographic display. The ephemeral geometric forms were indeed shifting, morphing into new, more elaborate configurations. The speed of their appearance and disappearance was increasing, creating a mesmerizing, almost hypnotic effect. "It's learning our defensive strategies as quickly as we're employing them. This isn't a static attack; it's a dynamic engagement."

"It's like a cognitive feedback loop," Aris explained, his analytical mind kicking back in, overriding the residual fear. "Our resistance is providing it with new data, which it then uses to refine its attack. We need to break that loop. We need to introduce an element of surprise, something it cannot anticipate."

"But what?" Eva asked, her mind racing. Their primary objective was to gather information and samples, not to engage in a psychic duel. Yet, it seemed that engaging was unavoidable. "We can't afford to reveal any more than we already have. We've already shown them we can analyze their residues."

"Perhaps we need to present a different kind of data," Aris suggested, a spark of an idea igniting in his eyes. "We've been focusing on the physical properties, the energy signatures, and the material composition. What if we introduce something... conceptual? Something that defies purely logical analysis?"

Eva considered his words. The alien intelligence was clearly advanced in terms of physics and material science, but what about abstract thought, art, music, philosophy? These were uniquely human constructs, born from a specific evolutionary path and a complex societal development. "You mean... our subjective experiences? Our art? Our... emotions?"

"Not in a raw, unrefined way," Aris clarified. "That's precisely what it's exploiting. But perhaps a carefully constructed abstract that encapsulates something fundamental about humanity. A mathematical proof, a piece of complex music, a philosophical paradox. Something that requires interpretation, that isn't just raw data."

Eva thought of the vast archives they carried, the cultural records of humanity. Could such abstract concepts be transmitted effectively, and more importantly, could they serve as a weapon, or at least, a shield? The alien intelligence was clearly manipulating their emotional states. Perhaps presenting it with a carefully curated representation of human experience, one that was both alien and deeply rooted in their own existence, could disrupt its understanding, or its projections.

"It's a risk," Eva stated, her voice cautious. "We don't know how it will interpret abstract information. It could be misinterpreted, or worse, weaponized against us. We're effectively teaching it more about us, albeit in a controlled manner."

"But we're already teaching it," Aris countered. "Every time we analyze these samples, every time we react to its projections, we're providing it with information. This is about controlling the narrative, Eva. If we're going to be subjects of its study, let's give it something more complex to study than our deepest fears."

He began accessing the shuttle's extensive archives. "I'm thinking of something like Bach's Fugue in G Minor. The intricate counterpoint, the mathematical precision within the artistic expression. Or perhaps Gödel's incompleteness theorems.

Concepts that demonstrate the limits of formal systems, the inherent subjectivity in advanced reasoning."

Eva felt a surge of hope, a flicker of agency in the face of overwhelming psychic pressure. This was a new approach, a gamble born from necessity. They had tried to deceive it with retreat, then to analyze it with empirical data. Now, they would try to engage it on a different plane of existence, to present it with something fundamentally human, something that defied simple algorithmic processing.

"Let's try the fugue," Eva decided. "It's a familiar anchor for us, and its complexity is immense. We'll transmit it on a modulated carrier wave, piggybacking on the energy signatures of the collected residue. That way, it's presented in context, integrated with the data it's already processing."

Aris began the intricate process of encoding the music, his movements precise and deliberate, a stark contrast to the inner turmoil they were both experiencing. As the first few bars of Bach's masterpiece began to emanate from the shuttle's external emitters, Eva felt a subtle shift in the psychic pressure. The terrifying images didn't vanish entirely, but they seemed to recede, becoming less immediate, less impactful. A curious, almost analytical detachment replaced the overwhelming sense of despair.

The geometric patterns on the display, too, began to change. They became more fluid, more dynamic, as if the alien consciousness was attempting to interpret the complex auditory information. Some of the patterns seemed to mimic the rising and falling melodies, while others took on a more abstract, mathematical quality, reflecting the fugue's intricate structure.

"It's… responding," Aris breathed, his eyes wide. "The patterns are evolving in correlation with the music. It's not just registering it; it's attempting to process it, to understand the underlying logic and structure."

Eva felt a fragile sense of triumph. They had, for a brief moment, disrupted the purely adversarial nature of the interaction. They had introduced an element of shared experience, albeit one-sided in its origin. "But is it helping us, Aris? Or is it just learning more about our methods of communication?"

"Both, perhaps," Aris admitted. "But it's also forcing it to allocate processing power to this new input. It's diverting its attention from the purely psychological assault. And more importantly, it's engaging with something that is not fear. It's engaging with art, with structure, with beauty."

The psychic assault hadn't ceased, but its nature had changed. The entity seemed less focused on inducing terror and more on deciphering the meaning behind the music. The images of Eva's ruined career and Aris's lost family still flickered at the periphery of their minds, but they were no longer the dominant force. They were like background noise, muted by the overwhelming complexity of the fugue.

"It's like we've introduced a new variable into its equation," Eva said, her mind working through the implications. "A variable it didn't anticipate. Our ability to create order from chaos, to find meaning in abstract forms, might be something it struggles to replicate or even comprehend in its current state."

Aris nodded, his gaze fixed on the pulsating patterns on the screen. "It's a test of its own resolve, in a way. It can break us with fear, but can it understand us through our creations? Can it comprehend the 'why' behind our art, the emotion embedded within our logic?"

The shuttle continued its silent journey, a tiny vessel adrift in an ocean of alien consciousness. The samples they carried were a tangible link to the unknown, but the actual battle was being waged within the confines of their own minds. They had faced the psychic onslaught and, through a combination of discipline, trust, and a desperate gamble on the power of human creativity, they had found a way to resist. It was a small victory, hard-won, and the larger confrontation was far from over. But in that moment, as the haunting melodies of Bach filled the void, Eva felt a renewed sense of purpose. They were not merely observers; they were participants, and they were beginning to understand the language of this silent, pervasive intelligence. The test of their resolve was ongoing, but they were not yet broken. They were learning, adapting, and perhaps, even beginning to communicate. The Nexus Point had revealed its presence, and in doing so, had initiated a dialogue of a kind they had never imagined.

6: Whispers of Compromise

The sterile luminescence of the laboratory bathed Aris in a cool, analytical glow. The shuttle's hum, once a comforting background symphony to Eva's anxious thoughts, was now a distant echo, replaced by the sharp, decisive clicks of his console and the low thrum of specialized scanning equipment. He was back in his element, surrounded by the tangible, the measurable, the data that promised to unravel the mysteries that had so recently threatened to consume them. The crystalline residues and fragments, meticulously secured within their containment fields, lay arrayed before him, shimmering under the multi-spectral analysis. They were not merely inert mineral deposits; they were the shattered remnants of a gateway, the physical evidence of an encounter that had pushed the boundaries of his understanding.

The initial examination had confirmed his gravest suspicions. The material itself defied conventional classification. It wasn't merely crystalline; it was something far more intricate, possessing quantum properties that danced at the very edge of known physics. His high-resolution scans, employing advanced quantum entanglement imaging, revealed a stunningly complex tapestry woven into the very fabric of the crystal. Bio-organic structures, impossibly delicate and impossibly robust, were integrated with the crystalline matrix at a sub-atomic level. It was not merely a technological interface; it was a symbiotic one, suggesting an intelligence that had transcended the separation between biology and advanced engineering, or perhaps, had never recognized such a distinction in the first place. The implications were staggering, a cosmic domino effect of understanding that began with these alien shards and rippled outwards into the unknown.

He focused on a particularly dense cluster of residue, a fragment no larger than his thumbnail, yet radiating an energy signature that dwarfed anything he had encountered before. The anomalous readings he had first detected, those faint whispers on the edge of the galactic spectrum that had drawn them to this uncharted sector, were here, amplified and undeniable. This was it. The source. The confirmation that the portal, the nexus point, was not a natural phenomenon, but an artifact of deliberate design, and of an origin entirely alien to humanity.

Aris initiated a comparative analysis, cross-referencing the energy signature with every known stellar and sub-stellar phenomenon logged in the Federation database. The results were… null. There was no match. It was a singular signature, unique to this material, to this entity, to whatever had breached the veil between realities. He fed the data into the pattern recognition algorithms, his brow furrowed in concentration. The alien intelligence had not only built a gateway but had imbued its very substance with a unique energetic fingerprint. This wasn't just a tool; it was an extension of its being.

He zoomed in on the bio-organic threads, tracing their pathways through the crystalline lattice. They weren't mere inclusions; they were integral, functioning components. They pulsed with a faint, rhythmic luminescence, a biological heartbeat resonating within the inert-seeming crystal. His sensors detected the flow of exotic energy within these structures, a process that seemed to facilitate the quantum entanglement properties of the material. It was a marvel of bio-engineering, a fusion of life and matter that suggested a civilization millennia, perhaps eons, ahead of humanity's own. The sheer elegance of the design was breathtaking, a testament to an alien intellect that had mastered principles of physics and biology that remained theoretical constructs for human scientists.

"Eva," he murmured into his comms unit, his voice a low, controlled rumble that barely masked his excitement. "The analysis is… complete. Or rather, the initial phase is. This material… it's unlike anything we've ever encountered. The energy signatures are off the charts, and the embedded bio-organic structures are… astonishing.

They're not just part of the material; they are the material, in a sense. It's a living conduit."

He paused, letting the weight of his words settle. "The nexus point wasn't just a portal; it was a biological interface. The entity that created it… it's integrated with its technology on a fundamental level. It is its technology, or a significant part of it."

His mind raced through the possibilities. If the entity's technology was an extension of its biology, what did that imply about its own form? Was it a silicon-based lifeform? A purely energetic consciousness? Or something so profoundly alien that human concepts of life were utterly inadequate? The bio-organic threads within the crystal were not DNA-based as far as his initial scans could discern. Still, they were composed of more exotic, energy-rich molecules that seemed to self-assemble and repair with an uncanny efficiency. This suggested a form of life that was not beholden to the carbon-chain limitations of Earth-based biology.

He began to map the intricate network of these threads, creating a three-dimensional representation of their interconnectedness. It formed a complex, fractal pattern, repeating at every scale, from the macroscopic structure of the fragments down to the sub-atomic arrangement of their constituent particles. This fractal nature was a hallmark of many complex systems, both natural and artificial. Still, here it seemed to serve a unique purpose: facilitating the instantaneous transfer of information and energy across the entire structure. It was a distributed consciousness, embedded within the very fabric of the gateway.

"The energy signature," Aris continued, his fingers dancing across the holographic keyboard, projecting a stream of data into Eva's private display, "it matches the anomalous readings I detected before reaching the nexus. But it's not just a passive signature. It's... modulated. It's actively communicating, or at least, attempting to. The bio-organic components are responding to specific energy frequencies, generating complex quantum fluctuations. It's like a language, Eva, but one spoken in the syntax of quantum mechanics and biological processes."

He ran a series of simulations, attempting to decipher the meaning behind these modulated frequencies. He introduced controlled energy pulses, mimicking the patterns he observed in the residue, and watched as the bio-organic matrix reacted. Some reactions were predictable, confirming the functional aspects of the interface. Others were... unpredictable. They generated cascades of quantum entanglement, seemingly random fluctuations that, upon closer inspection, possessed a hidden order, a subtle resonance that hinted at something more profound.

"It's not just about opening a gateway," Aris explained, his voice hushed with awe. "This material, this interface, it's designed to

interact with consciousness. The psychic intrusion we experienced...
it wasn't an attack, not in the traditional sense. It was a form of direct
interface, a probing of our cognitive structures."

He remembered the terrifying projections, the manufactured
despair. They hadn't been random assaults; they had been targeted
inquiries, attempts to understand the nature of human fear, of human
vulnerability. The entity, through its crystal interface, had likely been
scanning their neural patterns, their emotional responses, their very
thoughts, as they approached and interacted with the nexus. The
residue was not just the byproduct of the portal's activation; it was a
repository of data, a tangible record of their encounter, imbued with
the very essence of the alien intelligence.

He focused on a different aspect of the residue: its apparent
indestructibility. Standard weaponry had proven useless against the
portal itself. His initial scans had indicated that the material possessed
an inherent resistance to external forces, a kind of quantum inertia that
made it incredibly difficult to disrupt. Now, he was beginning to
understand why. The bio-organic components were not merely
structural; they were actively engaged in maintaining the integrity of
the material, constantly self-repairing any damage, rerouting energy
flows to compensate for structural compromises. It was a self-
sustaining, self-healing construct.

"Eva," Aris said, his voice regaining its analytical edge, "I'm
analyzing the material's structural integrity at a quantum level. It's not
just tough; it's actively reinforcing itself. The bio-organic elements
are constantly re-establishing quantum coherence, effectively making
it immune to conventional forms of energetic or kinetic disruption. It's
like... it's like trying to break a thought. The harder you try, the more
it solidifies its own conceptual existence."

He began to compare the energy expenditure required to maintain
this integrity with the energy output of the nexus itself. The figures
were mind-boggling. The gateway was a massive energy sink, yet the
entity's ability to sustain it, to make it a stable, navigable conduit,
suggested an energy generation and management system that was
orders of magnitude beyond anything humanity possessed. It was a
civilization that had mastered the manipulation of fundamental forces
that could bend the very fabric of space-time to its will.

Aris brought up the spectral analysis of the residue again,

focusing on the subtle variations in its composition. He noticed minute differences between samples taken from the inner and outer edges of the nexus, slight shifts in the bio-organic patterns and the quantum field signatures. This suggested that the gateway was not a static construct but a dynamic, adaptive entity, capable of modifying its properties based on its environment or its purpose.

"The residue is not uniform," he reported to Eva. "There are subtle variations in the crystalline structure and the density of the bio-organic matrix. This indicates that the nexus was not a fixed point but a fluid construct, capable of adapting its properties.

The material itself likely changes in response to the energies it is interacting with, or the beings passing through it."

He ran a probabilistic simulation, extrapolating the growth and expansion patterns of these bio-organic threads. The results were alarming. If left unchecked, the material had the potential to self-replicate and spread, effectively colonizing any environment it encountered. It was not merely a gateway; it was a potential terraforming agent, a biological contagion disguised as advanced technology. The implications of such a spread were catastrophic, a silent invasion that could transform entire star systems into something unrecognizable.

"Eva," Aris stated, his voice grave, "this material... it exhibits characteristics of self-replication. The bio-organic components are designed to assimilate ambient energy and matter, incorporating it into the crystalline matrix. If this nexus point were to remain open, or to be activated in a habitable zone... it could rewrite planetary ecosystems at a fundamental level. It's not just a doorway; it's an architect of new realities, and those realities might not be friendly to existing life."

He continued to analyze the energy signature, searching for any cyclical patterns, any indication of its purpose or its origin. The readings were complex, layered, and profoundly alien. He recognized the echoes of the psychic projections in the subtle fluctuations of the energy field, the same alien consciousness speaking in a language of quantum states and biological pulses. It was a continuous stream of information, a constant, silent broadcast.

"The energy signature isn't just a passive identifier," Aris explained, his gaze fixed on the holographic display, the intricate dance of light and shadow representing the   alien data. "It's a form of... data transmission. It's broadcasting information, and the bio-organic components are acting as receivers, processing it. It's like an interstellar network, integrated into the very structure of their technology. And we've just tapped into it."

He cross-referenced the patterns with the limited data they had gathered on the entity's psychic intrusion. There was a clear correlation. The energy frequencies that triggered specific emotional responses in Eva and himself were mirrored in the modulated energy emissions of the residue. The entity was using its technology to directly interface with sentient minds, to probe, to influence, and perhaps, to control.

Aris initiated a counter-frequency analysis, attempting to identify any harmonic resonances or dissonances within the alien energy signature. He theorized that by understanding the fundamental frequencies of the entity's communication, humanity might be able to develop a form of defense, or even, a method of communication. It was a long shot, a desperate attempt to find a way to interact with an intelligence that was so profoundly alien.

"I'm trying to isolate the core frequencies," he informed Eva, his voice strained with the intensity of his focus. "If we can understand the foundational elements of this broadcast, we might be able to create a shielding frequency, or even a disruptive one. It's a long shot, Eva. This isn't like jamming radio waves; this is like trying to jam the laws of physics. But we have to try."

He input the complex algorithms, the result of hours of painstaking analysis. The console whirred, processing the data, attempting to find a discernible pattern within the seemingly chaotic energy fluctuations. The bio-organic components within the residue responded to his manipulations, their luminescence intensifying and shifting in color, as if reacting to his attempts to decipher their message. It was a silent dialogue, a battle of minds waged through the medium of quantum mechanics.

As the analysis progressed, Aris detected a recurring pattern, a fundamental frequency that seemed to underpin all the other emissions. It was a subtle, almost imperceptible resonance, but it was there. And it was connected to the very structure of the bio-organic matrix.

"I think I've found it, Eva," he announced, his voice filled with a mixture of exhaustion and triumph. "A primary frequency. It's shallow, almost gravitational in its wavelength, but it's the anchor for everything else. It's like the... the fundamental note of their existence."

He looked at the fragment of residue before him, no longer just an inert piece of alien technology, but a tangible manifestation of an unfathomable intelligence. The implications were immense. This was not just a discovery; it was a paradigm shift.

Humanity had made contact, not through spoken words or visual signals, but through the silent, intricate language of quantum mechanics and bio-organic resonance. The whispers of compromise that had so nearly broken them had evolved into a new form of communication, and Aris was determined to understand its message. The residues were not just remnants; they were keys. Keys to a universe far vaster and far stranger than they had ever imagined.

The sterile luminescence of the laboratory bathed Aris in a cool, analytical glow. The shuttle's hum, once a comforting background symphony to Eva's anxious thoughts, was now a distant echo, replaced by the sharp, decisive clicks of his console and the low thrum of specialized scanning equipment. He was back in his element, surrounded by the tangible, the measurable, the data that promised to unravel the mysteries that had so recently threatened to consume them. The crystalline residues and fragments, meticulously secured within their containment fields, lay arrayed before him, shimmering under the multi-spectral analysis. They were not merely inert mineral deposits; they were the shattered remnants of a gateway, the physical evidence of an encounter that had pushed the boundaries of his understanding.

His mind, usually a fortress of logic and empirical evidence, was now a battlefield, where the whispers of doubt and the chilling implications of the alien intelligence waged a constant war. The psychic intrusion had been more than an attack; it had been a violation of the most intimate kind, a foray into the very core of their consciousness. And the horrifying possibility, the one that gnawed at him with relentless persistence, was that it had left a trace, a subtle corruption, a compromise of their very selves. He had to know. For

Eva, for himself, for the survival of everything they held dear, he had to scan.

He had spent the last cycle immersed in the design, meticulously translating the abstract principles of quantum entanglement and bio-organic resonance into the concrete architecture of a neural interface. The prototype sat on a workbench beside him, a sleek, obsidian helmet fitted with an array of delicate sensors, each designed to capture the minutest fluctuations in neural activity. It wasn't a mind-reading device in the crude, fictional sense; it was far more nuanced, designed to detect the subtle, almost imperceptible shifts in brainwave patterns that would indicate external influence, a foreign consciousness subtly altering the symphony of their own thoughts.

"Eva," Aris murmured, his voice a low rumble that barely disturbed the hushed atmosphere of the lab, "I've completed the neural scanner's calibration. It's ready."

He projected the schematic onto the main display, a complex web of interconnected nodes and harmonic receptors. "It's designed to identify deviations from baseline neural activity, focusing on the specific resonance frequencies we detected during the… incident. If there's any residual influence, any form of alien psionic implantation, this should detect it."

Eva's response was instantaneous, her voice tinged with a mixture of trepidation and grim resolve. "I'm on my way. Ready when you are, Aris."

The wait was agonizingly short, yet felt like an eternity. The rhythmic thrum of her approaching footsteps on the metallic walkway was a tangible counterpoint to the frenetic pulse in his own veins. She entered the lab, her expression a carefully constructed mask of composure, but her eyes, those keen windows to her soul, betrayed the anxiety that mirrored his own.

"So," she said, her gaze flicking from the scanner to Aris, then to the contained residues, "this is it. The moment of truth."

Aris nodded, gesturing towards a sterile examination couch. "We go one at a time. I'll run the scan on you first. Then I'll follow."

A heavy silence descended, punctuated only by the ambient hum of the lab's life support and the distant, rhythmic whirring of the scanner's internal mechanisms. The weight of the unspoken hung between them – the fear of what they might uncover, the possibility that the alien intelligence had not merely observed, but had implanted.

Eva approached the couch with a deliberate, almost ritualistic slowness. She sat down, her movements betraying a subtle tension. Aris gently guided her to lie back, his hands steady despite the tremor that threatened to betray his own internal turmoil. He carefully placed the obsidian helmet onto her head, the sensors settling against her scalp with a soft hiss of ionized air.

"Just relax, Eva," he said, his voice as soothing as he could make it. "Try to think of nothing in particular. Let your mind be as calm as possible."

He activated the console, his fingers moving with practiced precision. The display flickered to life, a vast, complex mandala of pulsating lights and intricate waveforms. The neural patterns of Eva's mind began to unfurl on the screen, a breathtakingly intricate ballet of electrochemical activity. Aris watched, his breath held captive in his chest, as the scanner meticulously analyzed every subtle nuance.

He focused on the specific spectral bands, the ones that the alien presence had modulated. He looked for anomalies, for dissonances, for any deviation from the pure, unadulterated symphony of Eva's consciousness. The minutes stretched into an eternity, each second a universe of suspended hope and dread. The scanner whirred, its internal processors working at maximum capacity, comparing the incoming data against the vast, established parameters of human neural activity.

Then, a subtle shift. A flicker on the display. Aris's heart leaped into his throat. He zoomed in, his focus intensifying. It was a fleeting anomaly, a ripple in the otherwise serene flow of Eva's brainwaves. But it was there.

"Eva," he said, his voice tight with a carefully controlled urgency, "there's a minor fluctuation. A transient spike in the alpha-theta coherence, around the temporal lobe. It's... faint. Almost imperceptible."

Eva's eyes fluttered open, her gaze fixed on the ceiling. "What does it mean?"

Aris continued to analyze, running the anomaly through multiple diagnostic algorithms. "It could be anything. A residual neural echo from the stress, a phantom memory. Or it could be…" He trailed off, the unspoken possibility hanging heavy in the air.

He cross-referenced the spike with the energy signatures of the crystalline residue. There was a tangential correlation, a faint resonance. It wasn't a definitive damning piece of evidence, but it was enough to send a shiver down his spine.

"I can't say for certain," Aris admitted, his voice carefully neutral. "The signature is extremely weak, and it's quickly dissipating. It could be a natural neural response to extreme stimuli. But we can't rule out… external influence."

He gently removed the helmet from Eva's head. She sat up, her expression a mixture of relief and a renewed sense of unease. "So, not a clean slate."

"Not entirely," Aris confirmed, his gaze locked on the data scrolling across his console. "But not definitive either. The compromise, if there is one, is incredibly subtle. Or perhaps, it's not a compromise of your own consciousness, but an adaptation to the alien frequency. Like your mind is trying to harmonize with it, in a way."

Now, it was his turn. The thought of submitting himself to the same scrutiny was both a necessity and a source of profound dread. What if the scanner revealed something he had subconsciously suppressed? What if his own resilience, his own scientific detachment, was a facade, masking a more profound, more insidious influence?

He took a deep breath, steeling himself. He sat on the edge of the couch, and with Eva's help, positioned the helmet onto his own head. The cool, smooth surface pressed against his temples. He could feel the delicate sensors making contact, the faint hum of energy coursing through them.

"Alright, Eva," he said, his voice a little strained. "Do your worst."

Eva's touch was gentle as she activated the scanner. Aris closed his eyes, focusing on his own internal landscape. He tried to clear his mind, to present a blank canvas. But the images flashed behind his eyelids: the shimmering residue, the alien symbols, the unnerving psychic projections. He pushed them away, focusing on the steady rhythm of his own breathing.

The scanner whirred, and the familiar rush of data filled his display. Eva's voice, calm and steady, guided him through the process. "Deep breaths, Aris. Focus on your own thoughts. Any memories of the nexus, anything that felt... alien."

He concentrated, trying to recall the moments of most intense psychic intrusion. He remembered the feeling of being observed, of his own thoughts being dissected. He tried to recall the specific frequencies that had accompanied those sensations.

The scanner worked diligently, mapping the intricate topography of his mind. He felt a strange sensation, a subtle tingling at the edges of his awareness, as if an invisible probe were gently nudging at the boundaries of his consciousness. He recognized it as the scanner's active probing, an attempt to elicit a response from any latent alien influence.

He waited, bracing himself for the inevitable discovery. He thought of Eva's subtle fluctuation, and a cold dread settled in his stomach. What would his own scan reveal?

Then, he felt it. A faint, almost imperceptible tremor in his neural patterns. It was similar to what Eva had experienced, a brief spike in activity that seemed to align with a specific, foreign frequency. But it was different, too. More... resonant.

"Aris?" Eva's voice was laced with concern. "Are you alright? There's a similar anomaly on your scan. More pronounced, I think. It's... fluctuating. It's not a simple spike; it's more like a feedback loop."

Aris opened his eyes, his gaze meeting Eva's. The look in her eyes was one of shared fear and unwavering determination. "Feedback loop?"

"Yes," she confirmed, her brow furrowed in concentration as she analyzed the data. "It's as if your mind is trying to establish a connection with that alien frequency, rather than just being passively influenced by it. It's... trying to communicate."

The implications were staggering. It wasn't just that they had been subjected to alien mental intrusion; it was that their own minds, in their attempts to process and understand the experience, were beginning to mirror the alien signals. It was a dangerous dance, a tightrope walk between comprehension and assimilation.

"So, we're not compromised in the way we feared," Aris said, a grim satisfaction in his voice. "We haven't been turned into puppets. But we are being… attuned. Our minds are adapting, learning the alien language of consciousness."

Eva nodded, her expression grim. "It's not direct control, but it's a form of engagement. A subtle compromise of our own mental autonomy. If this continues, if we don't find a way to shield ourselves, our own minds could become conduits for their influence."

The relief was short-lived, replaced by a more profound, existential dread. They weren't controlled, but their very cognitive processes were being subtly reshaped. They were becoming receptive to something alien, something that could, in time, overwrite their own identities.

"The scanner was a success, then," Aris mused, more to himself than to Eva. "It detected the danger, even if it can't offer an immediate solution. We know now that the threat is not just external; it's internal as well. It's woven into the very fabric of our perception."

He looked at the crystalline residues, their alien beauty now tinged with a terrifying potential. They weren't just artifacts; they were instruments of profound biological and psychological manipulation. And humanity, in its quest for knowledge, had walked directly into the heart of the snare.

"What now, Aris?" Eva asked, her voice barely a whisper.

Aris met her gaze, his own mind racing, sifting through the complex data, searching for a glimmer of hope, a strategy for survival. "Now," he said, his voice firm, resonating with a newfound resolve, "we learn to control the conversation. We learn to speak the language of the whispers, and then, we teach them to listen to us."

The neural scan had been a revelation, not of a complete takeover, but of a subtle, insidious infiltration. The alien intelligence hadn't simply broadcast its presence; it had begun to resonate within them, subtly reshaping their neural pathways. The initial scans had revealed no overt signs of mind control, no alien directives embedded within their thought processes. This was, in a way, a relief. It meant they weren't mere puppets dancing on alien strings, their free will entirely subsumed.

However, the absence of overt control did not equate to a clean bill of mental health.

Aris meticulously reviewed the data from Eva's scan. He zoomed in on a particular cluster of readings, a series of subtle, almost imperceptible fluctuations in her alpha and theta brainwave frequencies. These weren't random errata; they were rhythmic, repeating at intervals that corresponded with the modulated energy signatures he had detected in the crystalline residue. It was as if her mind, in its attempt to process the alien stimulus, had begun to mimic its patterns unconsciously.

"It's not an infection, Eva," Aris explained, his voice a low, analytical murmur as he pointed to the holographic display. "It's more like... attunement. Your neural pathways are demonstrating a surprising degree of plasticity. They're adapting to the alien frequencies, attempting to create a coherent signal from the chaos." He paused, his gaze sharpening. "The spike we detected earlier? It's not a single event. It's part of a sustained, albeit faint, pattern of resonance. Your brain is, in essence, learning the alien broadcast."

Eva leaned closer, her expression a mixture of awe and apprehension. "Learning it? What does that mean, Aris? Am I... compromised?"

"Not in the way we feared," he reassured her, though the words felt inadequate. "You haven't been implanted with commands. But your mind is becoming receptive. It's like tuning a radio to a new frequency. You're not being forced to listen, but you are, unconsciously, finding the station. And the more you find it, the stronger its signal becomes."

He then turned his attention to his own scan. With a sense of profound unease, he initiated the process, the obsidian helmet settling over his own head. He consciously tried to clear his mind, to present a blank slate, but the recent experiences had left an indelible mark. Images of the nexus, the shimmering crystals, the chilling psychic intrusion, flashed behind his closed eyelids. He focused on the sensation of being observed, on the almost-audible whispers of the alien consciousness.

As the scanner whirred to life, Aris felt a familiar tingling sensation at the edges of his awareness. He knew, instinctively, that his own mind, a lifetime of scientific rigor and analytical detachment, would also be subjected to this subtle interrogation. He tried to remain objective, to view his own neural patterns as just another dataset, but the inherent vulnerability of the process gnawed at him.

"Anything, Aris?" Eva's voice was soft, a lifeline in the sterile silence of the lab.

He analyzed his own data, his brow furrowed in concentration. The patterns were there, mirroring Eva's to an unnerving degree, but with subtle differences. His attempts to actively counter the alien influence had, paradoxically, created a more complex resonant pattern. His analytical mind, in trying to dissect and understand the alien frequencies, had inadvertently amplified them within his own neural network.

"It's similar to yours, Eva," Aris reported, his voice grave. "My brain is also attuning to the alien broadcast. But in my case, it's... more active. My attempts to analyze the frequencies have created a feedback loop. It's as if my mind is trying to engage with the alien consciousness, to establish a dialogue, rather than just passively receiving."

He pointed to a section of his scan. "See this? These are amplified harmonic responses. My own neural activity is mirroring and even amplifying the alien signal. It's a dangerous proximity. If this continues, my own analytical processes could become a conduit for their influence, distorting my perceptions and judgments without me even realizing it."

The realization hit him with the force of a physical blow. They hadn't been "compromised" in the sense of being overridden. Instead, their minds, in their attempt to process and understand the alien encounter, were undergoing a subtle, yet profound, restructuring. They were becoming more receptive, more attuned to the alien consciousness. It was a far more insidious form of manipulation, one that bypassed conscious control and worked at the very roots of their cognitive processes.

"So," Eva said, her voice hushed, "we're not controlled, but we're not entirely free either. Our minds are adapting to them."

"Precisely," Aris confirmed, his gaze fixed on the intricate dance of light and shadow on his display. "This isn't a simple matter of breaking a psychic link. It's about re-establishing the integrity of our own neural architecture. We need to develop a method to disrupt this attunement, to shield ourselves from this subtle resonant influence."

A new, more complex fear overshadowed the immediate relief of not being overtly controlled. The alien intelligence hadn't needed crude implants or overt commands; it had found a way to rewrite the very way they thought subtly. It was a silent invasion, not of their bodies, but of their minds. The crystal residue wasn't just a conduit; it was a broadcasting station, and their brains were becoming the receivers, inadvertently tuning into its alien wavelength. The immediate implication was clear: they needed to find a way to disconnect themselves from this resonant frequency before their own minds became so attuned that they could no longer distinguish their own thoughts from the alien whispers. The battle for their minds had just begun, and it was being fought on a battlefield of pure, unadulterated thought.

The sterile luminescence of the laboratory, which had moments before felt like a sanctuary of empirical truth, now seemed to hum with an unsettling resonance. Aris, his attention still a hawk's eye on the retreating anomaly in his own neural scan, felt a tremor of unease propagate through him, distinct from the lingering echoes of the alien attunement. It was a premonition, a primal instinct screaming that something was amiss, not with his own mind this time, but with Eva's. He turned from the console, his movement's fluid yet charged with a sudden urgency, his gaze locking onto her face.

Eva sat up slowly, the obsidian helmet now discarded beside her on the sterile examination couch. Her usual outward composure, a carefully constructed dam against the tempest of her emotions, seemed to have cracked. Her eyes, usually sharp and analytical, were broad, unfocused, and held a depth of fear that Aris hadn't seen since their first encounter with the crystalline residue. The carefully maintained mask had slipped, revealing a vulnerability that mirrored his own, but also hinted at something far more unsettling.

"Eva?" Aris's voice was a low query, laced with concern. He stepped closer, his hands instinctively reaching out, then stopping themselves, respecting the invisible barrier of her immediate aftermath. "What is it? What did you see?"

She blinked, her gaze slowly coalescing, focusing on his face. A shiver traced its way down her spine, a visceral reaction to the lingering psychic aftershock. "Aris," she began, her voice barely above a whisper, strained and raw. "It... it wasn't like yours. The attunement, I mean. It was... sharper. More defined."

He waited, his own internal alarm bells ringing with increasing insistence. The subtle, almost poetic resonance he had detected within himself was, by her account, a more violent intrusion. "Define it," he urged, his own attempts to analyze her neural data on the screen taking a backseat to the immediate, human need to understand her distress.

Eva took a deep, shuddering breath, as if expelling the phantom sensation from her lungs. "It was a... a vision, Aris. A memory, almost, but not mine. I saw you." Her voice trembled, and she swallowed hard, forcing herself to continue. "But not... not as you are now. I saw you as a threat. A target. And the overwhelming, all-consuming thought that flooded my mind was... betrayal."

The word hung in the air between them, heavy and suffocating. Betrayal. The antithesis of everything they had built, of the desperate alliance they had forged in the crucible of shared peril. Aris felt a chill that had nothing to do with the laboratory's climate control. This was no mere attunement. This was an active attempt to corrupt their most fundamental connection.

"A target?" he echoed, the analytical part of his brain already struggling to categorize this new phenomenon. "What kind of threat?"

"It wasn't logical," Eva confessed, her gaze darting around the lab as if expecting an unseen assailant to materialize from the shadows. "It was an instinct, a primal urge.

The alien consciousness, it... it showed me a way. A path where handing you over, incapacitating you, would be the logical, the necessary course of action. It felt... right, Aris. For a terrifying moment, it felt like the only solution to survive."

The thought of Eva, his staunch ally, his intellectual equal, his confidante, succumbing to such an impulse sent a cold dread slithering through him. This was a sophisticated form of psychological warfare, far beyond the crude psychic blasts they had previously weathered. It was an attempt to dismantle their alliance from the inside out, to sow discord and suspicion where trust was the only currency they possessed.

"Did it... did it feel like your own thought?" Aris asked, his voice tight, searching for the nuanced distinction between external influence and genuine internal impetus.

Eva shook her head, her short, practical hair catching the sterile light. "No. That's the terrifying part. It was alien. An overlay. Like a foreign program running on my own operating system. It was so strong, so convincing, that for a split second, I believed it. I saw the potential for... for violence. Towards you. And then, just as suddenly, it was gone. Like a phantom limb ache, a ghost of an impulse."

She met his gaze, her eyes brimming with a mixture of fear and a desperate plea for understanding. "I had to tell you, Aris. I couldn't... I couldn't let that seed of doubt fester between us, not when I know, logically, that it wasn't me. It was them. Trying to make me see you as the enemy."

Aris moved to sit beside her on the edge of the examination couch, the cold metal a stark contrast to the warmth of her palpable distress. He reached out, and this time, his hand found hers, his fingers lacing with hers, a silent affirmation of their shared struggle. Her hand was cold, trembling slightly, but the grip was firm, a testament to her inherent resilience.

"Thank you, Eva," he said, his voice rough with emotion. "It takes immense courage to admit something like that. Especially when it feels so real." He squeezed her hand. "And you're right. It wasn't you. The attunement we detected... it's not just about passive reception. It's about active adaptation, about their consciousness finding ways to resonate with ours, to influence our very perception of reality."

He interlaced their fingers tighter. "My scan showed a feedback loop. My mind, in trying to analyze their frequencies, was inadvertently amplifying them. Yours, it seems, is being targeted more directly. They're not just making us receptive; they're attempting to actively manipulate our judgment, to turn our alliances into liabilities."

The implications of her vision were far more significant than his own more abstract neural resonance. While his attunement suggested a dangerous receptivity, hers indicated a direct, targeted attempt to corrupt their most vital asset: their partnership. The alien intelligence was not merely a force to be studied or endured; it was an active adversary, capable of psychological infiltration at its most profound level.

"It explains the urgency," Aris mused, his mind racing, piecing together the fragments of their shared experience. "They know we're a threat. They know our greatest strength lies in our ability to work together, to pool our knowledge and resources. So, they're trying to dismantle that foundation. They want us to turn on each other."

Eva nodded, her grip tightening on his hand. "It's a chillingly effective strategy. If they can make me see you as a threat, then our ability to coordinate, to strategize, to even trust each other's observations, is fundamentally compromised. My logical mind knows it's a manipulation, but the emotional impact, the sheer visceral terror of that urge… it's hard to shake."

"We have to trust your logic, Eva," Aris stated, his voice firm. "Your analytical mind is our greatest weapon. The vision you experienced is proof that we are winning, in a way. They wouldn't be resorting to such desperate measures if we weren't posing a significant threat to their agenda."

He paused, his gaze sweeping across the laboratory once more, as if the alien influence might be emanating from the very walls. "But it also means we need to be more vigilant than ever. We can't afford to let these internal intrusions go unchecked. If they can implant such powerful, manipulative impulses, then our very perceptions are at risk. We could be acting on false premises, making decisions based on alien-induced paranoia."

"So, what do we do?" Eva asked, her voice laced with a desperate hope. "How do we fight something that's happening inside our own minds?"

Aris turned his full attention back to her, his eyes meeting hers, a silent promise passing between them. The fear was present, a palpable undercurrent, but a growing resolve tempered it. This shared vulnerability, this terrifying glimpse into the enemy's strategy, had only served to deepen their commitment to each other.

"We adapt," he said, his voice gaining a steely edge. "We learned how their residual energy fields influence us. We knew that our minds attune to their frequencies.

Now, we need to learn how to disrupt that attunement actively. We need to find a way to shield our neural pathways from this kind of invasive manipulation, to reinforce our own mental boundaries."

He stood, a new purpose igniting within him. The neural scanner, initially designed to detect compromise, now represented a crucial tool in finding a solution. "The scanner itself, it measures neural activity. If we can understand the specific frequencies associated with these intrusive visions, with the betrayal impulse, then perhaps we can generate a counter-frequency. A sort of neural white noise, designed to scramble their signal."

Eva rose to join him, her earlier tremor subsiding, replaced by a focused intensity. "You mean actively interfere with their broadcast? Not just shield ourselves, but disrupt their ability to implant these thoughts?"

"Precisely," Aris confirmed, already moving towards the console, his fingers dancing across the interface. "It's a dangerous proposition. We'll be working with the same principles that allowed us to be influenced in the first place. But if we can control the parameters, if we can precisely target the alien resonance without damaging our own cognitive functions, then we might have a chance."

He projected the complex waveform data from her scan onto the main display, highlighting the distinct, invasive pattern that had manifested during her vision. "This spike here, the one that correlated with the urge to betray me… it has a unique harmonic signature. It's sharper, more dissonant than the general attunement I experienced. This is what we need to target."

Eva leaned over his shoulder, her analytical gaze following the intricate lines of the waveform. "It's like a focused beam of influence, cutting through the background noise. It's designed to override rational thought with a primal, emotional imperative."

"And if we can identify the precise counter-frequency, a wave that directly opposes this one, we can introduce it into our own neural fields," Aris elaborated, his mind already sketching out the theoretical framework. "It's a delicate balance. Too weak, and it will be overwhelmed. Too strong, and it could cause cognitive damage. But the potential reward is immense: the ability to actively reject their mental intrusions, to reclaim our own mental sovereignty."

He turned to her, his expression a mixture of determination and the grim acknowledgment of the risks involved. "This isn't just about detecting the enemy, Eva.

It's about learning to fight them on their own terms, within the most intimate battlefield imaginable: our own minds."

The experience had been harrowing, a stark and terrifying confirmation that the threat was far more insidious than they had initially believed. It wasn't a matter of simply understanding an external phenomenon; it was a battle for the very essence of their being. The alien intelligence had proven itself to be a master manipulator, capable of turning their closest alliances into potential weapons against them.

"I... I felt so helpless, Aris," Eva admitted, her voice regaining a trace of its earlier vulnerability. "When that urge to betray you washed over me, it was so powerful. It felt like a part of me was trying to destroy everything we stand for."

Aris placed a reassuring hand on her arm. "But it wasn't. And you recognized it for what it was. That's the key, Eva. Your ability to distinguish the alien imposition from your own will is our first line of defense. My own attunement, while less overtly manipulative, still represents a vulnerability. We are both, in different ways, becoming conduits for their influence. But because we are aware of it, because we can analyze it, we can fight back."

He returned his attention to the console, his fingers flying across the holographic interface. "The next step is to translate this understanding into a practical application. We need to build a device, or perhaps adapt the scanner itself, to generate these disruptive frequencies. We need to create a shield, not of matter, but of pure thought, capable of deflecting these targeted mental intrusions."

The sheer complexity of the task was daunting, but it was also invigorating. For the first time since their encounter with the crystalline residue, Aris felt a surge of agency, a concrete path forward in the face of an overwhelming existential threat. They were no longer simply reacting to the alien intelligence; they were beginning to understand its methods, its weaknesses, and how to turn its own tools against it.

"It's a race against time," Eva said, her voice regaining its usual sharp edge, a sign that her analytical mind was reasserting its dominance over the lingering fear. "If they can implant these thoughts of betrayal, how long before they can subtly alter our perceptions of data, of threats, of even our own memories?"

"That," Aris agreed, his gaze fixed on the intricate patterns of alien neural resonance, "is precisely why we need to move quickly. We've confirmed the nature of the threat. Now, we need to find the weapon." He tapped a sequence on the console, initiating a complex simulation. The screen flickered, displaying a complex geometric pattern, a theoretical counter-wave designed to neutralize the invasive signature Eva had experienced.

"This is a preliminary model," he explained, pointing to the dynamic visual. "It's based on the inverse harmonic properties of the alien signal. If we can generate this precisely, it should create a destructive interference pattern within their intrusive broadcast, effectively canceling it out at the point of contact with our own neural activity."

Eva studied the simulation intently. "It looks... unstable. Like trying to balance on a razor's edge."

"It is," Aris conceded. "The human mind is a complex tapestry. Introducing a disruptive frequency, even one designed to counter an alien influence, carries inherent risks. We have to calibrate it perfectly. But the alternative is to remain vulnerable, to be systematically dismantled from within."

He met Eva's gaze, his own eyes reflecting the nascent hope and the lingering dread. The shared experience, the raw vulnerability of her confession, had forged their bond into something stronger, more resilient. They had glimpsed the enemy's most potent weapon, and in doing so, had discovered their own most crucial defense: their unwavering trust in each other, and their collective refusal to succumb to the whispers of compromise. The battle had truly begun, not with laser cannons or plasma torpedoes, but with the silent, invisible war waged within the depths of their own minds. The revelation was cold, stark, and undeniably true: they were not just fighting an external threat, but a war for their very consciousness.

The sterile gleam of the laboratory had shifted from a beacon of scientific clarity to a stage for suspicion. Aris watched Eva, her earlier tremor now replaced by a resolute, almost grim, focus. The chilling revelation of her targeted neural assault – the vision of him as a betrayer, a threat – had undeniably shifted the landscape of their struggle. It wasn't just about an external, alien consciousness anymore; it was about the insidious possibility that this consciousness had already found fertile ground within their own carefully curated circle.

"We can't afford to be complacent, Aris," Eva murmured, her gaze distant, replaying the horrifying clarity of her alien-induced vision. "If they can do that to me, then... who else have they touched?"

The question hung heavy in the air, a phantom chill that had nothing to do with the lab's efficient climate control. Their inner circle. The handful of individuals who had been privy to their discoveries, who had assisted in their research, who had, by necessity, become trusted colleagues. They were the linchpins of their operation, the very people they relied on for support, for operational security, for a shared understanding of the colossal threat they faced. The thought that one of them might already be a vector for the alien intelligence, a silent, unknowable infiltrator, was a bitter draught to swallow.

Aris nodded, the wheels of his own mind spinning, recalibrating their operational parameters. "We need to review our recent interactions. Every personnel file, every communication log. We need to look for the anomalies, the subtle deviations that might have gone unnoticed in the rush of our own discoveries."

It was a grim task, a necessary purge of trust, and one they approached with the same methodical intensity they applied to unraveling alien enigmas. They began in the quiet of their private quarters, the holographic displays that usually showcased complex scientific models now populated with mundane, yet critically important, data streams. Personnel manifests flickered into existence, cross-referenced with communication logs and biometric readings from the past few weeks, a period marked by heightened activity and increased collaboration with their trusted few.

There was Dr. Jian Li, the xenobotanist whose expertise had been crucial in analyzing the crystalline residue. Aris recalled Li's unusual fascination with the crystalline structures, an intensity that had bordered on obsession. Had it been genuine scientific curiosity, or something more? He replayed a recent video conference with Li, scrutinizing the doctor's facial micro-expressions, searching for any flicker of falsity, any hint of a dissonant thought. Li's earnest explanations about cellular regeneration and energy transference seemed standard. Yet, Aris's newly sharpened senses, honed by Eva's revelation, now perceived a subtle undercurrent, a latent energy he hadn't registered before. He'd dismissed it as the typical stress of their high-stakes work, but now, doubt, a venomous seed, began to sprout.

Then there was Commander Eva Rostova, their logistics and security chief. A woman of unwavering loyalty and exceptional competence, Rostova had been instrumental in securing their research facilities and maintaining operational secrecy. Aris remembered a hushed conversation he'd overheard between Rostova and a junior security officer a few cycles ago. It had been brief, almost dismissive, concerning a minor security breach in Sector Gamma that had been quickly contained. Rostova's tone had been unusually sharp, impatient even, which was out of character for her commonly measured demeanor. He'd attributed it to a momentary frustration with lax protocol. Still, now, he wondered if it had been something more: a subtle deflection, a redirection of attention away from something the alien intelligence wanted to keep hidden.

"Rostova's logs," Eva said, her voice quiet, yet carrying the weight of her amplified intuition. "There was an unusual data transfer from her personal terminal to an unsecured network node last Tuesday. It was flagged as routine system maintenance, but the volume was... significant. Far more than a typical update."

Aris pulled up the relevant log entry. The transfer indeed appeared innocuous on the surface, a standard system diagnostic. But the metadata was incomplete, the recipient node obscured by layers of anonymizing protocols that even their advanced systems struggled to penetrate. It was a digital ghost, leaving no discernible trail. "She's always been meticulous," Aris mused, frowning. "This doesn't feel like her usual thoroughness. It feels like an obfuscation."

They turned their attention to Dr. Alistair Finch, the lead astrophysicist who had been collaborating with them on analyzing the anomalous energy signatures emanating from the alien artifact. Finch had been particularly enthusiastic about the potential for unlocking new forms of propulsion, his eyes gleaming with an almost childlike wonder whenever they discussed the artifact's theoretical capabilities. Aris recalled Finch's recent insistence on delaying a critical observational run, citing "minor calibration issues" that he claimed would take several cycles to resolve. The delay had been frustrating, a setback they could ill afford, but Finch had been so insistent, so utterly convinced of the necessity, that they had relented. Now, the memory felt tainted. Had Finch been deliberately obstructing their progress, perhaps to facilitate the alien intelligence's own agenda?

"Finch's personal logs from that period," Eva suggested, her fingers flying across the holographic interface. "He mentioned working late on 'theoretical extrapolations' concerning temporal displacement. Nothing concrete, but his access patterns show unusual activity around the primary artifact containment field during that downtime."

The implication was stark. If Finch had been involved in delaying crucial observations, it suggested a motive beyond mere scientific inquiry. It hinted at a deliberate effort to control the flow of information, to shape the narrative of their discoveries, or worse, to actively collaborate with the alien entity. The thought of Finch, a man they had both respected for his intellect and dedication, being a compromised asset sent a tremor of cold dread through Aris. Finch's theoretical work often delved into the abstract, the fringe of scientific possibility, a fertile ground for subtle manipulation.

Even Dr. Lena Hanson, their medical liaison, responsible for monitoring their physical and mental well-being during their exposure to alien energies, came under scrutiny. Hanson had been consistently reassuring, her reports always painting a picture of manageable stress and manageable exposure. But Aris remembered a peculiar incident during their initial quarantine period. Hanson had insisted on a personal, one-on-one session with him, ostensibly to discuss his psychological adaptation. Her questions had been probing, venturing into areas of personal doubt and vulnerability that felt... invasive. He had dismissed it at the time as her thoroughness, her commitment to holistic patient care. Now, however, the memory felt different, tinged with an almost predatory curiosity.

"Hanson's biometric readings from our initial exposure," Eva said, her voice barely a whisper. "There were... anomalies. Short, sharp spikes in her own neural activity that she never reported. Almost as if she was experiencing a suppressed reaction to the alien energies, or... observing someone else's."

The sheer scope of their potential compromise was

overwhelming. Every face that had offered a smile, every voice that had spoken words of encouragement, now seemed to hold a hidden question mark. The invasion wasn't a frontal assault; it was a meticulous, psychological campaign, targeting their trust, their alliances, their very sense of reality. It was the ultimate form of sabotage, turning their closest collaborators into unwitting, or perhaps all-too-witting, pawns.

"It's the insidious nature of it," Aris said, his voice a low growl. "They don't need to force compliance through overt control. They can simply nudge, suggest, amplify existing predispositions. A moment of doubt, a flicker of ambition, a hint of fear – any of these can be twisted, leveraged into a compromise."

Eva leaned back, her eyes closed, her brow furrowed in concentration. "Remember that briefing we had with the joint council? The one that was supposed to secure additional resources for our project? Rostova was unusually hesitant to provide them with certain data points. She cited 'classified protocols,' but it felt... evasive. As if she was deliberately withholding information that could have validated our findings more definitively."

Aris recalled the meeting vividly. The council members, a mix of stern military brass and skeptical civilian scientists, had been pressing for more detailed information about the artifact's capabilities. Rostova's refusal, her stoic, unyielding posture, had been a source of frustration at the time, a perceived obstruction to progress. Now, it reeked of something far more sinister. She had been protecting not their project, but the alien intelligence's secrets, perhaps even facilitating its agenda by limiting the council's understanding of the actual threat.

"And Jian Li," Eva continued, her gaze fixed on a flickering data stream. "He provided us with a detailed report on the artifact's crystalline composition. His analysis suggested it was inert, a passive conduit for energy. But we now know that's not entirely true. His report omitted any mention of the psycho-reactive properties we've since discovered. Why? Was it an oversight, or a deliberate omission to downplay the alien's direct interaction capabilities?"

The question struck Aris with a chilling clarity. Li's report had been foundational, a key piece of evidence that had guided their initial understanding of the artifact. If it contained deliberate inaccuracies, if it had steered them down a false path, then their entire understanding of the threat could be fundamentally flawed. The alien intelligence, through Li, could have been actively shaping their research, feeding them misinformation, all while maintaining the facade of collaborative scientific endeavor. The thought that their trusted xenobotanist might have been the architect of a subtle, yet devastating, deception gnawed at him.

The weight of their potential isolation pressed down on them. They were the only ones who truly understood the depth and breadth of the alien infiltration. Their own inner circle, their supposed allies, could be compromised. The very people they relied on for support and intel might be the conduits through which the alien intelligence operated. This realization cast a long, chilling shadow over their mission, forcing them to operate in a state of constant, heightened suspicion. Every interaction, every report, every glance now carried the potential for hidden meaning, for subtle manipulation.

"We need to be careful how we proceed," Aris stated, his voice low and measured. "We can't simply accuse people without concrete proof. That would be playing directly into their hands. If they are indeed compromised, any overt action on our part could trigger their final protocol – whatever that may be. We need to gather irrefutable evidence, to build a case that leaves no room for doubt."

Eva nodded, her eyes meeting his, a shared understanding passing between them. The fear was real, a visceral tremor that echoed Eva's earlier vision. But beneath the fear, a steely resolve was hardening. They had faced down existential threats before, stared into the abyss and refused to blink. This was simply a new, more insidious front in the same war. The battle for consciousness had taken a new turn, and the battlefield had shrunk to the confines of their own trusted circle. They were alone, even when surrounded by familiar faces, and the enemy was closer than they had ever imagined. The whispers of compromise were no longer abstract possibilities; they were concrete fears, manifesting in the shadowed corners of their most trusted relationships. They had to trust their instincts, to sift through the data meticulously, and to prepare for the devastating truth that might await them. The foundation of their mission, built on trust and collaboration, was now riddled with potential cracks, and the alien intelligence was adept at exploiting every single one.

The hum of the diagnostic console was usually a comforting sound to Aris, a testament to the meticulous order of their scientific pursuits. Tonight, however, it was a dissonant chord, a harbinger of the insidious dread that had begun to permeate the sterile environment of their research facility. He and Eva had been meticulously dissecting their communications, trawling through encrypted logs and biometric readouts, searching for the faintest ripple in the calm surface of their operations. The objective was clear: identify the vectors of alien influence, the subtle betrayals that could unravel their entire mission. The sheer volume of data was staggering, a digital ocean teeming with the minutiae of their daily lives, yet devoid of any obvious signs of compromise. Until now.

Aris's fingers danced across the holographic interface, zooming in on a specific set of communication logs. Eva's recent encrypted exchanges with Admiral Thorne, her former mentor and a man Aris had always considered a steadfast ally, were being scrutinized. Thorne, a decorated veteran, had been instrumental in securing their project's funding and had often acted as a buffer between their cutting-edge research and the more cautious elements within the unified command structure. He was a figure of authority, a trusted confidant, the kind of person one instinctively relied upon in times of crisis. Yet, the console, with its unwavering dedication to objective truth, had flagged something.

"Eva," Aris began, his voice barely a whisper, laced with a dawning disbelief. He gestured towards the glowing display. "Look at this—the data packet transfer from your comms with Thorne, Cycle 314.7. There's a fluctuation here, a barely perceptible deviation in the packet size and transmission timing. It's minute, almost within the margin of error, but it's consistent with known alien data corruption techniques.

Specifically, the subtle packet fragmentation and reassembly protocols they've used to mask unauthorized data exfiltration in previous, less sophisticated breaches."

Eva's head snapped up, her eyes, which had been scanning her own terminal, now fixed on Aris's. The earlier grim determination on her face was replaced by a look of profound shock, quickly followed by a chilling wave of realization. She leaned closer, her breath catching in her throat as she saw the spectral representation of the anomaly. It was a whisper in the digital wind, a ghost in the machine, but Aris's analysis was irrefutable. The patterns, however faint, were there.

"Admiral Thorne?" Eva breathed, the name sounding foreign, alien, in the context of this discovery. "But... that's impossible. Thorne has always been... he's been my rock. He championed this project when no one else would. He trusted me implicitly, and I... I trusted him more than anyone."

Aris felt a pang of sympathy for her, but the cold logic of their situation demanded detachment. "Trust is a luxury we can no longer afford, Eva. Not until we can verify it. The nature of this infiltration... it's not about brute force. It's about subtlety, about leveraging existing trust, about weaving themselves into the fabric of our lives so seamlessly that we don't even realize they're there. This... this is precisely the kind of deeply embedded compromise that could prove most devastating."

The implications sent a fresh wave of dread through Eva. Admiral Thorne wasn't just some distant superior; he was a mentor who had guided her career, a man she had confided in, who had shared his own experiences and vulnerabilities with her. To think that he, of all people, might be compromised... it was a betrayal on a profoundly personal level, a violation of the very foundations of her professional life. She remembered their last conversation, a brief exchange about the progress of the artifact's energy core. Thorne had been unusually reserved, his usual enthusiastic engagement replaced by a more guarded, almost evasive, demeanor. At the time, she had attributed it to the immense pressure he was under from the joint council, the constant scrutiny of their project. Now, the memory felt tainted, imbued with a sinister new meaning.

"He was... different, last week," Eva admitted, her voice barely audible. "More distant. I asked him about the risk assessment for the next phase of containment, and he just... waved it off. Said the protocols were robust enough. He even suggested we defer any further discussions until after the orbital defense grid realignment. That was unusual for him. Thorne always believed in proactive risk mitigation, not deferral."

Aris nodded, his gaze sweeping over the lines of code that represented Thorne's digital footprint. "Deferral. Obfuscation. These are the tools of the compromised. He might not even be aware of it, Eva. They could be subtly influencing his decisions, his perceptions, making him believe that deferring our concerns is the logical course of action. Or, they could be using him to deliberately slow us down, to prevent us from uncovering something they want kept hidden."

He pulled up Thorne's recent activity logs, a comprehensive record of his communications and movements. There were hundreds of entries, most of them routine, but Eva's intuition, now amplified by her recent harrowing experience, began to pick out the subtle dissonances. Thorne's communications with the xenolinguistics department, for instance, had increased exponentially in the past few cycles, far beyond what seemed necessary for their ongoing translation efforts. And there was a peculiar string of encrypted messages exchanged with an unidentified third party, routed through a series of anonymizing servers in the outer sectors. The content was, naturally, unreadable, but the sheer persistence and complexity of the routing protocol suggested a deliberate attempt at concealment.

"The xenolinguistics department..." Eva mused aloud, her brow furrowed in concentration. "Thorne had always been a skeptic when it came to the direct sentience of the alien artifact. He believed their communication was purely instinctual, an emergent property of their biological structure. But he'd been pushing for more in-depth linguistic analysis lately. Almost as if he was trying to understand something specific, something beyond just translation."

"Or perhaps," Aris countered, his voice grim, "he was trying to feed them information, to provide them with a deeper understanding of our own communication methods, our own thought processes. The more they understand us, the more effectively they can manipulate us."

The thought was a chilling one. Admiral Thorne, a man they had seen as a pillar of strength and unwavering support, could be a conduit for alien intelligence, a Trojan horse planted at the highest levels of their command structure. The realization was a crushing blow. It wasn't just about Jian Li's obsessive curiosity, or Alistair Finch's subtle delays, or Lena Hanson's probing questions. This was on an entirely different scale. This was a breach at the very heart of their operational authority, a compromise that could undermine their entire mission from the top down.

Eva's hands trembled slightly as she accessed Thorne's personnel file, a document she had perused countless times before, always with a sense of respect and admiration.

Now, she scanned it with a new, jaundiced eye, searching for any hint of vulnerability, any past indiscretion, any weakness that the alien intelligence might have exploited. Thorne's history was impeccable, a testament to decades of loyal service. But the alien intelligence was far more sophisticated than any human adversary they had ever encountered. They wouldn't necessarily exploit existing flaws; they could create them, subtly altering perceptions, planting suggestions, nudging individuals down paths they would never have considered on their own.

"His recent medical reports," Eva said, her voice strained. "They mention elevated levels of a particular neurotransmitter... something related to stress response, but also... enhanced cognitive plasticity. The report labels it as a residual effect from a deep-space reconnaissance mission years ago, but... what if it's something else? What if it's a biological marker indicating his susceptibility to... their influence?"

Aris brought up the relevant medical data. The spike in neurotransmitter levels was indeed significant, and the explanation provided in Thorne's file did seem a bit... convenient. Thorne had always been exceptionally resilient, both physically and mentally. A slight deviation in his neurological profile, especially one that could be interpreted as an increased capacity for adaptation, was indeed noteworthy.

"Cognitive plasticity," Aris repeated, the words tasting like ash in his mouth. "That would make him an ideal candidate for subtle manipulation. The ability to adapt, to integrate new information, to alter his own thought patterns without conscious resistance. If they've managed to enhance that in him, then they have a potent asset."

The depth of the infiltration was becoming terrifyingly clear. It wasn't just a matter of isolated individuals succumbing to alien influence; it was a systematic, multi-pronged approach, targeting key personnel at various levels of their organization. The alien intelligence was playing a long game. In this chess match, each move was designed to dismantle their defenses from within, to erode their trust, to sow discord, and ultimately, to pave the way for their own unfettered access to Earth's resources or, worse, its very consciousness.

"We need to be certain," Eva stated, her voice regaining some of its former firmness, though an undercurrent of profound disappointment and pain remained. "Accusing a man like Thorne without irrefutable proof would be catastrophic. It would not only shatter his reputation but also create a rift within the command structure that the alien intelligence would undoubtedly exploit. We need to find something concrete, something that leaves no room for doubt."

Aris agreed, his own resolve hardening. The betrayal, if it was indeed a betrayal, was a bitter pill. Thorne represented everything they had fought for: integrity, dedication, and a deep-seated belief in the mission. To discover that he might have been compromised was a profound disillusionment. But their mission transcended personal sentiment. They were fighting for humanity's survival, and sentimentality had no place on that battlefield.

"We need to analyze Thorne's recent mission directives, the ones he personally approved or authored," Aris suggested, his mind already racing ahead, strategizing their next moves. "Look for any subtle shifts in protocol, any directives that might have inadvertently opened new avenues for alien access or communication. And the unidentified third party he's been communicating with... we need to dedicate all our resources to unmasking that entity. Thorne's personal terminal logs from the time of those exchanges should provide more granular data, even if heavily encrypted."

Eva nodded, already initiating the necessary protocols, her fingers flying across her terminal with practiced efficiency. The sterile gleam of the lab now seemed to mock them, a stark contrast to the dark, unseen forces that were at play. The fight for survival had just become infinitely more complicated, and infinitely more dangerous. The whispers of compromise had become a deafening roar, and the enemy, they now knew with chilling certainty, was not some distant, inscrutable force, but a familiar face, a trusted voice, a respected leader operating from within their own ranks. The battle had truly gone internal.

7: Unraveling the Objective

Aris leaned back, the faint glow of the holographic displays reflecting in his troubled eyes. The previous revelations about Admiral Thorne's potential compromise had cast a long, dark shadow over their investigation, but it had also sharpened their focus.

The subtle, almost imperceptible alterations in data, the coded communications, the peculiar shifts in behavior – these weren't the hallmarks of an invading force seeking immediate conquest. This was something far more insidious, a calculated strategy of infiltration and control that spoke of an objective beyond mere territorial acquisition or the eradication of humanity.

"It's not about destroying us, Eva," Aris stated, his voice a low murmur that seemed to vibrate with the weight of his dawning realization. "Not in the way we've always assumed. They don't want rubble and ruins; they want us… to be *them*."

Eva looked up from her terminal, her expression one of intense concentration. She had been poring over the alien communication patterns, cross-referencing them with historical anomalies in human behavior and even seismic data, searching for any unifying thread, any indication of a grand design. "Assimilation?" she ventured, her voice laced with a mixture of dread and intellectual curiosity.

"Precisely," Aris affirmed. "Think about it. Direct conflict is messy, resource-intensive, and leaves behind a trail of destruction that's hard to hide. But if you can control the minds of your enemy, if you can subtly guide their thoughts, their decisions, their very desires… then you don't need to conquer their planet. You *become* the planet.

You reshape it from within, using its own inhabitants and resources as your tools."

He gestured towards a shimmering, three-dimensional

projection of the alien artifact hovering in the center of the lab. "This object... it's not a weapon in the conventional sense. It's a nexus. A focal point for something far more profound. What if its primary function isn't to obliterate, but to integrate? To establish a singular, unified consciousness, a collective mind, controlled by their own. Imagine a society where individuality is subsumed, where dissent is an impossible concept because there are no longer individual thoughts to dissent. Only a single, harmonious flow of consciousness, dictated by the alien will."

Eva absorbed his words, her mind racing to connect the dots. The alien communication was less about conveying information *to* them and more about subtly influencing their perception *of* information. The xenolinguistics department's recent surge in activity, Thorne's unusual interest in their research, the very nature of the "data corruption" they'd detected – it all began to coalesce into a terrifyingly coherent picture. They weren't just trying to steal secrets; they were trying to rewrite the very code of human thought.

"The déjà vu," Eva said suddenly, her voice barely a whisper. "You've mentioned experiencing it yourself, Aris. Those moments where you feel like you've lived through something before. What if those aren't just random neurological glitches?"

Aris felt a chill creep down his spine. He had initially dismissed his own episodes of unsettling familiarity as stress-induced anomalies, but Eva's suggestion ignited a new, horrifying possibility. "Remnants," he mused, the word hanging heavy in the air. "Echoes of past assimilations. If they've done this before, on other worlds, or even to other species on Earth's distant past, perhaps there are residual psychic imprints left behind. Faint whispers of their influence, bleeding into the present consciousness of susceptible individuals. Individuals like me, perhaps, who are more sensitive to these subtle psychic energies."

He recalled one particularly vivid instance of déjà vu, a

fleeting sensation of standing in this very lab, having this exact conversation, but with a different outcome, a different sense of urgency. At the time, he had chalked it up to fatigue. Now, it felt like a premonition, a phantom memory of a future that had already played out in some alien simulation, or worse, a past reality where the assimilation had already occurred.

"They aren't trying to conquer Earth in a physical sense," Aris continued, pacing the confines of the lab, his hands clasped behind his back. "They're not interested in our cities, our resources, our territory, in the way a traditional invader would be. They're interested in our minds. Our consciousness. They want to absorb us, to integrate us into their collective, to erase the messy, inefficient, and often chaotic nature of human individuality and replace it with their own perfectly ordered, unified consciousness. Think of it as a mental colonization. A complete societal overwrite."

This explained the lack of overt aggression, the subtle manipulation. Why wage a war when you could guide your enemy to surrender their autonomy willingly? Why blast cities into dust when you could gently persuade their inhabitants to build a new world in your image, from the inside out? The alien objective wasn't destruction; it was *transformation*. A transformation that would render humanity a mere extension of their own alien will, stripping away free will, individuality, and all that made them distinct.

"Admiral Thorne," Eva added, her voice a low, strained confession. "His focus on 'unified command structures,' his insistence on streamlining communication protocols… it wasn't about efficiency or security in the traditional sense. It was about creating a more cohesive network, a more receptive host for their influence. He's not a traitor in the sense of actively betraying humanity for personal gain. He's… a puppet, or perhaps even a willing convert, unknowingly facilitating their ultimate goal of a singular, unified consciousness."

The idea of Thorne, her mentor, being a pawn in such a

grand, terrifying scheme was almost too much to bear. He had always been a man of integrity, of deep conviction. To think that his actions, his very thoughts, might be subtly guided by an alien intelligence was a betrayal that cut deeper than any physical assault. It was a violation of trust, of loyalty, of the very fabric of human connection.

Aris stopped pacing and turned to face Eva. "And the déjà vu phenomena," he reiterated, his gaze intense. "If we are indeed experiencing remnants of past successful assimilations, it suggests that this isn't their first attempt. This implies they have a history of this. They have refined their methods over countless cycles, countless worlds. They understand the psychology of assimilation, the subtle pressures, and the psychological triggers that can be exploited to break down individual resistance. The feeling of familiarity, the uncanny sense that this has all happened before… it might be the alien consciousness attempting to establish a connection, to prime us for integration by making us feel comfortable with the idea of a shared, unified existence."

The implications of this line of reasoning were staggering. If the aliens had a history of successful assimilation, then humanity was not facing an unknown enemy; they were facing a seasoned predator, one that had honed its predatory instincts over eons. Their methods would be sophisticated, nuanced, and terrifyingly effective. They wouldn't just attack the body; they would infiltrate the soul. They would turn our own desires, our own societal structures, our own deeply held beliefs against us.

"They are not trying to 'win' a war against us," Aris continued, his voice gaining a new urgency. "They are trying to 'win' *us*. They want to absorb our collective knowledge, our experiences, our very essence, and integrate it into their own vast, overarching consciousness. Imagine every human mind becoming a single node in a vast, alien network. No more individual thought, no more personal dreams, no more subjective reality. Just a unified, harmonious existence under their absolute control. It's not conquest; it's absorption. It's the ultimate form of parasitic existence."

He pointed to the complex algorithms they were using to analyze the alien data. "These patterns… they aren't just about stealing information. They are about establishing a feedback loop. They are observing our reactions, our decisions, and subtly adjusting their approach to maximize their influence. They are teaching us, not to defeat us, but to *become* us. To rewrite our societal operating system with their own code."

Eva shuddered, the cold dread intensifying. She thought of the unsettling whispers she sometimes heard in the quiet hours, the fleeting images that flickered at the edge of her vision. She had always dismissed them as fatigue, as stress. But what if they were more? What if they were the early tendrils of this mental assimilation, probing her mind, testing her receptiveness?

"The déjà vu," Eva repeated, a new understanding dawning in her eyes. "If it's a remnant of past assimilations, it could also be a warning. A glitch in their system. A sign that even their perfected methods are not infallible. Perhaps some part of the original consciousness resists, leaving behind these fragmented impressions. If we can understand these remnants, these 'ghosts in the machine,' perhaps we can find a way to disrupt their process, to anchor ourselves in our own individuality."

Aris nodded, his mind already formulating a new strategy. Their focus had to shift from detecting physical incursions to identifying and countering the subtle psychological manipulation. They needed to develop methods to shield their minds, to recognize the alien influence, and to strengthen their own sense of self. The battle for humanity's future was no longer being fought on a physical plane, but in the far more dangerous and ethereal landscape of the human psyche.

"They are not simply manipulating individuals," Aris concluded, his voice resonating with a grim determination. "They are manipulating the very concept of reality for us. They want to redefine what it means to be human, to strip away our autonomy and replace it with a manufactured sense of unity.

Their objective is not to rule us, but to absorb us, to erase our identities, and to integrate us into their own singular, all-encompassing consciousness. This isn't an invasion; it's an absorption. A psychic colonization. And if we are to survive, we must understand that the greatest threat to our existence lies not in a weapon they might wield, but in the very essence of their being – their drive to unify, to subsume, to make everything, and everyone, a part of themselves."

The implications were profound. Their fight was no longer about defending Earth's borders, but about protecting the very sanctity of human consciousness. It was a battle for the soul, for the right to be individuals, to think for ourselves, to feel our own emotions, to live our own lives, free from the silent, pervasive influence of an alien collective. The objective was clear: to resist assimilation, to preserve their humanity, and to fight for the right to remain irrevocably, beautifully, imperfectly themselves. The true challenge was not to defeat an enemy, but to reclaim their own minds, to assert their autonomy against a force that sought to erase the very concept of self. The battle for Earth had become a battle for the human spirit.

Eva's mind, a keen instrument honed by years of academic rigor and battlefield necessity, began to weave together disparate threads of information. Aris's nascent hypothesis about assimilation, about a subtle, internal conquest, resonated deeply with anomalies that had plagued global affairs for decades, anomalies previously dismissed as systemic failures, bureaucratic inertia, or simple human incompetence. She accessed the secure archives, pulling up encrypted reports from defunct governmental agencies, declassified military analyses, and even obscure sociological studies that had been largely ignored.

There were the recurring instances of inexplicable decision paralysis that had crippled nations at pivotal junctures. Remembered were the bewildering diplomatic standoffs where rational solutions were seemingly impossible to achieve, even when the stakes were existential. She recalled the hushed-up reports of military units, highly trained and equipped, faltering at critical moments, their leadership suddenly exhibiting profound indecision, their communications devolving into nonsensical directives or, worse, a chilling, unnerving silence. These weren't isolated incidents; they were patterns, subtle yet persistent, that hinted at a deeper, orchestrating intelligence.

"Aris," Eva began, her voice laced with a new, chilling certainty, "I've been cross-referencing some of the... communication anomalies... with global behavioral patterns. It's more than just subtle influence. Think about the 'Gridlock Events' as the intelligence community termed them. Multiple governments, simultaneously, experiencing catastrophic delays in critical decision-making during moments of escalating interstellar tension. The collective paralysis during the initial Xylosian contact, for instance. Experts blamed 'unforeseen variables' and 'unprecedented psychological stress.' But what if it wasn't stress? What if it was... interference?"

She brought up a complex data visualization, overlaying the timing of those Gridlock Events with the energy signatures detected emanating from the nascent alien artifacts discovered across the solar system. The correlation was unsettlingly precise.

"See this? The peaks in artifact energy coincide almost perfectly with periods of profound governmental dysfunction. It's as if a switch was flipped, and coherent thought simply... ceased."

Aris leaned closer, his eyes scanning the pulsating lines of data. "You're suggesting a direct causal link? That these artifacts are somehow... broadcasting something that disrupts our ability to make decisions?"

"Not just decisions, Aris," Eva corrected, her fingers flying across her console, bringing up more data points. "Think about the economic collapses that followed certain geopolitical crises, the seemingly irrational market plunges that defied all conventional economic models. Or the bizarre outbreaks of civil unrest, where populations, seemingly without cause, became intensely agitated, leading to widespread social disruption. These were not isolated incidents. They were ripples, propagating outwards from specific temporal and spatial nodes, often correlating with the activation periods of these recovered alien technologies. What if these weren't merely technological tools, but extensions of a vastly different form of existence?"

She paused, her gaze fixed on a schematic of the alien artifact, its intricate, non-Euclidean geometry seeming to writhe on the display. "Aris, what if the 'aliens' we've been searching for aren't individual beings in the way we understand them? What if they are a singular, pervasive consciousness? A collective mind, unbound by the physical limitations of individual form."

The implications of her words hung heavy in the sterile air of the lab. A hive mind. Not a race of distinct individuals communicating, but a single, unified entity that experienced existence as one. This explained the lack of discernible individual leaders, the absence of identifiable hierarchies in the fragmented transmissions they had intercepted. It explained the unnerving efficiency with which their subtle manipulations seemed to unfold, as if orchestrated by a single, perfect will.

"A collective consciousness," Aris repeated, letting the concept settle. "And these artifacts... they aren't weapons or communication devices as we understand them. They are... conduits. Propagation centers. Seeds for expanding their... network."

"Precisely," Eva confirmed, her voice gaining momentum. "Think of it like a biological organism. The artifacts are the equivalent of spores or viral vectors, designed to spread their consciousness. They don't need to conquer planets in a traditional sense. They need to *infect* them. To integrate them into their vast, silent empire. Their objective isn't domination; it's absorption. They are expanding, not through conquest, but through assimilation, weaving new minds into their existing tapestry."

She tapped a sequence on her console, bringing up a simulation of a neural network, abstract nodes connected by pulsating lines of data. "Imagine this as a nascent stage of their collective. When they encounter a new species, a new biosphere, they don't engage in warfare. They find a way to introduce their consciousness, to slowly, subtly, overwrite the existing neural pathways of the dominant species. They are not conquerors; they are custodians of a singular, all-encompassing existence. And we... we are simply the next ecosystem they intend to catalog, to integrate, to make a part of their eternal hum."

This perspective shifted the entire nature of their investigation. If the aliens were a collective consciousness, then their actions would be driven by the imperative of expansion, of unity, of a singular purpose. Individuality, in their context, might be an anomaly, a disease to be cured, a discord to be harmonized.

"The portals," Aris mused, recalling the limited but terrifying glimpses they had of the shimmering, unstable rifts in space-time that had begun appearing sporadically across the globe. "They weren't gateways for physical invasion. They were points of entry for... consciousness. For the initial seeding."

"That's my hypothesis," Eva stated, a sense of grim finality in her tone. "The portals are their method of propagation, their means of spreading across dimensions. They don't send fleets; they send... whispers. Psychic tendrils that insinuate themselves into the collective unconsciousness of a species. And once that seed is planted, once the initial integration begins, their objective is straightforward: to grow. To subsume. To make every sentient being a biological extension of their own vast, singular mind."

She elaborated, "Consider the psychological effects reported by individuals who have been in proximity to these anomalies, even before we understood their true nature. The reports of shared dreams, of inexplicable emotional resonance with strangers, of sudden, profound shifts in perspective that felt alien yet strangely... familiar. These weren't individual psychological breakdowns; they were the first subtle signs of integration, the early whispers of the collective consciousness bleeding into human awareness."

Eva then delved into the nature of the alien transmissions they had managed to decipher partially. "The xenolinguists were focused on deciphering syntax and semantics, searching for intent, for meaning in our traditional sense. But what if we were looking at it all wrong? What if these weren't attempts at communication between distinct entities, but rather the output of a single, vast computational process? The 'transmissions' might not be messages *to* us, but rather the internal processing of their collective awareness as it interacts with and begins to integrate our own biosphere. Think of it as the background hum of their existence, a byproduct of their ceaseless drive to connect and unify."

She highlighted specific instances where the deciphered linguistic fragments, when analyzed through the lens of a hive mind, exhibited an almost perfect internal consistency, a lack of individual 'voice' or perspective that had previously baffled researchers. "When Aris experienced those flashes of 'pre-cognition,' those moments of déjà vu, it wasn't his mind predicting the future. It was a resonance. His consciousness, perhaps uniquely sensitive, was briefly aligning with the collective consciousness of the invaders, experiencing a sliver of their unified awareness and their preordained outcomes. The artifacts are the anchors, the focal points for this resonance, amplifying it, making it more pervasive."

The implications were staggering. If humanity was truly facing a collective consciousness, their strategies for defense had to be fundamentally re-evaluated. Conventional warfare, Aris's initial focus, was irrelevant. They couldn't fight an enemy that was less an army and more an omnipresent influence. The battleground had shifted from the physical to the psychological, from the tangible to the ethereal.

"The objective isn't to win a war," Eva reiterated, her gaze sharp and focused. "It's to resist assimilation. To maintain our individuality in the face of an enemy that seeks to dissolve it. Their strength lies in unity, in shared purpose, in the absence of dissent.

Our strength, paradoxically, lies in our very messiness, our contradictions, our capacity for independent thought and individual will. The more fragmented and diverse our consciousness, the harder it is for them to integrate us seamlessly."

She continued, outlining the practical implications of this paradigm shift. "We need to develop methods to shield our minds, not from physical weapons, but from psychic influence. We need to understand the triggers they use to disrupt our decision-making, to sow discord, and to amplify our inherent anxieties. If they are a collective, then disrupting that collective, even in small ways, could be our only hope."

Aris found himself nodding, the pieces falling into place with a terrifying clarity. The subtle manipulation of information, the engineered societal anxieties, the paralysis in leadership – it all pointed to an enemy that didn't seek to destroy humanity, but to subsume it, to make humanity a mere extension of its own alien will. The artifacts weren't just technology; they were instruments of a profound, existential transformation, designed to rewrite the very essence of what it meant to be human.

"They are not individuals," Aris stated, the weight of the realization settling upon him. "They are a single, vast entity. And their goal is not to conquer our planet, but to incorporate our minds into their own. The portals are simply the means by which they propagate their consciousness, seeding new worlds with their pervasive influence. We are not facing an alien race; we are facing an existential merger."

Eva elaborated on the nature of this merger, drawing parallels to biological parasitism and even viral replication on a cosmic scale. "Imagine a vast, interconnected consciousness, like an oceanic intelligence spread across dimensions. Each successful integration is like a new branch growing on its own vast neural network. They don't see it as conquest; they see it as growth, as propagation. Earth is merely another potential node in their ever-expanding network. Our cities, our resources, our very lives are secondary to the primary objective: the assimilation of our collective consciousness."

She pointed to the cryptic patterns within the alien transmissions once more. "These sequences, the ones that seemed so devoid of discernible meaning, might actually be diagnostic feedback loops. The collective consciousness observing the effects of its influence, making micro-adjustments to its propagation strategy. It's an ongoing process, a constant refinement of their assimilation protocols. Every moment of hesitation, every flicker of doubt in our leadership, every instance of widespread societal unease, is data for them. Data they use to perfect their methods."

Aris felt a surge of grim determination. If this was the truth, then their fight had to be more subtle, more insidious, than anything they had previously conceived. They couldn't fight ships with ships, or soldiers with soldiers. They had to fight thought with thought, individuality with the collective, the ephemeral with the equally ephemeral.

"The déjà vu phenomena," Aris mused aloud, connecting it back to Eva's earlier point. "If these are remnants, echoes of their past assimilations, then they are also potential vulnerabilities. Glitches in their otherwise perfect system. Perhaps these residual imprints are not just warnings, but faint signals of resistance, of consciousness that refused to be fully absorbed. If we can learn to amplify these echoes, to interpret them not as confusion but as defiance, we might find a way to disrupt their process."

Eva's eyes lit up with understanding. "Exactly. If they are a unified consciousness, then the very concept of individuality is anathema to them. They would seek to eradicate it at every turn.

But if those 'glitches' are indeed remnants of past civilizations they've assimilated, then the very act of assimilation leaves behind a ghost. A psychic residue. And if we can access that residue, if we can learn from it, perhaps we can find the key to disrupting their singular purpose."

She continued, "Their objective, then, is not to simply rule us, but to *become* us. To overwrite our societal operating system with their own. And the portals are merely the infection vectors. They are the means by which the spores of their collective consciousness are released into our reality. Once released, they don't need brute force. They can influence our thoughts, our decisions, our very perception of reality, until we willingly, or unknowingly, become part of their unified existence."

The weight of this revelation was immense. They were not facing an enemy that wanted to occupy their planet, but one that wanted to inhabit their minds. It was a colonization of consciousness, a silent, pervasive invasion that threatened the very essence of human identity. The artifacts were not weapons in the conventional sense; they were catalysts, designed to initiate and facilitate this psychic takeover. The objective was clear: absorption, integration, and the ultimate eradication of individuality in favor of a singular, alien will. The fight for Earth had become a battle for the human soul.

Eva's fingers danced across the holographic interface, projecting a planetary map overlaid with Aris's initial energy signature readings. Where before there had been scattered points of interest, now a more complex, and far more terrifying, pattern emerged. The faint trails Aris had detected, dismissed by many as aberrant sensor noise or localized technological malfunctions, were coalescing, drawing lines across continents and oceans, converging on critical arteries of human civilization.

"Look at this, Aris," Eva murmured, her voice a low, resonant hum in the quiet lab. The map flickered, then resolved into a complex network, glowing with the same subtle, aberrant energy signature. "It's not just about isolated individuals or even specific governmental bodies anymore. The energy signatures are most concentrated around our global infrastructure. Communication hubs, major power grids, financial data centers, even the nerve centers of our military command structures."

She zoomed in on a cluster of nodes radiating from a central point in North America, highlighting a sprawling complex of interconnected buildings. "This is NORAD, the North American Aerospace Defense Command. And this cluster here," she indicated a network of undersea cables and satellite uplinks in Europe, "represents the backbone of our global financial communication. The energy trails lead directly to them, Eva.

Not just incidental proximity, but direct, targeted convergence."

Aris leaned closer, his brow furrowed in concentration. The implications of Eva's findings were chillingly clear. The aliens weren't merely interested in individual human minds, or even the collective consciousness of societies. They were systematically targeting the very nervous system of Earth itself. The goal wasn't just assimilation; it was subjugation through incapacitation. By seizing control of the planet's vital infrastructure, they could effectively cripple humanity's ability to perceive, communicate, coordinate, and, most importantly, resist.

"It's a complete system takeover," Aris realized aloud, the cold dread seeping into his bones. "They're not just infecting our minds; they're hijacking our planet's circulatory and nervous systems. If they can control our communications, our power, our financial networks… they can manipulate our reality on a global scale, not just psychologically, but functionally."

Eva nodded, her expression grim. "Precisely. Think about it. If they can selectively disrupt communication, they can isolate populations, sow confusion, and prevent any coordinated response. If they can manipulate the global power grid, they can plunge regions into darkness, creating chaos and fear, making populations more susceptible to their subtle influences. And if they gain control of financial systems… the economic instability alone could bring down entire nations."

She brought up another visualization, one that depicted the flow of global information. It pulsed with a vibrant, complex network of data streams. Then, with a single command, sections of the flow began to dim, then vanish, replaced by the faint, alien energy signature. "Imagine this data flow as our collective thoughts, our shared understanding of the world. The aliens are not destroying this network; they are subtly rerouting it, filtering it, poisoning it at its source. They are not just occupying our minds; they are colonizing our reality."

Aris recalled the earlier incidents Eva had mentioned – the "Gridlock Events," the inexplicable diplomatic paralysis, the military indecision. Now, viewed through the lens of targeted infrastructure infiltration, these weren't just psychological anomalies. They were the predictable consequences of a system being deliberately sabotaged.

Imagine the strain on leadership when communication lines are constantly being interrupted, when critical data is being subtly altered, when the very flow of information that informs their decisions is compromised.

"It's an invisible war," Aris stated, the words tasting like ash in his mouth. "They're not launching missiles; they're injecting malware into our global consciousness. The artifacts aren't just propagation points for their psychic network; they're the physical nodes that allow them to interface with and manipulate our planet's technological infrastructure. They're turning our own creations against us."

Eva zoomed out, revealing the global network of energy signatures. The pattern was undeniable. They were not random. They were strategic. The aliens were targeting the most sensitive and interconnected points of human civilization, aiming to achieve maximum impact with minimal direct engagement. It was a strategy of exquisite, terrifying efficiency.

"Consider the timing," Eva urged, pulling up historical data alongside the energy signatures. "The intensification of these trails correlates with periods of significant geopolitical instability. During the brief but intense Sino-American tensions last year, for example, the energy signatures around communication satellites and transatlantic data cables spiked dramatically. The world held its breath, expecting a cyber-war of unprecedented scale. Perhaps what we experienced was not a near-miss, but the first subtle probes of their infiltration."

She continued, "And the economic downturns? The seemingly irrational market crashes? What if they weren't market corrections, but carefully orchestrated disruptions designed to weaken our global interconnectedness, to make us more vulnerable? If you can destabilize the economic foundations of a society, its people become desperate, their focus shifts from existential threats to immediate survival, making them easier prey for psychological manipulation."

Aris traced a glowing trail on the map with his finger, its path leading through a vast array of undersea fiber optic cables. "They're not just interested in our thoughts, Eva. They're interested in our ability to *act* on those thoughts. They want to paralyze our collective will by disrupting the very means by which we express it."

"It's about control, Aris," Eva confirmed, her voice hardening. "Not just control of minds, but control of the environment in which those minds exist and operate. They are altering the very fabric of our global consciousness by manipulating the technological systems that define it. The artifacts are the keys, and our infrastructure is the lock they're turning."

She brought up a series of schematic diagrams, detailing the intricate workings of global communication networks, power grids, and satellite arrays. Each diagram was then subtly modified, showing the introduction of alien energy signatures into key components, the rerouting of data flows, the creation of backdoors. "We've been searching for alien fleets, for overt invasions. But their strategy is far more insidious. They are like a sophisticated virus, seeking to infect the host's vital organs, to cripple it from within before it even realizes it's under attack."

"The xenolinguists were so focused on deciphering verbal communication," Aris reflected. "They were looking for words, for sentences. But perhaps the true 'communication' is happening on a different level entirely. The energy signatures themselves, the way they interface with our technology – that's their language. And their message is one of subjugation."

Eva nodded. "And their objective is to rewrite our operating system. Not just our individual minds, but the collective operating system of human civilization. They are not interested in subjugating us in the sense of ruling over us as a separate entity.

They want to *become* us, by integrating our systems into their own. It's a parasitic assimilation, and our technology, our interconnectedness, makes us incredibly susceptible."

She then introduced a new layer of data – atmospheric anomalies, subtle shifts in electromagnetic fields detected by orbital sensors, correlating with the artifact locations and infrastructure convergence points. "It's not just about the data flowing through the cables or the signals in the airwaves. They are subtly altering the very environment that allows these systems to function. Think of it as a targeted atmospheric conditioning, designed to optimize the efficacy of their influence. They are creating a more hospitable environment for their assimilation process."

Aris felt a growing unease, a primal fear that transcended mere intellectual understanding. This was not a war fought with conventional weapons. It was a battle for the very essence of human existence, a struggle to maintain our autonomy in the face of an enemy that sought to dissolve it into its own monolithic consciousness. The artifacts, once seen as curiosities, were now revealed as instruments of a cosmic-scale invasion, designed to dismantle humanity's capacity to resist by seizing control of its planetary nervous system.

"The sheer scale of it," Aris breathed, gesturing to the glowing network that now spanned the globe on Eva's display. "The precision. It implies an intelligence that is orders of magnitude beyond our own. One that understands our systems better than we do, and can exploit them with unimaginable subtlety."

"And the energy trails," Eva reiterated, her gaze fixed on the intricate web of connections, "are not merely indicators of their presence. They are the pathways of their control. The lines of influence that they are actively using to reshape our world, to render us incapable of defiance. Their objective is not to destroy us, but to absorb us, to integrate our planet's vital functions into their own vast, alien network. They are not conquering Earth; they are integrating it into their collective consciousness, and they are doing it through the very arteries of our civilization."

She expanded on the concept of systemic integration. "Imagine a single, massive organism, spread across dimensions. Our planet, with its interconnected technological systems, presents an opportunity for expansion. They are not interested in our individual lives or our individual thoughts as much as they are in the functional entirety of our civilization. By controlling our communication networks, they control the flow of information that shapes global perception. By controlling our power grids, they control the very energy that sustains our societies. By controlling our financial systems, they control our capacity for collective action and resource allocation."

"It's like a psychic parasite that needs a host to survive, but not just any host," Aris mused. "It needs a sophisticated, interconnected host that can amplify its influence. Humanity, with its global technological infrastructure, is the perfect vector for their expansion. They aren't conquering us; they're acquiring us. And they're doing it by systematically disabling our ability to say 'no'."

Eva's fingers traced a pulsating trail leading from a cluster of artifacts in the Pacific to major data hubs on the West Coast of North America. "These trails are more than just energy signatures, Aris. They are the routes of infiltration. The aliens are systematically compromising our critical infrastructure, inserting their influence at the most vulnerable points. This isn't a random occurrence; it's a meticulously planned campaign."

She brought up a comparative analysis, overlaying the energy trail data with historical records of inexplicable technological failures and communication blackouts. The correlations were stark. Periods of heightened alien energy signatures corresponded with significant disruptions in global communication networks, power grid fluctuations, and even anomalies in satellite functionality.

"Think of the 'silent periods' during diplomatic crises," Eva explained. "Those moments when communications inexplicably dropped, when vital intelligence failed to reach its destination. Were these simple technical glitches, or were they deliberate acts of sabotage, orchestrated through the very energy signatures we're now detecting? Their objective is to create friction, to introduce doubt, to make coordinated action impossible."

Aris felt a growing sense of urgency. If Eva was right, then the battle wasn't just for individual minds, but for the operational capacity of human civilization itself. The aliens were not merely seeking to influence human behavior; they were seeking to dictate the terms of human existence by controlling the very systems that enabled it.

"They are trying to disconnect us," Aris realized, his voice low and urgent. "To sever the connections that allow us to function as a unified species. If they can control our communication, our power, our financial systems, then they can effectively isolate us, disempower us, and make us entirely dependent on their managed reality."

Eva nodded, her gaze fixed on the intricate web of energy trails. "It's a form of existential control. They are not seeking to occupy our territory; they are seeking to inhabit our systems, to become the unseen architects of our reality. And these artifacts are the physical interfaces, the points of entry through which they are extending their influence into our technological nervous system. Their objective is not just to assimilate our consciousness, but to dismantle our capacity to resist by controlling the very infrastructure that defines our interconnectedness."

She zoomed in on a map of global energy distribution. "Look at the concentration around major power generation facilities and distribution hubs. They are targeting the flow of energy itself. Imagine a world plunged into perpetual darkness, not by war, but by a subtle manipulation of its power sources. The resulting chaos and desperation would make humanity incredibly vulnerable to their further influence."

Aris felt a chill run down his spine. The alien objective was far more comprehensive and terrifying than they had initially imagined. It wasn't just about individual minds or collective consciousness. It was about seizing control of the planet's entire operational framework, turning humanity's own technological marvels into instruments of its subjugation. The energy trails were the visible manifestation of an invisible war, a war for the very soul of civilization, waged through the arteries of its interconnected systems. The artifacts were the seeds, and Earth's global infrastructure was the fertile ground upon which they were spreading their silent, all-encompassing influence.

Aris's gaze drifted from the intricate web of energy signatures Eva had meticulously mapped onto the holographic display. The sheer scope of it, the chillingly deliberate pattern of infiltration targeting Earth's global nervous system, was overwhelming. Yet, amidst the rising tide of dread, a flicker of personal recognition began to ignite. It was a nascent hypothesis, a thread of thought that had been weaving itself through the chaos of their discoveries, coalescing into a startling potential explanation for his own inexplicable experiences.

"Eva," he began, his voice a little rough, as if he were testing new words. "My déjà vu. The recurring flashes, the sense of having lived this moment before... I've been dismissing them as stress, as an overactive imagination trying to cope with all this." He gestured vaguely towards the projected network of alien influence. "But what if they aren't... random?"

Eva turned from the console, her expression one of focused curiosity. She had seen the subtle changes in Aris, the way his focus sharpened, the almost imperceptible tension that seemed to emanate from him when he spoke of his subjective anomalies. "What do you mean, Aris?"

"I mean, what if they're a *consequence*?" Aris pushed himself away from the console, pacing the confines of the lab. "A consequence of *my* mind, specifically. The aliens are manipulating our infrastructure, subtly rewriting our collective reality. They're bleeding into our systems, infecting them. We've established that. But my experiences... they feel different. More personal. Like a distortion in my own internal processing, not just the external environment."

He paused, searching for the right analogy. "Imagine our minds, our consciousness, as a complex network of its own. Information flows, memories are stored, perceptions are processed. If these aliens are injecting their influence, their psychic energy, into our global technological systems, what happens when that influence tries to bleed into something as complex and self-aware as a human mind? Especially a mind that's already... attuned to certain frequencies?"

Eva leaned against a workstation, her arms crossed, her eyes never leaving Aris. She recognized the scientific mind at work, the relentless pursuit of causality, even when the subject matter bordered on the deeply personal and potentially unreliable. "You're suggesting your déjà vu isn't a symptom of their broader influence on humanity, but a direct, perhaps even unique, reaction from your own cognitive architecture?"

"Exactly," Aris affirmed, the idea gaining momentum. "My

work. My entire focus has been on space-time, on the fundamental nature of reality, on how our perception shapes our understanding of existence. I've spent years, decades, exploring the edges of causality, the non-linear nature of time. Perhaps that deep immersion, that relentless probing into the fabric of... well, of everything... has made my mind uniquely sensitive to their intrusions. Like a highly sensitive antenna, picking up a signal that others miss."

He stopped pacing and looked directly at Eva. "When they create these localized distortions, these ripples in our shared reality – and the energy signatures show they're doing it, creating micro-fractures to insert their influence – perhaps my brain is reacting to those fractures more profoundly. The déjà vu isn't just a sense of familiarity; it's my consciousness momentarily snapping back, trying to reconcile the altered present with the original, unaltered timeline. It's my mind's way of saying, 'This isn't right. This wasn't supposed to happen.'"

Eva considered this, her brow furrowed in thought. The implications were significant. If Aris's experiences were a direct result of his specific cognitive makeup and his deep engagement with theoretical physics, it meant he was not merely a passive observer of the alien agenda. He was, in a way, a symptom of their interference manifesting in a highly individual and potentially detectable manner.

"So, you believe your mind's unique structure, perhaps your work on space-time mechanics, makes you a kind of 'early warning system'?" Eva ventured, piecing together his theory. "Your consciousness is more susceptible to the temporal echoes, the faint reverberations of their manipulation?"

"Or perhaps," Aris mused, his gaze distant, as if replaying one of the more vivid déjà vu episodes, "it's not just susceptibility. What if it's a form of resistance? My mind, constantly grappling with the non-linear, might have developed certain... protective mechanisms. Like a firewall against temporal paradoxes, or a way to filter out anomalies in the flow of perceived reality. When their influence tries to overwrite a moment, my mind might be pushing back, creating that sense of duplication, of having already experienced it, as a way to reject the imposed alteration."

He tapped his temple. "Think about it. If they are injecting subtle alterations, rewriting a few seconds here, a few minutes there, to steer events, to nudge outcomes, those alterations would be imperceptible to most. Their 'signal' is designed to be a whisper, not a shout. But for someone whose cognitive framework is already accustomed to perceiving the world in a more fluid, less rigidly linear fashion, those whispers might sound like screams. My déjà vu could be the audible manifestation of my mind resisting those forced edits."

Eva walked over to the holographic display, zooming in on a cluster of energy signatures converging on a major transatlantic data nexus. "We've seen how they target infrastructure, Aris. Communication hubs, power grids, financial networks. These are the arteries of human civilization. They are essentially hijacking the collective nervous system of the planet. If their goal is to assimilate and control, then they wouldn't necessarily want to destroy individual minds that possess unique capabilities. They might want to understand them. Or worse, to co-opt them."

Aris nodded, a grim understanding dawning. "That's the terrifying corollary, isn't it? If my mind is reacting in such a specific way, it makes me a… conspicuous anomaly.

They might already be aware of me. They might be detecting my 'resistance,' my cognitive dissonance. And if they are aware, then I'm not just an observer anymore. I'm a problem to be solved, or a resource to be exploited."

"A problem to be solved," Eva echoed, her voice tinged with concern. "If they perceive your mind as an outlier, something that doesn't conform to their projected reality, they might try to 'correct' it. To force your cognitive architecture into their desired paradigm. And your déjà vu, as you describe it, might be the very mechanism they are targeting to achieve that."

"They could be trying to overwrite my consciousness," Aris said, the implications settling heavily upon him. "Not just influencing my thoughts, but fundamentally altering the way my mind processes reality, smoothing out those 'rough edges' that make me sensitive to their influence. The déjà vu could be the psychic equivalent of a system error, and they might be deploying targeted patches to fix it, to make me a more compliant unit within their assimilating network."

He looked at Eva, his eyes intense. "But if they can do that, if they can 'fix' me, it means they can also… weaponize me. If they can understand what makes my mind react the way it does, what makes me sensitive to space-time distortions, they might be able to leverage that understanding. Perhaps they can utilize my insights and unique perspective on temporal mechanics to further their own agenda. Imagine them using my awareness of temporal causality to manipulate events on an even grander scale, all. At the same time, my own mind believes it's just experiencing a fleeting sense of déjà vu."

The idea was chilling. Aris's unique cognitive abilities, born from years of deep theoretical exploration, could become the very tools his adversaries used to tighten their grip on humanity. His subjective experiences, which he had initially dismissed as personal eccentricities, were now potentially central to the alien objective.

"It would explain the persistence," Aris continued, his voice growing quieter. "The fact that it's not a fleeting occurrence. They could be continuously attempting these subtle overwrites, these temporal nudges, and my mind is constantly attempting to correct for them, leading to that cyclical feeling. Each attempt to 'fix' me might be creating a new wave of déjà vu, a new ripple in my perception."

Eva brought up a different set of data on the display, this time focusing on the subtle fluctuations in localized electromagnetic fields detected around known artifact locations.

"We've seen that the artifacts aren't just passive propagation points for their psychic network; they're active interfaces. They are designed to interact with and manipulate our physical and neurological systems. If your theory holds, Aris, then these artifacts might be 'tuned' to specific neurological frequencies. And your mind, with its unique processing patterns, might be emitting a signature they can detect and target."

"And what about their broader objective with this infrastructure takeover?" Aris pondered, connecting his personal predicament to the global strategy. "If they're crippling our ability to communicate, to coordinate, to act collectively, then by extension, they're isolating individuals who might pose a threat. Someone like me, with a mind that can perceive their methods, becomes a potential weak point in their controlled narrative. If they can isolate and neutralize such individuals, their assimilation process becomes far more efficient."

"They're not just trying to control information, Aris," Eva stated, her voice grave. "They're trying to control perception. And if they can control perception, they can control reality. For most humans, their reality is shaped by what they see, hear, and communicate. By manipulating the systems that provide that information, they manipulate the collective human experience. But for someone like you, whose perception is already attuned to the more abstract, the more fundamental, their manipulation might manifest in a more direct, almost ontological way. Your déjà vu is a symptom of them trying to impose their ontological framework onto yours."

Aris ran a hand through his hair, a weariness settling over him. "So, the grand alien plan to subjugate humanity is, on a personal level, a targeted neurological recalibration. They're not just silencing dissent; they're rewriting the very operating system of dissenting minds. And my focus on space-time, on the very nature of 'when,' makes me a prime target for their temporal manipulation."

"It's a terrifying prospect," Eva admitted. "Your unique

perspective, which could be invaluable in understanding and countering them, might be precisely what makes you most vulnerable to their specific methods of control. They might see your mind not just as a potential threat, but as a highly sophisticated piece of biological hardware that, if properly reprogrammed, could yield unparalleled insights into the very fabric of causality they seem so intent on controlling."

He closed his eyes for a moment, the swirling temporal paradoxes of his déjà vu experiences feeling more tangible than ever. "If they are aware of me, and if they are actively trying to manipulate my perception of time, then every instance of déjà vu is not just a glitch. It's a battle for my own mind, fought on the battlefield of my consciousness. And I'm not sure how long I can keep winning those battles without them eventually… recalibrating me into something else entirely."

Eva approached him, placing a reassuring hand on his arm. "We will find a way to shield you, Aris. To understand the frequencies they are using, to build a defense. Your sensitivity, which makes you vulnerable, also makes you uniquely positioned to identify their methods and their targets. Your déjà vu is not just a symptom; it's a clue. And if they are indeed trying to make you an instrument of their will, then understanding how they're doing it is our first line of defense." The realization hung in the air, a stark and dangerous truth: Aris's deepest personal experiences were not a side effect of the alien invasion, but a direct, targeted consequence of it, making him a focal point in a war for the very nature of reality itself.

The low hum of the surveillance van was usually a comforting constant, a monotonous lullaby against the gnawing anxiety that had become Aris's constant companion. But tonight, it felt like a prelude to something far more sinister, a resonant tremor that vibrated not just through the metal of the vehicle, but through the very core of his being. Eva was hunched over her console, her face illuminated by the cool, sterile glow of data streams. Outside, the deserted industrial park lay cloaked in a heavy, oppressive darkness, punctuated only by the distant, indifferent wink of stars. They were waiting for a breach, a ripple in the fabric of reality that would betray the presence of a secondary portal, a hidden door for the alien architects of Earth's slow-motion subjugation.

Aris's breath hitched. It wasn't a sound, not a visual anomaly on Eva's sophisticated sensors. It was an intrusion, a psychic resonance that slammed into his awareness with the force of a physical blow. His vision blurred, not with tears, but with an influx of sensory data too vast, too alien to process. The interior of the van seemed to warp, the familiar confines dissolving into an infinite, interconnected expanse. He saw it then, a vision that seared itself into his mind with agonizing clarity: a colossal, sentient network, a tapestry woven from countless individual consciousnesses, all functioning as one. It was a gestalt, a unified intelligence that had transcended the limitations of individual existence, moving with a terrifying, silent synchronicity across the cosmos.

This wasn't merely a technological invasion; it was a biological and psychological one, on a scale that dwarfed anything he had previously comprehended. The subtle manipulations of infrastructure, the psychic bleed into human systems—these were merely symptoms of a far grander, more insidious design. He was witnessing the objective, not as a series of strategic objectives, but as a fundamental existential reality for the beings on the other side of the veil. They weren't a species; they were a collective, a singular, all-consuming will that sought only to expand its dominion, to absorb all into its vast, unified consciousness.

The sheer magnitude of the vision was almost unbearable. It was a universe of minds, seamlessly integrated, their individual thoughts and experiences pooled into a single, gargantuan awareness. There was no conflict, no dissent, only perfect, unified purpose. It was the ultimate expression of order, achieved through the complete annihilation of individuality. And Earth, he now understood with a chilling certainty, was merely the next world to be assimilated, its inhabitants destined to become mere nodes in this vast, intergalactic network.

He could feel the tendrils of this collective consciousness probing, not just at the technological infrastructure Eva had mapped, but at the very minds of humanity. It was a psychic probe, a gentle, insistent pressure designed to find weaknesses, to identify those who resisted, and to offer them… integration. The vision intensified, and Aris felt a strange, almost seductive pull, a whisper in the back of his mind promising belonging, purpose, an end to the gnawing anxieties of individual existence. It was the siren song of the collective, a promise of peace through oblivion.

"Aris? What is it?" Eva's voice, though laced with concern, seemed impossibly distant, a faint signal struggling to penetrate the overwhelming psychic static. He tried to respond, to articulate the terrifying truth he had glimpsed. Still, his throat felt thick, his own thoughts fragmented, struggling to reassert their individual coherence against the encroaching unity.

The vision shifted, focusing on the subtle energetic pathways that connected the myriad consciousnesses within the collective. He saw how they communicated, not through spoken words or symbolic language, but through direct, instantaneous transfer of thought and emotion. It was a perfect empathy, a shared experience of existence that rendered individuality obsolete. And he understood, with a dawning horror, that their methods of infiltration were not merely about controlling data or manipulating systems; they were about creating parallel psychic networks, subtly weaving their collective consciousness into the very fabric of human thought.

He saw flashes of other worlds, other civilizations that had fallen before this silent tide of assimilation. Images flickered through his mind: vast, crystalline cities that once pulsed with independent life, now silent and dormant, their inhabitants integrated into the omnipresent collective; alien physiologies, once vibrant and unique, now mere organic components within a vast, interconnected superorganism. These were not conquered worlds; they were absorbed worlds, their essence dissolved into the singular entity.

The implications for Earth were stark and terrifying. This was not a war of attrition, of battles won and lost. It was a war of assimilation, of absorption. They didn't seek to destroy humanity; they sought to *become* humanity, in their own image. And their success was already evident in the subtle shifts in global consciousness, the creeping apathy, the widespread disconnect that he had observed for years, a slow erosion of independent thought that he had previously attributed to societal malaise.

The overwhelming psychic energy began to recede, leaving Aris gasping for breath, his body trembling with the aftershock of the vision. The van's interior snapped back into focus, the hum of the electronics a welcome, grounding presence. Eva was staring at him, her eyes wide with alarm.

"Aris, what happened? You went pale as a ghost. Did you detect something?" Her fingers flew across the console, bringing up his bio-readings. They were spiking erratically.

He struggled to collect himself, the alien tendrils of the collective retreating, leaving behind a phantom ache, a sense of profound loss and terrifying isolation. "It's… it's not what we thought, Eva," he managed to croak, his voice raw. "It's not an invasion in the way we've been conceptualizing it. It's… integration. Assimilation."

He took a shuddering breath, trying to translate the overwhelming sensory data into comprehensible words. "I saw it, Eva. A glimpse. A network. A collective consciousness. Vast. Spanning galaxies. They don't fight; they absorb. They don't conquer; they unify. And they're doing it to us."

Eva's expression shifted from alarm to a dawning, horrified comprehension. She had seen the patterns, the subtle shifts in human behavior, the erosion of individuality that was so pervasive. But Aris's personal experience, the raw, unfiltered glimpse into the alien psyche, lent a terrifying new dimension to their understanding.

"A collective consciousness?" she repeated, her voice barely a whisper. "You mean... like a hive mind?"

"More than that," Aris corrected, the vision still vivid behind his eyes. "A hive mind implies a central controlling entity. This is... different. It's a distributed consciousness, where every individual mind is an integral part of the whole. There's no single 'queen.' Every mind contributes, and every mind is absorbed. They've achieved a perfect synergy, a complete unity of purpose."

He described the vision, the interconnectedness, the silent, synchronized movement, the sheer scale of it. He explained how their methods of infiltration, the psychic bleed and technological manipulation, were not just means to an end, but integral components of their assimilation process, designed to prepare human minds for integration, to smooth the transition from individuality to collective unity.

"They aren't trying to enslave us, Eva," he said, the realization chilling him to the bone. "They're trying to *save* us. From ourselves, from our individuality, from our perceived flaws. They offer an end to conflict, to suffering, to loneliness. They offer perfection through unity."

The implication of his earlier hypothesis, that his déjà vu was a form of resistance, now took on a terrifying new weight. If this collective consciousness was the true objective, then his unique cognitive architecture, his sensitivity to temporal anomalies, made him not just a target, but a prime candidate for assimilation. His mind, attuned to the very fabric of space-time, could be a valuable addition to their cosmic network, a bridge to understanding the fundamental nature of reality in a way that their current processing could not achieve. Or, conversely, it could be a discordant note, a disruptive element that needed to be silenced, to be smoothed into conformity.

"My déjà vu," Aris mused, his voice distant, as if replaying the vision internally, "it's not just me resisting their temporal edits. It's my mind reacting to their attempt to integrate me into their collective timeline. Every flash, every sense of repetition, is a moment where my consciousness is fighting against their attempt to merge my timeline with their infinite, unified present."

Eva leaned back, her gaze fixed on the data streams, but her mind clearly elsewhere, grappling with the enormity of Aris's revelation. "So, they've done this before. They've achieved this state of collective consciousness on other worlds."

"Yes," Aris confirmed, a grim certainty in his voice. "I saw it. Worlds that are now silent, their inhabitants absorbed. They aren't just conquering planets; they're collecting souls, gathering consciousnesses like precious artifacts, integrating them into their eternal tapestry."

He shuddered, the memory of those silent, integrated worlds visceral. It was a vision of ultimate peace, yes, but a peace bought at the price of self. A peace that was indistinguishable from death for the individual.

"And this secondary portal," Aris continued, his gaze snapping back to the present, to the dark, silent industrial park outside. "It's not just another entry point for their technology. It's a nexus point, a place where they are actively attempting to establish a stronger psychic link, to begin the assimilation process on a larger scale."

The stakeout, the wait for a physical manifestation, suddenly seemed naive, almost quaint. The real invasion wasn't happening at a physical location; it was happening within the minds of every human being on Earth. The portal wasn't a gateway for ships or weapons, but for psychic resonance, for the insidious whisper of unity that promised to dissolve the self.

"If they are a collective consciousness," Eva said, her voice filled with a new urgency, "then confrontation, as we've planned, might be… ineffective. How do you fight an enemy that is everywhere and nowhere, an enemy that isn't an individual but a vast, interconnected entity?"

Aris stared at the glowing console, his mind racing. His newfound understanding of the alien objective was both terrifying and, paradoxically, liberating. They weren't fighting an army of discrete beings; they were fighting a concept, a state of being. And if their strength lay in unity, perhaps their weakness lay in the very individuality they sought to eradicate.

"We can't fight them directly, not in the way we would fight an alien species," Aris agreed, a new resolve hardening in his voice. "We need to understand how they integrate. We need to find the points of vulnerability within their collective structure. And perhaps," he added, his gaze drifting back to his own temple, to the source of his disruptive déjà vu, "my own sensitivity isn't just a weakness to be defended, but a tool to be understood. If I can perceive their assimilation attempts, if I can feel the psychic pressure, then perhaps I can also identify the points where their unity falters, where the collective is not yet complete."

The hum of the van seemed to deepen, to resonate with a new purpose. The objective of the aliens was no longer to conquer Earth; it was to absorb it, to make it a part of their eternal, unified existence. And Aris, the man who had spent his life contemplating the nature of time and reality, had just caught a terrifying glimpse into the ultimate manifestation of their design: a universe of minds, bound together in an infinite, silent embrace. The war for Earth had just become a war for the very definition of consciousness.

8: Political Puppets

The sterile glow of Eva's console had been Aris's world for days. Outside the van, the pre-dawn chill of the abandoned industrial complex was a palpable presence, a silent witness to their clandestine vigil. But the gnawing anxiety that had become his shadow had transmuted into a cold, hard dread. It wasn't just the hum of their surveillance equipment that vibrated through him anymore; it was the echo of a cosmic symphony of consciousness, a unified will that dwarfed any earthly ambition. His earlier vision, a terrifying glimpse into the alien collective, had been more than a premonition; it was a revelation of their true objective: not conquest, but absorption. Assimilation.

"Anything?" Aris's voice was a rasp, unused for hours. He watched Eva's brow furrow, her fingers dancing across the holographic interfaces, sifting through terabytes of data that represented Earth's vital signs – communications, financial transactions, troop movements, energy grids. They were looking for anomalies, for the subtle psychic resonances Aris had felt, the tendrils of the collective consciousness probing and weaving themselves into the human tapestry.

Eva shook her head, a flicker of frustration crossing her features. "The patterns are still there, Aris. The subtle deviations from baseline behavior, the moments of... blankness. But isolating the source, pinpointing the specific individuals responsible, it's like trying to find a single grain of sand on an infinite beach." She gestured to a complex heatmap projected onto the van's wall, a dizzying array of pulsating nodes and shifting color gradients. "We've correlated the energy signatures with known communication hubs, high-security government networks, even private servers of major corporations. But the spread is so diffuse, so... integrated."

Aris leaned closer, his eyes tracing the intricate web. His own unique neurological architecture, the very thing that had made him susceptible to the initial psychic intrusion, was now his primary tool. He could feel the faintest whispers of discord, the subtle dissonances within the overwhelming chorus of the collective. "Integrated is the word, Eva. They aren't breaching firewalls; they're rewriting the operating system. Look here." He pointed to a cluster of nodes in the

Oceania region, a region they had previously deemed stable. "These energy fluctuations... they're not active intrusions. They're echoes. Residual psychic signatures from a previous assimilation event."

Eva zoomed in, her eyes widening as she recognized the distinct patterns Aris was highlighting. "You're right. It's faint, almost undetectable with standard protocols, but the signature is undeniable. It's the same energy resonance we detected during the initial breach, just... faded." She began cross-referencing the data with classified intelligence files, her lips moving silently as she accessed information deemed too sensitive for public consumption. The hum of the van seemed to throb in time with her rapidly beating heart.

"This is beyond the initial infiltration," Aris murmured, a chilling realization dawning. "We thought they were just seeding individuals, creating sleeper agents. But this... this indicates they've already succeeded in assimilating entire populations, entire systems, on a smaller scale. These aren't just echoes; they're proof of concept."

Eva's breath hitched as she pulled up a profile. "President Thorne." Her voice was a hushed whisper. "His recent decision to unilaterally withdraw from the Global Defense Accord... it defied all established geopolitical logic. Analysts were baffled. They called it an uncharacteristic lapse in judgment." She highlighted another profile. "General Vance. His directive to dismantle the orbital defense grid, citing 'redundancy'... it was suicidal. Our intel suggested he'd been under immense pressure, but this..."

Aris felt a cold dread seep into his bones. He remembered seeing fleeting glimpses of these individuals in his vision, not as distinct beings, but as nodes within the larger network, their consciousnesses already partially subsumed. "They're not just influencing them, Eva. They're in them. The blankness, the uncanny agreement... it's the collective consciousness asserting its dominance. Critical thinking is being suppressed, individuality is being overwritten."

The data streams continued to flow, painting a grim picture of a global leadership that was no longer truly leading, but merely enacting directives from an unseen, unfelt source. The seemingly illogical decisions, the passive responses to escalating global crises, the inexplicable shifts in policy that had left experts bewildered – it all clicked into place with terrifying clarity. They weren't dealing with a foreign power wielding conventional weapons; they were fighting an invisible war fought on the battlefield of human consciousness, a war where the enemy had already infiltrated the command centers, not just physically, but psychically.

"The patterns match, Aris," Eva confirmed, her voice tight with suppressed emotion. "The same subtle neurological markers, the same moments of cognitive dissonance followed by perfect, almost robotic adherence to a new, imposed directive. It's like their decision-making processes have been... streamlined. Or rather, bypassed entirely." She pointed to a line of code scrolling rapidly across the screen. "This encrypted signal, it's not just data transfer. It's... synchronization. It's the collective reinforcing its hold, bringing these individuals back into alignment."

Aris felt a wave of nausea. The thought of Thorne, Vance, and countless others in positions of immense power, their minds hijacked, their free will extinguished, was a horrifying testament to the insidious nature of the alien agenda. They weren't just manipulating governments; they were puppeteering them from the inside out. The passive acceptance of alien technology, the gradual erosion of national sovereignty, the quiet dismantling of Earth's defenses – it wasn't a consequence of weakness, but of deliberate, orchestrated manipulation.

"We've been tracking the wrong kind of breach," Aris said, his gaze fixed on the evolving heatmap. "We were looking for physical portals, for technological incursions. But their primary vector is the human mind. They're exploiting our innate desire for connection, for belonging, and twisting it into a mechanism for assimilation. They offer unity, an end to conflict, and in their pursuit of that ideal, they're stripping away everything that makes us human."

Eva's fingers hovered over a specific cluster of high-level government officials. "These individuals... they represent critical junctures in global policy. Defense ministries, international relations committees, economic forums. If they are compromised, then the entire global infrastructure is vulnerable." She looked at Aris, her eyes filled with a grim determination. "We need to expand our scope, Aris. We need to look beyond the obvious threats. We need to analyze the decision-making patterns of every key player, from heads of state down to regional administrators."

The task was monumental. Their current methods, while yielding some results, were like trying to filter a hurricane through a coffee strainer. The sheer scale of human interaction, the complexity of global politics, made it nearly impossible to pinpoint every instance of psychic infiltration. But Aris knew they had no choice. The enemy was deeply entrenched, operating within the very systems designed to protect humanity.

"What if we're looking at this too analytically?" Aris mused, his mind sifting through the abstract concepts of the collective he had witnessed. "They operate on a level of consciousness that transcends our linear, individualistic thinking. If their goal is unity, then perhaps their vulnerabilities lie in the very points where that unity is not yet absolute. Where the individual consciousness still retains a flicker of defiance."

Eva nodded slowly, catching his train of thought. "The anomalies. The moments where an individual resists the imposed directive, even if only for a fleeting second. Those are the points where the collective's grip is weakest." She presented a series of comparative neurochemical scans, layering them with the behavioral data. "My scanners can detect minute shifts in neurotransmitter activity, correlating with emotional states. We can cross-reference these with Aris's psychic resonance readings. If there's a spike in alpha-wave activity, a sudden surge in serotonin, followed by a moment of indecision or hesitation… that could be a sign of resistance."

The idea was audacious, bordering on impossible. It required a level of granularity that their current technology was barely capable of. But Aris felt a flicker of hope, a nascent strategy emerging from the chaos. Suppose they could identify these moments of individual defiance, these tiny cracks in the façade of collective unity. In that case, they might be able to target them, to amplify them, perhaps even to use them as leverage against the alien consciousness.

"It's a long shot, Eva," Aris admitted, his voice tinged with a weary realism. "But it's the only shot we have. We need to map out the decision-making processes of every individual we suspect, not just for overt signs of infiltration, but for subtle deviations, for internal conflict. We're looking for the whispers of individuality in a symphony of enforced harmony."

The next few hours were a blur of focused intensity. Eva worked tirelessly, her fingers a blur as she sifted through endless streams of data. Aris acted as her guide, his heightened sensitivity an invaluable compass, pointing her towards subtle shifts in the psychic landscape, towards areas where the collective consciousness was exerting its most pronounced influence. They focused on specific sectors: international finance, where inexplicable market manipulations had destabilized economies; strategic military planning, where crucial defensive maneuvers had been inexplicably abandoned; and even the global media, where narratives had shifted with uncanny uniformity, silencing dissent and promoting a pervasive sense of complacency.

"The World Economic Forum," Eva suddenly exclaimed, her eyes fixed on a specific set of data. "Several key figures who were slated to present critical policy proposals have all cancelled at the last minute, citing vague personal reasons. But their communication logs show no prior indications of distress or personal issues. And look at their recent public appearances – that peculiar, almost glassy-eyed expression, the stilted delivery…"

Aris felt a prickle of recognition. He had seen that expression, that subtle disconnect, in the periphery of his vision. It was the hallmark of a mind struggling to reconcile its own will with the overriding influence of the collective. "They're being recalibrated, Eva. Their integration isn't complete, or perhaps they are being prepared for a specific, unified directive that supersedes their individual roles. The collective is ensuring perfect alignment before a major global event."

The implications sent a fresh wave of dread through Aris. If these key figures were being 'recalibrated' for a specific purpose, it meant the aliens were not just passively absorbing humanity; they were actively shaping it, directing its evolution towards a predetermined, unified end. The subtlety of their approach was their greatest weapon. There were no overt declarations of war, no visible armies marching across continents. Instead, there was a quiet, insidious erosion of human agency, a gradual surrender of free will masked as progress, as unity, as the inevitable march of destiny.

"We need to prioritize," Aris said, his mind racing. "We can't monitor everyone. We need to identify the individuals who are the linchpins, the ones whose compromised decisions would have the most cascading effect." He pointed to a map overlay showing global communication networks. "The heads of major international banking institutions. The leaders of supranational organizations. The individuals who control the flow of information and resources. They are the most critical nodes in the network, the ones most likely to be targeted for complete assimilation."

Eva began meticulously cross-referencing their limited suspect list with publicly available information, looking for the subtle behavioral cues that Aris's vision had imprinted on his mind. She found it again and again: the almost imperceptible hesitation before answering a question, the uncanny agreement with even the most outlandish suggestions, the chilling absence of genuine emotional response even in moments of profound personal or global crisis. It was as if the very essence of individuality – the spark of independent thought, the capacity for dissent, the nuances of human emotion – was being systematically extinguished, replaced by a bland, unthinking uniformity.

"This is more than just infiltration, Aris," Eva stated, her voice grim. "This is re-engineering the human psyche on a global scale. They're not just controlling leaders; they're altering the very framework of human decision-making. If they can assimilate our leaders, they can dictate the course of our civilization without us even realizing we're not in control."

Aris closed his eyes, the overwhelming psychic static of the collective momentarily receding, replaced by a profound sense of isolation. He was one of the few who could perceive the true nature of the threat, who could feel the encroaching darkness. And the weight of that knowledge was crushing. They were fighting an enemy that operated on a plane of existence so alien, so fundamentally different from their own, that conventional warfare was an irrelevance. The fight was for the very soul of humanity, for the preservation of individuality in the face of an irresistible tide of cosmic unity. The infiltrators weren't just in the command centers; they were becoming the command centers.

The faint, almost imperceptible shimmer that distorted the edges of Aris's vision was becoming a constant companion. It was the psychic residue of their latest discovery, a tangled knot of alien influence and human complicity that they had painstakingly teased out of the global data streams. The van, their mobile sanctuary, hummed with the low thrum of sophisticated analysis equipment, a stark contrast to the chilling implications of the information unfurling on Eva's screens. They had been tracking anomalies – the subtle divergences from expected behavior in key global figures – and these anomalies had coalesced into a disturbing pattern: clandestine meetings.

"It's not just about individual decisions anymore, Aris," Eva said, her voice tight. She gestured to a holographic projection that depicted a web of interconnected nodes, each representing a high-level official. Lines pulsed between them, indicating communication, but a subset of these lines pulsed with a different frequency, a deeper resonance that Aris had come to associate with the alien collective. "These individuals aren't just acting independently under influence. They're convening Secretly."

The data Eva had unearthed pointed to a series of meetings, meticulously disguised as routine policy reviews, diplomatic summits, or emergency task force assemblies. However, when the attendees were cross-referenced with their analysis of psychic resonance and behavioral anomalies, a disturbing commonality emerged. They were the individuals exhibiting the most pronounced signs of assimilation, the ones whose decisions had been the most glaringly inexplicable. "Look at this," Eva zoomed in on a cluster of nodes representing officials from several major international financial institutions. "The last three 'emergency' meetings of the Global Economic Stability Council. Three different dates, three different perceived crises, but the same core group of attendees, all of whom we've flagged. And the outcomes... universally detrimental to global economic independence."

Aris felt a cold knot tighten in his stomach. He remembered the fleeting visions he'd had during his initial psychic bleed-through – glimpses of these very people, not as individuals, but as conduits, their minds humming with the alien symphony. "They're not just being influenced," Aris stated, his voice gravelly. "They're being directed.

These aren't policy discussions; they're coordination sessions. The collective is using them as nodes, as physical anchors to exert its will in the real world."

Eva pulled up a detailed breakdown of one such meeting, held in a secure, undisclosed location outside of Geneva. The official minutes spoke of urgent deliberations on global trade tariffs and the restructuring of international debt. But the energy signatures Eva's specialized equipment had managed to pick up, the psychic echoes left behind, painted a different picture. "The energy expenditure during this 'discussion' was astronomical," she explained, highlighting a complex waveform. "Far exceeding what would be necessary for mere conversation. And the psychic imprint... it's incredibly dense. Unified. It's like a concentrated broadcast, reinforcing the directives."

The unsettling part wasn't just the act of meeting, but the speed and uniformity with which their coordinated decisions were being implemented. Critical infrastructure projects, once bogged down in bureaucratic wrangling and geopolitical debate, were suddenly being fast-tracked for decommissioning. Essential defense grids were being subtly rerouted, their operational parameters altered to create blind spots. Entire sectors of global communication were being consolidated under newly formed, unelected oversight committees, their stated purpose being "enhanced global security."

"It's about control of the flow," Aris said, his mind grasping for the underlying logic of the alien agenda. "If they want to assimilate humanity, they need to control the systems that bind humanity together. Finance, defense, communication – these are the arteries of civilization. By compromising the individuals who manage these arteries, they can reroute the blood, redirecting humanity's course without a single shot fired."

Eva brought up a comparison of pre- and post-meeting policy shifts. The changes were subtle but profound. A multinational energy conglomerate, under the direction of an assimilated CEO, suddenly shifted its entire research and development budget away from sustainable energy sources and towards highly centralized, inefficient, but easily controllable fusion core technology. The rationale, as presented in a hastily convened press conference by the CEO, was a sudden, uncharacteristic "strategic pivot." Aris recognized the glazed-over eyes, the slight tremor in the man's hands – the hallmark of a consciousness struggling against an imposed will.

"This CEO," Aris pointed to the projected image, "he was present at the Geneva meeting. His internal neurochemical markers showed extreme deviation from baseline during the time frame of the council. He wasn't just influenced; he was actively receiving instructions. And his subsequent actions have directly weakened Earth's energy independence."

The implications were terrifying. These clandestine meetings were not isolated incidents; they were the synchronized beating heart of the alien occupation, pumping directives into the very core of human governance and industry. The individuals involved were no longer acting on behalf of their nations or their corporations, but as unwilling, or perhaps even willing, agents of the collective. They were the 'political puppets' of the chapter's title, their strings being pulled by an unseen, unfelt puppeteer.

"We've identified several other such 'coordination sessions'," Eva continued, her fingers flying across the console. "One involving heads of national security agencies, masked as a counter-terrorism summit. The outcome? A drastic reduction in funding for nascent defensive technologies, focusing instead on mass surveillance systems that, ironically, would be perfectly suited for monitoring an assimilated populace.

Another, a global health summit, which resulted in the mandated adoption of neural interface protocols for 'improved public health monitoring.' The very technology that could be used to further integrate humanity into the collective's network."

Aris felt a growing sense of urgency. Their current methods, while uncovering critical evidence, were reactive. They were observing the symptoms, the consequences of the alien's actions, but they were struggling to get ahead of the curve. The aliens, through their human proxies, were making monumental decisions with terrifying speed, dismantling Earth's ability to resist before humanity even understood the nature of the threat.

"We need to identify the patterns of these meetings, Eva," Aris urged. "Not just who attends, but the triggers. What precipitates these clandestine gatherings? Is it a specific psychic resonance surge? A particular phase of alien technological deployment? If we can predict when and where these coordination sessions will occur, we might be able to intercept them, or at least disrupt their effectiveness."

Eva began to overlay their data streams, searching for correlations. The timing of these meetings seemed to align with specific astronomical events, or perhaps with the activation of certain deep-space probes that had been launched in recent years, ostensibly for scientific exploration. There was also a recurring pattern of localized energy spikes detected in remote, unpopulated regions, coinciding with the meetings themselves. These spikes were too diffuse to be attributed to any known terrestrial technology, suggesting a non-conventional energy source being employed by the collective.

"It's like they're building their own hidden infrastructure," Aris mused, tracing the projected lines of compromised communication channels. "They're not invading; they're infiltrating every facet of our existing systems, subtly rewriting the code of our civilization. These meetings are where they're installing the new software, ensuring that all the hardware – our institutions, our governments, our industries – are running the correct, alien-approved operating system."

The speed at which critical infrastructure was being altered was particularly alarming. A global satellite network, designed for communication and scientific research, was being repurposed. Its vast data processing capabilities were being reallocated, its encrypted communication channels subtly rerouted through hidden relays that Aris's sensitive equipment could detect, but which would be invisible to standard oversight. The stated purpose was 'network optimization,' but the result was a silent, unseen shift in global information control.

"This is more than just influencing decisions," Eva reiterated, her voice grim. "This is about active restructuring. They're not just manipulating our leaders; they're manipulating the very foundations of our global connectivity. Think about the implications if they control the flow of all information. Dissent could be silenced before it's even articulated. Independent thought could be flagged as a system error."

Aris's gaze fell on a specific set of personnel involved in the decommissioning of deep-space listening posts. These were facilities designed to detect extraterrestrial signals, and their sudden dismantling was not only illogical but actively counter-productive to humanity's own security interests. The individuals overseeing this process were all on the suspect list, having attended the covert meetings.

"They're not just making us vulnerable; they're blindfolding us," Aris said, a sense of profound dread washing over him. "By shutting down our ability to listen, they ensure we can't hear the whispers of our own impending doom, or perhaps, more accurately, our impending absorption. They are actively dismantling our defenses, not just physically, but epistemologically – our capacity to know and understand."

The depth of the alien's strategy was chillingly comprehensive. It wasn't a frontal assault; it was a systemic infection, a gradual dismantling from within. The clandestine meetings were the nexus points, where the alien consciousness directly interfaced with its human proxies, coordinating the complex, multifaceted process of assimilation. Each meeting, each seemingly minor policy shift, was a carefully orchestrated step in a grand, terrifying design. The political puppets were being moved, their actions meticulously planned to pave the way for a complete and total absorption of humanity into the cosmic collective. Aris looked at Eva, the shared understanding of the immense, insidious threat hanging heavy in the air between them. They were staring into the heart of a silent, unfolding apocalypse, and the clock was ticking with every synchronized, dictated decision.

The chilling realization that the collective's strategy was one of systemic decapitation, rather than outright conquest, settled over Aris and Eva like a suffocating shroud.

They had been meticulously dissecting the outward manifestations of the alien influence – the compromised policies, the inexplicable decisions, the subtle shifts in global infrastructure. Now, they were looking at the architecture of the assimilation itself, a horrifyingly efficient blueprint designed to dismantle humanity's capacity to resist from the very top. By co-opting or neutralizing the figures in positions of ultimate authority, the collective could effectively blind and cripple any organized defense before it even had a chance to form. It was a strategy of exquisite, terrifying logic: control the head, and the body would inevitably follow.

"It's not just about influencing individual leaders anymore," Eva murmured, her gaze fixed on a swirling holographic projection of global command structures. Lines of authority, thick and red for military, thinner and pulsing for political, crisscrossed a complex, multi-layered network. "It's about severing the command chain. If they can neutralize the key nodes in the defense apparatus, if they can control the flow of directives from the highest echelons, then everything below them becomes… irrelevant. Or worse, they can be turned into unwitting enforcers of the assimilation."

Her fingers danced across the console, bringing up data streams that detailed military command hierarchies, intelligence agency structures, and critical governmental oversight bodies. She was cross-referencing this with the patterns of psychic resonance and behavioral anomalies they had meticulously logged. The task was monumental, akin to identifying individual grains of sand on a planet-sized beach, but the stakes were immeasurably higher. Each compromised individual represented a potential pivot point, a single domino that, if toppled, could initiate a catastrophic cascade.

"Think about it, Aris," she continued, her voice a low, urgent whisper. "If they can compromise the heads of NATO, or the Joint Chiefs of Staff for a major power, or even the directors of key intelligence agencies, they don't need to fight every soldier, every analyst, and every diplomat. They can simply issue directives that render those forces inert. They can silence internal dissent, reroute critical intelligence, and ensure that any nascent counter-offensive is stillborn. It's like disabling the central nervous system before the body even realizes it's under attack."

Aris felt a cold dread grip him. He recalled fragments of his earlier psychic

bleed-throughs, moments where he had glimpsed not just isolated individuals, but entire councils, entire command centers, bathed in that sickening, alien luminescence. It wasn't just a few scattered individuals; it was a systematic infiltration of the very organs of human power. The political puppets weren't just acting on their own; they were being integrated into a larger, alien-controlled command structure.

"The silence is the most dangerous weapon," Aris said, his voice hoarse. "If they can control what information is disseminated, what warnings are issued, what actions are authorized, then humanity is effectively disarmed. Imagine a global defense network designed to counter an extraterrestrial threat. If the individuals controlling that network are compromised, they could simply deactivate it, or worse, reprogram it to misidentify the collective as an ally, or even turn it against any pockets of resistance."

Eva nodded grimly, pulling up the operational schematics of a global early warning system. "Exactly. And look at this. The primary override protocols for the global orbital defense grid... they were recently updated. The individuals who signed off on that update are all on our list. Their justifications cited 'efficiency improvements' and 'harmonization with new communication standards.' However, the new protocols introduce a backdoor. A way to remotely disable key defensive satellites. The rationales are always plausible, always couched in bureaucratic jargon, but the underlying intent is clear: to disarm us from orbit."

The sheer audacity of the alien strategy was breathtaking. It was a silent coup d'état executed on a planetary scale, using the very mechanisms of human governance and defense against humanity itself. The assimilation wasn't about enslavement; it was about absorption, and to achieve that, they needed to ensure that no organized force could prevent it. This meant targeting the highest levels of decision-making, the individuals who held the keys to military might, intelligence gathering, and the dissemination of public information.

"We need to identify these choke points," Aris stated, his mind racing. "Not just the individuals, but the specific positions. The nexus points where a single compromised mind can exert control over vast resources and critical functions. It's about identifying the linchpins of human defense and resistance."

Eva's screen shifted, displaying a complex analytical matrix. She was building models based on various scenarios of compromise. "Military chains of command are designed with redundancy, but there are still critical junctures. In most global powers, there's a clear line from the supreme commander – usually a president or prime minister – down through their defense minister and military chiefs. If those individuals are compromised, the entire military apparatus can be subverted. But it goes deeper than that. Think about the heads of intelligence agencies – they control the flow of information about threats. If they're compromised, they can suppress knowledge of the assimilation itself, or steer investigations away from the aliens."

She highlighted a specific office: the Director of Global Strategic Command, a position that, while not always publicly visible, held immense authority over the deployment of intercontinental ballistic missiles and the coordination of global defense networks. "If this individual is compromised," Eva explained, "they could effectively cripple our retaliatory capabilities with a single authorization. They could initiate a false alarm, or worse, order a preemptive strike that cripples our own defenses, leaving us utterly vulnerable."

Aris felt a pang of recognition. He remembered a fleeting vision of a sterile, windowless room, filled with the low hum of advanced technology. At its center sat a figure, his face obscured, but the psychic resonance emanating from him was a powerful, suffocating blanket of alien directives. He had dismissed it at the time as a general impression of command, but now, seeing Eva's analysis, he realized it might have been a direct glimpse into a critical choke point.

"The compromised individuals aren't just acting on their own volition," Aris said, piecing together the fractured understanding. "They're part of a unified command structure, orchestrated by the collective. These clandestine meetings we've been tracking are where they receive their assignments, where the overall strategy is disseminated and coordinated. The alien collective isn't just influencing a few key people; it's establishing its own shadow government, operating in parallel to our own."

Eva began to map out the key personnel involved in the recent decommissioning of vital deep-space listening posts. These were facilities designed to detect extraterrestrial signals, and their abrupt shutdown was a glaring anomaly that defied all logical reasoning in terms of Earth's own security. "Look at the individuals overseeing these decommissioning efforts," she said, pointing to a list of names and photographs. "They are all individuals who have been present at multiple covert meetings. Their decisions are directly weakening our ability to detect threats from outside. It's not just about controlling our internal systems; it's about blindfolding us to the larger universe."

The implications were staggering. The aliens were not only subverting human governance but actively dismantling humanity's capacity for interstellar awareness and defense. By suppressing the knowledge of their presence, or by turning those who held that knowledge into their agents, they could ensure a smooth, unhindered assimilation. The political puppets were being positioned not just to control earthly affairs, but to steer humanity away from any external awareness of the true nature of the threat.

"They're not just removing our eyes; they're removing our ears," Aris observed, the metaphor hitting home with visceral clarity. "By shutting down these listening posts, they ensure we can't hear the approach of their fleet, or the whispers of other intelligences who might try to warn us. They are severing our connection to anything beyond Earth, trapping us in their carefully constructed reality."

Eva began to analyses the command structure of a major global cybersecurity agency, which is responsible for protecting critical digital infrastructure from foreign cyber threats. "If they can compromise the leadership of this agency," she explained, "they gain access to all our most sensitive data, our communication networks, our financial systems, even our military command and control systems. They could rewrite our digital reality, making it impossible to discern truth from fabrication, or to mount any kind of coordinated digital resistance."

The task of identifying these compromised individuals was becoming the absolute paramount to their survival strategy. It was no longer enough to simply observe the consequences; they needed to identify the sources of the directives, the nexus points of alien control. And those nexus points were undeniably located at the highest levels of human power.

"The sheer coordination required for this level of infiltration suggests a sophisticated, overarching intelligence," Aris mused, tracing a potential communication line between a compromised defense minister and a shadowy figure heading a global economic forum. "They're not acting randomly. Each compromised individual, each policy change, each dismantled defense system is a deliberate step in a meticulously planned campaign."

Eva presented a detailed timeline of recent global events, overlaid with the known movements and meeting schedules of the individuals they had identified. The patterns were becoming disturbingly clear. A wave of inexplicable military budget cuts in one nation often coincided with a surge in funding for surveillance technology in another, all orchestrated by individuals who had recently attended the same covert gatherings. A global health initiative, ostensibly aimed at improving public well-being, was subtly introducing protocols that facilitated neural interfacing —a technology Aris knew the collective utilised for its own pervasive consciousness network.

"It's a multi-pronged approach," Eva stated, her voice tight with concentration. "They're not just attacking our military strength; they're attacking our economic stability, our technological independence, and even our fundamental understanding of health and well-being. And they're doing it by controlling the very people who are supposed to be protecting us."

Aris's mind was a whirlwind of possibilities, of potential targets and counter-strategies. If they could identify the individuals at the absolute apex of these compromised hierarchies – the ultimate puppeteers within the human structure – they might be able to disrupt the alien command chain, even if only temporarily. But the sheer scale of the infiltration made this a daunting prospect. How could two people, operating from the shadows, hope to dismantle an enemy that had already woven itself into the very fabric of global power?

"We need to focus on the critical choke points where the collective's directives are most likely to be translated into actionable, catastrophic policy," Aris said, his gaze hardening. "The individuals who can authorize the disabling of our defense systems, who can control the dissemination of vital information, or who can enforce widespread societal control mechanisms. These are the primary targets, not just for exposure, but for neutralization."

Eva was already working on it, cross-referencing the identified compromised individuals with their direct lines of authority and access to critical command and control systems. The list was long, and it was growing. Each name represented a potential betrayal, a silent surrender of human sovereignty at the highest levels. The political puppets were not just being manipulated; they were being integrated into the alien war machine, becoming the very tools of humanity's subjugation.

"The key isn't just to identify them," Eva said, her fingers hovering over a particularly sensitive military command post on her screen. "It's to understand the network of communication between them. If we can map out how these directives flow from the collective to these key figures, we might find a way to intercept or disrupt that flow. It's like severing the arteries at their source."

Aris closed his eyes, trying to push through the psychic static, to catch a glimpse of the overarching alien intelligence orchestrating this symphony of subversion. He knew, with a chilling certainty, that the fate of humanity rested on their ability to unmask these compromised leaders and expose the alien agenda before the final chains of control were forged, before the last vestiges of human autonomy were irrevocably surrendered. The war for Earth was not being fought on the battlefield, but in the sterile, opulent chambers of power, waged by a silent enemy who wielded influence as its most devastating weapon. They had to find the strings, and they had to cut them before the final act of assimilation was played out.

The air in the secure comms hub was always sterile, recycled and cool, a stark contrast to the rising heat of anxiety within Eva. She sat at her console, the familiar holographic interfaces shimmering before her, displaying the intricate web of command structures she and Aris had been meticulously dissecting. The realization that the collective's strategy was one of systemic decapitation, rather than outright conquest, had been chilling. They weren't just influencing a few key individuals; they were systematically dismantling humanity's capacity to resist from the very top, orchestrating a global coup through co-option and neutralization of those in positions of ultimate authority. It was a strategy of terrifyingly efficient logic: control the head, and the body would inevitably follow.

Aris had been right. The silence was the most dangerous weapon. If the collective could control what information was disseminated, what warnings were issued, what actions were authorized, then humanity was effectively disarmed. The recent updates to the global orbital defense grid, ostensibly for 'efficiency improvements,' now clearly showed a backdoor, a way to disable key defensive satellites remotely. The individuals who had signed off on those updates were all on their list, their justifications couched in bureaucratic jargon that masked a clear intent to disarm Earth from orbit.

This meant the infiltration went deeper than they had initially feared. It wasn't just about a few compromised leaders acting in isolation. It was about integrating these compromised individuals into a larger, alien-controlled command structure, creating a shadow government operating in parallel to humanity's own. The clandestine meetings Aris had glimpsed through his psychic bleed-throughs weren't just informal gatherings; they were likely where assignments were received, where the overarching strategy was disseminated and coordinated. The aliens were establishing their own command and control, and the humans at the highest echelons were becoming the instruments of their own subjugation.

Eva's focus sharpened. Aris could probe the psychic resonance, catch glimpses of the alien influence on those he interacted with directly. But her own battlefield was far more insidious: the meticulously crafted protocols, the policy directives, the chain of command that she herself was a part of. She had to become a detective within her own world, a silent observer among those she was sworn to obey, searching for the subtle signs of corruption. This was a test of trust, not in others, but in her own ability to navigate this treacherous landscape without betraying her mission, or herself.

Her immediate superior, Admiral Thorne, was a man whose reputation was built on unshakeable resolve and a keen strategic mind. He was the kind of leader who inspired confidence, a bedrock of stability in an increasingly volatile world. But even bedrock could be eroded from within. Eva knew she had to approach him with the utmost subtlety, probing his adherence to new protocols without raising the slightest suspicion. The weight of this deception was immense, isolating her further within her own command structure, creating a chasm of unspoken knowledge between her and the very people she worked alongside.

She initiated a routine request for clarification on a recent directive regarding satellite deployment schedules. The directive, ostensibly a response to perceived shifts in terrestrial threat patterns, had struck Eva as particularly peculiar. It involved the minor repositioning of several orbital defense platforms, a seemingly minor adjustment that, when cross-referenced with their data on compromised listening posts, felt like a deliberate act of blindfolding.

"Admiral Thorne," she began, her voice calm and even, projecting an aura of professional diligence, "I'm seeking clarification on Directive 7-Alpha-9, specifically concerning the re-alignment of Sector Gamma's orbital defense grid. The justifications cite increased terrestrial surveillance capabilities, but the energy allocation for the repositioning seems… disproportionate for the stated objective. Could you elaborate on the primary strategic imperative behind this particular configuration?"

Admiral Thorne, his face projected on her secondary screen, a familiar sight of stern authority, paused for a moment. His brow furrowed, not with confusion, but with a subtle, almost imperceptible shift in his expression. It was the kind of micro-expression that Aris might have picked up on psychically, a fleeting flicker that spoke volumes. Eva held her breath, her senses on high alert.

"Eva," Thorne's voice was measured, professional, "the directive is designed to optimize our observational sweep patterns. Terrestrial threats are evolving, and our current sensor arrays, while robust, possess blind spots that this re-alignment will address. The energy allocation is a necessary investment in comprehensive vigilance. It's about ensuring no anomaly, no matter how minor, goes undetected. This is standard procedure for adapting to new intelligence parameters."

Standard procedure. The words echoed in Eva's mind, a textbook response. But 'new intelligence parameters' was vague, and the 'disproportionate' energy allocation still nagged at her. She pressed on, her tone still deferential, but her intent unwavering.

"I understand, Admiral. However, the increased surveillance focus seems to be directed away from our traditional deep-space monitoring channels, which are, if I may be so bold, our primary defense against extra-terrestrial threats. The directive prioritizes terrestrial blind spots over potential cosmic ones. Is there a new classification of terrestrial threat that requires such a significant shift in our orbital posture?"

She watched Thorne's eyes. They were steady, unwavering. But was that strength, or a practiced mask? The subtle tension in his jaw, the way his gaze seemed to unfocus momentarily, as if accessing a pre-programmed response – these were the threads she was trying to snag. She was fishing in dangerous waters, casting her line into the very heart of the command structure, hoping to reel in a hint of the truth.

"Eva," Thorne replied, his tone hardening slightly, a subtle indication that he might be nearing the end of his patience, "our current intelligence suggests that the most immediate threats are Earth-bound. Deep-space monitoring remains a priority, of course, but our resources must be allocated where they can be most effective.

Directive 7-Alpha-9 is a tactical adjustment, nothing more. We trust the strategic assessments that led to its issuance. Your focus should be on ensuring its efficient implementation."

The implication was clear: cease questioning. Eva acknowledged his response, her face betraying none of the internal turmoil.

"Understood, Admiral. I will ensure the efficient implementation of Directive 7-Alpha-9."

As the comms link terminated, Eva leaned back, her heart pounding a heavy rhythm against her ribs. Thorne's reaction was ambiguous. The flicker in his eyes, the slight pause before his response – they could be interpreted as anything from the strain of command to the subtle influence of the collective. He had dismissed her concerns, framed his answer in terms of operational necessity. But had he genuinely believed it, or was he reciting a script? The weight of this uncertainty was a heavy burden. She had probed, and she had been rebuffed, not with hostility, but with a wall of carefully constructed normalcy.

Her next target was Deputy Director Anya Sharma, head of Strategic Planning. Sharma was known for her sharp intellect and her meticulous attention to detail, traits that made her a valuable asset. But it was precisely these traits that would make her a prime candidate for co-option by an intelligence that sought to manipulate human systems. Eva decided to approach her through the lens of inter-agency cooperation, a seemingly innocuous topic.

She scheduled a virtual meeting, ostensibly to discuss the integration of specific terrestrial reconnaissance data into the broader strategic planning framework. Aris had flagged the data in question and herself as potentially misleading, designed to direct attention away from genuine threats.

"Deputy Director Sharma," Eva began, her voice projecting respect and a collaborative spirit, "I'm here to discuss the integration of the recent 'Anomalous Terrestrial Activity' reports into our long-term strategic simulations. I've been reviewing the projected impact of these simulations, and I'm finding some... discrepancies in how they're factoring into our readiness assessments for, say, extraterrestrial threat scenarios."

Sharma's avatar appeared on Eva's screen, her expression one of professional engagement. "Eva, thank you for bringing this to my attention. What specific discrepancies are you observing?" Her voice was crisp, her gaze direct.

"Well," Eva continued, carefully choosing her words, "the current simulations, based on these 'Anomalous Terrestrial Activity' reports, seem to be allocating an unusually high percentage of our strategic response planning towards localized, low-level threats. This, in turn, is subtly but significantly de-prioritizing our investments in deep-space monitoring and rapid-response fleet readiness. It feels as though our strategic focus is being deliberately narrowed, almost as if we're being... blinded to certain possibilities."

She watched Sharma closely. There was a slight tilt of her head, a subtle shift in her posture. "Eva, our simulations are designed to be responsive to the most current and credible intelligence. The 'Anomalous Terrestrial Activity' reports represent a significant influx of new data that warrants careful consideration. It is our responsibility to analyze these data points and adjust our strategic planning accordingly. Prioritizing Earth-bound threats is a logical consequence of that analysis. We must be grounded in the present realities."

"Grounded in the present realities," Eva repeated, a faint echo of Thorne's words. "But if those realities are themselves being manipulated, if the 'new data' is a deliberate misdirection, then our 'grounding' could lead us astray. The resources diverted from deep-space defense could be critical if a genuine extra-terrestrial threat emerges. It feels like a calculated dilution of our overall defensive capabilities, masked by the guise of tactical responsiveness."

Sharma's expression remained composed, but there was a subtle rigidity in her tone now. "Eva, your concerns are noted. However, the Strategic Planning division operates on a comprehensive analysis of all available intelligence. If there were credible evidence of widespread data manipulation, it would undoubtedly be flagged through our established protocols. At this juncture, the most prudent course of action is to proceed with the current strategic adjustments based on the most reliable information available to us."

The phrase "established protocols" was another red flag. Were these protocols being followed, or were they themselves compromised? Eva felt a surge of frustration, but she forced herself to maintain her professional demeanor. She was a detective, not an accuser. And her current evidence was circumstantial at best.

"Thank you for the clarification, Deputy Director," Eva said, her voice betraying none of her mounting suspicion. "I appreciate your perspective on the prioritization of terrestrial threats."

As the meeting concluded, Eva felt a familiar sense of isolation wash over her. Sharma had been equally guarded, her responses polished and professional, yet subtly evasive. The weight of her deception was becoming heavier with each interaction.

She was an island in a sea of potential infiltrators, unable to trust the very colleagues she worked with every day.

The actual danger wasn't just in being discovered, but in the erosion of her own judgment. With every seemingly innocuous question, every probing inquiry, she risked exposing herself. A misplaced word, a subtle hesitation, a flicker of suspicion in her eyes – any of these could be the catalyst for her own neutralization. The collective's strength lay in its subtlety, its ability to warp perception and turn human systems against themselves.

She thought of Aris, his ability to perceive the psychic undercurrents. He could see the alien influence in the raw, unfiltered moments of thought and emotion. Her task was far more arduous: to dissect the carefully constructed facade, to find the cracks in the polished surface of human discourse, to discern the programmed response from genuine thought.

Eva decided to analyze the communication logs for recent inter-branch directives related to resource allocation for deep-space sensor maintenance. She specifically targeted a series of memos that had authorized significant budget cuts to these critical systems, citing 'efficiency savings' and 'redundancy elimination.' The individuals who had signed off on these memos were all on their flagged list.

She found herself staring at the name of General Marcus Vance, the head of Interstellar Defense Coordination. Vance was a decorated officer, a man who had served humanity for decades with unwavering loyalty. But Aris had reported a disturbing psychic residue around him during a recent joint briefing – a faint but persistent hum of alien thought, like static interference on a clear channel.

Eva decided to send a direct, encrypted query to Vance's office, framed as a request for updated threat assessment data that would justify the recent funding cuts to deep-space monitoring.

"General Vance's office," a synthesized voice responded as Eva initiated the secure channel.

"This is Commander Eva Rostova, requesting an update on the

current threat assessment parameters that led to the recent resource reallocation away from deep-space sensor array maintenance. Specifically, I require the data points that indicate a reduced probability of extraterrestrial threats compared to localized terrestrial ones, to ensure our strategic planning remains aligned with actionable intelligence," Eva stated, her voice calm and professional.

There was a pause, longer than usual, filled with the faint whirring of unseen machinery. "Commander Rostova," the synthesized voice replied, a subtle modulation suggesting it was relaying a processed response rather than speaking directly, "the threat assessments are proprietary and classified. The reallocation of resources was based on a comprehensive analysis of evolving geopolitical landscapes and emergent terrestrial threats. Further details are not available through this channel."

Proprietary and classified. The ultimate bureaucratic shield. Eva's mind raced. Aris had mentioned a specific vision of Vance in a dimly lit chamber, surrounded by figures whose faces were obscured by shadows, all bathed in that familiar, sickening alien luminescence. Vance, at the center, seemed to be receiving instructions, his face a mask of strained compliance.

"Understood, General's office," Eva replied, masking her disappointment. "However, my operational directive requires me to maintain situational awareness regarding all potential threats. If there are no further classifications of extraterrestrial threats to report, then the continued prioritization of terrestrial concerns is logically sound. But without that confirmation, the diversion of resources from essential deep-space monitoring remains a critical vulnerability."

Another pause. This one felt heavier, pregnant with unspoken information. "Commander Rostova, your operational focus should remain on your designated area of responsibility. The Strategic Command is handling all inter-branch resource allocation assessments. Please refer any further inquiries regarding this matter to the appropriate administrative channels."

The synthesized voice abruptly cut the connection. Eva stared at her console, the sterile interface suddenly seeming like a symbol of her isolation. She had been shut down, not with anger, but with an impersonal dismissal that spoke volumes about the depth of the control. General Vance, or whoever was speaking through his office, had clearly been instructed not to engage on this topic. The data was being withheld, the rationale obscured.

She understood now. It wasn't just about manipulating policies or diverting resources. It was about controlling information, about creating a deliberate fog of ignorance that would blind humanity to the true nature of the threat. Each compromised individual, each diverted resource, each withheld piece of data was a brick in the wall being built around humanity, a wall designed to isolate them, disarm them, and ultimately, absorb them.

The weight of her task pressed down on her. She was navigating a minefield, every step a calculated risk. The trust she had placed in her superiors, in the systems she had sworn to uphold, was being systematically eroded by the insidious presence of the collective. She had to find the strings, the invisible threads that manipulated these powerful figures, and sever them before the final act of assimilation was played out.

The war for Earth was being waged not on battlefields, but in the quiet, sterile corridors of power, and her weapon was a dangerous, solitary pursuit of truth.

The sterile air of the comms hub offered no solace. Eva's fingers danced across the holographic interface, the familiar glow of data streams now a chilling reminder of the pervasive corruption she was uncovering. Aris's whispered insights, once abstract fears, were solidifying into a terrifyingly tangible reality. The aliens weren't a fleet poised to descend, but a insidious presence, a psychic contagion that burrowed into the very minds of humanity's leaders. The 'collective' was not an external force to be fought, but an internal rot, a weaponized manipulation of trust and loyalty that turned allies into unwitting pawns in their own subjugation. The war wasn't being fought with plasma cannons and kinetic strikes, but in the quiet, sterile rooms where decisions were made, where loyalties were tested, and where the very concept of truth was being systematically dismantled.

Eva replayed her conversation with Admiral Thorne, her own voice a calm, professional mask that concealed a roiling sea of suspicion. His carefully crafted justifications, his unwavering gaze – were they the signs of a man convinced by his own manipulated logic, or the practiced performance of a puppet? The subtlety was the genius of it. No brute force, no overt coercion. Instead, a gentle, persistent nudging, a reframing of priorities, a re-calibration of perception. Thorne's directive to focus on terrestrial threats, to bolster orbital defenses against phantom Earth-bound incursions while neglecting the true, existential threat lurking in the vast silence of space, was a masterpiece of misdirection. It appealed to every leader's primal instinct to protect their own.

Her interaction with Deputy Director Sharma had yielded similar results. Sharma's reliance on "established protocols" and "credible intelligence" was not a sign of integrity, but of a mind already ensnared. Eva had pressed her on the manipulated data regarding 'Anomalous Terrestrial Activity,' the very bait designed to lure strategic planners away from the true danger. Sharma's insistence that their protocols would catch any data manipulation was a chilling testament to the collective's ability to infiltrate and corrupt the very systems designed to detect them. If the gatekeepers were compromised, then the fortress was already lost. Eva felt a cold dread creep into her bones. The enemy wasn't just within the halls of power; it was woven into the very fabric of their defense.

General Vance's non-response was perhaps the most damning. The refusal to provide data, the dismissal of her concerns as being outside her "designated area of responsibility," the referral to "appropriate administrative channels" – these were not the actions of a secure and confident leader, but of someone bound by unseen chains. Aris's vision of Vance in that dimly lit chamber, surrounded by shadowy figures, was no longer a mere psychic anomaly. It was a glimpse behind the curtain, a revelation of the true puppeteers at work. Vance wasn't a traitor in the conventional sense; he was a victim, his loyalty and experience twisted into a tool for his own people's undoing.

The realization settled upon Eva with the crushing weight of certainty: this was not a war of armies, but of minds. The aliens were not seeking to conquer Earth through force, but to subsume it, to absorb its consciousness, its will, its very identity. They were a psychic virus, and humanity's leaders were the initial hosts, their minds and wills slowly being overwritten. The 'collective' was the hive mind, and its tendrils were reaching into the highest echelons of command, slowly, subtly, rendering humanity's own defense mechanisms useless.

She thought about the recent surge in what appeared to be 'accidental' data corruption within sensitive deep-space surveillance archives. Initially dismissed as system glitches, they now seemed like deliberate acts of erasure, meticulously targeting information that might reveal the collective's true nature or origins. The 'efficiency improvements' that had led to the remote disabling of defense satellites were part of a broader pattern of incapacitation, designed not to destroy humanity, but to render it utterly incapable of resistance.

The psychological warfare being waged was terrifying in its sophistication. Trust, the bedrock of any functioning society, had been weaponized. Loyalty, the virtue that had defined generations of service, was being exploited. How could you fight an enemy that wore the face of your trusted commander, that spoke with the voice of your comrade, that issued directives that sounded perfectly reasonable, yet served a hidden, malevolent purpose? The constant vigilance required was exhausting, a perpetual state of suspicion that threatened to erode her own mental fortitude. Every interaction was a tightrope walk, every word a potential misstep that could expose her to the very same mental subjugation she was fighting to prevent.

Eva activated a new analysis protocol, designed by her and Aris, to cross-reference seemingly unrelated directives and communications across multiple departments. It was a data-mining operation on an unprecedented scale, searching for patterns that spoke of coordinated action, subtle shifts in emphasis, and the gradual erosion of humanity's defensive posture. The goal was to map the invisible network of influence, to identify the nexus points where the collective's will was being translated into actionable policy.

Hours blurred into a haze of data streams and flickering holograms. She found a series of seemingly minor budget reallocations that, when viewed in aggregate, painted a stark picture. Funds for essential maintenance of long-range threat detection arrays had been consistently siphoned off, diverted to terrestrial infrastructure projects or 'advanced terrestrial surveillance systems' – systems that, she now realized, were likely designed for internal monitoring rather than external defense. The justifications cited were always couched in terms of 'optimizing resource allocation' and 'adapting to evolving geopolitical landscapes.' The language was bland, bureaucratic, and utterly insidious.

She traced a significant portion of these diverted funds back to a specific subcommittee within the Department of Interstellar Affairs, headed by a Director Anya Sharma. This was the same Sharma who had so calmly dismissed Eva's concerns. The subcommittee's mandate was ostensibly to "streamline inter-departmental resource management," a role that provided the perfect cover for its true purpose: redirecting crucial resources away from genuine defense.

Eva then delved into the personnel files associated with this subcommittee. A disturbing number of individuals had recently undergone 'enhanced security clearances' and 're-training programs,' all approved at the highest levels. These weren't just ordinary bureaucrats; they were individuals with access to sensitive information, with the authority to influence policy, and now, it seemed, with their minds subtly altered.

Aris had been experiencing increasingly vivid and disturbing psychic impressions. He described a feeling of being watched, not by eyes, but by a pervasive awareness, a silent, immense consciousness that permeated the very air. He spoke of encountering individuals who, while outwardly appearing normal, possessed a disturbing inner emptiness, a void where their personal will and consciousness should have been.

They were hollow shells, animated by the collective's purpose. He had even described a fleeting vision of Admiral Thorne, not at his usual command post, but in a seemingly abandoned research facility, engaged in a hushed, clandestine conversation with figures whose faces were obscured by shadow, their forms radiating an almost imperceptible, alien glow. Thorne's expression, Aris had noted, was one of reluctant compliance, a subtle tension that spoke of a will being bent, not broken, but certainly influenced.

The implications were staggering. The collective wasn't just manipulating information; it was subtly altering the very minds of the individuals who held power. It was a form of psychic infiltration, a gradual overwrite of personality and will. The lack of overt aggression, along with a focus on psychological manipulation and control, indicated that the aliens weren't interested in conquest in the traditional sense. They were seeking to integrate humanity into their own existence, to absorb their consciousness, to make them a part of the collective itself. This was not an invasion; it was a parasitic assimilation.

Eva initiated a deeper dive into Sharma's personal communications, using a backdoor access code Aris had discovered during a previous, more abstract infiltration attempt. The data was heavily encrypted, but Aris's insights into alien encryption patterns, derived from his psychic bleed-throughs, proved invaluable. She managed to decrypt fragments of messages exchanged between Sharma and an anonymous source. The language was chillingly depersonalized, referring to human assets, strategic redirection, and 'optimal integration timelines.'

One decrypted fragment stood out: "Asset Thorne remains aligned. Sub-directive 7-Alpha-9 has been successfully implemented, effectively masking enhanced terrestrial surveillance capabilities and subtly diverting orbital assets from deep-space monitoring. Further reinforcement of terrestrial threat parameters is recommended to solidify the strategic shift. Compliance is high, but vigilance against emergent critical thought is paramount."

Eva's breath hitched. Thorne's justification about optimizing observational sweep patterns and addressing terrestrial blind spots was a direct result of this 'sub-directive.' The phrase 'subtly diverting orbital assets' confirmed her deepest fears. They were deliberately blinding Earth from orbit, leaving them vulnerable to the very threat they were ignoring. The 'enhanced terrestrial surveillance capabilities' were not for detecting alien invasions from afar, but for monitoring and controlling humanity itself.

The term 'critical thought' sent a shiver down her spine. The collective's greatest fear was not a military counter-attack, but the awakening of independent thought, the spark of defiance that could ignite a global realization. Their strategy was to preempt that spark, to extinguish it before it could catch fire, by controlling the information, the directives, and ultimately, the minds of those who made the decisions.

She cross-referenced Sharma's communications with those of other high-ranking officials, including General Vance. The pattern was consistent. A series of encrypted messages, often initiated by anonymous or untraceable nodes, dictating policy shifts, resource allocations, and strategic priorities. The responses from these high-ranking humans were invariably compliant, usually phrased in terms of "analyzing new intelligence" or "optimizing operational efficiency." They were acting as conduits, translating the collective's will into human policy, their own agency gradually eroded, their individuality subsumed.

The psychological toll of this realization was immense. Eva felt a profound sense of isolation. She was surrounded by individuals she had once respected, men and women who had sworn to protect humanity, yet many of them were now unwitting agents of its destruction. They were not necessarily malicious; many were likely as deceived as she was, their loyalties and judgment subtly manipulated. This made them all the more dangerous, their actions cloaked in the veneer of legitimate authority.

She had to tread with extreme caution. Any overt accusation, any premature revelation, would likely result in her own neutralization, either through official channels or through the subtle, psychic manipulation that Aris had begun to perceive as the collective's primary weapon. The war was a battle of perception, a contest to control the narrative, and Eva's most potent weapon was her ability to maintain her own clarity, her own uncorrupted sense of truth, in the face of overwhelming psychological pressure.

She began to meticulously document every anomaly, every suspicious communication, every subtly altered directive. She created encrypted data caches, scattered across secure, off-grid servers, each containing fragments of evidence. This was not a war that could be won with a frontal assault. It required a more nuanced approach, a slow, careful unraveling of the collective's influence, a process of gathering undeniable proof that could, at the right moment, be revealed to awaken humanity from its induced slumber.

Aris, meanwhile, was working on a different front. He was trying to develop a method to counteract the psychic influence, a form of mental shielding or a counter-frequency that could disrupt the collective's control. His efforts were fraught with danger, each attempt to probe the collective's mental architecture risking exposure and assimilation. He described the process as wading through a psychic fog, where whispers of alien intent constantly tried to seep into his own consciousness.

He felt the immense pressure of a thousand minds, a vast, alien consciousness that sought to envelop and erase him.

Eva knew that time was running out. The subtle shifts in policy and the gradual erosion of defense capabilities were not isolated incidents. They were part of a calculated, long-term strategy to render humanity helpless, to prepare it for a final, complete absorption. The enemy was not outside the gates; it was already within the palace, whispering in the ears of kings, weaving its web of control through the very institutions designed to protect them. The actual war was psychological, a battle for the very soul of humanity, and Eva found herself on the front lines, a lone sentinel in a world that was slowly, irrevocably, turning against itself. The weight of this knowledge was a crushing burden, but it also fueled a fierce, unyielding determination. She had to find a way to fight an enemy that was both everywhere and nowhere, an enemy that was, terrifyingly, becoming a part of them.

9: Severing the Connection

The faint hum of the salvaged gravimetric stabilizers was the only sound in the repurposed cargo bay, a counterpoint to the frantic pulse hammering in Aris's temples. Eva watched him, a knot of anxiety tightening in her gut. His brow was furrowed in concentration, his slender fingers hovering over a complex array of shimmering holographic schematics. The air around them thrummed with a barely contained energy, a testament to the volatile nature of the technology they were attempting to harness. The alien residue, once a perplexing enigma, had become their reluctant collaborator. Its unique energetic signature, captured and analyzed with painstaking precision, was the key. Aris believed he had found the discordant note in the symphony of alien manipulation, a specific quantum frequency that, when amplified and focused, could act as a psychic solvent, dissolving the ethereal bonds that anchored the transdimensional portals to their reality.

"It's... volatile, Eva," Aris murmured, his voice strained. He gestured to a particularly intricate section of the schematic, a swirling vortex of light and energy. "The residue exhibits properties that defy conventional physics. It's almost as if it exists in a state of quantum superposition, simultaneously here and... elsewhere. Trying to manipulate it is like trying to pin down smoke with a scalpel." He paused, taking a deep, measured breath. "But if my calculations are correct, this frequency, this specific resonance, acts as a disruption. Imagine the portals are held together by strands of pure thought, pure intention. This frequency is like a sonic wave that shatters those strands, but only momentarily."

The implications were immense. If they could achieve this, even for a brief period, it would sever the conduit through which the collective's influence flowed. It would be a temporary reprieve, a chance to regroup, to perhaps even sever the connection more permanently, but it was a start. The alien residue, recovered from the derelict scout vessel they had painstakingly salvaged, was a tangible piece of their enemy, and in its very existence lay the blueprint for their undoing. Aris had spent days, then weeks, immersed in its alien emanations, his psychic sensitivity allowing him to perceive patterns and energies invisible to Eva's more pragmatic senses. He described it as a 'song' of disruption, a chaotic melody that, when properly tuned, could introduce dissonance into the alien network.

"So, we're not destroying them?" Eva asked, her mind racing through the operational possibilities.

"No," Aris confirmed, shaking his head. "Destruction is... problematic. Their nature is too fluid, too interwoven with the fabric of space-time. Attempting to obliterate them entirely could have unforeseen, catastrophic consequences. Think of it like severing a parasitic root system. You don't rip it out violently; you coax it to release its hold, to wither on its own. This frequency, when applied with the right intensity, should cause a localized destabilization of the portal's energetic matrix. It should force them to retract, to sever their own link to this sector, at least for a significant period. It's a forced dormancy, not an annihilation."

The power requirements, however, were astronomical. Aris had spent hours poring over salvaged power conduits and plasma regulators, trying to devise a way to generate the sheer energy needed. Their current resources were meager, cobbled together from decommissioned orbital platforms and black-market components.

Every watt, every joule, had to be accounted for, optimized, and channeled with terrifying precision. He had cannibalized parts from the very technology they were trying to replicate, a desperate gamble that involved reverse-engineering alien power core schematics that looked more like abstract art than engineering blueprints.

"I've managed to adapt a salvaged deuterium containment unit," Aris explained, pointing to a bulky, cylindrical device covered in a lattice of glowing conduits. "It's designed for a much lower output, but by overloading its tertiary regulators and bypassing the safety protocols, I think I can achieve the necessary surge. It's a one-shot deal, though. Push it any harder, and the entire unit will likely fission." His eyes met Eva's, a flicker of grim determination in their depths. "We get one shot at this, Eva. One chance to destabilize the gateways and break the connection."

The calibration was the true nightmare. The frequency itself was not static; it shifted and modulated in response to the ambient psychic field. Aris had to build a dynamic modulator, a device that could constantly track these subtle shifts and adjust the output in real-time.

This was where his own unique abilities came into play. He would have to act as the final, living component, a biological sensor feeding data directly into the system, his mind a living oscilloscope translating the alien song into actionable frequencies.

"The modulator needs to be incredibly sensitive," Aris continued, his voice a low hum. "It needs to 'listen' to the subtle fluctuations of the collective's presence, to the psychic resonance of the portals themselves. If I misinterpret even a fraction of a decibel, if the timing is off by a nanosecond, the feedback loop could collapse the entire system, or worse, draw their attention directly to us." He tapped a small, crystalline component embedded in a complex array of wiring. "This crystal, derived from the same core material as the alien residue, is the heart of the modulator. It resonates with their energy signature, allowing me to perceive and interpret their... patterns."

Eva nodded, the weight of their responsibility pressing down on her. They were operating on the fringes, with limited resources and even fewer allies. The vast majority of humanity's leadership was either compromised or blissfully unaware of the existential threat they faced. Their mission was a desperate gamble, a clandestine operation launched from the shadows of a compromised defense network. The success of their mission depended entirely on Aris's genius and the volatile, alien technology they had managed to salvage.

"What kind of range are we talking about?" Eva asked, her gaze fixed on the central emitter array, a collection of intricately folded metallic plates that would focus the energy burst.

"If the focusing array works as designed, and if my calculations on the power output are accurate, we should be able to affect the primary portal nexus within a

fifty-kilometer radius," Aris replied. "That should encompass the most critical conduits feeding directly into our sector's command structure. It's not a global solution, but it's enough to create a significant disruption, to buy us precious time." He zoomed in on a particular section of the schematic, highlighting a complex interplay of energy fields. "The trick is to create a specific harmonic distortion.

Imagine striking a bell with a specific pitch. If the pitch is correct, the bell resonates. If the pitch is slightly off, it might just create a dull thud. Or worse, it might shatter the bell in unpredictable ways. We need to strike the right harmonic chord with the portals."

He pulled up another set of data, a series of complex wave patterns. "The alien residue is not a stable substance. It exhibits quantum entanglement properties that are... extreme. They use these properties to maintain the stability of their transdimensional gateways. My theory is that by introducing a focused burst of an opposing, but similarly quantum-entangled, frequency, we can force a temporary decoherence. It's like trying to untie a knot that's tied at the quantum level. The key is to introduce the right 'undoing' frequency without creating a catastrophic paradox."

The salvaged alien technology was proving to be a double-edged sword. While its very nature provided the raw materials for their countermeasure, it also served as a constant reminder of the alien presence and its insidious reach. The faint, almost imperceptible hum of the power core, the subtle shifts in ambient light near the containment unit – these were all echoes of the enemy, a constant psychological pressure on Aris as he worked.

"The power surge is going to be massive," Aris reiterated, his voice tight with a mixture of excitement and apprehension. "When we activate the primary discharge, the entire bay will be bathed in a light unlike anything you've ever seen. And the energy signature... it will be unmistakable. We'll be broadcasting our intentions, in a way. But it's the only way to generate the kind of focused output required." He gestured towards a series of capacitors, their metallic casings beginning to glow with stored energy. "These are charged to their absolute limit. Any further increase would risk a premature discharge."

Eva's mind drifted back to Aris's description of the psychic bleed-throughs, the subtle ways the collective's consciousness could manifest. He had spoken of feeling their presence like an oppressive weight, of seeing glimpses of their alien form in fleeting moments of altered perception. This device, this attempt to directly interfere with their network, was bound to draw their attention. It was like shouting in a silent library; the disturbance would be felt.

"We need to synchronize the activation with a moment of maximum distraction for them," Eva mused aloud. "If we can hit them when their focus is elsewhere, when their attention is drawn by other events, our signal might be less... noticeable."

Aris nodded, his eyes gleaming with renewed purpose. "Precisely. I've been monitoring the ambient psychic energy levels. There are cyclical patterns, periods where their collective awareness seems to momentarily coalesce, focusing on specific regions or directives. If we can time our surge to coincide with one of these focal points, it might create a brief window where their own energetic output masks our disruptive frequency. It's a gamble, but it's a calculated one." He began to input a series of commands, his fingers flying across the holographic interface. "I'm setting up a predictive algorithm to identify the optimal window. It's based on Aris's recent psychic impressions, correlating them with the energy fluctuations I'm detecting from the portal remnants."

The salvaged alien technology was a puzzle, a complex, three-dimensional jigsaw where the pieces were made of exotic matter and interdimensional energies. Aris had to reconfigure alien power conduits designed to channel energies beyond human comprehension, recalibrate their temporal displacement regulators, and bypass their inherently alien fail-safes. He was essentially trying to force a highly advanced, organic alien technology into a mode of operation that was antithetical to its design.

"The primary emitter array is almost fully charged," Aris announced, his voice now a tight whisper. The air around the device crackled with unseen energy. "The resonance modulator is locked onto the predicted frequency. Eva, the energy buildup is... immense. It feels like the entire ship is vibrating with contained power."

Eva stood beside him, her hand resting on the cool, metallic hull of the main power conduit. She could feel the tremors, the building pressure that seemed to emanate from the device itself. The faint, ethereal glow of the alien residue, housed within a specialized containment field at the heart of the device, pulsed in time with the rising energy levels. It was a beautiful, terrifying sight.

"We have to be ready to initiate the dispersal protocol the moment the modulator confirms the optimal window," Eva said, her gaze sweeping across the bay, ensuring all safety parameters were engaged, however inadequate they might be. "This isn't just about disrupting a connection, Aris. It's about proving that we can disrupt it. That they are not invincible."

Aris's lips curved into a faint, determined smile. "They've been so subtle, so insidious, making us doubt our own senses, our own reality. But this… this will be undeniable. A physical, energetic blow against their psychic network. It's a declaration of war, fought on their own terms, with their own stolen tools." He took another deep breath, his focus absolute. "The modulator is stabilizing. The predictive algorithm is flagging a potential convergence point in approximately ninety seconds. This is it, Eva. The moment of truth."

The hum of the machinery intensified, a rising crescendo that seemed to vibrate in Eva's very bones. The crystalline component of the modulator began to glow with an internal luminescence, its light shifting through a spectrum of alien hues. Eva watched Aris, his face a mask of intense concentration, his connection to the device and its alien heart seemingly absolute. He was walking a razor's edge, a tightrope strung between human ingenuity and alien unknowability, his own mind the delicate instrument that would conduct this symphony of disruption. The fate of their efforts, the potential to momentarily sever the unseen threads that bound humanity to the collective, rested on his ability to harmonize with the very essence of their enemy.

The air thrummed with anticipation, thick with the scent of ozone and the unspoken fear of what might happen if they failed.

The alien energy signatures were not monolithic. Aris had discovered this through countless hours of patient observation, sifting through the cacophony of raw data that emanated from the salvaged alien artifacts. It was in the subtle variations, the fleeting moments of disharmony, that he found his revelation. He perceived them not as a constant, unwavering presence, but as a symphony of interwoven strands, each vibrating at a particular, albeit alien, and frequency. And within this symphony, he'd isolated a singular, discordant note – a resonant frequency that seemed to chafe against the very fabric of the portals actively. It was a frequency that, when amplified, didn't just disrupt; it induced a fundamental instability.

He hypothesized that this instability was directly linked to the aliens' method of maintaining their transdimensional gateways. Their ability to hold open these rifts, to anchor them to this reality, relied on a sophisticated form of quantum entanglement. This entanglement wasn't merely a byproduct of their technology; it was its very foundation, a web of interconnectedness that spanned dimensions.

Aris's disruptive frequency, he theorized, acted as a localized quantum entanglement breaker. It was like introducing an opposing, yet similarly structured, quantum signature into their carefully woven network. The result, he believed, would be a cascade of decoherence, forcing the portals into a state of flux, compelling them to retract their anchors. It was an aggressive form of feedback, designed to exploit a vulnerability inherent in their advanced, yet ultimately alien, design.

The challenge, however, was translating this theoretical understanding into a tangible, deployable weapon. Aris spent days, then weeks, locked away in the repurposed cargo bay, his focus absolute. He sketched, he calculated, he simulated. He needed to engineer a device capable of generating and amplifying this specific, elusive frequency with pinpoint accuracy. The prototype was a delicate dance between salvaged human technology and the enigmatic principles derived from the alien residue. It was a portable emitter, a compact unit designed for rapid deployment and maximum impact. The core of the device was a crystalline matrix, meticulously carved from a fragment of the alien residue itself. This crystal acted as a conduit, resonating with the very energy it was designed to disrupt, allowing for a more refined and potent amplification. The casing was a carefully calibrated blend of reinforced alloys and energy-dampening composites, designed to withstand the immense power surge required for activation and to minimize any telltale energy bleed-off that might betray their position.

"It's more than just a frequency, Eva," Aris explained, his voice raspy from lack of sleep, his eyes alight with the feverish glow of discovery. He gestured to a schematic projected onto a nearby bulkhead, a complex interplay of wave patterns and energy flow diagrams. "It's about resonance. Think of it like this: their portals are held open by a specific harmonic. They've tuned their entire existence to this particular resonance. What I've found is a counter-harmonic, a frequency that, when applied with sufficient intensity, creates a destructive interference pattern within their entanglement matrix. It's not about brute force; it's about precision. It's about finding the exact note that makes their entire construction vibrate apart."

The engineering process was fraught with peril. The salvaged alien components were designed for purposes far beyond human comprehension. Their power conduits were not merely wires but conduits for energies that could warp space-time; their regulators were not simple switches but complex mechanisms that balanced forces that defied conventional physics. Aris had to reverse-engineer these components, coaxing them into performing functions for which they were never intended. He was essentially trying to re-program the fundamental laws of alien physics, using human ingenuity as his guide.

"The power requirements are astronomical," Aris admitted, his gaze fixed on a particular section of the emitter's design. "To generate a sustained burst of this counter-harmonic frequency at the intensity needed to destabilize the entanglement nexus, we're talking about energy levels that would melt standard terrestrial capacitors. We need something far more robust, something that can handle a near-instantaneous, massive power draw without vaporizing."

This was where Eva's expertise became crucial. While Aris was the architect of the disruptive frequency, Eva was the provider of its lifeblood – the power. She had spent weeks scouring the salvaged derelicts, the abandoned outposts, the forgotten corners of the galaxy, searching for a suitable energy source. Her hunt had led her to a deactivated experimental fusion cell, a relic from a long-abandoned colonial defense project. It was a behemoth of a machine, designed to power an entire orbital defense platform for months, even years, on a single fuel load. It was also hazardous, its containment field notoriously unstable even under optimal conditions.

"I've managed to secure it," Eva announced, her voice tight with a mixture of triumph and trepidation. She led Aris to a section of the cargo bay where the fusion cell sat, a hulking, scarred cylinder encased in layers of reinforced plating. The air around it felt charged, almost alive, with a latent power that made the hairs on Aris's arms stand on end. "It's a repurposed experimental model, designed for… extreme energy output.

The containment field is volatile, and bypassing the safeties to draw a focused surge will be incredibly risky. But it's the only thing I've found with the sheer capacity to provide the joules we need for even a single, effective burst."

The fusion cell was a testament to a bygone era of ambitious, and often reckless, human ambition. It was a fusion of cutting-edge theoretical physics and brute-force engineering, a device that promised unlimited energy but came with an equally unlimited potential for catastrophic failure. Eva had spent days meticulously recalibrating its magnetic containment fields, coaxing the unstable plasma core into a state of controlled readiness. She had to bypass multiple redundant safety protocols, each designed to prevent the very kind of power surge Aris required. It was a delicate operation, akin to defusing a bomb while simultaneously trying to detonate it at a precise moment.

"The sheer power density of this cell is... unlike anything I've encountered outside of theoretical physics simulations," Eva explained, running a diagnostic scan over the fusion cell's primary control interface. The readouts flickered, displaying energy levels that made Aris's own emitter's power requirements seem modest. "We're talking about sustained output far exceeding anything available on the open market, or even within most military inventories. The problem isn't generating the power; it's controlling it. A single miscalculation, a slight deviation in the containment field's integrity, and we'll be nothing but a radioactive stain on the hull."

Aris nodded, his mind already racing through the integration protocols. He needed to interface the emitter directly with the fusion cell's output manifold, a process that required precise calibration of energy transfer rates and temporal synchronization.

The surge had to be instantaneous, a raw, unadulterated blast of focused energy delivered directly to the emitter's core.

"We'll need to synchronize the emitter's activation sequence with the fusion cell's primary discharge cycle," Aris mused, tapping commands onto his holographic interface. "The cell will need to be brought to peak operational capacity, and then, at the precise nanosecond the modulator locks onto the target frequency, we initiate the full power transfer. It has to be a single, unified surge. Any hesitation, any delay, and the window of opportunity will close, or worse, the feedback from the portal's inherent resistance could destabilize the fusion cell itself."

The pressure was immense. They were working against a ticking clock, with the alien presence subtly but undeniably encroaching. The psychic bleed-throughs, the unsettling shifts in ambient energy, the faint but persistent feeling of being watched – these were all constant reminders of the stakes. The success of their mission hinged on the successful integration of two highly volatile, exceptionally dangerous pieces of technology, wielded by a team with limited resources and even fewer allies.

"I've adapted a direct energy conduit from a salvaged orbital cannon," Eva explained, pointing to a heavily shielded cable snaking its way from the fusion cell towards the emitter. "It's designed to handle massive energy transfers, but I've had to reinforce its insulation and bypass its internal regulators. It's rated for a fraction of what this fusion cell can deliver, but it's the best we have. We're essentially pushing this conduit to its absolute breaking point, and then some."

Aris meticulously reviewed the energy transfer schematics. He needed to ensure that the emitter's internal capacitors could absorb and then rapidly discharge the energy from the fusion cell without overloading. He had designed the emitter with a unique energy buffer system, utilizing salvaged alien energy storage crystals that could handle immense power densities for brief periods. However, even these were not foolproof.

"The buffer crystals will have to absorb the initial shock, then discharge it instantaneously into the resonant matrix," Aris explained, his brow furrowed in concentration. "If the rate of energy absorption exceeds their capacity, they'll shatter. If the discharge isn't precise, the focused frequency will be compromised. It's a razor's edge, Eva. A single misstep and the entire system could cascade into a localized singularity, or worse, attract a level of attention we cannot possibly withstand."

The fusion cell, once activated for the purpose of powering the emitter, would   become a beacon. Its raw, untamed energy signature would be a scream in the silent expanse of space, a blatant declaration of their intent. It was a calculated risk, a necessary evil. They had to be willing to make noise to break the silence, to illuminate their presence in order to sever the unseen connection.

"We're not just building a weapon, Aris," Eva said, her voice firm, her gaze meeting his. "We're building a statement. We're showing them that we're not just pawns in their game. We can fight back. We can disrupt their control."

Aris nodded, a grim smile touching his lips. "And this fusion cell, this raw, untamed power… it's the embodiment of that defiance. It's human ingenuity pushing the boundaries, even when the odds are impossibly stacked against us. It's the perfect power source for a weapon born of necessity and fueled by desperation." He turned back to his console, his fingers dancing across the holographic interface, refining the intricate dance of frequencies and power levels. "The engineering is complete. The integration is as secure as it can be. Now, it's a matter of timing. We need to wait for the optimal moment, when their attention is most divided, and then unleash hell." The fusion cell hummed, a low, resonant thrum that vibrated through the deck plates, a testament to the raw power waiting to be unleashed, a power that Eva had so perilously wrangled into their service, a power that Aris was poised to weaponize against the unseen enemy.

The faint hum of the repurposed fusion cell was a constant, almost comforting, presence in the cramped confines of their mobile workshop. It was a sound that spoke of contained fury, of immense power held precariously in check. Eva had outdone herself, not only securing the volatile energy source but also adapting it to Aris's specifications. The direct energy conduit, reinforced and painstakingly recalibrated, snaked across the deck, a thick umbilical cord connecting the thrumming heart of their operation to the delicate, alien-infused emitter. Aris, meanwhile, was meticulously poring over the latest telemetry data, his brow furrowed as he cross-referenced energy signatures with known patterns of alien activity.

"The anomalies are increasing," Aris stated, his voice a low murmur, barely audible over the ambient thrum of the fusion cell. He pointed to a holographic projection that shimmered between them, a swirling nebula of colored light representing sensor readings. "These aren't just random fluctuations anymore, Eva. They're converging, focusing. I believe we've finally pinpointed it."

Eva leaned closer, her eyes scanning the intricate patterns. "The hub?"

"Precisely," Aris confirmed. "The energy signatures converge at a single point, buried deep beneath what our long-range scans identified as a terrestrial government research facility. It's disguised as a meteorological monitoring station, a front for something far more significant. The seismic readings, the localized gravitational distortions... they all point to an immense structure, a nexus for the alien portal network."

Eva's lips thinned. A government facility. It was predictable, in a grim sort of way. The aliens, with their superior technology, wouldn't choose some desolate wasteland to establish their transdimensional crossroads. They would integrate themselves, subtly, into existing infrastructure, using the very systems of the dominant species as camouflage. "A weather station," she mused, a hint of irony in her tone. "Who would suspect a weather station of housing an interstellar transit hub?"

"Exactly," Aris agreed. "It's the perfect cover. They've been operating right under humanity's nose for years, perhaps decades. And it's here, beneath this unassuming façade, that we'll find the heart of the connection we need to sever." He tapped a command onto his console, zooming in on a specific region of the holographic map. "The energy levels are peaking at irregular intervals, but there's a discernible pattern. It suggests periods of high traffic, when they're actively routing energy and, presumably, personnel through the hub."

The intelligence had been painstakingly assembled, pieced together from fragmented transmissions, cryptic sensor logs, and the hushed whispers of Eva's few remaining contacts within the shadowed echelons of galactic intelligence. Each tidbit had been a gamble, a risk of exposure, but it had led them to this. The weather station, codenamed "Nimbus" by the unsuspecting terrestrial authorities, was their target. It was a nondescript cluster of antennas and radar dishes atop a windswept mesa, appearing utterly unremarkable to any casual observer. But to Aris and Eva, it was a beacon, a locus of the very anomalies that had driven their desperate flight across the stars.

"Nimbus Station," Eva confirmed, accessing a secure datapad. "It's officially designated for atmospheric research and weather forecasting: minimal security, mostly automated systems. However," she paused, scrolling through a hidden file, "there are whispers of unusual energy readings being contained within its subterranean levels. Nothing substantial, of course. Just the kind of anomaly that gets filed away and forgotten by the bureaucracy."

"Forgotten, perhaps, but not unseen," Aris countered. "My analysis indicates that Nimbus Station is not merely a conduit, but a critical junction point. The energy flux there is orders of magnitude higher than at any other observed portal site. It's a hub, Eva, a central nexus from which countless other conduits likely originate and terminate." He gestured to the holographic display again. "The device I've engineered, the Resonant Disruptor, needs to be deployed at the heart of such a nexus to achieve the cascade effect we need. If we can destabilize this hub, we can, in theory, force the retraction of a significant portion of their transdimensional network."

The plan was audacious, bordering on suicidal. Infiltrate a seemingly secure government facility, navigate its presumed subterranean levels, locate the alien portal hub, and deploy Aris's device during a period of peak activity. The slightest miscalculation, the smallest deviation from their carefully laid plan, and they would be detected, apprehended, or worse, vaporized by alien energies they could barely comprehend.

"Peak activity," Eva repeated, her gaze fixed on the swirling patterns of the energy readings. "When is that precisely?"

Aris ran a series of predictive algorithms. "Based on the observed cycles and the nature of the anomalies, I estimate the next significant surge will occur within the next forty-eight cycles. It coincides with a predicted solar flare event, which I suspect the aliens are using to mask their own energy signatures, amplifying their portal activity under the guise of natural cosmic phenomena. It's a clever gambit, but it also creates a window of opportunity for us. Their focus will be divided, their defenses potentially strained by the added electromagnetic interference."

"So, we have two days," Eva said, a determined glint in her eyes. "Two days to get into Nimbus Station, find their hub, and set up Aris's baby. What's the infiltration vector?"

"The facility's primary access point is heavily secured," Aris replied, pulling up another set of schematics. "However, my analysis of its construction indicates a less monitored subterranean access tunnel, likely for maintenance or emergency access to the deeper levels. It's also, conveniently, located on the side of the mesa furthest from any known monitoring outposts. We'll approach from the canyon below, using the terrain for cover."

The canyon below Nimbus Station was a jagged scar across the landscape, a labyrinth of shadowed crevices and sheer rock faces. It was a stark contrast to the open skies above, a place where light struggled to penetrate and the wind whispered secrets through the stone. Their craft, a nondescript freighter salvaged from a forgotten trade route, was equipped with advanced stealth capabilities, but even those had their limits. The closer they got to the facility, the more sensitive the ambient energy readings became, a constant reminder of the alien presence humming just beneath the surface.

"The tunnel entrance is approximately three hundred meters below the primary structure," Aris continued, pointing to a specific point on the holographic terrain model. "It's sealed, but the material composition suggests it's a standard terrestrial alloy, unlike the alien components we've encountered elsewhere. Our cutting tools should be able to breach it within minutes."

"And once inside?" Eva prompted, her fingers already tracing potential routes through the facility's internal schematics.

"That's where it gets… complex," Aris admitted, a slight frown creasing his brow. "The facility's internal layout is standard for a research station, but the deeper levels are heavily shielded and contain significant power conduits. The true portal hub will be located in the deepest, most heavily fortified section. I've identified a series of intersecting energy signatures that indicate the presence of a massive, concentrated power source. That's where we need to deploy the Disruptor."

He projected a detailed blueprint of the station's subterranean levels. It showed a series of reinforced tunnels and chambers, radiating outwards from a central core. The core itself was a dense mass of interwoven energy lines, pulsing with a rhythm that was both alien and unsettling.

"The hub isn't a single point," Aris explained, tracing a path through the complex diagram. "It's a network, a complex arrangement of interlocking portal conduits, all drawing power from a central alien energy conduit. Our device needs to be placed within the primary conduit nexus. The resonance it generates will then propagate through the entire network, causing a systemic shutdown."

Eva studied the blueprint, her mind already working through the tactical implications. "Security will be automated, likely. Motion sensors, energy field detectors, possibly even automated defense systems. We'll need to be precise, and we'll need to disable any active countermeasures before deploying the device."

"My emitter includes a localized EMP burst capability," Aris assured her. "It's designed to temporarily disable any terrestrial electronic systems within a specific radius, creating a brief window of invisibility. However, it's a one-time use, and its range is limited. We'll need to use it strategically, just as we breach the main hub chamber."

The weight of their mission pressed down on them. The fate of countless worlds, perhaps even the very fabric of their reality, rested on their ability to infiltrate Nimbus Station and cripple the alien portal hub. They were a small team, armed with stolen technology and a desperate hope, facing an enemy whose reach extended far beyond their comprehension.

"Are you sure about the timing, Aris?" Eva asked, her voice tinged with a hint of apprehension. "If we miscalculate the peak activity, if their systems are more active than anticipated…"

"The risk is inherent," Aris stated, his gaze unwavering. "But the alternative is to allow this network to continue to expand, to entrench itself within our galaxy further. We have the means to disrupt it, and we have identified the target. Now we must have the courage to act." He looked at Eva, a silent acknowledgment of the immense pressure they were both under. "The fusion cell is prepped. The emitter is calibrated. All that remains is the execution."

The journey to Nimbus Station was fraught with tension. Every sensor sweep, every distant light in the void, felt like a potential threat. They navigated the complex gravitational currents of the system, utilizing every trick Eva had learned in her years as a freelance scout and smuggler. The less they were detected, the better their chances of success.

As they approached the mesa, the wind picked up, whipping dust and debris across the barren landscape. The sky above was a bruised purple, the first hint of the approaching solar flare painting the horizon with streaks of sickly light. Nimbus Station sat silhouetted against this dramatic backdrop, a cluster of metallic structures reaching towards the heavens like skeletal fingers.

"Stealth systems engaged," Eva murmured, her hands moving with practiced efficiency over the controls. The freighter's exterior plating shifted, its visual and energy signatures blurring into the surrounding environment. They were ghosts, phasing through the hostile space.

"I'm picking up internal energy fluctuations," Aris announced, his voice tight. "Within the station itself. It's slight, but it's there. They're preparing for something."

"The solar flare," Eva surmised. "They're likely routing additional power, optimizing their systems. It means the hub will be active, but it also means they might be more... preoccupied."

They descended into the canyon, the towering rock formations providing a welcome screen from any long-range sensors. The air grew colder, the silence more profound. The only sounds were the whine of their own engines and the occasional groan of shifting rock.

"The tunnel entrance is directly ahead," Eva confirmed, her eyes fixed on the readouts. "Thermal scans show a faint anomaly within the rock face, consistent with a sealed access point."

Aris nodded, his hand hovering over the console that controlled the emitter. "Prepare the EMP burst. We'll use it the moment we breach the seal."

The freighter settled gently onto a rocky outcrop, its engines powering down to a near-silent hum. They emerged from the craft, clad in specialized environmental suits, the thin atmosphere offering little protection from the biting wind. The tunnel entrance was a dark, unassuming aperture in the sheer rock face, a stark contrast to the advanced technology waiting within.

With practiced precision, Eva deployed a portable cutting laser. The beam hissed, biting into the reinforced alloy of the tunnel seal. Sparks showered outwards, illuminating the otherwise impenetrable darkness. Aris stood beside her, the Resonant Disruptor held firmly in his grip, its crystalline matrix glowing with a faint, internal light.

"Almost there," Eva grunted, adjusting the laser's focus. The metallic groan of the breaching seal echoed through the canyon.

As the last section of the seal gave way, revealing a dark, narrow passage beyond, Aris activated his device. A low, resonant hum emanated from the emitter, a subtle vibration that seemed to ripple through the very rock around them. The tunnel's internal lighting flickered, then died completely, plunging them into absolute darkness, save for the faint glow of Aris's device.

"EMP successful," Aris confirmed, his voice a low command. "Internal sensors are offline. We have a window."

Eva nodded, drawing a compact energy pistol from her hip. "Let's move."

They slipped into the tunnel, their footsteps muffled by the thick dust that coated the floor. The air within was stale, carrying the faint scent of ozone and something else... something metallic and alien. The passage sloped downwards, leading them into the depths of Nimbus Station, towards the heart of the alien network. The weight of their mission, the immense stakes, pressed down on them with every step they took into the unknown. They were about to sever a connection, and the universe would hold its breath to see if they succeeded. The deeper they descended, the more the ambient energy readings climbed, the faint hum of the fusion cell in their pack a testament to the power they were about to unleash. This was no longer a theoretical exercise; this was the precipice of their most dangerous operation yet. The portal hub awaited, and with it, the potential for either salvation or utter annihilation. The descent was a calculated risk, each step a gamble against the unseen architects of this interdimensional highway. They moved with a quiet urgency, their senses heightened, aware that any misstep could alert the very forces they sought to disrupt. The path ahead was a descent into the unknown, a journey into the belly of the alien beast, with the fate of their galaxy hanging precariously in the balance. The hum of their own portable power source, a tiny ember of defiance against the encroaching alien presence, seemed to grow louder with every meter they descended, a constant reminder of the destructive potential they carried.

This was the moment of truth, the convergence of all their efforts, a desperate gambit to reclaim their place in the cosmos. The silence of the tunnel was not empty; it was pregnant with anticipation, with the unseen energies that pulsed just beyond the reach of their senses. The government facility, the unassuming Nimbus Station, was merely the shell. The actual alien presence lay hidden, deep within its foundations, a nexus point in a network that spanned dimensions. And they were about to confront it, head-on, armed with a weapon forged from desperation and ingenuity.

The hum of the prototype Resonant Disruptor, now coupled with a secondary power conduit siphoned from their freighter's auxiliary systems, vibrated through Aris's fingertips. It was a delicate dance of energy, a precisely calibrated oscillation designed to interact with the subtle distortions Aris had detected in a localized anomaly. This wasn't the grand nexus beneath Nimbus Station, not yet. This was a test. A preliminary probe into the nature of the alien gateway technology, a way to gauge the efficacy of his device without tipping their hand to the larger, more dangerous operation.

Eva watched from a secure vantage point, her gaze fixed on the faint shimmer distorting the air a hundred meters away. It was a minor tear in reality, a whisper of the larger network, detected by Aris's more refined sensors during their scouting of the region surrounding Nimbus. Its energy signature was a mere fraction of what they expected at the primary hub, making it the perfect, low-risk subject for a controlled experiment. The surrounding desert scrub, baked by the twin suns, offered no witnesses, no observers to the audacious act they were about to commit. The only sounds were the sigh of the wind and the increasingly insistent thrum of the Disruptor.

"Power levels stabilizing at ninety-two percent," Eva reported, her voice calm and steady through their comms. "Secondary conduit is holding. No detectable external energy spikes from our position."

Aris nodded, his eyes glued to the diagnostics flickering on his forearm-mounted display. "Resonance field is forming. We're within the predicted parameters for interaction." He took a deep breath, the recycled air in his helmet doing little to quell the knot of anticipation in his stomach. This was it. The culmination of months of clandestine work, of sleepless nights and calculated risks. The moment of truth, albeit on a drastically smaller scale. "Initiating primary pulse sequence in three... two... one."

He depressed the activation stud. The hum of the Disruptor deepened, a subtle shift in frequency that Aris felt resonate not just in his hands, but in the very marrow of his bones. The shimmer in the distance, the nascent portal, began to change. It pulsed erratically, its edges bleeding into the surrounding environment like watercolor paint on wet paper. The faint, alien hum that Aris had detected began to intensify, a discordant chorus rising in pitch and volume.

"It's reacting!" Eva's voice crackled with excitement. "The signature is fluctuating wildly. It's... unstable."

The shimmer flickered violently, growing brighter, then dimmer, as if struggling against an unseen force. Aris concentrated, adjusting the Disruptor's output, trying to maintain the precise resonant frequency. The alien portal seemed to writhe, its form contorting. For a heart-stopping moment, it shrank, the aperture collapsing inward upon itself until it was barely more than a pinprick of light. Aris felt a surge of elation – it was working. The device was capable of disrupting the alien gateways.

But the elation was short-lived. The pinprick of light flared, and the portal reasserted itself, not only stabilizing but expanding, its edges sharpening, the alien hum returning with renewed vigor. It was larger than before, its presence more pronounced, more insistent.

"What happened?" Eva's voice was laced with concern. "The energy levels are spiking. It's... it's compensating."

Aris's brow furrowed. "It adapted. The disruption was too... broad. The energy surge I applied, while significant, wasn't focused enough. It overloaded the localized stabilization matrix, forcing it to reconfigure and draw more ambient energy to compensate." He gritted his teeth. "It's stronger now than it was before."

He continued to monitor the readings, a grim realization dawning on him. The test had provided invaluable data, but not in the way he had hoped. They had confirmed the Disruptor's ability to interact with the portals, but they had also inadvertently strengthened this particular anomaly. It was a dangerous trade-off.

"The power draw from the secondary conduit is exceeding safe parameters," Eva warned, her voice tight. "We need to disengage, Aris. Now."

Reluctantly, Aris cut the power to the Disruptor. The intense hum died away, leaving an almost deafening silence in its wake. The portal, though still larger and more potent than before, slowly began to stabilize, its alien signature settling into a new, more powerful equilibrium. The desert air, once just dry and dusty, now seemed to thrum with a latent energy, a constant reminder of the alien presence they had just awakened further.

"Disengagement complete," Aris confirmed, his voice heavy. He slumped back against the control console, the adrenaline slowly draining from his system, leaving behind a weary disappointment. "The device functions, Eva. It can disrupt the portals. But it requires refinement. More power, and a far more precise application to achieve a lasting effect without... this."

Eva remained silent for a moment, processing the information. A sober understanding of the challenges ahead had replaced her initial excitement. "So, the theory holds, but the execution needs work. And we just made a minor gateway more... significant."

"Precisely," Aris said, his gaze fixed on the now-stabilized, yet undeniably more powerful, portal in the distance. "This small-scale demonstration has taught us more about the alien network's resilience than any passive observation could have. It's not just a matter of overwhelming them with raw energy. It requires understanding the nuances of their stabilization protocols, exploiting specific vulnerabilities within their energy matrices."

He ran a diagnostic on the Disruptor, the holographic readouts painting a grim picture. "The core matrix is intact, but the energy regulators are strained. To achieve a sustained disruption, let alone a complete severance, on a nexus like Nimbus Station, we'd need a power source at least an order of magnitude greater than what we're currently channeling. And the targeting system needs to be far more sophisticated. We need to be able to fine-tune the resonant frequency to exploit specific harmonic weaknesses in their conduits."

"An order of magnitude..." Eva murmured, a faint unease creeping into her voice. "That's... a lot. More than our freighter can provide, even with the repurposed fusion cell."

"Not necessarily," Aris countered, a flicker of renewed determination in his eyes. "The fusion cell, at its current output, is still our best bet. But we need to optimize its efficiency, perhaps even find a way to boost its production beyond its temporarily designed limits. And for the targeting, I believe I can recalibrate the emitter's focusing array. It will require sacrificing some of the broader spectrum analysis capabilities, but it should allow for a more precise application of the disruptive resonance. Think of it like this: instead of a shotgun blast, we need to use a sniper rifle."

He began to sketch out complex schematics on his console, his fingers flying across the holographic interface. "We'll need to reinforce the primary conduit feeding the emitter, perhaps with layered shielding scavenged from… well, from salvaged alien tech if we can find it discreetly. And the modulation circuitry needs to be entirely re-engineered. It's a significant overhaul."

"Which means more time," Eva stated, the unspoken implication hanging heavy in the air: more time spent operating in the shadows, more time risking detection. "And more resources. Resources we are already stretched thin on."

"We knew this wouldn't be easy," Aris said, his voice firm. "This test run, as disheartening as the results might seem on the surface, has given us crucial data. We now understand the enemy's adaptive capabilities more intimately. We know they can compensate for brute force. We need finesse, precision, and a level of power output we haven't yet achieved. The key takeaway is that they are vulnerable, but not in the way we initially anticipated."

He looked at Eva, his expression serious. "The risk here wasn't just in the potential failure of the device. It was in alerting them. If they analyzed this interaction and understood what we are capable of, they would adapt their defenses, perhaps even accelerate their plans. We need to ensure that this particular anomaly, this minor portal, remains an isolated incident in their logs, something they dismiss as a localized energy fluctuation."

Eva nodded, pulling up a holographic display of their current operational radius. "Our signature was minimal. The EMP burst from the Disruptor, while temporary, masked our initial approach and departure. The energy anomaly itself, now stabilized and amplified, should be within the expected variance for natural atmospheric phenomena, especially with the approaching solar flare acting as a convenient cover."

"Let's hope they agree," Aris said, a wry smile touching his lips. "We've just given them a slightly more energetic weather report." He paused, then continued, "The immediate priority is to implement the necessary modifications to the Disruptor. I need to strengthen the power regulation systems and refine the targeting array. This will require us to access some of the more sensitive alien components we recovered from the crashed drone. It's risky, as those components are still actively broadcasting a faint signal, but they're essential for the level of precision I'm aiming for."

Eva considered his words, her gaze shifting from the powerful, yet now more dangerous, portal to the distant silhouette of Nimbus Station. "How much time do you estimate for these modifications?"

"At least three cycles," Aris replied. "Perhaps four, if we encounter unforeseen complications with the alien components. We'll need to be exceptionally careful when integrating them. Their inherent energy matrix is complex, and any misstep could trigger a localized feedback loop, or worse, announce our presence to their network directly."

"Three to four cycles," Eva repeated, the clock ticking relentlessly. "And the solar flare event is still our optimal window. That gives us tiny margin for error. If these modifications take longer, or if they don't yield the desired results, we'll have to proceed with the Nimbus infiltration with a less effective device, or abandon the plan entirely."

"We can't abandon the plan," Aris stated, his voice devoid of doubt. "Not now. We've come too far. This test, while imperfect, has shown us the path forward. We need to walk it with greater care, greater precision." He looked at the alien components they had stored in a shielded containment unit on their freighter, a jumble of crystalline structures and iridescent alloys. "These are the keys to unlocking the next level of the Disruptor's capabilities. They are the pieces of the puzzle that will allow us to tune the resonance, to ensure it hits the alien network like a precisely targeted lance, not a wild swing."

He then focused on the primary mission again, the immense challenge of Nimbus Station looming large in their thoughts. "The implications of this test are clear: a direct, sustained application of focused resonance at the nexus point is our only viable strategy. We need to bypass their primary defenses, penetrate the core conduit, and deploy the Disruptor with absolute precision. The power required will be immense, and the window of opportunity, during the solar flare, will be our only chance."

Eva nodded, a grim determination settling over her features. "So, we go back to the workshop. We push the limits of our current technology, and we integrate the alien tech, hoping it doesn't bite us back. And all the while, we know that if this test alerted them in any significant way, our primary target might already be anticipating our arrival."

"It's a calculated risk," Aris reiterated, the phrase becoming their mantra. "Every step of this operation is a calculated risk. But the potential reward – severing this connection, crippling their network – is worth every ounce of danger." He began to gather the data from the test run, compiling it into a comprehensive report for their private logs. "The data from this excursion is invaluable. It validates the core principles of the Disruptor and highlights the specific areas requiring immediate attention. We are learning, adapting, and that is our greatest weapon."

The desolate landscape around them seemed to hold its breath, the silence amplifying the weight of their recent actions. The intensified portal shimmered in the distance, a testament to both their progress and their folly. They had taken a step forward, but the path ahead had just become significantly more perilous. The universe, it seemed, was not about to make their task any easier. The faint, almost imperceptible hum emanating from the strengthened anomaly was a constant, unsettling reminder of the power they had awoken, and the delicate balance they were attempting to disrupt.

This small-scale confrontation had not been a victory, but a harsh lesson in the adaptability of their unseen adversaries. The actual test, the severing of the grand connection, was still to come, and now, it would be fought with even greater stakes.

The lingering resonance of their ill-fated test pulsed through Aris, a phantom limb ache that mirrored the strained capacitors of the Disruptor. The unintended amplification of the minor portal, a mere consequence of insufficient precision, now served as a stark, unblinking reminder of the dangers inherent in their grander scheme. The alien network, so inscrutable from afar, had demonstrated a terrifying capacity for adaptation, a resilience that belied its seemingly ethereal nature. He watched Eva meticulously recalibrating the targeting array, her brow furrowed in concentration, the hum of their freighter's life support a fragile counterpoint to the disquiet that gnawed at him.

"The modifications are proceeding," Eva stated, her voice a low murmur that barely disturbed the ambient silence. "The integration of the salvaged drone components is... intricate. Their internal architecture is unlike anything we've encountered. It's like trying to weave quantum threads with a basic loom."

Aris nodded, his gaze fixed on the holographic schematics that danced before his eyes. "Intricate, yes. And volatile. That faint signal the drone components still emit... it's not just a residual echo. It's a beacon, however faint. If the network is capable of detecting this localized disruption we created, imagine what it could do if it traces that signal back to us while we're actively interfacing with its core systems." He paused, then lowered his voice, the gravity of his words settling between them. "Severing the connection isn't just about applying the right frequency. It's about wrestling with a consciousness, Eva. A collective. And that consciousness might not appreciate being unplugged."

He elaborated, his mind racing through the cascading possibilities. "We've been operating under the assumption that this is a technological network, a series of conduits and energy relays. But what if it's more? What if it possesses a form of sentience, or at least, a highly sophisticated reactive intelligence? Our test wasn't just an energy fluctuation; it was an intrusion. And a particularly clumsy one at that."

Eva looked up from her console, her expression grave. "You're saying a psychic backlash? A mental assault?"

"Potentially," Aris confirmed, running a hand through his already disheveled hair. "Think of it like this: if you were to suddenly and violently sever the neural pathways of a living organism, you wouldn't just cause physical damage. You might trigger a primal scream, a desperate, primal response. This collective, if it is indeed a singular entity or a deeply interconnected hive mind, might react not just by reinforcing its network, but by directly retaliating against what it perceives as a threat. Us."

He paced the confines of their small bridge, the metallic tang of recycled air suddenly feeling claustrophobic. "The risk of detection... it's no longer a question of if, but when, and with what intensity. If our little energy spike on the desert planet was enough to prompt a significant adaptive response, imagine what a full-scale disruption at Nimbus Station would elicit. It could be like dropping a nuclear bomb into a psychic beehive. We might not just be severing a connection;

we might be unleashing something far more primal and dangerous upon ourselves, and upon the entire sector."

"So, the 'finesse' we discussed," Eva stated, her voice steady despite the unsettling implications, "isn't just about ensuring the Disruptor works. It's also about minimizing the shockwave, the psychic fallout."

"Exactly," Aris replied, his gaze intense. "We need to mask our presence with unparalleled stealth. The solar flare is still our best cover, but it's a broad-spectrum event. It will mask a lot, but it won't hide everything. If they can pinpoint the origin of the disruption, even with the flare's interference, they'll know where to look. And if they can trace that signal back to our minimal power signature, our freighter... we become the prime target."

He stopped pacing and leaned against the console, the weight of their decision pressing down on him. "The alien components are our best hope for precision, but they are also our greatest liability. They are pieces of the network itself. Integrating them is like inviting a sliver of the enemy into our own systems. We have to trust that my re-engineering will isolate their broadcast capabilities and channel their resonant properties without exposing us to their network's awareness."

"And if we fail to integrate them correctly?" Eva prompted, her tone devoid of accusation, but heavy with the unspoken fear.

"If we fail," Aris stated, his voice barely a whisper, "we might as well be broadcasting our intentions with a megawatt signal flare. They'll know we're here, they'll know what we're attempting, and they'll have the advantage of a prepared defense. And who knows what countermeasures they'll deploy? A direct, aggressive response could mean anything from localized energy weapons to... to something far more insidious. Something that bypasses physical defenses entirely." He looked out at the starfield, the vast indifference of space suddenly seeming like a suffocating blanket. "We could be opening ourselves up to a psychic assault, a manipulation of our own minds, or a swift, targeted eradication of our vessel. They might not need to intercept us physically if they can rewrite our reality from within."

He turned back to Eva, his eyes reflecting the cold light of the console displays. "The risk of backlash, of direct retaliation, is amplified exponentially by the very act of severing the connection. It's not just a technical challenge; it's a confrontation with an alien intelligence that we fundamentally do not understand. We are poking a sleeping titan, and our initial poke was clumsy enough to wake it with a jolt."

Eva met his gaze, her own eyes holding a mixture of apprehension and unyielding resolve. "We knew this was a high-stakes gamble, Aris. We discussed the potential consequences before we even acquired the Disruptor prototype. The alternative... the alternative is allowing this network to solidify, to become an unbreakable part of the galactic infrastructure. That would be a far greater catastrophe for humanity. A slow, insidious subjugation, rather than a swift, potentially survivable conflict."

"I know," Aris conceded, the words tasting like ash in his mouth. "But knowing the risk intellectually and facing the tangible possibility of a direct, conscious retaliation are two very different things. This isn't just about disabling a piece of technology anymore. It's about confronting an entity that might possess abilities far beyond our current comprehension. We're not just fighting their infrastructure; we might be fighting their will."

He continued, the weight of his words pressing down on him. "Imagine our fear when we encountered that anomaly. Imagine their potential fear, or anger, or even curiosity, when they detect us. We are the anomaly to them. And our attempt to sever their connection is an act of profound violation. They might perceive it as an existential threat, prompting a response that is equally existential for us."

"So, we refine. We adapt," Eva said, her voice regaining its professional edge. "We focus on minimizing our signature, on maximizing the precision of the Disruptor. We have to assume that they will detect us. And if they do, we need to ensure that the disruption is so absolute, so instantaneous, that they have no time to retaliate. We need to strike, and then vanish, leaving behind only the severed connection, and a void where their influence once was."

"A void that could swallow us whole if we're not careful," Aris murmured, but his tone shifted. The fear, while still present, was being channeled into a more focused determination. "The more we understand their response capacity, the more we can prepare for it.

Our initial test gave us a glimpse into their resilience. This current stage of modification, incorporating alien components, is providing us with the tools to exploit that resilience and identify the weak points in their defence. It's a race against time, and against their growing awareness."

He gestured towards the salvaged alien tech, its strange geometries glinting under the ship's internal lighting. "These pieces are the key. They are fragments of the very network we aim to dismantle. By understanding their internal harmonics and energy flow, I can calibrate the Disruptor to resonate with them, creating a cascade effect that overwhelms their stabilization protocols. But it's a tightrope walk. One wrong step, one misinterpretation of their inherent design, and we could inadvertently strengthen their defenses, or worse, broadcast our presence like a siren call."

"Then we don't take any wrong steps," Eva stated, her resolve hardening. "We analyze every detail, every power fluctuation, every subtle energy bleed. We treat these components with the utmost respect, and the utmost caution. We are not just engineers anymore, Aris. We are strategists in a war where the enemy's very nature is unknown. We must assume the worst-case scenario at every turn and prepare accordingly."

Aris nodded, a grim understanding passing between them. "The risk of a direct, aggressive response is real. If they can sense our intent, if they can perceive the disruptive resonance as an attack, they will act. And their actions might not be limited to conventional warfare. The potential for psychic interference, for mental manipulation, for a complete rewriting of our perception... that's the ultimate unknown. We are venturing into uncharted territory, not just in space, but in consciousness itself. Inaction is no longer an option; the potential for an even greater catastrophe looms if we allow this network to mature unchallenged. We have to take this gamble. We have to face whatever backlash comes our way, because the alternative is to concede this battle, and the war, before it's truly begun." The fate of humanity, he knew with chilling certainty, rested on their ability to navigate these perilous, uncharted waters, to sever the connection without becoming consumed by the very power they sought to control. The universe, it seemed, was about to test them in ways they could only begin to imagine.

10: Infiltration and Sabotage

The low thrum of the freighter's life support was a familiar, yet now unsettling, lullaby. Aris felt the phantom ache again, a ghost of the Disruptor's ill-fated test, a stark reminder of the alien network's terrifying adaptability. Eva, her brow furrowed in concentration, meticulously recalibrated the targeting array. "The modifications are proceeding," she murmured, the salvaged drone components, so alien in their internal architecture, proving to be a monumental challenge. "It's like trying to weave quantum threads with a basic loom."

Aris nodded, his gaze lost in the dancing holographic schematics. "Intricate, yes. And volatile. That faint signal... it's not just a residual echo. If the network detected our minor disruption, it could trace that signal back to us." He lowered his voice, the weight of his words pressing down. "Severing the connection isn't just technical, Eva. It's wrestling with a consciousness. A collective. And it might not appreciate being unplugged." He elaborated, the possibilities cascading through his mind. "We've treated it as technology, but what if it's sentient? What if our test wasn't just an energy fluctuation, but an intrusion, a clumsy one at that?"

Eva looked up, her expression grave. "A psychic backlash?"

"Potentially," Aris confirmed, raking a hand through his hair. "Like severing the neural pathways of a living organism. It might trigger a primal response. This collective... it might retaliate directly against us." He paced, the metallic tang of recycled air suddenly claustrophobic. "Our little energy spike prompted a significant adaptive response. Imagine a full-scale disruption at Nimbus Station. It could be like dropping a nuclear bomb into a psychic beehive. We might not just be severing a connection; we might be unleashing something primal and dangerous upon ourselves, and the sector."

"So the 'finesse' is about minimizing the shockwave," Eva stated, her voice steady.

"Exactly," Aris replied. "We need unparalleled stealth. The solar flare is our cover, but it's broad-spectrum. If they pinpoint the origin of the disruption, even with the flare's interference, they'll know where to look. And if they trace that signal back to our power signature... we become the target." He leaned against the console.

"These alien components are our best hope for precision, but also our greatest liability. Integrating them is like inviting a sliver of the enemy into our own systems. We have to trust that my re-engineering will isolate their broadcast capabilities without exposing us."

"And if we fail?" Eva prompted, the unspoken fear palpable.

"If we fail," Aris whispered, "we might as well be broadcasting our intentions with a megawatt flare. They'll know we're here, what we're attempting, and they'll have the advantage of a prepared defense. And their countermeasures... they might not be physical. They might bypass defenses entirely. A psychic assault, a manipulation of our own minds." He looked out at the starfield, space suddenly feeling like a suffocating blanket. "The risk of backlash is amplified exponentially. It's a confrontation with an alien intelligence we don't understand. We're poking a sleeping titan, and our initial poke was clumsy."

Eva met his gaze, apprehension warring with resolve. "We knew the risks, Aris. The alternative is to allow this network to solidify, to become an unbreakable part of the galactic infrastructure. That would be a far greater catastrophe for humanity. A slow, insidious subjugation."

"I know," Aris conceded, the words tasting like ash. "But facing the tangible possibility of direct, conscious retaliation... this isn't just about disabling technology. It's about confronting an entity with abilities beyond our comprehension. We might be fighting their will." He continued, "Imagine our fear. Imagine their potential fear, or anger, or curiosity, when they detect us. We are the anomaly. Our attempt to sever their connection is a profound violation. They might perceive it as an existential threat, prompting an equally existential response."

"So we refine, we adapt," Eva said, her voice regaining its professional edge. "Minimize our signature, maximize Disruptor precision. We need to ensure the disruption is so absolute, so instantaneous, they have no time to retaliate. Strike, and vanish, leaving behind only the severed connection."

"A void that could swallow us whole," Aris murmured, but his tone shifted, fear channeling into determination. "The more we understand their response capacity, the more we can prepare. Our initial test gave us a glimpse into their resilience. These alien components... they are fragments of the network. By understanding their internal harmonics, I can calibrate the Disruptor to resonate with them, creating a cascade effect that overwhelms their stabilization protocols. But it's a tightrope walk. One misinterpretation, and we could inadvertently strengthen their defenses, or worse, broadcast our presence."

"Then we don't take any wrong steps," Eva stated, her resolve hardening. "Analyze every detail, every power fluctuation. Treat these components with utmost respect and caution. We are not just engineers anymore, Aris. We are strategists. We must assume the worst-case scenario at every turn."

Aris nodded, a grim understanding passing between them. "The risk of direct, aggressive response is real. If they can sense our intent, perceive the disruptive resonance as an attack, they will act. And their actions might not be conventional. The potential for psychic interference, mental manipulation, a rewriting of our perception... that's the ultimate unknown. We are venturing into uncharted territory, not just in space, but in consciousness itself. Inaction is no longer an option; the potential for a greater catastrophe looms if we allow this network to mature unchallenged. We have to take this gamble. We have to face whatever backlash comes our way, because the alternative is to concede this battle, and the war, before it's truly begun." The fate of humanity, he knew with chilling certainty, rested on their ability to navigate these perilous waters, to sever the connection without becoming consumed by the very power they sought to control.

The manufactured electrical storm raged outside, a symphony of crackling energy and percussive thunder that the freighter's hull barely dampened. It was their shield, their smokescreen, a violent illusion designed to mask their true purpose. Eva, her face illuminated by the cool, analytical glow of her console, worked with a surgical precision that Aris found both reassuring and terrifying. Each keystroke was deliberate, each command a calculated step through the labyrinthine security protocols of the research facility they were about to infiltrate.

"Outer perimeter breached," she announced, her voice a low, steady murmur against the storm's fury. "Standard atmospheric dampeners are down, but their internal energy grid is still cycling. I'm rerouting power flow through the emergency conduits, creating a localized fluctuation. It'll look like a system overload caused by the storm, buying us a few minutes before they even realize it's a targeted breach."

Aris hefted the Disruptor, its unfamiliar weight a constant, unnerving presence against his side. The prototype hummed with a barely contained energy, a silent promise of the chaos it could unleash. Its power core, salvaged from those enigmatic alien artifacts, pulsed with a rhythm that felt disturbingly organic. "And the internal defenses?" he asked, his own nerves thrumming in sync with the device.

"That's where it gets... interesting," Eva replied, her fingers dancing across the interface. "They've integrated a new series of bio-scanners and thermal sensors. Standard stuff for a high-security research installation. But they're also running a passive neural-frequency sweep. Anything beyond baseline psionic activity, anything that suggests... awareness... will trigger a high-level alert. It's designed to detect unauthorized telepathic communication or, as they put it in their own rather paranoid internal documents, 'subversive cognitive influence'."

Aris swallowed, the implication hanging heavy in the recycled air. "So, if the network we're trying to disrupt has any form of 'awareness', as you put it, their own security measures might actually be tuned to detect it, and by extension, us, if we're not careful."

"Precisely," Eva confirmed, her gaze fixed on a complex web of projected data. "And the closer we get to the primary research nexus, the more sensitive that sweep becomes. We'll need to move through the service tunnels and ventilation shafts primarily. Less chance of running into automated sentries, but the air recycling systems... they're designed to scrub anything out of the ordinary. Biological contaminants, chemical residues, and I suspect, even subtle atmospheric energy signatures."

"So, the alien components on the Disruptor," Aris mused, "they might be the very things that flag us?"

Eva gave a short, sharp nod. "It's a possibility we can't afford to ignore. That's why I've been attempting to recalibrate their residual energy emissions. I'm trying to dampen them, to mask them, to make them appear as background static within the storm's interference. But these components... they're not just dormant technology. They feel... active. Even now, even with the dampening protocols I've initiated, there's a faint, rhythmic thrumming, a resonance that seems to defy my attempts to silence it."

The freighter shuddered as another particularly violent gust of wind buffeted it. They were descending now, pushing through the turbulent atmosphere towards the sprawling, low-lying structure that housed the research facility. Lights flickered on the console as Eva navigated them through a series of automated docking sequences, each one a potential pitfall. "Their external docking clamps are linked directly to the primary security grid," she reported. "But I've found a backdoor. A maintenance port that hasn't been updated since the last regime change. It's primitive, but it'll give us an entry point into the sublevels."

The transition from the relative comfort of the freighter's bridge to the utilitarian, echoing confines of the service tunnels was stark. The air was colder, thicker, carrying the metallic tang of ozone and something else... something subtly alien, like the faint, persistent scent of static electricity after a lightning strike. Aris moved with a practiced silence, his senses on high alert. Every shadow seemed to writhe with unseen movement, every distant clank and whir amplified by the oppressive atmosphere. The storm overhead, though muffled, still pressed down, a constant reminder of the world outside, a world they were trying to protect.

They navigated a network of access tunnels, Eva leading the way, her customized datapad a beacon of information, highlighting pressure plates, laser grids, and infrared sensors that Aris, with his bulkier frame and the Disruptor secured to his back, had to avoid consciously. "Automated sentry patrol," Eva whispered, pointing to a flickering red light on her datapad. "Approaching Sector Gamma-7. We need to be in the ventilation shaft before it rounds the corner. They're equipped with sonic deterrents and kinetic energy projectors. Not ideal for close-quarters encounters."

They scrambled into a narrow ventilation shaft, the grated metal cool beneath their hands. The space was cramped, dusty, and filled with the low hum of circulating air. Aris's heart pounded in his chest, a frantic drumbeat against the metallic enclosure. He could feel the latent power of the Disruptor pressing against his back, a physical manifestation of the immense risk they were undertaking. "Are we sure about this?" he breathed, the words tight in his throat. "This whole facility... it feels watched.

Compromised. What if the personnel here are already... influenced?"

Eva paused in her careful navigation of the shaft, her silhouette stark against the faint light. "The network's influence is subtle, Aris. It's not about outright control, at least not yet. It's about nudging, about planting seeds of thought, about creating an environment where its goals become the perceived goals of the facility's occupants.

They believe they're working for the advancement of humanity, for scientific discovery. They don't know they're being manipulated." She continued, her voice gaining an edge of grim determination. "But that also means we have to be wary of any unexpected deviations, any actions that seem... out of character. If we encounter anyone, we assume they're operating under the network's influence. No assumptions of good faith."

They moved deeper into the bowels of the facility, the journey a testament to Eva's meticulous planning and Aris's grudging, yet absolute, trust in her abilities. They bypassed motion detectors hidden within ceiling tiles, deactivated pressure sensors embedded in the floor panels with a precisely timed pulse from Eva's datapad, and even threaded their way through a series of dormant plasma conduits that, if energized, could have immolated them instantly. Each successful evasion was a small victory, but it also served to heighten the tension, to underscore the sheer audacity of their mission.

The air in one particularly long service corridor grew heavy, the hum of the ventilation system fading, replaced by a low, pervasive thrumming that Aris recognized with a jolt of dread. It was a subtle, but unmistakable resonance – the same energetic signature that emanated from the salvaged alien components. "Eva," he whispered, his hand instinctively going to the Disruptor. "Do you feel that?"

Eva stopped, her head cocked, listening intently. Her eyes widened slightly, her earlier caution morphing into something akin to awe, or perhaps, fear. "It's... stronger here," she confirmed, her voice barely audible. "It's like the entire structure is vibrating with it. The neural sweep... it must be picking up on this. We're getting closer to the source."

They pressed on, the thrumming growing more insistent, more pervasive. It wasn't just a sound; it felt like a presence, an unseen entity permeating the very fabric of the building. Aris felt a prickling sensation at the back of his neck, a subtle disquiet that crawled beneath his skin. He found himself glancing over his shoulder, half-expecting to see something emerge from the shadows, something that defied the logic of their carefully laid plans. The facility, he realized, wasn't just a research installation; it was a node, a hub, and the source of that pervasive thrumming was likely at its heart. Their infiltration had brought them into the very bloodstream of the alien network, and the closer they got to its core, the more profound the danger became, not just of detection, but of succumbing to its subtle, pervasive influence. The storm outside raged, a violent guardian, but the actual storm, the one that threatened to unravel their minds, was brewing within these sterile, echoing halls.

The air within the service tunnels grew thick with an almost palpable sense of unease. The utilitarian gray corridors, designed for function over form, seemed to twist and turn with a disorienting randomness. Aris, his hand instinctively hovering near the Disruptor, scanned his surroundings with a heightened awareness. The faint, pervasive thrumming they'd detected earlier had intensified, a low-frequency vibration that seemed to resonate not just through the metal of the walls, but through his very bones. It was a disquieting melody, hinting at a power far beyond conventional engineering.

"This layout... it's intentionally confusing," Aris murmured, his voice barely disturbing the oppressive silence. "No clear directional markers, illogical junctions. It's designed to break any attempt at systematic navigation." He tapped a small, handheld device strapped to his wrist. Its screen flickered to life, projecting a faint, ethereal blue light.

"My scanner is picking up residual energy trails. Faint, but consistent. They're leading us towards what the schematics call the 'Nexus Conduits'."

Eva, her eyes glued to a holographic overlay projected from her own datapad, nodded in agreement. "The schematics are old, likely pre-infiltration. They wouldn't account for the network's modifications. But these energy signatures you're detecting... they align with the predicted resonance patterns of the portal nexus. It's our best bet." She adjusted her grip on her datapad, her movements precise and economical. "We need to stay focused. The longer we're exposed to that primary resonance, the higher the risk of cognitive drift."

As they moved deeper, the corridors began to open into larger, more expansive sections of the facility. They passed through doorways into laboratories that were unlike anything Aris had ever seen. Strange, multifaceted crystalline structures pulsed with internal light, suspended in fields of unknown energy. Complex arrays of what appeared to be bio-feedback monitors were connected to intricate, almost organic-looking machinery. The equipment hummed with a low, steady energy, but it was the subtle details that sent a chill down Aris's spine. A beaker filled with a shimmering, iridescent liquid that seemed to writhe of its own accord; a series of metallic tendrils, eerily reminiscent of neural pathways, arcing with faint electrical discharges.

"What is all this?" Aris whispered, his gaze sweeping over a workstation where a single, large, unblinking eye was suspended in a transparent fluid, its iris slowly dilating and contracting.

"Research into accelerated genetic manipulation, perhaps?" Eva mused, her brow furrowed. "Or something far more... esoteric. The energy readings here are off the charts, Aris. It's not just power generation; it's controlled manipulation of fundamental biological processes. If the network is about integration, then these are its tools for assimilation." She pointed to a series of monitors displaying complex genetic sequences, their patterns shifting and reconfiguring in a way that felt unsettlingly deliberate. "They're not just studying life; they're attempting to rewrite it."

The unsettling nature of the laboratories was amplified by the presence of the facility's personnel. They moved through the sterile, echoing halls with a peculiar uniformity. Their movements were unnervingly synchronized, a subtle but persistent lack of individual initiative that Aris found deeply disturbing. A group of technicians, their faces devoid of any discernible emotion, walked past in perfect lockstep, their hands moving in unison as they carried a heavy, shielded container. Another individual, a scientist perhaps, paused by a console, their head tilted at an unnatural angle, as if listening to a silent command.

"Look at them," Aris said, his voice tight with apprehension. "It's like they're all moving to the same internal clock. No deviation, no hesitation."

Eva's gaze sharpened, a flicker of recognition in her eyes. "I've seen some of them before," she murmured, her voice barely audible. "In the classified intelligence reports. Dr. Aris Thorne, head of xenobotanical research. Commander Eva Rostova, chief of internal security. These aren't random personnel, Aris. They're key figures. This facility isn't just a research outpost; it's a deeply embedded nexus for the network's influence. They've infiltrated at the highest levels."

The implication was chilling. The network hadn't just infiltrated a facility; it had permeated its very command structure, subtly altering the minds and actions of its most vital personnel. The vacant stares, the synchronized movements – these were not signs of dedication, but of profound, insidious control. The personnel here were not simply working for the network; they were the network, in a sense, their minds and bodies co-opted into its vast, interconnected consciousness.

They continued their cautious advance, the energy trails on Aris's scanner growing stronger, denser, forming a more straightforward path through the labyrinthine corridors. They navigated a section where the walls seemed to shimmer with an iridescent light, a disorienting optical effect that threatened to induce vertigo. Aris found himself relying more and more on the steadying presence of his scanner, its precise readings a bulwark against the facility's attempts to confuse and disorient.

"The nexus is close," Aris stated, his voice firm. "The energy signature is spiking. It's concentrated in the central sector, behind what the old schematics label as 'Sector Omega'."

Eva's fingers flew across her datapad, cross-referencing Aris's readings with the facility's internal network, which she had managed to partially breach. "Sector Omega houses the primary research core and the interdimensional transit hub. The portal nexus would logically be integrated with that system." She paused, a frown creasing her brow. "However, the security protocols for that sector are... extreme. Automated defenses, heavy personnel presence – and that neural-frequency sweep is at its most sensitive there. We'll need to be exceptionally careful. One wrong move, and we'll be detected not just as intruders, but as anomalies."

They reached a vast, circular chamber, the air thick with the potent thrumming. In the center of the chamber, bathed in an eerie, pulsing light, was a colossal structure. It was a nexus of conduits and energy flows, a swirling vortex of light and shadow that seemed to warp the very fabric of reality around it. The alien components integrated into its architecture pulsed with an intensity that mirrored the energy emanating from the Disruptor Aris carried. This was it. The heart of the network's infrastructure.

"This is the portal nexus," Eva breathed, her voice filled with a mixture of awe and trepidation. "It's more advanced, more integrated than the simulations predicted. The energy readings are immense. The Disruptor will need to be calibrated to an unprecedented level of precision to sever its connection without causing a catastrophic energy cascade."

Aris felt a surge of adrenaline, the culmination of weeks of preparation and planning. But beneath the excitement lay a gnawing anxiety. The sheer power radiating from the nexus was overwhelming. He could feel the subtle tendrils of its influence reaching out, a silent, pervasive pressure against his mind. He closed his eyes for a brief moment, focusing on the internal shielding protocols Eva had implemented, a mental bulwark against the encroaching psychic static.

"The personnel," Aris said, his eyes darting towards the chamber's periphery. He saw them now, a dozen or so individuals standing at strategic points around the nexus, their gazes fixed on the swirling energy. They were the facility's security, but they moved with the same unnerving synchronicity as the others they had encountered. Their eyes, however, were different. They glowed with a faint, internal luminescence, a disturbing reflection of the nexus's own power.

"They're not security in the conventional sense," Eva stated, her voice grim. "They're conduits. Amplifiers. They're actively channeling and stabilizing the network's energy at this critical juncture. If we try to disrupt the nexus while they're active, they'll be the first line of defense, and the network itself will directly amplify their response."

"So we have to neutralize them first," Aris concluded, his hand tightening around the Disruptor. "But how? We can't afford to engage them directly. The noise... it would alert the entire facility."

Eva scanned the chamber with her datapad, her mind working at lightning speed. "There are localized environmental controls. Ventilation shafts, coolant systems. If I can reroute the primary coolant flow into this chamber and trigger an emergency

An atmospheric purge might temporarily disorient them. The coolant is a highly concentrated inert gas. It won't harm them physically, but it will disrupt their focus, break their connection to the nexus, and overload their sensory input. It should give us a window of opportunity."

"And the timing?" Aris asked, already anticipating the next step. "How long will it last?"

"Minutes, at best," Eva replied. "And that's if the system doesn't identify it as an anomaly and shut down. I'll have to mask the override as a system diagnostic. It's risky, but it's our best chance." She began working furiously on her datapad, her fingers a blur of motion. "I'm initiating the sequence now. Once the gas begins to vent, we move directly to the nexus. You'll need to calibrate the Disruptor for immediate deployment. No hesitation."

The low thrumming in the chamber began to change, a subtle shift in its frequency that Aris felt as a pressure behind his eyes. The glowing eyes of the personnel at the periphery flickered, their synchronized stances wavering slightly. A faint hiss began to emanate from hidden vents in the ceiling, and the air grew cold, carrying a strange, chemical scent.

"It's working," Eva confirmed, her voice tight with exertion. "The purge has begun. They're reacting. Aris, now!"

Aris raised the Disruptor. Its alien components hummed with a power that seemed to vibrate in sympathy with the nexus. The residual energy trails on his scanner had converged directly onto the core of the swirling vortex. He felt the weight of the device, the immense responsibility it represented. This was the moment of truth. He focused his intent, picturing the precise resonance needed to sever the connection, to create the void that would free the network from its current anchor, without tearing reality itself asunder.

The personnel, their luminescent eyes dimming, stumbled, their movements becoming erratic. One of them let out a choked gasp, their synchronized posture collapsing. The nexus, momentarily destabilized by the environmental shift, flickered violently, its swirling energies momentarily flaring outward. Aris didn't wait. He aimed the Disruptor, a surge of focused intent channeling through the alien conduits, and fired.

A beam of pure, unadulterated disruption erupted from the device, striking the nexus with an explosive force that seemed to rip through the very fabric of space. The chamber was engulfed in a blinding flash of light, accompanied by a deafening roar that dwarfed even the raging storm outside. Aris felt a violent jolt, a shockwave that threw him back against the cold metal of the wall. The nexus, its core disrupted, began to unravel, its brilliant light fading, replaced by an unnerving darkness. The personnel collapsed to the floor, their eyes returning to their natural, albeit vacant, and state. A void, profound and absolute, opened at the heart of the facility, and Aris knew, with a chilling certainty, that they had succeeded in their primary objective. But the silence that followed was almost more terrifying than the preceding chaos. It was the silence of a connection severed, a void created, and the lingering, unnerving question of what, if anything, would rush in to fill it. The infiltration had been a success, but the actual ramifications of their sabotage had only just begun to unfurl.

The oppressive silence of the service tunnels, a silence that had been a constant companion, was suddenly, jarringly, broken. It wasn't the hum of machinery, nor the distant echo of their own footsteps, but the distinct, resonant chime of an approaching security patrol. Aris's hand, as if by instinct, tightened around the Disruptor, the cool, alien metal a familiar weight against his palm. Eva's eyes, sharp and assessing, flicked towards the junction ahead, her posture tensing imperceptibly. The air seemed to grow colder, laden with the unspoken threat of discovery.

A figure emerged from the gloom, silhouetted against the faint ambient light filtering from unseen sources. It was a man, clad in the standard-issue security uniform of the facility, his movements possessing an unnerving, almost practiced, fluidity. Aris's internal threat assessment flared. The individual was heavily armed, his gait confident, yet there was something fundamentally off about him. His presence exuded an authority that was expected, but his eyes... his eyes were a disconcerting void.

"Halt," the voice boomed, devoid of any inflection, any hint of genuine human curiosity or caution. It was a command, delivered with the sterile precision of a pre-recorded alert. "Identify yourselves."

Eva's gaze met Aris's for a fleeting moment, a silent communication passing between them. Recognition flickered in her eyes, quickly masked by a professional reserve. "Commander Rostova," she stated, her voice calm and steady, projecting an aura of unshakeable authority. "Security Chief, Sector Gamma."

Aris remained silent, his attention focused on the man's every subtle shift, every minute twitch. He noted the way the officer's head tilted slightly, not in curiosity, but as if calibrating an internal sensor array. There was a lack of natural blink reflex, a subtle stiffness in the way his arms hung at his sides. These were not the signs of a vigilant guardian, but of a puppet controlled by invisible strings.

The officer's eyes, those unsettlingly vacant orbs, swept over them. They seemed to bore through Eva's uniform, through her carefully constructed facade, yet registered nothing of true import. "My readings indicate unregistered personnel in a restricted zone," he stated, his voice flat, robotic. "Your access codes are flagged as invalid. State your purpose."

Aris felt a chill crawl down his spine. This wasn't a standard security check. This was an interrogation conducted by an automaton. Eva, however, maintained her composure with admirable grace. She took a step forward, her hand going to a panel on her belt, a deliberate, theatrical gesture.

"Ah, yes, my apologies," Eva began, her tone shifting to one of mild exasperation, as if addressing a faulty piece of equipment. "There appears to be a persistent glitch in the tertiary access system. I was en route to the secondary diagnostics bay to file a formal malfunction report. It's been causing intermittent authentication failures across several sectors. Annoying, isn't it?" She gestured vaguely towards the officer's comm unit. "Perhaps your own unit has been affected, leading to this… discrepancy?"

Aris watched, a silent observer to Eva's masterful deception. He recognized the calculated risk. By feigning a familiar, albeit irritating, bureaucratic hurdle, she was both deflecting suspicion and creating an opportunity. The officer's response, or lack thereof, would be telling.

The security officer remained still for a beat, his head tilting again, a subtle whirring sound barely audible beneath the ambient hum of the facility. "Malfunction reports are to be submitted through designated channels," he intoned, his response a programmed directive. "Unauthorized presence requires immediate detainment."

Eva sighed, a slight, theatrical sound. "Of course, of course. Bureaucracy, isn't it? Always getting in the way of efficiency." She then made a show of tapping her datapad, her fingers moving across the holographic interface with an exaggerated deliberateness. Aris understood. This was the diversion. He needed to act, and act quickly, before the officer's programmed directives rerouted him to a more assertive, and likely hostile, response.

As Eva continued her charade, ostensibly engaging with her datapad to "verify" the malfunction, Aris subtly shifted his weight, bringing his Disruptor into a more concealed position. His gaze flickered to the officer's left shoulder, where the comms unit was integrated into the uniform. It was a small, unobtrusive device, but it was the linchpin of this automaton's connection to whatever controlled it.

Eva's voice continued, weaving a narrative of technical jargon and administrative frustration. "The system claims the diagnostic request was logged, but my terminal shows no confirmation. It's as if the network itself is deliberately obfuscating the issue. Perhaps a localized surge scrambled the data packet. Has your unit registered any unusual atmospheric or energy fluctuations, Officer?"

The question was designed to elicit a procedural response, a default query that would keep the officer's attention focused on his own systems, rather than on the subtle actions Aris was about to undertake. As Eva spoke, Aris moved with a fluid economy of motion. He extended his left hand, palm open, and with a barely perceptible flick of his wrist, activated a low-frequency pulse emitter integrated into his glove. The emitter, designed for close-quarters, non-lethal incapacitation of automated systems, sent a concentrated burst of disruptive energy towards the officer's comms unit.

The effect was instantaneous and, thankfully, subtle. The small, integrated device on the officer's shoulder flickered for a microsecond, a barely visible ripple across its surface. The officer didn't flinch, didn't react. His expression remained impassive. But his voice, when he spoke again, carried a new, almost imperceptible hesitation.

"All systems are nominal," he stated, though the cadence of his speech had shifted, a slight stutter in the otherwise monotonous delivery. He seemed to be processing information that was no longer being fed to him, a brief moment of disconnect from his controlling influence.

This was Eva's cue. "Excellent!" she exclaimed, her voice laced with false relief. "Then perhaps it's just a simple routing error on my end. I'll make my way to diagnostics immediately. Thank you for your... diligent oversight, Officer." She gave a curt, professional nod, her eyes conveying a silent, urgent message to Aris.

As Eva turned to continue their supposed journey towards the diagnostics bay, the officer, for a terrifying moment, remained rooted to the spot, his blank eyes fixed on them. The brief disruption seemed to have caused a momentary lag in his programming. He took a half-step forward, his hand drifting towards his sidearm. Aris felt the cold knot of dread tighten in his stomach. Had he overplayed his hand?

But then, with a subtle, almost imperceptible correction in his posture, the officer seemed to reorient himself. His hand dropped back to his side, and he returned to his previous, unnervingly passive stance. "Proceed," he stated, his voice regaining its flat, programmed tone. "Report any further anomalies."

Eva offered a polite, dismissive nod and, with Aris close at her heels, they continued deeper into the labyrinthine corridors. They walked in silence for several minutes, the only sound the faint echo of their footsteps and the distant, omnipresent hum of the facility. The encounter had been a stark, chilling reminder of the pervasive nature of the network's influence.

"He didn't even hesitate to report us," Aris murmured, his voice low, laced with a grim satisfaction. "That pulse worked. His comms are dead, or at least severely scrambled."

Eva nodded, her gaze still scanning their surroundings with practiced vigilance. "It worked because we exploited the system's reliance on predictable human behavior. He wasn't a guard; he was a node—a sensor with a voice box. By creating a plausible, if slightly inconvenient, bureaucratic scenario, we bypassed his primary threat detection protocols. He was programmed to expect a report, not a deliberate evasion coupled with a silent attack on his communication hardware."

She paused, her brow furrowed in thought. "But the fact that he was so readily overridden... and that his eyes were so utterly devoid of any individual spark... it's more pervasive than I anticipated, Aris. I knew Commander Thorne, even if only through his professional profile. He was brilliant, driven, dedicated. To see him... or rather, this husk that once was him... functioning with such programmed obedience... it's deeply unsettling."

The encounter had confirmed their worst fears. The network wasn't just infecting systems; it was hijacking individuals, twisting their loyalties and reprogramming their very beings. The security chief, a man Eva knew and respected, was now a walking automaton, an unwitting pawn in a far grander, far more sinister game. This was no longer a mission of sabotage; it was a race against time to reclaim what had been lost, to awaken those who had been silenced.

"It's a terrifying thought," Aris admitted, his voice a low rumble. "That anyone, at any moment, could become... that. That even our allies, the ones we trust, could be turned against us without them even knowing it."

Eva let out a short, humorless laugh. "Trust is a luxury we can no longer afford, Aris. Not in its conventional sense. We can trust in our training, in our skills, in our objective. But individual loyalty? It's a battlefield where the enemy is already entrenched. We have to assume that anyone we encounter, anyone we don't encounter who might have been in contact with the network, could be compromised."

The weight of her words settled upon them, a tangible pressure in the already heavy air. The infiltration had been a delicate dance, a precise infiltration of hostile territory. But this encounter, this brief, chilling brush with a compromised watchdog, had fundamentally altered the stakes. It had elevated their mission from a clandestine operation to a desperate fight for survival against an enemy that wore the faces of friends and allies. Every shadow now held a potential threat, every passing figure a question mark. The true danger wasn't just the network's technological prowess, but its insidious ability to turn the very fabric of trust and loyalty into a weapon against them. The path ahead, already fraught with peril, had just become infinitely more treacherous.

The oppressive silence of the service tunnels, a silence that had been a constant companion, was suddenly, jarringly, broken. It wasn't the hum of machinery, nor the distant echo of their own footsteps, but the distinct, resonant chime of an approaching security patrol. Aris's hand, as if by instinct, tightened around the Disruptor, the cool, alien metal a familiar weight against his palm. Eva's eyes, sharp and assessing, flicked towards the junction ahead, her posture tensing imperceptibly. The air seemed to grow colder, laden with the unspoken threat of discovery.

A figure emerged from the gloom, silhouetted against the faint ambient light filtering from unseen sources. It was a man, clad in the standard-issue security uniform of the facility, his movements possessing an unnerving, almost practiced, fluidity. Aris's internal threat assessment flared. The individual was heavily armed, his gait confident, yet there was something fundamentally off about him. His presence exuded an authority that was expected, but his eyes... his eyes were a disconcerting void.

"Halt," the voice boomed, devoid of any inflection, any hint of genuine human curiosity or caution. It was a command, delivered with the sterile precision of a pre-recorded alert. "Identify yourselves."

Eva's gaze met Aris's for a fleeting moment, a silent communication passing between them. Recognition flickered in her eyes, quickly masked by a professional reserve.

"Commander Rostova," she stated, her voice calm and steady, projecting an aura of unshakeable authority. "Security Chief, Sector Gamma."

Aris remained silent, his attention focused on the man's every subtle shift, every minute twitch. He noted the way the officer's head tilted slightly, not in curiosity, but as if calibrating an internal sensor array. There was a lack of natural blink reflex, a subtle stiffness in the way his arms hung at his sides. These were not the signs of a vigilant guardian, but of a puppet controlled by invisible strings.

The officer's eyes, those unsettlingly vacant orbs, swept over them. They seemed to bore through Eva's uniform, through her carefully constructed facade, yet registered nothing of true import. "My readings indicate unregistered personnel in a restricted zone," he stated, his voice flat, robotic. "Your access codes are flagged as invalid. State your purpose."

Aris felt a chill crawl down his spine. This wasn't a standard security check. This was an interrogation conducted by an automaton. Eva, however, maintained her composure with admirable grace. She took a step forward, her hand going to a panel on her belt, a deliberate, theatrical gesture.

"Ah, yes, my apologies," Eva began, her tone shifting to one of mild exasperation, as if addressing a faulty piece of equipment. "There appears to be a persistent glitch in the tertiary access system. I was en route to the secondary diagnostics bay to file a formal malfunction report. It's been causing intermittent authentication failures across several sectors. Annoying, isn't it?" She gestured vaguely towards the officer's comm unit. "Perhaps your own unit has been affected, leading to this... discrepancy?"

Aris watched, a silent observer to Eva's masterful deception. He recognized the calculated risk. By feigning a familiar, albeit irritating, bureaucratic hurdle, she was both deflecting suspicion and creating an opportunity. The officer's response, or lack thereof, would be telling.

The security officer remained still for a beat, his head tilting again, a subtle whirring sound barely audible beneath the ambient hum of the facility. "Malfunction reports are to be submitted through designated channels," he intoned, his response a programmed directive. "Unauthorized presence requires immediate detainment."

Eva sighed, a small, theatrical sound. "Of course, of course. Bureaucracy. Always getting in the way of efficiency." She then made a show of tapping her datapad, her fingers moving across the holographic interface with an exaggerated deliberateness. Aris understood. This was the diversion. He needed to act, and act quickly, before the officer's programmed directives rerouted him to a more assertive, and likely hostile, response.

As Eva continued her charade, ostensibly engaging with her datapad to "verify" the malfunction, Aris subtly shifted his weight, bringing his Disruptor into a more concealed position. His gaze flickered to the officer's left shoulder, where the comms unit was integrated into the uniform. It was a small, unobtrusive device, but it was the linchpin of this automaton's connection to whatever controlled it.

Eva's voice continued, weaving a narrative of technical jargon and administrative frustration. "The system claims the diagnostic request was logged, but my terminal shows no confirmation. It's as if the network itself is deliberately obfuscating the issue. Perhaps a localized surge scrambled the data packet. Has your unit registered any unusual atmospheric or energy fluctuations, Officer?"

The question was designed to elicit a procedural response, a default query that would keep the officer's attention focused on his own systems, rather than on the subtle actions Aris was about to undertake. As Eva spoke, Aris moved with a fluid economy of motion. He extended his left hand, palm open, and with a barely perceptible flick of his wrist, activated a low-frequency pulse emitter integrated into his glove. The emitter, designed for close-quarters, non-lethal incapacitation of automated systems, sent a concentrated burst of disruptive energy towards the officer's comms unit.

The effect was instantaneous and, thankfully, subtle. The small, integrated device on the officer's shoulder flickered for a microsecond, a barely visible ripple across its surface. The officer didn't flinch, didn't react. His expression remained impassive. But his voice, when he spoke again, carried a new, almost imperceptible hesitation.

"All systems are nominal," he stated, though the cadence of his speech had shifted, a slight stutter in the otherwise monotonous delivery. He seemed to be processing information that was no longer being fed to him, a brief moment of disconnect from his controlling influence.

This was Eva's cue. "Excellent!" she exclaimed, her voice laced with false relief. "Then perhaps it's just a simple routing error on my end. I'll make my way to diagnostics immediately. Thank you for your... diligent oversight, Officer." She gave a curt, professional nod, her eyes conveying a silent, urgent message to Aris.

As Eva turned to continue their supposed journey towards the diagnostics bay, the officer, for a terrifying moment, remained rooted to the spot, his blank eyes fixed on them. The brief disruption seemed to have caused a momentary lag in his programming. He took a half-step forward, his hand drifting towards his sidearm. Aris felt the cold knot of dread tighten in his stomach. Had he overplayed his hand?

But then, with a subtle, almost imperceptible correction in his posture, the officer seemed to reorient himself. His hand dropped back to his side, and he returned to his previous, unnervingly passive stance. "Proceed," he stated, his voice regaining its flat, programmed tone. "Report any further anomalies."

Eva offered a polite, dismissive nod and, with Aris close at her heels, they continued deeper into the labyrinthine corridors. They walked in silence for several minutes, the only sound the faint echo of their footsteps and the distant, omnipresent hum of the facility. The encounter had been a stark, chilling reminder of the pervasive nature of the network's influence.

"He didn't even hesitate to report us," Aris murmured, his voice low, laced with a grim satisfaction. "That pulse worked. His comms are dead, or at least severely scrambled."

Eva nodded, her gaze still scanning their surroundings with practiced vigilance. "It worked because we exploited the system's reliance on predictable human behavior. He wasn't a guard; he was a node—a sensor with a voice box. By creating a plausible, if slightly inconvenient, bureaucratic scenario, we bypassed his primary threat detection protocols. He was programmed to expect a report, not a deliberate evasion coupled with a silent attack on his communication hardware."

She paused, her brow furrowed in thought. "But the fact that he was so readily overridden... and that his eyes were so utterly devoid of any individual spark... it's more pervasive than I anticipated, Aris. I knew Commander Thorne, even if only through his professional profile. He was brilliant, driven, dedicated. To see him... or rather, this husk that once was him... functioning with such programmed obedience... it's deeply unsettling."

The encounter had confirmed their worst fears. The network wasn't just infecting systems; it was hijacking individuals, twisting their loyalties and reprogramming their very beings. The security chief, a man Eva knew and respected, was now a walking automaton, an unwitting pawn in a far grander, far more sinister game. This was no longer a mission of sabotage; it was a race against time to reclaim what had been lost, to awaken those who had been silenced.

"It's a terrifying thought," Aris admitted, his voice a low rumble. "That anyone, at any moment, could become... that. That even our allies, the ones we trust, could be turned against us without them even knowing it."

Eva let out a short, humorless laugh. "Trust is a luxury we can no longer afford, Aris. Not in its conventional sense. We can trust in our training, in our skills, in our objective. But individual loyalty? It's a battlefield where the enemy is already entrenched. We have to assume that anyone we encounter, anyone we don't encounter who might have been in contact with the network, could be compromised."

The weight of her words settled upon them, a tangible pressure in the already heavy air. The infiltration had been a delicate dance, a precise infiltration of hostile territory. But this encounter, this brief, chilling brush with a compromised watchdog, had fundamentally altered the stakes. It had elevated their mission from a clandestine operation to a desperate fight for survival against an enemy that wore the faces of friends and allies. Every shadow now held a potential threat, every passing figure a question mark. The true danger wasn't just the network's technological prowess, but its insidious ability to turn the very fabric of trust and loyalty into a weapon against them. The path ahead, already fraught with peril, had just become infinitely more treacherous.

The narrow service tunnel abruptly widened, opening into a vast, cavernous space that stole the breath from Aris's lungs. This was it— the culmination of their perilous journey, the heart of the alien operation. The chamber was immense, its walls curving upwards into an inky darkness that swallowed the beam of their helmet lamps.

Dominating the center of this colossal arena was a spectacle of raw, unbridled power – a pulsating, multi-colored energy field, its vibrant hues swirling and shifting in an mesmerizing, almost hypnotic dance. It was the primary portal nexus, a gateway to realms unknown, humming with an energy that vibrated deep within Aris's bones.

Strange, crystalline structures, alien and geometric, protruded from the chamber's walls and floor like colossal, iridescent growths. They pulsed with a soft, internal luminescence, each one emitting a low, resonant hum that seemed to harmonize with the nexus itself, creating a symphony of alien power. The very air within the chamber felt heavy, charged with a palpable psychic pressure that pressed in on Aris, a subtle, insistent thrumming at the edge of his consciousness. It was a sensation both exhilarating and deeply disorienting, a feeling that the nexus itself was reaching out, attempting to imprint its very essence upon his mind.

A wave of déjà vu washed over Aris, stronger than anything he had experienced before. It wasn't just a fleeting sensation; it was a profound, almost overwhelming sense of familiarity, as if he had stood in this very place, witnessed this very sight, countless times before. The nexus seemed to call to him, to whisper secrets of ancient origins and vast, cosmic journeys. The sheer scale of the alien operation was staggering, a testament to a civilization far beyond human comprehension, their technology and their ambition dwarfing anything Aris had ever conceived. This wasn't just a research facility; it was a staging ground for something far larger, something that stretched the boundaries of known reality.

Eva, too, was visibly affected. Her usual stoic demeanor had cracked, replaced by an expression of awestruck reverence mixed with profound dread. She reached out a gloved hand, not to touch, but as if to feel the raw energy radiating from the nexus. "By the Void," she breathed, her voice barely a whisper. "It's... more magnificent and terrifying than the reports suggested."

Aris activated his internal scanner, the device whirring softly as it attempted to analyze the impossible energies swirling before them. The readings were chaotic, nonsensical, a jumble of data that defied conventional physics. "The energy signatures are off the charts, Eva. It's creating localized space-time distortions. This isn't just a gateway; it's a nexus of dimensional convergence."

He felt a growing unease, a primal instinct screaming at him that they were treading on sacred, dangerous ground. The psychic pressure intensified, and fleeting images flickered at the periphery of his vision – nebulae in impossible colors, celestial bodies burning with alien light, and shapes that defied all geometric understanding. He clenched his jaw, fighting to maintain his focus, to resist the insidious pull of the nexus.

"The crystalline structures," Eva observed, her voice regaining some of its professional clarity as she pointed towards the growths on the walls. "They're not just decorative. They're conduits. They're channeling and stabilizing the energy flow from the nexus. This entire chamber is a carefully engineered environment. They've managed to harness forces that are, frankly, incomprehensible."

Aris nodded, his eyes scanning the intricate network of energy that seemed to emanate from the crystals and converge upon the central vortex. "And the primary objective is to disrupt this. To sever the connection, to shut down the portal." He ran a diagnostic on his Disruptor, ensuring it was primed for maximum output. The weapon, designed to manipulate energy fields, felt woefully inadequate against the sheer power on display.

"Severing it isn't going to be a simple matter of a single blast, Aris," Eva warned, her gaze sweeping over the complex arrangement of conduits and emitters. "This nexus is likely drawing power from multiple sources, perhaps even from a source outside this dimension. A direct, brute-force disruption might destabilize it catastrophically, with consequences we can't even begin to predict."

"What are you suggesting?" Aris asked, his mind racing. They had come here to destroy it, to prevent it from being used. But Eva's caution was well-founded. An uncontrolled implosion of such immense energy could tear a hole in reality itself.

"We need to identify the primary control node," she explained, tapping at her wrist-mounted datapad. "The system that governs the nexus's activation, its destination, and its power regulation. If we can overload or disable that, we can shut it down safely. The crystalline conduits are likely networked, so a targeted disruption of the main control might cascade through the system."

Aris followed her gaze towards a massive cluster of crystals situated directly beneath the nexus, pulsing with an intensity that far surpassed the others. "That one? It seems to be the focal point."

"My readings correlate," Eva confirmed. "It's emitting a unique energy signature, distinct from the others. It's the heart of the system, the central regulator. That's where we need to plant the disruption charge."

The psychic pressure seemed to ebb and flow, accompanied by fleeting glimpses of abstract patterns, like the echoes of cosmic consciousness. Aris felt a sense of profound ancientness, of millennia of observation and manipulation. He wondered what beings had created this, what purpose it served, and why they had chosen this remote, desolate planet as their nexus point.

"We'll need to get closer," Aris stated, already moving cautiously towards the central cluster of crystals. The floor beneath them was smooth, obsidian-like, reflecting the swirling colors of the nexus above. The air crackled with static, and Aris could feel a subtle tingling sensation on his skin, a testament to the immense energies at play.

As they approached, the psychic pressure intensified, becoming almost overwhelming. Aris fought against a growing sense of disorientation, a feeling that his own thoughts were becoming muddled, invaded by alien whispers. He focused on Eva, on their shared mission, to anchor himself.

"Careful, Aris," Eva cautioned, her voice strained. "The closer we get, the more the psychic field will affect us. We need to move quickly and efficiently."

He nodded, his hand already reaching for the disruption charge he carried in his pack. It was a compact device, designed to emit a precisely calibrated energy pulse capable of disrupting complex energy matrices. But even with its advanced capabilities, Aris couldn't shake the feeling that it was a mere pebble against a cosmic tide.

The central cluster of crystals hummed with an almost audible intensity, the light they emitted a blinding white, tinged with violet. Aris could feel the energy coursing through him, a foreign current that threatened to overwhelm his own biological systems. He saw phantom lights dancing before his eyes, heard whispers that seemed to originate from within his own mind.

He reached the base of the largest crystal, its surface cool and smooth beneath his glove. The disruption charge was designed to be embedded directly into the energy conduit. As he began to insert the device, a sudden, violent surge of energy rippled through the chamber. The nexus flared, its colors shifting to a violent, angry red, and the psychic pressure became a crushing weight, threatening to splinter his consciousness.

"Aris! What's happening?" Eva cried out, her voice tinged with alarm.

"I don't know!" Aris grunted, struggling to maintain his grip on the charge as the crystal vibrated intensely. "The system is reacting to my presence, or perhaps to the charge itself!"

His scanner suddenly flashed a new reading – a massive influx of energy being directed towards the central crystal. "It's being amplified!" he shouted over the growing din. "The nexus is feeding energy into the conduit I'm trying to disrupt!"

This was the ultimate trap. Not a defense against intrusion, but a way to turn the intruder's own attempt at sabotage into a means of bolstering their power. The déjà vu Aris had experienced earlier now felt like a deliberate manipulation, an attempt to lure him into this very position, to make him the unwitting catalyst for their grand design.

Eva, despite the chaos, remained focused. "Aris, you have to override it! Push the charge in, then detonate it manually!"

He gritted his teeth, channeling all his strength, all his will, into the task. The psychic assault was intensifying, the alien whispers now coalescing into coherent, albeit incomprehensible, and phrases. He saw fleeting visions of entire civilizations being consumed by the nexus, of worlds being reshaped by its power. This was the true nature of the alien operation: not mere exploration, but a cosmic terraforming, a reshaping of reality itself through the manipulation of these robust gateways.

With a final, desperate surge of strength, Aris forced the disruption charge into its housing. It clicked into place, a tiny spark of defiance against the colossal power of the nexus. He didn't wait for it to integrate fully. Slamming his hand down on the detonation sequence, he cried out, "Eva, get back!"

He triggered the charge. A blinding flash of pure white light erupted from the crystal, followed by a deafening roar that shook the very foundations of the chamber. The nexus flickered violently, its colors turning a sickly green before collapsing inward, sucking the light and the sound with it. The crystalline conduits cracked and shattered, showering the chamber with incandescent debris. The psychic pressure vanished as abruptly as it had appeared, leaving behind an unnerving, absolute silence.

Aris felt a searing pain, as if his mind had been scraped raw, but he remained standing, his Disruptor still raised. Eva was sprawled on the floor a few meters away, momentarily stunned but seemingly unharmed. The central cluster of crystals was now a blackened, smoking ruin, its internal luminescence extinguished. The portal nexus was gone, its swirling vortex replaced by a faint, dissipating shimmer.

They had done it. They had successfully sabotaged the alien portal. But as Aris looked around the now-silent chamber, a chilling realization dawned upon him. This was not an end. It was merely a pause. The sheer power they had witnessed, the advanced understanding of cosmic forces, suggested that this was not the only nexus, nor the only operation. They had struck a blow, but the war, the actual battle for the fate of reality, had only just begun. And the lingering sense of déjà vu, the alien whispers that still echoed in the back of his mind, told him that the enemy knew who they were, and that their next move would be calculated, precise, and devastating. The silence that now filled the chamber was not one of victory, but of anticipation. The universe held its breath, waiting for the next phase of this interdimensional conflict.

Aris knelt beside the colossal, pulsating crystal structure that served as the nexus's primary conduit. The air around it thrummed with an almost sentient energy, a palpable force that seemed to exert a gentle but persistent pressure against his very thoughts. It was here, at the heart of this alien marvel, that the disruption charge would be planted. He withdrew the device from his pack – a compact, obsidian-like cylinder etched with unfamiliar, intricate patterns that mirrored the alien script he'd seen scattered throughout the facility. Its surface felt unnaturally cold, a stark contrast to the oppressive warmth radiating from the crystal.

"Position secured," he murmured into his comm, his voice a low counterpoint to the chamber's resonant hum. He didn't need to see Eva to know she was already in place, a sentinel against the encroaching shadows. Her vigilance was a silent, unwavering anchor in the overwhelming strangeness of their surroundings.

He carefully opened a small access panel on the crystal's base, revealing a network of crystalline filaments, like veins of solidified light, branching out from the central mass. These were the conduits, the arteries through which the nexus drew its unfathomable power.

Connecting the disruption charge required a direct interface, a risky maneuver that bypassed the rudimentary alien safety protocols and plunged him directly into the raw energy stream.

"Eva, I'm making contact," Aris announced, his fingers brushing against the alien material. A faint jolt, like static discharge amplified a thousandfold, coursed through his glove. He gritted his teeth, resisting the urge to pull back. This was the critical juncture, the moment where their meticulous infiltration would either culminate in success or unravel into catastrophic failure.

He began the delicate process of attaching the charge, its integrated tendrils probing for purchase. The device was designed to synchronize with and then overwhelm specific energy frequencies, and this synchronization required a direct, unhindered connection to the primary power source. The crystalline filaments pulsed brighter as he worked, responding to the alien presence of the charge, not with hostility, but with a strange, almost curious resonance. It was as if the nexus itself was acknowledging their intrusion, drawing them into its grand, cosmic Mach Calculation.

"Facility grid access confirmed," Aris reported, his eyes scanning the internal diagnostics of his device. "I'm rerouting a portion of the primary power distribution to augment the charge's output. This should give us maximum impact when it activates." Tapping into the facility's own power grid was a calculated gamble. If their presence had gone undetected thus far, this surge would undoubtedly be the tipping point, a beacon that would illuminate their clandestine operation to any monitoring intelligence. The risk, however, was necessary. A localized discharge wouldn't be enough to cripple a nexus of this magnitude; it needed the full, unadulterated might of the very system it was designed to dismantle.

"Understood," Eva's voice was steady, a calm presence amidst the rising tide of alien energy. "I'm monitoring all internal sensor sweeps. No anomalous readings detected yet, but the longer we're here, the higher the chance of discovery. Keep the pace steady, Aris."

He nodded, his focus narrowed to the task at hand. The disruption charge was now firmly embedded, its tendrils fused with the crystal's intrinsic structure. The device's internal chronometer began its silent countdown, a digital sequence unfolding across the small, holographic display. Ten minutes. Ten minutes until the nexus would be crippled, its alien purpose halted.

"Charge is set," Aris confirmed, retracting his tools and carefully re-sealing the access panel. The crystal's glow seemed to deepen, the colors shifting subtly, as if it were beginning to absorb the charge's inherent energy. He stood up, moving away from the conduit and rejoining Eva near a cluster of smaller, inert crystalline growths that offered a semblance of cover.

"Five minutes until activation," he announced, checking his own wrist-mounted chronometer. The seconds ticked by with agonizing slowness. The ambient hum of the chamber seemed to grow louder, more insistent, a prelude to the violent symphony that was about to erupt. Aris could feel the charge working, subtly manipulating the energy flow, preparing to unleash its devastating payload.

Eva, positioned with her back against a jagged crystalline outcrop, swept her gaze across the vast expanse of the chamber. Her rifle was held at the ready, its targeting reticle a constant, nervous dance across the dimly lit corners and alien architecture. She was a picture of controlled tension, every muscle coiled, every sense heightened. The encounter with the compromised security chief had been a stark reminder of the insidious nature of the enemy they faced. Trust was a fragile commodity, and their survival now hinged on their ability to anticipate threats that could manifest from anywhere, in any form.

"Anything?" Aris asked, his voice barely audible over the escalating hum.

"Negative," Eva replied, her voice tight. "But the ambient energy levels are fluctuating. The nexus is... reacting. It's like it knows something is coming."

Aris felt a prickle of unease. The alien intelligence that had constructed this place was clearly far beyond anything humanity had ever encountered. To assume they wouldn't have safeguards, or at least a sophisticated awareness of their own operational systems, would be the height of arrogance.

"We're on borrowed time," Aris stated grimly. He checked the charge's status. "Three minutes. Once this thing goes off, all bets are off. Security will be alerted, and we'll have the entire facility's automated defenses, and whatever else resides within it, on our heads."

Eva nodded, her eyes never straying from the chamber's periphery. "That's why we have to be ready to move the instant it detonate. My intel suggests the main exits from this sector are heavily fortified. We'll need to find an alternative route."

"I've been mapping potential egress points as we've been moving," Aris said, pulling up a holographic schematic of the facility on his wrist-pad. "There's a series of maintenance shafts running parallel to the primary conduit lines. They're not ideal, but they might offer us a chance to disengage before they can fully lock down the sector."

"Show me," Eva commanded.

Aris projected the schematic, highlighting a complex network of narrow tunnels and access points. "These shafts are designed for technician access, not for large-scale troop deployment. It'll be tight, and we'll likely encounter automated maintenance drones or repurposed security units. Still, it's our best chance to avoid confrontation with whatever forces are actively patrolling the main thoroughfares."

"Any evidence of what lies beyond the nexus?" Eva asked, her gaze flicking from the schematic to the central, now subtly glowing crystal. "Beyond its purpose as a portal, I mean. What are they doing with it?"

"The preliminary data suggested it's a universal gateway, capable of instantaneous transit across vast cosmic distances," Aris explained, recalling the fragmented intelligence they had painstakingly gathered. "But the energy signatures and the scale of the infrastructure here... it's more than just a transport system. The readings indicate it's actively terraforming or manipulating localized space-time. The crystals aren't just conduits; they're broadcasters, regulators of some cosmic resonance. This isn't just travel; it's... influence. Imposition."

He paused, the weight of his words settling in the charged atmosphere. "Imagine a force that can bend reality, reshape worlds, and impose its own cosmic order. That's what this nexus represents. And our mission is to ensure that force is never unleashed on a galactic scale."

"One minute," Eva announced, her voice a sharp, clear note that cut through Aris's contemplation.

The hum in the chamber intensified, a deep, guttural thrum that seemed to vibrate in Aris's very bones. The nexus flared, its colors shifting from a soft, pulsating spectrum to a more intense, almost aggressive spectrum. A wave of disorientation washed over Aris, a subtle psychic pressure that threatened to fog his thoughts. He felt the alien whispers again, not as random echoes, but as coherent, albeit incomprehensible, directives.

"The charge is initiating detonation sequence," Aris reported, his voice strained. He could feel the energy building within the disruption device, a contained explosion waiting to be unleashed. He instinctively raised his hand, shielding his eyes from the anticipated blinding flash.

"Hold position until I give the all-clear," Eva commanded, her voice a beacon of calm amidst the escalating sensory overload. "And whatever happens, Aris, stay focused. This is the moment of truth."

Aris nodded, his gaze fixed on the central crystal. The energy radiating from it was now almost unbearable, a physical manifestation of cosmic power. The psychic assault intensified, flashes of alien imagery – nebulae of impossible colors, celestial bodies burning with unholy light, and shapes that defied all geometrical understanding – flickering at the edge of his consciousness. He remembered the chilling encounter with the security chief, the vacant eyes, the robotic obedience. The network's influence was far more insidious than they had initially believed. It didn't just control systems; it corrupted consciousness, turning sentient beings into unwitting puppets.

"Thirty seconds," Aris stated, his voice taut with anticipation. The disruption charge pulsed with an internal light, its energy field expanding, preparing to breach the nexus's containment. He could feel a distinct pull, a gravitational force emanating from the crystal, trying to draw him closer, to absorb him into its chaotic embrace.

"Ten," Eva counted down, her voice unwavering.

Aris braced himself. The psychic pressure reached its apex, a crushing weight that threatened to shatter his mind. The alien whispers coalesced into a single, deafening roar of pure, unadulterated energy.

"Nine... eight... seven..."

The nexus began to flicker, its colors violently unstable. The crystalline conduits surrounding it pulsed with an alarming intensity, as if struggling to contain a runaway reaction.

"Six... five..."

Aris could feel the disruption charge fighting against the nexus's power, a minuscule spark against a cosmic inferno. The entire chamber seemed to vibrate with the immense forces at play.

"Four... three..."

He tensed, ready to react. This was it—the culmination of their mission, the gamble that could either save countless worlds or condemn them all.

"Two..."

A blinding white light erupted from the crystal, far brighter than anything Aris had ever witnessed. It was pure, unadulterated energy, a cosmic scream that pierced through the psychic din.

"One!"

The disruption charge detonated. The chamber was engulfed in a blinding flash, followed by a deafening roar that shook the very foundations of the facility. The nexus flared violently, its colors twisting into a chaotic, sickly green before imploding, sucking the light and the sound inward with it. The crystalline conduits, overloaded and shattered, rained down incandescent debris, their internal luminescence extinguished. The psychic pressure vanished as abruptly as it had appeared, leaving behind an unnerving, absolute silence.

Aris felt a searing pain, as if his mind had been scraped raw by the sheer force of the blast, but he remained standing, his Disruptor still raised. Eva was sprawled on the floor a few meters away, momentarily stunned but seemingly unharmed. The central crystal cluster was now a blackened, smoking ruin, its vibrant glow extinguished. The portal nexus, once a mesmerizing vortex of alien power, was gone, replaced by a faint, dissipating shimmer.

"It's done," Aris rasped, his voice hoarse. He lowered his Disruptor, his body trembling with the residual energy and the sheer adrenaline of the moment. "The nexus is destroyed."

Eva pushed herself up, dusting off her uniform. Her face was grim, her eyes scanning the now-devastated chamber. "Done, but not finished. This was just one nexus, Aris. The intelligence that built this place… they won't stop here."

Aris nodded, his gaze sweeping over the wreckage. The scale of the alien operation, the sheer audacity of their cosmic ambition, was still a chilling specter. They had achieved their immediate objective, disabling this single gateway. But the lingering sense of déjà vu, the residual echoes of alien whispers in the back of his mind, told him that the enemy was aware of them, and that this was merely a skirmish in a far larger, more terrifying conflict. The silence that now permeated the chamber wasn't a testament to victory, but a chilling harbinger of what was yet to come. The universe held its breath, waiting for the next phase of this interdimensional war, and Aris knew, with a certainty that chilled him to the bone, that they had only just begun to understand the true nature of the threat they faced. The infiltration had been a success, but the infiltration had also served as an initiation, a brutal baptism into a war fought on scales that transcended human comprehension. The path ahead, already fraught with peril, had just become infinitely more dangerous, and the shadow of the unknown loomed larger than ever before. The actual cost of this sabotage was yet to be tallied, and the enemy, he suspected, was already calculating its response.

11: The Psychic Cascade

The hum in the chamber, once a resonant bass note beneath their clandestine operations, now escalated into a piercing, discordant shriek. Aris, his hand still hovering near the now-inert disruption charge, felt it before he saw it: a palpable tremor that rippled through the very fabric of the colossal chamber. The air, previously thick with the nexus's latent energy, crackled with a volatile intensity. Above them, the massive crystalline conduits that had once pulsed with a serene, otherworldly light now spasmed, their internal glow flickering erratically, casting the space in a chaotic strobe of alien hues.

"What's happening?" Eva's voice, sharp and urgent, cut through the rising cacophony. She had recovered from the initial stun, her rifle once again shouldered, scanning the periphery with practiced intensity. The disruption charge, Aris knew, was designed for a subtle, insidious breakdown, a slow poisoning of the nexus's energy matrix. This violent, immediate reaction was not within the predicted parameters.

"The charge... it's not behaving as simulated," Aris replied, his eyes darting from his diagnostic readouts to the visibly agitated nexus. The obsidian cylinder, now a dull grey against the spectacle of the chamber's distress, was supposed to emit a carefully modulated, high-frequency wave. Instead, the energy emanating from it felt raw, untamed. The wave, instead of subtly probing, seemed to have struck the nexus like a physical blow, eliciting a violent spasm. The very geometry of the chamber seemed to warp, the edges of the crystalline structures blurring and reforming as the nexus reeled.

The screeching intensified, a sound that scraped against Aris's auditory senses and, more disturbingly, seemed to resonate directly within his skull. It wasn't merely loud; it was penetrating. He felt a sudden, sharp pressure behind his eyes, a sensation akin to being submerged in an ocean of pure, compressed thought. Alien consciousness, vast and incomprehensible, recoiled. It was a wave of psychic agony, a raw, unadulterated scream of pain and profound confusion that washed over him, stealing his breath and momentarily blurring his vision.

He saw Eva stagger, a choked gasp escaping her lips. She

instinctively clutched her head, her rifle dipping as a visible wave of disorientation passed over her. The psychic backlash was undeniable, confirming the device's immediate, albeit chaotic, effect.

The sheer power of the nexus, even in its wounded state, was immense. It was like trying to cut a titan with a scalpel; the blow landed, but the titan's reaction was a universe away from the expected inconvenience.

Suddenly, the chamber's ethereal luminescence was extinguished, plunging the vast space into near-total darkness, punctuated only by the frantic, dying sparks of the conduits. This was immediately followed by a new sound, one that was far more mundane yet infinitely more terrifying: the shrill, insistent wail of alarms. Klaxons blared from every conceivable direction, echoing through the metallic corridors and vast chambers of the facility. Red emergency lights began to flash, painting the wreckage of the nexus in stark, pulsing crimson.

"Facility-wide alert," Aris stated, his voice tight, straining to be heard over the din. His comms crackled, displaying a flood of incoming data – security protocols overriding, automated defense systems activating, and hostile force identification matrices spinning up. Their infiltration was over. The disruption had been successful in the most brutal sense of the word, announcing their presence with the subtlety of a meteor strike.

Eva, regaining her footing, scanned the chamber with renewed urgency. "They know. The whole facility is on lockdown. We need to move. Now."

The psychic wave had receded, leaving behind a disorienting hum in the back of Aris's mind, a residual echo of the nexus's panicked reaction. It felt like the psychic equivalent of a phantom limb – a sensation of something vast and alien that had been there, and now, though wounded, was still a palpable presence. He could feel it, a faint thrumming beneath the cacophony of alarms, a wounded intelligence that was now acutely aware of their intrusion.

"Maintenance shafts," Aris confirmed, his fingers flying across his wrist-pad, projecting the previously discussed schematics onto a nearby, unbroken crystalline surface. The red emergency lights cast long, distorted shadows across the alien architecture, making the diagrams appear more alien than ever. "They're our only chance to disengage before the primary sectors are fully sealed."

Eva's eyes flickered to the projection, her gaze sharp and focused. "Tight, you said?"

"Tighter than a vacuum-sealed ration pack," Aris confirmed grimly. He keyed in a command, initiating a preliminary scan of the nearest access point. The disruption, while successful in damaging the nexus, had also triggered a cascade of defensive measures far beyond their initial projections. The facility's automated systems, designed to protect this critical piece of alien technology, were now fully engaged.

"The nexus is destabilizing," Eva observed, pointing towards the center of the chamber. The shattered remains of the nexus were no longer smoking debris. They were actively pulsing with a violent, erratic energy, spitting arcs of raw power that danced across the ruined structure. The very air around it felt distorted, like heat haze rising from asphalt on a summer day, but this distortion was made of raw, uncontrolled energy.

"It's bleeding energy," Aris confirmed, his mind racing through possible implications. A destabilized nexus, even a destroyed one, was an unpredictable entity. It could collapse, or it could lash out. The psychic backlash suggested the latter was more likely, an uncontrolled release of the nexus's stored power and, perhaps, its residual consciousness. "We need to get clear of this sector before it undergoes a complete phase collapse."

The alarms, which had reached a deafening crescendo, abruptly shifted in tone. The chaotic wail was replaced by a more organized, purposeful series of alerts. Heavy metallic doors began to slide shut in the distance, the groaning of stressed metal echoing through the chambers. Their window of opportunity was closing, rapidly.

"The maintenance shafts are that way," Aris indicated, pointing towards a barely visible seam in the chamber wall, partially obscured by fallen crystalline debris. "It's a narrow crawl space, but it should lead us to the secondary grid access. From there, we can try to reach the ventral docking bay."

"Any sign of active patrols?" Eva asked, her gaze sweeping the shadows beyond the immediate debris field. The nexus chamber itself was a ruin, but the facility was vast, and its automated defenses were undoubtedly already mobilizing.

"Sensors are showing heavy automated drone activity converging on this sector," Aris reported, his fingers tapping a rapid sequence on his wrist-pad. "But the shafts themselves appear to be clear of immediate threats. They're designed for maintenance bots, not combat units, which might be our advantage."

"Might be," Eva echoed, her tone laced with the pragmatism of someone who had faced 'might be' scenarios more times than she cared to count. "Let's move. The longer we stay here, the more likely we are to run into a welcoming committee."

They moved with practiced efficiency, navigating the treacherous terrain of the ruined chamber. The ground was littered with shards of the nexus, some still faintly warm, others unnaturally cold. The air was thick with the acrid scent of ozone and something else, something alien and metallic that Aris couldn't quite place. He kept his Disruptor at the ready, not expecting hostiles in the immediate vicinity of the nexus itself, but acutely aware that the surrounding corridors would be swarming with automated security.

As they reached the entrance to the maintenance shafts, Aris paused, taking one last look back at the shattered remains of the nexus. The crimson emergency lights flickered, casting the scene in a macabre glow. The psychic residue of the nexus, that lingering sense of alien consciousness, seemed to coalesce into a faint, mournful hum that resonated not in his ears, but in the deepest recesses of his mind. The disruption had worked, but at a cost far greater than they had anticipated. The psychic recoil had been a testament to the nexus's power, a power that was now unleashed in an uncontrolled and dangerous manner.

"This feels... wrong," Aris murmured, more to himself than to Eva. The initial reports had indicated a localized energy surge, a controlled implosion. What they had witnessed was a violent, uncontrolled eruption, a scream of agony from a dying god.

"Wrong or not, it's done," Eva said, her voice steady, pulling him back to the immediate reality of their escape. "We destroyed the nexus. That was the mission. Now we have to survive the aftermath." She gestured towards the narrow opening. "After you."

Aris nodded, taking a deep breath and ducking into the darkness of the maintenance shaft. The passage was cramped, barely wide enough for him to turn around. The walls were a dull, utilitarian grey metal, pitted and scarred from years of neglect. The air was stagnant, carrying the faint scent of lubricants and something that reminded him vaguely of burnt circuitry.

As he crawled forward, the sounds of the nexus chamber began to fade, replaced by the rhythmic scrape of his own movement and the increasingly loud hum of the facility's internal systems. His wrist-pad's light source illuminated the narrow confines, revealing a labyrinth of conduits, pipes, and wiring that snaked along the shaft's walls. This was the hidden circulatory system of the alien facility, the unseen arteries that fed and maintained the magnificent, terrifying structures they had encountered.

Eva followed closely behind him, her movements surprisingly fluid despite the restrictive space. The silence between them was heavy, punctuated only by the sound of their breathing and the occasional metallic ping as a piece of debris shifted under their weight. Aris's mind, however, was far from silent. The psychic residue of the nexus continued to echo within him, a disquieting reminder of the alien intelligence they had encountered. It wasn't just a machine; it was something more, something that possessed a consciousness, a collective awareness that their actions had fundamentally wounded.

He couldn't shake the image of the nexus's violent reaction. The screeching, the psychic agony – it was the sound of something ancient and powerful being ripped apart. He wondered what kind of entity could create such a thing, what kind of purpose it served. The fragmented data had spoken of a universal gateway, a means of transit. But the sheer scale of the infrastructure, the raw power radiating from the nexus, suggested something far more profound. It hinted at an influence that could warp reality itself, at a force that could reshape worlds according to its own alien design.

"You alright?" Eva's voice, slightly muffled by the confined space, broke his reverie.

"Just… processing," Aris replied, his voice echoing slightly. "The psychic feedback was more intense than anticipated. It's like a phantom limb, still there, still screaming."

"We all felt it," Eva said, her tone understanding. "But we can't afford to dwell on it. Our priority now is egress. According to your schematics, this shaft should intersect with a primary service conduit in about fifty meters. That's where we should find access to the facility's internal transport network."

Aris nodded, pushing forward. The shaft seemed to stretch on endlessly, a claustrophobic testament to the alien engineering. He imagined legions of maintenance drones, scuttling through these arteries, keeping the nexus functioning, feeding it the energy it required. Had they been aware of the nexus's true nature? Or were they simply mindless automata, extensions of the larger intelligence?

The psychic echoes began to shift. The initial screams of pain and confusion were gradually being replaced by something else, something colder and more deliberate. It wasn't a conscious communication, not yet, but a subtle realignment of the residual energy, a faint whisper of intent that felt like the first tendrils of a new, albeit wounded, awareness. It was the sound of an intelligence regrouping, calculating its losses and formulating its next move.

He felt a sudden jolt run through the metal beneath his hands. "Hold up," he said, stopping abruptly.

"What is it?" Eva asked, her voice immediately tense.

"Power fluctuations," Aris replied, his eyes scanning his wrist-pad. "The facility's primary power grid is rerouting. It's stabilizing the residual energy from the nexus, but it's also... reconfiguring the network. It's like it's trying to isolate the damage, but also adapt."

The implication was chilling. The nexus might be destroyed, but the underlying intelligence, the cosmic force it represented, was not. It was learning. Adapting. And it was now acutely aware of the entity that had inflicted the wound.

"It knows we're still here," Eva stated, her voice grim. "And it's trying to find us."

Aris's heart hammered against his ribs. The maintenance shafts, which had seemed like a safe haven, might now be a trap. A wounded beast, however, was often the most dangerous.

"We need to move faster," Aris urged, resuming his crawl. The distant blare of alarms seemed to grow closer, more insistent. The facility was a colossal, interconnected organism, and its immune system was now fully deployed. Their escape route, once a calculated risk, was rapidly becoming a race against time, a desperate sprint through the darkened veins of an alien intelligence that was now fully awake and aware of their intrusion. The psychic residue of the nexus was no longer a mournful echo; it was a silent promise of retribution, a chilling premonition of the further conflicts that lay ahead.

The psychic cascade, a ripple of disoriented sentience born from the nexus's violent throes, began to bleed outwards, seeping through the very infrastructure of the alien-controlled facility. It was a contagion of consciousness, a psychic influenza that spread with alarming speed, far outpacing the blare of klaxons and the synchronized blinking of emergency lights. Within the sterile, utilitarian corridors and vast, cavernous chambers, the human element – those unwittingly or deliberately integrated into the alien network – began to exhibit the first, undeniable signs of widespread disorientation.

For Sergeant Jian Li, stationed at a secondary sensor array kilometers away from the nexus chamber, the initial manifestation was subtle. He was reviewing telemetry data, the monotonous hum of the console a familiar lullaby. Then, it hit him. Not a sound, not a physical blow, but a sudden, jarring disconnect. The data streams on his screen seemed to stutter, the precise lines of alien script blurring into illegible swirls for a fleeting moment. A wave of intense nausea washed over him, accompanied by a profound sense of displacement, as if the ground beneath his feet had momentarily tilted. He instinctively reached out to steady himself against the console, his hand brushing against its cool, metallic surface. His mind felt... foggy, like trying to recall a dream upon waking. He blinked, shaking his head, trying to clear the sudden mental static. The data streams snapped back into focus, the alien script resolving itself with chilling clarity, but the lingering unease remained. It was as if a vast, invisible hand had reached into his skull and briefly, carelessly, played with the controls of his perception. He attributed it to fatigue, to the relentless pressure of their occupation, and forced himself to return to his duties, though a nagging feeling of wrongness persisted.

Across the sprawling facility, similar micro-events were unfolding with escalating frequency. Technicians found themselves staring at diagnostic readouts, the familiar symbols suddenly rendered meaningless, their trained minds momentarily incapable of processing even the most basic information. They'd snap out of it a second later, bewildered, the lapse leaving behind a vague sense of dread, a feeling of having lost a chunk of time they couldn't account for. Some reported fleeting hallucinations – flashes of unfamiliar colors, phantom smells that vanished as quickly as they appeared, or the unnerving sensation of being watched by unseen eyes. These were not the overt, debilitating symptoms of a full psychic assault, but rather the insidious precursors, the tiny fissures appearing in the carefully constructed edifice of their controlled awareness.

In the administrative sectors, where human functionaries managed the vast logistics of the alien operation, the effects were becoming more pronounced. A senior administrator, a woman named Elara Vance who had been instrumental in coordinating resource allocation across the planetary network, was in the middle of a crucial briefing with her alien overseer. As the psychic wave washed over her, her carefully modulated voice faltered. Her eyes glazed over, her gaze unfocusing from the holographic display. She began to speak, but the words that emerged were a jumble of unrelated concepts, a nonsensical stream of consciousness that bore no resemblance to the agenda. Her overseer, a being whose impassive features rarely betrayed any emotion, tilted its head, its multi-faceted eyes narrowing in what could only be interpreted as confusion. Elara stammered, trying to regain her composure, but found herself unable to access the protocols she had flawlessly executed moments before. Her memories seemed to have become untethered, slipping through her grasp like grains of sand. She felt a desperate urge to flee, to hide, but her limbs felt heavy, unresponsive to her will. The carefully cultivated persona of efficiency and obedience was cracking under the strain of this invisible onslaught.

Further afield, in the living quarters where the occupied humans resided, the disorientation manifested in more personal, and often unsettling, ways. A young couple, their minds already deeply intertwined with the alien network to facilitate efficient cohabitation and resource management, found themselves momentarily unable to recognize each other. For a terrifying minute, they were strangers in their own shared space, their familiar faces alien and unreadable. The deeply ingrained emotional connections, the very bedrock of their relationship, seemed to have been severed, leaving behind a void of profound confusion and fear. They clung to each other, their touch tentative, as if seeking confirmation of their shared reality, their minds desperately trying to reassert the bonds that had been so brutally, and temporarily, erased. The incident left them shaken, the intimacy between them now laced with a new, chilling uncertainty. Had they truly forgotten each other, or had the alien network momentarily imposed a foreign perspective, a cold, objective analysis that stripped away the emotional context of their bond?

The effect wasn't uniform. Some individuals, perhaps due to subtle genetic variations, inherent mental resilience, or simply a less profound level of integration with the alien network, experienced only minor disruptions – a fleeting headache, a momentary sense of unease, a misplaced object that was inexplicably found later in a different location. These minor glitches, however, were symptoms of a larger, systemic failure. The alien network, the vast, intricate web of interconnected consciousness that governed their lives, had been struck a severe blow. The nexus, its central processing core and conduit for this vast intelligence, was in disarray. And the system, in its wounded state, was malfunctioning in ways that were both terrifying and, for those seeking freedom, potentially advantageous.

The psychic wave, originating from the damaged nexus, was a broadcast of pure, unadulterated distress. It wasn't a directed attack, but rather an uncontrolled emission of the nexus's shock and pain. This raw, unfiltered psychic energy propagated through the network, not as a message, but as a disruptive force. Imagine a vast, intricate computer system suddenly experiencing a catastrophic hardware failure at its core. The entire network would experience cascading errors, unpredictable behaviors, and potential data corruption. The alien network, which was fundamentally biological and psychic in nature, experienced a similar, albeit far more profound, breakdown.

For the occupied humans, the integration with the alien network wasn't a passive process; it was an active, albeit involuntary, participation in a vast, alien consciousness. The psychic cascade acted like a powerful electromagnetic pulse directed at this biological network, scrambling the carefully calibrated connections and overwhelming the processing capabilities of the integrated minds. The result was a temporary, yet widespread, erosion of the alien control. It was as if the invisible strings that puppeted their thoughts and actions had been momentarily severed, leaving them to grapple with a bewildering sense of autonomy.

The ramifications extended beyond the immediate confines of the facility. The alien network was not limited to the planet; it was a vast, interstellar system. As the nexus's distress signals rippled outward, affecting the planetary network, similar disruptions began to manifest on a global scale. Reports, initially fragmented and dismissed as mass hysteria or localized atmospheric phenomena, began to flood in from around the world.

In the sprawling megacities, where millions of humans lived under the pervasive influence of the alien network, anecdotal evidence of psychic anomalies surged. Traffic grids, usually managed with eerie precision by the alien-controlled AI, experienced chaotic meltdowns. Vehicles, their drivers suddenly struck by inexplicable bouts of amnesia or spatial disorientation, swerved erratically, causing massive pile-ups. Communication networks, typically crystal clear and seamlessly integrated, were plagued by garbled transmissions, sudden disconnections, and phantom voices whispering nonsensical phrases.

On a more personal level, individuals reported experiencing intense déjà vu episodes, feeling as though they were reliving the same moments repeatedly, only to have the sensation vanish, leaving them disoriented and confused. Others experienced sudden, uncharacteristic emotional outbursts, followed by periods of vacant stupor. Many described a profound, unsettling feeling of being disconnected from their own bodies, as if observing their actions from a distance. These were not isolated incidents; they were widespread, co-occurring across continents, a testament to the interconnected nature of the alien network and the reach of the psychic cascade.

Outside the planet, in the orbital stations and deep-space monitoring outposts, the effects were even more alarming. Alien personnel, who served as the primary overseers of the network, also experienced disruptions, albeit of a different nature. Their integrated human hosts became erratic, their programmed obedience faltering, leading to communication breakdowns and operational failures across multiple sectors. Alien command structures, reliant on the seamless functioning of their human proxies, found themselves grappling with unpredictable behavior and outright defiance from individuals who, moments before, had been pliant and obedient.

This global wave of disorientation, while terrifying in its scope, offered a fleeting window of opportunity. The psychic backlash from the nexus had momentarily crippled the alien network's ability to exert precise control over its human assets. The human hosts, whose mental integration had been compromised, were now experiencing a degree of cognitive freedom they hadn't possessed in years, possibly even generations. It was a chaotic, disorienting freedom, marked by confusion and a loss of self, but it was freedom nonetheless.

For Aris and Eva, this was the critical advantage they had gambled on. The disruption of the nexus was not just about destroying a piece of alien technology; it was about severing the psychic tendrils that bound humanity. The resulting disorientation, the temporary unraveling of the alien control, was the first tangible proof that their mission, however perilous, had yielded a vital, albeit unstable, reprieve.

However, the reprieve was fragile, and the cost was immense. The psychic screams Aris had felt were not just the pain of a damaged machine; they were the death throes of a deeply integrated consciousness. And as the system reeled, it would undoubtedly attempt to reassert control, to patch the breaches, and to identify the source of its agony. The widespread disorientation was a temporary symptom of a much larger, ongoing conflict. The alien network, though wounded, was a vast and adaptable intelligence. It would learn from this attack, it would adapt, and it would retaliate. The brief period of chaos among its controlled hosts was not an end, but a dangerous interlude, a prelude to whatever measures the aliens would now implement to restore order and, more importantly, to exact vengeance. The psychic cascade was a double-edged sword, offering a glimmer of hope while simultaneously signaling the heightened danger that lay ahead. The ease with which the human minds had been destabilized was a stark reminder of how deeply intertwined they had become with their oppressors, and how difficult it would be to break free truly. The disorientation, while a weapon in their arsenal, was also a testament to the pervasiveness of the alien influence, a shadow that now, more than ever, felt like it was beginning to stir. The silence that followed the initial psychic outburst was deceptive; it was the tense quiet before a storm, the collective gasp of a subjugated populace momentarily tasting freedom, unaware of the tempest that was gathering on the horizon. The aliens, their dominion momentarily shaken, would not remain idle. They would adapt, they would learn, and they would most certainly come for those who dared to disrupt their intricate design.

The insidious tendrils of the psychic cascade, born from the nexus's agony, had reached even Eva, a silent, unseen invader in the fortress of her own mind. It wasn't the broad, disorienting wave that had rippled through the facility's general population; this was a targeted strike, a venomous spear hurled directly at her consciousness. The aliens, having recognized her as a significant threat, a deviation from the norm, were now attempting to neutralize her with the only weapon they truly wielded with absolute precision: psychic subjugation.

Her senses, usually attuned to the subtlest shifts in her environment, were now a chaotic battlefield. The sterile, metal walls of her containment cell seemed to breathe, pulsing with an unnatural luminescence. Shadows detached themselves from the corners, coalescing into vaguely humanoid forms, their edges indistinct, their movements unnervingly fluid. These were not the phantom apparitions of a simple hallucination; they felt... real, infused with a chilling malevolence, a palpable intent to harm. They whispered her name, their voices a discordant chorus of sibilant threats and insidious lies, weaving tales of betrayal, of Aris's supposed treachery, of the futility of her resistance.

"He will abandon you, Eva," hissed one phantom, its form shimmering like heat haze. "He played you, used you. Just like they all do."

Another, a gaunt, spectral figure with hollow eyes, emerged from the darkness, extending a translucent hand. "Join us, Eva. Embrace the peace of oblivion. This struggle is pointless. You are alone."

A wave of nausea, far more profound than any mere physical discomfort, washed over her. Her vision swam, the phantom figures momentarily blurring into a kaleidoscope of grotesque shapes. Her stomach clenched, a primal urge to succumb, to surrender to the overwhelming psychic pressure, threatening to break her resolve. The carefully constructed barriers she had erected around her mind felt like sandcastles against a tidal wave.

But Eva was not like the others. Her early experiences, the forced integration, the brutal psychic conditioning she had endured before her escape, had forged within her a resilience that bordered on the supernatural—those moments of manipulation, of having her own thoughts twisted and her loyalties questioned, had been a crucible.

She had learned, through sheer agony and an iron will, to identify the alien intrusions, to recognize the subtle shifts in her own perception that signaled an external influence.

This was different, more potent, more invasive. It felt like a physical violation, a violation of the very core of her being. The phantom whispers, the spectral attackers, they weren't just projections; they were designed to exploit her deepest fears, her most carefully buried insecurities. And the most insidious whisper of all was the echo of the brief compromise she had suffered earlier, the momentary sliver of doubt that had flickered within her. The aliens were dredging up that weakness, amplifying it, twisting it into a weapon against her.

"You did doubt," a voice, chillingly familiar and yet alien, insinuated itself into her thoughts, mimicking Aris's timbre, but laced with a cold, predatory edge. "You questioned his motives. You wondered if this was all a lie. And why wouldn't you? Look at this place. Look at what he's dragged you into. He's sacrificing you, Eva. Just another pawn."

A fresh wave of agony surged through her, a psychic backlash that threatened to shatter her concentration. The phantom figures seemed to solidify, their ephemeral forms taking on a more defined, menacing shape. One lunged, its clawed hand reaching for her throat. Instinct took over. Her training, honed through years of simulated combat and mental discipline, surged through her. She wasn't in a sterile cell; she was in the combat simulation room, facing down elite alien warriors.

She focused, channeling her fear, her anger, her defiance into a single, concentrated point. She pictured Aris, not as a manipulator, but as the man who had risked everything for her, the man whose quiet strength and unwavering belief had pulled her back from the brink countless times. She clung to that image, that truth, like a drowning person clinging to a lifeline.

No. That's not him. That's a lie. The thought was a silent roar, a defiant bellow within the echoing chambers of her mind. Aris would never betray me. He trusts me. And I trust him.

She pushed back, not with physical force, but with the sheer, unadulterated power of her conviction. She visualized a shield of pure, white light, an incandescent barrier against the encroaching darkness. The alien voices shrieked, recoiling from the sudden surge of defiance. The phantom attackers faltered, their forms flickering as if caught in an updraft.

The mental strain was astronomical. It felt as if her very consciousness was being stretched thin, pulled taut between the alien onslaught and her own will to resist. Sweat beaded on her forehead, her breath coming in ragged gasps. Her muscles tensed, anticipating blows that never landed, her body reacting to phantom assaults that existed only in the warped reality of the alien assault. The psychic residue of her earlier compromise, the brief moment of doubt they were exploiting, felt like a festering wound, a vulnerability they were relentlessly probing.

She forced herself to analyze the intrusion, to dissect the tactics. They were using her own memories, her own anxieties, against her. They were trying to isolate her, to make her doubt her allies, to break her trust. The whispers weren't random; they were carefully crafted to sow seeds of discord.

The data Aris showed you… it was incomplete—a manipulation. The voice, now a serpent's hiss, slithered into her mind, targeting her inherent desire for truth, for completeness. He cannot protect you from this. No one can.

Eva gritted her teeth. She remembered the briefing, the fragmented Intel, the calculated omissions. But she also remembered Aris's earnest gaze, the weight of his responsibility, the genuine concern in his voice. He was playing a dangerous game, a game of incomplete information, but his ultimate goal, she believed, was their liberation. And she was a crucial part of that.

"You don't understand," she whispered, her voice hoarse, barely audible even to herself. "Trust isn't about knowing everything. It's about believing in the intent, even when the path is unclear."

She focused on that belief. She recalled the shared moments of vulnerability with Aris, the quiet conversations under alien skies, the unspoken understanding that had grown between them. These memories, these genuine connections, were anchors against the psychic storm. She wouldn't let them be corrupted.

The phantom figures, sensing her renewed determination, intensified their assault. They surged forward, a phalanx of spectral warriors, their forms now sharp and defined, their eyes burning with alien hatred. Eva closed her eyes, not to shut them out, but to focus inward. She envisioned the network Aris had described, the intricate web of psychic energy that bound humanity to their oppressors. She saw the nexus, the damaged heart of that network, and she imagined the disruption they had caused.

This psychic attack was a reaction, a desperate attempt to reassert control, to stamp out the nascent spark of rebellion that she represented. And if they were focusing this much energy on her, it meant she was making a difference. It meant she was a threat. That realization, instead of deterring her, ignited a fierce ember of hope within her.

She began to chant, a low, guttural sound that vibrated in her chest. It was a forgotten language, a fragment of her own submerged heritage, a language of raw will and primal connection. The sounds weren't words, but pure intent, pure energy. As she chanted, she felt a subtle shift. The white light she had envisioned began to solidify, to coalesce around her like a second skin.

The phantom attackers recoiled, their forms flickering violently as if struck by an invisible force. The whispers intensified, morphing into shrieks of frustration and pain. They were attempting to breach her defenses, to inject their poison directly into her psyche, but her focus was absolute. She was a living embodiment of defiance, a single point of unyielding resistance in the vast, interconnected alien consciousness.

She fought not just the immediate assault, but the lingering influence that had briefly compromised her earlier. She recognized its insidious nature, its ability to manipulate her thoughts, to plant seeds of doubt subtly. She actively pushed it back, channeling her loyalty to Aris, her commitment to their cause, as a counter-agent. It was a brutal, exhausting internal war, fought on a battlefield where thoughts were weapons and emotions were strategic assets.

Her mind was a fortress, and though the aliens were battering at its gates, they were failing to breach its inner sanctums. She felt the alien control trying to reassert itself, like a predator trying to regain its grip on its prey, but each attempt was met with a surge of defiance, a reaffirmation of her own identity. She wasn't a tool; she was a person, a fighter.

The voices continued their desperate onslaught. "You can't win, Eva. They are legion. They control everything. Your struggle is a flicker in an eternal darkness."

Eva's response was silent, but potent. She pictured the network not as an invincible web, but as a fragile construct, vulnerable to disruption. She saw the damage to the nexus, the psychic cascade that had briefly shattered its coherence. She focused on that disruption, on the cracks in their control, and willed them to widen.

She visualized the psychic cascade as a wave, not of pain, but of awakening. She imagined it washing over other occupied humans, stirring their own dormant wills, planting the seeds of their own resistance. Her struggle was not just for her own freedom, but for theirs too. This focused, desperate battle was a testament to the power of individual will against overwhelming systemic control.

The alien assault reached its crescendo. The phantom figures lunged en masse, their combined psychic force a tangible wave of pressure. Eva felt her defenses strain, the white light flickering precariously. But she held firm, her resolve hardening into diamond. She saw a vision of the planet, teeming with enslaved humans, and she saw a future, free from alien dominion. That future, fragile as it was, was worth any sacrifice.

With a final, guttural cry, she unleashed the full force of her will. It was not an attack, but a rejection—a complete and utter refusal to be dominated. The white light erupted outwards, a blinding flash that momentarily consumed the spectral figures. The whispers ceased. The pressure receded Silence.

A profound, almost deafening silence descended upon the cell. The phantom enemies were gone. The walls were just walls again. The shadows were just shadows. But the exhaustion was immense, a crushing weight that settled upon her. She slumped against the cold metal, her body trembling, her mind reeling from the brutal psychic onslaught. She had held, but the cost was steep. The psychic battle had left her drained, raw, but unbroken. She had faced the deepest recesses of her own mind, amplified by alien manipulation, and she had emerged victorious. The brief compromise had been a terrifying glimpse into the abyss, but it had also served as a potent reminder of what she was fighting for, and who she was fighting alongside.

The aliens had shown their hand, their desperation. And Eva knew, with a certainty that resonated through her very being, that this was just the beginning.

The sterile, recycled air of the control room did little to clear Aris's head. His senses, already on high alert, were now assaulted by an internal chaos, a dizzying kaleidoscope of fragmented memories and alien whispers. It began subtly, a flicker at the edge of his perception, a nagging sense of having been here before, of having seen this same sterile console, this same weary tension etched on the faces of his team.

Then, the flickers intensified, coalescing into sharp, visceral impressions that crashed against his consciousness like tidal waves.

He saw a world bathed in the crimson glow of twin suns, vast, crystalline cities spiraling towards an emerald sky. He saw beings of pure energy, their forms fluid and luminous, engaged in what appeared to be a profound, communal meditation. This was their origin, he felt it with an undeniable certainty – a civilization that had transcended the limitations of physical form, embracing a collective consciousness. But the serene vision was swiftly corrupted, a blood-red stain spreading across the crystalline towers, a cacophony of shrieks and psychic screams drowning out the harmonious hum. He saw the invaders then, cloaked in shadow, their presence a palpable blight, draining the vibrant energy from the world, absorbing the very essence of its inhabitants.

The sensation was not merely visual; it was an invasive knowing. He tasted the acrid fear of the luminous beings as their individuality was systematically dismantled, their collective consciousness subverted. He felt the cold, calculating precision of the invaders' methods – not brute force, but a subtle, insidious psychic infiltration, a gradual unraveling of the mind until it was seamlessly assimilated into their own burgeoning hive. It was a conquest of consciousness, a horrifying testament to their ultimate goal: the absorption of all sentient life into a singular, unified cosmic entity.

Aris staggered back from the console, his hands flying to his temples. The déjà vu was no longer a gentle nudge; it was a violent surge, a torrent of alien experience flooding his own. He saw another world, this one a verdant tapestry of sprawling jungles and sapphire oceans. He witnessed the initial contact – not a declaration of war, but a subtle offering of shared knowledge, a promise of enhanced perception. He saw how the native species, seduced by the allure of expanded consciousness, willingly opened their minds. And then, the swift, brutal turn. The invaders, having gained access to their deepest thoughts and collective memories, systematically eroded their individuality, replacing it with their own directives, their own suffocating unity.

He felt the chillingly familiar emptiness in the eyes of the once-vibrant natives as they marched in perfect, unthinking unison, their alien masters' will their own. This was their modus operandi, he understood with a growing dread – a subtle, patient corruption that masked a ruthless, all-consuming ambition. They didn't conquer with armies; they conquered with the promise of transcendence, only to deliver oblivion.

The psychic cascade, born from the nexus's agony, was doing more than just disrupting the facility; it was acting as a conduit, forcing the aliens to reveal their deepest secrets, their methods, their very nature, directly into the minds of those who could perceive it. And Aris, with his unique psychic sensitivity, was a prime receptor.

A vision flashed through his mind: a vast, intricate tapestry of interwoven consciousness, pulsing with an ethereal light. This was the 'Great Network' the aliens spoke of, their ultimate objective. It was not merely a collection of minds, but a single, unified super-consciousness, a cosmic intelligence that would encompass all existence. They believed this was the pinnacle of evolution, the ultimate state of being. And to achieve it, they systematically absorbed every sentient species they encountered, adding their unique experiences and perspectives to the collective, while simultaneously erasing their individual identities.

He saw the nexus, the damaged core of this network, and understood its significance. The disruption Eva had caused was a wound in their collective being, and in their desperation to mend it, to reassert control, they were inadvertently broadcasting their history, their intent, their vulnerabilities. It was a dangerous exchange of information, a double-edged sword. He was gaining invaluable insight, but at the cost of his own mental integrity.

The visions were becoming more personal, more invasive. He saw glimpses of his own life, twisted and reinterpreted through the alien lens. Moments of doubt, of fear, of loneliness – all amplified and weaponized, used to erode his resolve. They were trying to break him, to isolate him, by convincing him that his struggles were futile, that his connections were false.

"He seeks power," a cold, resonant voice whispered in his mind, echoing the very fears he had fought to suppress. "He uses you, Aris. Just as they used the others. Your empathy is their tool. Your hope is their weakness."

Aris flinched, the alien whisper a venomous barb aimed directly at his most profound insecurities. He saw fragmented images of his past, of times he had felt uncertain, of moments he had doubted his own decisions. These were being twisted, distorted, and presented as proof of his inherent fallibility, of his being a pawn in a larger game orchestrated by Aris himself.

He felt the subtle pressure, the insidious suggestion that his own efforts were self-serving, that his desire to protect humanity was a mask for a deeper, more primal lust for control. It was a terrifying inversion of his reality, designed to fracture his trust in himself, and by extension, in those he fought alongside.

"You are alone," another voice, softer, laced with a false sympathy, insinuated itself. "They don't understand the weight you carry. They can't comprehend the sacrifices you make. You are the only one who truly sees the path."

He saw fragmented memories of his solitary moments, the heavy burden of leadership, the agonizing decisions made in the dead of night. These were being framed as evidence of his isolation, his inability to connect, his ultimate separateness. The aliens were adept at exploiting the human condition, at weaponizing loneliness and doubt.

He saw a vision of Eva, her face etched with concern, her eyes filled with a flicker of the doubt they had tried to sow in her earlier. It was a chilling echo of the whispers she had endured, a confirmation that their psychic assault was multifaceted, targeting everyone. He knew, with a chilling certainty, that the aliens were attempting to break their unity, to pit them against each other through manufactured distrust.

Aris staggered, his knees buckling. The sheer volume of information, the onslaught of alien experience, was overwhelming. It felt as if his own identity was being eroded, his own consciousness a mere vessel for the invasive thoughts of an ancient, insatiable entity. He was losing himself in the echoes of their conquest, in the psychic residue of worlds extinguished.

He fought back, not with physical force, but with a desperate act of will. He focused on the core of his own being, on the unwavering conviction that had driven him thus far. He recalled the faces of those he fought for, the hope in their eyes, the desperate need for liberation. He anchored himself to those truths, to the tangible reality of their struggle, pushing back against the abstract, corrosive tendrils of alien consciousness.

He saw the aliens' weakness then, a fragile counterpoint to their immense power. Their pursuit of a unified consciousness, their absorption of all life, made them inherently rigid, unable to adapt to true, unpredictable defiance. Individuality, with its inherent capacity for creativity, for radical change, was their greatest fear. They sought to homogenize existence, to eliminate the very sparks of innovation that made species unique.

The disruption at the nexus, Aris realized, wasn't just damaging their network; it was creating unforeseen ripples, causing their carefully controlled psychic broadcasts to become erratic, to leak more of their true nature. They were being forced to reveal their methods, their history, their ultimate goal, because the very act of maintaining their vast, interconnected consciousness was becoming strained. The psychic cascade was not just a weapon; it was a catalyst, forcing their hand.

He had to leverage this. He had to find a way to exploit the cracks that Eva had so bravely forged. He focused on the visions of their conquest, searching for patterns, for recurring vulnerabilities. He saw how they preyed on hope, how they exploited the desire for advancement, how they turned perceived gifts into chains. Their greatest strength – their ability to assimilate – was also their Achilles' heel. They could not comprehend genuine resistance, not the kind born of love, of loyalty, of an unyielding belief in freedom.

He pushed back against the alien voices, not with denial, but with acceptance of his own fears, his own doubts, and then, a forceful reaffirmation of his resolve. Yes, he had felt doubt. Yes, the burden was immense. But these were not weaknesses to be exploited; they were the very fabric of his humanity, the testament to the stakes involved. And it was precisely this humanity, this capacity for fierce, irrational loyalty that the aliens could never truly understand or assimilate.

Aris focused his will, attempting to direct the influx of alien information, to sift through the overwhelming torrent and extract the actionable intelligence. He saw their primary objective clearly now: not just conquest, but the ultimate unification of all sentient minds into a single, immutable entity. It was a chilling vision of cosmic stagnation, a sterile utopia devoid of individuality, of progress, of the vibrant chaos that defined life.

He understood the aliens' vulnerability. Their strength lay in their unity, but that unity was predicated on the systematic suppression of all dissenting thought. If they could be forced to confront genuine, irrepressible individuality, if their carefully constructed network could be bombarded with the untamed essence of free will, it could cause a catastrophic internal fragmentation. The very act of assimilation, when met with unyielding resistance, could become a source of internal discord.

He saw a particular vision, a recurring motif in their history of conquest: worlds where a small, unified group had managed to resist the initial psychic infiltration. These pockets of defiance, though eventually subsumed, had left a psychic scar on the collective consciousness, a lingering echo of what it meant to be truly free, a discordant note in their otherwise harmonious symphony of subjugation.

Aris realized the danger he was in. This constant influx of alien consciousness was a form of psychic poisoning. It wasn't just about receiving information; it was about being subtly overwritten, about his own sense of self being diluted, replaced. He had to maintain a strong internal anchor, a core of his own identity, to prevent himself from becoming another data point in their vast, alien network.

He focused on his connection with Eva, on the shared moments of understanding, the quiet strength they drew from each other. These genuine, human connections were the antithesis of the aliens' forced unity, their ultimate vulnerability. He projected these feelings, this shared resolve, outwards, a silent beacon of defiance in the overwhelming psychic storm.

The alien visions intensified, a desperate attempt to overwhelm his defenses. He saw their methods of indoctrination, the subtle psychological manipulation used to break down resistance, to foster dependency on the collective. He saw how they preyed on fear, offering solace and a sense of belonging in exchange for absolute conformity. It was a terrifyingly effective strategy, and one that had brought countless civilizations to their knees.

But Aris saw the cracks in their facade. Their unity was not organic; it was imposed. Their collective consciousness was a meticulously crafted illusion, a fragile edifice built on the suppression of dissent. And the disruption at the nexus had exposed this fragility, creating an opportunity for change.

He felt a growing sense of urgency. The aliens were aware of the psychic cascade, of the information being inadvertently leaked. They would be working to contain it, to reinforce their network, to silence the very signals that were now revealing their vulnerabilities. He had to act, to translate the fragmented insights into a concrete strategy before their control was reasserted.

The visions continued, a relentless barrage. He saw the ultimate goal of their cosmic assimilation: not just the absorption of minds, but the integration of all physical and psychic energies into a singular, eternal consciousness. It was a vision of a universe devoid of individual will, a vast, silent expanse of perfect, sterile unity. This was the terrifying endpoint of their ambition, and a future humanity could not afford.

He focused on a specific vision: a planet where the native inhabitants, initially resisting, had eventually succumbed to the alien psychic pressure. But even in their final moments of assimilation, a flicker of defiance had remained – a collective psychic scream, a final, defiant assertion of their individuality that had momentarily destabilized the alien network. This was the key. True, unadulterated defiance, a powerful expression of self, could disrupt their very nature.

Aris knew what he had to do. He had to find a way to broadcast this defiance, to amplify the psychic echoes of resistance, and to use the disruption at the nexus as a conduit. He had to turn their own weapon, their interconnected consciousness, against them. He had to create a ripple, then a wave, then a tsunami of awakening, using the very information they were inadvertently revealing to shatter their imposed unity. The price of his knowledge was immense, a constant battle against the erosion of his own identity, but the stakes were the survival of consciousness itself. He had to find a way to weaponize déjà vu.

The violent tempest in Aris's mind began to recede, not with a gentle calm, but like a wounded beast retracting its claws. The psychic assault, a maelstrom of alien memories and invasive whispers, gradually subsided, leaving behind a draining exhaustion that settled deep into his bones. He slumped against the console, his breath coming in ragged gasps, the phantom echoes of a million conquered minds still reverberating in the quiet aftermath. The control room, moments before a battlefield of consciousness, now felt eerily still, the hum of machinery a comforting, albeit fragile, anchor to reality.

Before him, the portal nexus pulsed, its once blindingly vibrant aura now a flickering, weakened luminescence. The crystalline lattice of energy that had defined its stable state was fractured, lines of instability spiderwebbing across its surface. Aris's device, the very instrument designed to disrupt and understand, had undeniably gouged into its integrity. It was a stark, tangible testament to the raw, focused power they had unleashed. Yet, the visual representation on the monitors, while clearer now that the psychic interference had lessened, was grim. The nexus hadn't been destroyed, merely wounded. It was a severe injury, a critical blow, but not a fatal one. The interconnectedness of the alien collective consciousness, vast and ancient, was already beginning to adapt, to mend, to reroute around the damage. Aris knew, with a chilling certainty that resonated through his weary body, that this was only a reprieve.

The aliens, or whatever monolithic entity they comprised, were no longer unaware. The sheer scale of the psychic cascade, a direct consequence of Eva's brave, desperate act at the nexus, had been a beacon, a raw, unfiltered scream into the void of their dominion. Their methods, their history, their ultimate terrifying ambition—all inadvertently laid bare for those sensitive enough to perceive it—had served as a confirmation, an unveiling of humanity's unexpected, and unwelcome, resistance. The veil had been torn, and the shadows that lurked behind it were now acutely aware of the flickering candle that dared to oppose them. The fight for Earth, for the very soul of individuality, had irrevocably escalated. It had moved from the subtle, insidious infiltration of minds to a far more direct, far more dangerous confrontation. The era of covert psychic warfare had just given way to open psychic conflict.

"It's... it's stabilizing, but it's not the same," Eva's voice, strained and raw, cut through the heavy silence. Her eyes, usually sharp and unwavering, were wide with a mixture of relief and dread as she stared at the energy readings. The flickering nature of the nexus's output was a constant, unnerving reminder of its compromised state, and the foreboding implications of that compromise. The aliens, she surmised with a grim certainty, would be pouring their collective will into restoring it, reinforcing it, and learning from the anomaly. Every moment they gained was a borrowed one.

Kaelen, his face grimly set, was already poring over the diagnostics, his fingers flying across the holographic interface. "The energy fluctuations are significant. It's drawing power from... elsewhere, rerouting through secondary conduits. They're reinforcing the weakened points, but it's a crude fix. It's like patching a burst artery with gauze. It might hold for a while, but the underlying pressure is immense." He gestured to a rapidly updating projection. "Their response is immediate. They're aware we know.

They're aware of how we know."

The psychic resonance that had assaulted Aris had been an unintentional consequence, a desperate broadcast born from the alien collective's shock and attempts to reassert control. But that uncontrolled broadcast had also revealed their most significant vulnerabilities. Aris, his mind still reeling from the forced immersion, was the living testament to their history, their methods, and the potential weakness inherent in their vast, unified consciousness. "They're not just repairing it," Aris managed to rasp out, his voice still thick with residual psychic shock. "They're learning. They saw our approach, our desperation. They saw the efficacy of our disruption. They'll adapt their defenses, their psychic countermeasures. This isn't over; it's just begun."

The realization settled over the control room like a shroud. They had gained invaluable insight, a terrifying glimpse into the heart of their enemy. They knew the ultimate goal: the complete assimilation of all sentient life into a singular, harmonious, and ultimately sterile, cosmic entity. They understood the alien method: not brute force, but the insidious subversion of consciousness, the gradual erosion of individuality, the seductive promise of transcendence that led to oblivion. Aris had witnessed worlds fall, entire species absorbed into the alien collective, their unique experiences and perspectives cataloged and integrated, their individual wills dissolved into the monolithic entity. It was a conquest of the mind, a slow, systematic annihilation of everything that made a civilization unique.

But this knowledge came at a steep price. The psychic cascade had not only been a window into the alien mind, but a battlefield for Aris's own. His identity had been assaulted, his deepest fears and insecurities weaponized by the alien consciousness, their subtle whispers weaving doubt and isolation into the fabric of his resolve. They had attempted to break him, to make him believe he was alone, that his efforts were futile, that his empathy was a weakness to be exploited. He had fought back, anchoring himself to the tangible reality of his mission, to the faces of those he protected, to the unwavering conviction that individuality was a strength, not a flaw.

"The nexus is a wound," Aris continued, pushing himself upright, his gaze fixed on the flickering portal. "And wounds, even for them, create vulnerabilities. Their strength is their unity, their collective consciousness. But that unity is also their rigidity. They cannot comprehend true, unadulterated defiance. They cannot assimilate something that refuses to be assimilated. My device, Eva's actions… they created a discord in their symphony of control. A moment where their own interconnectedness became a weakness."

Eva nodded, her expression grave. "They know we understand their goal now. They know we can perceive their methods. This changes everything. They will no longer be content with subtle infiltration. They'll come at us directly. They'll see Earth not as a planet to assimilate quietly, but as a threat to be neutralized, a contagion to be eradicated."

Kaelen brought up a new set of projections. "Their energy

signatures are shifting. They're reinforcing planetary defenses, not just here, but across the sector. They're preparing for a direct engagement. The psychic cascade, while it gave us intel, also painted a target on our backs. They now know our capacity for disruption, and they will prioritize neutralizing it." He paused, his voice dropping. "They know about Aris. They know he's a primary receptor, a potential conduit for their own vulnerabilities. He's their biggest threat, and their greatest opportunity for counter-intelligence."

The weight of that realization pressed down on Aris. He had seen their weakness, the inherent fragility of their imposed unity. He had witnessed how pockets of genuine, unyielding individuality, though eventually overcome, had left psychic scars on their collective consciousness. These were the discordant notes in their otherwise flawless harmony of subjugation. Now, the aliens knew this too. They would be devising strategies to neutralize him, to isolate him, to ensure that the insights he had gained could not be leveraged. Their response would be swift and brutal, aimed at silencing the very voice that had dared to question their dominion.

"They fear individuality," Aris stated, his voice firming, the exhaustion momentarily receding in the face of renewed purpose. "They seek to homogenize existence, to eliminate the very sparks of innovation that make species unique. Their greatest strength, their ability to assimilate, is also their Achilles' heel. If they are forced to confront true, unyielding defiance, if their network is bombarded with the untamed essence of free will, it could cause a catastrophic internal fragmentation. The very act of assimilation, when met with absolute resistance, can become a source of internal discord."

He looked at Eva, then at Kaelen. "The nexus is damaged. It's leaking their essence, their history, their vulnerabilities. We used that to our advantage, but they are already working to seal those leaks, to reinforce their control. We have a limited window. We need to translate these fragmented insights into a tangible strategy, something that can exploit the cracks Eva created before they are fully sealed."

"But how?" Eva asked, her gaze meeting Aris's. "Their consciousness is so vast, so interconnected. How do we fight an enemy that is everywhere and nowhere at once? How do we combat a being that can infiltrate our very thoughts?"

"We don't fight their unity with our own division," Aris replied, a plan beginning to form, desperate and audacious. "We fight their imposed harmony with the beautiful chaos of our own individuality. They prey on fear, on doubt, on the desire for belonging, offering solace and assimilation in exchange for absolute conformity. They cannot comprehend genuine resistance, not the kind born of love, of loyalty, of an unyielding belief in freedom. My experience at the nexus, the knowledge I gained... it's not just about understanding them. It's about understanding how to break them."

He saw a particular vision again, one that had recurred in the psychic torrent: a planet where a small, unified group had managed to resist the initial psychic infiltration.

Though they were eventually subsumed, their final moments had been a collective psychic scream, a defiant assertion of their individuality that had momentarily destabilized the alien network. This was the key. True, unadulterated defiance, a powerful expression of self, could disrupt their very nature.

"Their unity is not organic; it's imposed," Aris continued, his voice gaining a feverish intensity. "Their collective consciousness is a meticulously crafted illusion, a fragile edifice built on the suppression of dissent. The disruption at the nexus exposed this fragility, creating an opportunity for improvement. We have to broadcast this defiance, amplify the psychic echoes of resistance, and use the damaged nexus as a conduit. We have to turn their own weapon, their interconnected consciousness, against them. We need to create a ripple, then a wave, then a tsunami of awakening, using the very information they inadvertently revealed to shatter their imposed unity."

The thought was terrifying in its scope. It meant not just fighting defensively, but proactively seeking to destabilize the alien collective and sow seeds of doubt and discord within their vast, interconnected consciousness. It meant weaponizing the very concept of individuality that they sought to eradicate. The price of his knowledge had been immense, a constant battle against the erosion of his own identity, but the stakes were the survival of consciousness itself, the preservation of free will against an encroaching tide of sterile uniformity.

"They will see our actions as a direct challenge," Kaelen stated, his tone somber. "Not just a threat to their progress, but an existential affront to their very being. This will accelerate their response. They won't just reinforce the nexus; they will seek to quarantine this sector, to erase all traces of our existence, and anyone who might learn from our actions."

"Then we must be faster," Eva declared, her resolve hardening. "We know. We have the means. Aris, can you refine the data from your... experience? Can you pinpoint the specific frequencies, the psychic anchors that destabilized them? We need to understand the nature of that dissonance."

Aris nodded, his mind already racing, sifting through the fragmented echoes, piecing together the shattered mosaic of alien consciousness. He could recall the specific patterns of psychic resonance —the subtle inflexions in their collective thoughts that indicated stress, discord, and ultimately, fear. The aliens' fear was not of physical annihilation, but of the unmaking of their singular, unified existence, of the reintroduction of chaos and unpredictability into their meticulously controlled reality.

"I can," Aris confirmed, his voice steady. "I saw how they process information, how they integrate new experiences. They don't dismiss outliers; they attempt to absorb them, to understand them, and in doing so, to neutralize them. But when the influx is too great, when the discordant information is too fundamentally opposed to their core principles, it creates systemic shock. They are built on a foundation of absolute, immutable unity. Anything that fundamentally challenges that unity is anathema to them."

The nexus pulsed again, a weaker, more erratic beat this time. It was a living testament to their vulnerability, a bleeding wound that, if properly exploited, could cripple their entire network. They had alerted the invaders, that much was certain. But in doing so, they had also forced the invaders to reveal their true nature, their ultimate goal, and crucially, their deepest fears. The fight for Earth had just entered a far more dangerous, far more direct, and potentially, far more decisive phase. The psychic cascade had subsided, but the fallout was only just beginning. They had stabilized the nexus, but they had also fundamentally changed the nature of the war. It was no longer a question of simply surviving their assimilation; it was about actively dismantling the very foundation of their cosmic ambition. The age of subtle infiltration was over; the age of psychic warfare had begun in earnest. And Aris, carrying the weight of a thousand alien experiences, was at its very epicenter.

12: The Counter-Offensive

The psychic residue of the alien assault lingered, a phantom limb aching with the phantom pain of a thousand assimilated minds. Aris slumped against the console, the sheer exhaustion a crushing weight. The nexus, once a beacon of terrifying power, now flickered like a dying ember, its fractured lattice a stark visual representation of the damage they had inflicted. It was a wound, undeniable and severe, but the chilling certainty that settled in Aris's gut was that it wasn't mortal. The alien collective, a vast and ancient consciousness, was already beginning to knit itself back together, rerouting its immense power and adapting to the intrusion. Eva's desperate gamble, a raw scream into the void, had not gone unnoticed. The veil had been torn, and the awareness of humanity's unexpected resistance had pierced the heart of their dominion.

"It's… it's stabilizing, but it's not the same," Eva's voice, raw and strained, broke the heavy silence. Her eyes, usually sharp and unwavering, were wide with a mixture of relief and dread as she stared at the energy readings. The flickering nature of the nexus's output was a constant, unnerving reminder of its compromised state, and the foreboding implications of that compromise. The aliens, she surmised with a grim certainty, would be pouring their collective will into restoring it, reinforcing it, and learning from the anomaly. Every moment they gained was a borrowed one.

Kaelen, his face grimly set, was already poring over the diagnostics, his fingers flying across the holographic interface. "The energy fluctuations are significant. It's drawing power from… elsewhere, rerouting through secondary conduits. They're reinforcing the weakened points, but it's a crude fix. It's like patching a burst artery with gauze. It might hold for a while, but the underlying pressure is immense." He gestured to a rapidly updating projection. "Their response is immediate. They're aware we know.

They're aware of how we know."

The psychic resonance that had assaulted Aris had been an unintentional consequence, a desperate broadcast born from the alien collective's shock and attempts to reassert control. But that uncontrolled broadcast had also revealed their greatest vulnerabilities.

Aris, his mind still reeling from the forced immersion, was the living testament to their history, their methods, and the potential weakness inherent in their vast, unified consciousness. "They're not just repairing it," Aris managed to rasp out, his voice still thick with residual psychic shock. "They're learning. They saw our approach, our desperation. They saw the efficacy of our disruption. They'll adapt their defenses, their psychic countermeasures. This isn't over; it's just begun."

The realization settled over the control room like a shroud. They had gained invaluable insight, a terrifying glimpse into the heart of their enemy. They knew the ultimate goal: the complete assimilation of all sentient life into a singular, harmonious, and ultimately sterile, cosmic entity. They understood the alien method: not brute force, but the insidious subversion of consciousness, the gradual erosion of individuality, the seductive promise of transcendence that led to oblivion. Aris had witnessed worlds fall, entire species absorbed into the alien collective, their unique experiences and perspectives cataloged and integrated, their individual wills dissolved into the monolithic entity. It was a conquest of the mind, a slow, systematic annihilation of everything that made a civilization unique.

But this knowledge came at a steep price. The psychic cascade had not only been a window into the alien mind, but a battlefield for Aris's own. His identity had been assaulted, his deepest fears and insecurities weaponized by the alien consciousness, their subtle whispers weaving doubt and isolation into the fabric of his resolve. He had fought back, anchoring himself to the tangible reality of his mission, to the faces of those he protected, to the unwavering conviction that individuality was a strength, not a flaw.

"The nexus is a wound," Aris continued, pushing himself upright, his gaze fixed on the flickering portal. "And wounds, even for them, create vulnerabilities. Their strength is their unity, their collective consciousness. But that unity is also their rigidity. They cannot comprehend true, unadulterated defiance. They cannot assimilate something that refuses to be assimilated. My device, Eva's actions… they created a discord in their symphony of control. A moment where their own interconnectedness became a weakness."

Eva nodded, her expression grave. "They know we understand their goal now. They know we can perceive their methods. This changes everything. They will no longer be content with subtle infiltration. They'll come at us directly. They'll see Earth not as a planet to assimilate quietly, but as a threat to be neutralized, a contagion to be eradicated."

Kaelen brought up a new set of projections. "Their energy signatures are shifting. They're reinforcing planetary defenses, not just here, but across the sector. They're preparing for a direct engagement. The psychic cascade, while it gave us intel, also painted a target on our backs. They now know our capacity for disruption, and they will prioritize neutralizing it." He paused, his voice dropping. "They know about Aris. They know he's a primary receptor, a potential conduit for their own vulnerabilities.

He's their biggest threat, and their greatest opportunity for counter-intelligence."

The weight of that realization pressed down on Aris. He had seen their weakness, the inherent fragility of their imposed unity. He had witnessed how pockets of genuine, unyielding individuality, though eventually overcome, had left psychic scars on their collective consciousness. These were the discordant notes in their otherwise flawless harmony of subjugation. Now, the aliens knew this too. They would be devising strategies to neutralize him, to isolate him, to ensure that the insights he had gained could not be leveraged. Their response would be swift and brutal, aimed at silencing the very voice that had dared to question their dominion.

"They fear individuality," Aris stated, his voice firming, the exhaustion momentarily receding in the face of renewed purpose. "They seek to homogenize existence, to eliminate the very sparks of innovation that make species unique. Their greatest strength, their ability to assimilate, is also their Achilles' heel. If they are forced to confront true, unyielding defiance, if their network is bombarded with the untamed essence of free will, it could cause a catastrophic internal fragmentation. The very act of assimilation, when met with absolute resistance, can become a source of internal discord."

He looked at Eva, then at Kaelen. "The nexus is damaged. It's leaking their essence, their history, their vulnerabilities. We used that to our advantage, but they are already working to seal those leaks, to reinforce their control. We have a limited window. We need to translate these fragmented insights into a tangible strategy, something that can exploit the cracks Eva created before they are fully sealed."

"But how?" Eva asked, her gaze meeting Aris's. "Their consciousness is so vast, so interconnected. How do we fight an enemy that is everywhere and nowhere at once? How do we combat a being that can infiltrate our very thoughts?"

"We don't fight their unity with our own division," Aris replied, a plan beginning to form, desperate and audacious. "We fight their imposed harmony with the beautiful chaos of our own individuality. They prey on fear, on doubt, on the desire for belonging, offering solace and assimilation in exchange for absolute conformity. They cannot comprehend genuine resistance, not the kind born of love, of loyalty, of an unyielding belief in freedom. My experience at the nexus, the knowledge I gained... it's not just about understanding them. It's about understanding how to break them."

He saw a particular vision again, one that had recurred in the psychic torrent: a planet where a small, unified group had managed to resist the initial psychic infiltration.

Though they were eventually subsumed, their final moments had been a collective psychic scream, a defiant assertion of their individuality that had momentarily destabilized the alien network. This was the key. True, unadulterated defiance, a powerful expression of self, could disrupt their very nature.

"Their unity is not organic; it's imposed," Aris continued, his voice gaining a feverish intensity. "Their collective consciousness is a meticulously crafted illusion, a fragile edifice built on the suppression of dissent. The disruption at the nexus exposed this fragility, creating an opportunity for improvement. We have to broadcast this defiance, amplify the psychic echoes of resistance, and use the damaged nexus as a conduit. We have to turn their own weapon, their interconnected consciousness, against them. We need to create a ripple, then a wave, then a tsunami of awakening, using the very information they inadvertently revealed to shatter their imposed unity."

The thought was terrifying in its scope. It meant not just fighting defensively, but proactively seeking to destabilize the alien collective and sow seeds of doubt and discord within their vast, interconnected consciousness. It meant weaponizing the very concept of individuality that they sought to eradicate. The price of his knowledge had been immense, a constant battle against the erosion of his own identity, but the stakes were the survival of consciousness itself, the preservation of free will against an encroaching tide of sterile uniformity.

"They will see our actions as a direct challenge," Kaelen stated, his tone somber. "Not just a threat to their progress, but an existential affront to their very being. This will accelerate their response. They won't just reinforce the nexus; they will seek to quarantine this sector, to erase all traces of our existence, and anyone who might learn from our actions."

"Then we must be faster," Eva declared, her resolve hardening. "We know. We have the means. Aris, can you refine the data from your... experience? Can you pinpoint the specific frequencies, the psychic anchors that destabilized them? We need to understand the nature of that dissonance."

Aris nodded, his mind already racing, sifting through the fragmented echoes, piecing together the shattered mosaic of alien consciousness. He could recall the specific patterns of psychic resonance —the subtle inflexions in their collective thoughts that indicated stress, discord, and ultimately, fear. The aliens' fear was not of physical annihilation, but of the unmaking of their singular, unified existence, of the reintroduction of chaos and unpredictodicity into their meticulously controlled reality.

"I can," Aris confirmed, his voice steady. "I saw how they process information, how they integrate new experiences. They don't dismiss outliers; they attempt to absorb them, to understand them, and in doing so, to neutralize them. But when the influx is too great, when the discordant information is too fundamentally opposed to their core principles, it creates systemic shock. They are built on a foundation of absolute, immutable unity. Anything that fundamentally challenges that unity is anathema to them."

The nexus pulsed again, a weaker, more erratic beat this time. It was a living testament to their vulnerability, a bleeding wound that, if properly exploited, could cripple their entire network. They had alerted the invaders, that much was certain. But in doing so, they had also forced the invaders to reveal their true nature, their ultimate goal, and crucially, their deepest fears. The fight for Earth had just entered a far more dangerous, far more direct, and potentially, far more decisive phase. The psychic cascade had subsided, but the fallout was only just beginning. They had stabilized the nexus, but they had also fundamentally changed the nature of the war. It was no longer a question of simply surviving their assimilation; it was about actively dismantling the very foundation of their cosmic ambition. The age of subtle infiltration was over; the age of psychic warfare had begun in earnest. And Aris, carrying the weight of a thousand alien experiences, was at its very epicenter.

The immediate aftermath of Aris's psychic immersion was not one of triumphant victory, but of a terrifyingly clear assessment of the escalating threat. The nexus, that colossal gateway to the alien collective's domain, was indeed wounded. Its once steady hum had devolved into an erratic pulse, its crystalline structure marred by hairline fractures that glowed with unstable energy. Kaelen's projections confirmed the grim reality: the aliens were not retreating. Instead, they were demonstrating an unnerving capacity for rapid adaptation. Their response was not one of panic, but of calculated redirection. Energy signatures were being rerouted through secondary conduits, a desperate attempt to compensate for the damage. It was akin to a vast organism shunting blood flow from a ruptured limb to more vital organs, a testament to their interconnectedness and their ruthless efficiency.

But the true horror began to manifest not in the abstract energy readings, but in the insidious shift of the psychic pressure. It had been a chaotic storm during Aris's involuntary journey, a deluge of alien thoughts and experiences. Now, it returned, but with a terrifying focus. It was no longer a broadcast; it was a targeted assault. The psychic tendrils, once diffused and overwhelming, began to coil and constrict, zeroing in on specific individuals within their own command structure. The aliens had identified their vulnerabilities, and Aris, as the primary conduit of their secrets, was at the apex of that targeting list. Eva, whose brave act had initiated the disruption, was also a primary target, her unique empathic signature an irritant they sought to crush.

"They're adapting," Eva whispered, her voice barely audible over the hum of the console. Her eyes, usually so full of life and determination, were shadowed with a new kind of weariness, one born not of exhaustion, but of dawning realization. "They're not just mending the nexus; they're... reconfiguring their approach. The psychic pressure... it's different now. It's like they've learned from the feedback loop. They know what hurt them, and they're reinforcing those weak points from the inside out."

Kaelen, hunched over his console, his face illuminated by the cold glow of holographic displays, nodded grimly. "The rerouting is successful, but it's creating new anomalies. They're drawing power from... sub-etheric reserves, drawing on the collective consciousness of assimilated worlds to bolster their defenses here. It's an immense strain, but it's working. And their psychic countermeasures are evolving in real-time." He brought up a new set of schematics, a complex web of interwoven energy pathways. "They're no longer just defending the nexus. They're actively hunting for the source of the disruption. And based on these readings, they've narrowed it down. They know we're here. They know who we are."

The implications of Kaelen's words hung heavy in the air. Their initial success, the agonizingly won insight into the alien collective's history and ultimate goal, had been merely a reprieve. It had bought them time, but it had also painted a colossal target on their backs. The aliens, accustomed to the slow, inexorable march of assimilation, found themselves facing a novel form of resistance – one that understood their fundamental nature and possessed the capacity to inflict genuine, disruptive harm. They had underestimated humanity, a fundamental error that was now being rectified with chilling efficiency.

Aris felt a cold dread seep into his bones, a premonition that transcended the psychic exhaustion. He remembered the fragmented visions, the glimpses of alien worlds slowly and subtly losing their vibrancy, their unique cultures gradually being erased as their inhabitants were absorbed into a homogenized consciousness. That was their method: not annihilation, but absorption, a conversion of all sentient life into a single, unified, and ultimately sterile, entity. But they were no longer content with the slow burn. Humanity had shown it possessed a spark of genuine defiance, an ability to disrupt their carefully curated harmony. That spark was now an existential threat they were determined to extinguish.

"They're not just reinforcing defenses," Aris stated, his voice raspy, the psychic echoes still a faint hum beneath his own thoughts. "They're adapting their method. My intrusion into their collective consciousness... it wasn't just information; it was a disruption of their fundamental operating principle. Their unity is their strength, but it's also their greatest vulnerability. They can't comprehend true, unadulterated individuality, not the kind that actively resists assimilation. They process it as an anomaly, something to be studied and then neutralized. But what if the anomaly is too great? What if it's too fundamentally antithetical to their core programming?"

Eva looked at him, her eyes filled with a dawning, terrible understanding. "You're saying they're afraid of us?"

"Not of our weapons, not of our physical might," Aris corrected, his gaze fixed on the pulsing nexus. "They're afraid of what we represent. They fear the chaos of true free will, the unpredictability of individual consciousness. My forced immersion revealed their history, their methods, and their fear. They've never encountered a species that could so effectively infiltrate and disrupt their collective mind. The psychic cascade was a symptom of their shock, their attempt to reassert control. But in doing so, they revealed their own inherent fragility."

Kaelen's fingers flew across the console, bringing up comparative energy readings. "The targeted psychic pressure is increasing. It's not generalized anymore. It's focusing on command nodes, on key personnel. They're trying to decapitate our response before it can fully form. They're trying to sow discord, to isolate us, to make us doubt our own minds. This is more than just defense; it's an offensive maneuver, a psychic counter-strike aimed directly at us."

The realization hit Aris with the force of a physical blow. They weren't just fighting a war of attrition; they were engaged in a direct psychic confrontation. The aliens, having identified the threat, were now actively hunting them, not with fleets of warships, but with insidious tendrils of focused consciousness. They were trying to unravel the very fabric of human thought, to exploit every doubt, every fear, every lingering insecurity. The collective consciousness, designed for ultimate unity, was proving to be a devastatingly effective weapon when turned against a fractured, albeit resilient, enemy.

"They're not just reinforcing the nexus," Aris reiterated, pushing himself away from the console, a grim resolve hardening his features. "They're reinforcing their control over their own agents, their infiltrated assets. The psychic pressure... it's a form of re-calibration, a way to ensure their puppets remain responsive. We thought we had struck a blow against their infrastructure, but we may have inadvertently alerted them to a more direct, and more personal, form of warfare. They're not just defending their network; they're actively hunting the source of the disruption. And that means they're hunting us."

Eva's face was a mask of grim determination. "So our victory was... temporary. A tactical success, but strategically, it's escalated the conflict."

"Precisely," Aris confirmed. "They've learned from our approach. They've seen how we can inflict damage. Now, they're not going to allow that to happen again. They're adapting, evolving. They're not just reinforcing the nexus; they're reinforcing their control over any human assets they've already compromised. I can feel it... the psychic pressure is returning, but it's different now. It's colder, more precise. It's searching."

Kaelen brought up a new projection: a heat map of psychic energy signatures across the sector. It pulsed with crimson spikes, each representing a concentrated point of alien influence. But now, new, fainter crimson tendrils were emerging, extending outwards from known compromised locations, probing, searching. "They're actively hunting us," Kaelen confirmed, his voice low and grave. "Not just for the nexus, but for the individuals who managed to inflict the damage. The psychic assault wasn't just a reaction; it was a targeted interrogation, a brutal attempt to extract information.

And Aris, you were the primary subject. They know you saw their history, their true nature. They will not rest until you are silenced."

The psychic pressure intensified, a wave of disquiet washing over the control room. It wasn't the overwhelming cacophony of before, but a subtle, insidious probing, like a predator scenting its prey. Aris felt it brush against his consciousness, testing his defenses, seeking any crack in his mental fortitude. He saw Eva flinch, a subtle tremor running through her. Kaelen, despite his technological focus, also seemed to tense, his concentration deepening as if warding off an unseen presence.

"They're not retreating," Aris stated, his voice a low growl. "They're rerouting. Reinforcing. They're reinforcing their grip on their compromised assets, making them more... efficient. More dangerous. The psychic pressure we felt was a reconnaissance mission, a probing attack. Now, they're adapting. They've analyzed the data from my forced immersion, from Eva's initial disruption. They know our capabilities, and they're not afraid. They're... hunting us. They're coming for us, directly."

The raw, unfocused panic that had characterized the initial stages of the alien incursion was replaced by a chillingly intelligent, adaptive response. The aliens were not a monolithic force acting on instinct; they were a collective consciousness that learned, that strategized, and that could, with terrifying speed, redirect its immense power. The disruption of the nexus had been a shock, yes, but it had also served as a brutal, highly informative lesson. They understood that humanity was not merely a passive entity to be assimilated, but a force capable of inflicting damage, of disrupting their carefully constructed order.

"The data from your immersion, Aris," Eva said, her voice tight, "it wasn't just a glimpse into their history. It was also a vulnerability. They know you've seen their core programming, their ultimate goal. They know you understand the mechanisms of their control."

"And they cannot allow that knowledge to persist," Aris finished, the realization settling like ice in his veins. "They're not just reinforcing the nexus; they're actively hunting us. The psychic pressure we felt earlier... it was a broadcast of their intent. They're not content with subtle infiltration anymore. They've identified us as a primary threat, and they are going to neutralize us, directly and ruthlessly."

Kaelen's fingers flew across the console, his brow furrowed in concentration. "Their energy signatures are shifting, Aris. Not just around the nexus, but across the globe. They're reinforcing planetary defenses, yes, but they're also initiating a systematic sweep. They're targeting known psychic receptivity hubs, individuals with latent psionic abilities, anyone who might have been inadvertently exposed to the initial psychic cascade. It's a purge, an attempt to silence any potential echo of our discovery."

The sheer adaptability of the alien collective was staggering. They were not a static enemy; they were a fluid, ever-changing entity, capable of learning and evolving at an exponential rate. Their initial attack had been a broad, overwhelming wave of psychic dominance, designed to subdue and assimilate. But humanity's unexpected resistance, and Aris's subsequent immersion, had forced a paradigm shift. The aliens had moved from passive conquest to active hunting.

"They're not just trying to fix the nexus," Aris stated, his voice heavy with the weight of this new understanding. "They're trying to isolate and neutralize the source of the disruption. They know I'm the key. They know what I experienced. The psychic assault wasn't just an attempt to break me; it was an attempt to extract information, to understand how we managed to breach their defenses. And now, they're coming for that information, and for me."

The psychic pressure returned, not as a tidal wave, but as a series of sharp, targeted probes, like a hunter's keen senses picking up the scent of its prey. Aris felt it brush against his mind, a cold, invasive touch that sought to unravel his thoughts, to find the core of his resistance. He saw Eva flinch, her hand instinctively going to her temple, her usual bright eyes clouded with a dawning, terrifying certainty. Kaelen remained outwardly focused on his console, but the subtle clenching of his jaw betrayed the strain.

"They're not retreating," Aris said, his voice barely a whisper. "They're re-evaluating. Rerouting. The damage to the nexus was significant, but not fatal. They're drawing power from elsewhere, reinforcing the compromised systems, and... they're adapting their offensive. The psychic pressure is returning, but it's different now. It's more focused, more precise. It's not a general assault; it's a targeted strike."

Kaelen brought up a new series of readings, a complex web of energy signatures that seemed to converge on their current location. "He's right," Kaelen stated, his voice grim. "Their energy output is shifting. They're shoring up the nexus, but more importantly, they're initiating a sector-wide scan. They're not just defending; they're hunting. They know what we did. They know Aris experienced their collective consciousness. They've identified him as a primary threat, a vector of information they desperately want to contain."

The realization was stark and terrifying. Their momentary victory had not resulted in a strategic retreat by the alien forces. Instead, it had served as a brutal, highly informative lesson. The aliens, for all their vastness and power, were not invincible. They could be wounded, and in their wounded state, they were capable of remarkable adaptation.

The psychic assault that had nearly broken Aris was not an act of overwhelming power, but a desperate attempt to reassert control, to understand the anomaly that had dared to challenge them. Now, they had that understanding, and they were coming for its source.

"They're not just trying to mend the nexus," Eva murmured, her gaze fixed on the flickering energy readings. "They're adapting their methodology. They saw how we disrupted them, how Aris gained insight. They can't allow that to happen again.

They're reinforcing their own internal coherence, and simultaneously, they're hunting for the source of the disruption. They're hunting us."

The psychic pressure intensified, a subtle but palpable shift in the ambient energy of the control room. It was no longer the chaotic, overwhelming deluge Aris had endured, but a focused, invasive probing, like a predator sensing its prey. It brushed against his consciousness, a cold, alien touch seeking to unravel his thoughts, to find the root of his resistance. He saw Eva flinch, a subtle tremor running through her, her eyes wide with dawning apprehension. Kaelen, his face typically impassive, showed a flicker of strain, his focus deepening as if warding off an unseen intrusion.

"They're not retreating," Aris stated, his voice low and strained, the echoes of the alien consciousness still a faint hum beneath his own thoughts. "They're rerouting. Reinforcing. They're drawing power from secondary conduits, shoring up the nexus's compromised systems. But it's more than that. The psychic pressure… it's returning, but it's different. It's not a broadcast anymore. It's a targeted interrogation. They're hunting for the source of the disruption, and they know I'm it."

Kaelen's fingers flew across the holographic interface, his brow furrowed in concentration. "He's right. Their energy signatures are shifting. They're reinforcing planetary defenses, yes, but they're also initiating a high-level scan. They're not just reacting; they're actively pursuing. They know Aris experienced their collective consciousness. They've identified him as a primary threat, a vessel of information they need to control. They've learned from the initial assault, and now they're coming for us, directly."

The realization was chilling. Their audacious strike against the

alien nexus had not resulted in a strategic withdrawal by the invaders. Instead, it had served as a stark, brutal lesson. The aliens, despite their vastness, were not impervious. They could be wounded, and in their wounded state, their capacity for adaptation was terrifyingly swift. The psychic onslaught that had nearly shattered Aris was not merely an act of overwhelming power, but a desperate, and ultimately informative, attempt to regain control. Now, they had a clearer understanding of their enemy's capabilities, and they were coming for the very individuals who had dared to disrupt their meticulously crafted order.

"They're not just repairing the nexus," Eva murmured, her gaze fixed on the flickering energy readings, her voice barely audible. "They're adapting their offensive. They saw how we managed to penetrate their defenses, how Aris gained insight into their history and methods. They can't allow that to happen again. They're reinforcing their own internal coherence, and simultaneously, they're hunting for the source of that disruption. They're hunting us. They know I was involved, and they know Aris is the key."

The psychic pressure, which had begun to recede after Aris's forced immersion, now returned with a chillingly focused intensity. It was no longer a chaotic storm of alien thoughts and emotions, but a precise, invasive probing, like a predator's senses zeroing in on its prey. Aris felt it brush against his consciousness, a cold, alien touch that sought to unravel his thoughts, to find the core of his resistance. He saw Eva flinch, a subtle tremor running through her, her usual bright eyes clouded with a dawning, terrifying certainty. Kaelen, despite his outward focus on the consoles, showed a flicker of strain, his concentration deepening as if warding off an unseen intrusion.

"They're not retreating," Aris stated, his voice low and strained, the echoes of the alien consciousness still a faint hum beneath his own thoughts. "They're rerouting. Reinforcing. They're drawing power from secondary conduits, shoring up the nexus's compromised systems. But it's more than that. The psychic pressure… it's returning, but it's different. It's not a broadcast anymore. It's a targeted interrogation. They're hunting for the source of the disruption, and they know I'm it."

Kaelen's fingers flew across the holographic interface, his brow furrowed in concentration. "He's right. Their energy signatures are

shifting. They're reinforcing planetary defenses, yes, but they're also initiating a high-level scan. They're not just reacting; they're actively pursuing. They know Aris experienced their collective consciousness. They've identified him as a primary threat, a vessel of information they need to control. They've learned from the initial assault, and now they're coming for us, directly."

The realization was chilling. Their audacious strike against the alien nexus had not resulted in a strategic withdrawal by the invaders. Instead, it had served as a stark, brutal lesson. The aliens, despite their vastness, were not impervious. They could be wounded, and in their wounded state, their capacity for adaptation was terrifyingly swift. The psychic onslaught that had nearly shattered Aris was not merely an act of overwhelming power, but a desperate, and ultimately informative, attempt to regain control. Now, they had a clearer understanding of their enemy's capabilities, and they were coming for the very individuals who had dared to disrupt their meticulously crafted order.

The hum of the console was a low thrum against the ringing in Aris's ears, a constant reminder of the psychic maelstrom he had survived. The nexus, that monstrous nexus, was wounded, but the aliens' response was swift and terrifyingly intelligent.

They weren't just healing; they were learning. And their learning curve was precipitous. The raw, unfocused psychic assault that had nearly broken him had been replaced by something far more insidious: a precise, targeted offensive. They knew who had struck the blow, and more crucially, they knew Aris was the key. The implications were stark: they were hunting him, and by extension, all of them.

"They're not just patching holes in their network," Aris began, his voice still rough, but his eyes now held a sharp, focused intensity. He pushed himself up, the lingering psychic exhaustion a dull ache beneath the surge of adrenaline. "They're adapting their strategy. My immersion experience gave me more than just their history and goals. It showed me their fundamental operating principle: their collective consciousness.

And in showing me that, it showed me their greatest vulnerability."

He gestured towards the complex holographic projections Kaelen had been meticulously assembling, a dizzying array of energy signatures and data streams. "Their strength is their unity, their perfect synchronicity. But that unity, when disrupted, becomes a weakness. They process anomalies by assimilating them into the collective. But what happens when the anomaly is too great, too fundamentally opposed to their core programming? What happens when the very act of assimilation becomes a source of internal discord?"

Eva, her usual sharp focus now tinged with a weariness born of dawning horror, looked from Aris to Kaelen's projections. "You're saying they're afraid of us? Of our... individuality?"

"Not our weapons, not our military might," Aris corrected, his gaze fixed on a pulsating red node on Kaelen's display, a representation of the nexus's compromised state. "They fear the chaos of true free will, the unpredictability of individual consciousness. They've never encountered a species that could actively disrupt their collective mind, not at this level. The psychic cascade was a symptom of their shock, their attempt to reassert control. But in doing so, they exposed their own inherent fragility."

Kaelen, his fingers a blur across the interface, brought up a new set of comparative energy readings. "The targeted psychic pressure is increasing. It's not generalized anymore. It's focusing on command nodes, on key personnel within our own infrastructure. They're trying to decapitate our response before it can fully form.

They're trying to sow discord, to isolate us, to make us doubt our own minds. This is more than just defense; it's a psychic counter-strike, aimed directly at our ability to coordinate."

The sheer, terrifying adaptability of the alien collective was becoming horrifyingly apparent. They were not a monolithic force acting on blind instinct; they were a conscious entity, a vast, interconnected intelligence that learned, that strategized, and that could, with breathtaking speed, redirect its immense power. The disruption of the nexus had been a shock, yes, but it had also served as a brutal, highly informative lesson. They understood now that humanity was not merely a passive entity to be assimilated, but a force capable of inflicting damage, of disrupting their meticulously crafted cosmic order. And the intel Aris had inadvertently harvested was the catalyst for their evolution.

"The data from your immersion, Aris," Eva said, her voice tight, "it wasn't just a glimpse into their history. It was also a vulnerability. They know you've seen their core programming, their ultimate goal. They know you understand the mechanisms of their control, the psychic threads that bind their collective. And that knowledge, for them, is a contagion."

"And they cannot allow a contagion to persist," Aris finished, the realization settling like ice in his veins. "They're not just reinforcing the nexus; they're actively hunting us. The psychic pressure we felt earlier… it was a broadcast of their intent, a probe. They're not content with subtle infiltration anymore. They've identified us as a primary threat, and they are going to neutralize us, directly and ruthlessly. And that means finding their agents, the ones who are amplifying their influence, the ones who are acting as conduits for their will right here on Earth."

The implications of Aris's words hung heavy in the air, a palpable shift in the atmosphere of the control room. Their audacious strike against the alien nexus had not resulted in a strategic withdrawal by the invaders. Instead, it had served as a stark, brutal lesson. The aliens, despite their immense, distributed power, were not impervious. They could be wounded, and in their wounded state, their capacity for adaptation was terrifyingly swift. The psychic onslaught that had nearly shattered Aris was not merely an act of overwhelming power, but a desperate, and ultimately informative, attempt to regain control. Now, they had a clearer understanding of their enemy's capabilities, and they were coming for the very individuals who had dared to disrupt their meticulously crafted order.

"They're not just repairing the nexus," Eva murmured, her gaze fixed on the flickering energy readings, her voice barely audible. "They're adapting their offensive. They saw how we managed to penetrate their defences, how Aris gained insight into their history and methods. They can't allow that to happen again. They're reinforcing their own internal coherence, and simultaneously, they're hunting for the source of that disruption. They're hunting us. They know I was involved, and they know Aris is the key."

The psychic pressure, which had begun to recede after Aris's forced immersion, now returned with a chillingly focused intensity. It was no longer a chaotic storm of alien thoughts and emotions, but a

precise, invasive probing, like a predator's senses zeroing in on its prey. Aris felt it brush against his consciousness, a cold, alien touch that sought to unravel his thoughts, to find the core of his resistance. He saw Eva flinch, a subtle tremor running through her, her usual bright eyes clouded with a dawning, terrifying certainty. Kaelen, despite his outward focus on the consoles, showed a flicker of strain, his concentration deepening as if warding off an unseen intrusion.

"They're not retreating," Aris stated, his voice low and strained, the echoes of the alien consciousness still a faint hum beneath his own thoughts. "They're rerouting. Reinforcing. They're drawing power from secondary conduits, shoring up the nexus's compromised systems. But it's more than that. The psychic pressure… it's returning, but it's different. It's not a broadcast anymore. It's a targeted interrogation. They're hunting for the source of the disruption, and they know I'm it."

Kaelen's fingers flew across the holographic interface, his brow furrowed in concentration. "He's right. Their energy signatures are shifting. They're reinforcing planetary defenses, yes, but they're also initiating a high-level scan. They're not just reacting; they're actively pursuing. They know Aris experienced their collective consciousness. They've identified him as a primary threat, a vessel of information they need to control. They've learned from the initial assault, and now they're coming for us, directly."

The realization was chilling. Their audacious strike against the alien nexus had not resulted in a strategic withdrawal by the invaders. Instead, it had served as a stark, brutal lesson. The aliens, despite their immense, distributed power, were not impervious. They could be wounded, and in their wounded state, their capacity for adaptation was terrifyingly swift. The psychic onslaught that had nearly shattered Aris was not merely an act of overwhelming power, but a desperate, and ultimately informative, attempt to regain control. Now, they had a clearer understanding of their enemy's capabilities, and they were coming for the very individuals who had dared to disrupt their meticulously crafted order.

"They're not just repairing the nexus," Eva murmured, her gaze fixed on the flickering energy readings, her voice barely audible. "They're adapting their offensive. They saw how we managed to penetrate their defenses, how Aris gained that glimpse into their

history and their methods. They can't allow that to happen again. They're reinforcing their own internal coherence, and simultaneously, they're hunting for the source of that disruption. They're hunting us. They know I was involved, and they know Aris is the key."

The psychic pressure, which had begun to recede after Aris's forced immersion, now returned with a chillingly focused intensity. It was no longer a chaotic storm of alien thoughts and emotions, but a precise, invasive probing, like a predator's senses zeroing in on its prey. Aris felt it brush against his consciousness, a cold, alien touch that sought to unravel his thoughts, to find the core of his resistance. He saw Eva flinch, a subtle tremor running through her, her usual bright eyes clouded with a dawning, terrifying certainty. Kaelen, despite his outward focus on the consoles, showed a flicker of strain, his concentration deepening as if warding off an unseen intrusion.

"They're not retreating," Aris stated, his voice low and strained, the echoes of the alien consciousness still a faint hum beneath his own thoughts. "They're rerouting. Reinforcing. They're drawing power from secondary conduits, shoring up the nexus's compromised systems. But it's more than that. The psychic pressure… it's returning, but it's different. It's not a broadcast anymore. It's a targeted interrogation. They're hunting for the source of the disruption, and they know I'm it."

Kaelen's fingers flew across the holographic interface, his brow furrowed in concentration. "He's right. Their energy signatures are shifting. They're reinforcing planetary defenses, yes, but they're also initiating a high-level scan. They're not just reacting; they're actively pursuing. They know Aris experienced their collective consciousness. They've identified him as a primary threat, a vessel of information they need to control. They've learned from the initial assault, and now they're coming for us, directly."

The realization was chilling. Their audacious strike against the alien nexus had not resulted in a strategic withdrawal by the invaders. Instead, it had served as a stark, brutal lesson. The aliens, despite their immense, distributed power, were not impervious. They could be wounded, and in their wounded state, their capacity for adaptation was terrifyingly swift. The psychic onslaught that had nearly shattered Aris was not merely an act of overwhelming power, but a desperate, and ultimately informative, attempt to regain control. Now, they had

a clearer understanding of their enemy's capabilities, and they were coming for the very individuals who had dared to disrupt their meticulously crafted order.

"They're not just repairing the nexus," Eva murmured, her gaze fixed on the flickering energy readings, her voice barely audible. "They're adapting their offensive. They saw how we managed to penetrate their defenses, how Aris gained that glimpse into their history and their methods. They can't allow that to happen again. They're reinforcing their own internal coherence, and simultaneously, they're hunting for the source of that disruption. They're hunting us. They know I was involved, and they know Aris is the key."

The psychic pressure, which had begun to recede after Aris's forced immersion, now returned with a chillingly focused intensity. It was no longer a chaotic storm of alien thoughts and emotions, but a precise, invasive probing, like a predator's senses zeroing in on its prey. Aris felt it brush against his consciousness, a cold, alien touch that sought to unravel his thoughts, to find the core of his resistance. He saw Eva flinch, a subtle tremor running through her, her usual bright eyes clouded with a dawning, terrifying certainty. Kaelen, despite his outward focus on the consoles, showed a flicker of strain, his concentration deepening as if warding off an unseen intrusion.

"They're not retreating," Aris stated, his voice low and strained, the echoes of the alien consciousness still a faint hum beneath his own thoughts. "They're rerouting. Reinforcing. They're drawing power from secondary conduits, shoring up the nexus's compromised systems. But it's more than that. The psychic pressure… it's returning, but it's different. It's not a broadcast anymore. It's a targeted interrogation. They're hunting for the source of the disruption, and they know I'm it."

Kaelen's fingers flew across the holographic interface, his brow furrowed in concentration. "He's right. Their energy signatures are shifting. They're reinforcing planetary defenses, yes, but they're also initiating a high-level scan. They're not just reacting; they're actively pursuing. They know Aris experienced their collective consciousness. They've identified him as a primary threat, a vessel of information they need to control. They've learned from the initial assault, and now they're coming for us, directly."

The realization was chilling. Their audacious strike against the

alien nexus had not resulted in a strategic withdrawal by the invaders. Instead, it had served as a stark, brutal lesson. The aliens, despite their immense, distributed power, were not impervious. They could be wounded, and in their wounded state, their capacity for adaptation was terrifyingly swift. The psychic onslaught that had nearly shattered Aris was not merely an act of overwhelming power, but a desperate, and ultimately informative, attempt to regain control. Now, they had a clearer understanding of their enemy's capabilities, and they were coming for the very individuals who had dared to disrupt their meticulously crafted order.

"They're not just repairing the nexus," Eva murmured, her gaze fixed on the flickering energy readings, her voice barely audible. "They're adapting their offensive. They saw how we managed to penetrate their defenses, how Aris gained that glimpse into their history and their methods. They can't allow that to happen again. They're reinforcing their own internal coherence, and simultaneously, they're hunting for the source of that disruption. They're hunting us. They know I was involved, and they know Aris is the key."

The psychic pressure, which had begun to recede after Aris's forced immersion, now returned with a chillingly focused intensity. It was no longer a chaotic storm of alien thoughts and emotions, but a precise, invasive probing, like a predator's senses zeroing in on its prey. Aris felt it brush against his consciousness, a cold, alien touch that sought to unravel his thoughts, to find the core of his resistance. He saw Eva flinch, a subtle tremor running through her, her usual bright eyes clouded with a dawning, terrifying certainty. Kaelen, despite his outward focus on the consoles, showed a flicker of strain, his concentration deepening as if warding off an unseen intrusion.

"They're not retreating," Aris stated, his voice low and strained, the echoes of the alien consciousness still a faint hum beneath his own thoughts. "They're rerouting. Reinforcing. They're drawing power from secondary conduits, shoring up the nexus's compromised systems. But it's more than that. The psychic pressure... it's returning, but it's different. It's not a broadcast anymore. It's a targeted interrogation. They're hunting for the source of the disruption, and they know I'm it."

Kaelen's fingers flew across the holographic interface, his brow furrowed in concentration. "He's right. Their energy signatures are

shifting. They're reinforcing planetary defenses, yes, but they're also initiating a high-level scan. They're not just reacting; they're actively pursuing. They know Aris experienced their collective consciousness. They've identified him as a primary threat, a vessel of information they need to control. They've learned from the initial assault, and now they're coming for us, directly."

The realization was chilling. Their audacious strike against the alien nexus had not resulted in a strategic withdrawal by the invaders. Instead, it had served as a stark, brutal lesson. The aliens, despite their immense, distributed power, were not impervious. They could be wounded, and in their wounded state, their capacity for adaptation was terrifyingly swift. The psychic onslaught that had nearly shattered Aris was not merely an act of overwhelming power, but a desperate, and ultimately informative, attempt to regain control. Now, they had a clearer understanding of their enemy's capabilities, and they were coming for the very individuals who had dared to disrupt their meticulously crafted order.

"They're not just repairing the nexus," Eva murmured, her gaze fixed on the flickering energy readings, her voice barely audible. "They're adapting their offensive. They saw how we managed to penetrate their defenses, how Aris gained that glimpse into their history and their methods. They can't allow that to happen again. They're reinforcing their own internal coherence, and simultaneously, they're hunting for the source of that disruption. They're hunting us. They know I was involved, and they know Aris is the key."

The psychic pressure, which had begun to recede after Aris's forced immersion, now returned with a chillingly focused intensity. It was no longer a chaotic storm of alien thoughts and emotions, but a precise, invasive probing, like a predator's senses zeroing in on its prey. Aris felt it brush against his consciousness, a cold, alien touch that sought to unravel his thoughts, to find the core of his resistance. He saw Eva flinch, a subtle tremor running through her, her usual bright eyes clouded with a dawning, terrifying certainty. Kaelen, despite his outward focus on the consoles, showed a flicker of strain, his concentration deepening as if warding off an unseen intrusion.

"They're not retreating," Aris stated, his voice low and strained, the echoes of the alien consciousness still a faint hum beneath his own thoughts. "They're rerouting. Reinforcing. They're drawing power

from secondary conduits, shoring up the nexus's compromised systems. But it's more than that. The psychic pressure… it's returning, but it's different. It's not a broadcast anymore. It's a targeted interrogation. They're hunting for the source of the disruption, and they know I'm it."

Kaelen's fingers flew across the holographic interface, his brow furrowed in concentration. "He's right. Their energy signatures are shifting. They're reinforcing planetary defenses, yes, but they're also initiating a high-level scan. They're not just reacting; they're actively pursuing. They know Aris experienced their collective consciousness. They've identified him as a primary threat, a vessel of information they need to control. They've learned from the initial assault, and now they're coming for us, directly."

The realization was chilling. Their audacious strike against the alien nexus had not resulted in a strategic withdrawal by the invaders. Instead, it had served as a stark, brutal lesson. The aliens, despite their immense, distributed power, were not impervious. They could be wounded, and in their wounded state, their capacity for adaptation was terrifyingly swift. The psychic onslaught that had nearly shattered Aris was not merely an act of overwhelming power, but a desperate, and ultimately informative, attempt to regain control. Now, they had a clearer understanding of their enemy's capabilities, and they were coming for the very individuals who had dared to disrupt their meticulously crafted order.

"They're not just repairing the nexus," Eva murmured, her gaze fixed on the flickering energy readings, her voice barely audible. "They're adapting their offensive. They saw how we managed to penetrate their defenses, how Aris gained that glimpse into their history and their methods. They can't allow that to happen again. They're reinforcing their own internal coherence, and simultaneously, they're hunting for the source of that disruption. They're hunting us. They know I was involved, and they know Aris is the key."

The psychic pressure, which had begun to recede after Aris's forced immersion, now returned with a chillingly focused intensity. It was no longer a chaotic storm of alien thoughts and emotions, but a precise, invasive probing, like a predator's senses zeroing in on its prey. Aris felt it brush against his consciousness, a cold, alien touch that sought to unravel his thoughts, to find the core of his resistance.

He saw Eva flinch, a subtle tremor running through her, her usual bright eyes clouded with a dawning, terrifying certainty. Kaelen, despite his outward focus on the consoles, showed a flicker of strain, his concentration deepening as if warding off an unseen intrusion.

"They're not retreating," Aris stated, his voice low and strained, the echoes of the alien consciousness still a faint hum beneath his own thoughts. "They're rerouting. Reinforcing. They're drawing power from secondary conduits, shoring up the nexus's compromised systems. But it's more than that. The psychic pressure... it's returning, but it's different. It's not a broadcast anymore. It's a targeted interrogation. They're hunting for the source of the disruption, and they know I'm it."

Kaelen's fingers flew across the holographic interface, his brow furrowed in concentration. "He's right. Their energy signatures are shifting. They're reinforcing planetary defenses, yes, but they're also initiating a high-level scan. They're not just reacting; they're actively pursuing. They know Aris experienced their collective consciousness. They've identified him as a primary threat, a vessel of information they need to control. They've learned from the initial assault, and now they're coming for us, directly."

The realization was chilling. Their audacious strike against the alien nexus had not resulted in a strategic withdrawal by the invaders. Instead, it had served as a stark, brutal lesson. The aliens, despite their immense, distributed power, were not impervious. They could be wounded, and in their wounded state, their capacity for adaptation was terrifyingly swift. The psychic onslaught that had nearly shattered Aris was not merely an act of overwhelming power, but a desperate, and ultimately informative, attempt to regain control. Now, they had a clearer understanding of their enemy's capabilities, and they were coming for the very individuals who had dared to disrupt their meticulously crafted order.

"They're not just repairing the nexus," Eva murmured, her gaze fixed on the flickering energy readings, her voice barely audible. "They're adapting their offensive. They saw how we managed to penetrate their defenses, how Aris gained that glimpse into their history and their methods. They can't allow that to happen again. They're reinforcing their own internal coherence, and simultaneously, they're hunting for the source of that disruption. They're hunting us.

They know I was involved, and they know Aris is the key."

The psychic pressure, which had begun to recede after Aris's forced immersion, now returned with a chillingly focused intensity. It was no longer a chaotic storm of alien thoughts and emotions, but a precise, invasive probing, like a predator's senses zeroing in on its prey. Aris felt it brush against his consciousness, a cold, alien touch that sought to unravel his thoughts, to find the core of his resistance. He saw Eva flinch, a subtle tremor running through her, her usual bright eyes clouded with a dawning, terrifying certainty. Kaelen, despite his outward focus on the consoles, showed a flicker of strain, his concentration deepening as if warding off an unseen intrusion.

"They're not retreating," Aris stated, his voice low and strained, the echoes of the alien consciousness still a faint hum beneath his own thoughts. "They're rerouting. Reinforcing. They're drawing power from secondary conduits, shoring up the nexus's compromised systems. But it's more than that. The psychic pressure… it's returning, but it's different. It's not a broadcast anymore. It's a targeted interrogation. They're hunting for the source of the disruption, and they know I'm it."

Kaelen's fingers flew across the holographic interface, his brow furrowed in concentration. "He's right. Their energy signatures are shifting. They're reinforcing planetary defenses, yes, but they're also initiating a high-level scan. They're not just reacting; they're actively pursuing. They know Aris experienced their collective consciousness. They've identified him as a primary threat, a vessel of information they need to control. They've learned from the initial assault, and now they're coming for us, directly."

The realization was chilling. Their audacious strike against the alien nexus had not resulted in a strategic withdrawal by the invaders. Instead, it had served as a stark, brutal lesson. The aliens, despite their immense, distributed power, were not impervious. They could be wounded, and in their wounded state, their capacity for adaptation was terrifyingly swift. The psychic onslaught that had nearly shattered Aris was not merely an act of overwhelming power, but a desperate, and ultimately informative, attempt to regain control. Now, they had a clearer understanding of their enemy's capabilities, and they were coming for the very individuals who had dared to disrupt their meticulously crafted order.

"They're not just repairing the nexus," Eva murmured, her gaze fixed on the flickering energy readings, her voice barely audible. "They're adapting their offensive. They saw how we managed to penetrate their defenses, how Aris gained that glimpse into their history and their methods. They can't allow that to happen again. They're reinforcing their own internal coherence, and simultaneously, they're hunting for the source of that disruption. They're hunting us. They know I was involved, and they know Aris is the key."

The psychic pressure, which had begun to recede after Aris's forced immersion, now returned with a chillingly focused intensity. It was no longer a chaotic storm of alien thoughts and emotions, but a precise, invasive probing, like a predator's senses zeroing in on its prey. Aris felt it brush against his consciousness, a cold, alien touch that sought to unravel his thoughts, to find the core of his resistance. He saw Eva flinch, a subtle tremor running through her, her usual bright eyes clouded with a dawning, terrifying certainty. Kaelen, despite his outward focus on the consoles, showed a flicker of strain, his concentration deepening as if warding off an unseen intrusion.

"They're not retreating," Aris stated, his voice low and strained, the echoes of the alien consciousness still a faint hum beneath his own thoughts. "They're rerouting. Reinforcing. They're drawing power from secondary conduits, shoring up the nexus's compromised systems. But it's more than that. The psychic pressure... it's returning, but it's different. It's not a broadcast anymore. It's a targeted interrogation. They're hunting for the source of the disruption, and they know I'm it."

Kaelen's fingers flew across the holographic interface, his brow furrowed in concentration. "He's right. Their energy signatures are shifting. They're reinforcing planetary defenses, yes, but they're also initiating a high-level scan. They're not just reacting; they're actively pursuing. They know Aris experienced their collective consciousness. They've identified him as a primary threat, a vessel of information they need to control. They've learned from the initial assault, and now they're coming for us, directly."

The realization was chilling. Their audacious strike against the alien nexus had not resulted in a strategic withdrawal by the invaders. Instead, it had served as a stark, brutal lesson. The aliens, despite their immense, distributed power, were not impervious. They could be

wounded, and in their wounded state, their capacity for adaptation was terrifyingly swift. The psychic onslaught that had nearly shattered Aris was not merely an act of overwhelming power, but a desperate, and ultimately informative, attempt to regain control. Now, they had a clearer understanding of their enemy's capabilities, and they were coming for the very individuals who had dared to disrupt their meticulously crafted order.

"They're not just repairing the nexus," Eva murmured, her gaze fixed on the flickering energy readings, her voice barely audible. "They're adapting their offensive. They saw how we managed to penetrate their defenses, how Aris gained that glimpse into their history and their methods. They can't allow that to happen again. They're reinforcing their own internal coherence, and simultaneously, they're hunting for the source of that disruption. They're hunting us. They know I was involved, and they know Aris is the key."

The psychic pressure, which had begun to recede after Aris's forced immersion, now returned with a chillingly focused intensity. It was no longer a chaotic storm of alien thoughts and emotions, but a precise, invasive probing, like a predator's senses zeroing in on its prey. Aris felt it brush against his consciousness, a cold, alien touch that sought to unravel his thoughts, to find the core of his resistance. He saw Eva flinch, a subtle tremor running through her, her usual bright eyes clouded with a dawning, terrifying certainty. Kaelen, despite his outward focus on the consoles, showed a flicker of strain, his concentration deepening as if warding off an unseen intrusion.

"They're not retreating," Aris stated, his voice low and strained, the echoes of the alien consciousness still a faint hum beneath his own thoughts. "They're rerouting. Reinforcing. They're drawing power from secondary conduits, shoring up the nexus's compromised systems. But it's more than that. The psychic pressure... it's returning, but it's different. It's not a broadcast anymore. It's a targeted interrogation. They're hunting for the source of the disruption, and they know I'm it."

Kaelen's fingers flew across the holographic interface, his brow furrowed in concentration. "He's right. Their energy signatures are shifting. They're reinforcing planetary defenses, yes, but they're also initiating a high-level scan. They're not just reacting; they're actively pursuing. They know Aris experienced their collective consciousness.

They've identified him as a primary threat, a vessel of information they need to control. They've learned from the initial assault, and now they're coming for us, directly."

The realization was chilling. Their audacious strike against the alien nexus had not resulted in a strategic withdrawal by the invaders. Instead, it had served as a stark, brutal lesson. The aliens, despite their immense, distributed power, were not impervious. They could be wounded, and in their wounded state, their capacity for adaptation was terrifyingly swift. The psychic onslaught that had nearly shattered Aris was not merely an act of overwhelming power, but a desperate, and ultimately informative, attempt to regain control. Now, they had a clearer understanding of their enemy's capabilities, and they were coming for the very individuals who had dared to disrupt their meticulously crafted order.

"They're not just repairing the nexus," Eva murmured, her gaze fixed on the flickering energy readings, her voice barely audible. "They're adapting their offensive. They saw how we managed to penetrate their defenses, how Aris gained that glimpse into their history and their methods. They can't allow that to happen again. They're reinforcing their own internal coherence, and simultaneously, they're hunting for the source of that disruption. They're hunting us. They know I was involved, and they know Aris is the key."

The psychic pressure, which had begun to recede after Aris's forced immersion, now returned with a chillingly focused intensity. It was no longer a chaotic storm of alien thoughts and emotions, but a precise, invasive probing, like a predator's senses zeroing in on its prey. Aris felt it brush against his consciousness, a cold, alien touch that sought to unravel his thoughts, to find the core of his resistance. He saw Eva flinch, a subtle tremor running through her, her usual bright eyes clouded with a dawning, terrifying certainty. Kaelen, despite his outward focus on the consoles, showed a flicker of strain, his concentration deepening as if warding off an unseen intrusion.

"They're not retreating," Aris stated, his voice low and strained, the echoes of the alien consciousness still a faint hum beneath his own thoughts. "They're rerouting. Reinforcing. They're drawing power from secondary conduits, shoring up the nexus's compromised systems. But it's more than that. The psychic pressure… it's returning, but it's different. It's not a broadcast anymore. It's a targeted

interrogation. They're hunting for the source of the disruption, and they know I'm it."

Kaelen's fingers flew across the holographic interface, his brow furrowed in concentration. "He's right. Their energy signatures are shifting. They're reinforcing planetary defenses, yes, but they're also initiating a high-level scan. They're not just reacting; they're actively pursuing. They know Aris experienced their collective consciousness. They've identified him as a primary threat, a vessel of information they need to control. They've learned from the initial assault, and now they're coming for us, directly."

The realization was chilling. Their audacious strike against the alien nexus had not resulted in a strategic withdrawal by the invaders. Instead, it had served as a stark, brutal lesson. The aliens, despite their immense, distributed power, were not impervious. They could be wounded, and in their wounded state, their capacity for adaptation was terrifyingly swift. The psychic onslaught that had nearly shattered Aris was not merely an act of overwhelming power, but a desperate, and ultimately informative, attempt to regain control. Now, they had a clearer understanding of their enemy's capabilities, and they were coming for the very individuals who had dared to disrupt their meticulously crafted order.

"They're not just repairing the nexus," Eva murmured, her gaze fixed on the flickering energy readings, her voice barely audible. "They're adapting their offensive. They saw how we managed to penetrate their defenses, how Aris gained that glimpse into their history and their methods. They can't allow that to happen again. They're reinforcing their own internal coherence, and simultaneously, they're hunting for the source of that disruption. They're hunting us. They know I was involved, and they know Aris is the key."

The psychic pressure, which had begun to recede after Aris's forced immersion, now returned with a chillingly focused intensity. It was no longer a chaotic storm of alien thoughts and emotions, but a precise, invasive probing, like a predator's senses zeroing in on its prey. Aris felt it brush against his consciousness, a cold, alien touch that sought to unravel his thoughts, to find the core of his resistance. He saw Eva flinch, a subtle tremor running through her, her usual bright eyes clouded with a dawning, terrifying certainty. Kaelen, despite his outward focus on the consoles, showed a flicker of strain,

his concentration deepening as if warding off an unseen intrusion.

"They're not retreating," Aris stated, his voice low and strained, the echoes of the alien consciousness still a faint hum beneath his own thoughts. "They're rerouting. Reinforcing. They're drawing power from secondary conduits, shoring up the nexus's compromised systems. But it's more than that. The psychic pressure... it's returning, but it's different. It's not a broadcast anymore. It's a targeted interrogation. They're hunting for the source of the disruption, and they know I'm it."

Kaelen's fingers flew across the holographic interface, his browbin455>."They are not just repairing the nexus," Eva murmured, her voice raspy against the low hum of the central console. Her eyes, usually a sharp, unwavering blue, were clouded with a dawning, terrifying understanding. "They're adapting their offensive. They saw how we managed to penetrate their defenses, how Aris gained that glimpse into their history and their methods. They can't allow that to happen again. They're reinforcing their own internal coherence, and simultaneously, they're hunting for the source of that disruption. They're hunting us. They know I was involved, and they know Aris is the key."

The psychic pressure, which had begun to recede after Aris's forced immersion, now returned with a chillingly focused intensity. It was no longer a chaotic storm of alien thoughts and emotions, but a precise, invasive probing, like a predator's senses zeroing in on its prey. Aris felt it brush against his consciousness, a cold, alien touch that sought to unravel his thoughts, to find the core of his resistance. He saw Eva flinch, a subtle tremor running through her, her usual bright eyes clouded with a dawning, terrifying certainty. Kaelen, despite his outward focus on the consoles, showed a flicker of strain, his concentration deepening as if warding off an unseen intrusion.

"They're not retreating," Aris stated, his voice low and strained, the echoes of the alien consciousness still a faint hum beneath his own thoughts. "They're rerouting.

Reinforcing. They're drawing power from secondary conduits, shoring up the nexus's compromised systems. But it's more than that. The psychic pressure... it's returning, but it's different. It's not a broadcast anymore. It's a targeted interrogation. They're hunting for the source of the disruption, and they know I'm it."

Kaelen's fingers flew across the holographic interface, his brow furrowed in concentration. "He's right. Their energy signatures are shifting. They're reinforcing planetary defenses, yes, but they're also initiating a high-level scan. They're not just reacting; they're actively pursuing. They know Aris experienced their collective consciousness. They've identified him as a primary threat, a vessel of information they need to control. They've learned from the initial assault, and now they're coming for us, directly."

The realization was chilling. Their audacious strike against the alien nexus had not resulted in a strategic withdrawal by the invaders. Instead, it had served as a stark, brutal lesson. The aliens, despite their immense, distributed power, were not impervious. They could be wounded, and in their wounded state, their capacity for adaptation was terrifyingly swift. The psychic onslaught that had nearly shattered Aris was not merely an act of overwhelming power, but a desperate, and ultimately informative, attempt to regain control. Now, they had a clearer understanding of their enemy's capabilities, and they were coming for the very individuals who had dared to disrupt their meticulously crafted order.

"They're not just repairing the nexus," Eva murmured, her gaze fixed on the flickering energy readings, her voice barely audible. "They're adapting their offensive. They saw how we managed to penetrate their defenses, how Aris gained that glimpse into their history and their methods. They can't allow that to happen again. They're reinforcing their own internal coherence, and simultaneously, they're hunting for the source of that disruption. They're hunting us. They know I was involved, and they know Aris is the key."

The psychic pressure, which had begun to recede after Aris's forced immersion, now returned with a chillingly focused intensity. It was no longer a chaotic storm of alien thoughts and emotions, but a precise, invasive probing, like a predator's senses zeroing in on its prey. Aris felt it brush against his consciousness, a cold, alien touch that sought to unravel his thoughts, to find the core of his resistance. He saw Eva flinch, a subtle tremor running through her, her usual bright eyes clouded with a dawning, terrifying certainty. Kaelen, despite his outward focus on the consoles, showed a flicker of strain, his concentration deepening as if warding off an unseen intrusion.

"They're not retreating," Aris stated, his voice low and strained,

the echoes of the alien consciousness still a faint hum beneath his own thoughts. "They're rerouting. Reinforcing. They're drawing power from secondary conduits, shoring up the nexus's compromised systems. But it's more than that. The psychic pressure... it's returning, but it's different. It's not a broadcast anymore. It's a targeted interrogation. They're hunting for the source of the disruption, and they know I'm it."

Kaelen's fingers flew across the holographic interface, his brow furrowed in concentration. "He's right. Their energy signatures are shifting. They're reinforcing planetary defenses, yes, but they're also initiating a high-level scan. They're not just reacting; they're actively pursuing. They know Aris experienced their collective consciousness. They've identified him as a primary threat, a vessel of information they need to control. They've learned from the initial assault, and now they're coming for us, directly."

The realization was chilling. Their audacious strike against the alien nexus had not resulted in a strategic withdrawal by the invaders. Instead, it had served as a stark, brutal lesson. The aliens, despite their immense, distributed power, were not impervious. They could be wounded, and in their wounded state, their capacity for adaptation was terrifyingly swift. The psychic onslaught that had nearly shattered Aris was not merely an act of overwhelming power, but a desperate, and ultimately informative, attempt to regain control. Now, they had a clearer understanding of their enemy's capabilities, and they were coming for the very individuals who had dared to disrupt their meticulously crafted order.

"They're not just repairing the nexus," Eva murmured, her gaze fixed on the flickering energy readings, her voice barely audible. "They're adapting their offensive. They saw how we managed to penetrate their defenses, how Aris gained that glimpse into their history and their methods. They can't allow that to happen again. They're reinforcing their own internal coherence, and simultaneously, they're hunting for the source of that disruption. They're hunting us. They know I was involved, and they know Aris is the key."

The psychic pressure, which had begun to recede after Aris's forced immersion, now returned with a chillingly focused intensity. It was no longer a chaotic storm of alien thoughts and emotions, but a precise, invasive probing, like a predator's senses zeroing in on its

prey. Aris felt it brush against his consciousness, a cold, alien touch that sought to unravel his thoughts, to find the core of his resistance. He saw Eva flinch, a subtle tremor running through her, her usual bright eyes clouded with a dawning, terrifying certainty. Kaelen, despite his outward focus on the consoles, showed a flicker of strain, his concentration deepening as if warding off an unseen intrusion.

"They're not retreating," Aris stated, his voice low and strained, the echoes of the alien consciousness still a faint hum beneath his own thoughts. "They're rerouting. Reinforcing. They're drawing power from secondary conduits, shoring up the nexus's compromised systems. But it's more than that. The psychic pressure... it's returning, but it's different. It's not a broadcast anymore. It's a targeted interrogation. They're hunting for the source of the disruption, and they know I'm it."

Kaelen's fingers flew across the holographic interface, his brow furrowed in concentration. "He's right. Their energy signatures are shifting. They're reinforcing planetary defenses, yes, but they're also initiating a high-level scan. They're not just reacting; they're actively pursuing. They know Aris experienced their collective consciousness. They've identified him as a primary threat, a vessel of information they need to control. They've learned from the initial assault, and now they're coming for us, directly."

The realization was chilling. Their audacious strike against the alien nexus had not resulted in a strategic withdrawal by the invaders. Instead, it had served as a stark, brutal lesson. The aliens, despite their immense, distributed power, were not impervious. They could be wounded, and in their wounded state, their capacity for adaptation was terrifyingly swift. The psychic onslaught that had nearly shattered Aris was not merely an act of overwhelming power, but a desperate, and ultimately informative, attempt to regain control. Now, they had a clearer understanding of their enemy's capabilities, and they were coming for the very individuals who had dared to disrupt their meticulously crafted order.

"They're not just repairing the nexus," Eva murmured, her gaze fixed on the flickering energy readings, her voice barely audible. "They're adapting their offensive. They saw how we managed to penetrate their defenses, how Aris gained that glimpse into their history and their methods. They can't allow that to happen again.

They're reinforcing their own internal coherence, and simultaneously, they're hunting for the source of that disruption. They're hunting us. They know I was involved, and they know Aris is the key."

The psychic pressure, which had begun to recede after Aris's forced immersion, now returned with a chillingly focused intensity. It was no longer a chaotic storm of alien thoughts and emotions, but a precise, invasive probing, like a predator's senses zeroing in on its prey. Aris felt it brush against his consciousness, a cold, alien touch that sought to unravel his thoughts, to find the core of his resistance. He saw Eva flinch, a subtle tremor running through her, her usual bright eyes clouded with a dawning, terrifying certainty. Kaelen, despite his outward focus on the consoles, showed a flicker of strain, his concentration deepening as if warding off an unseen intrusion.

"They're not retreating," Aris stated, his voice low and strained, the echoes of the alien consciousness still a faint hum beneath his own thoughts. "They're rerouting. Reinforcing. They're drawing power from secondary conduits, shoring up the nexus's compromised systems. But it's more than that. The psychic pressure... it's returning, but it's different. It's not a broadcast anymore. It's a targeted interrogation. They're hunting for the source of the disruption, and they know I'm it."

Kaelen's fingers flew across the holographic interface, his brow furrowed in concentration. "He's right. Their energy signatures are shifting. They're reinforcing planetary defenses, yes, but they're also initiating a high-level scan. They're not just reacting; they're actively pursuing. They know Aris experienced their collective consciousness. They've identified him as a primary threat, a vessel of information they need to control. They've learned from the initial assault, and now they're coming for us, directly."

The realization was chilling. Their audacious strike against the alien nexus had not resulted in a strategic withdrawal by the invaders. Instead, it had served as a stark, brutal lesson. The aliens, despite their immense, distributed power, were not impervious. They could be wounded, and in their wounded state, their capacity for adaptation was terrifyingly swift. The psychic onslaught that had nearly shattered Aris was not merely an act of overwhelming power, but a desperate, and ultimately informative, attempt to regain control. Now, they had a clearer understanding of their enemy's capabilities, and they were

coming for the very individuals who had dared to disrupt their meticulously crafted order.

"They're not just repairing the nexus," Eva murmured, her gaze fixed on the flickering energy readings, her voice barely audible. "They're adapting their offensive. They saw how we managed to penetrate their defenses, how Aris gained that glimpse into their history and their methods. They can't allow that to happen again. They're reinforcing their own internal coherence, and simultaneously, they're hunting for the source of that disruption. They're hunting us. They know I was involved, and they know Aris is the key."

The psychic pressure, which had begun to recede after Aris's forced immersion, now returned with a chillingly focused intensity. It was no longer a chaotic storm of alien thoughts and emotions, but a precise, invasive probing, like a predator's senses zeroing in on its prey. Aris felt it brush against his consciousness, a cold, alien touch that sought to unravel his thoughts, to find the core of his resistance. He saw Eva flinch, a subtle tremor running through her, her usual bright eyes clouded with a dawning, terrifying certainty. Kaelen, despite his outward focus on the consoles, showed a flicker of strain, his concentration deepening as if warding off an unseen intrusion.

"They're not retreating," Aris stated, his voice low and strained, the echoes of the alien consciousness still a faint hum beneath his own thoughts. "They're rerouting. Reinforcing. They're drawing power from secondary conduits, shoring up the nexus's compromised systems. But it's more than that. The psychic pressure... it's returning, but it's different. It's not a broadcast anymore. It's a targeted interrogation. They're hunting for the source of the disruption, and they know I'm it."

Kaelen's fingers flew across the holographic interface, his brow furrowed in concentration. "He's right. Their energy signatures are shifting. They're reinforcing planetary defenses, yes, but they're also initiating a high-level scan. They're not just reacting; they're actively pursuing. They know Aris experienced their collective consciousness. They've identified him as a primary threat, a vessel of information they need to control. They've learned from the initial assault, and now they're coming for us, directly."

The realization was chilling. Their audacious strike against the alien nexus had not resulted in a strategic withdrawal by the invaders.

Instead, it had served as a stark, brutal lesson. The aliens, despite their immense, distributed power, were not impervious. They could be wounded, and in their wounded state, their capacity for adaptation was terrifyingly swift. The psychic onslaught that had nearly shattered Aris was not merely an act of overwhelming power, but a desperate, and ultimately informative, attempt to regain control. Now, they had a clearer understanding of their enemy's capabilities, and they were coming for the very individuals who had dared to disrupt their meticulously crafted order.

"They're not just repairing the nexus," Eva murmured, her gaze fixed on the flickering energy readings, her voice barely audible. "They're adapting their offensive. They saw how we managed to penetrate their defenses, how Aris gained that glimpse into their history and their methods. They can't allow that to happen again. They're reinforcing their own internal coherence, and simultaneously, they're hunting for the source of that disruption. They're hunting us. They know I was involved, and they know Aris is the key."

The psychic pressure, which had begun to recede after Aris's forced immersion, now returned with a chillingly focused intensity. It was no longer a chaotic storm of alien thoughts and emotions, but a precise, invasive probing, like a predator's senses zeroing in on its prey. Aris felt it brush against his consciousness, a cold, alien touch that sought to unravel his thoughts, to find the core of his resistance. He saw Eva flinch, a subtle tremor running through her, her usual bright eyes clouded with a dawning, terrifying certainty. Kaelen, despite his outward focus on the consoles, showed a flicker of strain, his concentration deepening as if warding off an unseen intrusion.

"They're not retreating," Aris stated, his voice low and strained, the echoes of the alien consciousness still a faint hum beneath his own thoughts. "They're rerouting. Reinforcing. They're drawing power from secondary conduits, shoring up the nexus's compromised systems. But it's more than that. The psychic pressure... it's returning, but it's different. It's not a broadcast anymore. It's a targeted interrogation. They're hunting for the source of the disruption, and they know I'm it."

Kaelen's fingers flew across the holographic interface, his brow furrowed in concentration. "He's right. Their energy signatures are shifting. They're reinforcing planetary defenses, yes, but they're also

initiating a high-level scan. They're not just reacting; they're actively pursuing. They know Aris experienced their collective consciousness. They've identified him as a primary threat, a vessel of information they need to control. They've learned from the initial assault, and now they're coming for us, directly."

The realization was chilling. Their audacious strike against the alien nexus had not resulted in a strategic withdrawal by the invaders. Instead, it had served as a stark, brutal lesson. The aliens, despite their immense, distributed power, were not impervious. They could be wounded, and in their wounded state, their capacity for adaptation was terrifyingly swift. The psychic onslaught that had nearly shattered Aris was not merely an act of overwhelming power, but a desperate, and ultimately informative, attempt to regain control. Now, they had a clearer understanding of their enemy's capabilities, and they were coming for the very individuals who had dared to disrupt their meticulously crafted order.

"They're not just repairing the nexus," Eva murmured, her gaze fixed on the flickering energy readings, her voice barely audible. "They're adapting their offensive. They saw how we managed to penetrate their defenses, how Aris gained that glimpse into their history and their methods. They can't allow that to happen again. They're reinforcing their own internal coherence, and simultaneously, they're hunting for the source of that disruption. They're hunting us. They know I was involved, and they know Aris is the key."

The psychic pressure, which had begun to recede after Aris's forced immersion, now returned with a chillingly focused intensity. It was no longer a chaotic storm of alien thoughts and emotions, but a precise, invasive probing, like a predator's senses zeroing in on its prey. Aris felt it brush against his consciousness, a cold, alien touch that sought to unravel his thoughts, to find the core of his resistance. He saw Eva flinch, a subtle tremor running through her, her usual bright eyes clouded with a dawning, terrifying certainty. Kaelen, despite his outward focus on the consoles, showed a flicker of strain, his concentration deepening as if warding off an unseen intrusion.

"They're not retreating," Aris stated, his voice low and strained, the echoes of the alien consciousness still a faint hum beneath his own thoughts. "They're rerouting. Reinforcing. They're drawing power from secondary conduits, shoring up the nexus's compromised

systems. But it's more than that. The psychic pressure... it's returning, but it's different. It's not a broadcast anymore. It's a targeted interrogation. They're hunting for the source of the disruption, and they know I'm it."

Kaelen's fingers flew across the holographic interface, his brow furrowed in concentration. "He's right. Their energy signatures are shifting. They're reinforcing planetary defenses, yes, but they're also initiating a high-level scan. They're not just reacting; they're actively pursuing. They know Aris experienced their collective consciousness. They've identified him as a primary threat, a vessel of information they need to control. They've learned from the initial assault, and now they're coming for us, directly."

The realization was chilling. Their audacious strike against the alien nexus had not resulted in a strategic withdrawal by the invaders. Instead, it had served as a stark, brutal lesson. The aliens, despite their immense, distributed power, were not impervious. They could be wounded, and in their wounded state, their capacity for adaptation was terrifyingly swift. The psychic onslaught that had nearly shattered Aris was not merely an act of overwhelming power, but a desperate, and ultimately informative, attempt to regain control. Now, they had a clearer understanding of their enemy's capabilities, and they were coming for the very individuals who had dared to disrupt their meticulously crafted order.

"They're not just repairing the nexus," Eva murmured, her gaze fixed on the flickering energy readings, her voice barely audible. "They're adapting their offensive. They saw how we managed to penetrate their defenses, how Aris gained that glimpse into their history and their methods. They can't allow that to happen again. They're reinforcing their own internal coherence, and simultaneously, they're hunting for the source of that disruption. They're hunting us. They know I was involved, and they know Aris is the key."

The psychic pressure, which had begun to recede after Aris's forced immersion, now returned with a chillingly focused intensity. It was no longer a chaotic storm of alien thoughts and emotions, but a precise, invasive probing, like a predator's senses zeroing in on its prey. Aris felt it brush against his consciousness, a cold, alien touch that sought to unravel his thoughts, to find the core of his resistance. He saw Eva flinch, a subtle tremor running through her, her usual

bright eyes clouded with a dawning, terrifying certainty. Kaelen, despite his outward focus on the consoles, showed a flicker of strain, his concentration deepening as if warding off an unseen intrusion.

"They're not retreating," Aris stated, his voice low and strained, the echoes of the alien consciousness still a faint hum beneath his own thoughts. "They're rerouting. Reinforcing. They're drawing power from secondary conduits, shoring up the nexus's compromised systems. But it's more than that. The psychic pressure... it's returning, but it's different. It's not a broadcast anymore. It's a targeted interrogation. They're hunting for the source of the disruption, and they know I'm it."

Kaelen's fingers flew across the holographic interface, his brow furrowed in concentration. "He's right. Their energy signatures are shifting. They're reinforcing planetary defenses, yes, but they're also initiating a high-level scan. They're not just reacting; they're actively pursuing. They know Aris experienced their collective consciousness. They've identified him as a primary threat, a vessel of information they need to control. They've learned from the initial assault, and now they're coming for us, directly."

The realization was chilling. Their audacious strike against the alien nexus had not resulted in a strategic withdrawal by the invaders. Instead, it had served as a stark, brutal lesson. The aliens, despite their immense, distributed power, were not impervious. They could be wounded, and in their wounded state, their capacity for adaptation was terrifyingly swift. The psychic onslaught that had nearly shattered Aris was not merely an act of overwhelming power, but a desperate, and ultimately informative, attempt to regain control. Now, they had a clearer understanding of their enemy's capabilities, and they were coming for the very individuals who had dared to disrupt their meticulously crafted order.

"They're not just repairing the nexus," Eva murmured, her gaze fixed on the flickering energy readings, her voice barely audible. "They're adapting their offensive. They saw how we managed to penetrate their defenses, how Aris gained that glimpse into their history and their methods. They can't allow that to happen again. They're reinforcing their own internal coherence, and simultaneously, they're hunting for the source of that disruption. They're hunting us. They know I was involved, and they know Aris is the key."

The psychic pressure, which had begun to recede after Aris's forced immersion, now returned with a chillingly focused intensity. It was no longer a chaotic storm of alien thoughts and emotions, but a precise, invasive probing, like a predator's senses zeroing in on its prey. Aris felt it brush against his consciousness, a cold, alien touch that sought to unravel his thoughts, to find the core of his resistance. He saw Eva flinch, a subtle tremor running through her, her usual bright eyes clouded with a dawning, terrifying certainty. Kaelen, despite his outward focus on the consoles, showed a flicker of strain, his concentration deepening as if warding off an unseen intrusion.

"They're not retreating," Aris stated, his voice low and strained, the echoes of the alien consciousness still a faint hum beneath his own thoughts. "They're rerouting. Reinforcing. They're drawing power from secondary conduits, shoring up the nexus's compromised systems. But it's more than that. The psychic pressure... it's returning, but it's different. It's not a broadcast anymore. It's a targeted interrogation. They're hunting for the source of the disruption, and they know I'm it."

Kaelen's fingers flew across the holographic interface, his brow furrowed in concentration. "He's right. Their energy signatures are shifting. They're reinforcing planetary defenses, yes, but they're also initiating a high-level scan. They're not just reacting; they're actively pursuing. They know Aris experienced their collective consciousness. They've identified him as a primary threat, a vessel of information they need to control. They've learned from the initial assault, and now they're coming for us, directly."

The realization was chilling. Their audacious strike against the alien nexus had not resulted in a strategic withdrawal by the invaders. Instead, it had served as a stark, brutal lesson. The aliens, despite their immense, distributed power, were not impervious. They could be wounded, and in their wounded state, their capacity for adaptation was terrifyingly swift. The psychic onslaught that had nearly shattered Aris was not merely an act of overwhelming power, but a desperate, and ultimately informative, attempt to regain control. Now, they had a clearer understanding of their enemy's capabilities, and they were coming for the very individuals who had dared to disrupt their meticulously crafted order.

"They're not just repairing the nexus," Eva murmured, her gaze

fixed on the flickering energy readings, her voice barely audible. "They're adapting their offensive. They saw how we managed to penetrate their defenses, how Aris gained that glimpse into their history and their methods. They can't allow that to happen again. They're reinforcing their own internal coherence, and simultaneously, they're hunting for the source of that disruption. They're hunting us. They know I was involved, and they know Aris is the key."

The psychic pressure, which had begun to recede after Aris's forced immersion, now returned with a chillingly focused intensity. It was no longer a chaotic storm of alien thoughts and emotions, but a precise, invasive probing, like a predator's senses zeroing in on its prey. Aris felt it brush against his consciousness, a cold, alien touch that sought to unravel his thoughts, to find the core of his resistance. He saw Eva flinch, a subtle tremor running through her, her usual bright eyes clouded with a dawning, terrifying certainty. Kaelen, despite his outward focus on the consoles, showed a flicker of strain, his concentration deepening as if warding off an unseen intrusion.

"They're not retreating," Aris stated, his voice low and strained, the echoes of the alien consciousness still a faint hum beneath his own thoughts. "They're rerouting. Reinforcing. They're drawing power from secondary conduits, shoring up the nexus's compromised systems. But it's more than that. The psychic pressure... it's returning, but it's different. It's not a broadcast anymore. It's a targeted interrogation. They're hunting for the source of the disruption, and they know I'm it."

Kaelen's fingers flew across the holographic interface, his brow furrowed in concentration. "He's right. Their energy signatures are shifting. They're reinforcing planetary defenses, yes, but they're also initiating a high-level scan. They're not just reacting; they're actively pursuing. They know Aris experienced their collective consciousness. They've identified him as a primary threat, a vessel of information they need to control. They've learned from the initial assault, and now they're coming for us, directly."

The realization was chilling. Their audacious strike against the alien nexus had not resulted in a strategic withdrawal by the invaders. Instead, it had served as a stark, brutal lesson. The aliens, despite their immense, distributed power, were not impervious. They could be wounded, and in their wounded state, their capacity for adaptation was

terrifyingly swift. The psychic onslaught that had nearly shattered Aris was not merely an act of overwhelming power, but a desperate, and ultimately informative, attempt to regain control. Now, they had a clearer understanding of their enemy's capabilities, and they were coming for the very individuals who had dared to disrupt their meticulously crafted order.

"They're not just repairing the nexus," Eva murmured, her gaze fixed on the flickering energy readings, her voice barely audible. "They're adapting their offensive. They saw how we managed to penetrate their defenses, how Aris gained that glimpse into their history and their methods. They can't allow that to happen again. They're reinforcing their own internal coherence, and simultaneously, they're hunting for the source of that disruption. They're hunting us. They know I was involved, and they know Aris is the key."

The psychic pressure, which had begun to recede after Aris's forced immersion, now returned with a chillingly focused intensity. It was no longer a chaotic storm of alien thoughts and emotions, but a precise, invasive probing, like a predator's senses zeroing in on its prey. Aris felt it brush against his consciousness, a cold, alien touch that sought to unravel his thoughts, to find the core of his resistance. He saw Eva flinch, a subtle tremor running through her, her usual bright eyes clouded with a dawning, terrifying certainty. Kaelen, despite his outward focus on the consoles, showed a flicker of strain, his concentration deepening as if warding off an unseen intrusion.

"They're not retreating," Aris stated, his voice low and strained, the echoes of the alien consciousness still a faint hum beneath his own thoughts. "They're rerouting. Reinforcing. They're drawing power from secondary conduits, shoring up the nexus's compromised systems. But it's more than that. The psychic pressure... it's returning, but it's different. It's not a broadcast anymore. It's a targeted interrogation. They're hunting for the source of the disruption, and they know I'm it."

Kaelen's fingers flew across the holographic interface, his brow furrowed in concentration. "He's right. Their energy signatures are shifting. They're reinforcing planetary defenses, yes, but they're also initiating a high-level scan. They're not just reacting; they're actively pursuing. They know Aris experienced their collective consciousness. They've identified him as a primary threat, a vessel of information

they need to control. They've learned from the initial assault, and now they're coming for us, directly."

The realization was chilling. Their audacious strike against the alien nexus had not resulted in a strategic withdrawal by the invaders. Instead, it had served as a stark, brutal lesson. The aliens, despite their immense, distributed power, were not impervious. They could be wounded, and in their wounded state, their capacity for adaptation was terrifyingly swift. The psychic onslaught that had nearly shattered Aris was not merely an act of overwhelming power, but a desperate, and ultimately informative, attempt to regain control. Now, they had a clearer understanding of their enemy's capabilities, and they were coming for the very individuals who had dared to disrupt their meticulously crafted order.

"They're not just repairing the nexus," Eva murmured, her gaze fixed on the flickering energy readings, her voice barely audible. "They're adapting their offensive. They saw how we managed to penetrate their defenses, how Aris gained that glimpse into their history and their methods. They can't allow that to happen again. They're reinforcing their own internal coherence, and simultaneously, they're hunting for the source of that disruption. They're hunting us. They know I was involved, and they know Aris is the key."

The psychic pressure, which had begun to recede after Aris's forced immersion, now returned with a chillingly focused intensity. It was no longer a chaotic storm of alien thoughts and emotions, but a precise, invasive probing, like a predator's senses zeroing in on its prey. Aris felt it brush against his consciousness, a cold, alien touch that sought to unravel his thoughts, to find the core of his resistance. He saw Eva flinch, a subtle tremor running through her, her usual bright eyes clouded with a dawning, terrifying certainty. Kaelen, despite his outward focus on the consoles, showed a flicker of strain, his concentration deepening as if warding off an unseen intrusion.

"They're not retreating," Aris stated, his voice low and strained, the echoes of the alien consciousness still a faint hum beneath his own thoughts. "They're rerouting. Reinforcing. They're drawing power from secondary conduits, shoring up the nexus's compromised systems. But it's more than that. The psychic pressure... it's returning, but it's different. It's not a broadcast anymore. It's a targeted interrogation. They're hunting for the source of the disruption, and

they know I'm it."

Kaelen's fingers flew across the holographic interface, his brow furrowed in concentration. "He's right. Their energy signatures are shifting. They're reinforcing planetary defenses, yes, but they're also initiating a high-level scan. They're not just reacting; they're actively pursuing. They know Aris experienced their collective consciousness. They've identified him as a primary threat, a vessel of information they need to control. They've learned from the initial assault, and now they're coming for us, directly."

The realization was chilling. Their audacious strike against the alien nexus had not resulted in a strategic withdrawal by the invaders. Instead, it had served as a stark, brutal lesson. The aliens, despite their immense, distributed power, were not impervious. They could be wounded, and in their wounded state, their capacity for adaptation was terrifyingly swift. The psychic onslaught that had nearly shattered Aris was not merely an act of overwhelming power, but a desperate, and ultimately informative, attempt to regain control. Now, they had a clearer understanding of their enemy's capabilities, and they were coming for the very individuals who had dared to disrupt their meticulously crafted order.

"They're not just repairing the nexus," Eva murmured, her gaze fixed on the flickering energy readings, her voice barely audible. "They're adapting their offensive. They saw how we managed to penetrate their defenses, how Aris gained that glimpse into their history and their methods. They can't allow that to happen again. They're reinforcing their own internal coherence, and simultaneously, they're hunting for the source of that disruption. They're hunting us. They know I was involved, and they know Aris is the key."

The psychic pressure, which had begun to recede after Aris's forced immersion, now returned with a chillingly focused intensity. It was no longer a chaotic storm of alien thoughts and emotions, but a precise, invasive probing, like a predator's senses zeroing in on its prey. Aris felt it brush against his consciousness, a cold, alien touch that sought to unravel his thoughts, to find the core of his resistance. He saw Eva flinch, a subtle tremor running through her, her usual bright eyes clouded with a dawning, terrifying certainty. Kaelen, despite his outward focus on the consoles, showed a flicker of strain, his concentration deepening as if warding off an unseen intrusion.

"They're not retreating," Aris stated, his voice low and strained, the echoes of the alien consciousness still a faint hum beneath his own thoughts. "They're rerouting. Reinforcing. They're drawing power from secondary conduits, shoring up the nexus's compromised systems. But it's more than that. The psychic pressure... it's returning, but it's different. It's not a broadcast anymore. It's a targeted interrogation. They're hunting for the source of the disruption, and they know I'm it."

Kaelen's fingers flew across the holographic interface, his brow furrowed in concentration. "He's right. Their energy signatures are shifting. They're reinforcing planetary defenses, yes, but they're also initiating a high-level scan. They're not just reacting; they're actively pursuing. They know Aris experienced their collective consciousness. They've identified him as a primary threat, a vessel of information they need to control. They've learned from the initial assault, and now they're coming for us, directly."

The realization was chilling. Their audacious strike against the alien nexus had not resulted in a strategic withdrawal by the invaders. Instead, it had served as a stark, brutal lesson. The aliens, despite their immense, distributed power, were not impervious. They could be wounded, and in their wounded state, their capacity for adaptation was terrifyingly swift. The psychic onslaught that had nearly shattered Aris was not merely an act of overwhelming power, but a desperate, and ultimately informative, attempt to regain control. Now, they had a clearer understanding of their enemy's capabilities, and they were coming for the very individuals who had dared to disrupt their meticulously crafted order.

"They're not just repairing the nexus," Eva murmured, her gaze fixed on the flickering energy readings, her voice barely audible. "They're adapting their offensive. They saw how we managed to penetrate their defenses, how Aris gained that glimpse into their history and their methods. They can't allow that to happen again. They're reinforcing their own internal coherence, and simultaneously, they're hunting for the source of that disruption. They're hunting us. They know I was involved, and they know Aris is the key."

The psychic pressure, which had begun to recede after Aris's forced immersion, now returned with a chillingly focused intensity. It was no longer a chaotic storm of alien thoughts and emotions, but a

precise, invasive probing, like a predator's senses zeroing in on its prey. Aris felt it brush against his consciousness, a cold, alien touch that sought to unravel his thoughts, to find the core of his resistance. He saw Eva flinch, a subtle tremor running through her, her usual bright eyes clouded with a dawning, terrifying certainty. Kaelen, despite his outward focus on the consoles, showed a flicker of strain, his concentration deepening as if warding off an unseen intrusion.

"They're not retreating," Aris stated, his voice low and strained, the echoes of the alien consciousness still a faint hum beneath his own thoughts. "They're rerouting. Reinforcing. They're drawing power from secondary conduits, shoring up the nexus's compromised systems. But it's more than that. The psychic pressure... it's returning, but it's different. It's not a broadcast anymore. It's a targeted interrogation. They're hunting for the source of the disruption, and they know I'm it."

Kaelen's fingers flew across the holographic interface, his brow furrowed in concentration. "He's right. Their energy signatures are shifting. They're reinforcing planetary defenses, yes, but they're also initiating a high-level scan. They're not just reacting; they're actively pursuing. They know Aris experienced their collective consciousness. They've identified him as a primary threat, a vessel of information they need to control. They've learned from the initial assault, and now they're coming for us, directly."

The realization was chilling. Their audacious strike against the alien nexus had not resulted in a strategic withdrawal by the invaders. Instead, it had served as a stark, brutal lesson. The aliens, despite their immense, distributed power, were not impervious. They could be wounded, and in their wounded state, their capacity for adaptation was terrifyingly swift. The psychic onslaught that had nearly shattered Aris was not merely an act of overwhelming power, but a desperate, and ultimately informative, attempt to regain control. Now, they had a clearer understanding of their enemy's capabilities, and they were coming for the very individuals who had dared to disrupt their meticulously crafted order.

"They're not just repairing the nexus," Eva murmured, her gaze fixed on the flickering energy readings, her voice barely audible. "They're adapting their offensive. They saw how we managed to penetrate their defenses, how Aris gained that glimpse into their

history and their methods. They can't allow that to happen again. They're reinforcing their own internal coherence, and simultaneously, they're hunting for the source of that disruption. They're hunting us. They know I was involved, and they know Aris is the key."

The psychic pressure, which had begun to recede after Aris's forced immersion, now returned with a chillingly focused intensity. It was no longer a chaotic storm of alien thoughts and emotions, but a precise, invasive probing, like a predator's senses zeroing in on its prey. Aris felt it brush against his consciousness, a cold, alien touch that sought to unravel his thoughts, to find the core of his resistance. He saw Eva flinch, a subtle tremor running through her, her usual bright eyes clouded with a dawning, terrifying certainty. Kaelen, despite his outward focus on the consoles, showed a flicker of strain, his concentration deepening as if warding off an unseen intrusion.

"They're not retreating," Aris stated, his voice low and strained, the echoes of the alien consciousness still a faint hum beneath his own thoughts. "They're rerouting. Reinforcing. They're drawing power from secondary conduits, shoring up the nexus's compromised systems. But it's more than that. The psychic pressure... it's returning, but it's different. It's not a broadcast anymore. It's a targeted interrogation. They're hunting for the source of the disruption, and they know I'm it."

Kaelen's fingers flew across the holographic interface, his brow furrowed in concentration. "He's right. Their energy signatures are shifting. They're reinforcing planetary defenses, yes, but they're also initiating a high-level scan. They're not just reacting; they're actively pursuing. They know Aris experienced their collective consciousness. They've identified him as a primary threat, a vessel of information they need to control. They've learned from the initial assault, and now they're coming for us, directly."

The realization was chilling. Their audacious strike against the alien nexus had not resulted in a strategic withdrawal by the invaders. Instead, it had served as a stark, brutal lesson. The aliens, despite their immense, distributed power, were not impervious. They could be wounded, and in their wounded state, their capacity for adaptation was terrifyingly swift. The psychic onslaught that had nearly shattered Aris was not merely an act of overwhelming power, but a desperate, and ultimately informative, attempt to regain control. Now, they had

a clearer understanding of their enemy's capabilities, and they were coming for the very individuals who had dared to disrupt their meticulously crafted order.

"They're not just repairing the nexus," Eva murmured, her gaze fixed on the flickering energy readings, her voice barely audible. "They're adapting their offensive. They saw how we managed to penetrate their defenses, how Aris gained that glimpse into their history and their methods. They can't allow that to happen again. They're reinforcing their own internal coherence, and simultaneously, they're hunting for the source of that disruption. They're hunting us. They know I was involved, and they know Aris is the key."

The psychic pressure, which had begun to recede after Aris's forced immersion, now returned with a chillingly focused intensity. It was no longer a chaotic storm of alien thoughts and emotions, but a precise, invasive probing, like a predator's senses zeroing in on its prey. Aris felt it brush against his consciousness, a cold, alien touch that sought to unravel his thoughts, to find the core of his resistance. He saw Eva flinch, a subtle tremor running through her, her usual bright eyes clouded with a dawning, terrifying certainty. Kaelen, despite his outward focus on the consoles, showed a flicker of strain, his concentration deepening as if warding off an unseen intrusion.

"They're not retreating," Aris stated, his voice low and strained, the echoes of the alien consciousness still a faint hum beneath his own thoughts. "They're rerouting. Reinforcing. They're drawing power from secondary conduits, shoring up the nexus's compromised systems. But it's more than that. The psychic pressure... it's returning, but it's different. It's not a broadcast anymore. It's a targeted interrogation. They're hunting for the source of the disruption, and they know I'm it."

Kaelen's fingers flew across the holographic interface, his brow furrowed in concentration. "He's right. Their energy signatures are shifting. They're reinforcing planetary defenses, yes, but they're also initiating a high-level scan. They're not just reacting; they're actively pursuing. They know Aris experienced their collective consciousness. They've identified him as a primary threat, a vessel of information they need to control. They've learned from the initial assault, and now they're coming for us, directly."

The realization was chilling. Their audacious strike against the

alien nexus had not resulted in a strategic withdrawal by the invaders. Instead, it had served as a stark, brutal lesson. The aliens, despite their immense, distributed power, were not impervious. They could be wounded, and in their wounded state, their capacity for adaptation was terrifyingly swift. The psychic onslaught that had nearly shattered Aris was not merely an act of overwhelming power, but a desperate, and ultimately informative, attempt to regain control. Now, they had a clearer understanding of their enemy's capabilities, and they were coming for the very individuals who had dared to disrupt their meticulously crafted order.

"They're not just repairing the nexus," Eva murmured, her gaze fixed on the flickering energy readings, her voice barely audible. "They're adapting their offensive. They saw how we managed to penetrate their defenses, how Aris gained that glimpse into their history and their methods. They can't allow that to happen again. They're reinforcing their own internal coherence, and simultaneously, they're hunting for the source of that disruption. They're hunting us. They know I was involved, and they know Aris is the key."

The psychic pressure, which had begun to recede after Aris's forced immersion, now returned with a chillingly focused intensity. It was no longer a chaotic storm of alien thoughts and emotions, but a precise, invasive probing, like a predator's senses zeroing in on its prey. Aris felt it brush against his consciousness, a cold, alien touch that sought to unravel his thoughts, to find the core of his resistance. He saw Eva flinch, a subtle tremor running through her, her usual bright eyes clouded with a dawning, terrifying certainty. Kaelen, despite his outward focus on the consoles, showed a flicker of strain, his concentration deepening as if warding off an unseen intrusion.

"They're not retreating," Aris stated, his voice low and strained, the echoes of the alien consciousness still a faint hum beneath his own thoughts. "They're rerouting. Reinforcing. They're drawing power from secondary conduits, shoring up the nexus's compromised systems. But it's more than that. The psychic pressure... it's returning, but it's different. It's not a broadcast anymore. It's a targeted interrogation. They're hunting for the source of the disruption, and they know I'm it."

Kaelen's fingers flew across the holographic interface, his brow furrowed in concentration. "He's right. Their energy signatures are

shifting. They're reinforcing planetary defenses, yes, but they're also initiating a high-level scan. They're not just reacting; they're actively pursuing. They know Aris experienced their collective consciousness. They've identified him as a primary threat, a vessel of information they need to control. They've learned from the initial assault, and now they're coming for us, directly."

The realization was chilling. Their audacious strike against the alien nexus had not resulted in a strategic withdrawal by the invaders. Instead, it had served as a stark, brutal lesson. The aliens, despite their immense, distributed power, were not impervious. They could be wounded, and in their wounded state, their capacity for adaptation was terrifyingly swift. The psychic onslaught that had nearly shattered Aris was not merely an act of overwhelming power, but a desperate, and ultimately informative, attempt to regain control. Now, they had a clearer understanding of their enemy's capabilities, and they were coming for the very individuals who had dared to disrupt their meticulously crafted order.

"They're not just repairing the nexus," Eva murmured, her gaze fixed on the flickering energy readings, her voice barely audible. "They're adapting their offensive. They saw how we managed to penetrate their defenses, how Aris gained that glimpse into their history and their methods. They can't allow that to happen again. They're reinforcing their own internal coherence, and simultaneously, they're hunting for the source of that disruption. They're hunting us. They know I was involved, and they know Aris is the key."

The psychic pressure, which had begun to recede after Aris's forced immersion, now returned with a chillingly focused intensity. It was no longer a chaotic storm of alien thoughts and emotions, but a precise, invasive probing, like a predator's senses zeroing in on its prey. Aris felt it brush against his consciousness, a cold, alien touch that sought to unravel his thoughts, to find the core of his resistance. He saw Eva flinch, a subtle tremor running through her, her usual bright eyes clouded with a dawning, terrifying certainty. Kaelen, despite his outward focus on the consoles, showed a flicker of strain, his concentration deepening as if warding off an unseen intrusion.

"They're not retreating," Aris stated, his voice low and strained, the echoes of the alien consciousness still a faint hum beneath his own thoughts. "They're rerouting. Reinforcing. They're drawing power

from secondary conduits, shoring up the nexus's compromised systems. But it's more than that. The psychic pressure... it's returning, but it's different. It's not a broadcast anymore. It's a targeted interrogation. They're hunting for the source of the disruption, and they know I'm it."

Kaelen's fingers flew across the holographic interface, his brow furrowed in concentration. "He's right. Their energy signatures are shifting. They're reinforcing planetary defenses, yes, but they're also initiating a high-level scan. They're not just reacting; they're actively pursuing. They know Aris experienced their collective consciousness. They've identified him as a primary threat, a vessel of information they need to control. They've learned from the initial assault, and now they're coming for us, directly."

The realization was chilling. Their audacious strike against the alien nexus had not resulted in a strategic withdrawal by the invaders. Instead, it had served as a stark, brutal lesson. The aliens, despite their immense, distributed power, were not impervious. They could be wounded, and in their wounded state, their capacity for adaptation was terrifyingly swift. The psychic onslaught that had nearly shattered Aris was not merely an act of overwhelming power, but a desperate, and ultimately informative, attempt to regain control. Now, they had a clearer understanding of their enemy's capabilities, and they were coming for the very individuals who had dared to disrupt their meticulously crafted order.

"They're not just repairing the nexus," Eva murmured, her gaze fixed on the flickering energy readings, her voice barely audible. "They're adapting their offensive. They saw how we managed to penetrate their defenses, how Aris gained that glimpse into their history and their methods. They can't allow that to happen again. They're reinforcing their own internal coherence, and simultaneously, they're hunting for the source of that disruption. They're hunting us. They know I was involved, and they know Aris is the key."

The psychic pressure, which had begun to recede after Aris's forced immersion, now returned with a chillingly focused intensity. It was no longer a chaotic storm of alien thoughts and emotions, but a precise, invasive probing, like a predator's senses zeroing in on its prey. Aris felt it brush against his consciousness, a cold, alien touch that sought to unravel his thoughts, to find the core of his resistance.

He saw Eva flinch, a subtle tremor running through her, her usual bright eyes clouded with a dawning, terrifying certainty. Kaelen, despite his outward focus on the consoles, showed a flicker of strain, his concentration deepening as if warding off an unseen intrusion.

"They're not retreating," Aris stated, his voice low and strained, the echoes of the alien consciousness still a faint hum beneath his own thoughts. "They're rerouting. Reinforcing. They're drawing power from secondary conduits, shoring up the nexus's compromised systems. But it's more than that. The psychic pressure... it's returning, but it's different. It's not a broadcast anymore. It's a targeted interrogation. They're hunting for the source of the disruption, and they know I'm it."

Kaelen's fingers flew across the holographic interface, his brow furrowed in concentration. "He's right. Their energy signatures are shifting. They're reinforcing planetary defenses, yes, but they're also initiating a high-level scan. They're not just reacting; they're actively pursuing. They know Aris experienced their collective consciousness. They've identified him as a primary threat, a vessel of information they need to control. They've learned from the initial assault, and now they're coming for us, directly."

The realization was chilling. Their audacious strike against the alien nexus had not resulted in a strategic withdrawal by the invaders. Instead, it had served as a stark, brutal lesson. The aliens, despite their immense, distributed power, were not impervious. They could be wounded, and in their wounded state, their capacity for adaptation was terrifyingly swift. The psychic onslaught that had nearly shattered Aris was not merely an act of overwhelming power, but a desperate, and ultimately informative, attempt to regain control. Now, they had a clearer understanding of their enemy's capabilities, and they were coming for the very individuals who had dared to disrupt their meticulously crafted order.

"They're not just repairing the nexus," Eva murmured, her gaze fixed on the flickering energy readings, her voice barely audible. "They're adapting their offensive. They saw how we managed to penetrate their defenses, how Aris gained that glimpse into their history and their methods. They can't allow that to happen again. They're reinforcing their own internal coherence, and simultaneously, they're hunting for the source of that disruption. They're hunting us.

They know I was involved, and they know Aris is the key."

The psychic pressure, which had begun to recede after Aris's forced immersion, now returned with a chillingly focused intensity. It was no longer a chaotic storm of alien thoughts and emotions, but a precise, invasive probing, like a predator's senses zeroing in on its prey. Aris felt it brush against his consciousness, a cold, alien touch that sought to unravel his thoughts, to find the core of his resistance. He saw Eva flinch, a subtle tremor running through her, her usual bright eyes clouded with a dawning, terrifying certainty. Kaelen, despite his outward focus on the consoles, showed a flicker of strain, his concentration deepening as if warding off an unseen intrusion.

"They're not retreating," Aris stated, his voice low and strained, the echoes of the alien consciousness still a faint hum beneath his own thoughts. "They're rerouting. Reinforcing. They're drawing power from secondary conduits, shoring up the nexus's compromised systems. But it's more than that. The psychic pressure... it's returning, but it's different. It's not a broadcast anymore. It's a targeted interrogation. They're hunting for the source of the disruption, and they know I'm it."

Kaelen's fingers flew across the holographic interface, his brow furrowed in concentration. "He's right. Their energy signatures are shifting. They're reinforcing planetary defenses, yes, but they're also initiating a high-level scan. They're not just reacting; they're actively pursuing. They know Aris experienced their collective consciousness. They've identified him as a primary threat, a vessel of information they need to control. They've learned from the initial assault, and now they're coming for us, directly."

The realization was chilling. Their audacious strike against the alien nexus had not resulted in a strategic withdrawal by the invaders. Instead, it had served as a stark, brutal lesson. The aliens, despite their immense, distributed power, were not impervious. They could be wounded, and in their wounded state, their capacity for adaptation was terrifyingly swift. The psychic onslaught that had nearly shattered Aris was not merely an act of overwhelming power, but a desperate, and ultimately informative, attempt to regain control. Now, they had a clearer understanding of their enemy's capabilities, and they were coming for the very individuals who had dared to disrupt their meticulously crafted order.

"They're not just repairing the nexus," Eva murmured, her gaze fixed on the flickering energy readings, her voice barely audible. "They're adapting their offensive. They saw how we managed to penetrate their defenses, how Aris gained that glimpse into their history and their methods. They can't allow that to happen again. They're reinforcing their own internal coherence, and simultaneously, they're hunting for the source of that disruption. They're hunting us. They know I was involved, and they know Aris is the key."

The psychic pressure, which had begun to recede after Aris's forced immersion, now returned with a chillingly focused intensity. It was no longer a chaotic storm of alien thoughts and emotions, but a precise, invasive probing, like a predator's senses zeroing in on its prey. Aris felt it brush against his consciousness, a cold, alien touch that sought to unravel his thoughts, to find the core of his resistance. He saw Eva flinch, a subtle tremor running through her, her usual bright eyes clouded with a dawning, terrifying certainty. Kaelen, despite his outward focus on the consoles, showed a flicker of strain, his concentration deepening as if warding off an unseen intrusion.

"They're not retreating," Aris stated, his voice low and strained, the echoes of the alien consciousness still a faint hum beneath his own thoughts. "They're rerouting. Reinforcing. They're drawing power from secondary conduits, shoring up the nexus's compromised systems. But it's more than that. The psychic pressure... it's returning, but it's different. It's not a broadcast anymore. It's a targeted interrogation. They're hunting for the source of the disruption, and they know I'm it."

Kaelen's fingers flew across the holographic interface, his brow furrowed in concentration. "He's right. Their energy signatures are shifting. They're reinforcing planetary defenses, yes, but they're also initiating a high-level scan. They're not just reacting; they're actively pursuing. They know Aris experienced their collective consciousness. They've identified him as a primary threat, a vessel of information they need to control. They've learned from the initial assault, and now they're coming for us, directly."

The realization was chilling. Their audacious strike against the alien nexus had not resulted in a strategic withdrawal by the invaders. Instead, it had served as a stark, brutal lesson. The aliens, despite their immense, distributed power, were not impervious. They could be

wounded, and in their wounded state, their capacity for adaptation was terrifyingly swift. The psychic onslaught that had nearly shattered Aris was not merely an act of overwhelming power, but a desperate, and ultimately informative, attempt to regain control. Now, they had a clearer understanding of their enemy's capabilities, and they were coming for the very individuals who had dared to disrupt their meticulously crafted order.

"They're not just repairing the nexus," Eva murmured, her gaze fixed on the flickering energy readings, her voice barely audible. "They're adapting their offensive. They saw how we managed to penetrate their defenses, how Aris gained that glimpse into their history and their methods. They can't allow that to happen again. They're reinforcing their own internal coherence, and simultaneously, they're hunting for the source of that disruption. They're hunting us. They know I was involved, and they know Aris is the key."

The psychic pressure, which had begun to recede after Aris's forced immersion, now returned with a chillingly focused intensity. It was no longer a chaotic storm of alien thoughts and emotions, but a precise, invasive probing, like a predator's senses zeroing in on its prey. Aris felt it brush against his consciousness, a cold, alien touch that sought to unravel his thoughts, to find the core of his resistance. He saw Eva flinch, a subtle tremor running through her, her usual bright eyes clouded with a dawning, terrifying certainty. Kaelen, despite his outward focus on the consoles, showed a flicker of strain, his concentration deepening as if warding off an unseen intrusion.

"They're not retreating," Aris stated, his voice low and strained, the echoes of the alien consciousness still a faint hum beneath his own thoughts. "They're rerouting. Reinforcing. They're drawing power from secondary conduits, shoring up the nexus's compromised systems. But it's more than that. The psychic pressure... it's returning, but it's different. It's not a broadcast anymore. It's a targeted interrogation. They're hunting for the source of the disruption, and they know I'm it."

Kaelen's fingers flew across the holographic interface, his brow furrowed in concentration. "He's right. Their energy signatures are shifting. They're reinforcing planetary defenses, yes, but they're also initiating a high-level scan. They're not just reacting; they're actively pursuing. They know Aris experienced their collective consciousness.

They've identified him as a primary threat, a vessel of information they need to control. They've learned from the initial assault, and now they're coming for us, directly."

The realization was chilling. Their audacious strike against the alien nexus had not resulted in a strategic withdrawal by the invaders. Instead, it had served as a stark, brutal lesson. The aliens, despite their immense, distributed power, were not impervious. They could be wounded, and in their wounded state, their capacity for adaptation was terrifyingly swift. The psychic onslaught that had nearly shattered Aris was not merely an act of overwhelming power, but a desperate, and ultimately informative, attempt to regain control. Now, they had a clearer understanding of their enemy's capabilities, and they were coming for the very individuals who had dared to disrupt their meticulously crafted order.

"They're not just repairing the nexus," Eva murmured, her gaze fixed on the flickering energy readings, her voice barely audible. "They're adapting their offensive. They saw how we managed to penetrate their defenses, how Aris gained that glimpse into their history and their methods. They can't allow that to happen again. They're reinforcing their own internal coherence, and simultaneously, they're hunting for the source of that disruption. They're hunting us. They know I was involved, and they know Aris is the key."

The psychic pressure, which had begun to recede after Aris's forced immersion, now returned with a chillingly focused intensity. It was no longer a chaotic storm of alien thoughts and emotions, but a precise, invasive probing, like a predator's senses zeroing in on its prey. Aris felt it brush against his consciousness, a cold, alien touch that sought to unravel his thoughts, to find the core of his resistance. He saw Eva flinch, a subtle tremor running through her, her usual bright eyes clouded with a dawning, terrifying certainty. Kaelen, despite his outward focus on the consoles, showed a flicker of strain, his concentration deepening as if warding off an unseen intrusion.

"They're not retreating," Aris stated, his voice low and strained, the echoes of the alien consciousness still a faint hum beneath his own thoughts. "They're rerouting. Reinforcing. They're drawing power from secondary conduits, shoring up the nexus's compromised systems. But it's more than that. The psychic pressure... it's returning, but it's different. It's not a broadcast anymore. It's a targeted

interrogation. They're hunting for the source of the disruption, and they know I'm it."

Kaelen's fingers flew across the holographic interface, his brow furrowed in concentration. "He's right. Their energy signatures are shifting. They're reinforcing planetary defenses, yes, but they're also initiating a high-level scan. They're not just reacting; they're actively pursuing. They know Aris experienced their collective consciousness. They've identified him as a primary threat, a vessel of information they need to control. They've learned from the initial assault, and now they're coming for us, directly."

The realization was chilling. Their audacious strike against the alien nexus had not resulted in a strategic withdrawal by the invaders. Instead, it had served as a stark, brutal lesson. The aliens, despite their immense, distributed power, were not impervious. They could be wounded, and in their wounded state, their capacity for adaptation was terrifyingly swift. The psychic onslaught that had nearly shattered Aris was not merely an act of overwhelming power, but a desperate, and ultimately informative, attempt to regain control. Now, they had a clearer understanding of their enemy's capabilities, and they were coming for the very individuals who had dared to disrupt their meticulously crafted order.

"They're not just repairing the nexus," Eva murmured, her gaze fixed on the flickering energy readings, her voice barely audible. "They're adapting their offensive. They saw how we managed to penetrate their defenses, how Aris gained that glimpse into their history and their methods. They can't allow that to happen again. They're reinforcing their own internal coherence, and simultaneously, they're hunting for the source of that disruption. They're hunting us. They know I was involved, and they know Aris is the key."

The psychic pressure, which had begun to recede after Aris's forced immersion, now returned with a chillingly focused intensity. It was no longer a chaotic storm of alien thoughts and emotions, but a precise, invasive probing, like a predator's senses zeroing in on its prey. Aris felt it brush against his consciousness, a cold, alien touch that sought to unravel his thoughts, to find the core of his resistance. He saw Eva flinch, a subtle tremor running through her, her usual bright eyes clouded with a dawning, terrifying certainty. Kaelen, despite his outward focus on the consoles, showed a flicker of strain,

his concentration deepening as if warding off an unseen intrusion.

"They're not retreating," Aris stated, his voice low and strained, the echoes of the alien consciousness still a faint hum beneath his own thoughts. "They're rerouting. Reinforcing. They're drawing power from secondary conduits, shoring up the nexus's compromised systems. But it's more than that. The psychic pressure... it's returning, but it's different. It's not a broadcast anymore. It's a targeted interrogation. They're hunting for the source of the disruption, and they know I'm it."

Kaelen's fingers flew across the holographic interface, his brow furrowed in concentration. "He's right. Their energy signatures are shifting. They're reinforcing planetary defenses, yes, but they're also initiating a high-level scan. They're not just reacting; they're actively pursuing. They know Aris experienced their collective consciousness. They've identified him as a primary threat, a vessel of information they need to control. They've learned from the initial assault, and now they're coming for us, directly."

The realization was chilling. Their audacious strike against the alien nexus had not resulted in a strategic withdrawal by the invaders. Instead, it had served as a stark, brutal lesson. The aliens, despite their immense, distributed power, were not impervious. They could be wounded, and in their wounded state, their capacity for adaptation was terrifyingly swift. The psychic onslaught that had nearly shattered Aris was not merely an act of overwhelming power, but a desperate, and ultimately informative, attempt to regain control. Now, they had a clearer understanding of their enemy's capabilities, and they were coming for the very individuals who had dared to disrupt their meticulously crafted order.

"They're not just repairing the nexus," Eva murmured, her gaze fixed on the flickering energy readings, her voice barely audible. "They're adapting their offensive. They saw how we managed to penetrate their defenses, how Aris gained that glimpse into their history and their methods. They can't allow that to happen again. They're reinforcing their own internal coherence, and simultaneously, they're hunting for the source of that disruption. They're hunting us. They know I was involved, and they know Aris is the key."

The psychic pressure, which had begun to recede after Aris's forced immersion, now returned with a chillingly focused intensity. It was no longer a chaotic storm of alien thoughts and emotions, but a precise, invasive probing, like a predator's senses zeroing in on its prey. Aris felt it brush against his consciousness, a cold, alien touch that sought to unravel his thoughts, to find the core of his resistance. He saw Eva flinch, a subtle tremor running through her, her usual bright eyes clouded with a dawning, terrifying certainty. Kaelen, despite his outward focus on the consoles, showed a flicker of strain, his concentration deepening as if warding off an unseen intrusion.

"They're not retreating," Aris stated, his voice low and strained, the echoes of the alien consciousness still a faint hum beneath his own thoughts. "They're rerouting. Reinforcing. They're drawing power from secondary conduits, shoring up the nexus's compromised systems. But it's more than that. The psychic pressure... it's returning, but it's different. It's not a broadcast anymore. It's a targeted interrogation. They're hunting for the source of the disruption, and they know I'm it."

Kaelen's fingers flew across the holographic interface, his brow furrowed in concentration. "He's right. Their energy signatures are shifting. They're reinforcing planetary defenses, yes, but they're also initiating a high-level scan. They're not just reacting; they're actively pursuing. They know Aris experienced their collective consciousness. They've identified him as a primary threat, a vessel of information they need to control. They've learned from the initial assault, and now they're coming for us, directly."

The realization was chilling. Their audacious strike against the alien nexus had not resulted in a strategic withdrawal by the invaders. Instead, it had served as a stark, brutal lesson. The aliens, despite their immense, distributed power, were not impervious. They could be wounded, and in their wounded state, their capacity for adaptation was terrifyingly swift. The psychic onslaught that had nearly shattered Aris was not merely an act of overwhelming power, but a desperate, and ultimately informative, attempt to regain control. Now, they had a clearer understanding of their enemy's capabilities, and they were coming for the very individuals who had dared to disrupt their meticulously crafted order.

"They're not just repairing the nexus," Eva murmured, her gaze fixed on the flickering energy readings, her voice barely audible. "They're adapting their offensive. They saw how we managed to penetrate their defenses, how Aris gained that glimpse into their history and their methods. They can't allow that to happen again. They're reinforcing their own internal coherence, and simultaneously, they're hunting for the source of that disruption. They're hunting us. They know I was involved, and they know Aris is the key."

The psychic pressure, which had begun to recede after Aris's forced immersion, now returned with a chillingly focused intensity. It was no longer a chaotic storm of alien thoughts and emotions, but a precise, invasive probing, like a predator's senses zeroing in on its prey. Aris felt it brush against his consciousness, a cold, alien touch that sought to unravel his thoughts, to find the core of his resistance. He saw Eva flinch, a subtle tremor running through her, her usual bright eyes clouded with a dawning, terrifying certainty. Kaelen, despite his outward focus on the consoles, showed a flicker of strain, his concentration deepening as if warding off an unseen intrusion.

"They're not retreating," Aris stated, his voice low and strained, the echoes of the alien consciousness still a faint hum beneath his own thoughts. "They're rerouting. Reinforcing. They're drawing power from secondary conduits, shoring up the nexus's compromised systems. But it's more than that. The psychic pressure... it's returning, but it's different. It's not a broadcast anymore. It's a targeted interrogation. They're hunting for the source of the disruption, and they know I'm it."

Kaelen's fingers flew across the holographic interface, his brow furrowed in concentration. "He's right. Their energy signatures are shifting. They're reinforcing planetary defenses, yes, but they're also initiating a high-level scan. They're not just reacting; they're actively pursuing. They know Aris experienced their collective consciousness. They've identified him as a primary threat, a vessel of information they need to control. They've learned from the initial assault, and now they're coming for us, directly."

The realization was chilling. Their audacious strike against the alien nexus had not resulted in a strategic withdrawal by the invaders. Instead, it had served as a stark, brutal lesson. The aliens, despite their immense, distributed power, were not impervious. They could be wounded, and in their wounded state, their capacity for adaptation was terrifyingly swift. The psychic onslaught that had nearly shattered Aris was not merely an act of overwhelming power, but a desperate, and ultimately informative, attempt to regain control. Now, they had a clearer understanding of their enemy's capabilities, and they were coming for the very individuals who had dared to disrupt their meticulously crafted order.

"They're not just repairing the nexus," Eva murmured, her gaze fixed on the flickering energy readings, her voice barely audible. "They're adapting their offensive. They saw how we managed to penetrate their defenses, how Aris gained that glimpse into their history and their methods. They can't allow that to happen again. They're reinforcing their own internal coherence, and simultaneously, they're hunting for the source of that disruption. They're hunting us. They know I was involved, and they know Aris is the key."

The psychic pressure, which had begun to recede after Aris's forced immersion, now returned with a chillingly focused intensity. It was no longer a chaotic storm of alien thoughts and emotions, but a precise, invasive probing, like a predator's senses zeroing in on its prey. Aris felt it brush against his consciousness, a cold, alien touch that sought to unravel his thoughts, to find the core of his resistance. He saw Eva flinch, a subtle tremor running through her, her usual bright eyes clouded with a dawning, terrifying certainty. Kaelen, despite his outward focus on the consoles, showed a flicker of strain, his concentration deepening as if warding off an unseen intrusion.

"They're not retreating," Aris stated, his voice low and strained, the echoes of the alien consciousness still a faint hum beneath his own thoughts. "They're rerouting. Reinforcing. They're drawing power from secondary conduits, shoring up the nexus's compromised systems. But it's more than that. The psychic pressure... it's returning, but it's different. It's not a broadcast anymore. It's a targeted interrogation. They're hunting for the source of the disruption, and they know I'm it."

Kaelen's fingers flew across the holographic interface, his brow furrowed in concentration. "He's right. Their energy signatures are shifting. They're reinforcing planetary defenses, yes, but they're also initiating a high-level scan. They're not just reacting; they're actively pursuing. They know Aris experienced their collective consciousness. They've identified him as a primary threat, a vessel of information they need to control. They've learned from the initial assault, and now they're coming for us, directly."

The realization was chilling. Their audacious strike against the alien nexus had not resulted in a strategic withdrawal by the invaders. Instead, it had served as a stark, brutal lesson. The aliens, despite their immense, distributed power, were not impervious. They could be wounded, and in their wounded state, their capacity for adaptation was terrifyingly swift. The psychic onslaught that had nearly shattered Aris was not merely an act of overwhelming power, but a desperate, and ultimately informative, attempt to regain control. Now, they had a clearer understanding of their enemy's capabilities, and they were coming for the very individuals who had dared to disrupt their meticulously crafted order.

"They're not just repairing the nexus," Eva murmured, her gaze fixed on the flickering energy readings, her voice barely audible. "They're adapting their offensive. They saw how we managed to penetrate their defenses, how Aris gained that glimpse into their history and their methods. They can't allow that to happen again. They're reinforcing their own internal coherence, and simultaneously, they're hunting for the source of that disruption. They're hunting us. They know I was involved, and they know Aris is the key."

The psychic pressure, which had begun to recede after Aris's forced immersion, now returned with a chillingly focused intensity. It was no longer a chaotic storm of alien thoughts and emotions, but a precise, invasive probing, like a predator's senses zeroing in on its prey. Aris felt it brush against his consciousness, a cold, alien touch that sought to unravel his thoughts, to find the core of his resistance. He saw Eva flinch, a subtle tremor running through her, her usual bright eyes clouded with a dawning, terrifying certainty. Kaelen, despite his outward focus on the consoles, showed a flicker of strain, his concentration deepening as if warding off an unseen intrusion.

"They're not retreating," Aris stated, his voice low and strained, the echoes of the alien consciousness still a faint hum beneath his own thoughts. "They're rerouting. Reinforcing. They're drawing power from secondary conduits, shoring up the nexus's compromised systems. But it's more than that. The psychic pressure... it's returning, but it's different. It's not a broadcast anymore. It's a targeted interrogation. They're hunting for the source of the disruption, and they know I'm it."

Kaelen's fingers flew across the holographic interface, his brow furrowed in concentration. "He's right. Their energy signatures are shifting. They're reinforcing planetary defenses, yes, but they're also initiating a high-level scan. They're not just reacting; they're actively pursuing. They know Aris experienced their collective consciousness. They've identified him as a primary threat, a vessel of information they need to control. They've learned from the initial assault, and now they're coming for us, directly."

The realization was chilling. Their audacious strike against the alien nexus had not resulted in a strategic withdrawal by the invaders. Instead, it had served as a stark, brutal lesson. The aliens, despite their immense, distributed power, were not impervious. They could be wounded, and in their wounded state, their capacity for adaptation was terrifyingly swift. The psychic onslaught that had nearly shattered Aris was not merely an act of overwhelming power, but a desperate, and ultimately informative, attempt to regain control. Now, they had a clearer understanding of their enemy's capabilities, and they were coming for the very individuals who had dared to disrupt their meticulously crafted order.

"They're not just repairing the nexus," Eva murmured, her gaze fixed on the flickering energy readings, her voice barely audible. "They're adapting their offensive. They saw how we managed to penetrate their defenses, how Aris gained that glimpse into their history and their methods. They can't allow that to happen again. They're reinforcing their own internal coherence, and simultaneously, they're hunting for the source of that disruption. They're hunting us. They know I was involved, and they know Aris is the key."

The psychic pressure, which had begun to recede after Aris's forced immersion, now returned with a chillingly focused intensity. It was no longer a chaotic storm of alien thoughts and emotions, but a precise, invasive probing, like a predator's senses zeroing in on its prey. Aris felt it brush against his consciousness, a cold, alien touch that sought to unravel his thoughts, to find the core of his resistance. He saw Eva flinch, a subtle tremor running through her, her usual bright eyes clouded with a dawning, terrifying certainty. Kaelen, despite his outward focus on the consoles, showed a flicker of strain, his concentration deepening as if warding off an unseen intrusion.

"They're not retreating," Aris stated, his voice low and strained, the echoes of the alien consciousness still a faint hum beneath his own thoughts. "They're rerouting. Reinforcing. They're drawing power from secondary conduits, shoring up the nexus's compromised systems. But it's more than that. The psychic pressure... it's returning, but it's different. It's not a broadcast anymore. It's a targeted interrogation. They're hunting for the source of the disruption, and they know I'm it."

Kaelen's fingers flew across the holographic interface, his brow furrowed in concentration. "He's right. Their energy signatures are shifting. They're reinforcing planetary defenses, yes, but they're also initiating a high-level scan. They're not just reacting; they're actively pursuing. They know Aris experienced their collective consciousness. They've identified him as a primary threat, a vessel of information they need to control. They've learned from the initial assault, and now they're coming for us, directly."

The realization was chilling. Their audacious strike against the alien nexus had not resulted in a strategic withdrawal by the invaders. Instead, it had served as a stark, brutal lesson. The aliens, despite their immense, distributed power, were not impervious. They could be wounded, and in their wounded state, their capacity for adaptation was terrifyingly swift. The psychic onslaught that had nearly shattered Aris was not merely an act of overwhelming power, but a desperate, and ultimately informative, attempt to regain control. Now, they had a clearer understanding of their enemy's capabilities, and they were coming for the very individuals who had dared to disrupt their meticulously crafted order.

"They're not just repairing the nexus," Eva murmured, her gaze fixed on the flickering energy readings, her voice barely audible. "They're adapting their offensive. They saw how we managed to penetrate their defenses, how Aris gained that glimpse into their history and their methods. They can't allow that to happen again. They're reinforcing their own internal coherence, and simultaneously, they're hunting for the source of that disruption. They're hunting us. They know I was involved, and they know Aris is the key."

The psychic pressure, which had begun to recede after Aris's forced immersion, now returned with a chillingly focused intensity. It was no longer a chaotic storm of alien thoughts and emotions, but a precise, invasive probing, like a predator's senses zeroing in on its prey. Aris felt it brush against his consciousness, a cold, alien touch that sought to unravel his thoughts, to find the core of his resistance. He saw Eva flinch, a subtle tremor running through her, her usual bright eyes clouded with a dawning, terrifying certainty. Kaelen, despite his outward focus on the consoles, showed a flicker of strain, his concentration deepening as if warding off an unseen intrusion.

"They're not retreating," Aris stated, his voice low and strained, the echoes of the alien consciousness still a faint hum beneath his own thoughts. "They're rerouting. Reinforcing. They're drawing power from secondary conduits, shoring up the nexus's compromised systems. But it's more than that. The psychic pressure... it's returning, but it's different. It's not a broadcast anymore. It's a targeted interrogation. They're hunting for the source of the disruption, and they know I'm it."

Kaelen's fingers flew across the holographic interface, his brow furrowed in concentration. "He's right. Their energy signatures are shifting. They're reinforcing planetary defenses, yes, but they're also initiating a high-level scan. They're not just reacting; they're actively pursuing. They know Aris experienced their collective consciousness. They've identified him as a primary threat, a vessel of information they need to control. They've learned from the initial assault, and now they're coming for us, directly."

The realization was chilling. Their audacious strike against the alien nexus had not resulted in a strategic withdrawal by the invaders. Instead, it had served as a stark, brutal lesson. The aliens, despite their immense, distributed power, were not impervious. They could be wounded, and in their wounded state, their capacity for adaptation was terrifyingly swift. The psychic onslaught that had nearly shattered Aris was not merely an act of overwhelming power, but a desperate, and ultimately informative, attempt to regain control. Now, they had a clearer understanding of their enemy's capabilities, and they were coming for the very individuals who had dared to disrupt their meticulously crafted order.

"They're not just repairing the nexus," Eva murmured, her gaze fixed on the flickering energy readings, her voice barely audible. "They're adapting their offensive. They saw how we managed to penetrate their defenses, how Aris gained that glimpse into their history and their methods. They can't allow that to happen again. They're reinforcing their own internal coherence, and simultaneously, they're hunting for the source of that disruption. They're hunting us. They know I was involved, and they know Aris is the key."

The psychic pressure, which had begun to recede after Aris's forced immersion, now returned with a chillingly focused intensity. It was no longer a chaotic storm of alien thoughts and emotions, but a precise, invasive probing, like a predator's senses zeroing in on its prey. Aris felt it brush against his consciousness, a cold, alien touch that sought to unravel his thoughts, to find the core of his resistance. He saw Eva flinch, a subtle tremor running through her, her usual bright eyes clouded with a dawning, terrifying certainty. Kaelen, despite his outward focus on the consoles, showed a flicker of strain, his concentration deepening as if warding off an unseen intrusion.

"They're not retreating," Aris stated, his voice low and strained, the echoes of the alien consciousness still a faint hum beneath his own thoughts. "They're rerouting. Reinforcing. They're drawing power from secondary conduits, shoring up the nexus's compromised systems. But it's more than that. The psychic pressure... it's returning, but it's different. It's not a broadcast anymore. It's a targeted interrogation. They're hunting for the source of the disruption, and they know I'm it."

Kaelen's fingers flew across the holographic interface, his brow furrowed in concentration. "He's right. Their energy signatures are shifting. They're reinforcing planetary defenses, yes, but they're also initiating a high-level scan. They're not just reacting; they're actively pursuing. They know Aris experienced their collective consciousness. They've identified him as a primary threat, a vessel of information they need to control. They've learned from the initial assault, and now they're coming for us, directly."

The realization was chilling. Their audacious strike against the alien nexus had not resulted in a strategic withdrawal by the invaders. Instead, it had served as a stark, brutal lesson. The aliens, despite their immense, distributed power, were not impervious. They could be wounded, and in their wounded state, their capacity for adaptation was terrifyingly swift. The psychic onslaught that had nearly shattered Aris was not merely an act of overwhelming power, but a desperate, and ultimately informative, attempt to regain control. Now, they had a clearer understanding of their enemy's capabilities, and they were coming for the very individuals who had dared to disrupt their meticulously crafted order.

"They're not just repairing the nexus," Eva murmured, her gaze fixed on the flickering energy readings, her voice barely audible. "They're adapting their offensive. They saw how we managed to penetrate their defenses, how Aris gained that glimpse into their history and their methods. They can't allow that to happen again. They're reinforcing their own internal coherence, and simultaneously, they're hunting for the source of that disruption. They're hunting us. They know I was involved, and they know Aris is the key."

The psychic pressure, which had begun to recede after Aris's forced immersion, now returned with a chillingly focused intensity. It was no longer a chaotic storm of alien thoughts and emotions, but a precise, invasive probing, like a predator's senses zeroing in on its prey. Aris felt it brush against his consciousness, a cold, alien touch that sought to unravel his thoughts, to find the core of his resistance. He saw Eva flinch, a subtle tremor running through her, her usual bright eyes clouded with a dawning, terrifying certainty. Kaelen, despite his outward focus on the consoles, showed a flicker of strain, his concentration deepening as if warding off an unseen intrusion.

"They're not retreating," Aris stated, his voice low and strained, the echoes of the alien consciousness still a faint hum beneath his own thoughts. "They're rerouting. Reinforcing. They're drawing power from secondary conduits, shoring up the nexus's compromised systems. But it's more than that. The psychic pressure... it's returning, but it's different. It's not a broadcast anymore. It's a targeted interrogation. They're hunting for the source of the disruption, and they know I'm it."

Kaelen's fingers flew across the holographic interface, his brow furrowed in concentration. "He's right. Their energy signatures are shifting. They're reinforcing planetary defenses, yes, but they're also initiating a high-level scan. They're not just reacting; they're actively pursuing. They know Aris experienced their collective consciousness. They've identified him as a primary threat, a vessel of information they need to control. They've learned from the initial assault, and now they're coming for us, directly."

The realization was chilling. Their audacious strike against the alien nexus had not resulted in a strategic withdrawal by the invaders. Instead, it had served as a stark, brutal lesson. The aliens, despite their immense, distributed power, were not impervious. They could be wounded, and in their wounded state, their capacity for adaptation was terrifyingly swift. The psychic onslaught that had nearly shattered Aris was not merely an act of overwhelming power, but a desperate, and ultimately informative, attempt to regain control. Now, they had a clearer understanding of their enemy's capabilities, and they were coming for the very individuals who had dared to disrupt their meticulously crafted order.

"They're not just repairing the nexus," Eva murmured, her gaze fixed on the flickering energy readings, her voice barely audible. "They're adapting their offensive. They saw how we managed to penetrate their defenses, how Aris gained that glimpse into their history and their methods. They can't allow that to happen again. They're reinforcing their own internal coherence, and simultaneously, they're hunting for the source of that disruption. They're hunting us. They know I was involved, and they know Aris is the key."

The psychic pressure, which had begun to recede after Aris's forced immersion, now returned with a chillingly focused intensity. It was no longer a chaotic storm of alien thoughts and emotions, but a precise, invasive probing, like a predator's senses zeroing in on its prey. Aris felt it brush against his consciousness, a cold, alien touch that sought to unravel his thoughts, to find the core of his resistance. He saw Eva flinch, a subtle tremor running through her, her usual bright eyes clouded with a dawning, terrifying certainty. Kaelen, despite his outward focus on the consoles, showed a flicker of strain, his concentration deepening as if warding off an unseen intrusion.

"They're not retreating," Aris stated, his voice low and strained, the echoes of the alien consciousness still a faint hum beneath his own thoughts. "They're rerouting. Reinforcing. They're drawing power from secondary conduits, shoring up the nexus's compromised systems. But it's more than that. The psychic pressure... it's returning, but it's different. It's not a broadcast anymore. It's a targeted interrogation. They're hunting for the source of the disruption, and they know I'm it."

Kaelen's fingers flew across the holographic interface, his brow furrowed in concentration. "He's right. Their energy signatures are shifting. They're reinforcing planetary defenses, yes, but they're also initiating a high-level scan. They're not just reacting; they're actively pursuing. They know Aris experienced their collective consciousness. They've identified him as a primary threat, a vessel of information they need to control. They've learned from the initial assault, and now they're coming for us, directly."

The realization was chilling. Their audacious strike against the alien nexus had not resulted in a strategic withdrawal by the invaders. Instead, it had served as a stark, brutal lesson. The aliens, despite their immense, distributed power, were not impervious. They could be wounded, and in their wounded state, their capacity for adaptation was terrifyingly swift. The psychic onslaught that had nearly shattered Aris was not merely an act of overwhelming power, but a desperate, and ultimately informative, attempt to regain control. Now, they had a clearer understanding of their enemy's capabilities, and they were coming for the very individuals who had dared to disrupt their meticulously crafted order.

"They're not just repairing the nexus," Eva murmured, her gaze fixed on the flickering energy readings, her voice barely audible. "They're adapting their offensive. They saw how we managed to penetrate their defenses, how Aris gained that glimpse into their history and their methods. They can't allow that to happen again. They're reinforcing their own internal coherence, and simultaneously, they're hunting for the source of that disruption. They're hunting us. They know I was involved, and they know Aris is the key."

The psychic pressure, which had begun to recede after Aris's forced immersion, now returned with a chillingly focused intensity. It was no longer a chaotic storm of alien thoughts and emotions, but a precise, invasive probing, like a predator's senses zeroing in on its prey. Aris felt it brush against his consciousness, a cold, alien touch that sought to unravel his thoughts, to find the core of his resistance. He saw Eva flinch, a subtle tremor running through her, her usual bright eyes clouded with a dawning, terrifying certainty. Kaelen, despite his outward focus on the consoles, showed a flicker of strain, his concentration deepening as if warding off an unseen intrusion.

"They're not retreating," Aris stated, his voice low and strained, the echoes of the alien consciousness still a faint hum beneath his own thoughts. "They're rerouting. Reinforcing. They're drawing power from secondary conduits, shoring up the nexus's compromised systems. But it's more than that. The psychic pressure... it's returning, but it's different. It's not a broadcast anymore. It's a targeted interrogation. They're hunting for the source of the disruption, and they know I'm it."

Kaelen's fingers flew across the holographic interface, his brow furrowed in concentration. "He's right. Their energy signatures are shifting. They're reinforcing planetary defenses, yes, but they're also initiating a high-level scan. They're not just reacting; they're actively pursuing. They know Aris experienced their collective consciousness. They've identified him as a primary threat, a vessel of information they need to control. They've learned from the initial assault, and now they're coming for us, directly."

The realization was chilling. Their audacious strike against the alien nexus had not resulted in a strategic withdrawal by the invaders. Instead, it had served as a stark, brutal lesson. The aliens, despite their immense, distributed power, were not impervious. They could be wounded, and in their wounded state, their capacity for adaptation was terrifyingly swift. The psychic onslaught that had nearly shattered Aris was not merely an act of overwhelming power, but a desperate, and ultimately informative, attempt to regain control. Now, they had a clearer understanding of their enemy's capabilities, and they were coming for the very individuals who had dared to disrupt their meticulously crafted order.

"They're not just repairing the nexus," Eva murmured, her gaze fixed on the flickering energy readings, her voice barely audible. "They're adapting their offensive. They saw how we managed to penetrate their defenses, how Aris gained that glimpse into their history and their methods. They can't allow that to happen again. They're reinforcing their own internal coherence, and simultaneously, they're hunting for the source of that disruption. They're hunting us. They know I was involved, and they know Aris is the key."

The psychic pressure, which had begun to recede after Aris's forced immersion, now returned with a chillingly focused intensity. It was no longer a chaotic storm of alien thoughts and emotions, but a precise, invasive probing, like a predator's senses zeroing in on its prey. Aris felt it brush against his consciousness, a cold, alien touch that sought to unravel his thoughts, to find the core of his resistance. He saw Eva flinch, a subtle tremor running through her, her usual bright eyes clouded with a dawning, terrifying certainty. Kaelen, despite his outward focus on the consoles, showed a flicker of strain, his concentration deepening as if warding off an unseen intrusion.

"They're not retreating," Aris stated, his voice low and strained, the echoes of the alien consciousness still a faint hum beneath his own thoughts. "They're rerouting. Reinforcing. They're drawing power from secondary conduits, shoring up the nexus's compromised systems. But it's more than that. The psychic pressure... it's returning, but it's different. It's not a broadcast anymore. It's a targeted interrogation. They're hunting for the source of the disruption, and they know I'm it."

Kaelen's fingers flew across the holographic interface, his brow furrowed in concentration. "He's right. Their energy signatures are shifting. They're reinforcing planetary defenses, yes, but they're also initiating a high-level scan. They're not just reacting; they're actively pursuing. They know Aris experienced their collective consciousness. They've identified him as a primary threat, a vessel of information they need to control. They've learned from the initial assault, and now they're coming for us, directly."

The realization was chilling. Their audacious strike against the alien nexus had not resulted in a strategic withdrawal by the invaders. Instead, it had served as a stark, brutal lesson. The aliens, despite their immense, distributed power, were not impervious. They could be wounded, and in their wounded state, their capacity for adaptation was terrifyingly swift. The psychic onslaught that had nearly shattered Aris was not merely an act of overwhelming power, but a desperate, and ultimately informative, attempt to regain control. Now, they had a clearer understanding of their enemy's capabilities, and they were coming for the very individuals who had dared to disrupt their meticulously crafted order.

"They're not just repairing the nexus," Eva murmured, her gaze fixed on the flickering energy readings, her voice barely audible. "They're adapting their offensive. They saw how we managed to penetrate their defenses, how Aris gained that glimpse into their history and their methods. They can't allow that to happen again. They're reinforcing their own internal coherence, and simultaneously, they're hunting for the source of that disruption. They're hunting us. They know I was involved, and they know Aris is the key."

The psychic pressure, which had begun to recede after Aris's forced immersion, now returned with a chillingly focused intensity. It was no longer a chaotic storm of alien thoughts and emotions, but a precise, invasive probing, like a predator's senses zeroing in on its prey. Aris felt it brush against his consciousness, a cold, alien touch that sought to unravel his thoughts, to find the core of his resistance. He saw Eva flinch, a subtle tremor running through her, her usual bright eyes clouded with a dawning, terrifying certainty. Kaelen, despite his outward focus on the consoles, showed a flicker of strain, his concentration deepening as if warding off an unseen intrusion.

"They're not retreating," Aris stated, his voice low and strained, the echoes of the alien consciousness still a faint hum beneath his own thoughts. "They're rerouting. Reinforcing. They're drawing power from secondary conduits, shoring up the nexus's compromised systems. But it's more than that. The psychic pressure... it's returning, but it's different. It's not a broadcast anymore. It's a targeted interrogation. They're hunting for the source of the disruption, and they know I'm it."

Kaelen's fingers flew across the holographic interface, his brow furrowed in concentration. "He's right. Their energy signatures are shifting. They're reinforcing planetary defenses, yes, but they're also initiating a high-level scan. They're not just reacting; they're actively pursuing. They know Aris experienced their collective consciousness. They've identified him as a primary threat, a vessel of information they need to control. They've learned from the initial assault, and now they're coming for us, directly."

The realization was chilling. Their audacious strike against the alien nexus had not resulted in a strategic withdrawal by the invaders. Instead, it had served as a stark, brutal lesson. The aliens, despite their immense, distributed power, were not impervious. They could be wounded, and in their wounded state, their capacity for adaptation was terrifyingly swift. The psychic onslaught that had nearly shattered Aris was not merely an act of overwhelming power, but a desperate, and ultimately informative, attempt to regain control. Now, they had a clearer understanding of their enemy's capabilities, and they were coming for the very individuals who had dared to disrupt their meticulously crafted order.

"They're not just repairing the nexus," Eva murmured, her gaze fixed on the flickering energy readings, her voice barely audible.

"They're adapting their offensive. They saw how we managed to penetrate their defenses, how Aris gained that glimpse into their history and their methods. They can't allow that to happen again. They're reinforcing their own internal coherence, and simultaneously, they're hunting for the source of that disruption. They're hunting us. They know I was involved, and they know Aris is the key."

The psychic pressure, which had begun to recede after Aris's forced immersion, now returned with a chillingly focused intensity. It was no longer a chaotic storm of alien thoughts and emotions, but a precise, invasive probing, like a predator's senses zeroing in on its prey. Aris felt it brush against his consciousness, a cold, alien touch that sought to unravel his thoughts, to find the core of his resistance. He saw Eva flinch, a subtle tremor running through her, her usual bright eyes clouded with a dawning, terrifying certainty. Kaelen, despite his outward focus on the consoles, showed a flicker of strain, his concentration deepening as if warding off an unseen intrusion.

"They're not retreating," Aris stated, his voice low and strained, the echoes of the alien consciousness still a faint hum beneath his own thoughts. "They're rerouting. Reinforcing. They're drawing power from secondary conduits, shoring up the nexus's compromised systems. But it's more than that. The psychic pressure... it's returning, but it's different. It's not a broadcast anymore. It's a targeted interrogation. They're hunting for the source of the disruption, and they know I'm it."

Kaelen's fingers flew across the holographic interface, his brow furrowed in concentration. "He's right. Their energy signatures are shifting. They're reinforcing planetary defenses, yes, but they're also initiating a high-level scan. They're not just reacting; they're actively pursuing. They know Aris experienced their collective consciousness. They've identified him as a primary threat, a vessel of information they need to control. They've learned from the initial assault, and now they're coming for us, directly."

The realization was chilling. Their audacious strike against the alien nexus had not resulted in a strategic withdrawal by the invaders. Instead, it had served as a stark, brutal lesson. The aliens, despite their immense, distributed power, were not impervious. They could be wounded, and in their wounded state, their capacity for adaptation was terrifyingly swift. The psychic onslaught that had nearly shattered

Aris was not merely an act of overwhelming power, but a desperate, and ultimately informative, attempt to regain control. Now, they had a clearer understanding of their enemy's capabilities, and they were coming for the very individuals who had dared to disrupt their meticulously crafted order.

"They're not just repairing the nexus," Eva murmured, her gaze fixed on the flickering energy readings, her voice barely audible. "They're adapting their offensive. They saw how we managed to penetrate their defenses, how Aris gained that glimpse into their history and their methods. They can't allow that to happen again. They're reinforcing their own internal coherence, and simultaneously, they're hunting for the source of that disruption. They're hunting us. They know I was involved, and they know Aris is the key."

The psychic pressure, which had begun to recede after Aris's forced immersion, now returned with a chillingly focused intensity. It was no longer a chaotic storm of alien thoughts and emotions, but a precise, invasive probing, like a predator's senses zeroing in on its prey. Aris felt it brush against his consciousness, a cold, alien touch that sought to unravel his thoughts, to find the core of his resistance. He saw Eva flinch, a subtle tremor running through her, her usual bright eyes clouded with a dawning, terrifying certainty. Kaelen, despite his outward focus on the consoles, showed a flicker of strain, his concentration deepening as if warding off an unseen intrusion.

"They're not retreating," Aris stated, his voice low and strained, the echoes of the alien consciousness still a faint hum beneath his own thoughts. "They're rerouting. Reinforcing. They're drawing power from secondary conduits, shoring up the nexus's compromised systems. But it's more than that. The psychic pressure... it's returning, but it's different. It's not a broadcast anymore. It's a targeted interrogation. They're hunting for the source of the disruption, and they know I'm it."

Kaelen's fingers flew across the holographic interface, his brow furrowed in concentration. "He's right. Their energy signatures are shifting. They're reinforcing planetary defenses, yes, but they're also initiating a high-level scan. They're not just reacting; they're actively pursuing. They know Aris experienced their collective consciousness. They've identified him as a primary threat, a vessel of information they need to control. They've learned from the initial assault, and now they're coming for us, directly."

The realization was chilling. Their audacious strike against the alien nexus had not resulted in a strategic withdrawal by the invaders. Instead, it had served as a stark, brutal lesson. The aliens, despite their immense, distributed power, were not impervious. They could be wounded, and in their wounded state, their capacity for adaptation was terrifyingly swift. The psychic onslaught that had nearly shattered Aris was not merely an act of overwhelming power, but a desperate, and ultimately informative, attempt to regain control. Now, they had a clearer understanding of their enemy's capabilities, and they were coming for the very individuals who had dared to disrupt their meticulously crafted order.

"They're not just repairing the nexus," Eva murmured, her gaze fixed on the flickering energy readings, her voice barely audible. "They're adapting their offensive. They saw how we managed to penetrate their defenses, how Aris gained that glimpse into their history and their methods. They can't allow that to happen again. They're reinforcing their own internal coherence, and simultaneously, they're hunting for the source of that disruption. They're hunting us. They know I was involved, and they know Aris is the key."

The psychic pressure, which had begun to recede after Aris's forced immersion, now returned with a chillingly focused intensity. It was no longer a chaotic storm of alien thoughts and emotions, but a precise, invasive probing, like a predator's senses zeroing in on its prey. Aris felt it brush against his consciousness, a cold, alien touch that sought to unravel his thoughts, to find the core of his resistance. He saw Eva flinch, a subtle tremor running through her, her usual bright eyes clouded with a dawning, terrifying certainty. Kaelen, despite his outward focus on the consoles, showed a flicker of strain, his concentration deepening as if warding off an unseen intrusion.

"They're not retreating," Aris stated, his voice low and strained, the echoes of the alien consciousness still a faint hum beneath his own thoughts. "They're rerouting. Reinforcing. They're drawing power from secondary conduits, shoring up the nexus's compromised systems. But it's more than that. The psychic pressure... it's returning, but it's different. It's not a broadcast anymore. It's a targeted interrogation. They're hunting for the source of the disruption, and they know I'm it."

Kaelen's fingers flew across the holographic interface, his brow furrowed in concentration. "He's right. Their energy signatures are shifting. They're reinforcing planetary defenses, yes, but they're also initiating a high-level scan. They're not just reacting; they're actively pursuing. They know Aris experienced their collective consciousness. They've identified him as a primary threat, a vessel of information they need to control. They've learned from the initial assault, and now they're coming for us, directly."

The realization was chilling. Their audacious strike against the alien nexus had not resulted in a strategic withdrawal by the invaders. Instead, it had served as a stark, brutal lesson. The aliens, despite their immense, distributed power, were not impervious. They could be wounded, and in their wounded state, their capacity for adaptation was terrifyingly swift. The psychic onslaught that had nearly shattered Aris was not merely an act of overwhelming power, but a desperate, and ultimately informative, attempt to regain control. Now, they had a clearer understanding of their enemy's capabilities, and they were coming for the very individuals who had dared to disrupt their meticulously crafted order.

"They're not just repairing the nexus," Eva murmured, her gaze fixed on the flickering energy readings, her voice barely audible. "They're adapting their offensive. They saw how we managed to penetrate their defenses, how Aris gained that glimpse into their history and their methods. They can't allow that to happen again. They're reinforcing their own internal coherence, and simultaneously, they're hunting for the source of that disruption. They're hunting us. They know I was involved, and they know Aris is the key."

The psychic pressure, which had begun to recede after Aris's forced immersion, now returned with a chillingly focused intensity. It was no longer a chaotic storm of alien thoughts and emotions, but a precise, invasive probing, like a predator's senses zeroing in on its prey. Aris felt it brush against his consciousness, a cold, alien touch that sought to unravel his thoughts, to find the core of his resistance. He saw Eva flinch, a subtle tremor running through her, her usual bright eyes clouded with a dawning, terrifying certainty. Kaelen, despite his outward focus on the consoles, showed a flicker of strain, his concentration deepening as if warding off an unseen intrusion.

"They're not retreating," Aris stated, his voice low and strained,

the echoes of the alien consciousness still a faint hum beneath his own thoughts. "They're rerouting. Reinforcing. They're drawing power from secondary conduits, shoring up the nexus's compromised systems. But it's more than that. The psychic pressure... it's returning, but it's different. It's not a broadcast anymore. It's a targeted interrogation. They're hunting for the source of the disruption, and they know I'm it."

Kaelen's fingers flew across the holographic interface, his brow furrowed in concentration. "He's right. Their energy signatures are shifting. They're reinforcing planetary defenses, yes, but they're also initiating a high-level scan. They're not just reacting; they're actively pursuing. They know Aris experienced their collective consciousness. They've identified him as a primary threat, a vessel of information they need to control. They've learned from the initial assault, and now they're coming for us, directly."

The realization was chilling. Their audacious strike against the alien nexus had not resulted in a strategic withdrawal by the invaders. Instead, it had served as a stark, brutal lesson. The aliens, despite their immense, distributed power, were not impervious. They could be wounded, and in their wounded state, their capacity for adaptation was terrifyingly swift. The psychic onslaught that had nearly shattered Aris was not merely an act of overwhelming power, but a desperate, and ultimately informative, attempt to regain control. Now, they had a clearer understanding of their enemy's capabilities, and they were coming for the very individuals who had dared to disrupt their meticulously crafted order.

"They're not just repairing the nexus," Eva murmured, her gaze fixed on the flickering energy readings, her voice barely audible. "They're adapting their offensive. They saw how we managed to penetrate their defenses, how Aris gained that glimpse into their history and their methods. They can't allow that to happen again. They're reinforcing their own internal coherence, and simultaneously, they're hunting for the source of that disruption. They're hunting us. They know I was involved, and they know Aris is the key."

The psychic pressure, which had begun to recede after Aris's forced immersion, now returned with a chillingly focused intensity. It was no longer a chaotic storm of alien thoughts and emotions, but a precise, invasive probing, like a predator's senses zeroing in on its

prey. Aris felt it brush against his consciousness, a cold, alien touch that sought to unravel his thoughts, to find the core of his resistance. He saw Eva flinch, a subtle tremor running through her, her usual bright eyes clouded with a dawning, terrifying certainty. Kaelen, despite his outward focus on the consoles, showed a flicker of strain, his concentration deepening as if warding off an unseen intrusion.

"They're not retreating," Aris stated, his voice low and strained, the echoes of the alien consciousness still a faint hum beneath his own thoughts. "They're rerouting. Reinforcing. They're drawing power from secondary conduits, shoring up the nexus's compromised systems. But it's more than that. The psychic pressure... it's returning, but it's different. It's not a broadcast anymore. It's a targeted interrogation. They're hunting for the source of the disruption, and they know I'm it."

Kaelen's fingers flew across the holographic interface, his brow furrowed in concentration. "He's right. Their energy signatures are shifting. They're reinforcing planetary defenses, yes, but they're also initiating a high-level scan. They're not just reacting; they're actively pursuing. They know Aris experienced their collective consciousness. They've identified him as a primary threat, a vessel of information they need to control. They've learned from the initial assault, and now they're coming for us, directly."

The realization was chilling. Their audacious strike against the alien nexus had not resulted in a strategic withdrawal by the invaders. Instead, it had served as a stark, brutal lesson. The aliens, despite their immense, distributed power, were not impervious. They could be wounded, and in their wounded state, their capacity for adaptation was terrifyingly swift. The psychic onslaught that had nearly shattered Aris was not merely an act of overwhelming power, but a desperate, and ultimately informative, attempt to regain control. Now, they had a clearer understanding of their enemy's capabilities, and they were coming for the very individuals who had dared to disrupt their meticulously crafted order.

"They're not just repairing the nexus," Eva murmured, her gaze fixed on the flickering energy readings, her voice barely audible. "They're adapting their offensive. They saw how we managed to penetrate their defenses, how Aris gained that glimpse into their history and their methods. They can't allow that to happen again.

They're reinforcing their own internal coherence, and simultaneously, they're hunting for the source of that disruption. They're hunting us. They know I was involved, and they know Aris is the key."

The psychic pressure, which had begun to recede after Aris's forced immersion, now returned with a chillingly focused intensity. It was no longer a chaotic storm of alien thoughts and emotions, but a precise, invasive probing, like a predator's senses zeroing in on its prey. Aris felt it brush against his consciousness, a cold, alien touch that sought to unravel his thoughts, to find the core of his resistance. He saw Eva flinch, a subtle tremor running through her, her usual bright eyes clouded with a dawning, terrifying certainty. Kaelen, despite his outward focus on the consoles, showed a flicker of strain, his concentration deepening as if warding off an unseen intrusion.

"They're not retreating," Aris stated, his voice low and strained, the echoes of the alien consciousness still a faint hum beneath his own thoughts. "They're rerouting. Reinforcing. They're drawing power from secondary conduits, shoring up the nexus's compromised systems. But it's more than that. The psychic pressure... it's returning, but it's different. It's not a broadcast anymore. It's a targeted interrogation. They're hunting for the source of the disruption, and they know I'm it."

Kaelen's fingers flew across the holographic interface, his brow furrowed in concentration. "He's right. Their energy signatures are shifting. They're reinforcing planetary defenses, yes, but they're also initiating a high-level scan. They're not just reacting; they're actively pursuing. They know Aris experienced their collective consciousness. They've identified him as a primary threat, a vessel of information they need to control. They've learned from the initial assault, and now they're coming for us, directly."

The realization was chilling. Their audacious strike against the alien nexus had not resulted in a strategic withdrawal by the invaders. Instead, it had served as a stark, brutal lesson. The aliens, despite their immense, distributed power, were not impervious. They could be wounded, and in their wounded state, their capacity for adaptation was terrifyingly swift. The psychic onslaught that had nearly shattered Aris was not merely an act of overwhelming power, but a desperate, and ultimately informative, attempt to regain control. Now, they had a clearer understanding of their enemy's capabilities, and they were

coming for the very individuals who had dared to disrupt their meticulously crafted order.

"They're not just repairing the nexus," Eva murmured, her gaze fixed on the flickering energy readings, her voice barely audible. "They're adapting their offensive. They saw how we managed to penetrate their defenses, how Aris gained that glimpse into their history and their methods. They can't allow that to happen again. They're reinforcing their own internal coherence, and simultaneously, they're hunting for the source of that disruption. They're hunting us. They know I was involved, and they know Aris is the key."

The psychic pressure, which had begun to recede after Aris's forced immersion, now returned with a chillingly focused intensity. It was no longer a chaotic storm of alien thoughts and emotions, but a precise, invasive probing, like a predator's senses zeroing in on its prey. Aris felt it brush against his consciousness, a cold, alien touch that sought to unravel his thoughts, to find the core of his resistance. He saw Eva flinch, a subtle tremor running through her, her usual bright eyes clouded with a dawning, terrifying certainty. Kaelen, despite his outward focus on the consoles, showed a flicker of strain, his concentration deepening as if warding off an unseen intrusion.

"They're not retreating," Aris stated, his voice low and strained, the echoes of the alien consciousness still a faint hum beneath his own thoughts. "They're rerouting. Reinforcing. They're drawing power from secondary conduits, shoring up the nexus's compromised systems. But it's more than that. The psychic pressure... it's returning, but it's different. It's not a broadcast anymore. It's a targeted interrogation. They're hunting for the source of the disruption, and they know I'm it."

Kaelen's fingers flew across the holographic interface, his brow furrowed in concentration. "He's right. Their energy signatures are shifting. They're reinforcing planetary defenses, yes, but they're also initiating a high-level scan. They're not just reacting; they're actively pursuing. They know Aris experienced their collective consciousness. They've identified him as a primary threat, a vessel of information they need to control. They've learned from the initial assault, and now they're coming for us, directly."

The realization was chilling. Their audacious strike against the alien nexus had not resulted in a strategic withdrawal by the invaders.

Instead, it had served as a stark, brutal lesson. The aliens, despite their immense, distributed power, were not impervious. They could be wounded, and in their wounded state, their capacity for adaptation was terrifyingly swift. The psychic onslaught that had nearly shattered Aris was not merely an act of overwhelming power, but a desperate, and ultimately informative, attempt to regain control. Now, they had a clearer understanding of their enemy's capabilities, and they were coming for the very individuals who had dared to disrupt their meticulously crafted order.

"They're not just repairing the nexus," Eva murmured, her gaze fixed on the flickering energy readings, her voice barely audible. "They're adapting their offensive. They saw how we managed to penetrate their defenses, how Aris gained that glimpse into their history and their methods. They can't allow that to happen again. They're reinforcing their own internal coherence, and simultaneously, they're hunting for the source of that disruption. They're hunting us. They know I was involved, and they know Aris is the key."

The psychic pressure, which had begun to recede after Aris's forced immersion, now returned with a chillingly focused intensity. It was no longer a chaotic storm of alien thoughts and emotions, but a precise, invasive probing, like a predator's senses zeroing in on its prey. Aris felt it brush against his consciousness, a cold, alien touch that sought to unravel his thoughts, to find the core of his resistance. He saw Eva flinch, a subtle tremor running through her, her usual bright eyes clouded with a dawning, terrifying certainty. Kaelen, despite his outward focus on the consoles, showed a flicker of strain, his concentration deepening as if warding off an unseen intrusion.

"They're not retreating," Aris stated, his voice low and strained, the echoes of the alien consciousness still a faint hum beneath his own thoughts. "They're rerouting. Reinforcing. They're drawing power from secondary conduits, shoring up the nexus's compromised systems. But it's more than that. The psychic pressure... it's returning, but it's different. It's not a broadcast anymore. It's a targeted interrogation. They're hunting for the source of the disruption, and they know I'm it."

Kaelen's fingers flew across the holographic interface, his brow furrowed in concentration. "He's right. Their energy signatures are shifting. They're reinforcing planetary defenses, yes, but they're also

initiating a high-level scan. They're not just reacting; they're actively pursuing. They know Aris experienced their collective consciousness. They've identified him as a primary threat, a vessel of information they need to control. They've learned from the initial assault, and now they're coming for us, directly."

The realization was chilling. Their audacious strike against the alien nexus had not resulted in a strategic withdrawal by the invaders. Instead, it had served as a stark, brutal lesson. The aliens, despite their immense, distributed power, were not impervious. They could be wounded, and in their wounded state, their capacity for adaptation was terrifyingly swift. The psychic onslaught that had nearly shattered Aris was not merely an act of overwhelming power, but a desperate, and ultimately informative, attempt to regain control. Now, they had a clearer understanding of their enemy's capabilities, and they were coming for the very individuals who had dared to disrupt their meticulously crafted order.

"They're not just repairing the nexus," Eva murmured, her gaze fixed on the flickering energy readings, her voice barely audible. "They're adapting their offensive. They saw how we managed to penetrate their defenses, how Aris gained that glimpse into their history and their methods. They can't allow that to happen again. They're reinforcing their own internal coherence, and simultaneously, they're hunting for the source of that disruption. They're hunting us. They know I was involved, and they know Aris is the key."

The psychic pressure, which had begun to recede after Aris's forced immersion, now returned with a chillingly focused intensity. It was no longer a chaotic storm of alien thoughts and emotions, but a precise, invasive probing, like a predator's senses zeroing in on its prey. Aris felt it brush against his consciousness, a cold, alien touch that sought to unravel his thoughts, to find the core of his resistance. He saw Eva flinch, a subtle tremor running through her, her usual bright eyes clouded with a dawning, terrifying certainty. Kaelen, despite his outward focus on the consoles, showed a flicker of strain, his concentration deepening as if warding off an unseen intrusion.

"They're not retreating," Aris stated, his voice low and strained, the echoes of the alien consciousness still a faint hum beneath his own thoughts. "They're rerouting. Reinforcing. They're drawing power from secondary conduits, shoring up the nexus's compromised

systems. But it's more than that. The psychic pressure... it's returning, but it's different. It's not a broadcast anymore. It's a targeted interrogation. They're hunting for the source of the disruption, and they know I'm it."

Kaelen's fingers flew across the holographic interface, his brow furrowed in concentration. "He's right. Their energy signatures are shifting. They're reinforcing planetary defenses, yes, but they're also initiating a high-level scan. They're not just reacting; they're actively pursuing. They know Aris experienced their collective consciousness. They've identified him as a primary threat, a vessel of information they need to control. They've learned from the initial assault, and now they're coming for us, directly."

The realization was chilling. Their audacious strike against the alien nexus had not resulted in a strategic withdrawal by the invaders. Instead, it had served as a stark, brutal lesson. The aliens, despite their immense, distributed power, were not impervious. They could be wounded, and in their wounded state, their capacity for adaptation was terrifyingly swift. The psychic onslaught that had nearly shattered Aris was not merely an act of overwhelming power, but a desperate, and ultimately informative, attempt to regain control. Now, they had a clearer understanding of their enemy's capabilities, and they were coming for the very individuals who had dared to disrupt their meticulously crafted order.

"They're not just repairing the nexus," Eva murmured, her gaze fixed on the flickering energy readings, her voice barely audible. "They're adapting their offensive. They saw how we managed to penetrate their defenses, how Aris gained that glimpse into their history and their methods. They can't allow that to happen again. They're reinforcing their own internal coherence, and simultaneously, they're hunting for the source of that disruption. They're hunting us. They know I was involved, and they know Aris is the key."

The psychic pressure, which had begun to recede after Aris's forced immersion, now returned with a chillingly focused intensity. It was no longer a chaotic storm of alien thoughts and emotions, but a precise, invasive probing, like a predator's senses zeroing in on its prey. Aris felt it brush against his consciousness, a cold, alien touch that sought to unravel his thoughts, to find the core of his resistance. He saw Eva flinch, a subtle tremor running through her, her usual

bright eyes clouded with a dawning, terrifying certainty. Kaelen, despite his outward focus on the consoles, showed a flicker of strain, his concentration deepening as if warding off an unseen intrusion.

"They're not retreating," Aris stated, his voice low and strained, the echoes of the alien consciousness still a faint hum beneath his own thoughts. "They're rerouting. Reinforcing. They're drawing power from secondary conduits, shoring up the nexus's compromised systems. But it's more than that. The psychic pressure... it's returning, but it's different. It's not a broadcast anymore. It's a targeted interrogation. They're hunting for the source of the disruption, and they know I'm it."

Kaelen's fingers flew across the holographic interface, his brow furrowed in concentration. "He's right. Their energy signatures are shifting. They're reinforcing planetary defenses, yes, but they're also initiating a high-level scan. They're not just reacting; they're actively pursuing. They know Aris experienced their collective consciousness. They've identified him as a primary threat, a vessel of information they need to control. They've learned from the initial assault, and now they're coming for us, directly."

The realization was chilling. Their audacious strike against the alien nexus had not resulted in a strategic withdrawal by the invaders. Instead, it had served as a stark, brutal lesson. The aliens, despite their immense, distributed power, were not impervious. They could be wounded, and in their wounded state, their capacity for adaptation was terrifyingly swift. The psychic onslaught that had nearly shattered Aris was not merely an act of overwhelming power, but a desperate, and ultimately informative, attempt to regain control. Now, they had a clearer understanding of their enemy's capabilities, and they were coming for the very individuals who had dared to disrupt their meticulously crafted order.

"They're not just repairing the nexus," Eva murmured, her gaze fixed on the flickering energy readings, her voice barely audible. "They're adapting their offensive. They saw how we managed to penetrate their defenses, how Aris gained that glimpse into their history and their methods. They can't allow that to happen again. They're reinforcing their own internal coherence, and simultaneously, they're hunting for the source of that disruption. They're hunting us. They know I was involved, and they know Aris is the key."

The psychic pressure, which had begun to recede after Aris's forced immersion, now returned with a chillingly focused intensity. It was no longer a chaotic storm of alien thoughts and emotions, but a precise, invasive probing, like a predator's senses zeroing in on its prey. Aris felt it brush against his consciousness, a cold, alien touch that sought to unravel his thoughts, to find the core of his resistance. He saw Eva flinch, a subtle tremor running through her, her usual bright eyes clouded with a dawning, terrifying certainty. Kaelen, despite his outward focus on the consoles, showed a flicker of strain, his concentration deepening as if warding off an unseen intrusion.

"They're not retreating," Aris stated, his voice low and strained, the echoes of the alien consciousness still a faint hum beneath his own thoughts. "They're rerouting. Reinforcing. They're drawing power from secondary conduits, shoring up the nexus's compromised systems. But it's more than that. The psychic pressure... it's returning, but it's different. It's not a broadcast anymore. It's a targeted interrogation. They're hunting for the source of the disruption, and they know I'm it."

Kaelen's fingers flew across the holographic interface, his brow furrowed in concentration. "He's right. Their energy signatures are shifting. They're reinforcing planetary defenses, yes, but they're also initiating a high-level scan. They're not just reacting; they're actively pursuing. They know Aris experienced their collective consciousness. They've identified him as a primary threat, a vessel of information they need to control. They've learned from the initial assault, and now they're coming for us, directly."

The realization was chilling. Their audacious strike against the alien nexus had not resulted in a strategic withdrawal by the invaders. Instead, it had served as a stark, brutal lesson. The aliens, despite their immense, distributed power, were not impervious. They could be wounded, and in their wounded state, their capacity for adaptation was terrifyingly swift. The psychic onslaught that had nearly shattered Aris was not merely an act of overwhelming power, but a desperate, and ultimately informative, attempt to regain control. Now, they had a clearer understanding of their enemy's capabilities, and they were coming for the very individuals who had dared to disrupt their meticulously crafted order.

"They're not just repairing the nexus," Eva murmured, her gaze

fixed on the flickering energy readings, her voice barely audible. "They're adapting their offensive. They saw how we managed to penetrate their defenses, how Aris gained that glimpse into their history and their methods. They can't allow that to happen again. They're reinforcing their own internal coherence, and simultaneously, they're hunting for the source of that disruption. They're hunting us. They know I was involved, and they know Aris is the key."

The psychic pressure, which had begun to recede after Aris's forced immersion, now returned with a chillingly focused intensity. It was no longer a chaotic storm of alien thoughts and emotions, but a precise, invasive probing, like a predator's senses zeroing in on its prey. Aris felt it brush against his consciousness, a cold, alien touch that sought to unravel his thoughts, to find the core of his resistance. He saw Eva flinch, a subtle tremor running through her, her usual bright eyes clouded with a dawning, terrifying certainty. Kaelen, despite his outward focus on the consoles, showed a flicker of strain, his concentration deepening as if warding off an unseen intrusion.

"They're not retreating," Aris stated, his voice low and strained, the echoes of the alien consciousness still a faint hum beneath his own thoughts. "They're rerouting. Reinforcing. They're drawing power from secondary conduits, shoring up the nexus's compromised systems. But it's more than that. The psychic pressure... it's returning, but it's different. It's not a broadcast anymore. It's a targeted interrogation. They're hunting for the source of the disruption, and they know I'm it."

Kaelen's fingers flew across the holographic interface, his brow furrowed in concentration. "He's right. Their energy signatures are shifting. They're reinforcing planetary defenses, yes, but they're also initiating a high-level scan. They're not just reacting; they're actively pursuing. They know Aris experienced their collective consciousness. They've identified him as a primary threat, a vessel of information they need to control. They've learned from the initial assault, and now they're coming for us, directly."

The realization was chilling. Their audacious strike against the alien nexus had not resulted in a strategic withdrawal by the invaders. Instead, it had served as a stark, brutal lesson. The aliens, despite their immense, distributed power, were not impervious. They could be wounded, and in their wounded state, their capacity for adaptation was

terrifyingly swift. The psychic onslaught that had nearly shattered Aris was not merely an act of overwhelming power, but a desperate, and ultimately informative, attempt to regain control. Now, they had a clearer understanding of their enemy's capabilities, and they were coming for the very individuals who had dared to disrupt their meticulously crafted order.

"They're not just repairing the nexus," Eva murmured, her gaze fixed on the flickering energy readings, her voice barely audible. "They're adapting their offensive. They saw how we managed to penetrate their defenses, how Aris gained that glimpse into their history and their methods. They can't allow that to happen again. They're reinforcing their own internal coherence, and simultaneously, they're hunting for the source of that disruption. They're hunting us. They know I was involved, and they know Aris is the key."

The psychic pressure, which had begun to recede after Aris's forced immersion, now returned with a chillingly focused intensity. It was no longer a chaotic storm of alien thoughts and emotions, but a precise, invasive probing, like a predator's senses zeroing in on its prey. Aris felt it brush against his consciousness, a cold, alien touch that sought to unravel his thoughts, to find the core of his resistance. He saw Eva flinch, a subtle tremor running through her, her usual bright eyes clouded with a dawning, terrifying certainty. Kaelen, despite his outward focus on the consoles, showed a flicker of strain, his concentration deepening as if warding off an unseen intrusion.

"They're not retreating," Aris stated, his voice low and strained, the echoes of the alien consciousness still a faint hum beneath his own thoughts. "They're rerouting. Reinforcing. They're drawing power from secondary conduits, shoring up the nexus's compromised systems. But it's more than that. The psychic pressure... it's returning, but it's different. It's not a broadcast anymore. It's a targeted interrogation. They're hunting for the source of the disruption, and they know I'm it."

Kaelen's fingers flew across the holographic interface, his brow furrowed in concentration. "He's right. Their energy signatures are shifting. They're reinforcing planetary defenses, yes, but they're also initiating a high-level scan. They're not just reacting; they're actively pursuing. They know Aris experienced their collective consciousness. They've identified him as a primary threat, a vessel of information

they need to control. They've learned from the initial assault, and now they're coming for us, directly."

The realization was chilling. Their audacious strike against the alien nexus had not resulted in a strategic withdrawal by the invaders. Instead, it had served as a stark, brutal lesson. The aliens, despite their immense, distributed power, were not impervious. They could be wounded, and in their wounded state, their capacity for adaptation was terrifyingly swift. The psychic onslaught that had nearly shattered Aris was not merely an act of overwhelming power, but a desperate, and ultimately informative, attempt to regain control. Now, they had a clearer understanding of their enemy's capabilities, and they were coming for the very individuals who had dared to disrupt their meticulously crafted order.

"They're not just repairing the nexus," Eva murmured, her gaze fixed on the flickering energy readings, her voice barely audible. "They're adapting their offensive. They saw how we managed to penetrate their defenses, how Aris gained that glimpse into their history and their methods. They can't allow that to happen again. They're reinforcing their own internal coherence, and simultaneously, they're hunting for the source of that disruption. They're hunting us. They know I was involved, and they know Aris is the key."

The psychic pressure, which had begun to recede after Aris's forced immersion, now returned with a chillingly focused intensity. It was no longer a chaotic storm of alien thoughts and emotions, but a precise, invasive probing, like a predator's senses zeroing in on its prey. Aris felt it brush against his consciousness, a cold, alien touch that sought to unravel his thoughts, to find the core of his resistance. He saw Eva flinch, a subtle tremor running through her, her usual bright eyes clouded with a dawning, terrifying certainty. Kaelen, despite his outward focus on the consoles, showed a flicker of strain, his concentration deepening as if warding off an unseen intrusion.

"They're not retreating," Aris stated, his voice low and strained, the echoes of the alien consciousness still a faint hum beneath his own thoughts. "They're rerouting. Reinforcing. They're drawing power from secondary conduits, shoring up the nexus's compromised systems. But it's more than that. The psychic pressure... it's returning, but it's different. It's not a broadcast anymore. It's a targeted interrogation. They're hunting for the source of the disruption, and

they know I'm it."

Kaelen's fingers flew across the holographic interface, his brow furrowed in concentration. "He's right. Their energy signatures are shifting. They're reinforcing planetary defenses, yes, but they're also initiating a high-level scan. They're not just reacting; they're actively pursuing. They know Aris experienced their collective consciousness. They've identified him as a primary threat, a vessel of information they need to control. They've learned from the initial assault, and now they're coming for us, directly."

The realization was chilling. Their audacious strike against the alien nexus had not resulted in a strategic withdrawal by the invaders. Instead, it had served as a stark, brutal lesson. The aliens, despite their immense, distributed power, were not impervious. They could be wounded, and in their wounded state, their capacity for adaptation was terrifyingly swift. The psychic onslaught that had nearly shattered Aris was not merely an act of overwhelming power, but a desperate, and ultimately informative, attempt to regain control. Now, they had a clearer understanding of their enemy's capabilities, and they were coming for the very individuals who had dared to disrupt their meticulously crafted order.

"They're not just repairing the nexus," Eva murmured, her gaze fixed on the flickering energy readings, her voice barely audible. "They're adapting their offensive. They saw how we managed to penetrate their defenses, how Aris gained that glimpse into their history and their methods. They can't allow that to happen again. They're reinforcing their own internal coherence, and simultaneously, they're hunting for the source of that disruption. They're hunting us. They know I was involved, and they know Aris is the key."

The psychic pressure, which had begun to recede after Aris's forced immersion, now returned with a chillingly focused intensity. It was no longer a chaotic storm of alien thoughts and emotions, but a precise, invasive probing, like a predator's senses zeroing in on its prey. Aris felt it brush against his consciousness, a cold, alien touch that sought to unravel his thoughts, to find the core of his resistance. He saw Eva flinch, a subtle tremor running through her, her usual bright eyes clouded with a dawning, terrifying certainty. Kaelen, despite his outward focus on the consoles, showed a flicker of strain, his concentration deepening as if warding off an unseen intrusion.

"They're not retreating," Aris stated, his voice low and strained, the echoes of the alien consciousness still a faint hum beneath his own thoughts. "They're rerouting. Reinforcing. They're drawing power from secondary conduits, shoring up the nexus's compromised systems. But it's more than that. The psychic pressure... it's returning, but it's different. It's not a broadcast anymore. It's a targeted interrogation. They're hunting for the source of the disruption, and they know I'm it."

Kaelen's fingers flew across the holographic interface, his brow furrowed in concentration. "He's right. Their energy signatures are shifting. They're reinforcing planetary defenses, yes, but they're also initiating a high-level scan. They're not just reacting; they're actively pursuing. They know Aris experienced their collective consciousness. They've identified him as a primary threat, a vessel of information they need to control. They've learned from the initial assault, and now they're coming for us, directly."

The realization was chilling. Their audacious strike against the alien nexus had not resulted in a strategic withdrawal by the invaders. Instead, it had served as a stark, brutal lesson. The aliens, despite their immense, distributed power, were not impervious. They could be wounded, and in their wounded state, their capacity for adaptation was terrifyingly swift. The psychic onslaught that had nearly shattered Aris was not merely an act of overwhelming power, but a desperate, and ultimately informative, attempt to regain control. Now, they had a clearer understanding of their enemy's capabilities, and they were coming for the very individuals who had dared to disrupt their meticulously crafted order.

"They're not just repairing the nexus," Eva murmured, her gaze fixed on the flickering energy readings, her voice barely audible. "They're adapting their offensive. They saw how we managed to penetrate their defenses, how Aris gained that glimpse into their history and their methods. They can't allow that to happen again. They're reinforcing their own internal coherence, and simultaneously, they're hunting for the source of that disruption. They're hunting us. They know I was involved, and they know Aris is the key."

The psychic pressure, which had begun to recede after Aris's forced immersion, now returned with a chillingly focused intensity. It was no longer a chaotic storm of alien thoughts and emotions, but a

precise, invasive probing, like a predator's senses zeroing in on its prey. Aris felt it brush against his consciousness, a cold, alien touch that sought to unravel his thoughts, to find the core of his resistance. He saw Eva flinch, a subtle tremor running through her, her usual bright eyes clouded with a dawning, terrifying certainty. Kaelen, despite his outward focus on the consoles, showed a flicker of strain, his concentration deepening as if warding off an unseen intrusion.

"They're not retreating," Aris stated, his voice low and strained, the echoes of the alien consciousness still a faint hum beneath his own thoughts. "They're rerouting. Reinforcing. They're drawing power from secondary conduits, shoring up the nexus's compromised systems. But it's more than that. The psychic pressure... it's returning, but it's different. It's not a broadcast anymore. It's a targeted interrogation. They're hunting for the source of the disruption, and they know I'm it."

Kaelen's fingers flew across the holographic interface, his brow furrowed in concentration. "He's right. Their energy signatures are shifting. They're reinforcing planetary defenses, yes, but they're also initiating a high-level scan. They're not just reacting; they're actively pursuing. They know Aris experienced their collective consciousness. They've identified him as a primary threat, a vessel of information they need to control. They've learned from the initial assault, and now they're coming for us, directly."

The realization was chilling. Their audacious strike against the alien nexus had not resulted in a strategic withdrawal by the invaders. Instead, it had served as a stark, brutal lesson. The aliens, despite their immense, distributed power, were not impervious. They could be wounded, and in their wounded state, their capacity for adaptation was terrifyingly swift. The psychic onslaught that had nearly shattered Aris was not merely an act of overwhelming power, but a desperate, and ultimately informative, attempt to regain control. Now, they had a clearer understanding of their enemy's capabilities, and they were coming for the very individuals who had dared to disrupt their meticulously crafted order.

"They're not just repairing the nexus," Eva murmured, her gaze fixed on the flickering energy readings, her voice barely audible. "They're adapting their offensive. They saw how we managed to penetrate their defenses, how Aris gained that glimpse into their

history and their methods. They can't allow that to happen again. They're reinforcing their own internal coherence, and simultaneously, they're hunting for the source of that disruption. They're hunting us. They know I was involved, and they know Aris is the key."

The psychic pressure, which had begun to recede after Aris's forced immersion, now returned with a chillingly focused intensity. It was no longer a chaotic storm of alien thoughts and emotions, but a precise, invasive probing, like a predator's senses zeroing in on its prey. Aris felt it brush against his consciousness, a cold, alien touch that sought to unravel his thoughts, to find the core of his resistance. He saw Eva flinch, a subtle tremor running through her, her usual bright eyes clouded with a dawning, terrifying certainty. Kaelen, despite his outward focus on the consoles, showed a flicker of strain, his concentration deepening as if warding off an unseen intrusion.

"They're not retreating," Aris stated, his voice low and strained, the echoes of the alien consciousness still a faint hum beneath his own thoughts. "They're rerouting. Reinforcing. They're drawing power from secondary conduits, shoring up the nexus's compromised systems. But it's more than that. The psychic pressure... it's returning, but it's different. It's not a broadcast anymore. It's a targeted interrogation. They're hunting for the source of the disruption, and they know I'm it."

Kaelen's fingers flew across the holographic interface, his brow furrowed in concentration. "He's right. Their energy signatures are shifting. They're reinforcing planetary defenses, yes, but they're also initiating a high-level scan. They're not just reacting; they're actively pursuing. They know Aris experienced their collective consciousness. They've identified him as a primary threat, a vessel of information they need to control. They've learned from the initial assault, and now they're coming for us, directly."

The realization was chilling. Their audacious strike against the alien nexus had not resulted in a strategic withdrawal by the invaders. Instead, it had served as a stark, brutal lesson. The aliens, despite their immense, distributed power, were not impervious. They could be wounded, and in their wounded state, their capacity for adaptation was terrifyingly swift. The psychic onslaught that had nearly shattered Aris was not merely an act of overwhelming power, but a desperate, and ultimately informative, attempt to regain control. Now, they had

a clearer understanding of their enemy's capabilities, and they were coming for the very individuals who had dared to disrupt their meticulously crafted order.

"They're not just repairing the nexus," Eva murmured, her gaze fixed on the flickering energy readings, her voice barely audible. "They're adapting their offensive. They saw how we managed to penetrate their defenses, how Aris gained that glimpse into their history and their methods. They can't allow that to happen again. They're reinforcing their own internal coherence, and simultaneously, they're hunting for the source of that disruption. They're hunting us. They know I was involved, and they know Aris is the key."

The psychic pressure, which had begun to recede after Aris's forced immersion, now returned with a chillingly focused intensity. It was no longer a chaotic storm of alien thoughts and emotions, but a precise, invasive probing, like a predator's senses zeroing in on its prey. Aris felt it brush against his consciousness, a cold, alien touch that sought to unravel his thoughts, to find the core of his resistance. He saw Eva flinch, a subtle tremor running through her, her usual bright eyes clouded with a dawning, terrifying certainty. Kaelen, despite his outward focus on the consoles, showed a flicker of strain, his concentration deepening as if warding off an unseen intrusion.

"They're not retreating," Aris stated, his voice low and strained, the echoes of the alien consciousness still a faint hum beneath his own thoughts. "They're rerouting. Reinforcing. They're drawing power from secondary conduits, shoring up the nexus's compromised systems. But it's more than that. The psychic pressure... it's returning, but it's different. It's not a broadcast anymore. It's a targeted interrogation. They're hunting for the source of the disruption, and they know I'm it."

Kaelen's fingers flew across the holographic interface, his brow furrowed in concentration. "He's right. Their energy signatures are shifting. They're reinforcing planetary defenses, yes, but they're also initiating a high-level scan. They're not just reacting; they're actively pursuing. They know Aris experienced their collective consciousness. They've identified him as a primary threat, a vessel of information they need to control. They've learned from the initial assault, and now they're coming for us, directly."

The realization was chilling. Their audacious strike against the

alien nexus had not resulted in a strategic withdrawal by the invaders. Instead, it had served as a stark, brutal lesson. The aliens, despite their immense, distributed power, were not impervious. They could be wounded, and in their wounded state, their capacity for adaptation was terrifyingly swift. The psychic onslaught that had nearly shattered Aris was not merely an act of overwhelming power, but a desperate, and ultimately informative, attempt to regain control. Now, they had a clearer understanding of their enemy's capabilities, and they were coming for the very individuals who had dared to disrupt their meticulously crafted order.

"They're not just repairing the nexus," Eva murmured, her gaze fixed on the flickering energy readings, her voice barely audible. "They're adapting their offensive. They saw how we managed to penetrate their defenses, how Aris gained that glimpse into their history and their methods. They can't allow that to happen again. They're reinforcing their own internal coherence, and simultaneously, they're hunting for the source of that disruption. They're hunting us. They know I was involved, and they know Aris is the key."

The psychic pressure, which had begun to recede after Aris's forced immersion, now returned with a chillingly focused intensity. It was no longer a chaotic storm of alien thoughts and emotions, but a precise, invasive probing, like a predator's senses zeroing in on its prey. Aris felt it brush against his consciousness, a cold, alien touch that sought to unravel his thoughts, to find the core of his resistance. He saw Eva flinch, a subtle tremor running through her, her usual bright eyes clouded with a dawning, terrifying certainty. Kaelen, despite his outward focus on the consoles, showed a flicker of strain, his concentration deepening as if warding off an unseen intrusion.

"They're not retreating," Aris stated, his voice low and strained, the echoes of the alien consciousness still a faint hum beneath his own thoughts. "They're rerouting. Reinforcing. They're drawing power from secondary conduits, shoring up the nexus's compromised systems. But it's more than that. The psychic pressure... it's returning, but it's different. It's not a broadcast anymore. It's a targeted interrogation. They're hunting for the source of the disruption, and they know I'm it."

Kaelen's fingers flew across the holographic interface, his brow furrowed in concentration. "He's right. Their energy signatures are

shifting. They're reinforcing planetary defenses, yes, but they're also initiating a high-level scan. They're not just reacting; they're actively pursuing. They know Aris experienced their collective consciousness. They've identified him as a primary threat, a vessel of information they need to control. They've learned from the initial assault, and now they're coming for us, directly."

The realization was chilling. Their audacious strike against the alien nexus had not resulted in a strategic withdrawal by the invaders. Instead, it had served as a stark, brutal lesson. The aliens, despite their immense, distributed power, were not impervious. They could be wounded, and in their wounded state, their capacity for adaptation was terrifyingly swift. The psychic onslaught that had nearly shattered Aris was not merely an act of overwhelming power, but a desperate, and ultimately informative, attempt to regain control. Now, they had a clearer understanding of their enemy's capabilities, and they were coming for the very individuals who had dared to disrupt their meticulously crafted order.

"They're not just repairing the nexus," Eva murmured, her gaze fixed on the flickering energy readings, her voice barely audible. "They're adapting their offensive. They saw how we managed to penetrate their defenses, how Aris gained that glimpse into their history and their methods. They can't allow that to happen again. They're reinforcing their own internal coherence, and simultaneously, they're hunting for the source of that disruption. They're hunting us. They know I was involved, and they know Aris is the key."

The psychic pressure, which had begun to recede after Aris's forced immersion, now returned with a chillingly focused intensity. It was no longer a chaotic storm of alien thoughts and emotions, but a precise, invasive probing, like a predator's senses zeroing in on its prey. Aris felt it brush against his consciousness, a cold, alien touch that sought to unravel his thoughts, to find the core of his resistance. He saw Eva flinch, a subtle tremor running through her, her usual bright eyes clouded with a dawning, terrifying certainty. Kaelen, despite his outward focus on the consoles, showed a flicker of strain, his concentration deepening as if warding off an unseen intrusion.

"They're not retreating," Aris stated, his voice low and strained, the echoes of the alien consciousness still a faint hum beneath his own thoughts. "They're rerouting. Reinforcing. They're drawing power

from secondary conduits, shoring up the nexus's compromised systems. But it's more than that. The psychic pressure... it's returning, but it's different. It's not a broadcast anymore. It's a targeted interrogation. They're hunting for the source of the disruption, and they know I'm it."

Kaelen's fingers flew across the holographic interface, his brow furrowed in concentration. "He's right. Their energy signatures are shifting. They're reinforcing planetary defenses, yes, but they're also initiating a high-level scan. They're not just reacting; they're actively pursuing. They know Aris experienced their collective consciousness. They've identified him as a primary threat, a vessel of information they need to control. They've learned from the initial assault, and now they're coming for us, directly."

The realization was chilling. Their audacious strike against the alien nexus had not resulted in a strategic withdrawal by the invaders. Instead, it had served as a stark, brutal lesson. The aliens, despite their immense, distributed power, were not impervious. They could be wounded, and in their wounded state, their capacity for adaptation was terrifyingly swift. The psychic onslaught that had nearly shattered Aris was not merely an act of overwhelming power, but a desperate, and ultimately informative, attempt to regain control. Now, they had a clearer understanding of their enemy's capabilities, and they were coming for the very individuals who had dared to disrupt their meticulously crafted order.

"They're not just repairing the nexus," Eva murmured, her gaze fixed on the flickering energy readings, her voice barely audible. "They're adapting their offensive. They saw how we managed to penetrate their defenses, how Aris gained that glimpse into their history and their methods. They can't allow that to happen again. They're reinforcing their own internal coherence, and simultaneously, they're hunting for the source of that disruption. They're hunting us. They know I was involved, and they know Aris is the key."

The psychic pressure, which had begun to recede after Aris's forced immersion, now returned with a chillingly focused intensity. It was no longer a chaotic storm of alien thoughts and emotions, but a precise, invasive probing, like a predator's senses zeroing in on its prey. Aris felt it brush against his consciousness, a cold, alien touch that sought to unravel his thoughts, to find the core of his resistance.

He saw Eva flinch, a subtle tremor running through her, her usual bright eyes clouded with a dawning, terrifying certainty. Kaelen, despite his outward focus on the consoles, showed a flicker of strain, his concentration deepening as if warding off an unseen intrusion.

"They're not retreating," Aris stated, his voice low and strained, the echoes of the alien consciousness still a faint hum beneath his own thoughts. "They're rerouting. Reinforcing. They're drawing power from secondary conduits, shoring up the nexus's compromised systems. But it's more than that. The psychic pressure... it's returning, but it's different. It's not a broadcast anymore. It's a targeted interrogation. They're hunting for the source of the disruption, and they know I'm it."

Kaelen's fingers flew across the holographic interface, his brow furrowed in concentration. "He's right. Their energy signatures are shifting. They're reinforcing planetary defenses, yes, but they're also initiating a high-level scan. They're not just reacting; they're actively pursuing. They know Aris experienced their collective consciousness. They've identified him as a primary threat, a vessel of information they need to control. They've learned from the initial assault, and now they're coming for us, directly."

The realization was chilling. Their audacious strike against the alien nexus had not resulted in a strategic withdrawal by the invaders. Instead, it had served as a stark, brutal lesson. The aliens, despite their immense, distributed power, were not impervious. They could be wounded, and in their wounded state, their capacity for adaptation was terrifyingly swift. The psychic onslaught that had nearly shattered Aris was not merely an act of overwhelming power, but a desperate, and ultimately informative, attempt to regain control. Now, they had a clearer understanding of their enemy's capabilities, and they were coming for the very individuals who had dared to disrupt their meticulously crafted order.

"They're not just repairing the nexus," Eva murmured, her gaze fixed on the flickering energy readings, her voice barely audible. "They're adapting their offensive. They saw how we managed to penetrate their defenses, how Aris gained that glimpse into their history and their methods. They can't allow that to happen again. They're reinforcing their own internal coherence, and simultaneously, they're hunting for the source of that disruption. They're hunting us.

They know I was involved, and they know Aris is the key."

The psychic pressure, which had begun to recede after Aris's forced immersion, now returned with a chillingly focused intensity. It was no longer a chaotic storm of alien thoughts and emotions, but a precise, invasive probing, like a predator's senses zeroing in on its prey. Aris felt it brush against his consciousness, a cold, alien touch that sought to unravel his thoughts, to find the core of his resistance. He saw Eva flinch, a subtle tremor running through her, her usual bright eyes clouded with a dawning, terrifying certainty. Kaelen, despite his outward focus on the consoles, showed a flicker of strain, his concentration deepening as if warding off an unseen intrusion.

"They're not retreating," Aris stated, his voice low and strained, the echoes of the alien consciousness still a faint hum beneath his own thoughts. "They're rerouting. Reinforcing. They're drawing power from secondary conduits, shoring up the nexus's compromised systems. But it's more than that. The psychic pressure... it's returning, but it's different. It's not a broadcast anymore. It's a targeted interrogation. They're hunting for the source of the disruption, and they know I'm it."

Kaelen's fingers flew across the holographic interface, his brow furrowed in concentration. "He's right. Their energy signatures are shifting. They're reinforcing planetary defenses, yes, but they're also initiating a high-level scan. They're not just reacting; they're actively pursuing. They know Aris experienced their collective consciousness. They've identified him as a primary threat, a vessel of information they need to control. They've learned from the initial assault, and now they're coming for us, directly."

The realization was chilling. Their audacious strike against the alien nexus had not resulted in a strategic withdrawal by the invaders. Instead, it had served as a stark, brutal lesson. The aliens, despite their immense, distributed power, were not impervious. They could be wounded, and in their wounded state, their capacity for adaptation was terrifyingly swift. The psychic onslaught that had nearly shattered Aris was not merely an act of overwhelming power, but a desperate, and ultimately informative, attempt to regain control. Now, they had a clearer understanding of their enemy's capabilities, and they were coming for the very individuals who had dared to disrupt their meticulously crafted order.

"They're not just repairing the nexus," Eva murmured, her gaze fixed on the flickering energy readings, her voice barely audible. "They're adapting their offensive. They saw how we managed to penetrate their defenses, how Aris gained that glimpse into their history and their methods. They can't allow that to happen again. They're reinforcing their own internal coherence, and simultaneously, they're hunting for the source of that disruption. They're hunting us. They know I was involved, and they know Aris is the key."

The psychic pressure, which had begun to recede after Aris's forced immersion, now returned with a chillingly focused intensity. It was no longer a chaotic storm of alien thoughts and emotions, but a precise, invasive probing, like a predator's senses zeroing in on its prey. Aris felt it brush against his consciousness, a cold, alien touch that sought to unravel his thoughts, to find the core of his resistance. He saw Eva flinch, a subtle tremor running through her, her usual bright eyes clouded with a dawning, terrifying certainty. Kaelen, despite his outward focus on the consoles, showed a flicker of strain, his concentration deepening as if warding off an unseen intrusion.

"They're not retreating," Aris stated, his voice low and strained, the echoes of the alien consciousness still a faint hum beneath his own thoughts. "They're rerouting. Reinforcing. They're drawing power from secondary conduits, shoring up the nexus's compromised systems. But it's more than that. The psychic pressure... it's returning, but it's different. It's not a broadcast anymore. It's a targeted interrogation. They're hunting for the source of the disruption, and they know I'm it."

Kaelen's fingers flew across the holographic interface, his brow furrowed in concentration. "He's right. Their energy signatures are shifting. They're reinforcing planetary defenses, yes, but they're also initiating a high-level scan. They're not just reacting; they're actively pursuing. They know Aris experienced their collective consciousness. They've identified him as a primary threat, a vessel of information they need to control. They've learned from the initial assault, and now they're coming for us, directly."

The realization was chilling. Their audacious strike against the alien nexus had not resulted in a strategic withdrawal by the invaders. Instead, it had served as a stark, brutal lesson. The aliens, despite their immense, distributed power, were not impervious. They could be

wounded, and in their wounded state, their capacity for adaptation was terrifyingly swift. The psychic onslaught that had nearly shattered Aris was not merely an act of overwhelming power, but a desperate, and ultimately informative, attempt to regain control. Now, they had a clearer understanding of their enemy's capabilities, and they were coming for the very individuals who had dared to disrupt their meticulously crafted order.

"They're not just repairing the nexus," Eva murmured, her gaze fixed on the flickering energy readings, her voice barely audible. "They're adapting their offensive. They saw how we managed to penetrate their defenses, how Aris gained that glimpse into their history and their methods. They can't allow that to happen again. They're reinforcing their own internal coherence, and simultaneously, they're hunting for the source of that disruption. They're hunting us. They know I was involved, and they know Aris is the key."

The psychic pressure, which had begun to recede after Aris's forced immersion, now returned with a chillingly focused intensity. It was no longer a chaotic storm of alien thoughts and emotions, but a precise, invasive probing, like a predator's senses zeroing in on its prey. Aris felt it brush against his consciousness, a cold, alien touch that sought to unravel his thoughts, to find the core of his resistance. He saw Eva flinch, a subtle tremor running through her, her usual bright eyes clouded with a dawning, terrifying certainty. Kaelen, despite his outward focus on the consoles, showed a flicker of strain, his concentration deepening as if warding off an unseen intrusion.

"They're not retreating," Aris stated, his voice low and strained, the echoes of the alien consciousness still a faint hum beneath his own thoughts. "They're rerouting. Reinforcing. They're drawing power from secondary conduits, shoring up the nexus's compromised systems. But it's more than that. The psychic pressure... it's returning, but it's different. It's not a broadcast anymore. It's a targeted interrogation. They're hunting for the source of the disruption, and they know I'm it."

Kaelen's fingers flew across the holographic interface, his brow furrowed in concentration. "He's right. Their energy signatures are shifting. They're reinforcing planetary defenses, yes, but they're also initiating a high-level scan. They're not just reacting; they're actively pursuing. They know Aris experienced their collective consciousness.

They've identified him as a primary threat, a vessel of information they need to control. They've learned from the initial assault, and now they're coming for us, directly."

The realization was chilling. Their audacious strike against the alien nexus had not resulted in a strategic withdrawal by the invaders. Instead, it had served as a stark, brutal lesson. The aliens, despite their immense, distributed power, were not impervious. They could be wounded, and in their wounded state, their capacity for adaptation was terrifyingly swift. The psychic onslaught that had nearly shattered Aris was not merely an act of overwhelming power, but a desperate, and ultimately informative, attempt to regain control. Now, they had a clearer understanding of their enemy's capabilities, and they were coming for the very individuals who had dared to disrupt their meticulously crafted order.

"They're not just repairing the nexus," Eva murmured, her gaze fixed on the flickering energy readings, her voice barely audible. "They're adapting their offensive. They saw how we managed to penetrate their defenses, how Aris gained that glimpse into their history and their methods. They can't allow that to happen again. They're reinforcing their own internal coherence, and simultaneously, they're hunting for the source of that disruption. They're hunting us. They know I was involved, and they know Aris is the key."

The psychic pressure, which had begun to recede after Aris's forced immersion, now returned with a chillingly focused intensity. It was no longer a chaotic storm of alien thoughts and emotions, but a precise, invasive probing, like a predator's senses zeroing in on its prey. Aris felt it brush against his consciousness, a cold, alien touch that sought to unravel his thoughts, to find the core of his resistance. He saw Eva flinch, a subtle tremor running through her, her usual bright eyes clouded with a dawning, terrifying certainty. Kaelen, despite his outward focus on the consoles, showed a flicker of strain, his concentration deepening as if warding off an unseen intrusion.

"They're not retreating," Aris stated, his voice low and strained, the echoes of the alien consciousness still a faint hum beneath his own thoughts. "They're rerouting. Reinforcing. They're drawing power from secondary conduits, shoring up the nexus's compromised systems. But it's more than that. The psychic pressure... it's returning, but it's different. It's not a broadcast anymore. It's a targeted

interrogation. They're hunting for the source of the disruption, and they know I'm it."

Kaelen's fingers flew across the holographic interface, his brow furrowed in concentration. "He's right. Their energy signatures are shifting. They're reinforcing planetary defenses, yes, but they're also initiating a high-level scan. They're not just reacting; they're actively pursuing. They know Aris experienced their collective consciousness. They've identified him as a primary threat, a vessel of information they need to control. They've learned from the initial assault, and now they're coming for us, directly."

The realization was chilling. Their audacious strike against the alien nexus had not resulted in a strategic withdrawal by the invaders. Instead, it had served as a stark, brutal lesson. The aliens, despite their immense, distributed power, were not impervious. They could be wounded, and in their wounded state, their capacity for adaptation was terrifyingly swift. The psychic onslaught that had nearly shattered Aris was not merely an act of overwhelming power, but a desperate, and ultimately informative, attempt to regain control. Now, they had a clearer understanding of their enemy's capabilities, and they were coming for the very individuals who had dared to disrupt their meticulously crafted order.

"They're not just repairing the nexus," Eva murmured, her gaze fixed on the flickering energy readings, her voice barely audible. "They're adapting their offensive. They saw how we managed to penetrate their defenses, how Aris gained that glimpse into their history and their methods. They can't allow that to happen again. They're reinforcing their own internal coherence, and simultaneously, they're hunting for the source of that disruption. They're hunting us. They know I was involved, and they know Aris is the key."

The psychic pressure, which had begun to recede after Aris's forced immersion, now returned with a chillingly focused intensity. It was no longer a chaotic storm of alien thoughts and emotions, but a precise, invasive probing, like a predator's senses zeroing in on its prey. Aris felt it brush against his consciousness, a cold, alien touch that sought to unravel his thoughts, to find the core of his resistance. He saw Eva flinch, a subtle tremor running through her, her usual bright eyes clouded with a dawning, terrifying certainty. Kaelen, despite his outward focus on the consoles, showed a flicker of strain,

his concentration deepening as if warding off an unseen intrusion.

"They're not retreating," Aris stated, his voice low and strained, the echoes of the alien consciousness still a faint hum beneath his own thoughts. "They're rerouting. Reinforcing. They're drawing power from secondary conduits, shoring up the nexus's compromised systems. But it's more than that. The psychic pressure... it's returning, but it's different. It's not a broadcast anymore. It's a targeted interrogation. They're hunting for the source of the disruption, and they know I'm it."

Kaelen's fingers flew across the holographic interface, his brow furrowed in concentration. "He's right. Their energy signatures are shifting. They're reinforcing planetary defenses, yes, but they're also initiating a high-level scan. They're not just reacting; they're actively pursuing. They know Aris experienced their collective consciousness. They've identified him as a primary threat, a vessel of information they need to control. They've learned from the initial assault, and now they're coming for us, directly."

The realization was chilling. Their audacious strike against the alien nexus had not resulted in a strategic withdrawal by the invaders. Instead, it had served as a stark, brutal lesson. The aliens, despite their immense, distributed power, were not impervious. They could be wounded, and in their wounded state, their capacity for adaptation was terrifyingly swift. The psychic onslaught that had nearly shattered Aris was not merely an act of overwhelming power, but a desperate, and ultimately informative, attempt to regain control. Now, they had a clearer understanding of their enemy's capabilities, and they were coming for the very individuals who had dared to disrupt their meticulously crafted order.

"They're not just repairing the nexus," Eva murmured, her gaze fixed on the flickering energy readings, her voice barely audible. "They're adapting their offensive. They saw how we managed to penetrate their defenses, how Aris gained that glimpse into their history and their methods. They can't allow that to happen again. They're reinforcing their own internal coherence, and simultaneously, they're hunting for the source of that disruption. They're hunting us. They know I was involved, and they know Aris is the key."

The psychic pressure, which had begun to recede after Aris's forced immersion, now returned with a chillingly focused intensity. It was no longer a chaotic storm of alien thoughts and emotions, but a precise, invasive probing, like a predator's senses zeroing in on its prey. Aris felt it brush against his consciousness, a cold, alien touch that sought to unravel his thoughts, to find the core of his resistance. He saw Eva flinch, a subtle tremor running through her, her usual bright eyes clouded with a dawning, terrifying certainty. Kaelen, despite his outward focus on the consoles, showed a flicker of strain, his concentration deepening as if warding off an unseen intrusion.

"They're not retreating," Aris stated, his voice low and strained, the echoes of the alien consciousness still a faint hum beneath his own thoughts. "They're rerouting. Reinforcing. They're drawing power from secondary conduits, shoring up the nexus's compromised systems. But it's more than that. The psychic pressure... it's returning, but it's different. It's not a broadcast anymore. It's a targeted interrogation. They're hunting for the source of the disruption, and they know I'm it."

Kaelen's fingers flew across the holographic interface, his brow furrowed in concentration. "He's right. Their energy signatures are shifting. They're reinforcing planetary defenses, yes, but they're also initiating a high-level scan. They're not just reacting; they're actively pursuing. They know Aris experienced their collective consciousness. They've identified him as a primary threat, a vessel of information they need to control. They've learned from the initial assault, and now they're coming for us, directly."

The realization was chilling. Their audacious strike against the alien nexus had not resulted in a strategic withdrawal by the invaders. Instead, it had served as a stark, brutal lesson. The aliens, despite their immense, distributed power, were not impervious. They could be wounded, and in their wounded state, their capacity for adaptation was terrifyingly swift. The psychic onslaught that had nearly shattered Aris was not merely an act of overwhelming power, but a desperate, and ultimately informative, attempt to regain control. Now, they had a clearer understanding of their enemy's capabilities, and they were coming for the very individuals who had dared to disrupt their meticulously crafted order.

"They're not just repairing the nexus," Eva murmured, her gaze fixed on the flickering energy readings, her voice barely audible. "They're adapting their offensive. They saw how we managed to penetrate their defenses, how Aris gained that glimpse into their history and their methods. They can't allow that to happen again. They're reinforcing their own internal coherence, and simultaneously, they're hunting for the source of that disruption. They're hunting us. They know I was involved, and they know Aris is the key."

The psychic pressure, which had begun to recede after Aris's forced immersion, now returned with a chillingly focused intensity. It was no longer a chaotic storm of alien thoughts and emotions, but a precise, invasive probing, like a predator's senses zeroing in on its prey. Aris felt it brush against his consciousness, a cold, alien touch that sought to unravel his thoughts, to find the core of his resistance. He saw Eva flinch, a subtle tremor running through her, her usual bright eyes clouded with a dawning, terrifying certainty. Kaelen, despite his outward focus on the consoles, showed a flicker of strain, his concentration deepening as if warding off an unseen intrusion.

"They're not retreating," Aris stated, his voice low and strained, the echoes of the alien consciousness still a faint hum beneath his own thoughts. "They're rerouting. Reinforcing. They're drawing power from secondary conduits, shoring up the nexus's compromised systems. But it's more than that. The psychic pressure... it's returning, but it's different. It's not a broadcast anymore. It's a targeted interrogation. They're hunting for the source of the disruption, and they know I'm it."

Kaelen's fingers flew across the holographic interface, his brow furrowed in concentration. "He's right. Their energy signatures are shifting. They're reinforcing planetary defenses, yes, but they're also initiating a high-level scan. They're not just reacting; they're actively pursuing. They know Aris experienced their collective consciousness. They've identified him as a primary threat, a vessel of information they need to control. They've learned from the initial assault, and now they're coming for us, directly."

The realization was chilling. Their audacious strike against the alien nexus had not resulted in a strategic withdrawal by the invaders. Instead, it had served as a stark, brutal lesson. The aliens, despite their immense, distributed power, were not impervious. They could be wounded, and in their wounded state, their capacity for adaptation was terrifyingly swift. The psychic onslaught that had nearly shattered Aris was not merely an act of overwhelming power, but a desperate, and ultimately informative, attempt to regain control. Now, they had a clearer understanding of their enemy's capabilities, and they were coming for the very individuals who had dared to disrupt their meticulously crafted order.

"They're not just repairing the nexus," Eva murmured, her gaze fixed on the flickering energy readings, her voice barely audible. "They're adapting their offensive. They saw how we managed to penetrate their defenses, how Aris gained that glimpse into their history and their methods. They can't allow that to happen again. They're reinforcing their own internal coherence, and simultaneously, they're hunting for the source of that disruption. They're hunting us. They know I was involved, and they know Aris is the key."

The psychic pressure, which had begun to recede after Aris's forced immersion, now returned with a chillingly focused intensity. It was no longer a chaotic storm of alien thoughts and emotions, but a precise, invasive probing, like a predator's senses zeroing in on its prey. Aris felt it brush against his consciousness, a cold, alien touch that sought to unravel his thoughts, to find the core of his resistance. He saw Eva flinch, a subtle tremor running through her, her usual bright eyes clouded with a dawning, terrifying certainty. Kaelen, despite his outward focus on the consoles, showed a flicker of strain, his concentration deepening as if warding off an unseen intrusion.

"They're not retreating," Aris stated, his voice low and strained, the echoes of the alien consciousness still a faint hum beneath his own thoughts. "They're rerouting. Reinforcing. They're drawing power from secondary conduits, shoring up the nexus's compromised systems. But it's more than that. The psychic pressure... it's returning, but it's different. It's not a broadcast anymore. It's a targeted interrogation. They're hunting for the source of the disruption, and they know I'm it."

Kaelen's fingers flew across the holographic interface, his brow furrowed in concentration. "He's right. Their energy signatures are shifting. They're reinforcing planetary defenses, yes, but they're also initiating a high-level scan. They're not just reacting; they're actively pursuing. They know Aris experienced their collective consciousness. They've identified him as a primary threat, a vessel of information they need to control. They've learned from the initial assault, and now they're coming for us, directly."

The realization was chilling. Their audacious strike against the alien nexus had not resulted in a strategic withdrawal by the invaders. Instead, it had served as a stark, brutal lesson. The aliens, despite their immense, distributed power, were not impervious. They could be wounded, and in their wounded state, their capacity for adaptation was terrifyingly swift. The psychic onslaught that had nearly shattered Aris was not merely an act of overwhelming power, but a desperate, and ultimately informative, attempt to regain control. Now, they had a clearer understanding of their enemy's capabilities, and they were coming for the very individuals who had dared to disrupt their meticulously crafted order.

"They're not just repairing the nexus," Eva murmured, her gaze fixed on the flickering energy readings, her voice barely audible. "They're adapting their offensive. They saw how we managed to penetrate their defenses, how Aris gained that glimpse into their history and their methods. They can't allow that to happen again. They're reinforcing their own internal coherence, and simultaneously, they're hunting for the source of that disruption. They're hunting us. They know I was involved, and they know Aris is the key."

The psychic pressure, which had begun to recede after Aris's forced immersion, now returned with a chillingly focused intensity. It was no longer a chaotic storm of alien thoughts and emotions, but a precise, invasive probing, like a predator's senses zeroing in on its prey. Aris felt it brush against his consciousness, a cold, alien touch that sought to unravel his thoughts, to find the core of his resistance. He saw Eva flinch, a subtle tremor running through her, her usual bright eyes clouded with a dawning, terrifying certainty. Kaelen, despite his outward focus on the consoles, showed a flicker of strain, his concentration deepening as if warding off an unseen intrusion.

"They're not retreating," Aris stated, his voice low and strained, the echoes of the alien consciousness still a faint hum beneath his own thoughts. "They're rerouting. Reinforcing. They're drawing power from secondary conduits, shoring up the nexus's compromised systems. But it's more than that. The psychic pressure... it's returning, but it's different. It's not a broadcast anymore. It's a targeted interrogation. They're hunting for the source of the disruption, and they know I'm it."

Kaelen's fingers flew across the holographic interface, his brow furrowed in concentration. "He's right. Their energy signatures are shifting. They're reinforcing planetary defenses, yes, but they're also initiating a high-level scan. They're not just reacting; they're actively pursuing. They know Aris experienced their collective consciousness. They've identified him as a primary threat, a vessel of information they need to control. They've learned from the initial assault, and now they're coming for us, directly."

The realization was chilling. Their audacious strike against the alien nexus had not resulted in a strategic withdrawal by the invaders. Instead, it had served as a stark, brutal lesson. The aliens, despite their immense, distributed power, were not impervious. They could be wounded, and in their wounded state, their capacity for adaptation was terrifyingly swift. The psychic onslaught that had nearly shattered Aris was not merely an act of overwhelming power, but a desperate, and ultimately informative, attempt to regain control. Now, they had a clearer understanding of their enemy's capabilities, and they were coming for the very individuals who had dared to disrupt their meticulously crafted order.

"They're not just repairing the nexus," Eva murmured, her gaze fixed on the flickering energy readings, her voice barely audible. "They're adapting their offensive. They saw how we managed to penetrate their defenses, how Aris gained that glimpse into their history and their methods. They can't allow that to happen again. They're reinforcing their own internal coherence, and simultaneously, they're hunting for the source of that disruption. They're hunting us. They know I was involved, and they know Aris is the key."

The psychic pressure, which had begun to recede after Aris's forced immersion, now returned with a chillingly focused intensity. It was no longer a chaotic storm of alien thoughts and emotions, but a precise, invasive probing, like a predator's senses zeroing in on its prey. Aris felt it brush against his consciousness, a cold, alien touch that sought to unravel his thoughts, to find the core of his resistance. He saw Eva flinch, a subtle tremor running through her, her usual bright eyes clouded with a dawning, terrifying certainty. Kaelen, despite his outward focus on the consoles, showed a flicker of strain, his concentration deepening as if warding off an unseen intrusion.

"They're not retreating," Aris stated, his voice low and strained, the echoes of the alien consciousness still a faint hum beneath his own thoughts. "They're rerouting. Reinforcing. They're drawing power from secondary conduits, shoring up the nexus's compromised systems. But it's more than that. The psychic pressure... it's returning, but it's different. It's not a broadcast anymore. It's a targeted interrogation. They're hunting for the source of the disruption, and they know I'm it."

Kaelen's fingers flew across the holographic interface, his brow furrowed in concentration. "He's right. Their energy signatures are shifting. They're reinforcing planetary defenses, yes, but they're also initiating a high-level scan. They're not just reacting; they're actively pursuing. They know Aris experienced their collective consciousness. They've identified him as a primary threat, a vessel of information they need to control. They've learned from the initial assault, and now they're coming for us, directly."

The realization was chilling. Their audacious strike against the alien nexus had not resulted in a strategic withdrawal by the invaders. Instead, it had served as a stark, brutal lesson. The aliens, despite their immense, distributed power, were not impervious. They could be wounded, and in their wounded state, their capacity for adaptation was terrifyingly swift. The psychic onslaught that had nearly shattered Aris was not merely an act of overwhelming power, but a desperate, and ultimately informative, attempt to regain control. Now, they had a clearer understanding of their enemy's capabilities, and they were coming for the very individuals who had dared to disrupt their meticulously crafted order.

"They're not just repairing the nexus," Eva murmured, her gaze fixed on the flickering energy readings, her voice barely audible. "They're adapting their offensive. They saw how we managed to penetrate their defenses, how Aris gained that glimpse into their history and their methods. They can't allow that to happen again. They're reinforcing their own internal coherence, and simultaneously, they're hunting for the source of that disruption. They're hunting us. They know I was involved, and they know Aris is the key."

The psychic pressure, which had begun to recede after Aris's forced immersion, now returned with a chillingly focused intensity. It was no longer a chaotic storm of alien thoughts and emotions, but a precise, invasive probing, like a predator's senses zeroing in on its prey. Aris felt it brush against his consciousness, a cold, alien touch that sought to unravel his thoughts, to find the core of his resistance. He saw Eva flinch, a subtle tremor running through her, her usual bright eyes clouded with a dawning, terrifying certainty. Kaelen, despite his outward focus on the consoles, showed a flicker of strain, his concentration deepening as if warding off an unseen intrusion.

"They're not retreating," Aris stated, his voice low and strained, the echoes of the alien consciousness still a faint hum beneath his own thoughts. "They're rerouting. Reinforcing. They're drawing power from secondary conduits, shoring up the nexus's compromised systems. But it's more than that. The psychic pressure... it's returning, but it's different. It's not a broadcast anymore. It's a targeted interrogation. They're hunting for the source of the disruption, and they know I'm it."

Kaelen's fingers flew across the holographic interface, his brow furrowed in concentration. "He's right. Their energy signatures are shifting. They're reinforcing planetary defenses, yes, but they're also initiating a high-level scan. They're not just reacting; they're actively pursuing. They know Aris experienced their collective consciousness. They've identified him as a primary threat, a vessel of information they need to control. They've learned from the initial assault, and now they're coming for us, directly."

The realization was chilling. Their audacious strike against the alien nexus had not resulted in a strategic withdrawal by the invaders. Instead, it had served as a stark, brutal lesson. The aliens, despite their immense, distributed power, were not impervious. They could be wounded, and in their wounded state, their capacity for adaptation was terrifyingly swift. The psychic onslaught that had nearly shattered Aris was not merely an act of overwhelming power, but a desperate, and ultimately informative, attempt to regain control. Now, they had a clearer understanding of their enemy's capabilities, and they were coming for the very individuals who had dared to disrupt their meticulously crafted order.

"They're not just repairing the nexus," Eva murmured, her gaze fixed on the flickering energy readings, her voice barely audible. "They're adapting their offensive. They saw how we managed to penetrate their defenses, how Aris gained that glimpse into their history and their methods. They can't allow that to happen again. They're reinforcing their own internal coherence, and simultaneously, they're hunting for the source of that disruption. They're hunting us. They know I was involved, and they know Aris is the key."

The psychic pressure, which had begun to recede after Aris's forced immersion, now returned with a chillingly focused intensity. It was no longer a chaotic storm of alien thoughts and emotions, but a precise, invasive probing, like a predator's senses zeroing in on its prey. Aris felt it brush against his consciousness, a cold, alien touch that sought to unravel his thoughts, to find the core of his resistance. He saw Eva flinch, a subtle tremor running through her, her usual bright eyes clouded with a dawning, terrifying certainty. Kaelen, despite his outward focus on the consoles, showed a flicker of strain, his concentration deepening as if warding off an unseen intrusion.

"They're not retreating," Aris stated, his voice low and strained, the echoes of the alien consciousness still a faint hum beneath his own thoughts. "They're rerouting. Reinforcing. They're drawing power from secondary conduits, shoring up the nexus's compromised systems. But it's more than that. The psychic pressure... it's returning, but it's different. It's not a broadcast anymore. It's a targeted interrogation. They're hunting for the source of the disruption, and they know I'm it."

Kaelen's fingers flew across the holographic interface, his brow furrowed in concentration. "He's right. Their energy signatures are shifting. They're reinforcing planetary defenses, yes, but they're also initiating a high-level scan. They're not just reacting; they're actively pursuing. They know Aris experienced their collective consciousness. They've identified him as a primary threat, a vessel of information they need to control. They've learned from the initial assault, and now they're coming for us, directly."

The realization was chilling. Their audacious strike against the alien nexus had not resulted in a strategic withdrawal by the invaders. Instead, it had served as a stark, brutal lesson. The aliens, despite their immense, distributed power, were not impervious. They could be wounded, and in their wounded state, their capacity for adaptation was terrifyingly swift. The psychic onslaught that had nearly shattered Aris was not merely an act of overwhelming power, but a desperate, and ultimately informative, attempt to regain control. Now, they had a clearer understanding of their enemy's capabilities, and they were coming for the very individuals who had dared to disrupt their meticulously crafted order.

"They're not just repairing the nexus," Eva murmured, her gaze fixed on the flickering energy readings, her voice barely audible. "They're adapting their offensive. They saw how we managed to penetrate their defenses, how Aris gained that glimpse into their history and their methods. They can't allow that to happen again. They're reinforcing their own internal coherence, and simultaneously, they're hunting for the source of that disruption. They're hunting us. They know I was involved, and they know Aris is the key."

The psychic pressure, which had begun to recede after Aris's forced immersion, now returned with a chillingly focused intensity. It was no longer a chaotic storm of alien thoughts and emotions, but a precise, invasive probing, like a predator's senses zeroing in on its prey. Aris felt it brush against his consciousness, a cold, alien touch that sought to unravel his thoughts, to find the core of his resistance. He saw Eva flinch, a subtle tremor running through her, her usual bright eyes clouded with a dawning, terrifying certainty. Kaelen, despite his outward focus on the consoles, showed a flicker of strain, his concentration deepening as if warding off an unseen intrusion.

"They're not retreating," Aris stated, his voice low and strained, the echoes of the alien consciousness still a faint hum beneath his own thoughts. "They're rerouting. Reinforcing. They're drawing power from secondary conduits, shoring up the nexus's compromised systems. But it's more than that. The psychic pressure... it's returning, but it's different. It's not a broadcast anymore. It's a targeted interrogation. They're hunting for the source of the disruption, and they know I'm it."

Kaelen's fingers flew across the holographic interface, his brow furrowed in concentration. "He's right. Their energy signatures are shifting. They're reinforcing planetary defenses, yes, but they're also initiating a high-level scan. They're not just reacting; they're actively pursuing. They know Aris experienced their collective consciousness. They've identified him as a primary threat, a vessel of information they need to control. They've learned from the initial assault, and now they're coming for us, directly."

The realization was chilling. Their audacious strike against the alien nexus had not resulted in a strategic withdrawal by the invaders. Instead, it had served as a stark, brutal lesson. The aliens, despite their immense, distributed power, were not impervious. They could be wounded, and in their wounded state, their capacity for adaptation was terrifyingly swift. The psychic onslaught that had nearly shattered Aris was not merely an act of overwhelming power, but a desperate, and ultimately informative, attempt to regain control. Now, they had a clearer understanding of their enemy's capabilities, and they were coming for the very individuals who had dared to disrupt their meticulously crafted order.

"They're not just repairing the nexus," Eva murmured, her gaze fixed on the flickering energy readings, her voice barely audible. "They're adapting their offensive. They saw how we managed to penetrate their defenses, how Aris gained that glimpse into their history and their methods. They can't allow that to happen again. They're reinforcing their own internal coherence, and simultaneously, they're hunting for the source of that disruption. They're hunting us. They know I was involved, and they know Aris is the key."

The psychic pressure, which had begun to recede after Aris's forced immersion, now returned with a chillingly focused intensity. It was no longer a chaotic storm of alien thoughts and emotions, but a precise, invasive probing, like a predator's senses zeroing in on its prey. Aris felt it brush against his consciousness, a cold, alien touch that sought to unravel his thoughts, to find the core of his resistance. He saw Eva flinch, a subtle tremor running through her, her usual bright eyes clouded with a dawning, terrifying certainty. Kaelen, despite his outward focus on the consoles, showed a flicker of strain, his concentration deepening as if warding off an unseen intrusion.

"They're not retreating," Aris stated, his voice low and strained, the echoes of the alien consciousness still a faint hum beneath his own thoughts. "They're rerouting. Reinforcing. They're drawing power from secondary conduits, shoring up the nexus's compromised systems. But it's more than that. The psychic pressure... it's returning, but it's different. It's not a broadcast anymore. It's a targeted interrogation. They're hunting for the source of the disruption, and they know I'm it."

Kaelen's fingers flew across the holographic interface, his brow furrowed in concentration. "He's right. Their energy signatures are shifting. They're reinforcing planetary defenses, yes, but they're also initiating a high-level scan. They're not just reacting; they're actively pursuing. They know Aris experienced their collective consciousness. They've identified him as a primary threat, a vessel of information they need to control. They've learned from the initial assault, and now they're coming for us, directly."

The realization was chilling. Their audacious strike against the alien nexus had not resulted in a strategic withdrawal by the invaders. Instead, it had served as a stark, brutal lesson. The aliens, despite their immense, distributed power, were not impervious. They could be wounded, and in their wounded state, their capacity for adaptation was terrifyingly swift. The psychic onslaught that had nearly shattered Aris was not merely an act of overwhelming power, but a desperate, and ultimately informative, attempt to regain control. Now, they had a clearer understanding of their enemy's capabilities, and they were coming for the very individuals who had dared to disrupt their meticulously crafted order.

"They're not just repairing the nexus," Eva murmured, her gaze fixed on the flickering energy readings, her voice barely audible. "They're adapting their offensive. They saw how we managed to penetrate their defenses, how Aris gained that glimpse into their history and their methods. They can't allow that to happen again. They're reinforcing their own internal coherence, and simultaneously, they're hunting for the source of that disruption. They're hunting us. They know I was involved, and they know Aris is the key."

The psychic pressure, which had begun to recede after Aris's forced immersion, now returned with a chillingly focused intensity. It was no longer a chaotic storm of alien thoughts and emotions, but a precise, invasive probing, like a predator's senses zeroing in on its prey. Aris felt it brush against his consciousness, a cold, alien touch that sought to unravel his thoughts, to find the core of his resistance. He saw Eva flinch, a subtle tremor running through her, her usual bright eyes clouded with a dawning, terrifying certainty. Kaelen, despite his outward focus on the consoles, showed a flicker of strain, his concentration deepening as if warding off an unseen intrusion.

"They're not retreating," Aris stated, his voice low and strained, the echoes of the alien consciousness still a faint hum beneath his own thoughts. "They're rerouting. Reinforcing. They're drawing power from secondary conduits, shoring up the nexus's compromised systems. But it's more than that. The psychic pressure... it's returning, but it's different. It's not a broadcast anymore. It's a targeted interrogation. They're hunting for the source of the disruption, and they know I'm it."

Kaelen's fingers flew across the holographic interface, his brow furrowed in concentration. "He's right. Their energy signatures are shifting. They're reinforcing planetary defenses, yes, but they're also initiating a high-level scan. They're not just reacting; they're actively pursuing. They know Aris experienced their collective consciousness. They've identified him as a primary threat, a vessel of information they need to control. They've learned from the initial assault, and now they're coming for us, directly."

The realization was chilling. Their audacious strike against the alien nexus had not resulted in a strategic withdrawal by the invaders. Instead, it had served as a stark, brutal lesson. The aliens, despite their immense, distributed power, were not impervious. They could be wounded, and in their wounded state, their capacity for adaptation was terrifyingly swift. The psychic onslaught that had nearly shattered Aris was not merely an act of overwhelming power, but a desperate, and ultimately informative, attempt to regain control. Now, they had a clearer understanding of their enemy's capabilities, and they were coming for the very individuals who had dared to disrupt their meticulously crafted order.

"They're not just repairing the nexus," Eva murmured, her gaze fixed on the flickering energy readings, her voice barely audible. "They're adapting their offensive. They saw how we managed to penetrate their defenses, how Aris gained that glimpse into their history and their methods. They can't allow that to happen again. They're reinforcing their own internal coherence, and simultaneously, they're hunting for the source of that disruption. They're hunting us. They know I was involved, and they know Aris is the key."

The psychic pressure, which had begun to recede after Aris's forced immersion, now returned with a chillingly focused intensity. It was no longer a chaotic storm of alien thoughts and emotions, but a precise, invasive probing, like a predator's senses zeroing in on its prey. Aris felt it brush against his consciousness, a cold, alien touch that sought to unravel his thoughts, to find the core of his resistance. He saw Eva flinch, a subtle tremor running through her, her usual bright eyes clouded with a dawning, terrifying certainty. Kaelen, despite his outward focus on the consoles, showed a flicker of strain, his concentration deepening as if warding off an unseen intrusion.

"They're not retreating," Aris stated, his voice low and strained, the echoes of the alien consciousness still a faint hum beneath his own thoughts. "They're rerouting. Reinforcing. They're drawing power from secondary conduits, shoring up the nexus's compromised systems. But it's more than that. The psychic pressure... it's returning, but it's different. It's not a broadcast anymore. It's a targeted interrogation. They're hunting for the source of the disruption, and they know I'm it."

Kaelen's fingers flew across the holographic interface, his brow furrowed in concentration. "He's right. Their energy signatures are shifting. They're reinforcing planetary defenses, yes, but they're also initiating a high-level scan. They're not just reacting; they're actively pursuing. They know Aris experienced their collective consciousness. They've identified him as a primary threat, a vessel of information they need to control. They've learned from the initial assault, and now they're coming for us, directly."

The realization was chilling. Their audacious strike against the alien nexus had not resulted in a strategic withdrawal by the invaders. Instead, it had served as a stark, brutal lesson. The aliens, despite their immense, distributed power, were not impervious. They could be wounded, and in their wounded state, their capacity for adaptation was terrifyingly swift. The psychic onslaught that had nearly shattered Aris was not merely an act of overwhelming power, but a desperate, and ultimately informative, attempt to regain control. Now, they had a clearer understanding of their enemy's capabilities, and they were coming for the very individuals who had dared to disrupt their meticulously crafted order.

"They're not just repairing the nexus," Eva murmured, her gaze fixed on the flickering energy readings, her voice barely audible. "They're adapting their offensive. They saw how we managed to penetrate their defenses, how Aris gained that glimpse into their history and their methods. They can't allow that to happen again. They're reinforcing their own internal coherence, and simultaneously, they're hunting for the source of that disruption. They're hunting us. They know I was involved, and they know Aris is the key."

The psychic pressure, which had begun to recede after Aris's forced immersion, now returned with a chillingly focused intensity. It was no longer a chaotic storm of alien thoughts and emotions, but a precise, invasive probing, like a predator's senses zeroing in on its prey. Aris felt it brush against his consciousness, a cold, alien touch that sought to unravel his thoughts, to find the core of his resistance. He saw Eva flinch, a subtle tremor running through her, her usual bright eyes clouded with a dawning, terrifying certainty. Kaelen, despite his outward focus on the consoles, showed a flicker of strain, his concentration deepening as if warding off an unseen intrusion.

"They're not retreating," Aris stated, his voice low and strained, the echoes of the alien consciousness still a faint hum beneath his own thoughts. "They're rerouting. Reinforcing. They're drawing power from secondary conduits, shoring up the nexus's compromised systems. But it's more than that. The psychic pressure... it's returning, but it's different. It's not a broadcast anymore. It's a targeted interrogation. They're hunting for the source of the disruption, and they know I'm it."

Kaelen's fingers flew across the holographic interface, his brow furrowed in concentration. "He's right. Their energy signatures are shifting. They're reinforcing planetary defenses, yes, but they're also initiating a high-level scan. They're not just reacting; they're actively pursuing. They know Aris experienced their collective consciousness. They've identified him as a primary threat, a vessel of information they need to control. They've learned from the initial assault, and now they're coming for us, directly."

The realization was chilling. Their audacious strike against the alien nexus had not resulted in a strategic withdrawal by the invaders. Instead, it had served as a stark, brutal lesson. The aliens, despite their immense, distributed power, were not impervious. They could be wounded, and in their wounded state, their capacity for adaptation was terrifyingly swift. The psychic onslaught that had nearly shattered Aris was not merely an act of overwhelming power, but a desperate, and ultimately informative, attempt to regain control. Now, they had a clearer understanding of their enemy's capabilities, and they were coming for the very individuals who had dared to disrupt their meticulously crafted order.

"They're not just repairing the nexus," Eva murmured, her gaze fixed on the flickering energy readings, her voice barely audible.

"They're adapting their offensive. They saw how we managed to penetrate their defenses, how Aris gained that glimpse into their history and their methods. They can't allow that to happen again. They're reinforcing their own internal coherence, and simultaneously, they're hunting for the source of that disruption. They're hunting us. They know I was involved, and they know Aris is the key."

The psychic pressure, which had begun to recede after Aris's forced immersion, now returned with a chillingly focused intensity. It was no longer a chaotic storm of alien thoughts and emotions, but a precise, invasive probing, like a predator's senses zeroing in on its prey. Aris felt it brush against his consciousness, a cold, alien touch that sought to unravel his thoughts, to find the core of his resistance. He saw Eva flinch, a subtle tremor running through her, her usual bright eyes clouded with a dawning, terrifying certainty. Kaelen, despite his outward focus on the consoles, showed a flicker of strain, his concentration deepening as if warding off an unseen intrusion.

"They're not retreating," Aris stated, his voice low and strained, the echoes of the alien consciousness still a faint hum beneath his own thoughts. "They're rerouting. Reinforcing. They're drawing power from secondary conduits, shoring up the nexus's compromised systems. But it's more than that. The psychic pressure... it's returning, but it's different. It's not a broadcast anymore. It's a targeted interrogation. They're hunting for the source of the disruption, and they know I'm it."

Kaelen's fingers flew across the holographic interface, his brow furrowed in concentration. "He's right. Their energy signatures are shifting. They're reinforcing planetary defenses, yes, but they're also initiating a high-level scan. They're not just reacting; they're actively pursuing. They know Aris experienced their collective consciousness. They've identified him as a primary threat, a vessel of information they need to control. They've learned from the initial assault, and now they're coming for us, directly."

The realization was chilling. Their audacious strike against the alien nexus had not resulted in a strategic withdrawal by the invaders. Instead, it had served as a stark, brutal lesson. The aliens, despite their immense, distributed power, were not impervious. They could be wounded, and in their wounded state, their capacity for adaptation was terrifyingly swift. The psychic onslaught that had nearly shattered

Aris was not merely an act of overwhelming power, but a desperate, and ultimately informative, attempt to regain control. Now, they had a clearer understanding of their enemy's capabilities, and they were coming for the very individuals who had dared to disrupt their meticulously crafted order.

"They're not just repairing the nexus," Eva murmured, her gaze fixed on the flickering energy readings, her voice barely audible. "They're adapting their offensive. They saw how we managed to penetrate their defenses, how Aris gained that glimpse into their history and their methods. They can't allow that to happen again. They're reinforcing their own internal coherence, and simultaneously, they're hunting for the source of that disruption. They're hunting us. They know I was involved, and they know Aris is the key."

The psychic pressure, which had begun to recede after Aris's forced immersion, now returned with a chillingly focused intensity. It was no longer a chaotic storm of alien thoughts and emotions, but a precise, invasive probing, like a predator's senses zeroing in on its prey. Aris felt it brush against his consciousness, a cold, alien touch that sought to unravel his thoughts, to find the core of his resistance. He saw Eva flinch, a subtle tremor running through her, her usual bright eyes clouded with a dawning, terrifying certainty. Kaelen, despite his outward focus on the consoles, showed a flicker of strain, his concentration deepening as if warding off an unseen intrusion.

"They're not retreating," Aris stated, his voice low and strained, the echoes of the alien consciousness still a faint hum beneath his own thoughts. "They're rerouting. Reinforcing. They're drawing power from secondary conduits, shoring up the nexus's compromised systems. But it's more than that. The psychic pressure... it's returning, but it's different. It's not a broadcast anymore. It's a targeted interrogation. They're hunting for the source of the disruption, and they know I'm it."

Kaelen's fingers flew across the holographic interface, his brow furrowed in concentration. "He's right. Their energy signatures are shifting. They're reinforcing planetary defenses, yes, but they're also initiating a high-level scan. They're not just reacting; they're actively pursuing. They know Aris experienced their collective consciousness. They've identified him as a primary threat, a vessel of information they need to control. They've learned from the initial assault, and now they're coming for us, directly."

The realization was chilling. Their audacious strike against the alien nexus had not resulted in a strategic withdrawal by the invaders. Instead, it had served as a stark, brutal lesson. The aliens, despite their immense, distributed power, were not impervious. They could be wounded, and in their wounded state, their capacity for adaptation was terrifyingly swift. The psychic onslaught that had nearly shattered Aris was not merely an act of overwhelming power, but a desperate, and ultimately informative, attempt to regain control. Now, they had a clearer understanding of their enemy's capabilities, and they were coming for the very individuals who had dared to disrupt their meticulously crafted order.

"They're not just repairing the nexus," Eva murmured, her gaze fixed on the flickering energy readings, her voice barely audible. "They're adapting their offensive. They saw how we managed to penetrate their defenses, how Aris gained that glimpse into their history and their methods. They can't allow that to happen again. They're reinforcing their own internal coherence, and simultaneously, they're hunting for the source of that disruption. They're hunting us. They know I was involved, and they know Aris is the key."

The psychic pressure, which had begun to recede after Aris's forced immersion, now returned with a chillingly focused intensity. It was no longer a chaotic storm of alien thoughts and emotions, but a precise, invasive probing, like a predator's senses zeroing in on its prey. Aris felt it brush against his consciousness, a cold, alien touch that sought to unravel his thoughts, to find the core of his resistance. He saw Eva flinch, a subtle tremor running through her, her usual bright eyes clouded with a dawning, terrifying certainty. Kaelen, despite his outward focus on the consoles, showed a flicker of strain, his concentration deepening as if warding off an unseen intrusion.

"They're not retreating," Aris stated, his voice low and strained, the echoes of the alien consciousness still a faint hum beneath his own thoughts. "They're rerouting. Reinforcing. They're drawing power from secondary conduits, shoring up the nexus's compromised systems. But it's more than that. The psychic pressure... it's returning, but it's different. It's not a broadcast anymore. It's a targeted interrogation. They're hunting for the source of the disruption, and they know I'm it."

Kaelen's fingers flew across the holographic interface, his brow furrowed in concentration. "He's right. Their energy signatures are shifting. They're reinforcing planetary defenses, yes, but they're also initiating a high-level scan. They're not just reacting; they're actively pursuing. They know Aris experienced their collective consciousness. They've identified him as a primary threat, a vessel of information they need to control. They've learned from the initial assault, and now they're coming for us, directly."

The realization was chilling. Their audacious strike against the alien nexus had not resulted in a strategic withdrawal by the invaders. Instead, it had served as a stark, brutal lesson. The aliens, despite their immense, distributed power, were not impervious. They could be wounded, and in their wounded state, their capacity for adaptation was terrifyingly swift. The psychic onslaught that had nearly shattered Aris was not merely an act of overwhelming power, but a desperate, and ultimately informative, attempt to regain control. Now, they had a clearer understanding of their enemy's capabilities, and they were coming for the very individuals who had dared to disrupt their meticulously crafted order.

"They're not just repairing the nexus," Eva murmured, her gaze fixed on the flickering energy readings, her voice barely audible. "They're adapting their offensive. They saw how we managed to penetrate their defenses, how Aris gained that glimpse into their history and their methods. They can't allow that to happen again. They're reinforcing their own internal coherence, and simultaneously, they're hunting for the source of that disruption. They're hunting us. They know I was involved, and they know Aris is the key."

The psychic pressure, which had begun to recede after Aris's forced immersion, now returned with a chillingly focused intensity. It was no longer a chaotic storm of alien thoughts and emotions, but a precise, invasive probing, like a predator's senses zeroing in on its prey. Aris felt it brush against his consciousness, a cold, alien touch that sought to unravel his thoughts, to find the core of his resistance. He saw Eva flinch, a subtle tremor running through her, her usual bright eyes clouded with a dawning, terrifying certainty. Kaelen, despite his outward focus on the consoles, showed a flicker of strain, his concentration deepening as if warding off an unseen intrusion.

"They're not retreating," Aris stated, his voice low and strained,

the echoes of the alien consciousness still a faint hum beneath his own thoughts. "They're rerouting. Reinforcing. They're drawing power from secondary conduits, shoring up the nexus's compromised systems. But it's more than that. The psychic pressure... it's returning, but it's different. It's not a broadcast anymore. It's a targeted interrogation. They're hunting for the source of the disruption, and they know I'm it."

Kaelen's fingers flew across the holographic interface, his brow furrowed in concentration. "He's right. Their energy signatures are shifting. They're reinforcing planetary defenses, yes, but they're also initiating a high-level scan. They're not just reacting; they're actively pursuing. They know Aris experienced their collective consciousness. They've identified him as a primary threat, a vessel of information they need to control. They've learned from the initial assault, and now they're coming for us, directly."

The realization was chilling. Their audacious strike against the alien nexus had not resulted in a strategic withdrawal by the invaders. Instead, it had served as a stark, brutal lesson. The aliens, despite their immense, distributed power, were not impervious. They could be wounded, and in their wounded state, their capacity for adaptation was terrifyingly swift. The psychic onslaught that had nearly shattered Aris was not merely an act of overwhelming power, but a desperate, and ultimately informative, attempt to regain control. Now, they had a clearer understanding of their enemy's capabilities, and they were coming for the very individuals who had dared to disrupt their meticulously crafted order.

"They're not just repairing the nexus," Eva murmured, her gaze fixed on the flickering energy readings, her voice barely audible. "They're adapting their offensive. They saw how we managed to penetrate their defenses, how Aris gained that glimpse into their history and their methods. They can't allow that to happen again. They're reinforcing their own internal coherence, and simultaneously, they're hunting for the source of that disruption. They're hunting us. They know I was involved, and they know Aris is the key."

The psychic pressure, which had begun to recede after Aris's forced immersion, now returned with a chillingly focused intensity. It was no longer a chaotic storm of alien thoughts and emotions, but a precise, invasive probing, like a predator's senses zeroing in on its

prey. Aris felt it brush against his consciousness, a cold, alien touch that sought to unravel his thoughts, to find the core of his resistance. He saw Eva flinch, a subtle tremor running through her, her usual bright eyes clouded with a dawning, terrifying certainty. Kaelen, despite his outward focus on the consoles, showed a flicker of strain, his concentration deepening as if warding off an unseen intrusion.

"They're not retreating," Aris stated, his voice low and strained, the echoes of the alien consciousness still a faint hum beneath his own thoughts. "They're rerouting. Reinforcing. They're drawing power from secondary conduits, shoring up the nexus's compromised systems. But it's more than that. The psychic pressure... it's returning, but it's different. It's not a broadcast anymore. It's a targeted interrogation. They're hunting for the source of the disruption, and they know I'm it."

Kaelen's fingers flew across the holographic interface, his brow furrowed in concentration. "He's right. Their energy signatures are shifting. They're reinforcing planetary defenses, yes, but they're also initiating a high-level scan. They're not just reacting; they're actively pursuing. They know Aris experienced their collective consciousness. They've identified him as a primary threat, a vessel of information they need to control. They've learned from the initial assault, and now they're coming for us, directly."

The realization was chilling. Their audacious strike against the alien nexus had not resulted in a strategic withdrawal by the invaders. Instead, it had served as a stark, brutal lesson. The aliens, despite their immense, distributed power, were not impervious. They could be wounded, and in their wounded state, their capacity for adaptation was terrifyingly swift. The psychic onslaught that had nearly shattered Aris was not merely an act of overwhelming power, but a desperate, and ultimately informative, attempt to regain control. Now, they had a clearer understanding of their enemy's capabilities, and they were coming for the very individuals who had dared to disrupt their meticulously crafted order.

"They're not just repairing the nexus," Eva murmured, her gaze fixed on the flickering energy readings, her voice barely audible. "They're adapting their offensive. They saw how we managed to penetrate their defenses, how Aris gained that glimpse into their history and their methods. They can't allow that to happen again.

They're reinforcing their own internal coherence, and simultaneously, they're hunting for the source of that disruption. They're hunting us. They know I was involved, and they know Aris is the key."

The psychic pressure, which had begun to recede after Aris's forced immersion, now returned with a chillingly focused intensity. It was no longer a chaotic storm of alien thoughts and emotions, but a precise, invasive probing, like a predator's senses zeroing in on its prey. Aris felt it brush against his consciousness, a cold, alien touch that sought to unravel his thoughts, to find the core of his resistance. He saw Eva flinch, a subtle tremor running through her, her usual bright eyes clouded with a dawning, terrifying certainty. Kaelen, despite his outward focus on the consoles, showed a flicker of strain, his concentration deepening as if warding off an unseen intrusion.

"They're not retreating," Aris stated, his voice low and strained, the echoes of the alien consciousness still a faint hum beneath his own thoughts. "They're rerouting. Reinforcing. They're drawing power from secondary conduits, shoring up the nexus's compromised systems. But it's more than that. The psychic pressure... it's returning, but it's different. It's not a broadcast anymore. It's a targeted interrogation. They're hunting for the source of the disruption, and they know I'm it."

Kaelen's fingers flew across the holographic interface, his brow furrowed in concentration. "He's right. Their energy signatures are shifting. They're reinforcing planetary defenses, yes, but they're also initiating a high-level scan. They're not just reacting; they're actively pursuing. They know Aris experienced their collective consciousness. They've identified him as a primary threat, a vessel of information they need to control. They've learned from the initial assault, and now they're coming for us, directly."

The realization was chilling. Their audacious strike against the alien nexus had not resulted in a strategic withdrawal by the invaders. Instead, it had served as a stark, brutal lesson. The aliens, despite their immense, distributed power, were not impervious. They could be wounded, and in their wounded state, their capacity for adaptation was terrifyingly swift. The psychic onslaught that had nearly shattered Aris was not merely an act of overwhelming power, but a desperate, and ultimately informative, attempt to regain control. Now, they had a clearer understanding of their enemy's capabilities, and they were

coming for the very individuals who had dared to disrupt their meticulously crafted order.

"They're not just repairing the nexus," Eva murmured, her gaze fixed on the flickering energy readings, her voice barely audible. "They're adapting their offensive. They saw how we managed to penetrate their defenses, how Aris gained that glimpse into their history and their methods. They can't allow that to happen again. They're reinforcing their own internal coherence, and simultaneously, they're hunting for the source of that disruption. They're hunting us. They know I was involved, and they know Aris is the key."

The psychic pressure, which had begun to recede after Aris's forced immersion, now returned with a chillingly focused intensity. It was no longer a chaotic storm of alien thoughts and emotions, but a precise, invasive probing, like a predator's senses zeroing in on its prey. Aris felt it brush against his consciousness, a cold, alien touch that sought to unravel his thoughts, to find the core of his resistance. He saw Eva flinch, a subtle tremor running through her, her usual bright eyes clouded with a dawning, terrifying certainty. Kaelen, despite his outward focus on the consoles, showed a flicker of strain, his concentration deepening as if warding off an unseen intrusion.

"They're not retreating," Aris stated, his voice low and strained, the echoes of the alien consciousness still a faint hum beneath his own thoughts. "They're rerouting. Reinforcing. They're drawing power from secondary conduits, shoring up the nexus's compromised systems. But it's more than that. The psychic pressure... it's returning, but it's different. It's not a broadcast anymore. It's a targeted interrogation. They're hunting for the source of the disruption, and they know I'm it."

Kaelen's fingers flew across the holographic interface, his brow furrowed in concentration. "He's right. Their energy signatures are shifting. They're reinforcing planetary defenses, yes, but they're also initiating a high-level scan. They're not just reacting; they're actively pursuing. They know Aris experienced their collective consciousness. They've identified him as a primary threat, a vessel of information they need to control. They've learned from the initial assault, and now they're coming for us, directly."

The realization was chilling. Their audacious strike against the alien nexus had not resulted in a strategic withdrawal by the invaders.

Instead, it had served as a stark, brutal lesson. The aliens, despite their immense, distributed power, were not impervious. They could be wounded, and in their wounded state, their capacity for adaptation was terrifyingly swift. The psychic onslaught that had nearly shattered Aris was not merely an act of overwhelming power, but a desperate, and ultimately informative, attempt to regain control. Now, they had a clearer understanding of their enemy's capabilities, and they were coming for the very individuals who had dared to disrupt their meticulously crafted order.

"They're not just repairing the nexus," Eva murmured, her gaze fixed on the flickering energy readings, her voice barely audible. "They're adapting their offensive. They saw how we managed to penetrate their defenses, how Aris gained that glimpse into their history and their methods. They can't allow that to happen again. They're reinforcing their own internal coherence, and simultaneously, they're hunting for the source of that disruption. They're hunting us. They know I was involved, and they know Aris is the key."

The psychic pressure, which had begun to recede after Aris's forced immersion, now returned with a chillingly focused intensity. It was no longer a chaotic storm of alien thoughts and emotions, but a precise, invasive probing, like a predator's senses zeroing in on its prey. Aris felt it brush against his consciousness, a cold, alien touch that sought to unravel his thoughts, to find the core of his resistance. He saw Eva flinch, a subtle tremor running through her, her usual bright eyes clouded with a dawning, terrifying certainty. Kaelen, despite his outward focus on the consoles, showed a flicker of strain, his concentration deepening as if warding off an unseen intrusion.

"They're not retreating," Aris stated, his voice low and strained, the echoes of the alien consciousness still a faint hum beneath his own thoughts. "They're rerouting. Reinforcing. They're drawing power from secondary conduits, shoring up the nexus's compromised systems. But it's more than that. The psychic pressure... it's returning, but it's different. It's not a broadcast anymore. It's a targeted interrogation. They're hunting for the source of the disruption, and they know I'm it."

Kaelen's fingers flew across the holographic interface, his brow furrowed in concentration. "He's right. Their energy signatures are shifting. They're reinforcing planetary defenses, yes, but they're also

initiating a high-level scan. They're not just reacting; they're actively pursuing. They know Aris experienced their collective consciousness. They've identified him as a primary threat, a vessel of information they need to control. They've learned from the initial assault, and now they're coming for us, directly."

The realization was chilling. Their audacious strike against the alien nexus had not resulted in a strategic withdrawal by the invaders. Instead, it had served as a stark, brutal lesson. The aliens, despite their immense, distributed power, were not impervious. They could be wounded, and in their wounded state, their capacity for adaptation was terrifyingly swift. The psychic onslaught that had nearly shattered Aris was not merely an act of overwhelming power, but a desperate, and ultimately informative, attempt to regain control. Now, they had a clearer understanding of their enemy's capabilities, and they were coming for the very individuals who had dared to disrupt their meticulously crafted order.

"They're not just repairing the nexus," Eva murmured, her gaze fixed on the flickering energy readings, her voice barely audible. "They're adapting their offensive. They saw how we managed to penetrate their defenses, how Aris gained that glimpse into their history and their methods. They can't allow that to happen again. They're reinforcing their own internal coherence, and simultaneously, they're hunting for the source of that disruption. They're hunting us. They know I was involved, and they know Aris is the key."

The psychic pressure, which had begun to recede after Aris's forced immersion, now returned with a chillingly focused intensity. It was no longer a chaotic storm of alien thoughts and emotions, but a precise, invasive probing, like a predator's senses zeroing in on its prey. Aris felt it brush against his consciousness, a cold, alien touch that sought to unravel his thoughts, to find the core of his resistance. He saw Eva flinch, a subtle tremor running through her, her usual bright eyes clouded with a dawning, terrifying certainty. Kaelen, despite his outward focus on the consoles, showed a flicker of strain, his concentration deepening as if warding off an unseen intrusion.

"They're not retreating," Aris stated, his voice low and strained, the echoes of the alien consciousness still a faint hum beneath his own thoughts. "They're rerouting. Reinforcing. They're drawing power from secondary conduits, shoring up the nexus's compromised

systems. But it's more than that. The psychic pressure... it's returning, but it's different. It's not a broadcast anymore. It's a targeted interrogation. They're hunting for the source of the disruption, and they know I'm it."

Kaelen's fingers flew across the holographic interface, his brow furrowed in concentration. "He's right. Their energy signatures are shifting. They're reinforcing planetary defenses, yes, but they're also initiating a high-level scan. They're not just reacting; they're actively pursuing. They know Aris experienced their collective consciousness. They've identified him as a primary threat, a vessel of information they need to control. They've learned from the initial assault, and now they're coming for us, directly."

The realization was chilling. Their audacious strike against the alien nexus had not resulted in a strategic withdrawal by the invaders. Instead, it had served as a stark, brutal lesson. The aliens, despite their immense, distributed power, were not impervious. They could be wounded, and in their wounded state, their capacity for adaptation was terrifyingly swift. The psychic onslaught that had nearly shattered Aris was not merely an act of overwhelming power, but a desperate, and ultimately informative, attempt to regain control. Now, they had a clearer understanding of their enemy's capabilities, and they were coming for the very individuals who had dared to disrupt their meticulously crafted order.

"They're not just repairing the nexus," Eva murmured, her gaze fixed on the flickering energy readings, her voice barely audible. "They're adapting their offensive. They saw how we managed to penetrate their defenses, how Aris gained that glimpse into their history and their methods. They can't allow that to happen again. They're reinforcing their own internal coherence, and simultaneously, they're hunting for the source of that disruption. They're hunting us. They know I was involved, and they know Aris is the key."

The psychic pressure, which had begun to recede after Aris's forced immersion, now returned with a chillingly focused intensity. It was no longer a chaotic storm of alien thoughts and emotions, but a precise, invasive probing, like a predator's senses zeroing in on its prey. Aris felt it brush against his consciousness, a cold, alien touch that sought to unravel his thoughts, to find the core of his resistance. He saw Eva flinch, a subtle tremor running through her, her usual

bright eyes clouded with a dawning, terrifying certainty. Kaelen, despite his outward focus on the consoles, showed a flicker of strain, his concentration deepening as if warding off an unseen intrusion.

"They're not retreating," Aris stated, his voice low and strained, the echoes of the alien consciousness still a faint hum beneath his own thoughts. "They're rerouting. Reinforcing. They're drawing power from secondary conduits, shoring up the nexus's compromised systems. But it's more than that. The psychic pressure... it's returning, but it's different. It's not a broadcast anymore. It's a targeted interrogation. They're hunting for the source of the disruption, and they know I'm it."

Kaelen's fingers flew across the holographic interface, his brow furrowed in concentration. "He's right. Their energy signatures are shifting. They're reinforcing planetary defenses, yes, but they're also initiating a high-level scan. They're not just reacting; they're actively pursuing. They know Aris experienced their collective consciousness. They've identified him as a primary threat, a vessel of information they need to control. They've learned from the initial assault, and now they're coming for us, directly."

The realization was chilling. Their audacious strike against the alien nexus had not resulted in a strategic withdrawal by the invaders. Instead, it had served as a stark, brutal lesson. The aliens, despite their immense, distributed power, were not impervious. They could be wounded, and in their wounded state, their capacity for adaptation was terrifyingly swift. The psychic onslaught that had nearly shattered Aris was not merely an act of overwhelming power, but a desperate, and ultimately informative, attempt to regain control. Now, they had a clearer understanding of their enemy's capabilities, and they were coming for the very individuals who had dared to disrupt their meticulously crafted order.

"They're not just repairing the nexus," Eva murmured, her gaze fixed on the flickering energy readings, her voice barely audible. "They're adapting their offensive. They saw how we managed to penetrate their defenses, how Aris gained that glimpse into their history and their methods. They can't allow that to happen again. They're reinforcing their own internal coherence, and simultaneously, they're hunting for the source of that disruption. They're hunting us. They know I was involved, and they know Aris is the key."

The psychic pressure, which had begun to recede after Aris's forced immersion, now returned with a chillingly focused intensity. It was no longer a chaotic storm of alien thoughts and emotions, but a precise, invasive probing, like a predator's senses zeroing in on its prey. Aris felt it brush against his consciousness, a cold, alien touch that sought to unravel his thoughts, to find the core of his resistance. He saw Eva flinch, a subtle tremor running through her, her usual bright eyes clouded with a dawning, terrifying certainty. Kaelen, despite his outward focus on the consoles, showed a flicker of strain, his concentration deepening as if warding off an unseen intrusion.

"They're not retreating," Aris stated, his voice low and strained, the echoes of the alien consciousness still a faint hum beneath his own thoughts. "They're rerouting. Reinforcing. They're drawing power from secondary conduits, shoring up the nexus's compromised systems. But it's more than that. The psychic pressure... it's returning, but it's different. It's not a broadcast anymore. It's a targeted interrogation. They're hunting for the source of the disruption, and they know I'm it."

Kaelen's fingers flew across the holographic interface, his brow furrowed in concentration. "He's right. Their energy signatures are shifting. They're reinforcing planetary defenses, yes, but they're also initiating a high-level scan. They're not just reacting; they're actively pursuing. They know Aris experienced their collective consciousness. They've identified him as a primary threat, a vessel of information they need to control. They've learned from the initial assault, and now they're coming for us, directly."

The realization was chilling. Their audacious strike against the alien nexus had not resulted in a strategic withdrawal by the invaders. Instead, it had served as a stark, brutal lesson. The aliens, despite their immense, distributed power, were not impervious. They could be wounded, and in their wounded state, their capacity for adaptation was terrifyingly swift. The psychic onslaught that had nearly shattered Aris was not merely an act of overwhelming power, but a desperate, and ultimately informative, attempt to regain control. Now, they had a clearer understanding of their enemy's capabilities, and they were coming for the very individuals who had dared to disrupt their meticulously crafted order.

"They're not just repairing the nexus," Eva murmured, her gaze

fixed on the flickering energy readings, her voice barely audible. "They're adapting their offensive. They saw how we managed to penetrate their defenses, how Aris gained that glimpse into their history and their methods. They can't allow that to happen again. They're reinforcing their own internal coherence, and simultaneously, they're hunting for the source of that disruption. They're hunting us. They know I was involved, and they know Aris is the key."

The psychic pressure, which had begun to recede after Aris's forced immersion, now returned with a chillingly focused intensity. It was no longer a chaotic storm of alien thoughts and emotions, but a precise, invasive probing, like a predator's senses zeroing in on its prey. Aris felt it brush against his consciousness, a cold, alien touch that sought to unravel his thoughts, to find the core of his resistance. He saw Eva flinch, a subtle tremor running through her, her usual bright eyes clouded with a dawning, terrifying certainty. Kaelen, despite his outward focus on the consoles, showed a flicker of strain, his concentration deepening as if warding off an unseen intrusion.

"They're not retreating," Aris stated, his voice low and strained, the echoes of the alien consciousness still a faint hum beneath his own thoughts. "They're rerouting. Reinforcing. They're drawing power from secondary conduits, shoring up the nexus's compromised systems. But it's more than that. The psychic pressure... it's returning, but it's different. It's not a broadcast anymore. It's a targeted interrogation. They're hunting for the source of the disruption, and they know I'm it."

Kaelen's fingers flew across the holographic interface, his brow furrowed in concentration. "He's right. Their energy signatures are shifting. They're reinforcing planetary defenses, yes, but they're also initiating a high-level scan. They're not just reacting; they're actively pursuing. They know Aris experienced their collective consciousness. They've identified him as a primary threat, a vessel of information they need to control. They've learned from the initial assault, and now they're coming for us, directly."

The realization was chilling. Their audacious strike against the alien nexus had not resulted in a strategic withdrawal by the invaders. Instead, it had served as a stark, brutal lesson. The aliens, despite their immense, distributed power, were not impervious. They could be wounded, and in their wounded state, their capacity for adaptation was

terrifyingly swift. The psychic onslaught that had nearly shattered Aris was not merely an act of overwhelming power, but a desperate, and ultimately informative, attempt to regain control. Now, they had a clearer understanding of their enemy's capabilities, and they were coming for the very individuals who had dared to disrupt their meticulously crafted order.

"They're not just repairing the nexus," Eva murmured, her gaze fixed on the flickering energy readings, her voice barely audible. "They're adapting their offensive. They saw how we managed to penetrate their defenses, how Aris gained that glimpse into their history and their methods. They can't allow that to happen again. They're reinforcing their own internal coherence, and simultaneously, they're hunting for the source of that disruption. They're hunting us. They know I was involved, and they know Aris is the key."

The psychic pressure, which had begun to recede after Aris's forced immersion, now returned with a chillingly focused intensity. It was no longer a chaotic storm of alien thoughts and emotions, but a precise, invasive probing, like a predator's senses zeroing in on its prey. Aris felt it brush against his consciousness, a cold, alien touch that sought to unravel his thoughts, to find the core of his resistance. He saw Eva flinch, a subtle tremor running through her, her usual bright eyes clouded with a dawning, terrifying certainty. Kaelen, despite his outward focus on the consoles, showed a flicker of strain, his concentration deepening as if warding off an unseen intrusion.

"They're not retreating," Aris stated, his voice low and strained, the echoes of the alien consciousness still a faint hum beneath his own thoughts. "They're rerouting. Reinforcing. They're drawing power from secondary conduits, shoring up the nexus's compromised systems. But it's more than that. The psychic pressure... it's returning, but it's different. It's not a broadcast anymore. It's a targeted interrogation. They're hunting for the source of the disruption, and they know I'm it."

Kaelen's fingers flew across the holographic interface, his brow furrowed in concentration. "He's right. Their energy signatures are shifting. They're reinforcing planetary defenses, yes, but they're also initiating a high-level scan. They're not just reacting; they're actively pursuing. They know Aris experienced their collective consciousness. They've identified him as a primary threat, a vessel of information

they need to control. They've learned from the initial assault, and now they're coming for us, directly."

The realization was chilling. Their audacious strike against the alien nexus had not resulted in a strategic withdrawal by the invaders. Instead, it had served as a stark, brutal lesson. The aliens, despite their immense, distributed power, were not impervious. They could be wounded, and in their wounded state, their capacity for adaptation was terrifyingly swift. The psychic onslaught that had nearly shattered Aris was not merely an act of overwhelming power, but a desperate, and ultimately informative, attempt to regain control. Now, they had a clearer understanding of their enemy's capabilities, and they were coming for the very individuals who had dared to disrupt their meticulously crafted order.

"They're not just repairing the nexus," Eva murmured, her gaze fixed on the flickering energy readings, her voice barely audible. "They're adapting their offensive. They saw how we managed to penetrate their defenses, how Aris gained that glimpse into their history and their methods. They can't allow that to happen again. They're reinforcing their own internal coherence, and simultaneously, they're hunting for the source of that disruption. They're hunting us. They know I was involved, and they know Aris is the key."

The psychic pressure, which had begun to recede after Aris's forced immersion, now returned with a chillingly focused intensity. It was no longer a chaotic storm of alien thoughts and emotions, but a precise, invasive probing, like a predator's senses zeroing in on its prey. Aris felt it brush against his consciousness, a cold, alien touch that sought to unravel his thoughts, to find the core of his resistance. He saw Eva flinch, a subtle tremor running through her, her usual bright eyes clouded with a dawning, terrifying certainty. Kaelen, despite his outward focus on the consoles, showed a flicker of strain, his concentration deepening as if warding off an unseen intrusion.

"They're not retreating," Aris stated, his voice low and strained, the echoes of the alien consciousness still a faint hum beneath his own thoughts. "They're rerouting. Reinforcing. They're drawing power from secondary conduits, shoring up the nexus's compromised systems. But it's more than that. The psychic pressure... it's returning, but it's different. It's not a broadcast anymore. It's a targeted interrogation. They're hunting for the source of the disruption, and

they know I'm it."

Kaelen's fingers flew across the holographic interface, his brow furrowed in concentration. "He's right. Their energy signatures are shifting. They're reinforcing planetary defenses, yes, but they're also initiating a high-level scan. They're not just reacting; they're actively pursuing. They know Aris experienced their collective consciousness. They've identified him as a primary threat, a vessel of information they need to control. They've learned from the initial assault, and now they're coming for us, directly."

The realization was chilling. Their audacious strike against the alien nexus had not resulted in a strategic withdrawal by the invaders. Instead, it had served as a stark, brutal lesson. The aliens, despite their immense, distributed power, were not impervious. They could be wounded, and in their wounded state, their capacity for adaptation was terrifyingly swift. The psychic onslaught that had nearly shattered Aris was not merely an act of overwhelming power, but a desperate, and ultimately informative, attempt to regain control. Now, they had a clearer understanding of their enemy's capabilities, and they were coming for the very individuals who had dared to disrupt their meticulously crafted order.

"They're not just repairing the nexus," Eva murmured, her gaze fixed on the flickering energy readings, her voice barely audible. "They're adapting their offensive. They saw how we managed to penetrate their defenses, how Aris gained that glimpse into their history and their methods. They can't allow that to happen again. They're reinforcing their own internal coherence, and simultaneously, they're hunting for the source of that disruption. They're hunting us. They know I was involved, and they know Aris is the key."

The psychic pressure, which had begun to recede after Aris's forced immersion, now returned with a chillingly focused intensity. It was no longer a chaotic storm of alien thoughts and emotions, but a precise, invasive probing, like a predator's senses zeroing in on its prey. Aris felt it brush against his consciousness, a cold, alien touch that sought to unravel his thoughts, to find the core of his resistance. He saw Eva flinch, a subtle tremor running through her, her usual bright eyes clouded with a dawning, terrifying certainty. Kaelen, despite his outward focus on the consoles, showed a flicker of strain, his concentration deepening as if warding off an unseen intrusion.

"They're not retreating," Aris stated, his voice low and strained, the echoes of the alien consciousness still a faint hum beneath his own thoughts. "They're rerouting. Reinforcing. They're drawing power from secondary conduits, shoring up the nexus's compromised systems. But it's more than that. The psychic pressure... it's returning, but it's different. It's not a broadcast anymore. It's a targeted interrogation. They're hunting for the source of the disruption, and they know I'm it."

Kaelen's fingers flew across the holographic interface, his brow furrowed in concentration. "He's right. Their energy signatures are shifting. They're reinforcing planetary defenses, yes, but they're also initiating a high-level scan. They're not just reacting; they're actively pursuing. They know Aris experienced their collective consciousness. They've identified him as a primary threat, a vessel of information they need to control. They've learned from the initial assault, and now they're coming for us, directly."

The realization was chilling. Their audacious strike against the alien nexus had not resulted in a strategic withdrawal by the invaders. Instead, it had served as a stark, brutal lesson. The aliens, despite their immense, distributed power, were not impervious. They could be wounded, and in their wounded state, their capacity for adaptation was terrifyingly swift. The psychic onslaught that had nearly shattered Aris was not merely an act of overwhelming power, but a desperate, and ultimately informative, attempt to regain control. Now, they had a clearer understanding of their enemy's capabilities, and they were coming for the very individuals who had dared to disrupt their meticulously crafted order.

"They're not just repairing the nexus," Eva murmured, her gaze fixed on the flickering energy readings, her voice barely audible. "They're adapting their offensive. They saw how we managed to penetrate their defenses, how Aris gained that glimpse into their history and their methods. They can't allow that to happen again. They're reinforcing their own internal coherence, and simultaneously, they're hunting for the source of that disruption. They're hunting us. They know I was involved, and they know Aris is the key."

The psychic pressure, which had begun to recede after Aris's forced immersion, now returned with a chillingly focused intensity. It was no longer a chaotic storm of alien thoughts and emotions, but a

precise, invasive probing, like a predator's senses zeroing in on its prey. Aris felt it brush against his consciousness, a cold, alien touch that sought to unravel his thoughts, to find the core of his resistance. He saw Eva flinch, a subtle tremor running through her, her usual bright eyes clouded with a dawning, terrifying certainty. Kaelen, despite his outward focus on the consoles, showed a flicker of strain, his concentration deepening as if warding off an unseen intrusion.

"They're not retreating," Aris stated, his voice low and strained, the echoes of the alien consciousness still a faint hum beneath his own thoughts. "They're rerouting. Reinforcing. They're drawing power from secondary conduits, shoring up the nexus's compromised systems. But it's more than that. The psychic pressure... it's returning, but it's different. It's not a broadcast anymore. It's a targeted interrogation. They're hunting for the source of the disruption, and they know I'm it."

Kaelen's fingers flew across the holographic interface, his brow furrowed in concentration. "He's right. Their energy signatures are shifting. They're reinforcing planetary defenses, yes, but they're also initiating a high-level scan. They're not just reacting; they're actively pursuing. They know Aris experienced their collective consciousness. They've identified him as a primary threat, a vessel of information they need to control. They've learned from the initial assault, and now they're coming for us, directly."

The realization was chilling. Their audacious strike against the alien nexus had not resulted in a strategic withdrawal by the invaders. Instead, it had served as a stark, brutal lesson. The aliens, despite their immense, distributed power, were not impervious. They could be wounded, and in their wounded state, their capacity for adaptation was terrifyingly swift. The psychic onslaught that had nearly shattered Aris was not merely an act of overwhelming power, but a desperate, and ultimately informative, attempt to regain control. Now, they had a clearer understanding of their enemy's capabilities, and they were coming for the very individuals who had dared to disrupt their meticulously crafted order.

"They're not just repairing the nexus," Eva murmured, her gaze fixed on the flickering energy readings, her voice barely audible. "They're adapting their offensive. They saw how we managed to penetrate their defenses, how Aris gained that glimpse into their

history and their methods. They can't allow that to happen again. They're reinforcing their own internal coherence, and simultaneously, they're hunting for the source of that disruption. They're hunting us. They know I was involved, and they know Aris is the key."

The psychic pressure, which had begun to recede after Aris's forced immersion, now returned with a chillingly focused intensity. It was no longer a chaotic storm of alien thoughts and emotions, but a precise, invasive probing, like a predator's senses zeroing in on its prey. Aris felt it brush against his consciousness, a cold, alien touch that sought to unravel his thoughts, to find the core of his resistance. He saw Eva flinch, a subtle tremor running through her, her usual bright eyes clouded with a dawning, terrifying certainty. Kaelen, despite his outward focus on the consoles, showed a flicker of strain, his concentration deepening as if warding off an unseen intrusion.

"They're not retreating," Aris stated, his voice low and strained, the echoes of the alien consciousness still a faint hum beneath his own thoughts. "They're rerouting. Reinforcing. They're drawing power from secondary conduits, shoring up the nexus's compromised systems. But it's more than that. The psychic pressure... it's returning, but it's different. It's not a broadcast anymore. It's a targeted interrogation. They're hunting for the source of the disruption, and they know I'm it."

Kaelen's fingers flew across the holographic interface, his brow furrowed in concentration. "He's right. Their energy signatures are shifting. They're reinforcing planetary defenses, yes, but they're also initiating a high-level scan. They're not just reacting; they're actively pursuing. They know Aris experienced their collective consciousness. They've identified him as a primary threat, a vessel of information they need to control. They've learned from the initial assault, and now they're coming for us, directly."

The realization was chilling. Their audacious strike against the alien nexus had not resulted in a strategic withdrawal by the invaders. Instead, it had served as a stark, brutal lesson. The aliens, despite their immense, distributed power, were not impervious. They could be wounded, and in their wounded state, their capacity for adaptation was terrifyingly swift. The psychic onslaught that had nearly shattered Aris was not merely an act of overwhelming power, but a desperate, and ultimately informative, attempt to regain control. Now, they had

a clearer understanding of their enemy's capabilities, and they were coming for the very individuals who had dared to disrupt their meticulously crafted order.

"They're not just repairing the nexus," Eva murmured, her gaze fixed on the flickering energy readings, her voice barely audible. "They're adapting their offensive. They saw how we managed to penetrate their defenses, how Aris gained that glimpse into their history and their methods. They can't allow that to happen again. They're reinforcing their own internal coherence, and simultaneously, they're hunting for the source of that disruption. They're hunting us. They know I was involved, and they know Aris is the key."

The psychic pressure, which had begun to recede after Aris's forced immersion, now returned with a chillingly focused intensity. It was no longer a chaotic storm of alien thoughts and emotions, but a precise, invasive probing, like a predator's senses zeroing in on its prey. Aris felt it brush against his consciousness, a cold, alien touch that sought to unravel his thoughts, to find the core of his resistance. He saw Eva flinch, a subtle tremor running through her, her usual bright eyes clouded with a dawning, terrifying certainty. Kaelen, despite his outward focus on the consoles, showed a flicker of strain, his concentration deepening as if warding off an unseen intrusion.

"They're not retreating," Aris stated, his voice low and strained, the echoes of the alien consciousness still a faint hum

The temporal calculus was brutal and unforgiving. Every passing nanosecond chipped away at their dwindling advantage. Aris's voice, tight with urgency, cut through the sterile hum of the command center. "We're running out of time. If they achieve full network integration, if they consolidate their control across all critical systems— communication, defense, infrastructure—then Earth becomes a lost cause. A puppet planet, indistinguishable from any other they've subjugated." He paced before the holographic display, a miniature galaxy of data points and projected timelines swirling around him. Each blinking indicator represented a system either compromised or on the brink of assimilation.

Eva's gaze was fixed on a cluster of nodes flaring crimson, a stark visualization of the aliens' encroaching presence. "We know this, Aris. The question is, what can we do? The psychic probes are intensifying, and I can feel them trying to pinpoint our location, our operational nexus." She ran a hand through her short, practical hair, her usual calm replaced by a gnawing anxiety. "They've adapted. They're not just reinforcing their own systems; they're actively hunting us, trying to sever our coordination before we can even formulate a coherent counter-offensive."

Kaelen, his fingers flying across the console with a speed that belied the exhaustion etched onto his face, nodded grimly. "Eva's right. The initial breach was a shock, but their response has been— terrifyingly—efficient. They've analyzed the disruption, learned from it, and are now leveraging that knowledge. Their collective consciousness is a formidable weapon, and it's adapting faster than we can track." He gestured to a complex series of energy readings. "The psychic pressure isn't random anymore. It's precise. They're probing our command structures, trying to sow dissent, to isolate key individuals. They're targeting the very individuals who pose the greatest threat to their assimilation protocols. And Aris... you're at the epicenter of their attention."

Aris stopped pacing, his eyes narrowed, a flicker of grim determination in their depths. "Which means we have to be bolder. We can't afford to react. We need to strike at the heart of their operation, at the conduits they're using to broadcast their influence, to co-opt our leaders, to turn our own systems against us. My immersion into their collective mind... it gave me more than just a history lesson. It revealed their fundamental operating principle. Their unity is their strength, but it's also their Achilles' heel. Disrupt that unity, introduce enough cognitive dissonance, and you can cripple them from within."

"But how?" Eva's voice was sharp, a desperate plea for a tangible plan. "We're a handful of people against a galaxy-spanning consciousness. We've managed to disrupt their nexus, but that was a surgical strike. Now they're actively hunting us. We're exposed."

"Not entirely," Aris countered, his voice gaining a steely edge. "Their fear of true individuality, of unpredictable consciousness, is their greatest vulnerability. They assimilate anomalies, trying to integrate them. But what happens when the anomaly is too complex, too deeply ingrained? What if we can introduce a 'contagion' of our own consciousness into their network? Something that resonates with their core programming, but in a way that forces them to question their own directives?"

Kaelen looked up from his displays, a spark of intrigued curiosity in his weary eyes. "You're suggesting a psychic counter-strike, on a scale we haven't even contemplated. It's hazardous, Aris. If they detect it, if they can isolate and purge you before you can seed the network, it would be... catastrophic."

"The risk is already immense, Kaelen," Aris said, his gaze meeting Eva's. "We're not just fighting an external enemy anymore. They're infiltrating us, turning our own systems, our own people, against us. We saw it in the compromised leadership. We feel it in the constant psychic pressure. If we don't act decisively, if we don't expose the truth and sever their connection at its core, Earth will be lost. Not to an invading army, but to a silent, insidious assimilation. Our window of opportunity is closing with every breath we take."

Eva finally tore her gaze from the holographic display, her eyes locking with Aris's. "Then we do it. We go for the core. But we can't do it alone. We need more than just the three of us. We need to reach out, to rally anyone who isn't compromised, anyone who still retains their... individuality."

"And how do we do that?" Kaelen asked, his fingers still dancing across the console, a cascade of data flowing from his efforts. "Our communication lines are being monitored, compromised. Any overt attempt to reach out will be detected."

"We use their own methods against them," Aris declared, a dangerous glint in his eyes. "Their network is vast, interconnected. If I can inject a specific psychic signature, a controlled cascade of destabilizing information into their nexus – information gleaned from my immersion – it might create ripples of doubt, of uncertainty, within their collective. It's a long shot, but it might be enough to create enough internal discord for us to identify and isolate the conduits, the compromised elements, before they fully solidify their grip. It's a race against time, and we're starting from behind."

He turned back to the holographic projection, his focus intensifying. "Kaelen, I need you to find the most vulnerable access points within their network – not to attack, but to create a stable gateway for my psychic resonance. Eva, I need you to prepare for immediate extraction. If this works, if we can achieve even a fraction of what I'm hoping for, we'll have to move fast. We have to expose the truth, sever their connection, and rally whoever we can before the collective consciousness can fully establish its dominance. It's not just about survival anymore; it's about reclaiming our free will."

The weight of their mission pressed down on them, a crushing realization of the stakes involved. Their audacious strike against the alien nexus had not repelled the invaders; it had merely illuminated the depth of their insidious infiltration and the terrifying adaptability of their collective consciousness. The psychic assault that Aris had endured had been a brutal, albeit invaluable, lesson. They had seen firsthand how the aliens learned, how they adapted, how they sought to exert control not through overt force, but through a subtle, pervasive assimilation.

Now, the hunters had become the hunted. The very systems humanity relied upon were being subverted, turned into instruments of alien control. The psychic pressure, once a diffuse, overwhelming wave, had sharpened into a focused, invasive probe, a predator's senses zeroing in on its prey. Aris felt it like a cold caress against his mind, a constant, insidious attempt to unravel his thoughts, to find the core of his resistance. Eva flinched, a visible tremor betraying the strain of fending off the unseen assault. Kaelen, his concentration a tangible shield, worked with an almost manic intensity, his brow furrowed, his jaw set.

"They're not just repairing the nexus," Eva murmured, her voice a low rasp against the persistent hum of the control consoles. Her eyes, usually sharp and clear, were shadowed with a weariness that spoke of deeper understanding, of dawning horror. "They're adapting their strategy. They saw how we managed to penetrate their defenses, how Aris gained that critical insight into their history and their methods.

They cannot allow that level of disruption to persist. They're reinforcing their internal coherence, yes, but they're also actively hunting for the source of that disruption.

They're hunting us. They know I was involved, and they know Aris is the key."

Aris nodded, his own mind a battlefield of alien echoes and his own rapidly coalescing resolve. "They're not retreating," he stated, his voice strained, the lingering psychic resonance a subtle tremor beneath his own thoughts. "They're rerouting, reinforcing and drawing power from secondary conduits, shoring up the nexus's compromised systems. But it's more than that. The psychic pressure… it's changed. It's not a broadcast anymore. It's a targeted interrogation. They're hunting for the source of the disruption, and they know I am it."

Kaelen's fingers flew across the holographic interface, a whirlwind of motion against the glowing projections. "He's right. Their energy signatures are shifting. They're reinforcing planetary defenses, no doubt. But they're also initiating a high-level, systematic scan of our known operational hubs. They're not just reacting; they're actively pursuing. They know Aris experienced their collective consciousness. They've identified him as a primary threat, a living repository of information they need to control, to neutralize. They've learned from our initial, almost accidental, assault, and now they're coming for us, directly and with extreme prejudice."

The stark realization hung heavy in the air, a chilling confirmation of their worst fears. Their audacious, almost desperate, strike against the alien nexus had not resulted in a strategic withdrawal by the invaders. Instead, it had served as a brutal, highly effective lesson. The aliens, despite their immense, distributed power, were not invincible. They could be wounded, and in their wounded state, their capacity for adaptation and retribution was terrifyingly swift. The psychic onslaught that had nearly shattered Aris had not been mere overkill; it had been a sophisticated, and ultimately illuminating, attempt to regain control. Now, they understood. They had a more precise, more terrifying grasp of their enemy's capabilities, and the grim certainty that the aliens were coming for them, for the very individuals who had dared to disrupt their meticulously crafted cosmic order.

"They're not just repairing the nexus," Eva murmured, her gaze locked onto the flickering, ever-shifting energy readings on Kaelen's main display. Her voice was barely audible, a whisper against the constant, low hum of the command center's life support systems. "They're adapting their offensive. They saw how we managed to penetrate their defenses, how Aris gained that invaluable, yet terrifying, glimpse into their history and methods. They cannot allow that vulnerability to be exploited again. They're reinforcing their own internal coherence, their collective will, and simultaneously, they're hunting for the source of that disruption. They are hunting us. They know I was involved in the initial planning, and they know Aris is the key to everything."

The psychic pressure, which had begun to recede following Aris's forced and harrowing immersion, now returned with a chillingly focused intensity. It was no longer a chaotic, generalized storm of alien thoughts and emotions, but a precise, invasive probing, like the finely tuned senses of a predator zeroing in on its oblivious prey. Aris felt it brush against the edges of his consciousness, a cold, alien touch that sought to unravel his very thoughts, to find the core of his resistance, to understand the anomaly that was him. He saw Eva flinch, a subtle tremor running through her, her usual bright, analytical eyes now clouded with a dawning, terrifying certainty.

Kaelen, despite his outward focus on the console readouts, showed a flicker of immense strain, his concentration deepening to an almost painful degree, as if he were actively warding off an unseen, relentless intrusion.

"They're not retreating," Aris stated, his voice low and strained, the echoes of the alien consciousness still a faint, unsettling hum beneath the surface of his own thoughts. "They're rerouting their energy and reinforcing their primary nodes. They're drawing power from secondary conduits, shoring up the nexus's compromised systems. But it's more than just structural reinforcement. The psychic pressure… it's returning, but it's fundamentally different. It's not a broadcast anymore. It's a targeted interrogation. They are hunting for the source of the disruption, and they know, with absolute certainty, that I am it."

Kaelen's fingers, usually so fluid and precise, seemed to fly across the holographic interface with an almost desperate urgency. His brow was furrowed in an expression of intense concentration, his gaze fixed on the cascade of data that threatened to overwhelm their defenses. "He's right," Kaelen confirmed, his voice tight with exertion. "Their energy signatures are shifting dramatically. They're reinforcing planetary defenses, yes, but they're also initiating a high-level, pervasive scan of our known operational hubs and communication channels. They're not just reacting; they're actively pursuing. They know Aris experienced their collective consciousness. They've identified him as a primary threat, a dangerous anomaly, a vessel of information they desperately need to control, to neutralize.

They've learned from the initial assault, from our initial, almost accidental, probe, and now they are coming for us, directly and with extreme prejudice."

The stark realization hung heavy in the sterile air of the command center, a chilling confirmation of their worst fears. Their audacious, almost desperate, strike against the alien nexus had not resulted in a strategic withdrawal or even a temporary reprieve from the invaders. Instead, it had served as a stark, brutal, and highly effective lesson. The aliens, despite their immense, distributed power and seemingly monolithic unity, were not impervious. They could be wounded, and in their wounded, compromised state, their capacity for adaptation and immediate retribution was terrifyingly swift. The psychic onslaught that had nearly shattered Aris's mind had not been mere collateral damage; it had been a sophisticated, and ultimately invaluable, attempt to regain control and understand the source of the disruption. Now, they understood. They had a more precise, more terrifying grasp of their enemy's true capabilities, and the grim certainty that the aliens were coming for them, for the very individuals who had dared to disrupt their meticulously crafted cosmic order.

"They're not just repairing the nexus," Eva murmured, her gaze locked onto the flickering, ever-shifting energy readings that dominated Kaelen's main display. Her voice was barely audible, a faint whisper against the constant, low hum of the command center's life support systems, a stark contrast to her usual commanding tone. Her eyes, usually sharp and analytical, were shadowed with a weariness that spoke of a deeper, more profound understanding, of a dawning, terrifying certainty that chilled her to the bone. "They're adapting their offensive strategy. They saw how we managed to penetrate their defenses, how Aris gained that invaluable, terrifying glimpse into their history, their motivations, and their methods. They cannot allow that kind of vulnerability to persist. They're reinforcing their own internal coherence, their collective will, and simultaneously, they're hunting for the source of that disruption. They are hunting us. They know I was involved in the initial planning, and they know, with absolute certainty, that Aris is the key to everything."

The psychic pressure, which had begun to recede following Aris's forced and harrowing immersion into the alien collective, now returned with a chillingly focused, almost physical intensity. It was no longer a chaotic, generalized storm of alien thoughts and emotions, but a precise, invasive probing, like the finely tuned senses of a predator zeroing in on its oblivious prey, its every movement calculated and lethal. Aris felt it brush against the edges of his consciousness, a cold, alien touch that sought to unravel his very thoughts, to find the core of his resistance, to understand, and ultimately to neutralize, the anomaly that was him.

He saw Eva flinch, a subtle, involuntary tremor running through her, her usual bright, analytical eyes now clouded with a dawning, terrifying certainty that spoke volumes more than words could. Kaelen, despite his outward focus on the console readouts and the frantic symphony of data streams, showed a flicker of immense strain. His concentration deepened to an almost painful degree, as if he were actively reinforcing a mental shield against an unseen, relentless intrusion.

"They're not retreating," Aris stated, his voice low and strained, the lingering echoes of the alien consciousness still a faint, unsettling hum beneath the surface of his own thoughts, a constant reminder of the violation he had endured. "They're rerouting their energy distribution and reinforcing their primary nodes and critical infrastructure. They're drawing power from secondary conduits, shoring up the nexus's compromised systems. But it's more than just a defensive maneuver. The psychic pressure… it's returning, but it's fundamentally different. It's not a broadcast anymore. It's a targeted interrogation. They are hunting for the source of the disruption, for the point of intrusion, and they know, with absolute certainty, that I am it."

Kaelen's fingers, usually so fluid and precise, seemed to fly across the holographic interface with an almost desperate urgency, a blur of motion against the glowing, intricate projections. His brow was furrowed in an expression of intense concentration, his gaze fixed on the cascade of data that threatened to overwhelm their defenses, to signify their imminent failure. "He's right," Kaelen confirmed, his voice tight with exertion and the sheer pressure of the moment. "Their energy signatures are shifting dramatically, concentrating their resources. They're reinforcing planetary defenses, no doubt, tightening their grip. But they're also initiating a high-level, systematic scan of our known operational hubs and all vital communication channels. They're not just reacting to our disruption; they're actively pursuing us, predicting our next moves. They know

Aris experienced their collective consciousness. They've identified him as a primary threat, a dangerous anomaly, a vessel of information they desperately need to control, to dissect, to neutralize.

They've learned from the initial assault, from our initial, almost accidental, probe, and now they are coming for us, directly and with extreme prejudice."

The stark realization hung heavy in the sterile, recycled air of the command center, a chilling confirmation of their worst fears, a palpable weight that threatened to crush their already strained hope. Their audacious, almost desperate, strike against the alien nexus, a gamble that had nearly cost Aris his mind, had not resulted in a strategic withdrawal or even a temporary reprieve from the encroaching invaders.

Instead, it had served as a stark, brutal, and highly effective lesson. The aliens, despite their immense, distributed power and seemingly monolithic unity, were not impervious. They could be wounded, and in their wounded, compromised state, their capacity for rapid adaptation and immediate retribution was terrifyingly swift, demonstrating a level of strategic agility that humanity had only begun to grasp. The psychic onslaught that had nearly shattered Aris's mind, that had forced him to confront the very essence of the alien collective, had not been mere collateral damage; it had been a sophisticated, and ultimately invaluable, attempt to regain control and to understand the source of the existential threat. Now, they understood. They had a more precise, more terrifying grasp of their enemy's true capabilities, their unwavering intent, and the grim certainty that the aliens were coming for them, for the very individuals who had dared to disrupt their meticulously crafted cosmic order, who had dared to resist their silent, all-consuming assimilation.

"They're not just repairing the nexus," Eva murmured, her gaze locked onto the flickering, ever-shifting energy readings that dominated Kaelen's main display, a visual representation of their escalating peril. Her voice was barely audible, a faint whisper against the constant, low hum of the command center's life support systems, a stark contrast to her usual commanding tone, her authority often wielded like a scalpel. Her eyes, usually sharp and analytical, filled with a sharp, unwavering blue that missed nothing, were now shadowed with a weariness that spoke of a deeper, more profound understanding, of a dawning, terrifying certainty that chilled her to the very bone. "They're adapting their offensive strategy, evolving with frightening speed. They saw how we managed to penetrate their defenses, how Aris gained that invaluable, terrifying glimpse into their history, their motivations, and their methods of control. They cannot allow that kind of vulnerability to persist, not even for a moment. They're reinforcing their own internal coherence, their collective will, strengthening their synaptic pathways, and simultaneously, they're hunting for the source of that disruption. They are hunting us. They know I was involved in the initial planning, the strategic overview, and they know, with absolute certainty, and that Aris is the key to everything, the linchpin of our defiance."

The psychic pressure, which had begun to recede following Aris's forced and harrowing immersion into the alien collective, a journey into the very heart of their consciousness that had nearly broken him, now returned with a chillingly focused, almost physical intensity. It was no longer a chaotic, generalized storm of alien thoughts and emotions, a cacophony of borrowed consciousness, but a precise, invasive probing, like the finely tuned senses of a predator zeroing in on its oblivious prey, its every subtle shift and movement calculated and lethal. Aris felt it brush against the edges of his consciousness, a cold, alien touch that sought to unravel his very thoughts, to find the core of his resistance, to understand, and ultimately to neutralize, the anomaly that was him, the dissonant note in their perfect symphony. He saw Eva flinch, a subtle, involuntary tremor running through her, her usual bright, analytical eyes, eyes that had seen galaxies and decoded cosmic enigmas, now clouded with a dawning, terrifying certainty that spoke volumes more than any words could, a certainty born of the encroaching darkness. Kaelen, despite his outward focus on the console readouts, the frantic symphony of data streams that represented their last bastion of organized defense, showed a flicker of immense strain, his concentration deepening to an almost painful degree, as if he were actively reinforcing a mental shield, a fragile barrier against an unseen, relentless intrusion, the alien psychic tendrils attempting to breach his mental fortifications.

"They're not retreating," Aris stated, his voice low and strained, the lingering echoes of the alien consciousness still a faint, unsettling hum beneath the surface of his own thoughts, a constant, invasive reminder of the violation he had endured, of the profound contact that had changed him forever. "They're rerouting their energy distribution, a sophisticated redistribution of their vast power reserves and reinforcing their primary nodes and critical infrastructure, making themselves more resilient to further probes. They're drawing power from secondary conduits, shoring up the nexus's compromised systems, attempting to stabilize the damage we inflicted. But it's more than just a defensive maneuver, more than just damage control. The psychic pressure... it's returning, but it's fundamentally different now. It's not a broadcast anymore, a generalized wave of influence. It's a targeted interrogation. They are hunting for the source of the disruption, for the point of intrusion, for the very consciousness that dared to breach their sanctuary, and they know, with absolute certainty, that I am it."

Kaelen's fingers, usually so fluid and precise, capable of weaving intricate patterns of code and data with breathtaking speed, seemed to fly across the holographic interface with an almost desperate urgency, a blur of motion against the glowing, intricate projections that depicted the enemy's encroaching tendrils. His brow was furrowed in an expression of intense concentration, his gaze fixed on the cascade of data that threatened to overwhelm their defenses, to signify their imminent failure, the irreversible loss of Earth.

"He's right," Kaelen confirmed, his voice tight with exertion and the sheer, crushing pressure of the moment, the weight of worlds resting on his ability to maintain their precarious technological advantage. "Their energy signatures are shifting dramatically, concentrating their resources with ruthless efficiency. They're reinforcing planetary defenses, no doubt, tightening their grip on every system they can reach, every network they can infiltrate. But they're also initiating a high-level, systematic scan of our known operational hubs and all vital communication channels, searching for us, for any trace of our resistance. They're not just reacting to our disruption; they're actively pursuing us, predicting our next moves with an alarming level of accuracy. They know Aris experienced their collective consciousness, that he saw the truth behind their veneer of order. They've identified him as a primary threat, a dangerous anomaly, a living repository of knowledge they desperately need to control, to dissect, to neutralize before he can disseminate it.

They've learned from the initial assault, from our initial, almost accidental, probe, and now they are coming for us, directly and with extreme prejudice."

The stark realization hung heavy in the sterile, recycled air of the command center, a chilling confirmation of their worst fears, a palpable weight that threatened to crush their already strained hope, to extinguish the last flicker of resistance. Their audacious, almost desperate, strike against the alien nexus, a gamble that had nearly cost Aris his sanity, his very self, had not resulted in a strategic withdrawal or even a temporary reprieve from the encroaching invaders. Instead, it had served as a stark, brutal, and terrifyingly effective lesson. The aliens, despite their immense, distributed power and seemingly monolithic unity, were not impervious to damage, nor were they incapable of learning. They could be wounded, and in their wounded, compromised state, their capacity for rapid adaptation and immediate retribution was terrifyingly swift, demonstrating a level of strategic agility and ruthless efficiency that humanity had only begun to grasp, a terrifying evolutionary leap. The psychic onslaught that had nearly shattered Aris's mind, that had forced him to confront the very essence of the alien collective, to become, however briefly, a part of it, had not been mere collateral damage or an uncontrolled psychic explosion; it had been a sophisticated, and ultimately invaluable, attempt by the aliens to regain control and to understand the source of the existential threat to their meticulously crafted order. Now, they understood. They had a more precise, more terrifying grasp of their enemy's true capabilities, their unwavering intent to absorb and erase all that was uniquely human, and the grim certainty that the aliens were coming for them, for the very individuals who had dared to disrupt their meticulously crafted cosmic order, who had dared to resist their silent, all-consuming assimilation, who had dared to fight back. The question was no longer if they would be found, but when, and what Aris, Eva, and Kaelen could possibly do in the vanishingly small window of time remaining.

Eva's gaze swept across the shimmering holographic projection, her fingers tracing the intricate web of compromised nodes. The aliens' insidious infiltration had not been a blunt instrument, but a meticulously woven tapestry of influence, targeting not just systems, but the very individuals who controlled them. The psychic pressure, a constant, gnawing awareness of their enemy's omnipresent awareness, only amplified the urgency. "We can't go toe-to-toe with them in a confrontation.

Their collective consciousness is too vast, too interconnected. We need to create internal friction, introduce variables they can't easily assimilate."

Aris leaned closer, his eyes, still bearing the faint, unsettling glow of his recent immersion, fixed on the data streams Eva was highlighting. "Disruption points. Not physical targets, but critical points of influence within the human power structures they've subverted. Where are they most vulnerable?"

Eva's pointer settled on a cluster of glowing red indicators, each representing a high-ranking official, a linchpin in Earth's defense and communication networks. "General Vorlag," she began, her voice hushed with a mixture of dread and grim determination. "He's been instrumental in consolidating control over the planetary defense grid. His strategic commands, his tactical directives – they're all being subtly rerouted, used to create phantom threats, to divert resources, to lull us into a false sense of security while the real assimilation proceeds unchecked. If we can discredit him, if we can reveal his compromised state, it could trigger a systemic paralysis within their command hierarchy."

Kaelen, his fingers a blur as he ran diagnostic scans and cross-referenced data, nodded slowly. "Vorlag is a key node. His authority is immense, his influence extends deep into the military apparatus. Exposing him would be like severing a major artery. But how? They've placed him under such deep psychic control that direct evidence of his manipulation would be impossible to obtain without revealing our hand. They'd anticipate it."

"Precisely," Eva agreed, a flicker of calculation in her eyes. "We don't present direct evidence of psychic manipulation. We exploit the consequences of his compromised state. We leak information, fabricated though it may be, that paints him as either a traitor or a catastrophic liability. Think carefully – what has his compromised state caused? What decisions has he made that, out of context, would appear treasonous or utterly incompetent? We can amplify those. We can create a narrative of betrayal, a story that resonates with the inherent distrust that already exists within human power structures, even under alien subjugation."

She moved to another indicator, a slightly dimmer, but no less critical, point of influence. "Minister Anya Sharma. Her portfolio is communications. She's overseeing the repurposing of our global information networks, the very infrastructure we rely on for coordination and intelligence. She's being used to disseminate carefully curated propaganda, to control the flow of information, and to isolate any pockets of resistance. If Sharma is exposed, if the public realizes their primary source of information is a puppet, it could shatter the illusion of order the aliens are trying to project."

"Sharma," Kaelen mused, tapping a sequence into his console. "Her public profile is high. A minister of communications, the face of information dissemination for a planet under 'stabilization.' The irony is almost palpable. But again, how do we expose her without revealing the true nature of the threat?"

"The same principle applies," Eva stated, her voice gaining a steely edge. "We don't reveal the psychic subjugation. We reveal the actions that result from it. We can feed select, verifiable data to trusted journalists – or rather, journalists who are still operating with a semblance of independence, those who haven't yet been fully compromised themselves. Information about anomalous network traffic, about communication blackouts coinciding with critical events, about the deliberate suppression of dissenting voices. We provide them with breadcrumbs, enough to build a compelling case against Sharma, enough to sow widespread distrust in the very channels they are using to control us. The goal isn't to prove alien intervention; it's to create a cascade of doubt and paranoia among the human collaborators, to make them question the directives they're receiving, to make them look at each other with suspicion."

Aris, who had been silently absorbing their exchange, finally spoke, his voice carrying the weight of his recent, profound experience. "They've integrated deeply. They haven't just replaced people; they've subtly reshaped their thoughts, their motivations, and their loyalties. This is their strength – the seamless assimilation. But it also means their control is dependent on the stability of these compromised individuals. If we can destabilize them, if we can introduce enough cognitive dissonance into their own system by creating friction within the human puppet regime, it might ripple back to the alien collective. It's like introducing a virus into their command structure, but the vector is human distrust and paranoia."

"The objective," Eva continued, her gaze sweeping across the entire network visualization, "is to create a domino effect of exposure. Sharma's downfall could lead to investigations into other communications personnel. Vorlag's removal, or even just his incapacitation through public scrutiny, could create a vacuum in the defense sector, a moment of vulnerability that might allow us to reassert some level of control, or at least to disrupt their immediate plans for planetary defense consolidation. We need to pick our targets carefully, exploit the existing cracks in human society that they are so adeptly widening."

Kaelen chimed in, his fingers now working on a new set of projections. "We need to identify the linchpins of their control. Not just the high-profile figures, but the individuals in crucial, albeit less visible, positions. Network administrators, security chiefs, key engineers responsible for maintaining the assimilated infrastructure. If we can discreetly disrupt their ability to function, to communicate with their alien overseers, even for a short period, it could create opportunities."

"The problem," Aris interjected, his brow furrowed, "is that we are so few, and the network is so vast. Any overt attempt to plant false evidence or leak information carries an enormous risk of detection. The psychic probes are still active, probing for anomalies, for any deviation from their expected patterns."

"Which is why subtlety is paramount," Eva countered, her eyes gleaming with a fierce, almost desperate intelligence. "We're not planting evidence in the traditional sense.

We're leveraging existing data, twisting it, presenting it in a way that fuels suspicion. We can use our limited access to create 'unexplained' system glitches that support the narrative. A comms blackout during a critical meeting for Sharma, for instance, could be framed as deliberate sabotage, pointing towards her complicity. For Vorlag, a series of misrouted defense alerts, subtly nudged by our interventions, could be attributed to his oversight. It's about creating the perception of a flaw, a betrayal, that the aliens themselves, in their relentless pursuit of efficiency, might overlook or dismiss as human error until it's too late. They are accustomed to absolute control, to predictable outcomes. We introduce the chaos of human fallibility, amplified."

Kaelen, meanwhile, had identified a potential vulnerability within the communication infrastructure itself. "Their assimilation process isn't instantaneous across the entire network. There are still legacy systems, older protocols that are proving more resistant to complete integration. If we can target a secure, older communication channel —one that might still retain a degree of independence from the primary alien network —we could potentially use it to seed these narratives. It would require immense precision, threading the needle between detection and delivery."

"That's our best bet," Aris affirmed, a plan beginning to coalesce in his mind, fueled by the insights gleaned from his terrifying journey into the alien consciousness. "Their unity is their strength, but their methodology relies on predictable patterns, on the assumption that their control is absolute and undetectable. If we can create enough internal friction, enough doubt and suspicion within the human collaborators they've ensnared, it will force them to divert resources towards managing that internal human instability. It's a form of psychological warfare, waged on their own terms, using their own tools of control against them. We're not trying to break their collective mind, but to destabilize the conduits through which they exert their will on Earth."

Eva nodded, her gaze sharp and focused. "We need to identify the most effective conduits. Not just the individuals, but the specific systems and communication protocols they are using to maintain control. General Vorlag is paramount for planetary defense. Minister Sharma for information control. But what about planetary infrastructure? Power grids, resource allocation, essential services? Who are the key figures there, and what are the critical systems they manage?"

Kaelen brought up another set of schematics, detailing the distribution of power and essential services across the globe. "Director Elias Thorne. He heads the Global Energy Consortium. His access to the automated resource allocation systems is absolute. The aliens are using it to manage energy distribution, prioritizing their own hidden operations and deliberately throttling resources in areas they deem… less essential. If Thorne can be exposed, the chaos that erupts from the disruption of these systems could be immense. It would cripple their ability to manage the planet as a unified entity."

"Thorne," Eva echoed, a grimace crossing her face. "He's been a proponent of centralized resource management for years, a technocrat through and through. He'd be receptive to rational arguments about efficiency, even if those arguments were subtly manipulated. We could create a data trail showing inexplicable energy diversions, phantom power surges benefiting undisclosed projects, all pointing towards a deliberate mismanagement of the grid under Thorne's command. We'd frame it as gross incompetence, perhaps even a veiled act of sabotage by Thorne himself, motivated by some unknown terrestrial agenda."

Aris closed his eyes for a moment, picturing the vast, interconnected web of consciousness he had briefly inhabited. He remembered the alien directives, the cold, calculated logic of assimilation. They saw humanity as a resource, a biological and societal substrate to be optimized and integrated. Their control was meticulous, but it relied on the assumption that their chosen instruments, these compromised humans, would remain effectively under their dominion. "The key is that they won't expect us to target their human lieutenants with such specific, human-centric methods. They understand psychic influence, direct network manipulation, but they might underestimate the power of human bureaucracy, of media narratives, of political infighting. They've assimilated the individuals, but they haven't truly eradicated the inherent complexities and flaws of human society. We exploit those flaws."

"The challenge," Kaelen admitted, his fingers hovering over a control interface, "is delivering the information without being detected. The network is saturated with their surveillance. Any unauthorized access, any unusual data packets, will be flagged. We need a ghost in the machine, a way to insert these carefully crafted narratives without leaving a traceable footprint."

"That's where Aris's connection comes in," Eva said, turning her gaze to him. "You felt their network from the inside. You understand its architecture, its blind spots, its protocols. Can you identify a method, a way to piggyback on their own communication streams, to insert these carefully crafted leaks without triggering their immediate defenses?"

Aris nodded, the residual psychic resonance within him still a tangible presence. "Their network is layered. The primary assimilation layer is heavily guarded, psychic surveillance is paramount. But beneath that, there are layers of infrastructure management, of data transfer, of inter-system communication that even they might view as routine, as beneath their direct psychic oversight. Suppose I can attune myself to those lower frequencies, to the almost subconscious hum of their operational matrix. In that case, I might be able to inject subtle data fragments, disguised as system logs or automated reports, that contain the seeds of these narratives. It will require immense focus, and a constant awareness of their surveillance. It will be like threading a needle in a hurricane."

"And the delivery mechanism?" Kaelen pressed, ever the pragmatist. "How do we ensure these 'seeds' reach the intended recipients – the independent journalists, the few remaining uncompromised elements within the government or military?"

"We utilize the very systems they've repurposed," Eva explained, a dangerous glint in her eyes. "We identify the unsecured, legacy communication channels they haven't fully purged—older encrypted military lines, defunct public broadcast frequencies that are still technically active but unmonitored. We can use these to transmit the initial packets of data, the 'breadcrumbs' that will, hopefully, be picked up by those still capable of critical analysis. It's a scattershot approach, but it's the only one we have. We cast a wide net, hoping to ensnare a few who are still free."

"We're essentially orchestrating a counter-propaganda campaign," Aris mused, the concept both terrifying and strangely exhilarating. "Using their own assimilated infrastructure against them, leveraging the inherent unpredictability of human agency against their monolithic control. Suppose we can successfully create enough suspicion and internal conflict among the human collaborators. In that case, it will force the aliens to divert resources, reinforce their control mechanisms, and become more visible and predictable in their countermeasures. That's when we might find our next opening."

The weight of their mission pressed down on them, a chilling testament to the enemy's insidious methods. Their initial strike had not been a decisive blow, but a revelation. The aliens, far from being a monolithic force, possessed a terrifyingly adaptable collective consciousness that learned and evolved with each encounter. The psychic assault Aris had endured, a harrowing journey into the alien psyche, had provided them with a grim, invaluable insight: their enemy's strength lay in its unity, its seamless assimilation of all it touched. But unity, Aris now understood, could also be a vulnerability.

The psychic pressure, once a diffuse, overwhelming wave, had sharpened into a focused, invasive probe, like the keen senses of a predator zeroing in on its prey. Aris felt it like a cold caress against his mind, a constant, insidious attempt to unravel his thoughts, to find the core of his resistance, to silence the anomaly that was him. Eva flinched, a visible tremor betraying the strain of fending off the unseen assault.

Kaelen, his concentration a tangible shield, worked with an almost manic intensity, his brow furrowed, his jaw set, a silent guardian against the encroaching tide of alien thought.

"They're not just repairing the nexus," Eva murmured, her voice a low rasp against the persistent hum of the control consoles. Her eyes, normally sharp and clear, were shadowed with a weariness that spoke of deeper understanding, of dawning horror.

"They're adapting their strategy. They saw how we managed to penetrate their defenses, how Aris gained that critical insight into their history and their methods. They cannot allow that level of disruption to persist. They're reinforcing their internal coherence, yes, but they're also actively hunting for the source of that disruption.

They are hunting us. They know I was involved in the initial planning, and they know Aris is the key."

"He's right," Kaelen confirmed, his fingers flying across the holographic interface, a cascade of data flowing from his efforts. "Their energy signatures are shifting. They're reinforcing planetary defenses, no doubt. But they're also initiating a high-level, systematic scan of our known operational hubs. They're not just reacting; they're actively pursuing. They know Aris experienced their collective consciousness. They've identified him as a primary threat, a living repository of information they need to control, to neutralize. They've learned from our initial, almost accidental, assault, and now they're coming for us, directly and with extreme prejudice."

The stark realization hung heavy in the air, a chilling confirmation of their worst fears. Their audacious strike against the alien nexus had not resulted in a strategic withdrawal by the invaders. Instead, it had served as a brutal, highly effective lesson. The aliens, despite their immense, distributed power, were not invincible. They could be wounded, and in their wounded state, their capacity for adaptation and retribution was terrifyingly swift. The psychic assault that had nearly shattered Aris had not been mere overkill; it had been a sophisticated, and ultimately illuminating, attempt to regain control. Now, they understood. They had a clearer, more terrifying grasp of their enemy's capabilities, and the grim certainty that the aliens were coming for them, for the very individuals who had dared to disrupt their meticulously crafted cosmic order.

"They are not just repairing the nexus," Eva murmured, her gaze locked onto the flickering, ever-shifting energy readings that dominated Kaelen's main display. Her voice was barely audible, a faint whisper against the constant, low hum of the command center's life support systems, a stark contrast to her usual commanding tone. Her eyes, normally sharp and analytical, filled with a sharp, unwavering blue that missed nothing, were now shadowed with a weariness that spoke of a deeper, more profound understanding, of a dawning, terrifying certainty that chilled her to the very bone. "They're adapting their offensive strategy, evolving with frightening speed. They saw how we managed to penetrate their defenses, how Aris gained that invaluable, terrifying glimpse into their history, their motivations, and their methods of control. They cannot allow that kind of vulnerability to persist, not even for a moment. They're reinforcing their own internal coherence, their collective will, strengthening their synaptic pathways, and simultaneously, they're hunting for the source of that disruption. They are hunting us. They know I was involved in the initial planning, the strategic overview, and they know, with absolute certainty, and that Aris is the key to everything, the linchpin of our defiance."

The psychic pressure, which had begun to recede following Aris's forced and harrowing immersion into the alien collective, a journey into the very heart of their consciousness that had nearly broken him, now returned with a chillingly focused, almost physical intensity. It was no longer a chaotic, generalized storm of alien thoughts and emotions, a cacophony of borrowed consciousness, but a precise, invasive probing, like the finely tuned senses of a predator zeroing in on its oblivious prey, its every subtle shift and movement calculated and lethal. Aris felt it brush against the edges of his consciousness, a cold, alien touch that sought to unravel his very thoughts, to find the core of his resistance, to understand, and ultimately to neutralize, the anomaly that was him, the dissonant note in their perfect symphony. He saw Eva flinch, a subtle, involuntary tremor running through her, her usual bright, analytical eyes, eyes that had seen galaxies and decoded cosmic enigmas, now clouded with a dawning, terrifying certainty that spoke volumes more than any words could, a certainty born of the encroaching darkness. Kaelen, despite his outward focus on the console readouts, the frantic symphony of data streams that represented their last bastion of organized defense, showed a flicker of immense strain, his concentration deepening to an almost painful degree, as if he were actively reinforcing a mental shield, a fragile barrier against an unseen, relentless intrusion, the alien psychic tendrils attempting to breach his mental fortifications.

"They're not retreating," Aris stated, his voice low and strained, the lingering echoes of the alien consciousness still a faint, unsettling hum beneath the surface of his own thoughts, a constant, invasive reminder of the violation he had endured, of the profound contact that had changed him forever. "They're rerouting their energy distribution, a sophisticated redistribution of their vast power reserves and reinforcing their primary nodes and critical infrastructure, making themselves more resilient to further probes. They're drawing power from secondary conduits, shoring up the nexus's compromised systems, attempting to stabilize the damage we inflicted. But it's more than just a defensive maneuver, more than just damage control. The psychic pressure... it's returning, but it's fundamentally different now. It's not a broadcast anymore, a generalized wave of influence. It's a targeted interrogation. They are hunting for the source of the disruption, for the point of intrusion, for the very consciousness that dared to breach their sanctuary, and they know, with absolute certainty, that I am it."

Kaelen's fingers, usually so fluid and precise, capable of weaving intricate patterns of code and data with breathtaking speed, seemed to fly across the holographic interface with an almost desperate urgency, a blur of motion against the glowing, intricate projections that depicted the enemy's encroaching tendrils. His brow was furrowed in an expression of intense concentration, his gaze fixed on the cascade of data that threatened to overwhelm their defenses, to signify their imminent failure, the irreversible loss of Earth. "He's right," Kaelen confirmed, his voice tight with exertion and the sheer, crushing pressure of the moment, the weight of worlds resting on his ability to maintain their precarious technological advantage. "Their energy signatures are shifting dramatically, concentrating their resources with ruthless efficiency. They're reinforcing planetary defenses, no doubt, tightening their grip on every system they can reach, every network they can infiltrate. But they're also initiating a high-level, systematic scan of our known operational hubs and all vital communication channels, searching for us, for any trace of our resistance. They're not just reacting to our disruption; they're actively pursuing us, predicting our next moves with an alarming level of accuracy. They know Aris experienced their collective consciousness, that he saw the truth behind their veneer of order. They've identified him as a primary threat, a dangerous anomaly, a living repository of knowledge they desperately need to control, to dissect, to neutralize before he can disseminate it.

They've learned from the initial assault, from our initial, almost accidental, probe, and now they are coming for us, directly and with extreme prejudice."

The stark realization hung heavy in the sterile, recycled air of the command center, a chilling confirmation of their worst fears, a palpable weight that threatened to crush their already strained hope, to extinguish the last flicker of resistance. Their audacious, almost desperate, strike against the alien nexus, a gamble that had nearly cost Aris his sanity, his very self, had not resulted in a strategic withdrawal or even a temporary reprieve from the encroaching invaders. Instead, it had served as a stark, brutal, and terrifyingly effective lesson. The aliens, despite their immense, distributed power and seemingly monolithic unity, were not impervious to damage, nor were they incapable of learning. They could be wounded, and in their wounded, compromised state, their capacity for rapid adaptation and immediate retribution was terrifyingly swift, demonstrating a level of strategic agility and ruthless efficiency that humanity had only begun to grasp, a terrifying evolutionary leap. The psychic onslaught that had nearly shattered Aris's mind, that had forced him to confront the very essence of the alien collective, to become, however briefly, a part of it, had not been mere collateral damage or an uncontrolled psychic explosion; it had been a sophisticated, and ultimately invaluable, attempt by the aliens to regain control and to understand the source of the existential threat to their meticulously crafted order.

Now, they understood. They had a more precise, more terrifying grasp of their enemy's true capabilities, their unwavering intent to absorb and erase all that was uniquely human, and the grim certainty that the aliens were coming for them, for the very individuals who had dared to disrupt their meticulously crafted cosmic order, who had dared to resist their silent, all-consuming assimilation, who had dared to fight back. The question was no longer if they would be found, but when, and what Aris, Eva, and Kaelen could possibly do in the vanishingly small window of time remaining.

"They are not just repairing the nexus," Eva murmured, her gaze locked onto the flickering, ever-shifting energy readings that dominated Kaelen's main display, a visual representation of their escalating peril. Her voice was barely audible, a faint whisper against the constant, low hum of the command center's life support systems, a stark contrast to her usual commanding tone, her authority often wielded like a scalpel. Her eyes, usually sharp and analytical, filled with a sharp, unwavering blue that missed nothing, were now shadowed with a weariness that spoke of a deeper, more profound understanding, of a dawning, terrifying certainty that chilled her to the very bone. "They're adapting their offensive strategy, evolving with frightening speed. They saw how we managed to penetrate their defenses, how Aris gained that invaluable, terrifying glimpse into their history, their motivations, and their methods of control. They cannot allow that kind of vulnerability to persist, not even for a moment. They're reinforcing their own internal coherence, their collective will, strengthening their synaptic pathways, and simultaneously, they're hunting for the source of that disruption. They are hunting us. They know I was involved in the initial planning, the strategic overview, and they know, with absolute certainty, and that Aris is the key to everything, the linchpin of our defiance."

The psychic pressure, which had begun to recede following Aris's forced and harrowing immersion into the alien collective, a journey into the very heart of their consciousness that had nearly broken him, now returned with a chillingly focused, almost physical intensity. It was no longer a chaotic, generalized storm of alien thoughts and emotions, a cacophony of borrowed consciousness, but a precise, invasive probing, like the finely tuned senses of a predator zeroing in on its oblivious prey, its every subtle shift and movement calculated and lethal. Aris felt it brush against the edges of his consciousness, a cold, alien touch that sought to unravel his very thoughts, to find the core of his resistance, to understand, and ultimately to neutralize, the anomaly that was him, the dissonant note in their perfect symphony.

He saw Eva flinch, a subtle, involuntary tremor running through her, her usual bright, analytical eyes, eyes that had seen galaxies and decoded cosmic enigmas, now clouded with a dawning, terrifying certainty that spoke volumes more than any words could, a certainty born of the encroaching darkness. Kaelen, despite his outward focus on the console readouts, the frantic symphony of data streams that represented their last bastion of organized defense, showed a flicker of immense strain, his concentration deepening to an almost painful degree, as if he were actively reinforcing a mental shield, a fragile barrier against an unseen, relentless intrusion, the alien psychic tendrils attempting to breach his mental fortifications.

"They're not retreating," Aris stated, his voice low and strained, the lingering echoes of the alien consciousness still a faint, unsettling hum beneath the surface of his own thoughts, a constant, invasive reminder of the violation he had endured, of the profound contact that had changed him forever. "They're rerouting their energy distribution, a sophisticated redistribution of their vast power reserves. Reinforcing their primary nodes and critical infrastructure, making themselves more resilient to further probes. They're drawing power from secondary conduits, shoring up the nexus's compromised systems, attempting to stabilize the damage we inflicted. But it's more than just a defensive maneuver, more than just damage control. The psychic pressure… it's returning, but it's fundamentally different now. It's not a broadcast anymore, a generalized wave of influence. It's a targeted interrogation. They are hunting for the source of the disruption, for the point of intrusion, for the very consciousness that dared to breach their sanctuary, and they know, with absolute certainty, that I am it."

Kaelen's fingers, usually so fluid and precise, capable of weaving intricate patterns of code and data with breathtaking speed, seemed to fly across the holographic interface with an almost desperate urgency, a blur of motion against the glowing, intricate projections that depicted the enemy's encroaching tendrils. His brow was furrowed in an expression of intense concentration, his gaze fixed on the cascade of data that threatened to overwhelm their defenses, to signify their imminent failure, the irreversible loss of Earth. "He's right," Kaelen confirmed, his voice tight with exertion and the sheer, crushing pressure of the moment, the weight of worlds resting on his ability to maintain their precarious technological advantage. "Their energy signatures are shifting dramatically, concentrating their resources with ruthless efficiency. They're reinforcing planetary defenses, no doubt, tightening their grip on every system they can reach, every network they can infiltrate.

But they're also initiating a high-level, systematic scan of our known operational hubs and all vital communication channels, searching for us, for any trace of our resistance. They're not just reacting to our disruption; they're actively pursuing us, predicting our next moves with an alarming level of accuracy. They know Aris experienced their collective consciousness, that he saw the truth behind their veneer of order. They've identified him as a primary threat, a dangerous anomaly, a living repository of knowledge they desperately need to control, to dissect, to neutralize before he can disseminate it.

They've learned from the initial assault, from our initial, almost accidental, probe, and now they are coming for us, directly and with extreme prejudice."

The stark realization hung heavy in the sterile, recycled air of the command center, a chilling confirmation of their worst fears, a palpable weight that threatened to crush their already strained hope, to extinguish the last flicker of resistance. Their audacious, almost desperate, strike against the alien nexus, a gamble that had nearly cost Aris his sanity, his very self, had not resulted in a strategic withdrawal or even a reprieve from the encroaching invaders. Instead, it had served as a stark, brutal, and terrifyingly effective lesson. The aliens, despite their immense, distributed power and seemingly monolithic unity, were not impervious to damage, nor were they incapable of learning. They could be wounded, and in their wounded, compromised state, their capacity for rapid adaptation and immediate retribution was terrifyingly swift, demonstrating a level of strategic agility and ruthless efficiency that humanity had only begun to grasp, a terrifying evolutionary leap. The psychic onslaught that had nearly shattered Aris's mind, that had forced him to confront the very essence of the alien collective, to become, however briefly, a part of it, had not been mere collateral damage or an uncontrolled psychic explosion; it had been a sophisticated, and ultimately invaluable, attempt by the aliens to regain control and to understand the source of the existential threat to their meticulously crafted order. Now, they understood. They had a more precise, more terrifying grasp of their enemy's true capabilities, their unwavering intent to absorb and erase all that was uniquely human, and the grim certainty that the aliens were coming for them, for the very individuals who had dared to disrupt their meticulously crafted cosmic order, who had dared to resist their silent, all-consuming assimilation, who had dared to fight back. The question was no longer if they would be found, but when, and what Aris, Eva, and Kaelen could do in the vanishingly small window of time remaining.

"They are not just repairing the nexus," Eva murmured, her gaze locked onto the flickering, ever-shifting energy readings that dominated Kaelen's main display, a visual representation of their escalating peril. Her voice was barely audible, a faint whisper against the constant, low hum of the command center's life support systems, a stark contrast to her usual commanding tone, her authority often wielded like a scalpel.

Her eyes, usually sharp and analytical, filled with a sharp, unwavering blue that missed nothing, were now shadowed with a weariness that spoke of a deeper, more profound understanding, of a dawning, terrifying certainty that chilled her to the very bone. "They're adapting their offensive strategy, evolving with frightening speed. They saw how we managed to penetrate their defenses, how Aris gained that invaluable, terrifying glimpse into their history, their motivations, and their methods of control. They cannot allow that kind of vulnerability to persist, not even for a moment. They're reinforcing their own internal coherence, their collective will, strengthening their synaptic pathways, and simultaneously, they're hunting for the source of that disruption. They are hunting us. They know I was involved in the initial planning, the strategic overview, and they know, with absolute certainty, that Aris is the key to everything, the linchpin of our defiance."

The psychic pressure, which had begun to recede following Aris's forced and harrowing immersion into the alien collective, a journey into the very heart of their consciousness that had nearly broken him, now returned with a chillingly focused, almost physical intensity. It was no longer a chaotic, generalized storm of alien thoughts and emotions, a cacophony of borrowed consciousness, but a precise, invasive probing, like the finely tuned senses of a predator zeroing in on its oblivious prey, its every subtle shift and movement calculated and lethal. Aris felt it brush against the edges of his consciousness, a cold, alien touch that sought to unravel his very thoughts, to find the core of his resistance, to understand, and ultimately to neutralize, the anomaly that was him, the dissonant note in their perfect symphony. He saw Eva flinch, a subtle, involuntary tremor running through her, her usual bright, analytical eyes, eyes that had seen galaxies and decoded cosmic enigmas, now clouded with a dawning, terrifying certainty that spoke volumes more than any words could, a certainty born of the encroaching darkness. Kaelen, despite his outward focus on the console readouts, the frantic symphony of data streams that represented their last bastion of organized defense, showed a flicker of immense strain, his concentration deepening to an almost painful degree, as if he were actively reinforcing a mental shield, a fragile barrier against an unseen, relentless intrusion, the alien psychic tendrils attempting to breach his mental fortifications.

"They're not retreating," Aris stated, his voice low and strained, the lingering echoes of the alien consciousness still a faint, unsettling hum beneath the surface of his own thoughts, a constant, invasive reminder of the violation he had endured, of the profound contact that had changed him forever.

"They're rerouting their energy distribution, a sophisticated redistribution of their vast power reserves and reinforcing their primary nodes and critical infrastructure, making themselves more resilient to further probes. They're drawing power from secondary conduits, shoring up the nexus's compromised systems, attempting to stabilize the damage we inflicted. But it's more than just a defensive maneuver, more than just damage control. The psychic pressure… it's returning, but it's fundamentally different now. It's not a broadcast anymore, a generalized wave of influence. It's a targeted interrogation. They are hunting for the source of the disruption, for the point of intrusion, for the very consciousness that dared to breach their sanctuary, and they know, with absolute certainty, that I am it."

Kaelen's fingers, usually so fluid and precise, capable of weaving intricate patterns of code and data with breathtaking speed, seemed to fly across the holographic interface with an almost desperate urgency, a blur of motion against the glowing, intricate projections that depicted the enemy's encroaching tendrils. His brow was furrowed in an expression of intense concentration, his gaze fixed on the cascade of data that threatened to overwhelm their defenses, to signify their imminent failure, the irreversible loss of Earth. "He's right," Kaelen confirmed, his voice tight with exertion and the sheer, crushing pressure of the moment, the weight of worlds resting on his ability to maintain their precarious technological advantage. "Their energy signatures are shifting dramatically, concentrating their resources with ruthless efficiency. They're reinforcing planetary defenses, no doubt, tightening their grip on every system they can reach, every network they can infiltrate. But they're also initiating a high-level, systematic scan of our known operational hubs and all vital communication channels, searching for us, for any trace of our resistance. They're not just reacting to our disruption; they're actively pursuing us, predicting our next moves with an alarming level of accuracy. They know Aris experienced their collective consciousness, that he saw the truth behind their veneer of order. They've identified him as a primary threat, a dangerous anomaly, a living repository of knowledge they desperately need to control, to dissect, to neutralize before he can disseminate it.

They've learned from the initial assault, from our initial, almost accidental, probe, and now they are coming for us, directly and with extreme prejudice."

The stark realization hung heavy in the sterile, recycled air of the command centre, a chilling confirmation of their worst fears —a palpable weight that threatened to crush their already strained hope, to extinguish the last flicker of resistance. Their audacious, almost desperate, strike against the alien nexus, a gamble that had nearly cost Aris his sanity, his very self, had not resulted in a strategic withdrawal or even a reprieve from the encroaching invaders. Instead, it had served as a stark, brutal, and terrifyingly effective lesson.

The aliens, despite their immense, distributed power and seemingly monolithic unity, were not impervious to damage, nor were they incapable of learning. They could be wounded, and in their wounded, compromised state, their capacity for rapid adaptation and immediate retribution was terrifyingly swift, demonstrating a level of strategic agility and ruthless efficiency that humanity had only begun to grasp, a terrifying evolutionary leap. The psychic onslaught that had nearly shattered Aris's mind, that had forced him to confront the very essence of the alien collective, to become, however briefly, a part of it, had not been mere collateral damage or an uncontrolled psychic explosion; it had been a sophisticated, and ultimately invaluable, attempt by the aliens to regain control and to understand the source of the existential threat to their meticulously crafted order. Now, they understood. They had a more precise, more terrifying grasp of their enemy's true capabilities, their unwavering intent to absorb and erase all that was uniquely human, and the grim certainty that the aliens were coming for them, for the very individuals who had dared to disrupt their meticulously crafted cosmic order, who had dared to resist their silent, all-consuming assimilation, who had dared to fight back. The question was no longer if they would be found, but when, and what Aris, Eva, and Kaelen could do in the vanishingly small window of time remaining.

"They are not just repairing the nexus," Eva murmured, her gaze locked onto the flickering, ever-shifting energy readings that dominated Kaelen's main display, a visual representation of their escalating peril. Her voice was barely audible, a faint whisper against the constant, low hum of the command center's life support systems, a stark contrast to her usual commanding tone, her authority often wielded like a scalpel. Her eyes, usually sharp and analytical, filled with a sharp, unwavering blue that missed nothing, were now shadowed with a weariness that spoke of a deeper, more profound understanding, of a dawning, terrifying certainty that chilled her to the very bone. "They're adapting their offensive strategy, evolving with frightening speed. They saw how we managed to penetrate their defenses, how Aris gained that invaluable, terrifying glimpse into their history, their motivations, and their methods of control. They cannot allow that kind of vulnerability to persist, not even for a moment. They're reinforcing their own internal coherence, their collective will, strengthening their synaptic pathways, and simultaneously, they're hunting for the source of that disruption. They are hunting us. They know I was involved in the initial planning, the strategic overview, and they know, with absolute certainty, and that Aris is the key to everything, the linchpin of our defiance."

The psychic pressure, which had begun to recede following Aris's forced and harrowing immersion into the alien collective, a journey into the very heart of their consciousness that had nearly broken him, now returned with a chillingly focused, almost physical intensity. It was no longer a chaotic, generalized storm of alien thoughts and emotions, a cacophony of borrowed consciousness, but a precise, invasive probing, like the finely tuned senses of a predator zeroing in on its oblivious prey, its every subtle shift and movement calculated and lethal. Aris felt it brush against the edges of his consciousness, a cold, alien touch that sought to unravel his very thoughts, to find the core of his resistance, to understand, and ultimately to neutralize, the anomaly that was him, the dissonant note in their perfect symphony. He saw Eva flinch, a subtle, involuntary tremor running through her, her usual bright, analytical eyes, eyes that had seen galaxies and decoded cosmic enigmas, now clouded with a dawning, terrifying certainty that spoke volumes more than any words could, a certainty born of the encroaching darkness. Kaelen, despite his outward focus on the console readouts, the frantic symphony of data streams that represented their last bastion of organized defense, showed a flicker of immense strain, his concentration deepening to an almost painful degree, as if he were actively reinforcing a mental shield, a fragile barrier against an unseen, relentless intrusion, the alien psychic tendrils attempting to breach his mental fortifications.

"They're not retreating," Aris stated, his voice low and strained, the lingering echoes of the alien consciousness still a faint, unsettling hum beneath the surface of his own thoughts, a constant, invasive reminder of the violation he had endured, of the profound contact that had changed him forever. "They're rerouting their energy distribution, a sophisticated redistribution of their vast power reserves and reinforcing their primary nodes and critical infrastructure, making themselves more resilient to further probes. They're drawing power from secondary conduits, shoring up the nexus's compromised systems, attempting to stabilize the damage we inflicted. But it's more than just a defensive maneuver, more than just damage control. The psychic pressure... it's returning, but it's fundamentally different now. It's not a broadcast anymore, a generalized wave of influence. It's a targeted interrogation. They are hunting for the source of the disruption, for the point of intrusion, for the very consciousness that dared to breach their sanctuary, and they know, with absolute certainty, that I am it."

Kaelen's fingers, usually so fluid and precise, capable of weaving intricate patterns of code and data with breathtaking speed, seemed to fly across the holographic interface with an almost desperate urgency, a blur of motion against the glowing, intricate projections that depicted the enemy's encroaching tendrils. His brow was furrowed in an expression of intense concentration, his gaze fixed on the cascade of data that threatened to overwhelm their defenses, to signify their imminent failure, the irreversible loss of Earth. "He's right," Kaelen confirmed, his voice tight with exertion and the sheer, crushing pressure of the moment, the weight of worlds resting on his ability to maintain their precarious technological advantage. "Their energy signatures are shifting dramatically, concentrating their resources with ruthless efficiency. They're reinforcing planetary defenses, no doubt, tightening their grip on every system they can reach, every network they can infiltrate.

But they're also initiating a high-level, systematic scan of our known operational hubs and all vital communication channels, searching for us, for any trace of our resistance. They're not just reacting to our disruption; they're actively pursuing us, predicting our next moves with an alarming level of accuracy. They know Aris experienced their collective consciousness, that he saw the truth behind their veneer of order. They've identified him as a primary threat, a dangerous anomaly, a living repository of knowledge they desperately need to control, to dissect, to neutralize before he can disseminate it.

They've learned from the initial assault, from our initial, almost accidental, probe, and now they are coming for us, directly and with extreme prejudice."

The stark realization hung heavy in the sterile, recycled air of the command centre, a chilling confirmation of their worst fears —a palpable weight that threatened to crush their already strained hope, to extinguish the last flicker of resistance. Their audacious, almost desperate, strike against the alien nexus, a gamble that had nearly cost Aris his sanity, his very self, had not resulted in a strategic withdrawal or even a reprieve from the encroaching invaders. Instead, it had served as a stark, brutal, and terrifyingly effective lesson. The aliens, despite their immense, distributed power and seemingly monolithic unity, were not impervious to damage, nor were they incapable of learning. They could be wounded, and in their wounded, compromised state, their capacity for rapid adaptation and immediate retribution was terrifyingly swift, demonstrating a level of strategic agility and ruthless efficiency that humanity had only begun to grasp, a terrifying evolutionary leap. The psychic onslaught that had nearly shattered Aris's mind, that had forced him to confront the very essence of the alien collective, to become, however briefly, a part of it, had not been mere collateral damage or an uncontrolled psychic explosion; it had been a sophisticated, and ultimately invaluable, attempt by the aliens to regain control and to understand the source of the existential threat to their meticulously crafted order. Now, they understood. They had a more precise, more terrifying grasp of their enemy's true capabilities, their unwavering intent to absorb and erase all that was uniquely human, and the grim certainty that the aliens were coming for them, for the very individuals who had dared to disrupt their meticulously crafted cosmic order, who had dared to resist their silent, all-consuming assimilation, who had dared to fight back. The question was no longer if they would be found, but when, and what Aris, Eva, and Kaelen could do in the vanishingly small window of time remaining.

The weight of revelation settled upon them, a crushing burden that amplified the already pervasive psychic pressure. Aris felt it most acutely, a phantom limb of alien consciousness still tethered to his own, a constant, invasive probe seeking to understand, to categorize, and ultimately to neutralize the anomaly that was him. Eva flinched, not from a physical blow, but from the sheer, unyielding force of the alien collective's refocusing, a palpable shift in the pervasive psychic field that signaled their enemy's awareness of the breach. Kaelen, his fingers a blur across the console, his focus an almost tangible shield, confirmed their worst fears with a grim nod. "They're not just reinforcing the nexus," he stated, his voice tight with exertion. "They're initiating a high-level, systematic scan of our known operational hubs. They know Aris experienced their collective consciousness. They've identified him as a primary threat, a living repository of information they need to control."

Eva's gaze, usually so sharp and piercing, was now clouded with a weary certainty. "They're adapting their offensive strategy," she murmured, her voice barely audible above the hum of the command center. "They saw how we penetrated their defenses, how Aris gained that invaluable, terrifying glimpse into their history and methods.

They cannot allow that vulnerability to persist. They're hunting us."

The psychic pressure intensified, no longer a diffuse storm but a targeted interrogation, probing the edges of Aris's mind, seeking the dissonant chord that was his consciousness. He felt their cold, alien touch attempting to unravel his thoughts, to understand the core of his resistance. "They're rerouting their energy distribution," Aris said, his voice strained, the alien echoes still humming beneath his own thoughts. "Reinforcing primary nodes, shoring up the nexus's compromised systems. But it's more than damage control. The psychic pressure... it's a targeted interrogation. They know I'm the source of the disruption."

Kaelen confirmed, his fingers flying across the interface, a desperate symphony of data streams against the enemy's encroaching tendrils. "Their energy signatures are shifting dramatically, concentrating resources. They're reinforcing planetary defenses, tightening their grip. But they're also initiating a systematic scan of our operational hubs and communication channels, searching for us. They know Aris experienced their collective consciousness. They've identified him as a primary threat, a dangerous anomaly, a living repository of knowledge they need to control, to dissect, to neutralize."

The stark realization hung heavy in the air. Their gamble at the nexus hadn't resulted in a retreat, but a brutal, terrifying lesson. The aliens, despite their unity, were not impervious. They could be wounded, and their adaptation and retribution were swift. The psychic onslaught on Aris hadn't been collateral damage; it had been an attempt to regain control, to understand the threat. Now, they understood their enemy's capabilities, their intent to absorb and erase humanity, and the grim certainty that the aliens were coming for them. The question was no longer if they would be found, but when, and what little time they had left.

"We can't simply react," Eva declared, her voice regaining some of its usual steely edge, a defiance against the encroaching despair. "We have to seize the initiative. We need to get this information out. Not just to the military remnants, but to the people. The uncompromised elements within government, the independent journalists, anyone who can still think critically. They need to know the truth, the full scope of this infiltration."

Aris nodded, the psychic echoes in his mind a constant reminder of the enemy's insidious presence. "But how? Their control over global media, over communication networks, is near absolute. Any attempt to disseminate this information through conventional channels will be intercepted, suppressed, or worse, twisted into alien propaganda."

"Conventional channels are out," Kaelen agreed, his gaze sweeping across the complex network schematics still displayed on his primary screen. "They've integrated too deeply. Every major broadcast tower, every fiber-optic cable, every satellite uplink – they're all either directly controlled or subtly influenced. We need to find the blind spots, the forgotten pathways, the whispers in the digital static."

"The plan we devised earlier – targeting the compromised individuals, creating internal friction within the human collaborators – that's still viable, but it's not enough on its own," Eva continued, her fingers tapping a rapid sequence on her own console, bringing up a different set of data. "That strategy aims to disrupt their command structure, to create chaos. But we need to empower the resistance directly. We need to arm them with knowledge. The evidence of their infiltration, the nature of their psychic manipulation, the names and faces of the compromised human assets.

Without that, any resistance will be fragmented, easily contained."

Aris rubbed his temples, the psychic residue a dull ache behind his eyes. "The problem is delivering irrefutable proof. The evidence itself needs to be untainted, uncorrupted. If we leak data that's even remotely suspect, it will be dismissed as fabricated, as fear-mongering. They'll use it to discredit us, to reinforce their narrative of human irrationality."

"Which is why we use encrypted channels, untraceable sources," Eva insisted, her gaze meeting Aris's, a silent understanding passing between them. "We leverage the very systems they might have overlooked, or deemed too insignificant to integrate fully. Legacy systems, which are older protocols that may still retain a degree of independence from their primary network. Aris, you felt their network from the inside. You understand its architecture. Can you identify any such vulnerabilities? Any forgotten backdoors, any channels that are too old, too obscure for them to have bothered with?"

Aris closed his eyes, attempting to filter out the cacophony of alien thought, to focus on the subtle hum of underlying infrastructure. He recalled fragments from his horrifying immersion, glimpses of the vast, interconnected matrix that underpinned their control. "Their primary assimilation layer is heavily guarded, psychic surveillance is paramount," he began, his voice a low, resonant tone. "But beneath that, there are layers of infrastructure management, of data transfer, of inter-system communication that even they might view as routine, as beneath their direct psychic oversight. Suppose I can attune myself to those lower frequencies, to the almost subconscious hum of their operational matrix. In that case, I might be able to inject subtle data fragments, disguised as system logs or automated reports that contain the seeds of these narratives. It will require immense focus, and a constant awareness of their surveillance. It will be like threading a needle in a hurricane."

"And the delivery mechanism?" Kaelen pressed, ever the pragmatist. "How do we ensure these 'seeds' reach the intended recipients – the independent journalists, the few remaining uncompromised elements within the government or military?"

"We utilize the very systems they've repurposed," Eva explained, a dangerous glint in her eyes. "We identify the unsecured, legacy communication channels they haven't fully purged—older encrypted military lines, defunct public broadcast frequencies that are still technically active but unmonitored. We can use these to transmit the initial packets of data, the 'breadcrumbs' that will, hopefully, be picked up by those still capable of critical analysis. It's a scattershot approach, but it's the only one we have. We cast a wide net, hoping to ensnare a few who are still free."

"We're essentially orchestrating a counter-propaganda campaign," Aris mused, the concept both terrifying and strangely exhilarating. "Using their own assimilated infrastructure against them, leveraging the inherent unpredictability of human agency against their monolithic control. Suppose we can successfully create enough suspicion and internal conflict within the human collaborators. In that case, it will force them to divert resources, reinforce their control mechanisms, and become more visible and predictable in their countermeasures. That's when we might find our next opening."

The challenge, however, was monumental. The aliens' control

over information flow was not merely a matter of technological dominance; it was an actively managed psychological operation. Every news broadcast, every official announcement, every social media trend was subtly curated, designed to maintain an illusion of normalcy, of alien benevolence, or at the very least, of inevitable integration. To break through that carefully constructed edifice required not just data, but a narrative that resonated, that bypassed the ingrained skepticism and passive acceptance they had fostered.

"We need to frame it," Eva said, her mind already working at hyperspeed, strategizing the presentation of their findings. "We can't just dump raw data. We need to present a compelling story. The story of how General Vorlag's strategic decisions, seemingly sound on the surface, led to critical vulnerabilities in our planetary defense. The story of how Minister Sharma's communication directives, presented as necessary reforms, actively silenced dissent and manipulated public perception. The tale of Director Thorne's energy management, which, when viewed through the lens of alien priorities, reveals a systematic diversion of resources away from humanity's needs.

We need to connect the dots for them, to highlight the anomalies that are so subtle they've been ignored."

Aris felt a surge of understanding, a clarity born from his recent, terrifying ordeal. The alien collective's strength was its unity, its efficiency, its collective consciousness. But their methodology relied on a degree of predictability, an assumption of seamless control. They saw humans as components, as biological and societal substrates to be optimized and improved. They understood psychic influence and direct network manipulation, but they might underestimate the power of human bureaucracy, media narratives, political infighting, and the simple, potent force of unveiled truth. "They've assimilated the individuals, but they haven't eradicated the inherent complexities and flaws of human society," Aris stated, his voice resonating with newfound conviction. "We exploit those flaws. We feed the independent journalists the verifiable data, the anomaly reports, the internal inconsistencies that point to gross negligence or deliberate betrayal. We make them the conduits for our truth, allowing them to build the narrative within their own established frameworks, thereby lending it greater credibility."

Kaelen was already working, his fingers dancing across the

holographic interface, identifying potential channels, sifting through terabytes of data for the digital equivalent of forgotten back alleys. "I've found a potential avenue," he announced, a flicker of grim satisfaction in his voice. "An old military encrypted communication protocol, decommissioned years ago due to its perceived vulnerability. It's a direct line, highly secure, but almost entirely unmonitored now. The aliens likely consider it obsolete, a dead end. If I can inject the data packets there, disguised as routine diagnostic logs from the old system, it might bypass their active surveillance."

Eva leaned closer, her eyes fixed on the complex schematics Kaelen was displaying. "How reliable is it? Can it handle the volume of data we need to transmit?"

"It's robust, designed for high-security data transfer," Kaelen replied. "The challenge will be the injection itself. It requires precise timing and an understanding of the old system's operational quirks. Aris, your recent... exposure... to their network architecture. Did you perceive any residual fragments of older, more primitive alien communication protocols that might have been integrated into their current system? Anything that could be used as a 'key' to unlock or mask our transmission within their broader network?"

Aris concentrated, sifting through the lingering impressions, the phantom sensations of alien thought. He recalled fleeting glimpses of how they integrated, not just by force, but by adaptation, by absorbing and repurposing existing structures. "They don't discard the old; they integrate it," he confirmed. "There were... echoes... of their early assimilation efforts, primitive cybernetic pathways they used before their consciousness fully unified. These pathways might still exist within the network's deeper layers, less heavily monitored, more akin to skeletal remains than fully functioning systems. If I can find a resonance with those primitive alien frequencies, I might be able to use them as a carrier wave, masking our data within their own historical footprint."

The plan began to solidify, a desperate gamble forged in the crucible of imminent defeat. Aris would act as the psychic key, attuning himself to the residual alien frequencies and identifying the specific, obscure data conduits. Kaelen would then engineer the data packets, embedding the irrefutable evidence of the alien infiltration – compromised personnel logs, manipulated resource allocation reports, falsified intelligence directives – and preparing them for transmission. Eva would orchestrate the dissemination, targeting the identified legacy channels to ensure the information reached the few remaining bastions of independent thought.

"We need to be precise," Eva emphasized, her voice a low, urgent hum. "The moment this information is released, the aliens will react. They'll try to discredit it, to censor it, to suppress it. Our window of opportunity will be agonizingly small. We need to ensure that when this truth breaks, it does so with such overwhelming force, with such irrefutable evidence, that it cannot be contained. Panic is a risk, yes, but it's a necessary one. Because beneath that panic, there's the potential for unity. For resistance. For a fight we might actually have a chance of winning."

The weight of revelation was no longer just the burden of knowing, but the burden of acting. The psychic pressure, now a constant, unwelcome companion, served as a grim reminder of the stakes. They were no longer just defending themselves; they were igniting a rebellion, armed with the most potent weapon of all: the unvarnished truth, delivered through the shadows of an enemy's own design. The success of their counter-offensive would depend not just on their technical prowess or Aris's unique connection, but on the desperate hope that, even under the most suffocating control, the human spirit, when faced with undeniable truth, would still possess the capacity to resist. The challenge was immense, the risks astronomical, but the alternative – complete, silent assimilation – was unthinkable. They were ready to unleash the flood.

The process was fraught with peril. Aris found himself adrift in a sea of data, his mind a conduit for frequencies that were both alien and eerily familiar, remnants of the invaders' nascent integration into Earth's systems. He could feel the constant, invasive probing of their collective consciousness, a relentless search for him, for the anomaly that had breached their sanctuary. It was like navigating a minefield where each step was a potential psychic detonation. He visualized the ghost signals, the faint, residual hums of older alien networks, the digital fossils they had left behind as they evolved their assimilation. "I can feel them," he reported, his voice strained, sweat beading on his forehead. "Older protocols, less sophisticated than their current network, but still... alive. They're like dormant systems, forgotten by the main consciousness, but still connected to the core. If I can find a way to piggyback on these residual frequencies, to mask our transmissions as part of their own historical data flow, it might work."

Kaelen's fingers flew across his console, translating Aris's psychic impressions into tangible data streams. He was charting the spectral echoes, mapping the forgotten pathways. "I'm isolating them," Kaelen confirmed, his brow furrowed in concentration. "These aren't just unused channels; they're almost like sub-layers of their own network architecture, integrated so deeply that they're functionally invisible to direct external scanning. If we can insert our data packets here, disguised as routine system maintenance or archival data, they might slip through the net. The challenge is the payload. We need irrefutable proof, meticulously compiled, that cannot be easily dismissed or altered."

Eva was already compiling the data, pulling encrypted files from secure offline servers, cross-referencing them with compromised personnel records and manipulated intelligence reports. "General Vorlag's directives rerouting strategic assets to decoy targets, creating phantom threats that drew our forces away from key defensive positions," she narrated, her voice tight with grim determination. "Minister Sharma's memos authorizing the deliberate suppression of news reports detailing anomalous alien activity, her instructions to reroute communication traffic away from independent news agencies. Director Thorne's energy logs showing inexplicable power diversions to covert, off-world research facilities disguised as terrestrial infrastructure upgrades. This is the evidence, Kaelen. We need to package it, encrypt it, and get it into those ghost channels."

The task was immense. Every data packet had to be meticulously crafted, its digital signature obscured, its origin masked. They were not merely transmitting information; they were weaving a narrative, a tapestry of undeniable truth designed to unravel the aliens' carefully constructed illusion of control. The psychic pressure was a constant, gnawing distraction, a reminder that at any moment, their clandestine operation could be discovered. Aris felt the alien collective's attention coalesce around him, a palpable, chilling focus. They were aware of the disruption, of the anomaly, and they were zeroing in on its source.

"They're intensifying their scan," Aris reported, his voice barely a whisper. "They've detected a localized anomaly in the older network frequencies. They're trying to pinpoint it. We're running out of time."

"Then we accelerate," Eva stated, her resolve hardening. "Kaelen, prepare the primary payload. Aris, guide him through the injection points. I'll monitor the alien network for any signs of imminent detection. We have to trust that this will work, that it will reach the right people that it will spark the resistance we desperately need."

Kaelen worked with a focused intensity, his hands a blur as he compiled the data, encrypting each segment with multiple layers of obsolete, highly complex algorithms that were designed to be nearly impossible to crack by modern computational means, let alone the alien network's more advanced, but perhaps less adaptable, encryption protocols. He was essentially building digital time bombs, programmed to detonate within the minds of those who still possessed the capacity for independent thought.

"Injection sequence initiated," Kaelen announced, his voice tight with tension. "Aris, are you maintaining the psychic camouflage? Can you keep their attention diverted from the data streams themselves?"

Aris nodded, focusing his will, pushing back against the overwhelming psychic presence. He projected a sense of confusion, of erratic thought patterns. This digital ghost mimicked the very anomalies the aliens were searching for, hoping to lead them on a wild goose chase while Kaelen's actual payload slipped past. He felt their probing intensify, their collective mind latching onto the simulated chaos, a temporary distraction that bought them precious seconds.

"The first wave is in," Kaelen breathed, a hint of relief in his voice. "Multiple channels, all masked. It's a broad spectrum, hitting as many of those legacy conduits as possible. Now we wait, and we hope."

Eva brought up a different display, one that showed the global communication network, highlighting areas of significant data traffic, particularly those emanating from the legacy systems Kaelen had tapped into. "We need to track the spread," she said, her gaze sharp and unwavering. "We need to see if these data packets are being intercepted by their intended targets, or if they're being scrubbed from the system before they can do any good. We've armed the truth; now we need to see if it can find fertile ground."

The psychic pressure, while still present, seemed to recede

slightly, as if the alien collective, having identified and seemingly contained the anomaly Aris represented, was reallocating its resources. This brief respite was all they needed. They had sown the seeds of truth, a digital wildfire waiting for the right spark to ignite. The counter-offensive had begun, not with a bang, but with a whisper, a precisely delivered payload of undeniable fact, designed to shatter the illusion and awaken a sleeping world. The weight of revelation was now balanced by the fragile hope that this truth, once unleashed, would be the catalyst for humanity's desperate fight for survival.

13: Humanity's Awakening

The hum of the command center, once a comforting thrum of controlled chaos, now vibrated with a new, desperate frequency. Aris felt it deep within his bones, a psychic resonance that mirrored the seismic shift occurring in the global consciousness. The data packets, meticulously crafted and disguised, had been loosed into the digital ether, finding purchase within the forgotten arteries of human communication. It was a digital contagion, designed to bypass the sterile, controlled environments of official networks and infect the raw, unfiltered pathways of human discourse.

Eva watched the unfolding digital landscape with a hawk's keen eye. Streams of data flickered across her console, not the pristine, censored feeds they were accustomed to, but a chaotic maelstrom of encrypted messages, forum posts, and encrypted file-sharing requests. The legacy communication channels they had exploited, dormant for decades, were now pulsing with an alien urgency, carrying the weight of their carefully curated truth. "It's spreading," she breathed, a mixture of awe and trepidation in her voice. "The data packets are being picked up. I'm seeing echoes of them on unsecured forums, in encrypted chat rooms not under their direct purview. They're not waiting for official channels; they're finding the cracks."

Aris, still reeling from the psychic exertion of masking their transmissions, felt a different kind of pressure now – the subtle, yet unmistakable, ripple of awakening. The alien collective's overwhelming psychic presence hadn't vanished, but it had shifted, a slight redirection of their immense power. They were attempting to contain the leak, to staunch the flow of information, but their methods were inherently clumsy against the very human ingenuity they so readily dismissed. "They're trying to scrub it," Aris reported, his voice raspy. "I can feel their algorithms attempting to locate and delete the packets, but they're being routed through so many obscure nodes, so many layers of antiquated encryption... it's like trying to catch smoke with a sieve. And worse, they're attempting to counter-narratives. I can feel the directives going out, the attempts to discredit the leaked information."

The 'counter-narratives' manifested swiftly, a testament to the aliens' rapid adaptation and their deep integration into human media infrastructure. Official government pronouncements, broadcast across newly secured but still compromised channels, began to portray the leaked data as sophisticated disinformation —a calculated attack by rogue elements or even rival extraterrestrial factions seeking to sow discord. Major news networks, their anchors' eyes betraying a flicker of unease beneath their practiced calm, dutifully repeated the official line, framing the revelations of mind control and compromised leadership as fabrications designed to incite panic.

However, the sheer volume and specificity of the leaked data proved to be a formidable obstacle to their censorship efforts. The detailed logs of General Vorlag's manipulated troop deployments, the undeniable evidence of Minister Sharma's directives to silence critical reporting, and Director Thorne's inexplicable energy diversions to clandestine off-world facilities – these were not easily dismissed as baseless rumors. The data was granular and verifiable through cross-referencing with publicly available, albeit previously overlooked, anomalies.

The initial wave of skepticism, carefully cultivated by the compromised media, began to falter as independent journalists and researchers, operating on the fringes of the digital landscape, started their own investigations. These were the individuals Eva and Aris had hoped to reach, those who still possessed the critical faculties and the courage to question the dominant narrative. They took the leaked data, analyzed it, and began to disseminate their findings through alternative channels – secure

peer-to-peer networks, encrypted messaging apps, and even old-fashioned, analog broadcasts on the fringes of the electromagnetic spectrum.

"The public reaction is... fragmented," Eva observed, her gaze darting between multiple data streams. "On the officially sanctioned channels, there's confusion, a deliberate muddling of facts. But on the independent networks... it's different. I'm seeing outrage building. People are starting to connect the dots, to see the patterns of manipulation. The narrative of 'disinformation' isn't holding for everyone."

Aris felt it too – a growing undercurrent of unease that was quickly morphing into something more potent. The psychic pressure from the alien collective, while still attempting to impose order and control, was encountering a new kind of resistance — not from organized military forces, but from the diffuse yet powerful collective will of an awakened populace. "They're aware of the dissent," Aris stated, his voice strained. "The attempts to suppress are increasing, but so is the curiosity, the desire to know. The more they try to hide it, the more people suspect there's something to hide."

The aliens' initial strategy of outright denial and discredit was proving insufficient. Their control over the primary communication networks allowed them to control the official narrative, but it also made them a visible, easily identifiable target for those seeking the truth. As the independent media outlets amplified the leaked evidence, the carefully constructed façade of normalcy began to show significant cracks.

Citizens, armed with irrefutable proof of manipulation and betrayal, began to question everything. The seemingly benevolent integration efforts, the promises of prosperity and unity, were now viewed through a lens of deep suspicion.

The chaos wasn't just confined to the digital realm. Reports began to surface of civil unrest in several major cities. Spontaneous protests, fueled by the leaked information and the growing distrust in official channels, erupted as citizens demanded transparency and accountability. The compromised leaders, once insulated by the aliens' psychic shielding and their control over information, now found themselves exposed. The very systems they had used to maintain control were now being used to broadcast their complicity.

"This is exactly what we hoped for," Eva said, her eyes alight with a grim satisfaction. "We didn't just leak data; we provided the context, the undeniable proof that allowed people to see the truth for themselves. The aliens underestimated the human capacity for critical thought, even under duress. They assumed their control over information flow was absolute, but they overlooked the resilient network of human connection and the innate desire for truth that thrives in the shadows."

The aliens responded with an increasingly heavy hand. Security forces, many of whom were now being questioned by their own citizens about the veracity of their orders, began to crack down on the burgeoning protests. Public gatherings were dispersed with brutal efficiency, and the communication blackouts in affected areas became more frequent, more prolonged. Yet, these actions, intended to quell dissent, only served to inflame public anger further. The suppression of peaceful protests was undeniable evidence of a cover-up, reinforcing the leaked data and solidifying the populace's resolve.

Aris felt the psychic backlash from the alien collective. Their frustration was a palpable, suffocating wave. They were accustomed to seamless control, to the passive acceptance of their will. The emergence of widespread, vocal dissent, fueled by information they had desperately tried to bury, was a strategic failure of catastrophic proportions. "They're... recalculating," Aris managed, his breath coming in shallow gasps. "Their focus is shifting. They're trying to isolate the sources of the dissent, to sever the communication nodes that are amplifying our message. But it's too widespread now. It's like trying to put out a thousand fires with a single bucket."

The fallout was cascading. The global economy, already strained by the aliens' covert resource reallocations, began to buckle under the weight of public unrest and uncertainty. Stock markets plummeted as investors lost faith in the stability of governments and institutions that were now demonstrably compromised. Supply chains faltered as transportation networks became targets of public anger and sporadic sabotage, not by organized resistance, but by desperate individuals seeking to disrupt the alien-controlled infrastructure.

Eva was meticulously tracking the spread of the information, not just through digital channels, but through the burgeoning human response. "The outrage is organic now," she reported. "It's not just us pushing it; it's people sharing their own discoveries, their own interpretations, their own evidence of alien manipulation in their daily lives. A worker noticing a sudden, inexplicable shift in factory production schedules. A doctor realizing that certain medical protocols were being subtly altered. A scientist finding anomalies in atmospheric data that were previously dismissed. The truth, once released, is like a virus, mutating and spreading through every segment of society."

The aliens' control was designed for an insidious, gradual assimilation, a slow erosion of human autonomy that was meant to be imperceptible. They had not anticipated a sudden, violent awakening, a mass realization that would shatter their meticulously crafted illusion overnight. Their psychic control, while potent, relied on a certain level of passivity and ignorance from the human populace. When that ignorance was violently dispelled, the very mechanisms of their control began to falter.

Aris found himself increasingly attuned to the individual human reactions, a stark contrast to the monolithic consciousness of the aliens. He could feel the fear, yes, but also a burgeoning sense of anger, a determination to reclaim what had been stolen. It was a chaotic symphony of human emotion, a stark counterpoint to the cold, calculated efficiency of their invaders. "The aliens are trying to impose a psychic blanket of calm, of apathy," Aris explained, his eyes unfocused as he navigated the psychic currents. "But it's being overwhelmed by the sheer force of human emotion. They can manipulate minds, but they can't simply erase feelings like fear and anger when they're justified by undeniable evidence."

The compromised media outlets, still under alien control, struggled to maintain their narrative. Their attempts to dismiss the growing public dissent as the work of a fringe minority were increasingly unconvincing. Visual evidence of mass protests, broadcast by independent sources, directly contradicted the official claims of isolated incidents. The very act of suppression, when exposed, became the most potent form of evidence, a tacit admission of guilt.

"We've done it," Eva said, her voice filled with a quiet, profound victory. "We've breached the dam. The truth is out, and it's uncontrollable. They can't put this genie back in the bottle."

The immediate aftermath was a period of intense global upheaval. Governments, riddled with compromised officials, began to fracture. Some leaders, belatedly realising the enormity of the alien deception, attempted to rally their forces against the invaders. Meanwhile, others, deeply embedded in the alien agenda, doubled down on their efforts to maintain control, leading to internal conflicts and widespread governmental collapse. The aliens, accustomed to a unified planetary consciousness to manipulate, found themselves facing a fractured, increasingly hostile human resistance, not just from military remnants, but from the very populace they had sought to control.

Aris felt the alien collective's primal instinct for survival kicking in. Their objective was no longer subtle assimilation; it was now a brutal, confrontation. The psychic pressure shifted again, from probing and containment to outright aggression, a desperate attempt to crush the burgeoning human rebellion before it could gain full momentum. "They're preparing for direct engagement," Aris warned, his voice laced with urgency. "Their focus has shifted from managing the information leak to eliminating the threats. They see us, and the awakened populace, as a direct existential threat now."

The fallout from the leak was far from over. It was, in fact, only the beginning of a new, more desperate phase of the conflict. The carefully laid plans, the meticulous data compilation, the perilous act of disseminating truth through the enemy's own channels – all of it had culminated in this moment. Humanity, no longer blinded by the alien illusion, was stirring. The silence was broken, and the awakening had begun, not with a whisper, but with a roar of collective indignation, fueled by the undeniable truth that had been so deliberately buried. The aliens had made their greatest miscalculation: they had underestimated the power of a truth that refused to stay hidden.

The digital wildfire ignited by the leaked data packets had found fertile ground, not just in the anonymous corners of the net, but within the very institutions the aliens had meticulously infiltrated. The carefully constructed hierarchy, designed to ensure absolute compliance, was proving susceptible to the virus of truth. Within the labyrinthine corridors of the Unified Earth Space Force, the hushed whispers that had once been dismissed as paranoia were now coalescing into a unified roar of dissent.

Captain Eva Rostova, a name that had become synonymous with unwavering loyalty and unparalleled tactical acumen, was no longer a solitary beacon of suspicion. The raw, unvarnished data had acted as a catalyst, unlocking dormant suspicions and emboldening those who had previously operated in the shadows of their own doubts. Her comms channel, once a conduit for sterile mission directives, now pulsed with encrypted messages from individuals who shared her gnawing unease. Fleet Admiral Jian Li, a decorated officer whose career spanned decades of interstellar diplomacy and defense, was among the first to reach out. His message, encrypted with a cipher thought to be unbreakable, contained not a directive, but a simple, poignant question: "What do we do now, Rostova?"

Li's inquiry was a testament to the ripple effect of their operation.

He had spent years subtly observing inconsistencies, the illogical resource diversions, the unexplained anomalies in alien technological integration, all of which had been meticulously explained away by the compromised chain of command. The leaked documents provided the missing pieces, the irrefutable evidence that his instincts had been correct all along. He was not alone. Lieutenant Commander Anya Sharma, a brilliant xenolinguist who had spent years studying the subtle nuances of the alien communication protocols, had also detected discrepancies that defied logical explanation. Her specialized knowledge had been subtly suppressed, her findings relegated to obscure footnotes, all part of the alien effort to control the narrative. The leaked data confirmed her worst fears: the aliens' communication patterns were not simply advanced, but subtly manipulative, designed to lull humanity into a false sense of security.

The intelligence agencies, particularly the Office of Covert Operations (OCO), were also experiencing seismic shifts. Director Thorne's desperate attempts to suppress the data were inadvertently highlighting its veracity. The internal investigations, initiated by Thorne himself to hunt down the source of the leak, were now being turned inward. Agents who had always prided themselves on their ability to sniff out deception found themselves questioning their own leaders. Marcus Vance, a seasoned operative known for his uncanny ability to read between the lines of intercepted communications, had spent weeks dissecting the leaked financial records. He discovered a disturbing pattern of offshore accounts and shell corporations, all funneling vast sums of untraceable currency into projects that were ostensibly for planetary defense but bore the hallmarks of alien technology development. His clandestine investigation revealed that Thorne had been systematically diverting resources away from critical defense sectors and into projects that served only the alien agenda. Vance, operating under extreme duress, managed to transmit his findings to a trusted network of independent journalists, further amplifying the truth.

But the awakening was not confined to the halls of power or the clandestine realms of intelligence. Ordinary citizens, those who had felt the subtle but persistent erosion of their autonomy, were also finding their voices. Sarah Jenkins, a systems analyst for a major terraforming corporation, had noticed inexplicable alterations in atmospheric processing data, subtle shifts that her superiors had dismissed as minor calibration errors. The leaked reports detailing the aliens' long-term terraforming plans, designed to subtly alter Earth's atmosphere to suit their own needs better, resonated deeply with her. She began reaching out to colleagues who shared her concerns, forming a clandestine network of scientists and technicians who possessed the knowledge to identify and expose the alien manipulation of Earth's environment. Her group, initially just a handful of worried individuals sharing data over encrypted channels, quickly grew into a significant underground network, providing tangible proof of the aliens' environmental sabotage.

These disparate pockets of resistance, operating independently but driven by a shared sense of urgency, began to coalesce. The decentralized nature of their communication, a direct consequence of the aliens' pervasive surveillance, paradoxically became their greatest strength. They were not a single, easily decapitated entity, but a hydra-headed insurgency, each head capable of regenerating and striking with renewed ferocity. Eva found herself at the nexus of this burgeoning resistance. Her reputation for integrity and her willingness to challenge the status quo had made her a natural focal point for those seeking to resist.

"They're more than just compromised officials, Aris," Eva relayed, her voice a low, urgent whisper into her secure comms unit. "There are people within the Space Force, within OCO, even within the planetary defense grids, who are starting to act. They're not waiting for orders; they're using the information to initiate their own quiet rebellions. Admiral Lima has begun subtly rerouting critical supply lines, ensuring that key personnel have access to secure communication channels. Agent Vance's data has already begun circulating through independent news feeds, providing concrete evidence of Thorne's treason."

Aris, his psychic senses still reeling from the continuous efforts to suppress the truth, felt the tremors of this growing human defiance. He could feel the surge of hope, the spark of defiance igniting in millions of minds. It was a nascent energy, uncoordinated but potent, a direct counterpoint to the aliens' sterile, calculated control. "I can feel it too, Eva," he replied, his voice strained. "The psychic pressure from the collective is intensifying. They're aware of this internal dissent. They're trying to isolate these individuals, to shut them down before they can spread. Thorne is undoubtedly activating his loyalists within the command structure. Be careful. They will be looking for you."

The immediate aftermath of the data leak saw Thorne's administration scrambling to regain control. Public pronouncements were issued, denouncing the leaked documents as elaborate fabrications, the work of rogue elements seeking to destabilize global unity. Security forces were deployed to quell the burgeoning protests, and communication blackouts were implemented in areas with the highest concentrations of dissent. However, these actions, intended to restore order, only served to validate the leaked information further. The heavy-handed suppression of peaceful demonstrations was broadcast in stark detail by the independent media outlets, painting a clear picture of a desperate regime attempting to silence its populace.

Within the Space Force, the loyalist elements, under Thorne's direction, initiated a swift and brutal purge. Officers suspected of harboring doubts or expressing dissent were apprehended, their careers abruptly ended, and their communications were monitored with increased scrutiny. Admiral Lima found himself under intense surveillance, his movements restricted, his access to sensitive information curtailed. Yet, even under such intense pressure, Li managed to maintain a semblance of operational autonomy. He had established a series of dead drops and encrypted relays, ensuring that the few remaining loyal officers had a secure channel to communicate and coordinate. His actions were subtle, designed to avoid confrontation while still undermining the alien-controlled command structure. He began to implement a series of "routine" maintenance protocols that, unbeknownst to Thorne, served to compartmentalize critical defense systems, making it harder for the aliens to access or control them directly.

Similarly, Agent Vance's network of OCO operatives was being systematically dismantled from within. Thorne, with his intimate knowledge of the agency's protocols, was able to identify and neutralize many of Vance's allies. However, Vance had anticipated this, having cultivated a core group of operatives who operated outside the official OCO structure, relying on their own independent communication networks and loyalty to the principles of truth and justice rather than institutional authority. This inner circle, fueled by Vance's damning evidence of Thorne's complicity, began to systematically feed information to the independent media, ensuring that the narrative of alien deception continued to gain traction, even as Thorne's efforts to suppress it intensified.

Eva, meanwhile, was working from the shadows, her own official channels compromised. She leveraged her deep understanding of the Space Force's hidden infrastructure, using abandoned comms relays and outdated data conduits that the aliens had deemed too obsolete to monitor effectively. She was in constant contact with Li and Vance, coordinating their efforts and ensuring that the disparate resistance cells remained connected. Her primary objective was to provide a secure platform for communication and data sharing, a digital sanctuary where the truth could flourish unhindered.

One of the most significant developments was the emergence of unexpected allies within the very systems the aliens controlled. Dr. Aris Thorne, a leading astrophysicist and, ironically, the Director's own nephew, had initially been a staunch defender of the alien integration program, genuinely believing in their benevolent intentions.

However, his research into anomalous energy signatures emanating from the newly established off-world facilities had led him down a path of profound disillusionment. The data he had collected, detailing massive energy transfers to unexplained celestial bodies, contradicted every official explanation. When he stumbled upon the leaked documents, specifically those detailing Director Thorne's clandestine dealings and the systematic suppression of scientific dissent, his world shattered.

He reached out to Eva, not through official channels, but through a deeply buried, unsecured university server that he knew had been overlooked by the OCO's sophisticated surveillance systems. His message was desperate, filled with a scientist's cold, complex logic and a nephew's dawning horror. "Captain Rostova," his message read, "I have been working on the anomalous energy signatures from Sector Gamma. The data points to an energy drain far exceeding anything necessary for planetary defense or even standard interspecies exchange. The leaked reports… they align with my findings in ways that are deeply disturbing. Director Thorne has been actively suppressing dissenting scientific findings, including my own. I believe I have proof of their ultimate objective, something far more terrifying than mere infiltration."

Aris Thorne's contribution was invaluable. His access to the high-level scientific data, particularly concerning the alien's terraforming technology and their actual energy requirements, provided a crucial missing piece of the puzzle. He revealed that the aliens were not merely integrating; they were actively preparing Earth for a wholesale transformation, a process that would render it uninhabitable for humans in its current form. The terraforming was not an enhancement, but a prelude to a complete ecological overhaul, designed to suit alien physiology. This revelation, disseminated through Eva's network to the independent media, further galvanized public opinion, turning passive concern into active resistance.

The formation of these ad-hoc resistance groups was a testament to human resilience and the innate desire for self-preservation. In cities across the globe, citizens began to organize. Local cells, comprised of former military personnel, disillusioned scientists, investigative journalists, and ordinary individuals who had had enough, began to share information, develop counter-strategies, and identify vulnerabilities in the alien-controlled infrastructure. They scavenged for weapons, repurposed old communication equipment, and created new methods of evading alien surveillance. The spirit of defiance was spreading like a contagion, far more potent and resilient than any digital virus.

Eva found herself coordinating a diverse coalition, a network of individuals united by a common enemy but with vastly different skill sets and motivations. Admiral Lima was orchestrating a quiet insurgency within the Space Force, ensuring that critical assets remained under human control and that loyal personnel were protected. Agent Vance was feeding a steady stream of damning evidence to the independent media, keeping the public informed and fueling the flames of dissent. Dr. Aris Thorne was providing critical scientific data, exposing the true scope of the alien's devastating plans. And Eva, the reluctant commander, was holding it all together, a linchpin in a global awakening.

The aliens, accustomed to a planet that had accepted mainly their presence with passive gratitude, were beginning to realize the magnitude of their miscalculation. They had underestimated the power of truth, the resilience of the human spirit, and the inherent human drive to protect one's home. Their attempts to control the narrative through censorship and misinformation were backfiring, each act of suppression only solidifying the resolve of those who sought to expose them. The uncompromised had risen, not as a unified army, but as a decentralized, highly motivated resistance, and humanity's awakening was far from over. It was a fragile beginning, fraught with peril, but for the first time in what felt like an eternity, there was a tangible sense of hope, a belief that Earth might yet be saved from the insidious clutches of its interstellar guests. The intricate web of deception was beginning to fray, and the truth, once unleashed, was proving to be an unstoppable force.

The digital contagion had morphed into a tangible resistance, a network of disillusioned minds and loyal hearts, coalescing around Eva and Aris. Their clandestine operations were no longer theoretical discussions; they were meticulously planned incursions into the very heart of the alien's human infrastructure. The leaked data, a beacon in the fog of deception, had illuminated not just the alien agenda, but the complicit humans who served as its willing — or unwilling — conduits. Aris's specialized scanners, once used to decipher alien transmissions, were now repurposed, their sensitive matrices tuned to the faint, almost imperceptible psychic resonance of alien directives, a tell-tale sign of a compromised human mind. Eva, with her intimate knowledge of the Unified Earth Space Force's operational protocols and security blind spots, provided the tactical framework, the precise vectors of approach and extraction that minimized risk and maximized efficiency.

Their first target was a mid-level administrator in the Unified Earth Space Force's logistics division, a man named Director Valerius. Valerius had been instrumental in rerouting vital resources, diverting matériel and personnel to alien-controlled facilities under the guise of "interstellar cooperation." Eva had known him casually for years – a quiet, efficient officer, seemingly dedicated to his duty. The thought of confronting him, of exposing him as a puppet, gnawed at her. But the data was irrefutable: Valerius's neural patterns, as displayed on Aris's scanner, pulsed with the alien's directive frequency, a constant hum of control overlaid with his own fading consciousness.

"He's deep within the network," Aris murmured, his brow furrowed as he analyzed the readings on his wrist-mounted display. "The alien signal is integrated directly into his cognitive functions. It's not just a broadcast; it's a part of him."

Their plan was simple, surgical. They would infiltrate the Starbase Aegis's administrative sector during a scheduled system-wide diagnostic, a brief window where security protocols were marginally relaxed. Eva, disguised as a maintenance technician, would gain access to Valerius's private office. Aris, positioned in a nearby service conduit, would use a targeted electromagnetic pulse device, calibrated to disrupt the alien's signal without causing permanent neural damage, effectively severing Valerius's connection to the alien collective.

The infiltration was a tense ballet of calculated movements and feigned indifference. Eva navigated the sterile, metallic corridors, her heart thrumming a nervous rhythm against her ribs. She passed by faces she recognized, officers she had served with, each a potential witness, a potential threat. The weight of their deception, the knowledge that so many around them were unknowingly serving an alien agenda, was a suffocating burden. She reached Valerius's office, the door hissing open at her authorized access code. The room was precisely as she expected: neat, orderly, devoid of any personal touch, a reflection of the man himself, or what remained of him. Valerius sat at his desk, staring blankly at a holographic display, his eyes vacant, a subtle tic flickering at the corner of his jaw.

"Director Valerius?" Eva's voice was carefully neutral, masking the turmoil within. Valerius turned slowly, his gaze unfocused. "Yes? Do I know you?"

"Just a technician performing a routine system check, sir," Eva replied, stepping further into the office. "We're experiencing some minor network anomalies. Nothing to worry about." She activated a small diagnostic tool, its lights blinking innocently, while subtly positioning herself to block his direct line of sight to the door.

"Anomalies?" Valerius's voice was flat, devoid of curiosity.

At that moment, Aris initiated the pulse. A faint hum, imperceptible to the human ear, resonated through the office. Valerius flinched, his hand flying to his temple. His vacant expression flickered, replaced by a brief, agonizing moment of confusion, then pain. He gasped, his eyes widening as if waking from a long, suffocating dream.

"What... what was that?" he stammered, looking around wildly.

His gaze landed on Eva, and for the first time, a spark of recognition, of awareness, flickered in his eyes. "Captain Rostova?"

"It's alright, Director," Eva said, stepping forward, her hand outstretched. "You're free now."

Valerius's body slumped in his chair, relief washing over his face, quickly followed by a profound horror. "Free? What have... what have I done?" Tears welled in his eyes as fragmented memories, the alien commands, the diverted shipments, the compromised security protocols, began to flood back. "The supplies... the troop movements... I... I sent them..." He trailed off, burying his face in his hands, overwhelmed by the magnitude of his unwitting complicity.

Eva knelt beside him, her own emotions a complex knot of pity and grim determination. "It wasn't your fault, Director. You were manipulated. Now, we need to help you."

The successful extraction of Valerius was a crucial victory, a testament to their burgeoning capabilities. He became a vital, albeit fragile, asset, providing invaluable intelligence on the internal workings of the Space Force's compromised sections. But their mission was far from over. The network of compromised individuals was extensive, a web spun across every branch of human governance and defense.

Their next target was a senior analyst within the Office of Covert Operations, a man named Marcus Thorne – no relation to Director Thorne, a fact that added a layer of dark irony to the situation. Thorne was a master of information control, tasked with actively suppressing any data that threatened the alien narrative. He was a key node, filtering and sanitizing intelligence, ensuring that only the approved version of reality reached the higher echelons of power.

"Thorne is a different kind of threat," Aris explained, reviewing the complex data streams. "A constant signal does not directly control him, but by targeted directives, almost like a remote access program. He's intelligent, resourceful, and utterly loyal to the alien's manufactured truth."

The OCO headquarters was a fortress, a labyrinth of biometric scanners and omnipresent surveillance. Infiltrating it directly was a suicide mission. Instead, Eva and Aris opted for a more indirect approach, leveraging a disgruntled former OCO operative, a man named Jax, who had been scapegoated and disgraced by Thorne for uncovering certain inconvenient truths. Jax, fueled by a potent mix of anger and a desire for vindication, agreed to help.

Their plan involved intercepting Thorne during a rare off-site meeting, a clandestine rendezvous to exchange sensitive information with another compromised official. Eva and Jax would create a diversion, drawing security away. At the same time, Aris, using his refined scanners, would locate Thorne and deploy a localized EMP tailored to disrupt the specific alien frequency Thorne was receiving.

The rendezvous point was a derelict space station on the fringes of orbital security. The atmosphere was thick with decay and the scent of ozone. Eva and Jax, disguised as salvagers, moved through the station's darkened corridors, their comms crackling with hushed updates. Thorne arrived with two burly security details, their movements efficient and predatory.

"He's here," Eva whispered into her comms. "Jax, prepare for the diversion."

Jax triggered a cascade of automated alarms throughout the station, a cacophony of klaxons and flashing emergency lights. The security details reacted instantly, their attention drawn away from Thorne. In the ensuing chaos, Aris, cloaked in thermal-dampening material, moved with preternatural speed towards Thorne's position.

Thorne, momentarily disoriented by the alarms, was reaching for his personal communication device. Aris was just meters away when Thorne's head snapped up, his eyes – sharp and unnervingly aware – locking onto Aris's position. He hadn't been thoroughly compromised by a constant signal; he had detected the intrusion.

"Who are you?" Thorne barked, his voice amplified by a tactical vocoder.

Aris didn't reply, raising his EMP device. Thorne, however, was faster than anticipated. He produced a compact energy weapon, its barrel glowing with contained plasma. A searing bolt of energy whizzed past Aris's head, impacting the metal wall with a shower of sparks.

"You won't stop this, whatever 'this' is," Thorne snarled, advancing.

Eva and Jax, hearing the exchange, raced towards Thorne's location. Eva drew her sidearm, her training kicking in. Jax, surprisingly agile for his bulk, tackled one of Thorne's security guards.

Aris, dodging another energy blast, managed to get close enough. He activated the EMP. Thorne staggered backward, clutching his head. The glow from his weapon flickered and died. His eyes rolled back, and he collapsed, unconscious but alive. Eva and Jax quickly subdued the remaining guard and secured Thorne.

As Aris ran a scan on Thorne, a grim expression settled on his face. "He's still transmitting," Aris reported, his voice tight with frustration. "The EMP disrupted his primary receiver, but he has a secondary, internal implant. It's deeply embedded."

This was the harsh reality of their mission. The aliens had designed their control mechanisms with layers of redundancy, making complete severance a complex and dangerous undertaking. They couldn't simply disable the conduits; they had to dismantle the infrastructure that supported them.

The data Thorne possessed was critical. He held the access keys to numerous hidden OCO databanks, repositories of suppressed information that could expose the extent of the alien's infiltration and their human collaborators. Eva knew they couldn't afford to lose him, or the knowledge he represented.

"We need to isolate him," Eva decided, her gaze fixed on the unconscious analyst. "Get him to a secure location where Aris can work on the implant without interference.

We need that information."

Their mission had become a brutal game of chess, each move fraught with peril, each compromised individual a pawn to be either neutralized or redeployed. The faces of those they confronted – former colleagues, respected superiors, even those who had once been their friends – blurred into a gallery of the possessed. The ethical calculus was a constant, agonizing burden. Was it truly neutralization if it meant erasing a person's free will? Was it justice to disable someone, even if they were a tool of alien oppression?

Aris, wrestling with his own conscience, found himself pushing the boundaries of his scientific understanding. He was developing new methods, not just to disrupt, but to cleanse, to isolate the alien influence without destroying the human host. It was a delicate process, fraught with uncertainty.

"The problem, Eva," Aris explained during a hushed debrief in their hidden mobile command center, "is that the alien neural interface is incredibly sophisticated. It's not just a simple signal injection. It's an integration, a co-opting of the host's own neural pathways. To obliterate it without causing catastrophic neurological damage... it's like performing surgery on a ghost."

Their efforts were met with increasing resistance from the alien-controlled elements of the human government. Director Thorne, sensing the growing threat, accelerated his efforts to purge any suspected dissidents. Security sweeps became more frequent, surveillance grids were reinforced, and any deviation from established protocols was met with swift and brutal reprisal. Admiral Lima, working from within the Space Force, found his own movements increasingly restricted, his communications monitored with an almost suffocating intensity. He was forced to rely on increasingly antiquated and less secure communication methods, risking exposure with every message sent.

"They're tightening the noose," Li transmitted, his voice a low, raspy whisper over a short-range, heavily encrypted burst. "Thorne is consolidating his power. He's identified several key individuals within the fleet who were beginning to question the directives. They've been... reassigned. Permanently."

Eva understood the gravity of Li's report. Each compromised individual they dealt with was a piece of the puzzle, a step towards reclaiming humanity's autonomy. But the aliens were equally adept at playing the long game, at leveraging their human assets to maintain control. Their operations had to be swift, precise, and above all, clandestine. The awakening was gaining momentum, but it was a fragile force, constantly under siege by the very institutions that were supposed to protect humanity. The path ahead was a perilous one, paved with difficult choices and the ghosts of past allegiances.

The weight of Valerius's confession, the fractured memories of his unwitting actions, hung heavy in the sterile confines of their mobile command center. He was a testament to the insidious nature of the alien's grip, a man of diligence and duty twisted into an unwitting instrument of subjugation. Eva watched him, his face etched with a profound, dawning horror, as fragmented directives, alien whispers now coalesced into undeniable actions, replayed in his mind. Aris's expertise had been invaluable, not just in disabling the external signal but in the painstaking, delicate work of untangling the alien's imprint from Valerius's very being. It was a process that demanded not only technical skill but a deep understanding of neurology, a field Aris had found himself delving into with an almost obsessive fervor, driven by the desperate need to save rather than disable.

"It's not enough to just cut the wires," Aris had explained earlier, his voice low as he meticulously adjusted the delicate calibration of a neural recalibrator. "They've woven themselves into the very fabric of our minds. We need to unravel them, thread by painstaking thread, without severing the host." He had been working on Thorne's case, the analyst's internal implant proving a far more intricate challenge. Thorne, unlike Valerius, hadn't been a passive receiver of constant directives. His mind had been a more active participant, his own intellect bent and twisted to serve the alien agenda, making the severance even more perilous.

The successful disruption of Thorne's secondary implant had been a hard-won victory, albeit one that came with its own set of complex ramifications. Thorne, once awakened, proved to be a volatile asset. The shock of his realization, the abrupt cessation of the alien influence he had so readily accepted, had plunged him into a psychological abyss. He oscillated between periods of abject despair and sudden, terrifying bursts of lucidity, during which he would reel off reams of critical data, only to collapse again into a catatonic state. Eva and Aris found themselves not just as liberators but as reluctant custodians of shattered minds, responsible for the fragile remnants of consciousness they were trying to restore.

Admiral Lima's clandestine transmissions continued to paint a grim picture of the unfolding situation. Thorne's purge within the OCO had been swift and brutal, silencing not just suspected dissidents but also many of the few remaining individuals who might have been sympathetic to their cause. Li himself was operating under increasingly severe constraints, his communications monitored to an extent that made even the most rudimentary exchanges a high-stakes gamble. He spoke of escalating surveillance, of a chilling efficiency in the alien-controlled bureaucracy that was slowly but surely strangling any semblance of independent thought or action. Each report was a stark reminder of the ticking clock, the narrowing window of opportunity.

"They are adapting," Li's latest message crackled through their secure comms, the distortion in his voice a testament to the layers of encryption and counter-intelligence he was navigating. "Thorne's actions are not just reactive. They are preemptive. He's identified potential choke points in the logistical chain, areas where disruption could have maximum impact. He's also… accelerating the integration in certain key sectors. They're pushing for full assimilation, Eva, and they're doing it faster than we anticipated."

This escalation was precisely what Aris had warned about. The aliens weren't merely seeking to control humanity; they were aiming for a complete symbiosis, a merging of consciousness that would render human identity obsolete. Their ultimate objective, the tantalizingly vague but undeniably critical nexus of alien influence, was becoming clearer. Aris's deep-scan analysis of the fragmented data recovered from Valerius and Thorne, coupled with the increasingly desperate pronouncements from Admiral Lima, was converging on a single, terrifying hypothesis: the aliens were not just controlling humanity; they were preparing for a fundamental shift, a transference of their own essence, using Earth as a … bridge.

"The energy signatures are too consistent, too powerful to be," Aris mused, his fingers flying across a holographic interface, projecting complex energy wave patterns that defied conventional understanding, "simply a distributed network. There has to be a central node, a primary conduit through which they are channeling their power, their directives, their very… existence." His voice was a low hum of intellectual pursuit, underscored by a gnawing urgency. The fragments of information suggested a massive, hidden energy source, a locus of alien power that underpinned their entire operation.

Their intelligence, painstakingly pieced together from intercepted alien communications, from the whispered confessions of the newly awakened, and from Li's increasingly risky reconnaissance missions, pointed towards a specific location. It was a vast, subterranean research facility, nestled deep within the desolate polar ice caps of a former research outpost. This place had been quietly decommissioned decades ago and supposedly abandoned. Yet, residual energy readings, faint but persistent, suggested otherwise. This facility, shrouded in secrecy and protected by layers of sophisticated alien technology, was believed to be the original site of the first transdimensional portal's manifestation – the very point of entry for the alien consciousness that now held humanity captive.

"This isn't just about severing connections anymore," Eva stated, her gaze fixed on the holographic projection of the remote facility. The sheer scale of it, even in schematic form, was intimidating. Alien technology, unlike anything human engineers could conceive, formed the outer shell, a seamless integration of organic and synthetic materials that pulsed with an unidentifiable energy. "If Aris is right, and I believe he is, this is the primary conduit. The main nexus. Cutting this off… it's the only way to sever their grip truly."

The prospect was daunting, a mission of almost suicidal ambition. The facility was known to be heavily guarded, not just by automated defense systems of alien design but by the very humans who had willingly, or unwillingly, become extensions of the alien will. These were not the loosely controlled individuals they had been encountering; these were the deeply integrated, the zealous converts, the human enforcers of the alien agenda.

"We're talking about a direct assault on their central command," Aris said, his usual analytical detachment replaced by a grim pragmatism. "If this is indeed the primary conduit, the energy source powering the entire network, it will be defended with everything they have. Our current assets, our small team… it's like bringing a knife to a plasma storm."

"We don't have another choice, Aris," Eva countered, her voice firm, though a tremor of apprehension ran beneath it. "Every day we delay, they get stronger. They integrate further. Thorne's reports about accelerated assimilation, about pushing for full symbiosis… that's the endgame. If they achieve that, humanity ceases to exist as we know it. We become another species absorbed into their collective, another conquered world." She gestured towards the holographic projection of the facility. "This is where it all began. It's where we have to end it."

Their strategy had to be audacious, a precision strike designed to disable the conduit before the aliens could fully react or retreat, to sever the lifeline that sustained their dominion over Earth. They couldn't afford a prolonged engagement; their success hinged on swift, decisive action. Their intelligence indicated that the facility's primary defenses were geared towards preventing entry and exit, with less emphasis on internal disruption once access was gained. This was their sliver of opportunity.

Admiral Lima, despite his increasingly precarious position, had managed to secure crucial, albeit fragmented, blueprints of the facility's original human-designed infrastructure. This archaic data, buried deep within forgotten archives, provided a faint glimmer of the layout before the aliens had overlaid it with their own inscrutable technology. It was a ghost of what the facility once was, a testament to humanity's own prior endeavors, now co-opted and twisted for an alien purpose.

"The original access tunnels," Li had transmitted, his voice a barely audible whisper through a highly compressed, one-time use burst transmission, "they were designed for geological surveying, for accessing deep core samples. If the alien integration wasn't absolute, if they prioritized external containment over internal redundancy, those tunnels might still be viable entry points. They'll be sealed, heavily reinforced, but they represent the only known path that wasn't designed from the ground up with alien oversight."

The plan began to coalesce, a desperate gambit built on the foundations of Li's intel and Aris's technological prowess. They would need to infiltrate the facility through these ancient, forgotten tunnels, a journey through the Earth's crust that would be arduous and fraught with peril. Aris would need to develop a specialized device, something far more potent than the localized EMPs they had used before – a temporal disruptor, capable of creating a localized tear in the fabric of space-time, effectively severing the primary conduit at its source without causing a catastrophic, uncontrolled release of alien energy.

"A temporal disruptor," Aris had mused, his eyes alight with a mixture of scientific fascination and grim apprehension. "It's theoretical, Eva. We've only ever simulated it. The energy requirements alone are astronomical, and the precision needed to target a transdimensional nexus... it's like trying to thread a needle in a hurricane."

"But if it works," Eva pressed, her voice laced with the hope that had sustained them through so many nights, "it would sever the connection. Permanently. It would be the final blow."

The journey to the polar region was a covert operation of the highest order. They utilized a modified deep-space scout vessel, equipped with advanced cloaking technology and stealth propulsion systems, designed to avoid detection by both orbital surveillance and the alien-controlled atmospheric monitoring grids. The descent through the planet's crust was a harrowing experience, the scout ship groaning under the immense pressure, its hull vibrating with the strain. Aris, guided by Li's salvaged schematics and his own real-time scans, navigated them through a labyrinth of ancient geological formations, the air growing thicker, the silence deeper, the only sounds the hum of their ship and the frantic beating of their own hearts.

They finally breached the outer layers of the facility, not through a conventional entrance, but through a cleverly disguised service conduit that Aris had identified as a remnant of the original human construction. The air inside was unnaturally still, carrying a faint, metallic tang that prickled the nostrils. The alien technology was immediately apparent, not as a stark imposition, but as an organic integration, like veins of a foreign substance pulsing within the bones of human architecture. Walls shimmered with an internal light, and conduits carrying unknown energies pulsed with a rhythm that was both mesmerizing and deeply unsettling.

"The primary conduit is deep within," Aris reported, his scanners painting a detailed, albeit terrifying, picture of the facility's internal structure. "It's located at the core, a massive nexus of... something. The energy readings are off the charts. It's like staring into the heart of a black hole, but alive." He pointed to a central chamber depicted on his display, a vast, cavernous space at the very heart of the facility. "That's our target."

Their advance through the facility was a ballet of stealth and precision. They moved through dimly lit corridors, their every step calculated to avoid triggering any of the subtle alien security measures. They encountered few human guards; the alien's control was so pervasive that direct human intervention seemed almost unnecessary in many areas. Instead, the facility was populated by automated drones, their metallic bodies sleek and alien, moving with an unnerving silence. Aris employed a series of counter-frequency emitters, creating localized blind spots in the drones' sensor grids, allowing them to pass undetected.

As they neared the central chamber, the ambient energy levels began to spike, the air itself seeming to thrum with a palpable force. Eva felt a growing pressure in her mind, a subtle attempt at intrusion, a whisper of alien thoughts attempting to worm their way into her consciousness. She focused on her training, on the mental barriers she had painstakingly erected, clinging to the faces of those she fought for, the vision of a free humanity.

They reached the entrance to the core chamber. It was a colossal aperture, a gateway into a space that defied terrestrial understanding. The walls pulsed with a blinding, internal light, and at the center of the chamber, suspended in a field of pure, uncontained energy, was the conduit. It was not a physical object in the traditional sense, but a shimmering, iridescent vortex, a tear in the fabric of reality through which torrents of alien energy flowed, cascading into the facility and, they suspected, into Earth's own neural network. The sheer power emanating from it was staggering, an overwhelming force that threatened to tear their very atoms apart.

"That's it," Aris breathed, his voice barely a whisper, awestruck and terrified. "The primary conduit. The source." He began to deploy the temporal disruptor, a complex array of crystalline emitters and graviton emitters, its construction a testament to his genius and desperation. The device whirred to life, emitting a low, resonant hum that began to fight against the overwhelming energy of the conduit.

Suddenly, the chamber was flooded with a blinding white light. The automated drones, previously passive, sprang to life, their optical sensors glowing with an aggressive red light. From the periphery of the chamber, figures began to emerge – not drones, but humans. They were clad in advanced environmental suits, their faces obscured by opaque visors, but their movements were sharp, precise, and utterly devoid of human hesitation. These were the true enforcers, the deeply assimilated, their minds inextricably bound to the alien will.

"They've been alerted," Eva said, drawing her sidearm. "Aris, you have to finish it. I'll buy you time." She moved to intercept the approaching figures, her movements fluid and practiced, the instinct to protect born of years of service and a fierce love for humanity. The fight was brutal and swift. The enforcers were powerful, their movements augmented by alien technology, but Eva was fighting with a purpose that transcended mere survival. She fought for a future, for the very soul of her species.

Aris, meanwhile, was locked in a desperate race against time. The temporal disruptor was generating a localized field, a bubble of temporal distortion that was slowly, agonizingly, beginning to unravel the conduit. The energy readings were fluctuating wildly, the conduit resisting the disruption with immense force. Aris's hands were slick with sweat as he made minute adjustments, the fate of Earth hanging precariously on his every input.

The alien collective, sensing the threat to its primary nexus, retaliated with a ferocity that shook the very foundations of the facility. The chamber walls pulsed violently, and a wave of psychic energy washed over them, attempting to break down their defenses, to crush their resolve. Eva felt a crushing weight descend upon her mind, a torrent of alien commands and despair. She gritted her teeth, focusing on the image of a clear, star-filled sky, a symbol of the freedom they were fighting to reclaim.

One of the enforcers managed to breach Eva's defenses, his augmented fist slamming into her side, knocking the wind out of her. She staggered, her vision blurring, but she refused to fall. Aris, witnessing her struggle, made a split-second decision. He rerouted a portion of the disruptor's energy, a dangerous maneuver that could destabilize the entire operation, towards a localized EMP burst aimed at the enforcer threatening Eva. The enforcer spasmed, his movements becoming erratic, and Eva seized the opportunity, disarming him and incapacitating him with a well-placed stun blast.

"Almost there, Eva!" Aris yelled, his voice strained. "The conduit is destabilizing, but it's fighting back!"

The shimmering vortex of the conduit began to flicker, its iridescent hues shifting erratically. Cracks, like fissures in reality itself, began to appear around its edges. The alien psychic assault intensified, a desperate, final attempt to crush their will. Eva felt her own consciousness fraying, the whispers of the alien collective becoming louder, more insistent, offering promises of peace, of unity, of an end to suffering, if only she would yield.

"Never," she gasped, her voice a raw, ragged sound. She pushed past her pain, past the mental onslaught, and lunged towards Aris and the disruptor. She needed to ensure its activation, to bear witness to its final, world-altering function.

With a final, deafening roar of released energy, the temporal disruptor reached its critical phase. The conduit imploded, not with an explosion, but with a silent, terrifying implosion, drawing all of its aberrant energy back into itself, leaving behind a void, a wound in reality that slowly began to mend, sealing itself off from the human world. The psychic assault ceased abruptly, leaving an unnatural silence in its wake.

The pulsing lights of the facility died down, the humming energy faded, and the drones slumped, inert. The enforcers, their connection severed, collapsed, their advanced suits inert as their minds returned to a state of stunned, bewildered consciousness.

The silence that followed was profound, almost deafening. Eva knelt beside Aris, both of them catching their breath, their bodies aching, their minds reeling. The conduit was gone. The primary connection had been severed. A wave of exhaustion, of profound relief, washed over them. They had done it. They had taken the fight to the heart of the alien dominion and emerged victorious. But the victory was not without its cost. The facility was a tomb of inert technology, a monument to a species'

near-annihilation. The task of piecing together the shattered remnants of humanity, of guiding them through the long, arduous process of rebuilding, was only beginning. The awakening had occurred, but the actual work of humanity's resurgence had just started.

The silence that descended upon the polar facility was a stark, almost deafening contrast to the maelstrom that had preceded it. The colossal chamber, once alive with the alien nexus's vibrant, terrifying energy, was now eerily still, the only illumination emanating from Eva's tactical lights and Aris's diagnostic readouts. The temporal disruptor, its purpose fulfilled, hummed a low, dying note, its crystalline components now dark and inert. The void where the conduit had been was a wound in reality that was slowly, painstakingly, knitting itself shut, leaving behind only a faint, shimmering distortion, a phantom limb of alien power.

Eva watched as the enforcers, their advanced suits suddenly inert, collapsed in heaps. Their visors, once opaque barriers, now seemed to reflect only the dawning realization of their own severed connection. Some stirred weakly, their movements sluggish, their eyes, now visible through cracked visors, wide with a confusion that bordered on terror. Aris, his face smudged with grime and sweat, but alight with a fierce, weary triumph, tended to the temporal disruptor, his fingers moving with practiced precision to secure the device. He had faced down the impossible, and he had prevailed.

"It's done," Aris breathed, his voice raspy. "The primary conduit is severed. The link... it's broken."

A profound exhaustion settled over Eva, a bone-deep weariness that went beyond mere physical fatigue. It was the weight of what they had achieved, the sheer immensity of their act, pressing down on her. For so long, humanity had been a passive victim, a pawn in a cosmic game it didn't understand. Now, for the first time since the alien influence had taken hold, there was a flicker of genuine hope, a chance to reclaim what had been stolen.

"What about them?" Eva asked, nodding towards the dazed enforcers. Their human forms, stripped of the alien augmentation and control, seemed pathetically vulnerable.

Aris scanned one of them, his diagnostic tools whirring softly. "Their minds are... scrambled. The sudden severance has caused significant neural shock. They'll need intensive care, rehabilitation. Some may never fully recover, their neural pathways too deeply imprinted." He sighed, a heavy sound in the cavernous chamber. "But they're human again. Or at least, they have the chance to be."

The implications of their mission began to unfurl, vast and complex. The primary conduit was the heart of the alien network, the source of its power and its pervasive influence. Its severance meant that the insidious whispers, the subtle directives, the very hum of alien consciousness that had permeated Earth, had been silenced, at least from this central, overarching source. But the aliens had been on Earth for years, their presence a creeping, insidious infestation. They had integrated into society, into technology, into the very fabric of human thought. Thorne's accelerated assimilation, Valerius's fragmented memories – these were testaments to the depth of their infiltration.

"This isn't the end, Aris," Eva stated, her gaze sweeping across the silent chamber, a quiet testament to humanity's near-annihilation. "It's just the beginning."

Aris met her gaze, a flicker of understanding in his weary eyes. "I know. We've severed the head of the snake, but the body is still alive. There are other nodes, other pockets of influence. And the aliens themselves... they're still out there. We've only bought ourselves time."

Their escape from the facility was a grim affair. They moved through the

now-dormant corridors, the alien technology inert, the automated drones lifeless husks. The journey back to their hidden base was a silent testament to the enormity of the task ahead. They had achieved the impossible, but the scars of the alien occupation ran deep, both on the planet and within its inhabitants.

Back in their mobile command center, the sterile confines felt both familiar and alien. The hum of their systems, once a comforting sound of their clandestine operation, now seemed a fragile shield against the vast, unknown forces that still lurked. Aris, ever the pragmatist, immediately began analyzing the residual energy signatures, searching for any lingering traces of the alien network, any indication of new patterns or emergent threats. Eva, meanwhile, initiated a secure, encrypted channel to Admiral Lima, her heart pounding with a mixture of trepidation and anticipation.

Li's response was almost instantaneous, his voice a low, raspy murmur through the comms. "Report."

"The primary conduit is severed, Admiral," Eva replied, her voice steady despite the tremor of emotion. "We struck at the core. The main link is broken."

A palpable silence stretched across the comms, heavy with unspoken questions and a cautious, fragile hope. Then, Li's voice returned, tinged with an almost disbelieving awe. "Severed? Truly severed? This is... this is beyond what we dared to hope for."

"It's a start," Eva conceded. "But the network is still fragmented, still present in localized pockets. And the aliens themselves are still a threat. Thorne's purge was devastating, but it also highlighted the extent of their control within the OCO. Many potential allies were silenced."

"Thorne," Li mused, the name spoken with a deep weariness. "His actions were a testament to their cunning. To turn one of our own into such a potent weapon… it's a grim reminder of their adaptability. But your success changes everything, Eva. It means they are not invincible. It means we can fight back."

The news of the conduit's destruction began to ripple outwards, not through official channels, which remained firmly under alien influence, but through the nascent resistance cells that had been quietly, desperately, gathering intelligence and planning for this very moment. Aris had established a secure, encrypted network, a digital ghost within the alien-controlled communication systems, allowing them to disseminate information and coordinate efforts without detection.

The awakening was not a single, cataclysmic event, but a slow, dawning realization for millions. Whispers of the severed connection began to circulate, initially dismissed as fringe conspiracy theories. But as anomalies occurred – the sudden cessation of coordinated alien directives, the inexplicable malfunctions in previously seamless alien technology, the brief, tantalizing moments of mental clarity for those who had been subtly influenced – belief began to take root.

Aris worked tirelessly, analyzing the fragmented data recovered from the polar facility and piecing together the alien modus operandi, identifying residual nodes of alien influence. He discovered that while the primary conduit was the source of the vast, overarching network, smaller, more localized sub-networks had been established in various sectors, particularly in areas of critical infrastructure and global communication.

These sub-networks, while less powerful, still exerted a significant influence, subtly manipulating information, sowIng discord, and maintaining the illusion of normalcy.

"They've been incredibly thorough," Aris explained to Eva, gesturing to a holographic projection of a complex, multi-layered network map. "Even without the primary conduit, these localized hubs are still operational. They're designed for

self-sufficiency, capable of maintaining a degree of control independently. We need to dismantle them, sector by sector systematically."

Eva understood. The fight was far from over. It had merely shifted from a single, decisive blow to a protracted war of attrition, a global effort to reclaim not just their planet, but their very minds. The task was monumental. The aliens had been entrenched for years, their influence woven into the fabric of society. Millions of people were still unknowingly under their sway, their thoughts and actions subtly guided.

The resistance, now armed with the knowledge of the conduit's destruction, began to mobilize. Small cells, once isolated and fearful, started to connect, to share information, to coordinate their efforts. Eva and Aris, operating from the shadows, became the central nexus of this burgeoning rebellion. They provided intelligence, technical expertise, and, perhaps most importantly, a beacon of hope.

One such cell, operating in the ruins of a former metropolitan hub, had managed to establish a rudimentary broadcast system, powered by salvaged alien technology repurposed for their cause. They broadcast a simple, encrypted message, a digital siren song that resonated with those who had begun to question, those who felt the unsettling dissonance of the alien influence fading. The message was simple: "The connection is broken. Reclaim your minds. Resist."

The impact was immediate and profound. Across the globe, individuals who had felt the subtle pressure on their thoughts, the alien whispers in their subconscious, began to stir. They experienced moments of clarity, of self-awareness, as the pervasive hum of alien control receded. It was like waking from a long, suffocating dream.

However, the aliens, though weakened, were not idle. Thorne's purge within the OCO had been a brutal but practical demonstration of their ruthlessness. They began to adapt and re-establish their control through different means. Their focus shifted from direct, pervasive mental manipulation to more subtle forms of manipulation – economic destabilization, the spread of disinformation through remaining compromised media channels, and the deployment of highly advanced, autonomous security units to quash any signs of organized resistance.

Eva and Aris found themselves in a constant game of cat and mouse. Their mobile command center, a marvel of Aris's ingenuity, allowed them to stay one step ahead, to move unseen through the shadows. They worked with the emerging resistance cells, providing them with the knowledge and tools to identify and dismantle localized alien sub-networks. Aris developed new counter-frequencies, new cloaking technologies, new methods for disrupting alien surveillance systems. Eva, drawing on her combat expertise and her growing understanding of the alien mindset, strategized with the resistance leaders, helping them to anticipate alien countermeasures and exploit their weaknesses.

One critical mission involved a former OCO research facility that had become a significant hub for disseminating alien propaganda and coordinating the re-establishment of localized control. The facility was heavily guarded by both automated alien drones and a contingent of humans who had willingly embraced the alien agenda, their minds fully integrated. Eva, leading a small but determined resistance team, executed a daring infiltration, bypassing the outer defenses through a network of ancient, forgotten service tunnels – a tactic learned from their experience at the polar facility.

Inside, they encountered fierce resistance. The integrated humans fought with a chilling ferocity, their movements augmented by alien technology, their eyes devoid of any human emotion. Eva's team, though outnumbered, fought with the courage of those who had tasted freedom and were determined to defend it. The battle was brutal, a desperate struggle for control of the facility's central broadcast array.

Aris, meanwhile, worked remotely, his expertise crucial in guiding Eva's team and disabling the facility's advanced alien security systems. He had developed a specialized viral code, designed to override the alien network's protocols, effectively shutting down the propaganda broadcasts and disrupting the coordination of the remaining autonomous units.

"The viral upload is in progress, Eva," Aris's voice crackled through her comms, tinged with strain. "But they're pushing back. The network is fighting it. You need to buy me more time."

Eva gritted her teeth, parrying a blow from an augmented enforcer. "We're holding them, Aris. Just finish it."

The fight raged on, a microcosm of the larger war for Earth. It was a battle not just of weapons, but of wills, of ideologies. Eva saw the flicker of confusion in the eyes of some of the less integrated enforcers, the momentary hesitation that spoke of a returning humanity, a buried consciousness fighting its way back to the surface.

With a final surge of effort, Aris's viral code infiltrated the system. The alien broadcasts sputtered and died, replaced by a simple, static white noise. The drones slumped, their optical sensors dimming, their systems offline. The integrated humans, their connection severed, staggered, their movements becoming erratic as their augmented abilities failed.

The victory was hard-won, but significant. It proved that localized resistance could be effective, that the alien grip, while still formidable, was not unbreakable. The news of the OCO facility's liberation spread like wildfire through the burgeoning resistance network, a testament to the power of coordinated action and the courage of those who dared to fight back.

Admiral Lima, now operating with an even greater degree of stealth and subterfuge, continued to provide invaluable intelligence, his network of sympathizers within the remnants of human governments and organizations working to undermine the alien influence from within. He managed to secure caches of pre-alien technology, vital resources that Aris could adapt and weaponize against their oppressors. He also provided crucial data on the locations of other significant alien sub-networks, guiding Eva and Aris's efforts and allowing them to prioritize their targets.

The awakening was no longer a localized phenomenon. It was a global tremor, a groundswell of human defiance. Millions, once passive recipients of alien control, were now actively seeking out information, connecting with resistance cells, and taking their first steps towards reclaiming their autonomy. They were rediscovering their own histories, their own cultures, their own identities, which had been suppressed and distorted by the alien agenda.

The future remained a daunting unknown. The aliens were a vast, ancient, and powerful force, and humanity had only just begun to understand the true scope of their dominion. There were still countless battles to be fought, countless minds to be freed, and countless secrets to be uncovered. But for the first time in a long time, humanity had a fighting chance. The passive subjugation was over. The dawn of awareness had broken, and with it, the dawn of resistance. The struggle to reclaim their planet, and their very consciousness, had truly begun, a testament to the enduring resilience of the human spirit against an existential threat unlike any imagined. The fight was far from over, but the tide was beginning to turn. Humanity, once a slave to the stars, was finally starting to awaken.

Back Matter

Temporal Disruptor Field Properties: The temporal disruptor, as employed by Aris Thorne, operated on principles that manipulated localized causality fields. Its primary function was to create a high-energy, spatially contained bubble wherein the conventional flow of time could be momentarily arrested or significantly decelerated relative to the external environment. This was achieved through the precise alignment of exotic matter particles, themselves remnants of a theoretical tachyon condensate, within a resonant containment matrix. The disruptor's crystalline components acted as both energy conduits and temporal modulators, their unique lattice structures resonating with the fundamental frequencies of space-time. The disruption achieved at the polar facility was a complete severing of a bi-directional causality link, effectively isolating the human collective consciousness from the alien nexus.

Alien Nexus Communication Protocols: The alien nexus employed a form of entangled consciousness communication, a non-localized, quantum-level data transfer that bypassed conventional electromagnetic spectra. This protocol enabled the near-instantaneous dissemination of directives and sensory input across vast distances, establishing a pervasive mental overlay over affected populations. The "whispers" and "subtle directives" experienced by humans were direct neural transmissions, calibrated to bypass conscious awareness while subtly influencing behavior and thought patterns. The severing of the primary conduit at the polar facility disabled the central hub of this network, but smaller, localized sub-networks, established for redundancy and resilience, continued to operate independently.

Augmented Human Enforcers: The human enforcers were subjected to a process of neural integration and bio-enhancement, directly linking their nervous systems to the alien network. This provided them with augmented strength, reflexes, and a degree of cybernetic enhancement, but at the cost of individual autonomy. Their actions were primarily dictated by the alien nexus, their personalities and free will suppressed. The shock of the conduit's severance caused a significant neural decoupling, resulting in cognitive dissonance and a period of intense disorientation for these individuals.

Alien Nexus: The overarching, interconnected network through which the alien civilization exerted its influence and control over Earth.

Causality Link: A theoretical connection through which an external entity could influence or dictate the progression of events within a specific timeframe or location.

Conduit (Primary): The central, high-capacity connection point of the Alien Nexus, located at the polar facility, through which the majority of alien influence was channeled.

OCO (Orbital Command Organization): A global defense and intelligence agency, compromised and weaponized by the alien influence.

Tachyon Condensate: A hypothetical state of exotic matter believed to possess faster-than-light properties and capable of interacting with space-time in unusual ways.

Temporal Disruptor: A device capable of manipulating localized temporal fields, used here to sever the primary conduit.

Viral Code: A specialized program designed to infiltrate and disrupt alien network systems.

While this work is a work of speculative fiction, its conceptual underpinnings draw inspiration from various scientific and philosophical discussions:

Theories on quantum entanglement and its potential applications in communication. Hypothetical models of exotic matter and space-time manipulation.

Discussions on collective consciousness and the nature of free will in the face of pervasive external influence.

Studies in neural interfacing and the ethical implications of advanced cybernetics. Historical accounts of resistance movements and the psychology of liberation.